ACCURSED

G JOHANSON

Published by Kharon Publishing

Cover illustration by Douglas Mullen

Chapter 1 – Leaving Home – Attempt Two

"Are you in or out?"

James Grey had barely set foot into the work premises before his employer, Bob Grant, asked this question. Bob's office was humbleness itself, a sharp contrast to his large home, though he spent so little time there that the size was immaterial. Bob ran a gardening business, built up from scratch and originally a one man operation before the years took their toll and now he had three employees who did most of the physical work. Unfortunately times were hard and with the war three years old and still going strong he found that customers were in short supply. Initially work had picked up as they obtained several short term jobs mowing lawns and basic gardening as housewives called on their services when their menfolk went away, but that didn't last long (even though they charged peanuts for this, with money at a premium most learnt to do the job themselves). He was still able to rely on regular state assignments but it looked increasingly likely that he was going to have to let one of the boys go and as the youngest and most recent employee, Dick Pike would be the sacrificial lamb, depending entirely on what answer James Grey gave him. Grey was less than a year older than Pike, and had just turned 18 and had attended his physical examination for entry into the army yesterday. The Marines had rejected his application a year earlier so, despite Grey's eagerness to serve his country, his army career was not assured.

"Both. In the army and out of the business," Grey said, beaming with pride. "I'll work today as agreed, 'til ten at night if I have to to get the work finished."

Bob shook his hand and patted his shoulder, pleased for him as Grey had made it plain how much he wanted this. "Get yourself off home. Make the most of your time off. You'll be paid for the week."

Grey shook his head. "I've got two weeks yet before basic training. Besides, I want to see this project through. I can't expect Dick to do it all himself."

"I was planning on working with him. It's up to you. You can go home with a full week's pay or if you want you can finish off today."

"I'll finish today, boss. I'd better load up the pickup and call on Dick and get started, unless you're not going to be around tonight…"

"Not if you finish at 10 I won't be. Sit down, I'll make a brew. Dick can wait half an hour for his lift – he'll be grateful his job's safe," Bob said, filling the kettle as Grey sat down.

"I'll have to come back another day anyway, to see Greg. Are you going to pair them up again?" Grey said, referring to Bob's oldest employee, in age and length of service. Greg had trained Grey when he started exactly a year ago, and as

Grey had proven himself a fast learner with a maturity beyond his years he was quickly trusted to complete assignments on his own. Dick was a shiftier character and kept his job because he had good crack and when he chose to knuckle down he worked hard, hard enough to make up for the moments when he slackened off. Unfortunately Dick and Greg had proven completely incompatible and Dick had quickly been assigned to work with Grey instead.

"That depends. You've worked with him for a good while now. Is he ready to fly solo?"

"Yeah," Grey nodded without hesitation. The true answer was probably not but Grey gave him the benefit of the doubt.

"How are your parents?"

"They're fine. They've had a lot of time to get used to the idea. They know how much I want this."

"We all know that! End it quickly, will you? A couple more years like this and I'll be my sole employee again."

"With your contacts you're guaranteed to stay afloat."

"Staying afloat doesn't cut it with the wife. She has expensive tastes. I need to thrive again to satisfy her. Tip for the future, Jim. Get involved in an industry that can profiteer from the war," Bob said, his comments tongue in cheek. If the war really did ruin him it would be a different matter but he knew he would weather the storm. Grey had found him an ideal first boss – relaxed, unassuming, a good-natured sort who talked to him as an equal.

"I was hoping to get back into this game."

"Your job will be waiting for you, if you want it."

"If it is, then great, but I know that things change. If you find you need to take on more staff and when I come back you don't need anyone else I wouldn't want to take another man's job from him."

"If I do hire anyone else, which is unlikely at the moment, I'll let them know straight up that they're only filling in."

"Make your plans based on your business needs. I say I want to get back into gardening, and I do because I love the work. The thing is though, I don't have any concrete plans for what follows the war. I'm so focused on this, that the future beyond that ...who knows. Best take me out of the equation, Bob."

Bob passed Grey his mug and sat down across from him and supped his drink. "The furthest you've travelled before this is Illinois, right?"

Grey grinned and said, "Yep. Chicago, and that felt a long way away. Just before I got this job I thought about spending the waiting year travelling across the States."

"That's something I've wanted to do for the last 30 years but life's practicalities have always gotten in the way. You can always do that when you come back."

"That's why I don't want to make concrete plans. For the next x years plus six months my life is structured for me so I have no decisions to worry about until after."

"You're a bright lad. You might get a responsible position."

Grey grimaced and said, "Having other men's lives under my command – that's not for me. I know my limitations." Killing was going to be hard enough and the prospect of sending his own men into danger was an impossibility.

"You undersell yourself," Bob said encouragingly.

"Privates are the backbone of the army," Grey said, taking pride in what many might consider the lowest rank, which was technically correct, but the role was still damned important and all that he aspired for in his military career. He was no career soldier; his job was to get trained, get sent overseas and help end the war and keep the peace if necessary, though this held less interest, then get straight back to civilian life. "I'm satisfied to help form that spine."

Dick Pike pointed at his watch as he saw Grey finally approach at the agreed rendezvous point. "What kept you?" he said as he got in, pretending to be irate, his manner humorous.

"The bossman. Take it up with him because he's keeping you on. I managed to scrape in this time, so good news all round," Grey said positively.

"Well, good news for me. You might change your mind in six months time when you're sleeping in a foxhole," Dick quipped, in no rush to follow Grey and serve his country.

"I hope to be fighting quicker than that."

"Did you ask him about me working alone?"

"Yeah. I lied and said you were ready for it so – don't quote me on this, but I reckon that's how he'll play it."

"Thank fuck for that," Dick said, greatly relieved at this. While Grey was as blinkered as Greg when it came to getting on with the job, he let Dick get on with it without censure, unlike Greg, who was completely humourless and a total stickler for the rules.

"If we can finish off today this is my last day. Shit. Sorry, mate, I think you're going to be working with Greg," Grey said. He had been so fixated on joining up that he had not given this matter sufficient thought and now he suddenly realised a major flaw. "You're going to need to get your own wheels fast."

Dick thought this over, looking for a way round it before exclaiming, "Fuck! It's worse than that – Bob'll finish me and get a guy in who can find his own way around the city."

Grey shook his head and said calmly, trying to pacify him, "I couldn't drive when Bob took me on and it didn't put him off."

"I should have been better prepared. This is your last day. So what am I doing tomorrow?"

"Nothing's lined up so just go to the office in the morning and see what's up."

"Another part-time week. That could be useful. I can use the time to get some wheels. If I had the dough."

"I tell you what. You can look after this for me. Don't show off to your mates in it. It's dented and scratched enough as it is." Grey made the offer after a moment's consideration. His warning would be wasted on Dick who would be pulling off three point turns at three in the morning and cruising everywhere with scant regard for his own safety or anyone else's. Even taking this into account, Dick needed the vehicle and he was able to help him out. His parents were not interested in taking up driving and his friends either had their own wheels or had their sights set on something better than his rusty pickup.

"Seriously?" Dick said, disbelieving that Grey would be prepared to practically write off his beloved vehicle. It was not perfect but it was his first set of wheels and he cherished it.

"When I come back I'm reclaiming it. You're only borrowing it, and you have to maintain it. Nobody else wants it so it's better off being used than blocking my parents' view."

"I'm broke at the moment, with these part-time weeks. I can't give you much for it."

Grey shook his head. "You don't need to. As I say, I'm lending it to you – I want this dream machine back."

"I know. If you weren't driving I'd shake your hand, Mr Grey. You're a scholar and a gent," Dick said effervescently.

"Before you get carried away, I'm going to need it until I go away, so you will probably have to work with Greg for a bit. At least he's punctual."

"Yeah, I'll say that for him. Don't worry about this beast, Jimmy; I'll take good care of it. It's not quick enough for me to try and race my mates so you don't have to worry about anything like that."

"You can disrespect me, but don't talk bad about the pickup," Grey joked. "Just be as careful as you can be."

"I can't imagine why you doubt me," Dick said, playing the innocent, well aware that his numerous anecdotes about his escapades had given Grey good cause to worry and made his offer downright foolish.

"It's probably just as well I won't be making any decisions for a while," Grey said. Changing the subject he said, "How did it go yesterday?"

"She was giving me the evil eye yesterday so I had to work without cigarette breaks. We'll be finished today, easy."

"Bob said he dropped you off and picked you up. He might do that for the next fortnight. I reckon you and Greg could start again and work together without conflict but I know I'd want to stand on my own two feet and go it alone and I know you feel the same."

Mrs Saunders was the kind of customer that Bob Grant had long relied on – wealthy and with no desire to be self-sufficient. With her husband away she had decided that her vast back garden, which quickly resembled wasteland, needed a complete overhaul and she came up with grand designs involving a patio and path, reducing the lawn substantially so that maintenance would be less of a problem. Her husband would hate it but he had already been gone a year and by not asking him she could pretend she thought he would like this surprise. Grey took great pride in his work and when Mrs Saunders had gone over her ideas he had been doubtful that they would look good but as it approached completion he had to admit that her vision was coming together well. She'd trusted him when it came to which plants and flowers to plant to complete the aesthetics while she was more interested in which areas to pave, creating a spiral design. Over half of this project had been more like working on a building site rather than gardening and Grey and Dick had managed this aspect well and the end was in sight. Over the last week she had proven to be a prickly customer for Bob's workers but as she saw the project take shape and develop better than even she had envisioned she calmed down a little, though would still not invite the workers into the house. As it was the final day she brought out some tea and biscuits for them on their lunch break and left them to it.

"Weak as piss," Dick said after his first sip when she was just out of earshot.

Grey repressed his laughter and said, “The biscuits are tasty. Give her credit, she's warmed to us.”

“As much as an owner can to her slaves. Tell us a bit more about yesterday then.”

“I think I've given you the gist.”

“In five months time I'll be getting the same treatment. Is the short arm examination a myth or do they…”

“They do. I already knew about that but you still feel like saying ‘Back off, buddy’. It's probably even less fun for the poor docs who have to process us all. It's not painful and everyone has to go through it. Just close your eyes and imagine Lynn Merrick doing...on second thoughts that's a lame idea, because if you react wrong to that you'll be going nowhere.”

“Thanks, that's my strategy sorted. You still as keen to get out there.”

“Absolutely. Look at the films that are coming out, the recruitment ones especially that show it as a very civilised, enjoyable campaign. How could I not be sold on that? If it's not that perfect I might change my mind. I'm joking by the way,” Grey said, as Dick was looking at him as though he was taking him seriously.

“I know, but I still can't see what the draw is for you. I'll go if I'm drafted, but I won't break my neck to.”

“It's got to be done, mate. Evil still thrives. Evil that you couldn't make up, suffering that you can't put into words. I may be just one man, but that's one more against evil. Even one person increases the odds.”

“I wouldn't like to give you your odds. It's…”

“It's pot luck. I know that. All I can do is train hard and be the best soldier that I can. The odds are slightly better for me than for most,” Grey said cryptically.

“Huh? Your running?”

Grey nodded, letting him believe that was it. Grey had learnt long ago that absolute honesty led to dark places – necessity required a level of dishonesty that did not sit comfortably with him. He was reckless in mentioning his odds, scratching the surface of the ‘forbidden’ topic, broaching a subject he wouldn't expand on. Lately he'd been getting careless – there were enough eyes boring into him, scrutinising his behaviour without him giving clues. Perhaps it was because he was leaving Keokuk – he did want to return and if he didn't watch his step that option would not be available.

“This should be an Olympic Year and they took my chance of a medal from me. This is personal, Dick, and I plan on showing the ‘Master Race’ that there's Americans much fitter than them, too quick to be killed,” Grey said hyperbolically, putting on the smokescreen to cover up his error of judgement. When he trained regularly he was one of the best 5000 metre runners in the state and probably in the top 100 for the country – even a Bronze in the Olympics was highly unlikely. “It won't be the first time Hitler's been embarrassed by an American athlete.”

“We'll have to go out for a drink before you go.”

“I'm going to be spending next week training flat out so I'm going out next Saturday as the farewell drinks session. You're more than welcome.”

“I'll be there.”

Grey had been cajoled by his friends into making a big night of his farewell. All he wanted was a quiet night at his local where he would drink up to his usual limit, five pints over two hours. An all night pub crawl where they would be plying drink down his throat all night...he was loose-lipped enough sober all of a sudden and this concerned him. Everyone knew he preferred smoking to drinking and he clung to the thin hope that he could convince them to treat him to cigars over booze. Now those odds were slim...

Mid-afternoon Grey called Mrs Saunders out to the garden to see the finished product, and after she requested one alteration, which took close to an hour, Grey called her out again and she gushed over her new garden.

"It's wonderful. You've captured exactly what I had in my mind. I'll recommend you to my friends," she said effusively.

"Please do," Grey said, leading the conversation with her as Dick stood back as she had made it clear she thought little of him. She recognised that Grey was well-mannered and respectful, whereas his apprentice had a noticeable attitude about him. "If you need any more work done as a previous customer you'll go straight to the front of the queue."

"Wait here," she said, returning to the house, her brow heavy as she left them.

"What now?" Dick muttered, noticing the sudden change in her mood. "She's already paid – let's get out of here."

"Do you want to start loading up? I'll help you in a minute."

Mrs Saunders came back out clutching a small sum of money, which Dick espied from afar, having a hawk's eye when it came to anything involving cash. She was glad Dick was out of earshot putting their things away as she felt awkward enough. "You've done a good job here. I know this is your last job before you go overseas and I'd like to give you a little extra..."

"There's no need..."

"I knew you'd say that, and that makes me want to do this. It's only five dollars, James. Treat yourself," she said insistently.

"It would go straight to Mr Grant. We don't pocket tips. I'm just glad you're pleased with the finished product."

"I'm absolutely delighted. I'll be inviting over everyone I know to see it. I'll be offended if you don't take it."

Grey took the money reluctantly and halved it with Dick as he drove off, with Dick making innuendos about how he'd got the money for 'services rendered'. Grey knew Bob wouldn't take the money and broke his own rule this once. He could get a stash of butts with that to tide him over for a month or two. Bob had left the office by the time they arrived back (he only spent a couple of hours a day there and they often were too late back to see him on the evening) and Grey unloaded the pickup for the last time. He'd feel nostalgic about this – this small moment would become a big moment later, he could feel it as he finished his last minutes at work. With Bob gone Dick wasn't sure what he was supposed to do Wednesday but he didn't mention it to Grey (he'd just have to get the bus in and see what Bob had lined up) who surveyed the yard, the three sheds and the small office.

"It'll still be here when you get back," Dick said, reading his thoughts.

Grey smiled and said, "Come on, I'll drop you off. It's getting late and you don't have a lie-in tomorrow."

After taking Dick home Grey did not arrive back home until quarter to eight. While Grey lived in a better locale than Dick, who lived in a rough part of town, Dick's mother and stepfather's house was considerably bigger than the Grey family home. Grey parked outside the small terraced house, which was just a little off the centre of town; close enough to walk to the town while far enough away that their nights were quiet. 'My odds are better than most' – he imagined if he'd made that slip-up to his parents, who would have responded very differently to Dick. One thing he could be sure of was that even if he drank 20 gallons of whisky he'd still never mention that topic to them.

Grey kicked his boots off at the door and announced his presence. His mother came to the hall to greet him and said, "I'll put your dinner in now. It's going to take 50 minutes so I can rustle you up a snack first while you have a bath."

"It's all right. I've got some chips in my room. I'll eat them while I wait for the bath to fill."

"Was it your last day?"

"Yep. We finished a bit later than we anticipated but we got the job done and she was overjoyed. You don't need to make me breakfast in the morning. I'm sleeping in," Grey grinned.

"I might still prepare you something. I'd better get started," Shirley said, turning round and heading for the kitchen as Grey went upstairs. He was a grown man now but she still waited on him hand and foot, doting on her only child. Even if he hadn't been doomed to go to war she would have been the same as at least James accepted her ministrations gratefully, even if he would have preferred to look after himself, while her husband Abner demanded to be waited on yet rarely showed appreciation. She walked through the lounge to access the kitchen and passed Abner who sat on the couch reading – she didn't expect him to break away from his book to greet James but she wished he could have at least shouted a greeting. "It was his last day," she said.

"He said it would be," Abner said, considering her news old hat.

"He said it might be. Mrs Saunders was pleased. She's a very particular woman. He's done well there."

"I thought you didn't know her?" Abner said, never once making eye contact with his wife.

"Hilary knows her sister. And James has said that she's a perfectionist."

"She's the customer, she's entitled to be."

Shirley sighed and left him to it and turned the oven on. This once she didn't want to bite her tongue and she stood in the doorway and said, "James didn't criticise her."

Abner looked up and said, "What are you going on about?"

"Never mind," Shirley said, unsure herself what she was twittering on about. She only had 13 days left with her son, 12 really as today was practically over, and she was working for 7 of them. She got on well with her boss at the department store and considered asking for some leave. Normally she only worked two mornings a week and one Saturday a month (the limited hours had been what persuaded Abner to let her take the job in the first place four years ago) but one of the poor girls in another department had been bereaved, in the damned war, and she had ended up taking on two of her shifts until she was ready to return. If she could just have the last Friday off to spend a special day with him then she'd work Doreen's shifts for her the rest of the year if necessary. She could only find excuses to stay in the kitchen for so long and eventually returned to the living room and sat on the sofa. Abner always sat on the hardbacked chair closest to the fire; James always sat on the other chair leaving her alone on the sofa. She stood back up again and walked to the smallest bookcase in the room, the only one of the four bookcases that contained books for herself or her son. The other books were all her husband's and while he let others read them, Shirley and James rarely did so as he complained about the condition of them if they were not pristine. Abner was an academic man who had been forced to cut his studies short when she had fallen pregnant; while he claimed to like his job, as wages clerk at a large factory manufacturing refrigerators, Shirley knew his ambitions had once been grander than that.

For a short time Abner had projected his ambitions onto his son, before it became apparent that living his dreams vicariously through him was not going to work. Once he would have supported him through college; as things turned out when James dropped out of school Abner only made a half-hearted protest, going through the motions as he recognised that further education was a waste of time. James was slightly better than average, as demonstrated in his standing in the class tests, intelligent enough for Abner to support him still were it not for other things. Those other issues made an academic or clerical career unlikely and manual work was what he was suited for.

Shirley sat at the dining table in the kitchen with James as he ate, filling her in on the minutiae of his day to his transfixed audience; even he found it pretty boring stuff but he knew she liked to hear about his day and he tried to make it lively for her so at least one of them found it interesting. Shirley remembered she had some news to tell him and she called into the next room, "Abner, do you want to tell him about Frank?"

Abner came through and stood by the table. "Your uncle and cousin are coming to stay next Friday. Dolores and her family will be joining us for a meal."

"We're going out for a meal. I wouldn't want to cook for that many," Shirley joked. "Everybody wants to give you a good send-off."

"Can we make it Joe's?" Grey asked. Joe's had the widest seafood variety in Keokuk and Grey preferred fish to anything, looking forward to every Friday.

"That's where we booked," Abner said. "Make no other plans for next Friday."

"Bar Saturday I've got no plans. I'm a man of leisure now, Dad."

"Not for long," Abner said, leaving them to it.

Shirley noted how pleased her son seemed at the news that they'd booked Joe's, and she knew why. She liked to give him a varied diet and would only cook fish once or maybe twice a week. For this last fortnight that could change. As he tucked into his beef dinner she said, "Shall I pop to the fish market tomorrow?"

Grey nodded keenly, brought up not to speak with his mouth full. After a drink he said, "Bob's given me a bit extra and I got a tip today so splash out."

"My treat."

Grey shook his head. "It's to go in my stomach. You can't even stand the smell. So how long are Frank and Fred stopping?" he said loudly, looking to the living room.

"Friday afternoon through to the next morning. He'd like to stop longer if it wasn't for work," Abner replied.

"That's good enough. I would have gone to see them if they weren't coming," Grey said – in a way he would have preferred to visit his uncle at his pub.

"Now you don't need to. If you're at a loose end tomorrow I can think of a few things around here that need doing."

"Can't talk, Dad, I'm eating," Grey said, signalling to his mother what he thought of that idea by shaking his head. He returned to talking to his mother, saying, "I'll be going out myself tomorrow so I could always hit the market."

"It's as easy for me to go after work."

"Yeah, you don't want to go before and have them through the back all day."

"To be honest the smell wouldn't be worse than Helen's perfume. I know she's trying to attract admirers but really."

"Which one's Helen again?"

"The tall one with the plait. You gave her a lift home once. She wasn't wearing it then."

"I guess I'm off her radar."

"I wish that was true. She asks about you a lot. I've had to tell her you're seeing someone to shut her up." While Shirley liked Helen she considered her far too old for her son at 24 and too flirty by far.

"Maybe I should pop by tomorrow to pick you up," Grey teased.

"There's no need. I might be home before you get up."

"That's quite possible." Grey finished off every morsel from his plate and walked to the sink and rinsed his plate and cutlery.

"Would you like a dessert?" Shirley asked.

"I'm absolutely stuffed," Grey said, patting his stomach. "That was a big bag of chips I had up there and the portions you dispense are a lot bigger than what I'm going to have to get used to."

"You know you shouldn't eat..."

"Before a bath," Grey said, finishing the oft repeated sentence for her. "Most old wives tales have some truth about them but that one doesn't hold water for me. Thank you, that was delicious. I'm looking forward to tomorrow's dinner already."

"Which we should be able to eat together at a decent time."

Grey nodded and walked through to the living room and sat in his usual seat. He looked at the cover of the book his father was reading, something about economics, and as talking about what he was reading would be a conversational dead end he said, "After the meal once the ladies and Fred are back home I'd like it if the three of us could go out for a drink." He had always got on well with his Uncle Frank, a far more relaxed man than his father, and in his brother's company Abner loosened up a little.

Abner put his book down and said, "I imagine Frank would be keen. Let's see what the time is first. We're going to be eating at 7:30."

Shirley came through and sat on the sofa and said to Abner, "We're going to have fish a little more often this week."

"He can, but I'll stick with my meat. It's steak night tomorrow."

"What about crab? You like that," Grey suggested.

"Not as much as steak. You can't be fussy in the army, son. You have to eat what they give you, every morsel in case the next meal is a long time coming."

"It was my suggestion," Shirley said.

"If you cook him fish every night he won't be bothered about going to the restaurant, will he?" Abner said, his specious argument flooring Shirley who gave up.

"I'm not a fussy eater – I pretty much lick the plate clean every night, fish or not. Steak's good, Mom, stick with that."

"You can have what you want as long as it's not imposed on me," Abner said. "Anyway, I'm off to bed. Good night."

They both bade him good night and after he left them Shirley said, "I forgot I promised him steak. Maybe Thursday?"

"That's fine," Grey said, not bothered in the slightest apart from feeling a sliver of anger at seeing her upset.

"Okay. Good night, son," she said, kissing his cheek as she headed for bed less than a minute after Abner. Grey closed his eyes and felt guilty at his thoughts. All of the other men he had talked to about serving over the years, including some bizarre conversations conducted stark bollock naked on Monday as it became closer to reality for them, had all stressed how much they would miss their family and home. He did not feel the same.

Coach Stone recognised his former student from a distance, used to seeing his charges from afar as he had them run umpteen laps until he was satisfied and cross country marathons on occasion, sending them to a friend's farm where they had to see his friend to confirm they had gone the distance before making their way back. Grey walked across leisurely, smiling at him as Coach Stone ran on the spot, indicating to him that he should be running to him and Grey decided he might as well, sprinting across to him.

"You've lost a bit of speed there, Grey," Coach Stone said, looking back to the track where three teenage girls were running laps.

"I put that down to these pants, Coach. I knew I'd find you here."

"I can rustle you up a kit if you want to get out there."

"Better not, else I'll have no excuses to fall back on. I've still been training, but mostly weight training and…"

"You've filled out, bulked up too much for a long distance runner. You're built more like a sprinter now."

"Not at all. Where's the fun in sprinting? The race is over before you've begun, there's no sizing up your competitors, no time to enjoy it – no burn either so I suppose that's one good thing. I'm still quick, just not competition level. The added strength should prove more useful, 'cause those kitbags are meant to be heavy."

"You in this time?" Coach Stone asked, turning to look at him again. He knew how important this was to Grey who had quit his training prior to his 17th birthday when he was supposed to have been joining the Marines before they rejected his application, claiming to be over quota. Coach Stone had been prepared to take him back but Grey had declined, explaining that he would be leaving in a year anyway and with work leaving his free time to a minimum he wanted to spend it unwinding rather than pushing himself to the limit for competitions he wouldn't be around to enter.

"I passed the medical Monday with flying colours. With the training I received here I knew it was only a formality. The relentless hikes you sent us on will make the marches over there seem like a walk in the park," Grey said breezily.

"When you meet your drill instructor you will realise how mild-mannered I've been."

"I'll take that bet. I heard Dylan's already gone over," Grey said, referring to another of Coach Stone's protégés.

"About nine months ago now. I see his father around town. He likes it by all accounts. Navy. Where are you going?"

"Germany."

"No, which branch?"

"The Army. It seems pointless wasting my speed in the air or on a ship."

"I don't think it's a race, but it'll do you no harm neither. Good luck, son," Coach Stone said and he shook his hand.

"Thanks, Coach. I hope you go easier on these girls than you did on us," Grey said, looking at the girls who continued circling the track.

"That wouldn't be doing them any favours. The theory is they won't be taken from me by this inconvenient conflict that's already cost me my best," Coach Stone said, explaining why he'd opted to train girls for the first time in over 25 years of coaching.

"How old are they?"

"15 and 13. I don't coach the one lagging at the back. She's friends with the older one and I let her come out and practice with them but she's no contender and she knows that herself. I have high hopes for the 15 year old. She's called Katie Cash."

"I think I have seen her run before at a meet. Another long distance runner, right?"

Coach Stone nodded. "She has real potential. Her focus is fantastic."

"I'd better make sure this war ends soon then so she doesn't get distracted."

"I don't think anything would distract her. Not boys...not yet anyway."

Grey chuckled. "That's going to be funny, how you handle that."

"It won't be a factor; she wants to be a champ. More than you or Dylan, obviously."

"There's many ways of being a champ."

"I know. I respect your choice, though you'll never be atop a podium now."

Grey shrugged. "True, but I wanted this more. When you look at the sporting legends who're already serving..."

"It's had to take a back seat. The one positive thing is that women's athletics could receive more attention – these girls have proved pluckier than any boys I've ever trained," Coach Stone said, having surprised himself with how involved he had become with his two charges. Initially he had thought he was slumming it somewhat by taking on girl students and his attitude quickly changed. He'd take on boy trainees again, after the war or even sooner if the right candidate presented himself, but he would not be as nurturing with the boys as he was with these girls.

"I can see they're giving it their all."

"Bar the one at the back, but she's not one of mine," he reiterated, disassociating himself from her. "When do you go?"

"A week on Monday. I don't know what to do with myself. It's the same as a race. Doing it's fine, but waiting is brutal. That's why I'm checking out my old haunts, trying to keep myself busy. I shouldn't have quit work so early."

"If you've got time to kill why don't you go in and get changed and see how quick you are at 5k now with a bit more meat on your bones?"

"I can be a cautionary example to your girls of what happens if you stop training. For old times' sake, but don't expect the old pace."

Coach Stone pulled his girls off the track when Grey came back out and had them cool down as Grey limbered up. Grey remembered that he liked to protect his runners and that he would alter training times to ensure they trained without any other competition – a year ago he would have outgunned them though this was not necessarily true now. He started off around the track at a brisk pace, contemplating how many times he'd ran circuits here – it was remarkable all of the runners here hadn't run a groove into the track. He was never quite good enough for the Olympic trials and had to push himself when competing at state level meets to even stay with the pack, victory at even this level an unobtainable dream. Even so, despite the fact an Olympic medal was never a possibility, this calling had been a blessing to him. He took pride in that he was the best in Keokuk at his chosen distance. At a time when he really needed it he became one of the school sporting heroes, for his running primarily and he was also a permanent fixture on the school baseball team. Baseball was his ultimate dream as he had been a devoted fan for as far back as he could remember, yet he wasn't quite good enough to turn professional though still played regularly for an amateur side. He enjoyed the sociable side of baseball, though as he ran laps he remembered how the solitary aspect of running also struck a chord. Here he could be alone with his thoughts theoretically, or at least give the spirits his undivided attention. One came through after four laps, and Grey knew at once this guy would be no problem, his voice calm.

How do, fella? You're running laps I hear?

Yep. Another eight to go with my coach scrutinising me. The name's James Grey, amateur medium and very amateur athlete. American as you can probably hear while you sound English, mate.

That I am. Or was? I guess I should use the past tense.

We're talking now so don't. Don't disregard yourself or think negatively. This is your last stop before Heaven – so many people are dying at once the route gets congested and you need a little help finding your way, that's all. What's your name, pal?

Peter Summers. I didn't make it off, Crete, James. That's the luck of the draw, he said without bitterness.

I hope I can be as magnanimous in your shoes.

I hope you never have to find out. How old are you?

18, just.

Wait for them to call you up.

I start serving my country in 12 days time.

It's hard for me to think of any advice to help you because words don't cut it. You can't really prepare for it. Get as fit and lean as you can and then just try your best. It does get easier. I don't know whether being a medium will make it easier or harder for you.

I hope easier. How old are you, Peter?

32. It's better us older blokes snuff it then the young boys like yourself but it doesn't always work out like that. Survival's 20 per cent skill, 80 per cent luck.

They're steep odds.

Sorry. I'm not trying to dishearten you.

You're not. I've been waiting for this too long for anything or anyone to deter me. But I respect what you're saying – you're a veteran, you know what you're talking about.

That doesn't mean I know anymore about it than you – the troops often know the least about what's going on. If you get stationed in Blighty keep your grubby mitts off the English girls. We all know what you Yanks are like.

That's the risk of leaving your ladies unattended. The odds you were quoting before sum up my luck with the ladies so you don't have to worry about me on that score. Is there a Mrs Summers?

*Several. I was married, yes. We have three boys. Dying's not that hard, James, but leaving your loved ones…*he trailed off, unable to finish the sentence.

Maybe that's why it's better that young men fight, without ties. Do you have any messages that you'd like passed on?

Best not. It would only scare them. So how long have you been doing this?

Over half my life. I should be better at it, shouldn't I?

You're doing grand. You handle a voice in your head better than I would.

I didn't originally.

You were a kid. You still are now. You were an infant then – how did this happen?

Your guess is as good as mine. Now I take it as a blessing. I've met thousands of remarkable people who I would never have known otherwise.

Thousands?

Not hundreds of thousands. More like 4 figures, 3000. This was a lie, the figure closer to 30,000 and Grey had to be careful not to think this for when in contact with spirits they often heard stray thoughts. One second he'd be staring at a pinup girl and then a murder victim would be in his head and he had to quickly stop thinking any lustful thoughts, privacy a very rare thing for him.

That's a lot.

It's generally a quick conversation. For example, if you want, if you're sure you don't want me passing on any messages I can send you on your way now, to peace. Anyone who you've known who's passed over will be there to greet you.

I…I guess it's better than this nothing existence. If I didn't want to go could you keep me present so that I could find out how my family are?

I could try.

You don't want to be lumbered with me for months, do you?

I have been in contact with some spirits for years. Some have real trouble finding their way; I sense you could find peace now if you wanted. Honestly, Peter, I don't mind. Having a veteran present could come in handy.

After contemplating his options for a few minutes Peter said, *Release me. I'll end up asking you to say something to them from me and they don't need any more grief. Be careful, James. Try and find another veteran who can help you better than me.*

Coach Stone walked to the finish line where Grey stood hunched over and he patted his back and said, "Well, on the bright side, no one died. Do you want to know your time?"

"Was I over a minute out?"

While talking to his coach Grey tried continuing the conversation with Peter Summers, saying, *It's completely your choice. I think it's the right one, but you have to be sure.*

Let me go.

"48 seconds outside your best. Considering you haven't been training properly there may still be hope for you. If you want you can ask me if I'll take you on again when you come back."

Enjoy your rest, Peter. You've earned it. And with that he was gone.

"Will you take me on again when I come back?"

"I mean ask me then, and well you know it."

"I've got a stitch from hell. Baseball's the easy option over this."

"You ran through it. That fortitude will serve you well. Let's not rule out '48."

Grey woke up late after another interrupted night's sleep, after another bout of nightmares about the war. This time the dream he remembered most was particularly chilling, playing on his real fears as his ship was sunk and even when he managed to ascend to the deck and escape going down with the ship, he found himself in shark infested waters. Travelling to the front scared him more than action. In peacetime a cruise would be fun; not so when they were a target and he was powerless to do anything to change the outcome. Talking to spirits wasn't going to be useful in such an instance. Soldiers were supposed to be plagued by bad nightmares after the fighting, not before.

Grey found that he was going through cigarettes at an alarming rate and walked into the city to buy some more butts from the tobacconist. The owner, Cliff, knew him well and joked that he would struggle without his custom. Grey bought five packs and treated himself to two cigars and told Cliff that should tide him over for the night. On his way home he ran into Daisy Lovell, almost bumping into her as he lit up, the peak of his hat obscuring his vision as he looked down to light a cigarette. Daisy lived a street away and had been in Grey's class at school. He'd had a thing for her for years and they had dated briefly two years back, their relationship quickly fizzling out amicably.

"Sorry, Daisy, in a world of my own there."

"That's nothing new. Were you going to leave without saying goodbye?" she said, affecting offence.

"I wouldn't dare. I wouldn't want to run into you in a field hospital in a bad mood."

"I'm finishing my education first. You see, I'm sensible."

"Sometimes. You're still going to join up too though, yeah?"

Daisy nodded. "If you guys haven't ended it first, yes. I guess craziness isn't confined to the male gender."

Grey chuckled. "How's John?"

"He must have injured his hand. I send letters to him at a rate of 4 to 1 return."

"An injured hand? That's a good one. I'll use that myself."

"You write to your mother regular. It's hard waiting for news."

"Not as hard as writing letters. I've already warned my folks I won't be flooding the letterbox. As long as I write them and tell them I'm okay once a month they're cool with that. You'll be sending novels through the post to John and that'll be why he's not replying so quick, 'cause he'll be spending all his time reading your essays."

"Please! You jabber on yourself plenty."

"Not in print. Not with my parents either."

"At least pretend you're going to miss them."

"I will. I'll miss everybody. Still, it seems near enough everybody else is going over there too so I won't be too homesick with so many familiar faces about. It's not goodbye anyway. It's Auf Wiedersehen."

"You still want to go to Germany? James, you don't get a choice which theatre you fight in. You can choose air, land or sea but not destination."

"It'll be Germany. If not I'll find a way to make it be."

Daisy shook her head and said, "What's the difference?"

"Come on, you've heard me speak out about the German government for nearly 10 years. I was boring you guys with politics in the playground when the Nazis were portrayed in a pretty good light over here."

"I acknowledge that."

"I was spitting in the wind then – I made my case poorly, but I knew it was so wrong then and things are getting worse, big time worse, as we speak. That's where I need to be."

"What do you read to find out all this?"

"Yank, but I always feel a fraud. As of ten days time I can read it legitimately."

"You didn't read Yank 10 years ago."

"What is this, the Spanish Inquisition?"

"I bet anything you end up in the Pacific. That's where we're needed too, James. It's more personal to me."

"Is that because of John?"

"Partly. Pearl Harbor too. You must remember me crying for days."

"I was ill around that time. I didn't go out for weeks – not because of that, I just had a virus. It was a rubbish Christmas all around, that year."

"Let's hope this one's better. You take care of yourself, James, otherwise you may run into Nurse Lovell where you least expect it."

"That's me having nightmares for the foreseeable," Grey said and Daisy tapped his arm lightly. "You'll have to curb those violent urges before you join the nursing profession."

"And you're going to have to conjure some up. I know you're a gentle soul, James. It won't come easy."

"I've wanted this for too long to let anything stand in my way. I'll get through it, just like you'll breeze through your training. I'm going in as a Private and I'll be leaving as one too. It wouldn't surprise me if you end up Matron Lovell by the time it's all over."

"Fingers crossed. You'll be in my prayers."

"Thank you. As soon as I find out when you go I'll do the same for you – I don't want to waste prayers on you while you're still safe in Keokuk. Seriously, you take care too, Daisy. I couldn't do your career for all the money in the world," Grey said with admiration, admitting his stomach was too weak for the task.

"Just remember to write your mother a lot," Daisy said, embracing him. John wouldn't like her hugging her ex but he didn't need to know and she decided that James Grey needed it.

"I promise. Scouts honour," Grey said, very appreciative of the gesture, though he hugged her back loosely, aware that this was done from friendship.

Daisy pulled away from him and said, "I'll see you around, I guess."

"If all goes well sooner rather than later. Auf Wiedersehen, Daisy."

"Auf Wiedersehen, James," Daisy said, taking her leave.

Grey watched her walk away and took a deep draw from his cigarette and thought of what could have been. Daisy Lovell was one of a short line of girls with whom he had formed fledgling relationships that never got out of first gear. Out of neutral, if he was being honest. Daisy was nicer than most though, which made the fact that they never took off harder. He'd tried his best, but after four dates she kept postponing the fifth before finally telling him she had accepted a date with another. She was upfront and kind in how she told him and he took the news well superficially. He couldn't blame her – having one foot in the real world and the other in the spirit world often meant that he straddled neither successfully.

Uncle Frank was a gregarious figure, as different from his brother as it was possible to be, and he hugged Grey as he opened the door to him. Frank's son, Fred, was with him, though at 14 he was disinclined to hug anyone and Grey recognised this and shook his hand.

"Is it all right if I park out front? I know that's where you normally have your pickup," Frank said, ready to move if required.

"It's gone."

"I thought you loved that vehicle," Frank said, taking a seat in the lounge.

"I still do. I've lent it to a colleague. I won't need it for a while. I was planning on visiting you two before I heard you were coming," Grey said, sitting down with them as Shirley put the kettle on. "At least this way you've had the day off school, Fred."

"You had the right idea getting out," Fred said, academically challenged and completely disinterested in study.

"James might be going back, Fred," Shirley said from the kitchen.

"Maybe," Grey said while mouthing 'No way' before shaking his head vigorously, amusing his guests. "You've made it here in good time. Was the traffic quiet?"

"There wasn't much on the road at all. Fred twists if I don't put my foot on the gas."

"I remember when I've took you out in the pickup you always wanted to test the top speed. When you get behind the wheel you're going to be a regular speed demon," Grey said, knowing this as fact as he had once let Fred drive the pickup on a quiet road and he had quickly spun it out of control. Frank also occasionally let his son drive when they went out of town on wasteland and Fred always chose speed over caution. His ex-wife would go mad if she knew this but Frank indulged him and knew what a difficult age Fred was at, still a boy but desperate to become a man. The war made it harder as Fred wanted to fight and had to wait his turn while seeing his peers leave. With Frank owning and living in a pub with Fred staying with him except for alternate weekends, it would have been easy for Fred to start drinking sneakily and Frank chose to let his son start drinking at 13, though this was something else that had to be kept secret from Sheila.

"I'll have to get a fast car first. I've seen tractors quicker than your two's wheels," Fred joked.

"Go and see if your aunt wants any help."

"You should pay penance for that one. The pickups sacred," Grey said.

"I could probably walk quicker," Fred said as he walked through to the kitchen.

"Insolent, isn't he?" Frank said with a smile and he sat forward in his chair to be closer to Grey and said quietly, "He mentioned about your leaving to his mother and she's decided to come."

"Okay. I'm not too sure where she can stay," Grey said. With Fred sharing his room and Frank sleeping on the sofa there was nowhere else available in the small terraced house.

"She's heading back home after. The rat's driving her but he's not coming to the meal. I'll try and control myself because I don't want to ruin your send-off," Frank said, still bitter two years after his acrimonious divorce. They had both been unhappy for a while but he still found her adultery unforgivable.

"Don't worry about me, but I think you should keep a level head for Fred, 'cause he's stuck in the middle."

"I'll try my best. It's the Grey curse, a hot temper. You seem to have escaped it, James – Fred hasn't."

Grey shrugged. "I guess going over there I'll find out what I'm made of."

"You'll do grand, we all know that. Even Sheila, who's coming because she does care about you. What are you thinking, lending your pickup out? Never lend anything of that magnitude unless to family or close friends."

"He needed it. I trust him."

"I hope this war doesn't turn you into a bitter old cynic like me and your father."

"It won't turn me old. Everything else is up in the air, unpredictable, and that's how I like it."

Frank drove his son and his brother's family to Joe's where they met up with Shirley's sister, Dolores Howard, and her husband, Skip, and their two daughters, 19 year old, Geraldine, and 17 year old Phyllis. Geraldine was married and still lived at home as her husband had gone to fight. Even though the Howard's lived in Keokuk they were not especially close to the Greys and only met at holidays or special occasions like this one. Grey sat next to Geraldine and Fred and he asked her about Brian and she quickly fled the table in tears.

"Did I say something wrong?" Grey said, looking to the Howards.

"She's a complete crybaby. Ignore her, we're all bored of it," Phyllis said.

Dolores stood up to go and see to her daughter and said to Grey before she left, "You haven't said anything wrong. She's just a bit sensitive about Brian. It's their three month anniversary today."

"That's not a proper anniversary, Mother," Phyllis said, earning a black look from her mother before she went to console her daughter in the toilets, closely followed by Shirley.

"Any tips for how I could make the marines?" Fred asked Grey.

"I'm the wrong person to ask. I didn't make the grade. Work on your fitness and don't appear too desperate. That's where I'd say I went wrong."

"Are you trying to get out there too, son?" Skip Howard asked Fred.

"None of them want to stay," Frank said. "He's only 14, so he's got a while to wait yet."

"Let's hope the war's over by then," Abner said.

"It will be. I guarantee it," Grey said with bravado.

"I'm holding you to that," Frank said.

"That gives me a deadline of July '46. Easy," Grey said.

"How about by the time I'm 18?" Phyllis said.

"Three months? I might still be in training then. I can't promise that one."

Sheila Bockwinkel snuck up behind Grey and tapped him on the shoulder and said, "Surprise!"

"You're going to have to be more alert than that in the field," Skip said amusedly.

"Aunt Sheila's a bit less dangerous than snipers," Grey said, accepting a gift-wrapped present from her gratefully.

"I wouldn't say that," Frank said under his breath to Abner who sat beside him.

"You shouldn't have," Grey said.

"Nonsense," Sheila said, kissing Fred's cheek as she looked at the abundance of spare seats and she asked, "Do I have a free choice of seat?"

"This is your seat here, Ma," Fred said, pointing to the seat next to him.

"Just open it later, James. It's nothing flash. It's just some thermal socks, which I know is a present most young men would rather not receive, but I hear that soldiers in the field find these very useful," Sheila said. "Did Fred go to school this morning, Frank?"

"This took priority," Frank said.

"I thought we agreed that he'd go in the morning…never mind. So where are Shirley and the other girls?" Sheila said, looking around the table.

"Geraldine's husband has gone to war recently and I put my foot in it," Grey said.

"He just asked how he was. She's pathetic," Phyllis said.

"That's enough, Phyll," Skip said sternly.

"Have you ordered yet?" Sheila asked.

"Just. I'll call the waiter over for you," Fred offered. Sheila finished giving her order as the ladies emerged with Geraldine visibly puffy-eyed.

"I'm sorry," Grey said. "We don't have to talk about anything like that all night."

"I'm sorry. I'm very emotional lately. Three of his friends died last week. I don't want to ruin your night so I'm going to go home…" Geraldine said.

"No, there's no need," Grey said.

"I need to. Good luck, James," Geraldine said, reaching down and hugging him before he had a chance to stand up.

"Do you mind driving her?" Dolores asked Skip.

"Ask them to keep my steak warm. I shouldn't be long," Skip said, leaving with his daughter as Shirley and Dolores took their places.

"These are hard times for everyone," Sheila observed sadly.

"She takes everything to heart," Dolores said. "She's very sensitive."

"So is James," Shirley said.

"Mom, I'm trying to project a tough soldier image – that doesn't help," Grey said.

"Well this won't either, because I know you don't mind if I move from next to you, Frank, to sit next to my son and sister," Shirley said.

"If you want to play musical chairs, Shirley, I'm not going to stop you," Frank replied.

"Remember that he can feed himself," Abner said to his wife.

"They don't always hit their mouths though, do they, Shirley?" Sheila said. "Make sure you get a portrait taken in uniform, James. I like to see a man in uniform..."

"There's a shock," Frank said slyly.

Sheila heard her husband's dig and chose to ignore it, adding, "You'll look very smart, James."

"I haven't got my uniform yet," Grey said.

"When you get leave have a picture taken and make sure I get a copy," Sheila said.

"They don't get much leave nowadays, but I'll have one too," Dolores said.

"Okay, both my aunts are embarrassing me so anyone want another drink?" Grey asked.

"Keep your hand in your pocket, James, you're paying for nothing tonight," Frank said. Despite an undercurrent that existed between Frank and Sheila, the evening went well with Skip returning after half an hour. Towards the end of the evening Grey asked another innocuous question which caused a flashpoint as he asked Sheila how another of her nephews was finding the navy.

"He likes it. He's actually got leave coming up and he hasn't been there long so you'll probably be back with us again soon too. I don't think I told you that, did I, Frank. I didn't think you'd be interested seems as you didn't attend his farewell," Sheila said pointedly.

"I saw him and wished him well. There was no way I was spending an evening with your lover," Frank replied fierily.

"This isn't the place for this," Sheila said sourly.

"Agreed, so don't bring up things like that. Where is the rat at the moment then?"

"I have no idea who you mean."

"I think you do. Everybody else at the table knows."

"I think it's absolutely sick, how you try and paint me as the harlot in public, in front of our son."

"I never said anything about you, just the rat. I don't badmouth you in front of Fred," Frank said vehemently, believing this to be true as he tried not to though sometimes fell short.

Shirley was embarrassed at the scene and tried to change the subject, asking Phyllis, "So how's Butch?" Butch was the family dog, a golden retriever, and while Shirley was able to revive healthy conversation, the atmosphere was toxic and the night quickly ended. Sheila said her goodbyes at the restaurant, as did the Howards and when the Greys arrived home Abner and Shirley went straight to bed, as did Fred, depressed at the incident between his parents.

"Sorry, James," Frank said as they sat in the lounge, drinking a bottle of whisky between them. "I tried to bite my tongue."

"I'm just glad you all came. Who knows, by the time I'm back you two might have ceased all hostilities too."

"Not by '46. Fred's disappointed."

"That might be because you wouldn't let him drink. Fred's a tough customer. I don't think anything fazes him. I'm damned jealous."

"You'll be okay. I know Abner plays it cool, but he will miss you."

"Yeah, that impression comes over real strong," Grey said sarcastically. Withdrawing the comment he said, "It hasn't always been easy between us, but I know he cares. And obviously my mom will struggle."

"Make sure you write to her regularly."

"I reckon a lynch mob will come after me if I don't! I'm not good at letters though, Frank, so if I don't..."

"Don't worry about me. I'll find out how you're doing from your parents. You're welcome to write me but I understand you'll be busy."

"And then some. I meant what I said about the deadline. I don't want Fred to have to fight and I want it over before then anyway. There's death camps, there's horrific slaughter on the Russian front – it's got to end fast. At one point I even relished the situation with the Russians. I figured if Hitler and Stalin could slaughter each other that would be the perfect outcome but the genocide going on there quickly changed my mind. I'm rambling, aren't I? I'll let you get to bed, Frank."

"You're welcome to stop up. When I get tired I'll just pull the blanket over me but you can stop up in your own house."

"I'd best get some rest. Night, Frank," Grey said, deciding it was best he went to bed before he ended up saying too much as Frank made the perfect confidant, his sympathetic ear well trained from 23 years working in public houses. Fred was still awake when Grey went to bed and Grey said, "I told you I didn't mind if you had my bed. I don't mind the cot."

"I've got three years left in a comfortable bed. You haven't."

Grey could hear in Fred's voice that he had been crying. Grey felt it was best that he pretend he wasn't aware of this and instead he tried to cheer him up with nonsense of how within the next year he'd be sleeping in Hitler's comfortable bed after defeating him single-handedly.

Grey felt like crying himself when he awoke on Sunday morning. He had wanted to go out with his friends on his penultimate Saturday but they insisted it had to be the Saturday before he left and now he regretted it. It was all right for them – they didn't have hangovers and spirits to contend with simultaneously. He was prone to headaches at the best of times and this was not the best of times. There had only been a small group of them. Hodge and Gordon were there, the only school friends he kept in regular touch with, both still enrolled which made sense as they were both brighter than he was. Hodge was pretty much his best mate and was a straight A student destined for college unless the war got in the way. He met up with most of his baseball team late in the night, when his memories started to get hazy, though Felix Haines from the team was there all night. Dick Pike showed up too but he wasn't there all night, saying his goodbyes when he bumped into some of his mates.

Grey remembered there had been an altercation between a joker from his school who dropped out before he did, and Felix. Prichard had called him a loony, dating back to the 7th grade when Grey started going into regular trances, and made cracks about the army taking any old shit. Grey had handled it to his own satisfaction, telling Prichard to sign up quickly before the quality control improved, or something like that, only Felix preferred to handle it by decking Prichard. Felix was training to be a G-man and was already handy with his fists, which Grey always said would serve him well with his shady employers, joking though Felix hoped he could be heavy-handed in his work.

A bad memory struck Grey. His ex, Susan Hicks, had come into the pub with her new beau and Grey's friends had shouted at her to give him a goodbye kiss. She had too, a peck on his cheek (which was pretty much all he got out of her when they were dating), though this seemed under duress and Grey recalled fragments of arguments which he was not involved in. Susan was prettier than Daisy, though not as nice, and had seemed to appreciate that Grey had wheels and could drive her around (though she looked down on his pickup and when Grey had playfully told her not to slag off the wheels she gave him the silent treatment for a whole evening) rather than enjoying his company. He couldn't blame her for that...His friends all had her pegged as a user (Grey talked little of her with his parents and they never met), and Grey suspected as much himself from early on but the girl was stunning, which distracted him from any flaws. Grey didn't consider himself ugly; he was a decent enough height (6ft plus on tiptoes, 5'10 naturally), solidly built through his training with light brown hair and eyes on a youthful face that somehow didn't show the ravages of stress, but he was not in Sue's league. Ideally he needed to look better than he did to overcome the medium deficit – when it came to qualities girls looked for in their ideal partner, spiritualist abilities didn't top any polls Still, he'd scrub up well in his army uniform. They'd be like bees around honey then. And in the real world...

Grey forced himself to get up so as not to disappoint one woman who did care about him. If they'd gone out drinking last week he could have skipped church for one week. With this being his last service he had to attend and hope that no one noticed how hungover he was.

Shirley Grey looked down at her husband as he remained stationary, ignoring all of the hints she had given him over the last few days. Time was now running out and she realised he wasn't going to pleasantly surprise her and spring to his feet and shave and dress for church. The Sunday newspapers seemed more important and had his rapt attention.

"Are you sure you're not going to come, Abner?" she asked meekly.

Abner didn't bother to look at her, replying sternly, "I go to weddings, funerals and christenings. You know that."

"You go to the Christmas service too. This is another special occasion." She knew that, as this was James' last Sunday before he departed, Reverend West would mention him and she wanted to present a united front.

Abner grunted and Shirley gave up and put her coat on. "Lunch might be a little late," she said.

No response. She explained, "People will want to wish James well."

"You could still come straight home. He's old enough to make his way home alone."

Grey came downstairs and caught this last fragment of the conversation. He had tried once to change his father's treatment of his mother, a redundant gesture which she chastised him for and which earned him a good hiding from his father and he had long ago given up and no longer got involved. It was hard sometimes when his father was especially cutting with her but he would do his best to cheer her up and praise her to counteract the criticism. He was dressed in his Sunday best – he always made an effort with his appearance for church and knew this was especially important today. Reverend West had forewarned him that he would be making him the centre of attention, a role he did not covet by any means but he understood that he meant well and would play along.

"I'm going out for lunch so you don't need to wait for me, Mom," Grey said.

"Are you? I didn't know that," Shirley said, disappointed that she could not cook one last Sunday roast for him in case…

"There's still a few folk I haven't said goodbye to and I know where I can find them Sunday lunchtime," Grey improvised, simply because he wanted to stay out for a while.

"He goes Monday," Shirley said to those around her in the congregation as they waited for the service to begin.

"Get some of them for me!" Mr Wilkins said jovially, nudging him.

"Any particular number?" Grey said.

"A hundred will do."

"Be careful, James," Mrs Simpson said softly. He knew her advice came from the heart, from her personal experience when she was widowed in the previous global conflict.

"He's a sensible boy. He'll be all right," Mr Wilkins said, stating this as fact, succour for the frail women around him who would worry way too much about him.

"I'll be back before you even notice I've left," Grey said.

"You'll have chance to not even get over there. It won't be long now," Mr Wilkins said earnestly.

"I hope you're right," Shirley said. The conversation petered out as Reverend West took to the pulpit and proceeded to embarrass Grey for the length of the service, making him stand at the front throughout and compelling him to say a few words. It was a favourable audience, at least, though it was still unwelcome. He'd expected to be mentioned in the service, not be the service. He had nothing prepared to say to them and felt his brain turn to mush under their kind-eyed scrutiny. He held his hat in his hand, fiddling with it as he started,

"Right. Speeches aren't my strong point so I'll make this brief. I know a lot of you have relatives who are already serving, who somehow managed to avoid being ambushed like I have here," he joked, raising a titter. "Err, what am I trying to say, Reverend?"

"I don't know, it's your speech, James."

"Thanks a lot. I do mean that actually, I want to thank everybody here for making me feel a part of this community and for your support and good wishes. I'm not going off to do anything special. It's just something that needs to be done. I'll miss Keokuk – the baseball mainly. It's not forever though. It won't be long. I have it on good authority we're in the home stretch," he said, looking to Mr Wilkins. "Can I sit down now?"

Reverend West nodded and finished off the service. Afterwards Grey was bombarded with well-wishers, with Shirley remaining by his side proudly. While she still wished Abner was there, Grey was pleased he was not, aware that he would have given his hapless speech a harsh critique – he was internally cringing enough without somebody picking holes in it, though his audience had responded well to it, as choreographed to by Reverend West. After umpteen kisses, hugs and handshakes Grey was left in the church with his mother and the vicar, who asked for a private word. Shirley waited outside and before the reverend began, Grey said, making it clear in his tone of voice that he was jesting, "You could have shown some charity and given a drowning man some rope!"

"They wanted to hear your words. I know you don't like to be the centre of attention and I wanted to show you that you could handle it. You're stronger than you give yourself credit for."

"That's a whole year of solid training."

"Don't be facetious," Reverend West said, scolding him lightly. "Today was about you and it was about your mother too. She's very proud of you. Continue to make her proud."

"I'll do my best."

"I probably shouldn't have said that about being ambushed – though I was. He warned me he'd bring it up, but he didn't warn me he'd bring me up to the spotlight," Grey said to his mother as he walked her home.

"You handled it well, James, much better than I would."

"Come on. You're the one who treads the boards."

"Small roles in amateur dramatic plays isn't treading the boards," Shirley said modestly.

"It's more than I'd be able to do, and you are good at it."

"I haven't done a play for five years now."

"Is that how long it's been? That's something you can write me about then, your next project."

"No, I don't think…"

"You'll have more time now you don't have to wash fungi out of my grubby overalls. You'll only be cooking for two, you can cordon off my room – you'll have loads more time on your hands now you don't have to take care of me," Grey said, trying to motivate her to resume her hobby, which he knew she adored.

After walking his mother home Grey changed out of his Sunday best and went for a long run, one last look at all of the familiar streets. Even though being a medium gave a slight advantage to him, his survival prospects were still uncertain and he accepted that he might never be fortunate enough to return here. While deep in thought, and counselling a spirit at the same time, Grey almost got knocked down by a truck. The driver pipped his horn and Grey raised his hand in apology and carried on running. To be squashed flat on the eve of joining the Army in the biggest military campaign ever – that was the sort of ironic thing that would happen to him. He had to heed the lesson – stay alert.

Late at night Abner deigned to have a private word with his son, commanding Shirley to leave them alone.

"The moment is upon us. I truly believed the war would end before you came of age. I'm disappointed that they let it drag on so long," Abner said.

"They let him get too strong. If they'd acted when I wanted them to it wouldn't have come to this," Grey said.

"That's right, you always had Hitler's number. I didn't pay your views much credence. It's hard to respect a child's views on world politics, though your views have been proven correct and most of our esteemed leaders have been made to look like fools. You're a man now, son, and you can now fight for your beliefs."

"At long last. It's been a long time coming."

"Make sure you write regularly. It'll mean a lot to your mother."

"I will. I know we haven't always got on but I'll miss you too, Dad."

"Hmm. We'll miss you," Abner said awkwardly. "This'll be good for you. It'll be the making of you. When you do return, this will still be your home, though I will still expect you to follow my rules."

Grey internally sighed. Why give a lecture now? "Of course."

Abner shook his hand and bade him goodnight. Grey struggled to sleep that night, finally dropping off half an hour before his alarm rang. A neighbour was kindly driving him to the Training Centre, and after his daily ablutions Grey said goodbye to his parents, hugging his emotional mother and shaking his father's hand. They waved him off as the car drove away.

As the car turned the corner and Grey looked to the front again, his neighbour, Ted, said, "I bet that was hard."

"I've been waiting a year, Ted. That was hard. Bring on the Nazis. I couldn't be more ready."

CHAPTER 2 – READY, WILLING & ABLE?

James Grey's background in amateur athletics provided some preparation for his induction into the army as he experienced the highs and lows that his Replacement Training Centre had to offer, initially mainly highs as he wanted this more than he had wanted anything in his short life. The physical training was very strenuous and the camp instructors were very tough with them, the slightest error or wrong word producing a barrage of abuse and extra press-ups for all of the recruits from the captious drill instructors. The group quickly bonded under these conditions and after a few weeks the instructors remained demanding but were not so critical, starting to show traces of a human side.

Unlike many other raw recruits who trained alongside him, Grey did not show any particular aptitude in specific areas that could have led to him being used in specialised military work. He seemed bright and alert, but not especially intelligent. He was physically capable and active and proved himself to be an exceptional endurance runner. He had no mechanical experience, no combat experience and he expressed no desire to learn a particular trade in the army, preferring to be a private in the infantry to anything else and his superiors granted his wish. His keenness in everything he did was his main attribute, something his instructors said privately. He was calm and obedient and did not seem the type to buckle under pressure. They had faith in this recruit.

Grey trained alongside Iowans and other Midwesterners, and he was glad that two dozen men started divisional training at the same time as him so that he was not the only new boy. The older soldiers made them welcome and Grey felt at ease, making friends with the others easily for he was very sociable. He wasn't a joker like many of the others, his closest friend, Mick Downey, constantly making the others crack up, but he was talkative and cheerful with a profound interest in those around him and what they had to say. He was the only one who would sit and talk at length with Chris Crowe, considered by many to be the most tedious man they'd ever met, his monotonous voice making anything sound boring, yet Grey seemed to enjoy their chats.

Crowe was unpopular, but he was not hated or ostracised by his fellow soldiers. Grey was the first to earn that distinction. Crowe was boring but dependable and that was considered preferable to insanity. Grey had been with his unit a month, still based in Iowa, when the cracks started to show. The other soldiers noticed that he would go into trances. Over two days he went into seven extended trances, twice during field exercises. He was sent to the psychiatrist and Grey managed to convince him that he was sane and he had just been a little distracted by personal matters and he promised that it wouldn't happen again. He saw that his friends were now wary of him and he promised them too that it wouldn't recur.

Damned spirits. Grey's problem came down to the serious issue of whether being a soldier and being a medium were incompatible. He had believed otherwise, and now he questioned himself again as his gift threatened to stop him from serving his country. He could ignore Terry and Katarzyna and concentrate on his duties and try and socialise with his friends again, if he had any left. That option wasn't even a possibility – even though his own dream was jeopardised he couldn't turn his back on these two poor souls in need. He'd spent more than half of his life juggling both lives – why was it proving so hard now, when he wasn't even in combat yet?

The following week, midway through a conversation in the barracks, Grey stopped speaking and looked into space as he consoled Katarzyna again, trying to reassure her that her daughter would survive as troops were coming to liberate the camp. All eyes fell on him and he tried to perform as if nothing was wrong, talking to them, but distantly.

"What the fuck is the matter with you?" Downey said aggressively, angry with himself for having associated so closely with this freak.

"Nothing. I don't get why you're all staring at me."

"We're staring at you 'cause your head's in the clouds again." His act was convincing no one. It was obvious that he had zoned out again, even if it was only briefly this time.

"I'm just thinking of you lot. You must get sick of hearing my voice so sometimes I think about what's to come. We're going to war, that's..."

One of the more outspoken soldiers, Carter, said, "We're going to war. I'm not so sure you'll be coming with us. You need to see the psychiatrist again."

"You're overreacting."

"You are going to be a liability in combat. I don't want you watching my back 'cause you can't even see what's in front of you half the time," Carter said forcefully and he turned from him and talked to the others, intentionally freezing Grey out from future conversations. Some had felt that Carter's words were too harsh initially, but Grey zoned out three more times that day, convincing everyone that he did not belong in the unit. The more tolerant members of the unit might have kept patience with him if he had admitted he had a problem. Instead Grey made more of an effort to speak as he felt himself drifting off and it was obvious to everyone that he was tripping. He had to go.

Grey was adamant that he did not want to see any psychiatrists and he tried to rebuild friendships, to no avail. The other soldiers had all agreed that he was to be ignored until he requested to see a doctor – something that Grey would never do. Eventually they told their commanding officers everything and Grey found himself kicked out of his unit and in danger of being kicked out of the army. He had to run the gauntlet of four psychiatrists, each seeming to assume him mad until he proved he was sane. He was calm and composed and almost able to provide a satisfactory explanation for his catatonia. He stressed the normality of his life up until he enlisted – a simple existence in a quiet city, which he called the safest place in America. He suggested that his anticipation at what was to come, coupled with rumours of torturous atrocities inflicted on soldiers, had made him too pensive. He claimed to meditate regularly and said that in future he would confine meditating until he was alone or just before he went to bed. He convinced three of the four psychiatrists that he was mentally stable enough to remain a soldier, though he was told that he would be monitored and was given leave for two weeks.

Grey chose not to go home, instead finding cheap lodgings, and he filled the long days by wandering the streets and sitting in his room with plenty of time for 'meditation'. He had been counting down the days to his eighteenth birthday; such was his desperation to join the army and fight, and now, six weeks later, things were not as he had planned. To be almost drummed out of the army so quickly, after doing nothing to make a difference in the war, made him feel nauseous, completely worthless and very apprehensive as to how his new posting would turn out. He felt such shame at what had happened that he could not face his parents, especially as he suspected that they would agree with the general consensus of opinion about him. He talked to very few people during the fortnight as he tried to get his own head in order. He walked down the street, just another Joe, seemingly as normal as the next man, as he tried to prove to himself that he could fit in. He needed this too badly, close to being a broken man at 18 years old just at the threat of this being taken away from him. Maybe there was something wrong with him to be so obsessed with fighting in this war; even as a boy he had never dreamed of being a soldier and now it was his sole focus, something from which he doubted he'd derive pleasure, more of an imperative duty. If the war ended tomorrow and he never had to fight, then that was great and he'd have no regrets and he could try and work out what to do with his life; he could make his gardening job a profession for life, possibly travel, something he'd always wanted to do. As he knew the war had years left, all he could concentrate on was that. If they didn't let him fight he was going to find his own way over there…

During Grey's two weeks holiday a place had been found for him and he was sent on his way to join the rest of his company. Grey was surprised to learn that he was joining a company comprised mainly of New Yorkers and other Easterners, but he understood why his superiors had come to this decision. His name was mud in his old platoon and that bad reputation would spread and that was why he was sent far away. Word could reach his new company eventually – hopefully by then they would know him and believe him to be sane.

Grey travelled across the country to his new RTC in Pennsylvania, taking a deep breath before entering the grounds. Take two – there would be no third chance to get it right, he had to be a flawless soldier from this point on. Grey's paperwork was scrutinised by an officer at the gates before he was ushered inside and marched to an office in the main building where he was ordered to remain at attention until his captain was ready to see him. Grey waited in the empty room for over an hour before anyone joined him, two other men ordered in and made to stand at attention also within ten minutes of each other. While remaining at attention Grey talked to them and found out they were called Hobbs and Hill, and like him they were being transferred into the unit. In both cases Grey could imagine why they were being transferred, both seemingly easy targets for bullying and Grey wondered if things would be different in their new unit for any of them. Whatever happened, even if they couldn't integrate successfully into the new group, hopefully he could make friends with these two men at least. Even that didn't matter – all that mattered was that this time Grey managed to see active service.

Captain Walker entered shortly after; Grey heard him approach and instantly fell silent while Hill kept talking despite Grey signalling him to be quiet. Walker didn't reprimand them for talking, and looked at them each in turn fleetingly before he sat down at his desk and asked them who was who as he read notes on each of them. He made it plain to them immediately that his time was a precious commodity without raising his voice, telling Hill to cut to the chase when he launched into an anecdote when he had only asked for his name.

After Walker had reread their files he looked at them and said, "I haven't got time to talk to you one on one today. All I want to know is do you want to be here? If you're just here because they made you come then the door is behind you."

Grey was first to answer, saying, "I want to be a soldier and fight for our country as soon as possible, sir. The place I'd ideally like to be is Germany or Japan now, fighting them, but I know I need to finish my training first and go wherever the army sends me. I want to be here," Grey said compellingly.

Hill and Hobbs' answers were briefer, also stressing that they wanted to remain in the army. After getting kitted out again with clothes and equipment (which made a huge difference to Grey, who felt like a soldier again in the military garb) they joined their fellow recruits who were enjoying a rare break in their barracks. The barracks already had around two dozen men inside lying on bunks and playing cards and the new arrivals did not go unnoticed. They were invited to play cards and introductions were made, Grey being the spokesman for them all.

A gregarious figure came across, extending his hand to each of them and said, "The name's Fallon. Any of you fellas want to lay a bet anytime, my office is always open, my odds always good, all bets considered."

"Does that include Keokuk baseball games?" Grey asked.

"I cover some minor leagues, but that's taking the piss. Any real bets, you know where to find me."

Most of the troops were friendly, but not all. Dwight Hill was having more difficulty than most in adapting to being a soldier. He lacked basic common sense and was naturally clumsy, his gangly frame lacking co-ordination, which had not proved a big problem in his life up to now, but now appeared problematic to the officers. Hill himself did not think he had a problem, but this was a minority view and his natural, slack-jawed expression gave the other soldiers the measure of him as he entered and made him an immediate target of derision. He had short ginger hair (naturally curly though this was not so noticeable with his hair cropped), wide staring eyes with a long nose and protruding teeth and all of these features were commented on by a soldier lazing on a top bunk, glaring across at him. Hill did not verbally respond and instead blankly stared at him which made the insults worse and made others laugh at him and his bully began to turn threatening as Hill did not know when to look away.

"Quit staring at me, freak, or you'll be picking your teeth up off the floor," his tormentor said aggressively and he jumped from his bunk and squared up to an uncertain Hill, ready to lay into him. He gave height away to Hill, but he was wider and, he warranted, tougher.

Grey interceded, unwilling to see Hill beaten up unfairly by this belligerent thug. He walked to them before any blows had been exchanged and offered his hand to the bully to shake.

"I'm Grey and he's Hill," he said. "We're all in the same unit now and we're going to have to work together so let's not get off on the wrong foot, pal." He spoke amicably, not blaming the other man, simply trying to diffuse the situation and make things harmonious. They were not at war yet and he did not want them to battle amongst themselves.

"Fuck you!" the other man said aggressively in Grey's face. "You're in our unit," he said, emphasising 'our' possessively, letting them know that they were not accepted yet, if they ever would be. "If any of you are in my squad you'll be fucking regretting it."

"Ease up, Ray," another man said. He had been laughing at his pal's jokes as he had been funny at first, before he had lapsed into dudgeon and created an unpleasant atmosphere.

"Fucking pair of asses," Ray said, climbing back onto his bunk and Grey walked away, as did Dwight Hill, finding bunks for themselves, which they put their bulging kit bags on. The bully's behaviour had aggrieved him, but it was insufficient to fight over and he felt he had done the honourable thing by walking away. If he persisted he felt he could be provoked into acting differently. As Grey sorted through his bag, a low, deep voice from the bunk next to his said,

"That's Ray Pearce. He's always that welcoming." Grey saw that the man who said this to him had much darker skin than the rest of the platoon, potentially making him an outsider too, and he sat on his bunk facing him to address this.

"We're new. You have to expect it," Grey said tolerantly whilst implying subtly with a grimace that he would not always accept being talked to in such a manner or stand and let others be talked to like that.

"I'm Mexican. I always expect it," his neighbour said, sitting up to talk to him. He had seen Grey offer his hand to Pearce and he offered his hand to Grey, which he accepted at once, and they shook hands, consciously firmly in greeting. "Isdel Delgado. What's your full name?" He was a tall man, a very dark Mexican-American with a broad nose and large face with his hair cut much shorter than he liked.

"James Grey. Where are you from, Isdel?" Grey said. "You don't sound like you're from these parts."

"Phoenix, which is where I should be now. I wouldn't mind fighting this war, if it wasn't for the lousy timing. I was in my final year at medical school when I got the draft and that place won't be waiting for me when I get back," he grumbled.

"That's a tough break," Grey said sympathetically. "They should let you resume."

"They won't," Delgado said cynically, certain of this, "You're not local either. Where are you from?"

"Iowa. I'm just from plain old Keokuk and now I'm here," Grey said, looking around the quarters, expressing a wonder that he did not fully feel at the transition in his life. He was excited, that much was true, but he indicated that he had led a narrow, sheltered and uneventful existence up to now, which was not exactly true, his supernatural experiences adding another dimension to his life. It was not a conscious untruth. He saw Delgado seemed to want to talk to him and he asked more about him. "If you were in your final year you must be about 21?"

"23, pal, it takes longer than that. You're probably 18," Delgado said.

"Good guess. I wasn't at college or in a dream job – I liked my job but I like this one more – so for me coming here hasn't meant any disruption, so it's easier for me. I know the colleges sure aren't easy to get into," he said, praising Delgado.

"You're right there. By studying all of the hours I could as well as working nights, I kept on top of it," Delgado said. "Even if they do let me resume I reckon I'll have to take my last year again just to re-educate myself."

"It wasn't that long ago I left school and all of the stuff you learned goes real quick, doesn't it? If you've got any books with you I wouldn't mind helping you study. Gives me something to do to keep myself out of trouble."

"I've got a couple, but I'll wait until my knowledge starts to fade. These conditions aren't the best to concentrate in anyway." Delgado knew his return was no foregone conclusion, which made it hard for him to find the motivation to study. Instead he talked with this refreshingly friendly (though Delgado sensed his friendliness could ultimately become excessive) newcomer, telling him of his parents and how they had worked long hours in demeaning jobs, scrimping and saving for him to get him through college. He had wanted to support them when he got his degree and now he felt he might never get the chance and it grieved him. Something about Grey's kind eyes and agreeable demeanour made Delgado tell him all of this so quickly and Grey listened attentively, maintaining eye contact. Grey said the right things back to him, telling him that he was certain he'd get the chance to treat them as they deserved. He had noted the reverence with which Delgado had talked of his parents and he encouraged him to talk more of them as he was receptive and he could tell it would be beneficial to Delgado. Delgado had some friends in the platoon, but they deliberately kept a certain distance, preferring him as a minor friend rather than as their best buddy. Grey did not have this prejudice and talked to Delgado of his own parents, who were also both hard workers, though not the solid grafters that Delgado's parents were, the Delgados' solid slog rewarded with a pittance of a wage.

Bearing in mind what Delgado was studying, Grey said, "Did you think about joining the medical corps?"

"Yes," Delgado blasted, the matter a contentious issue.

"At least it's a free holiday," Grey said cheerfully. While he understood Delgado's resentment he did not want to look to the negative. Such an attitude before they had even left American shores was not conducive to victory. "I've always wanted to see the world."

"I guess that's one way of looking at it," Delgado said, forcing a smile. While he was a pessimistic soldier, he was not unremittingly negative and he did not want to bring this young, good-natured optimist down. "My mother's family are from Spain so I would love to go there just to send my parents a postcard. I can't see us going there, mind."

"No, I think it's occupied Europe or the Far East for us. Maybe you could take a detour on the way back to see relatives," Grey suggested.

"I've no relatives there now. My grandparents immigrated to America, but my mother would love to go there and see her parents' land and I'd like to do it for her."

"My father's grandparents came from Ireland so I might stand a slim chance of going to my forefathers' land but I can tell it would mean more to you to go to Spain so I hope that does happen," he said cordially.

"We don't get any choices, Grey," Delgado said. "From here on in we go where they say and do what they want." His frustration would not completely let up even when he tried. He heard how downbeat he sounded and he added with a little more optimism, "Going there's just a pipe dream. It probably won't happen, but we'll see. I doubt you'll be in luck with Ireland either. They're not exactly taking a stand, are they? The centre of Europe beckons us, my friend."

Delgado did not know how accurate his words were as Europe was indeed beckoning Grey constantly. The unofficial word was that their unit would be shipping out soon to try to reach Germany through a ground force invasion, a formidable task, but there was much ebullient confidence and bravado in the unit regarding this unconfirmed rumour.

"That's okay, there are places there I want to see. I hope we see Rome and the Colosseum and the Swiss Alps – that won't happen, will it?" Grey said, realising that, as a neutral country, they would not be going there.

"It might. The Alps aren't just in Switzerland, they're in Austria too. This is going to be your holiday of a lifetime, Grey," Delgado said with a queer grin as he lay back down on his bunk thinking how much this naïve soldier had to learn. Delgado was a rookie too, but he knew things of life and he felt that Grey's optimism would unfortunately perish in time, quicker than it should.

Grey only slept for around two hours that night, plagued by insomnia, as usual. A cold shower helped invigorate him, Grey feeling full of energy as his platoon were taken on a long morning run, Grey at the front with five others at the end (he felt he could have outpaced them and finished well ahead and opted not to as it wasn't a competition). His sergeant, Cloisters, seemed impressed by his display and Grey sought to impress with all aspects of his training, including the parts he found trickier, like target practice. At close range he was passable; when it came to long distance shooting he couldn't master looking through the sights and neither hand was steady enough. He had to improve quickly, Grey inferior to most of the other men in this regard, but willing it to happen wouldn't make it so and Grey tried to get as many hours of practice on the range as permitted.

The inability to shoot straight further than 10 metres was a major stumbling block to his goal, though he tried not to dwell on it as it was social problems that saw him drummed out of his last unit and Grey endeavoured to make sure that history did not repeat itself. His genuine interest in people and eagerness to make friends in his new unit saw him attempting to converse with everyone, with mixed results. He was too voluble for some, too damned keen to know everything about them, which sometimes came across like prying. His behaviour had little to do with what had happened in his past unit – while he made sure not to lapse into long silences, everything else was how he would always act, Grey keen to help others and the better he knew them the easier this was.

Grey found two potential good buddies, Isdel Delgado and Jake Baker, the only man in the platoon younger than Grey. Grey spent more time with Delgado then he did with Jake Baker as Baker had what Grey wanted, a tight knit circle of friends which he fraternized with. There was his easygoing elder brother Harvey, their close friend Frankie Fanelli and Harvey and Fanelli's pal Stephen

Macmurray whose presence had been responsible for Grey and Jake Baker's friendship. Jake Baker was a moralist and clashed with Macmurray who came from the same part of New York as the brothers and who Jake viewed as dissolute, an intemperate adulterer. Macmurray was irascible by nature and did not take criticism well, violent when challenged, especially concerning his marriage, and Harvey was stuck in the middle of this feud and often Jake would storm off from them which was how he and Grey started talking. As well as being obsessive baseball fanatics and amateur players, both were keen athletes and had competed to represent their state, neither exceeding this stage, Jake competing at 200m while Grey was a long distance runner, the 5000m being his best event. Baseball formed the staple of their conversation, with Grey talking at length to him enthusiastically on the topic with some ribbing, as they supported different teams, before Jake's brother came to take him back into the fold. Grey found he could relate easily to Jake Baker and appreciated his attempts to bring him into his group (unfortunately impossible as both Macmurray and Fanelli disliked him), but he was closer to Delgado. Although he dwelled on where he should have been, his heart was still on their mission and Grey knew he was committed and would not be a weak link. He was going to hear his grievances, but he suspected that if Delgado were offered a discharge, despite what he might say, he would not take it. Delgado fought in the barracks against Kowalski, a man goaded by Pearce to fight the 'spick' and Grey had intervened and took a punch to the face from an incensed Delgado (unintentionally, Delgado aiming for Kowalski when Grey came between them). Delgado apologised later but told him not to get in his way when the red mist descended on him. Grey would not promise that he would not intervene as he hated bullying (not that Delgado was the type to tolerate being bullied), and he reminded Delgado that it was fighting that got him kicked out of his last unit. Once he had calmed down he heeded his words and the strange squabble seemed to cement their friendship further, which was enduring as the bruising on Grey's ear subsided. Delgado was different to the rest of them, more educated yet assumed to be mentally inferior, and, crucially, he was not white. Grey seemed the quintessential American young male, as average as they come. He was not, but his differences were under the surface.

Cloisters eventually found time to talk to Grey, having deliberately waited a few days to give him time to observe him. Cloisters looked to be around 40 and had fair features and the strongest New York accent Grey had ever heard. Cloisters was gruff even when dealing with the men individually but he was not mean and while he asked personal questions, it was just to learn more of his troop and he had a crude wit which was cutting and used sparingly. Grey reached to shake his hand during his chat with him, a formality that Grey always observed, and Cloisters shook it and said, "So you got kicked out of your original unit?" This was not a criticism, merely an observation.

"That's correct, sir."

"So how do you think you're settling into this happy group?"

"Very well, Sarge. Coming in late, I admit I had a few apprehensions, but they seem a decent bunch and I already feel accepted as part of the unit," Grey said openly, feeling relaxed as he talked with him unlike some who were intimidated under his scrutiny, as it was clear he was examining them, his eyes fixed on his subject. Cloisters was quick to accept men who had been expelled from other units, glad to give fresh starts to those who needed them, but he liked to know why. Hill came across like a backwards yokel, Hobbs was effeminate, Delgado was Mexican and brawled when provoked (and bellyached way too much about where he'd rather be, as though he was the only person whose life had been interrupted) and in each instance Cloisters could recognise how they had come to be removed from their original units. Grey was different and he was different because he appeared so average; he was no deviant, minority or malcontent and he appeared perfectly sane. The truth was that he appeared to be one of the most obedient and respectful soldiers in the platoon and Cloisters saw that and, as such, responded positively to him. He saw him as a very amiable, obliging man who did step into the breach to try to keep the peace (before Cloisters interceded, far more effective at it with his bellowing and punishments for undisciplined behaviour) and Cloisters made fun of him about this. He told Grey that a good nickname for him would be nursemaid as he was always trying to cheer others up and be overly helpful.

"It wouldn't be the worst thing I've been called, though I think that name may be better suited to someone else," Grey said, smiling at the jest but not wishing to become a joke. "I'm just a private, sir. It's the sergeants who feed, clothe and provide us with somewhere to kip," he said, making out that Cloisters fulfilled the role of a nursemaid.

"Yeah, I'm your nursemaid 'cause I'm doing my job, but you're the squad's voluntary nursemaid, Grey, and I'm pleased that you are. I don't want you to stop doing what you're doing because you are helping some of them like Hill and the poor kid fucking needs it. You can stay as Grey till I come up with another idea," Cloisters said, giving him a reprieve, only ribbing him a little.

Grey had trouble sleeping again that night, with what felt like litres of sweat dripping off him, and he gave up trying in the early hours and pulled on his trousers and grabbed his smokes and headed for the door.

"Where the hell you going?" a voice said as Grey walked past the rows of beds.

"I can't sleep in this hothouse. I need some air."

"Grouser Grey. It's all adding up now," the voice said spitefully, condemning him, even though he didn't know him at all, Grey having no idea who the person was.

"Just go to sleep, bud. I'll come back once I've cooled down," Grey said disarmingly, not looking for an argument and keen not to make a bad impression on his new unit.

Grey smoked by the entrance to the barracks, no one around to notice him. He would go inside if anyone appeared, aware that at this stage in his army career he could be reprimanded and punished for anything, even the heinous crime of being unable to sleep. His insomnia had not been so bad over the past few days, and compared to other people's problems he knew it was completely insignificant, incomparable to Micky Quinlan's plight...

I'm still ablaze

You're not. You're holding on to the memory of the pain. It's not happening now, I swear.

You can't feel what I feel.

I know that there is no pain on this level, Grey said firmly for the benefit of Micky as he tried to calm him down.

When were you last shoved in a furnace?

What they did to you was despicable. I have no experience of suffering of that kind. My experience is with spirits, many of whom have suffered and none of them can feel pain or sensation of any kind.

I'm telling you that I can. I can still smell my smouldering flesh.

Sensations like smell aren't unheard of. I mean more the senses of touch, of feeling.

Logically I agree with you. A mind without a body shouldn't feel the body's pain, but I feel it, a white-hot searing pain.

Let's look at granting you peace quickly then, Micky, then it'll be gone, Grey said. This was a new development to him, the notion of pain on the spirit plane, and he hoped that Micky was mistaken and he tried to release his spirit when he found he had company, Stafford joining him on the step. Grey had had to learn years ago to conduct two conversations simultaneously, and despite all of his years of doing so he was still not adept at it. He couldn't do two things at once well; he couldn't read a book and listen to the radio, his attention focusing on whichever was more interesting, and it was the same here, Grey trying his best to make both conversations fluid and struggling.

"Are you trying to wangle a discharge too?" Stafford asked. Grey had got the measure of him quickly, Stafford the most hated man in the unit (for which Grey pitied him, understanding how that felt), Stafford a slacker looking to get out of the army.

"No," Grey said quickly and forcefully

"You sleep with that on?" Stafford said, looking at Grey's dog tags.

"The cross or the dog tags?"

"The dog tags."

"I never take them off. This way I can never lose them, because it's a certainty I would otherwise. I've wanted to wear the whole uniform, including the dog tags, for that long that I'd sleep in the whole get up if it wasn't such a sweat lodge through there."

"You will soon enough, in combat. Not me. I'm not going to go and get my head blown off. Any tips for how to get discharged? How did you get thrown out of your first unit?"

Grey grimaced at the question, a thorny topic to him, and he said, "I won't lie and say that it might not be as bad as you think over there. It's worse than we all expect, but someone has to go and fight. It's completely your choice whether you fight or not; I would recommend fighting, because either way you'll have battles to face. Fight this way and at least when the war's over so are your troubles. The other way – that's a lifelong stigma."

"I'm not bothered what people think of me."

"Fair enough. If you're absolutely certain then tell the sergeant you don't want to fight and I'm sure you won't have to," Grey said. Unlike the other men in the barracks Grey felt no revulsion at Stafford's stance and did not consider him a coward and gave him the best advice he could think of.

"I've tried that. Cloisters is a jerk. He says he's determined to make me toe the line."

"He's been okay with me."

"You follow the rules, that's why."

"He's going to come down on you hard if you challenge him – that's the norm in the army. It would be nice to be asked politely to go about our duties rather than being hollered at, but as soldiers being prepared for imminent combat I can understand that the rod of iron approach is necessary."

Stafford shook his head. "You think just like the rest of them."

"Maybe I do." Grey shrugged and said, "All I'm giving is my point of view. That doesn't mean I can't understand where you're coming from. I wasn't coerced into this – if anything it feels like people are conspiring to try and stop me from this, because of my age and…other stuff."

"What is this other stuff? That's the sort of information I could use."

"It won't help you. You're in the opposite position to me, being forced into doing something you don't want to do, so…persevere until you achieve your goal," Grey said, the words sticking in his craw somewhat as he endorsed Stafford's decision. To him Stafford's goal seemed the wrong choice and Grey felt Stafford was damaging his future irreparably, yet he still encouraged him to do his best to be discharged because that was Stafford's dream.

"I could be discharged tomorrow if I wanted. I want to know how to be discharged without consequences, without serving any time."

Grey wouldn't give him the advice that would help him here, as Grey considered nothing worse than being thought of as insane and could not recommend that Stafford pretended to be so, even though that tactic would almost definitely work.

"I won't wear my fucking dog collar in bed. You know why we wear the dog tags? If that doesn't persuade you that you should get out of this, then nothing will. Even they think our chances of coming home, or our bodies even being recognisable, are slim," Stafford grumbled.

"We won't realistically all survive. It's better for families to have their loved ones identified."

"Fuck our families. What about us?"

"A lot of wars are just territorial pissing contests. This isn't though, this is different…I'm sorry, I don't know your first name."

"They're never used here, that's why. Eric."

"Pleased to meet you, Eric," Grey said, shaking his hand. "My name's James Grey, if you don't already know."

"You're young, aren't you?"

"18. Jake Baker's the only one younger than me here, I think, at least in our platoon. Yourself?"

"24. You could get out of this easily. They don't normally send them so young. I wish I was in your position."

"I wanted to come and it's not like I could get on with my life while waiting to be drafted. The waiting's the worst part. We'll all feel better once we've done something, experienced combat for the first time."

"Apart from the ones who get blown to bits. It might be you."

"I try not to think about that."

"How can you not? You're just a kid and you're looking at this in a very childlike way. Don't run yourself ragged for Cloisters and the rest because at the end of the day you're a dime a dozen to all of them. This is going to be hell."

Grey nodded. "We've got no choice. We either fight or tolerate evil."

Stafford shook his head. "I always thought we weren't getting involved in this. That's what the politicians told us for years."

"They were wrong. I've thought that from the start. I wanted them to do something about Nazi Germany before the war," Grey said resolutely. Stafford realised he had misjudged Grey; he was more of a zealot and warmonger than the others, though at least, unlike them, he was not critical of him.

"The politics of this don't interest me, James. My priority is keeping my head on my shoulders. That no one else seems to feel the same way makes me wonder if I'm awash in a sea of madmen."

"All we can do is try our best to do the right thing."

"What does that mean?" Stafford said defensively.

"I'm not having a go. What the right thing is is different to everyone. Good luck, Eric," Grey said, heading back inside, his cigarette burnt away and Micky at peace, Grey feeling cooler now.

"We didn't think you'd be coming back." Grey recognised that voice as he walked back into the barracks. That was Pearce, pushing the right buttons, cowardice an accusation that Grey found hard to tolerate.

"Give it a rest. I wanted a smoke – it's hardly the crime of the century."

"You're new here and you follow our rules as well as theirs."

"I might be new, but I'm not a dog you can kick around. We can be friends, enemies, or strangers. I'd sooner try for friends but it's your choice."

"Watch your mouth, Grey. You talk to me like that again and I'll knock your teeth out."

"Will you two fight tomorrow and get this sorted and shut up so the rest of us can get to sleep," Macmurray said grumpily.

"I'll take that pissant on," Pearce said, up for the suggestion.

"This is my second unit. I can't afford to get into any more trouble so I'm not going to risk my place in the army over chickenshit like this. You must have too much time on your hands, Pearce, to be so interested in what I'm up to," Grey said, walking away from him back to his sweat drenched bed.

Grey didn't sleep at all and was first into the shower block and was finishing shaving as Pearce came in with two of his friends, Greene and Bradshaw, and Pearce threw a jug of water into Grey's face, saturating him.

Grey stared at him and said, unfazed, "I'm about to shower anyway in a minute so you've picked the worst time to do that if you wanted to make an impact. In a couple of months people will be trying to kill me in combat, so a jug of water being thrown in my face is nothing compared to that. Disrespectful, yes, but that's the kind of man you are. I don't want to feud with you but I can only extend the olive branch so many times. Anything else?"

"One thing," Pearce said smugly, looking at his two henchmen who grabbed an arm each, restraining Grey as Pearce produced a razor blade.

"What, you're washing and shaving me?" Grey said, feigning indifference, not even attempting to get free, pretending the situation did not daunt him remotely. "I'm kinda concerned you might want to help me shower."

"I've warned you about that mouth before!" Pearce said mercurially. He only intended to use the blade for show, to make Grey piss himself, and talk like that tempted him to make some superficial cuts.

Macmurray, Fanelli and the two Baker brothers entered the showers and broke up the scene. Macmurray pushed Pearce into a wall and confiscated his blade. "I told you two to fight to sort this out. Men use fists and fight one on one, Pearce," Macmurray said. While he was not Grey's biggest fan he took his side in this instance.

"You and your goons get out of here," Harvey said, kicking Greene in the backside as they slunk off. "You all right, Grey?"

"Yeah, he was bluffing."

"We'll be your witnesses if you report it," Jake said, to the displeasure of the other three.

"Nah, I don't want to do that. I appreciate the offer. Pearce is just jealous because all the best baseball teams come from my city, that's what I think it's about," Grey said to Jake.

"He must have whacked you on the head before we came in. You're delusional," Jake said.

"Don't report him, Grey – he'll think himself important and love the attention if you did and would turn it round with the others and make it bite you on the ass. If he does anything like that again tell us and we'll sort it…if you tell pretty much anyone out there they'll deal with him too. You might be the new guy but nobody would think that was acceptable," Harvey said. Grey appreciated the offer but knew he had to fight his own battles and when it came to Pearce he would have to try and raise his tolerance levels. He would have far more legitimate enemies to deal with soon enough.

"Mind if I join you, Eric?" Grey said, sitting down opposite Stafford with his lunch, out of breath from a vigorous morning's training where he had pushed himself very hard.

"Don't be stupid, James. Breaking bread with me will make you as popular with this lot as if you said you wanted to suck off Hitler," Stafford said, appreciative of the gesture. He didn't expect Grey to talk to him when others were around, and as most had sent him to Coventry weeks earlier he thought it best that Grey did not visibly associate with him, thinking of Grey's standing in the unit. Grey knew that talking to Stafford wasn't going to help him integrate quicker into the unit, but he couldn't let another day pass without anyone speaking to Stafford bar his critical instructors and sergeant.

"I wouldn't mind blowing him away, to kingdom come with a bazooka," Grey said humorously. "The image you've given me has put me off my lunch."

"You'll have to develop a stronger stomach quickly then, James, to prepare you for what you will be seeing all around you."

"I'm working on it. I know that bayoneting a sandbag or shooting targets isn't preparation for killing a man; it's just preparation for using weapons. I'm not fooling myself that this is going to be easy. It's going to be a baptism of fire."

"That's one thing in your favour over the rest of them. You accept it's going to be hard," Stafford said.

"They all do too, even if they don't say it. You looking forward to the weekend?" Grey said, the group having learnt first thing that they would be given a three day furlough starting Friday.

"Not at all. When Cloisters pulled me to one side he told me I had to stay here."

"Tough break. I've only just arrived so I'll probably have to stay as well," Grey said, less disappointed about it than Stafford. While he did want to head to New York and see the Big Apple, Jake inviting him back to stay at his family home (which would prove a squeeze, with both Baker brothers and Frankie Fanelli staying in Mrs Baker's small house), if he couldn't go at least it gave him more time to train.

"He loved telling me," Stafford said bitterly.

"Maybe if you go a bit faster on the runs and put in a little more effort he might change his mind," Grey said, wishing he'd worded his advice better as he heard it back.

"I can't be bought that easily. They probably figure I wouldn't report back, and at the moment I doubt that I would. They should give you leave, the amount of effort you put in. What are your plans? Don't hang around here to keep me company. You should make the most of any leave."

"I'm probably going into New York, watch some crap baseball, have a game myself, see the city, dry in the day and drunk at night. Have you ever thought of having a talk with the Sarge to try and resolve this issue between you?"

"The League of Nations couldn't resolve our problems – of course they can't resolve anything."

"Diplomacy doesn't work when dealing with fascists."

"Then it's pointless me trying it with Cloisters."

"Okay, Eric," Grey said, trying to close the topic and move onto something trivial, Stafford eventually allowing him to do this, descending from his soapbox after a few more antiwar statements. Jake Baker approached Grey later in the day and addressed his bad choice of dining companion.

"Stafford's bad news. You should stay away from him."

"That's not an option. He's one of us."

"He isn't. He doesn't want to be."

"Everyone grumbles," Grey said, downplaying Stafford's recalcitrance.

"Not like him. A lot of us are worried about what it's going to be like over there and the last thing anyone wants to hear is him saying that our eyes and dicks are going to be obliterated by machineguns. He saps morale."

"I hear what you're saying. I would sooner he didn't go on like that too. But he does and that's something we all have to live with – we all have bad habits and quirks."

"It's beyond that! Look, your friend Delgado doesn't want to go yet because he wants to be studying, but he doesn't play scaremonger or try and weasel his way out of service like Stafford. No one's supposed to talk to him."

Grey sighed and said, "I can't promise that I won't from time to time."

"Be careful. Pearce may be the biggest dick in our platoon, but he has no sway. The ones that do don't have any problems with you at the moment but if they keep seeing you with Stafford that might change."

Grey heeded his warning and said, "Okay. I'll talk to him a bit less than I otherwise would have." He didn't like compromising in this way but he couldn't risk being drummed out of this unit too, though he would not completely blank Stafford like Jake suggested – he didn't wear the cross around his neck for decoration. Grey had thought Jake's warning was a little paranoid and he quickly learnt that was not the case when Fudd asked for a private word.

"We've noticed you're still talking to Stafford. You're like me, Grey, a chronic yakker, but Stafford is off-limits. We've sent him to Coventry and for that to work we all have to be on the same page. One in, all in. If you're talking with him 'cause you haven't made enough friends yet then we'll sort that," Fudd said, his offer of helping Grey to integrate sincere. It was tempting, as Grey knew that Fudd was capable of helping him, gregarious Elmer 'Fudd' Rhodes the lynchpin of his squad and the whole platoon it seemed, with his two best buddies almost as popular. Their senior officers called the shots outside of the barracks but amongst the troops Fudd had tremendous influence. Grey felt it was fortunate that he was mostly good-natured, though his contempt for Stafford was extreme.

Grey's conscience would not allow him to accept this offer and against his better judgement he said, "Thanks for the offer, Fudd, but as a Christian I can't turn my back on him."

Fudd shook his head. "Talk about missing the point. We can't turn our backs on him either because we know he won't be covering it. We're not asking you to do anything to him. Just don't talk to him 'til he gets the message. You think sending him to Coventry is bad? Things could get a lot worse for him."

"I don't want to go against the crowd but I feel strongly on this. Let me make it clear that I don't share Stafford's views at all. The thing is I wouldn't isolate anyone, not even Pearce."

"The incident with the razor was going to be sorted too. Not now if you take this stance. For all of his faults, Pearce treats Stafford the way the rest of us do."

"He's a bully so he would. This is the sort of stuff he loves."

"It's torture for him, because Pearce loves to mouth off against him and he can't, because he goes with the group. Tell you what. We'll give you a week's grace to make your decision, and this is only because you're a kid, too young to know better."

"Trouble is I know my mind won't change over a week, a month, period."

"Being sent to Coventry would be harder for you than it is for Stafford. Think about it," Fudd threatened. No one had rolled out the red carpet for Grey since his arrival but Fudd had been welcoming enough and Grey knew he would be a bad person to have for an enemy because of the sway he held. Going with the tide this time was the wise option; despite this he couldn't turn on the underdog.

Cloisters allowed Grey to spend more time on the range and one of the older soldiers, Lol Shaw, volunteered to help him. Lol Shaw had been a keen huntsman since he was a boy and was a good shot and his very quiet nature belied a very philanthropic man, Lol Shaw as keen to help others as Grey; he was just less vocal about it. He was patient with Grey and admonished him for putting himself down for his lack of shooting prowess, pointing out to Grey that he had only undergone 9 weeks training compared to the 15 weeks that most of the rest of the division had received. At the end of their training, when it was time for dinner, Lol told Grey that he didn't mind helping him improve his shooting whenever necessary, an offer Grey told him he would hold him to. With his help Grey thought that he might make the grade, if not as a marksman, as a half decent shot.

Grey and Lol Shaw were late into the mess hall, and upon entering Jake Baker shouted at Grey that he'd saved a place for him, his expression dark. Grey suspected he knew the reason for that, spotting that Jake was sitting removed from his brother and friends, indicating he had fallen out with Macmurray again. As he sat down with his food Jake said, "Bad news, James. Pearce's palled up with Hartmann."

Grey did not see how this was such a big problem as Jake made out. Hartmann seemed fine to him, a soldier who got on with most people without having formed his own group yet – they were not all as lucky as Jake to have their own tightknit subgroups yet. "Hartmann's okay."

"That won't last now. They've already trashed your bed and hidden all of Hill's things."

"I guess that's the advantage of travelling light," he mused, realising that if he'd had anything to destroy they would have done so. "Pranks like that at my expense don't bother me. They'd better give Hill his stuff back before he gets into trouble, mind."

"It's not his kit, just his personal stuff."

"That's maybe worse. I'll give them two days to have their fun and then if they still haven't turned it over I'll have to gear up for another argument with Raymond Pearce."

"That's what he'll want. Hartmann is a professional boxer and Pearce will use him as muscle to throw his weight around. He's going to be insufferable now."

Grey grasped Jake's point now, Hartmann a perfect heavy for Pearce, a heavyweight who looked capable of inflicting considerable damage, though Grey gave him the benefit of the doubt, saying, "I don't see Hartmann doing that."

"You haven't known Pearce as long as I have. He's total venom."

"I'm not sure about that. He's..." Grey oohed and aahed for a milder way of putting it, the mildest, still accurate description he could come up with being, "...he's trouble."

Hill's things were returned to him after a few hours, and despite a little more attitude from Pearce, Grey didn't notice a huge difference in the atmosphere. Even though he really wanted to go to New York, Grey declined the offer, instead accepting an invitation from Lol Shaw to join him on a hunting expedition. Grey appreciated Lol's offer, the trip for Grey's benefit, and as Lol didn't mind Delgado coming along too Grey had to spend his furlough this way. Delgado couldn't go back to Phoenix for three days and he was glad to go on the hunting trip to get out of the barracks for a few days. Grey found shooting animals hard (the deer in his sights had done nothing to him, killing it seeming unnecessary) and it made him concerned as to how he would fare with a human being in his sights. He forced himself to kill, though he was happy to let Lol skin and cook his kill. Delgado skinned his own kills, prompting Grey to ask him if he was sure he hadn't been hunting before.

"This is my first time hunting, but I've dissected that many cadavers that this is nothing to me."

"I guess that'll be useful, that you're used to seeing dead bodies," Grey said.

"Hopefully. If Stafford carries on as he has been you may see one before we leave the US," Delgado said, Stafford pushing the wrong buttons in too many people, acting far too awkwardly.

"Why hasn't Cloisters kicked him out?" Grey asked, looking to both Delgado and Lol.

Lol shook his head, concentrating on his cooking over a small fire and he said, "I stay out of these things."

"Cloisters doesn't believe in failure. That's why he gets all the rejects from other units, like us two," Delgado said, his deprecation only in jest.

"You two will be fine. You're a very good shot, Isdel, and you're getting better, James," Lol said encouragingly.

"Killing that deer has helped. I've only ever been fishing before, not hunting and I've proved to myself I can shoot something. I won't be watching Bambi again, mind," Grey said light-heartedly.

"A person is a big step up," Delgado pointed out. "Lol's right though, you'll do all right. If you can endure Pearce you can endure anything."

Three days after returning back to their RTC their journey began (to Stafford's desperate fury, Stafford feeling that he was running out of time to avoid active service). Shipping out from the East Coast confirmed to most of them that they were heading to the European front. When they saw how many other soldiers were boarding the ship ahead of them, Delgado joked to Grey, "I'd better be getting my own cabin or I'll want a refund."

"Hey, our treatment's been substandard from the get go – one thing I have to say for the army, they're consistent," Stafford moaned. "Sardines in a tin can, waiting to be opened by a German shell."

Stafford felt a sharp pain in his lower back as someone punched him. He turned around and saw Cloisters, who said furiously, "Shut the fuck up, Stafford! Don't fuck with me now; I'm not in the mood."

Cloisters was more intense than usual, shouting as he tried to organise his men and get them to where they needed to go, name-calling any that got in his way as they boarded the ship, irrespective of rank. Grey found he was surprisingly calm as they entered dangerous waters, his crossing spent calming down two claustrophobic men. Grey found this benefited him, as dispelling their fears distracted him from his own, and actions like these redeemed him in the eyes of most of the platoon for consorting with Stafford. Talking to Stafford was still a black mark against his name but it was understood that Grey did so because he was a do-gooder, and that he was not a malcontent like Stafford, and they wouldn't chase him out of the unit for it. Grey now knew his platoon and liked most of them and was still making an effort to get on with those who were indifferent or hostile towards him. Fates willing, there was time for him to get on with them all.

Grey wandered off from the others to try and have a private conversation with an old friend, taking in some bracing sea air, extremely refreshing after spending so long in the stuffy quarters.

You're making a mistake.

Time will tell. I truly think that I'm doing the right thing.

So did I and look what war did to me – and what I did in war.

The difference is that you fought for something you didn't believe in. I'm not sure I could have fought and killed under those circumstances. This war is a rare thing, a war where good and evil are clearly defined.

You'll still be taking lives and don't try to convince me that every one of your foes is evil.

I know they're not. I hate to use the word evil to describe anyone. If we don't act though, Linus, then many will die – legion have already and I don't mean just in combat.

Others will volunteer to kill; I guarantee you that. Why did you have to volunteer?

It's my duty. My country's at war and so am I.

How does that attitude make you any different to the Germans?

It doesn't. We are very similar, only their leaders are much worse than ours. Their actions are despicable and I need to help as much as I can to put a stop to them. I'm not becoming arrogant – I know I can do very little; I'm not a significant player like you were during your war.

I cannot be a party to this. Thank you for your time and patience, James, but I will not be contacting you until this is over.

Why? I won't tell you what's going on if you prefer. You still need help. Without me you'll be alone.

A state I'm used to. Good luck.

"You get shellshock after you've fought, fuckwit," Pearce said, laughing at Grey who had almost been in a trance.

"I wanted some time by myself to think about things. What do you want anyway?" Grey said defensively. He had been doing so well at masking it and now he was caught out again and by the person least likely to be discreet. Fortunately for him the other soldiers thought that Pearce was being his usual mean-spirited self and paid little attention to him. It was a close call and Grey vowed to learn from it.

Arriving in England they were placed in a training camp and Cloisters became stricter with them than he had been back home, putting them through frequent drills and checking they understood how to use their weaponry properly and that they were maintaining it. Sergeant Wilson, who commanded the squad that comprised of the Baker clique, Hartmann, Hobbs and four other men, was a quiet man who was happy to defer to Cloisters and their lieutenant, conserving his energy for the action while Sergeant Blakey kept his squad, the third and final of their platoon, separate from the others as much as possible, acting as though he were in competition with the others. Their camp was close to a town and Captain Walker occasionally gave them dispensation to venture into town. They largely kept as a unit, taking over a dance hall and wooing the local girls who were quite bowled over by the GI's, much to the local men's annoyance. Grey bore the brunt of one of the local's objections to the invasion of the Yanks, as his spirit tore strips off him. This was a rare case in which the spirit could see Grey (this was only the fourth time Grey had encountered such a spirit and these instances always made him edgy) and those around him and he took great exception to the Americans and the way the English girls responded.

Why do you think there are so few of our men here?

The war. I understand where you're coming from. You're seeing us literally waltz in and try our luck with your ladies. We're not trying to rub your noses in it. We're all on the same side, pal.

I am not your pal, the spirit said with contempt.

And I'm not some Romeo here to pick up a skirt and then leave her high and dry. I kinda wish I was. It might make life more fun. I'm probably the most harmless guy here, regarding your ladies' virtue. I say harmless but I'm half distracted which is making my dancing even worse. I've stood on this poor girl's foot three times so far this dance so I think she'll be throwing in the towel before round two. There were only two girls I wanted to get to know better and one of them was snagged away while I was practising my patter in my head and the other declined my advances. A novel experience for me, hearing a girl swear. That gives you an idea how emphatic her refusal was. I know you have noble intentions regarding these girls.

Unlike you lot.

Okay, you consider this a negative. However, there is a positive. We're raiding the dancehalls tonight, and tomorrow or the day after that, we'll be called to action, making sure these girls don't end up getting their shins kicked by jackboots. I think you may be in the minority with how you feel about our presence. I'm not discrediting how you feel. I'm saying that most of the guys and gals on the street have welcomed us with open arms. Impeccable manners and I don't mean the gentry...we haven't been rubbing shoulders with them! The folks who have nothing yet would give you all that they had. I'm touched by it. If the roles were reversed and you guys were in our country I'm sure we'd make you feel at home too.

I don't have a problem with you being in my country. I have a problem with your off duty activity.

"I'm right here, Jim," the girl (and her name was already gone from his memory) said as she noticed how disinterested he appeared. "Dancing's not your thing, is it?"

"Nope. Sorry about your feet," Grey said, ending the dance prematurely as his partner had clearly had enough of him. "Thanks for..."

She was already walking away shaking her head as she rejoined her friends. Delgado stuck to drinking instead of women and Grey joined him by the wall.

"Not your type, Grey?" Delgado asked, sensing no interest from Grey, and he noticed that Grey's partner (who knew she was his second choice, after the town tart turned him down) positively snarled when she rejoined her friends.

"Her shoes were too dainty and she'd need thick boots to have lasted much longer. That's my dancing quota filled for the year."

"That blonde over there looks more receptive," Delgado said encouragingly. "What do you think?"

Grey looked at the girl, whose appearance lay somewhere between pretty and plain and he felt no attraction and simply smiled politely at her in acknowledgement and looked away. He was in no position to be choosy yet he was very particular and as the two beauties weren't going to be draped around him he lost interest in the whole dance. "She's pretty enough," Grey said, underwhelmed though still trying to be gallant, "but I'll spare her the bruises."

"Don't you get down. If you lose your cheerfulness what hope have the rest of us got?" Delgado said, acknowledging Grey's ever-present alacrity was missing when he should have been at his happiest like the rest of the eager, concupiscent troop. Granted, Delgado was also not dancing or mingling with the girls, but he was still having a good time, unlike Grey who had seemed happier at camp. "What's up?" Delgado said, keen to help him, disliking seeing him so.

"I'm not in the mood for dancing, I guess. I reckon we should blow this joint and go somewhere else."

"There's a pub over the road," Delgado said and they told the others where they were going and were told by some that they would join them later after they'd had their fun. The taste of beer felt sweet to Grey and it hardly touched the sides and he ordered another. As soon as he left the dancehall and the 'unprotected' English ladies the spirit left him alone.

"I was keen to have a look out," Grey said to Delgado at the bar, "and I was looking forward to seeing the girls but I couldn't see any for me." This was the problem, how remote he had felt while looking at a sea of girls who were all wrong for him at a glance. The girls seemed sweet but they were wholly inappropriate for him and he found it difficult being around a horde of women who were all over his friends while he stood like a voyeur, odd man out yet again. He lacked the energy to make the effort – he'd have to force the patter tonight and even if the chase was successful the end result wouldn't lift his spirits much so he hardly tried at all.

"The others are hardly fussy and that's why they all found someone," Delgado said, neither criticising the girls or the soldiers, just explaining why they all paired up which he understood. "I stood back because I prefer to date Spanish women. The English roses just don't do it for me, and you are obviously more discerning than the rest of them. If we have a few pints I might go back and change my mind."

"Good on them I say," Grey said, lifting his pint to toast them, "but I didn't see the girl for me. There was two beauties there who drew my eye. Even if they had lowered themselves to dance with me, and that's a big if, it wouldn't have worked out, because it was purely physical. Attraction on my part, revulsion on theirs, but no meeting of minds like how I know it can be. I already have a dream girl in my head, Isdel, and she wasn't there."

"Aha. Your heart's already spoken for," Delgado said, thinking he understood. "I'm guessing she's some sweetheart from your home town."

"No, it's more of a fantasy. A young Chinese woman, Kaia Yang, clever as they come and real sweet," Grey said, talking spiritedly.

"So is this a real girl you know?" Delgado said, trying to comprehend what he was saying.

"No, not exactly. You must think I'm talking gibberish," Grey said, shaking his head.

"No, mate, I don't. I don't know what you're talking about, but that doesn't mean I think you're blithering on. I reckon that you could do with hitting it off with one of the girls back there, though," Delgado said, thinking that might be better for his friend than dwelling on this mysterious girl who he couldn't ascertain as to whether she was real or imaginary.

"Not tonight, pal," Grey said, unswayable on this. He could not contemplate sex with what they had to face and the thoughts that were swirling around his mind made him sombre though he tried not to let it seep out. "You might have company though," Grey said, looking at a face that came into view in the lounge, which was visible through a serving hatch. Delgado looked to where Grey's eyes were indicating and he saw a young dusky girl around 18. She smiled at Delgado, seeing she had caught his attention, and she looked downwards demurely and a little embarrassed as she awaited service. Her skin was a very pale brown tone and her hair long and straight. Her features were very Caucasian, her ethnicity indeterminable, but Grey presumed she was Hispanic.

Delgado found her visage very acceptable and he nodded approval to Grey and asked him if he would be all right on his own. If his friend needed him he would stay, but Grey patted his back and said, "I'm not alone." It was a strange thing to say but his big grin encouraged Delgado to go for it. Grey watched discreetly and saw there was a middle-aged large woman with the girl and he could hear her saying things to Delgado as he tried to approach her daughter with offers of a drink. It transpired that she was this girl's mother; a single mother who was harsh with any would be lotharios who tried to put her daughter in the same position, and there was some resentment displayed with regard to his ethnicity as she lumped him in with her absent lover. Delgado still tried to talk to the girl despite this termagant and eventually he managed to persuade her to come to the dance hall with him, mainly because she felt sorry for him after her mother's vitriolic outbursts against him. Grey saw them leave the pub together and Delgado waved at Grey who waved back and ordered another pint. He did not want to return to camp drunk, but he felt like he was going mad and needed this escape from his thoughts. Kaia was not there in his mind to help him, having long departed, and the current crop of abundant voices were detrimental, a deafening chorus building to a crescendo when they docked. The other men needed sex or simply female companionship and a sight of skirt as a treat and morale booster before the battle. Grey needed inebriation. Jake Baker and his brother Harvey entered the pub hollering at each other and Grey tried to diffuse the tension, offering them both a drink, which they accepted, and Grey soon learnt what the problem was without having to ask.

"Will you just let Mac get on with it, bro? Cut the guy some slack," Harvey said, irate at what he saw as his brother's pettiness. Harvey was six years older than his brother at 24 and a good deal more tolerant of others shortcomings. He knew that Macmurray was prone to drinking and philandering, but he didn't care what kind of husband he was; he cared what sort of a friend he was. He found Mac to be a jovial, fun guy who he trusted implicitly and who he appreciated for suffering his brother out of consideration for him because he knew his hot-tempered friend wanted to deck him for his judgemental disapproval. Despite Jake's little digs and tacit provocation, Harvey wouldn't stand for his little brother being beaten up even if he deserved it, but he wanted the carping to stop. Jake looked up to his brother deferentially and was prepared to obey him out of respect, yet he would not stop criticising Macmurray while he kept acting like a bachelor unless his brother point-blank ordered him to, which he had not done yet, Harvey preferring to talk it through before laying down the law. Harvey knew his brother would toe the line if told to forcibly as it was understood that he was in charge of him, but he was reluctant to play that card.

"What about Myrtle? She doesn't deserve this. We're not even at war yet and his pants are already round his ankles," Jake countered, swigging his drink down in an angry, violent gesture. "If we'd been at war and shot at then I guess the guy could be stressed and I could overlook it, but we haven't faced any combat yet and he's already unfaithful."

"It's not up to you to overlook! You could be having your end away if you hadn't been so interested in trying to tear him away from his partner. It didn't work, you know the dames go mad for Mac, and that pretty little redhead who you were smooching with has lost interest in you after you broke off from her to go and talk to him about his kid. If you come back with me now I reckon I could spin her a yarn to give you a shot, but then you'll have to just fucking stick with her because you can't blow off a chick twice. What do you say, Grey?" Harvey said, surprised by his silent brooding, as Grey looked out into space.

"Hmm? Live for the moment, Jake. Take your chance. You don't have to approve of what Macmurray's doing, and I'm not saying I do, but the best thing you can do is not to get involved. I know that it rises up in you and you feel you have to say something; come and talk to me at those times," Grey said, forcing himself to respond though he was inclined to be silent, feeling uncharacteristically reticent.

"I do that already. You know she loves the fucking bones of him and he treats her like shit," Jake said to Harvey, upset for Myrtle and that no one else could comprehend what was so wrong with Macmurray's behaviour.

"That's between man and wife, not between fellow soldiers. The best of it is, Grey, that I know he doesn't even want Myrtle," Harvey said, pointing at his brother. If Jake had desired Myrtle then he felt this would be some sort of excuse for his resentment at what he perceived as her maltreatment, only this was not the case.

"I know, he just doesn't like seeing anyone treated badly, which is kind of like our whole mission," Grey said, supporting Jake's point of view though he had a lot of time for Harvey, the more agreeable and sociable of the two brothers. Grey wanted solitude, but he felt he had to help these two sort out their problems. "Macmurray's only been away from his wife for a couple of months. After a couple of years he might grow to miss her and when he gets back it'll be a whole new start so the best thing to do is try to be his friend instead of lecturing him. He might change naturally or through gentle encouragement."

"Couple of years? Talk like that and I'll be the one who needs encouragement!" Harvey said airily. Sensing his brother was somewhat pacified Harvey put his arm around his shoulder and led him back to the dance. Grey was glad to be alone at the bar, his solitude only lasting a few minutes. Hill and two others who had blown it by being too forward joined him for a drink and ended up having to aid him back to camp.

Back at the camp in their quarters he awoke in the middle of the night feeling queasy and threw up by his bed in the barracks, awaking several with the violence of his vomiting. He made it to the latrines where he kept spewing and where a bleary-eyed Delgado joined him. Delgado had seen it was Grey who was ill and because it was his friend he was there to help, touching his shoulder and asking if he was all right.

"Yep. Get back to bed. Sorry for waking you," Grey said apologetically, feeling like an idiot.

"I'll be back in a minute," Delgado said and, taking a bucket and mop with him, he cleaned up Grey's mess in the barracks and he returned to his side.

"How did it go," Grey asked as he leaned by the sink, drinking water from the tap to take the foul taste from his mouth as he had momentarily stopped vomiting.

"It went well. We didn't do it; we just talked and danced. She's called Nina. I got her address," Delgado said, satisfied with how the evening had panned out. She was not the girl for him forever more (and not at all Hispanic as it transpired), but with everything so uncertain he was happy to have a temporary companion for the duration of their stay at the camp.

"It sounds like a success. Go back to bed, Isdel, I'll be all right," Grey said, feeling a nuisance. "I'll be up a while yet and there'll be drill at six."

"Exactly. There's not much point going back to sleep," Delgado said (it was just after three), not about to desert his post yet. "Besides, I don't think you are all right. You've been down all night. Is it just the push that's coming?" Delgado said, trying to get to the heart of the matter.

Grey shook his head. "I am thinking about that, but that's not it." Grey felt unable to share the truth with him even though he thought highly of him and he said, "I expected too much from our foray into town and I got a bit disappointed. I think I was just due a downer, but I'll make sure I have my next one on military duty and not on leave," Grey said, forcing himself to be jolly.

"That's the spirit. Have a long face on their shift, not yours."

"If the Sarge sees what state I'm in I'm not going to get another chance to go to town in a while. I didn't mean to get that drunk. I don't know if it's the same for you, but I haven't had any for that long that it went straight to my head," Grey said, recovering physically and feeling a little better mentally.

"Well, I only had one pint and then I tried my luck. How many did you have after I left?" Delgado asked.

"If you can't remember that's a sign that it's a fair few I guess. By the time the Sarge sees me I'll look all right. You never know, he might go easy on us after last night," Grey said hopefully.

"After giving us a night off the leash he'll be doubly vigorous. That's not what you want to hear, but you know it's true," Delgado said amiably. "There's not long to go so he's going to keep training us hard. I don't think we are going to get the chance to see all the sights of England, amigo," Delgado said, referring to the invasion that they all suspected would be happening soon and life changing for all. It was a crucial day in history and they knew they stood on the precipice of it and would actively determine the outcome, which was exciting and nerve-wracking to them.

"We will. There's always the return trip. I think we'll end up travelling more miles than Phileas Fogg," Grey said, thinking of all the places they had talked of that they wanted to go to which Grey had tagged on to be done on their triumphant return.

"Yes, and it'll take double the time it took him. When this war – which for us hasn't really started yet – when it is all over I'm going to go straight back," Delgado said, talking seriously, a little wistful at the thought of home and his parents who he might never see again.

"Yeah, 'cause you're going to march into the university and complete your degree so you have to. I can go sightseeing and I will. Maybe I'll send you a postcard from Spain."

"Nah, you won't have time. You'll be too busy getting blotto at the bars for correspondence," Delgado joked, making out Grey was a chronic drunk and wastrel.

"You may be right. If I have no one to clean up my sick I might stop. Thanks for that."

"Yeah, well, don't make a habit of it. Pearce and some of them are grumbling through there, but most of them are telling them to shut their traps. It's no big deal," Delgado said supportively. Grey had undergone a difficult night, but it was light and he could see the bright side even though potentially dark days loomed. The dark horizons did not stretch so far now and even in the shadows Grey could make out light in the distance. There was hope and it renewed him.

Grey completed his rigorous training the next morning without grumbling and he had returned to his natural public face, that of smiling geniality and buoyancy. Looking on the bright side seemed to be for the best for the morale of others and himself and there were already enough others expressing doubts and reservations without him joining in. He did get to see a lot of England thanks to a long train journey from the Northwest down to the Southern coast. The train maintained a steady speed and did not make any stops and this scenic journey was fascinating for the impressionable Grey who could find wonder and beauty in obscure things whilst others played cards to pass the time. Grey sat by himself on his bag, watching the passing countryside with a wide grin, thoughtful and introspective, but not withdrawn as he talked to the others most of the time and this once he was savouring the travelling, only occasionally making sociable comments. It was beauteous for several reasons and the reason that especially touched Grey and made him elated was its freedom. It was not subjugated, it had not been occupied, and to him that felt spiritually good.

After an initial stumbling block due to his ethnicity, Delgado was now friendly with quite a few of the platoon who were finding themselves re-evaluating their opinions about ethnic minorities after spending time with Delgado. He was not quite as integrated as Grey, Grey more sociable to a probing degree (which irritated some), while Delgado was more cool and less intense, often standing back and giving others peace which he liked to be given also. Grey was too interested in the others' welfare, which was beneficial to those who were troubled and wanted to discuss their fears, but was not to everyone's liking…

"Grey's an ass. He's not a complete ass, but he's too much. If I've got any problems I'll talk to you guys about it, my pals, or even Cloisters or the padre, but not fucking Grey, sniffing around trying to get into my skull. He's a fucking busybody," Macmurray said. He spoke in aggression, but did so amusingly and Fanelli laughed at the truths uttered in his diatribe, which he agreed with. Harvey thought his comments a little uncharitable though amusing, but repressed his laughter to a half smile because of his brother's presence as he knew Jake liked Grey.

"He's looking out for people and that makes him an asshole?" Jake Baker said defensively.

"I've talked to the fucking doctors about how I'm feeling and I don't see his certificate. He's…" He nudged Fanelli for the word he was searching for.

"Intrusive," Fanelli offered and Macmurray nodded even though it wasn't the word he was thinking of, but was more apt. Fanelli was a quiet soldier who came to life in his core group and hated any intruders trying to ingratiate themselves with him.

"Intrusive, yeah. To use medical jargon, a fucking screwball," Macmurray said, exaggerating his dislike at Grey for comic effect.

"With Pearce and you on his back I pity him," Jake Baker said, expressing contempt at Macmurray, lumping him in with Pearce

"He's got you to hold his hand or, from the way you're carrying on, his pecker," Macmurray countered. Jake Baker reacted to this with an angry flash of his eyes, his expression blackening further as Macmurray grinned derisively at him.

"Next one of you two to speak gets a punch from me," Harvey Baker said sternly, preventing anything from kicking off. "Grey's harmless, he's just not used to living with a group of men," Harvey said, making allowances for Grey while conceding that his behaviour could be annoying.

"It's like having a broad in here with us. Even Myrtle doesn't ask that many questions," Macmurray said, sighing to convey his exasperation at Grey's ways.

"Yeah, but he's not as bad as he was. I haven't seen him ask you many questions lately, Mac," Harvey said, finding this amusing as he recalled past question and curt answer sessions.

"I'm fucking gutted, I tell ya," Macmurray joked.

Macmurray's irritation was echoed by Pearce and he tried to taunt him about this, calling him a busybody and asking him if he was going to go into another trance, but Grey mostly shrugged it off and the majority of the group just thought that he was a would-be Salvo. It was only Delgado who noticed that, infrequent as it was, he was prone to deep contemplation and that something painful existed beneath the surface, the cheery mask not a perfect fit. While Delgado had started spending a lot of time with the more mature members of the group he still tried to make time to try and teach the keen Grey chess (his father had given up trying to teach him years ago and Grey remembered little) on a small travel set. It was better keeping him occupied on his breaks this way then letting him fall in with Stafford, and Delgado had a hunch that he needed to keep a close eye on James Grey. Something about why he left his first unit didn't ring true...

Arriving at the South coast they were led by Cloisters to a marshalling centre where they mingled with tens of thousands of other soldiers. Seeing all of the other soldiers and hearing that there were thousands more at other centres along the Southern coast, they knew that action and invasion was imminent, a matter of days.

Chapter 3 – Welcome to France

She had known of his approach long before he knocked on her large double doors at the front of her secluded country manor, her inbuilt radar informing her in advance as it always did, an especially useful talent in occupied France. For him it was some trek, all of it walked. His legs were too weak and uncoordinated now to risk a bicycle, especially along this unworn, solitary and scenic route. Laura lived six miles out of the town with no nearby neighbours and while it suited her to be so remote that she was nearly off the map, the journey did not suit Georges. This countryside ramble through undergrowth and steep climbs was for adventurous children or young lovers and he was neither now. At 79 he felt too old for this, but he had persevered and he arrived, sitting down in a grassy knoll before knocking, a chance to recapture his breath, his male pride forbidding him from knocking on her door breathless. He was a run-down old man and he could not help that, but he could prevent her seeing him so exhausted and he did so.

She was at the door shortly after he knocked, smiling at him as she realised why he had paused. While he looked sprightly enough (for his age) standing in her doorway, his aura revealed the truth rather than his casing and she saw how frail he was. His hair was mostly gone save for large white wavy clumps at the sides and his eyes seemed narrower and his lids heavy and the bags under his eyes more pronounced, blacker. His face was sallow and his body thinner than the last time she saw him which was only months ago, though he had not quite wasted away yet, still weighing a healthy amount for his shrinking height of 5ft 7 (which she had commented upon the last time she saw him). He was smartly dressed in black suit and tie with white shirt; his typical attire but he would never turn up at her door unless he was very presentable. He held up a small bouquet of posies he had arranged which she took as she invited him in and she put them in water as he sat down in her lounge. The room was large, as were most in this renovated farmhouse (the building was extensively restored by Georges in his youth, which now felt like a lifetime ago, and had been regularly maintained by him before Laura came back to stay), and the décor bright with Laura opting to keep things minimalist, keeping her rooms spacious, and there were only two comfortable chairs in her first sitting room that faced each other at an angle. Laura fetched him an unsolicited glass of water which he consumed with ease (she knew the journey would have left him parched) and she sat down gazing at him. She commented on the fine quality of the posies, that were obviously handpicked (unquestionably by his hands), and he complimented her on her fine garden which he had observed, a shrubbery of vibrant colours covering the sort of large area normally reserved for wheat or other crops. Both knew there was something more important to be said, but she did not want to rush him and he was deliberately taking his time, waiting for the right moment. He was polished enough at small talk and she waited patiently and when he mentioned about his creaking joints, jovially deprecating himself, she took the opportunity to discuss his health.

"You have seen better days. The journey here must have been like an expedition to you." There was a sharp edge to her voice and words as she stared at him with a slight smile. He was used to her ways and knew her mockery was a term of affection and he was not offended and he said,

"I had to see your beauty – you roused me as always – and I had to gaze upon you again, especially with you being so close." He spoke tenderly and reverently and added, "I know you like your peace, but I hoped you'd indulge me one last time."

"You're always welcome here, old friend," she said seriously, his company something she could easily bear, especially for the little time he had left. He was no nuisance to her even if she might imply it, and he understood her better than most. Laura was unknown to most, not a villager or a Frenchwoman, known only as the mysterious Englishwoman who owned a huge chunk of land which she did not use to its full potential. She was not at all integrated into the local farming community, most being unable to recognise her if they saw her and she had struck up little dialogue with those she had seen. She knew far more about them than they knew of her and this was how she liked it, preferring to catch them unawares rather than learn of them through discourse where they would likely present false fronts for her amusement even though the essence of them – their true nature – was far more fascinating than the show.

Those that had seen her had not forgotten her. She possessed the looks of a 30 year old and she had a solid frame with wide shoulders, a heavy chest curving inward to large hips and long fleshed legs. Her auburn hair was today tied into a plait that she had draped down her chest, the length exceeding her bosom. Her narrow greyish-blue eyes kept staring at Georges as she looked at him on several levels, estimating his life span. Above her eyes her thin eyebrows were high on her forehead and her long nose was thin, as were her lips. Her cheekbones were defined and she had a calm nobility about her in her voice which made her authoritative and made people pay attention to her.

"It's strange – I still felt young for so long even after the world had decided that I was aged. It's in these last few months that the years have caught me up. Today I feel young again, invigorated and in sync with the elements," he said boldly. "Your company agrees with me. It's a tonic I could permanently use."

"You can stay here, Georges, or I can take you back to Scotland as a guest. I think you're a little too long in the tooth for anything else," she said, smiling wider as she said this.

Georges chuckled at this and nodded, "True, true. I can't keep pace with the elderly mesdames let alone the mademoiselle who exhausted me in my prime.

My only regret from my whole life is that you didn't say yes 50 years ago," he said seriously, his eyes indicating this with the humorous twinkle gone. It quickly returned as he said, "I understand why now. I wouldn't have seen 40!"

"You overestimate yourself. I would have said 35. I would say no to an old fool just like I did to a young fool, but I would rather not have to say no and I would be far more tempted by the debilitated geriatric," she said, a combination of ridicule (partly for fun and to control his ardour) and deep affection. His age and condition were of amusement to her as she had seen him in his youth before the ravages of time and she knew he did not mind her ribbing him as she did care for him. She wished he was not dying, the imminence of his death depressing her. He was her oldest and dearest friend and she had seen little of him since the occupation and she knew there would be little opportunity to see much more of him.

"That's succour for my 'frail' heart. I know you're humouring me and I appreciate it," he said, knowing he still stood no chance with her. "I envy Jock for having been so loved by you. Do you think you will ever marry again? I'm not asking for myself, I promised to myself that I would never pester you with another unwelcome proposal and this body is coming to the end after a good run." He purely wanted to know what the future held for her which interested him greatly and she knew there was no ulterior motive behind his question. As her former lover she knew that his feelings for her exacerbated his curiosity, but it was a valid question for a friend to ask.

"No. Did you never consider marrying another?" she said, suspecting the answer would be negative.

"It wouldn't have been fair on the girl to live under such an imposing shadow. Our years together and our enduring friendship – I hold that very dear to my heart," he said solemnly, putting his hand to his chest. These treasured times were enough to content him, having loved and lost her better than having never known her.

"Bachelorhood suits you. You have a lot of love and it is better in your case unshackled and spread rather than being confined to one as it would have been," she said, knowing how focused he would have been on his love (her) and she felt the charitable, compassionate things that he had done were a better legacy he was leaving and what she felt he was meant for.

"I care for the boy a lot. That's partly why I'm here," Georges said, approaching the crux of his visit. He had wanted to see her one last time desperately, that was true, but the reason for his visit was twofold. She noticed hesitancy from him, indicating he might ask her to do something trying. She said tentatively,

"Go on."

"I'm dying. I don't mind; I've had a great run. I am very concerned about what I'm leaving behind. The group should survive without me, though it might be hard for them at first. Their power levels are very low. I worry for Konah's welfare after I die," he said gravely.

"Old man, I'll help you and the boy, your whole group if you wish, leave the country, but I will not get involved in this war. It has nothing to do with me and I won't even for you," she said adamantly.

"I would never ask you to join the group. I know that is not your way. If you are averse to aiding them in any way I understand, only if you could please point them in the right direction after I'm gone – if you could see them once and talk to them. Hearing you talk would prove inspirational," Georges said, compromising as he had wanted to ask her to become heavily involved and he now saw how steely her resolve was to stay neutral. She was not angry with him, but she was fiercely opposed to the suggestion so he adapted and reduced his plea. Despite his desperation he did not want to pressurise her and hoped she would heed his wishes without feeling forced, as he did not want that to be her last memory of him.

"They're – you're playing a dangerous game best left to the generals and their tanks and toys. No, I will not help them and I think it's time you stopped," she said, thinking him an imbecile for how heavily he was involved as the leader of what sounded like a ragtag bunch of resistance 'fighters'.

"Would that I had the choice to stop fighting as I would dearly love to accede to your wishes but, alas, I am compelled to fight this fight. I apologise for asking," he said penitently, wishing he had not bothered her with this.

"Don't. You must follow your own heart, Georges. You are going to stay and have a meal with me and I won't let you refuse that," she said, giving him no choice in the matter. "It's an occasion that merits vintage," she said, knowing it was the last time she would see him.

"We'll toast your health, not mine," Georges joked heartily, able to smile about what he faced, as did Laura, but he could not smile at the thought of his group without him. The Nazis would destroy them and he had so little time left to help them and he felt so weak now.

In honour of her guest Laura gave the rooster the chop instead of the roaming hens and Georges said to the cockerel as he stood outside with Laura who wielded the axe, "I'll be joining you soon, cocky." The cockerel was dead before he knew what happened, Laura very able with the axe, and she cooked Georges a fine dinner and sat with him around the dining table as night drew in and they began to eat. The dining room was to the rear of the house and looked out to a now sparsely populated forest, many of the trees felled before Laura purchased the land. Laura poured out the vintage from her wine cellar, the best she had, and Georges savoured the taste, swirling it round in his mouth. He was no connoisseur, but he knew what he liked and this wine was fine, better than any from his small collection. He talked a little more of his resistance group without hinting for help (and none was offered) and Laura laughed at the descriptions of some of their escapades, attempting tasks which seemed so rudimentary which they had still bungled. Georges was not laughing as he told the stories, not finding their failures that humorous, until Laura set him off laughing and he saw the funny side, but he knew things had to improve. He would not be there to see if they did and he would have to hope for the best.

Georges began the inevitable reminisces of their past well into the meal, holding back as long as he could, and this once Laura was also keen to relive their past in what was her last opportunity with him. They had been together for four years in the 1890's and they had been happy times and in retrospect seemed even more splendid than they were at the time. She had ended it and she still knew that she had been right to do so, yet she remembered those times fondly and vividly, as did he, Georges even able to describe exactly what outfits she wore on every occasion that they discussed. He seemed blissfully happy as he gave detailed descriptions of her and amid all of his gushing praise she complimented him a few times lightly, enough to swell his head. They drank some more after the meal in the sitting room and as it grew late she suggested that he should stay at hers and retire for the night. He knew this meant a separate bedroom and no impropriety and he graciously declined.

"If I stay I would never wish to leave and there is much that must be done. You know that after what I told you of my people," he said, smiling, having noticed how amused she had been by those stories. "I am renewed in strength now – enough for what I must do at least," he said, crediting her with his revitalisation.

"It is very late and dark. If you must return I can see you back safely, but it's your choice, Georges."

"I must go," he said, standing up, his joints creaking as he did so. Laura stood up and walked with him to the front door and she looked at him. This was their final farewell, but he did not presume to kiss her and he waited till a hand was proffered which he kissed softly and briefly as he held the soft underside of her smooth hand, her soft palm. "I have faith that you will be well, but I would advise you to leave this tumultuous continent for smoother pastures. Farewell, my goddess, and thank you for the years you graced me with," he said, opening the door, ready to leave.

"Farewell, Georges," she said and the old man was gone, giving her a broad smile as he walked away and a wave as he reached as far as she could see which she reciprocated. She would have told him to take it easy but the old dotard would not do things differently. She was not reliant on him and was not in love with him anymore; she would still miss the daft old codger. Despite this she wished that he had days left rather than weeks, as she wanted his life to come to a natural end. Old man or not, the Nazis would mercilessly dissect him if they found out what he was up to.

You in the same boat as me? a youthful, seemingly English voice said to Grey.

Probably not. When I was born it was a difficult birth. They thought I was stillborn at first and I was declared so initially then after a few minutes I was brought back, which is my theory as to why I can communicate on this plane.

Come again?

Just talking crap, kid, don't worry about it. Other people can stop breathing and then recover and they don't hear spirits. What's your name, pal?

Max. Are you a Yank?

I can proudly say that I am. The name's Grey. The first name's Jimmy but I'm in the army now and that's never used.

It would have been the navy for me.

You Brits have had a good navy for centuries. That's how you colonised the world. Nobody could ever accuse me of having sea legs. How old are you, Max?

At the time of my death, 13. Guess it is an unlucky number, huh? Max said without bitterness, seeming an upbeat character, all things considered.

For a long time. It goes back to The Last Supper, that superstition. I'm a medium, Max, which means I can help you.

I reckon you're too late for that. The bombers struck my home a long time ago.

We've been hearing about the Blitz for a long time back home. Plus I've heard from a lot of spirits too. We all respect how you guys have got on with it in very difficult circumstances.

There's nothing else you can do, is there? Evacuation – I don't think so! Max said emphatically. *I wasn't going nowhere without my ma. My family don't do the countryside.*

I'm a city boy too, Max, I know what you mean.

Whereabouts?

Keokuk. Not quite as well known as some other American cities.

Where the hell's that?

Iowa. The Midwest. We're one of the farming states, but our cities are the same as yours.

No city can be as good as London.

If things had been different I would have loved to have spent my summer amongst you Cockneys. I'll make sure to visit someday to see your city for myself. I've gotta admit, you've got great history, this side of the Atlantic.

We used to own you.

You used to own near enough everywhere once. We grew out of it quick and stood on our own two feet.

You Yanks should have come and helped us out quicker.

You've got me there, Max. Couldn't agree more. It's not too late now. Things are changing as we speak.

How do you mean?

We're doing something that will make the front page. We're wading through the sea on a French beach as we speak.

No way!

Gospel.

Are they putting up much of a fight?

We've got good numbers. It's not just us Yanks – your men are here too.

Have you taken any out yet?

The artillery's doing most of the work until we get ashore. I'm more bothered about the cold water rather than the Jerries – they warned me I'd get shot at when I signed up but they didn't mention being submerged in icy, freeze your nuts off, water, Grey joked.

Makes them less of a target. Do you think this time you'll make a foothold? Dunkirk or Waterloo?

Waterloo's the Napoleon defeat, right?

Victory, mate, victory.

Of course, for you it was. Waterloo then.

Watch out for the mines.

I'm choosing to believe that the mined beach stories are rumours.

Why wouldn't they booby-trap the beach? They'd know you're coming at some stage.

The French coast is vast so they won't have mined everywhere.

They've had enough time to.

I'm on your side, remember, so humour me about the mines. I've wanted us to act for years, and now the moment has arrived so maybe our image may improve with you Brits?

Nah, you'll hog all the glory now.

You guys are just mad that we threw off the shackles. Hollywood will make out we did it ourselves but this soldier won't, scouts honour.

We'll see. I know you're not a general or major. I still want you to make sure they execute the bombers at the end of it. Me and my ma are just two of their victims – the total number must be millions.

It's more like thousands, I think, Max.

Nah, millions, honestly. They're blowing up women and kids in their beds. They don't deserve to live.

I can see why you feel that way. It's not the most ethical thing to do.

It's cowardly and evil.

Both sides do it, and the bombers are only following orders. Misguided orders. I don't know, wars make people do things they shouldn't, force impossible choices.

Our home was nowhere near any military targets. They wanted to slaughter some Brits, and they got us, kipping in our beds. Big brave men.

Well…the leaders, Hitler, Goering, Himmler – they'll be executed, that's a certainty. There'll be no Napoleonic exile for them, I can guarantee that.

What method do you think they'll use?

There'll be a trial first, probably in the States…though that depends who breaks through first, 'cause I don't think the Russians will hand them to us if they prove quicker. The tales I hear from that front, Max – I'll stick to the cold water here.

That's true cold, over there.

In more ways than one.

So is it proving really easy?

Grey paused and said with bravado, *Haven't you heard? Us Yanks are fearless.*

They all say you're better at putting girls in the pudding club than fighting.

We've gotta burn off that surplus energy somehow. Bear with me, mate. I'll talk to you in a few minutes.

Okay. Is something wrong?

It's getting a bit trickier. Nothing to worry about. I just need to concentrate a bit more.

I'll leave you to it. I don't want to do anything to stop you from taking a few out for me. Thanks for the good news. What's the date?

June the 6th.

'43?

'44.

Time passes weird here. Good luck then and try and keep up with us 'Tommies'.

I only need a few minutes. Don't break contact.

You don't need the distraction. You've got a job to do.

There's another guy talking to me who has some tactical information. I gather you can't hear him. That's why I'm a little slow to respond to both of you, that and being dropped on my head as a kid. I don't want you going anywhere yet though, Max, so we'll just carry on. We need to get you beyond this stage.

What does that mean?

It's time for you to go to Heaven. I can help with that, if you are willing.

Why now?

There's so many spirits active at the moment if we don't try it soon we may not be able to find each other again.

You stand out. I'll be able to contact you.

There's what seems to be tens of thousands – maybe millions – so let's stay talking.

You said you wanted me to break off.

No, I wanted you to remain, just for us not to talk for a minute. It doesn't matter, ignore that. Right, we were talking about the fate of Hitler and his cronies. If they are taken to the States, probably electric chair.

That would be incredible. Hanging's too clean and a firing squad is too quick. I'm in favour of that.

The queue to flick the switch is going to be endless.

Grey.

That's my name.

I was too young to join up, otherwise I'd be fighting now. What does it feel like? I've heard stories off my mates on leave, but most of it sounded bull.

I'm hardly a veteran. My war is starting right now. It's going to be tough but that's the job. As long as we get through today everything else will be all right. It feels like it's going well. They can't fight a war on two fronts, so if this front proves viable then the Nazis are finished.

You seen any dead yet?

Grey replied emphatically, *Yeah.*

Any of your friends?

Let's talk more about you. Why are you so sure that your mother didn't survive?

I died instantly. I felt sudden agony and then nothing. It must have been a direct hit.

How about your father?

Let's talk about something else. He's not important.

Okay. I gather you've been on the spirit plane for over a year so I may have to help you along, sort of like steering you to the right path. I won't do it without your permission.

Why am I stuck?

It happens for a variety of reasons. Generally it's if someone dies suddenly or when there's unresolved business. If you die before your time. It's cases like yours that are the true tragedy of war – at least I've got to adulthood, so if I was struck down now I couldn't complain.

How old are you?

18

That's only 5 years older than me. 4 if it's '44, like you say. So what do you reckon my unresolved business is?

I think you needed to know that your country is going to be all right. That's why we're talking today on this momentous day, because the bombing campaigns, the threat of invasion – that's all over. Great Britain is safer today than it has been for years, because from this point forth Hitler's going to be so stretched that even a contortionist couldn't cover every base. Attacking your country is not going to be one of his priorities anymore. Defending his empire, then defending his country when that fails, then defending his life, so that's three triple failures he has to look forward to.

This is a good day, isn't it? What are you complaining about the cold for? This is…this is the beginning of the end.

It's the beginning of a bright new future. Take care, Max, Grey said as Max found his own way to the light. Grey was glad for him, though had to move on as others vied for his attention. Max's description seemed better than Grey's; this looked more like the beginning of the end, where the four horsemen wouldn't have seemed out of place. It was undoubtedly the most difficult day he had ever faced, and the day was still young. After a shaky start, where all confidence evaporated from him, he managed to hold it together by thinking of the big picture and this sense of duty got him through the morning. He had dreamed of handling his first taste of combat with aplomb and he realised early on that surviving it would suffice. The sickening boat ride early in the morning was endurable and even wading ashore with his troop he still felt capable. His stomach churned and he panicked but he managed to find the resolve and courage to continue even as he saw those around him shot down, some from his unit by snipers on the beach, machine guns cutting so many men down, including Stafford. Grey strained to contact his spirit, to no avail. Grey believed what he said to Max, that Allied victory was now assured; unfortunately that day was a long way off, and there would be a long fight ahead. If he survived he'd lose years of his life to this campaign, unless it could somehow be accelerated. It would have to be accelerated – even if he survived, too many days like this would wipe years off his lifespan.

The dead bodies disturbed him, though the worst sights were the almost dead. Looking at some of them it was hard not to retch; they needed succour, solace and Grey was glad that he had other duties which excused him from this task. Most were still and quiet, while others made anguished screams…Isdel was a stronger man than he for wanting to be a medic, a harder job impossible to imagine. The wounds were too hard to look at, Grey unable to imagine how much pain his comrades were suffering – the spirits described it but it had the most impact visually.

It was an epic moment in history. Movies would be made of this, books would be written, yet nothing would convey the morning, not even the newsreel footage being shot. How the fuck were they going to edit that to make it palatable to the general public? His war had only just begun, yet whatever followed would pale into insignificance next to the beach assault. Waking up on Mars like John Carter would have felt no stranger than this, an air of unreality present throughout.

He had wanted Hitler forcibly removed from power for a long time, years before the war, and as such he was a strong advocate of America's participation in the war. Now, he wavered. Was any cause worth this level of sacrifice? The generals who had formulated this plan and approved it, knowing the likely casualties…surely sleep was now a thing of the past for them? Even with no other choice and the whole greater good excuse that was a heavy burden for any man's conscience. Many years had passed since the follies of the Great War, of thousands of men being forced to go over the top to certain death, yet this opening salvo was no different. They'd gained a toehold so maybe there was a fractional difference. The phrase 'Be careful what you wish for' reverberated around Grey's aching head. He had been desperate to come; now he was desperate to be anywhere but here. This shit needed to be over soon.

Grey tried to rouse himself. The self-pity and especially the fear had to be tamed. He emerged without a scratch from that…was there a word for that? He was lucky. They were at war – he was being naïve expecting no blood to be spilt. It was the volume that perturbed him as there proved to be no safety in numbers. Get this hard, hard day out of the way and it would be downhill all the way, one way or another. Grey's special powers gave him the knowledge that they had caught the enemy unaware – imagine if they had been fully prepared for them, how, impossibly, things would have been even worse for them? His brain remained hyperactive and he knew he had to stop thinking so much and just get on with business. His life was no more valuable than those who perished so far today and he had to fight his fear which urged self-preservation and actively seek to make a difference, utilising his power for more than saving his own skin. If anything his life was less important than many of the casualties for he had no children, nobody dependent on him; grit your teeth and get on with it, man.

Mike Aspinall, a fellow American soldier who didn't survive the day was handling death better than Grey was handling life and Grey was glad for his company.

It's small consolation at this precise moment but in time your sacrifice will seem worth it. The whole greater good, big picture thing is that what we're doing here today will change the world, for the better. At the moment it seems strange that any cause could be worth a man's life but once some distance is between us and this day we'll know it's true. It seems so unfair to be struck down immediately but…

But what?

We can help each other, Mike. Keep talking to me, take my mind off this, and I can help you find peace.

You sound calm.

Yeah? I must be a better bluffer than I figured. Wanna know something scary?

Go for it.

It doesn't matter.

You've got to say now.

So far the losses are better than projected. Across the campaign, as a whole.

That's good, isn't it?

Absolutely. Ignore me. This moment's catching me out. I like to talk the talk about being desperate to fight and now I'm learning that walking the walk is a billion times harder. Considering my powers should make me more acclimatised to death than most I'm proving damned squeamish. I've known this was going to be hard and still wanted it to come sooner. I just hope and pray we can get the job done quickly, mate. The Nazis are fallible. This has to work.

It's still a huge gamble.

Ten years too late in my opinion. Better late than never. Don't get me wrong, Mike, I couldn't be more committed to this. First battle still scares the shit out of you.

You wouldn't be human if it didn't.

I think I'm keeping my anxiety internal. How did you find the buildup to all of this?

I was okay. Calmer than most. I didn't see this coming. I figured the odds of my being killed first time out would be remote.

Were you one of the first waves?

Yep.

I'm not. It increases your chances, I've discovered, coming out later. A couple from my platoon have been hit but at the front it's whole platoons wiped out.

I guess we got the short straw. Are our bodies getting trampled?

Not if we can help it. The formation's gone to hell so…thanks to a German spirit I know where their troops are. In this chaos I won't be able to get that across so should I just go there and hope others follow my lead?

What's your rank?

Private.

There's your answer.

Yet I know exactly where they are.

Try and get that across.

I can't explain how I know that. As long as I don't stray too far away I should be able to get away with it…

Grey was not able to make that much of an impact without completely abandoning his position and as he felt he was getting too far away he returned without making a significant contribution. He tried informing some other soldiers where they had to strike in the distance and the number of men they faced to a mixed reaction. Cloisters was waiting for Grey when he returned and he pulled him to one side for a word.

Cloisters stared Grey hard in the eye and said, "Believe it or not there is some sort of organisation here, and platoons are meant to stick together. This once I'll let it slide 'cause you were putting yourself forward, getting overkeen."

"I could see where the threat was. I figured the quicker they were dealt with the more men might get to go home."

"That'd be okay, if you'd been slightly out of position. You were miles out, and that made me take my eye off the ball, watching you. That happens again then we have a problem. By that I mean you have a problem."

"It won't happen again."

"I was impressed with you out there, Grey, apart from that. I suspected that in battle you might have stuck by the weak ones or the fallen like a mother hen, trying to carry them through it at the expense of your own duties. You didn't though, you were determined and you did well." This was genuine praise and Grey appreciated it.

"I figured the best way I could help the others would be to try and beat the Jerries as quickly as possible. Holding their hands wouldn't help them in battle, Sarge, I know that. Defeating as many of the enemy as possible is the best way I can help them here," Grey said, having given the matter some thought. "After the battle I can see how they are then to try and help them."

"Well put. Keep that focus, Grey, and you and me are going to get on," Cloisters said, liking his attitude.

"I would like to make a request, Sarge," Grey said apprehensively.

"Go on," Cloisters said cautiously, staring at him hard again.

"I want to be positioned at the front. I want to be fighting now. I think I can help the others." Grey felt he was being wasted in his current position and wanted to be where the fighting continued.

"Our unit's not there though, is it? It's fine to be eager and you'll get your chance, but for now just fall in." Cloisters was impressed with his zeal and knew Grey would not need to be patient; once they had regrouped they were set to continue fighting until further notice.

Grey rejoined the others and he saw that a few had fallen and he was nudged by Delgado who was feeling exhilarated and out of breath. "Where'd you go?" Delgado asked. "We thought you were going to march all the way to Berlin!" He was not accusing Grey of cowardice in his desertion of his troop, lightly joking with him regarding his zeal to get into the heart of the action and in the utmost danger.

"In time we will. By that time there might not be much for me to see, but that's where we have to get soon," Grey said determinedly.

"I'll settle for not being driven out of France," Delgado said moderately, not being presumptuous of where they stood. Grey noticed how heavily Delgado was breathing, almost hyperventilating, and he focused on him again, aware that he had been neglectful of those he considered friends, through necessity, and until he fought again he would not overlook that duty.

"How you doing? You okay?" Grey asked Delgado.

"Yeah," Delgado said, nodding. "I'm overdosing on adrenaline, but I'm all right. I know how lucky I am so I'm not going to bellyache today. What do you think of France then?" he said as though they were tourists.

"A little crowded for my tastes," Grey said, joking with him, "and some of the other visitors aren't too friendly. Apart from that, it passes muster."

"You're welcome to Europe, Grey. America sounds damned sweet at the moment," Delgado said, trying to recapture his breath. "That was definitely something I will never forget."

"You can't describe it," Grey said to him, feeling that no one could. "How can anyone put that into words?"

"I won't be writing my folks and telling them what that was like," Delgado said, not wanting to upset them. He had felt like he was waiting to be chopped down and he had felt helpless even with his weapon in his hand, as though whether he lived or died was down to chance. By nature Delgado was not a fatalist, as he liked to think he could change things as society in some ways radically needed changing, but now he was not so sure.

"Don't repress it though. When you get back, do tell them," Grey said, advising him not to keep his parents at arm's length even for their own good as he felt it would be better for Isdel to share his experiences with them. Grey had kept many things from his parents and it had damaged his relationship with them.

"When I get back I might tell my father, but not in a letter," Delgado said, appreciating Grey's input.

"Yellow-bellied chickenshit," Pearce said to Grey abusively, having also noticed him leaving the unit and never letting an opportunity pass to denigrate others.

Grey turned to look at Pearce, a man who had tried over the last few weeks to irk him and received little reaction and in an aerated state Grey let loose and fired at him, "I volunteered for this war and I fought hard in that battle. We're at war now and we've all got enough on our plates without your piddling fucking bullshit. You can think what the hell you like, but keep your ignorant views in that narrow mind of yours." He spoke cantankerously; ready for a fight if that was the only way to stop this troublemaker from unsettling everyone with his malignant nature. This paroxysm was most unlike Grey and made Pearce back away, though his surly expression revealed that there would be repercussions.

"That's the first time I've heard you swear," Delgado said, smiling disarmingly, trying to calm him down.

"It won't be the last," Grey said, questioning his outburst. Pearce was out of line, but perhaps he was too. "We're going to win this war, Isdel," Grey said resolutely, looking back at the carnage again, at the nightmare that every man who survived would remember every day for the rest of their lives, a blood bath that seemed impossible to categorise as success, yet which was the first step to victory. Just the first step, at least for him, and surviving that had seemed a miracle and his blood ran cold as he realised that his chances of surviving the war were a lot slimmer than he had originally thought.

Grey had another chance to fight later that day against the tanks and the Panzer units, their position by no means assured and the liberation of France a long way away. As he fought, the chorus of voices in his head that guided him grew quieter and he could hear one individual.

Can anyone hear me? a voice asked, bewildered by his predicament.

I hear you. I think I recognise your voice. What's your name, pal?

Teddy Murphy, Murph. Is that Grey? Get the docs, Grey, something's seriously wrong with me.

Murph, this is going to be hard for you to accept, and I am very sorry to have to tell you this, but you must have fallen. You were unlucky, Murph. I remember seeing you in training back in England and you were ten times the soldier that I am but today has just been like a lottery as to who lived and died. Some platoons look to have been nearly wiped out. I'm sorry, Grey said sadly. Grey wanted to make him feel better about his passing and praised him (while Grey would have lied to make him feel better, the praise was genuine) and made it clear that today had all been down to chance, not skill.

Stop fucking about and get me some help! he said angrily.

Grey said Teddy's name and inwardly sighed as he thought as to how he could gently convince him. *You're not in any pain now, correct?*

I can't feel my body, it must be fucked, but I'm alive in some form. Might not be if you don't get me some fucking help! There was desperation in Murph's voice as he clutched at straws.

What's the last thing you remember?

Pearce is right, you are a freak. Get someone else to talk to me, he said, losing patience with Grey.

Teddy, you know how many men are out here, yet I'm the only one you can talk to. Doesn't that strike you as odd?

You're one queer bastard, Grey. Dead? That would make you dead too if you're talking to me.

I can see why you'd think that. Have you ever heard of mediums, people who talk to the departed?

Yeah, old crones with a screw loose. Not 18 year old soldiers.

I guess someone's messed up somewhere then because I've been given these powers and I want to use them to help you. A girl likely would have fared better.

Guys generally aren't so hot at communication. I try my best. Scary, huh, that this is my best? Have you any messages you want to give your loved ones and I'll see they receive them?

I'll tell them myself. You stay away from my wife and kid, he said fiercely and then, his tone turning a little sombre, I'm not dead.

Until you accept it and find peace you'll remain in this state. I want to help you find release, Murph. Talk to me about your family.

We accepted you into our company, Grey, and most of us gave you a chance and now you're proving us wrong by turning the screw into me. I'm begging you, stop torturing me and get me some help.

I don't mean to cause you further distress. I've been a medium for many years now, Teddy, and I still hate this, being the bearer of bad news. We didn't know each other that well so I can understand why you're reluctant to believe me. What I meant by the last thing you remember is the last thing you remember before your senses changed, when you could see and hear or can you still see and hear? Some in your condition can.

I can't see or hear. Or smell, come to that. Is your first name Jake? Get me some help, Jake.

The noise is still deafening now and you can't hear anything. That is because…

I can hear you clear as day. I can just about make out some other voices – some of them are women, which is a bit screwy – must be Hobbsy. My hearing is damaged, but I can hear a little bit. You must have a loud voice.

Does that tally with your memories of me?

I don't have many memories of you, Grey! You mean nothing to me, do you get that? Murph was irate with Grey as he began to realise that his insane and eerie explanation was likely the truth.

Grey gave him a few minutes to calm down and said to him sympathetically, *Again, I'm sorry. In your position I doubt I'd want to hear from me.*

I was shot in the chest. I went down in the water and then the pain stopped and I went blind and couldn't feel my body. That was my death? he said, accepting it and wanting confirmation.

Yes. The good news is that your current state is temporary. Once you accept it, which you seem close to doing, then you will find release.

You mean Heaven? he said hopefully.

Uh-huh, Grey equivocated. He believed that the spirits went to Heaven, but did not know it for certain.

Okay. That would be better than this. Okay, Grey, what do you want me to do?

Tell me about your family. Do you want some time to think of some messages for them?

How the hell do I say goodbye to them? he snapped. He softened and said, *Mildred's my wife and she thought I wouldn't come back. We've only been married for a year. She's just a girl, not a woman yet*

Motherhood and marriage would mature her I would think.

You don't know Mildred. She doesn't have a clue how to manage anything. Without me she won't be able to cope. She couldn't wash clothes until I taught her.

In these difficult times we'll all learn that we're more capable than we believe. I might even earn my fellow soldiers' respect, Grey said light-heartedly.

This is a war, Grey, not a miracle. Maybe it is a miracle – can you bring me back? he asked, suddenly desperately hopeful.

That's way beyond my power, sorry. What's your child called?

Nathan. Mildred tried to wean him on water at first until the landlady intervened. They won't be all right without me. It's my duty to be there for them. They'll have no kind of a life without me. His voice began to tremble as he said sorrowfully, *I can't leave them, Grey. I don't care what the Jerries are doing to Europe; I shouldn't have left my family. They're going to be scrimping and saving for the next 15 years at least. I was going to provide for them and give them good lives and now they'll be living in one-bedroomed dives. Mildred and Nathan are not equipped for the hard life.*

At least you were married. She'll receive…

What she'll get won't cover lodgings, food and clothing. Our families are a dead loss and our friends are poorer than us. My friends, Millie's so timid she won't talk to anyone. She's scared of her own shadow and now she's going to have to live in the slums where she'll get ripped to shreds. Fuck me, how could I leave them?

I give you my word that if I survive I will check on them, as a friend only, nothing untoward, I swear.

I know you wouldn't take advantage. I hardly know you, but I trust your integrity over my friends back home.

Thank you, Murph, Grey said, appreciating the compliment.

Please check on them and if you can, help her out. You know what? Being dead and somehow still being here – I can almost accept that, but not that I'm talking to you. You're…?

I'm the last person you'd expect. It should be your loved ones who receive you and through me they will. Think long and hard over what messages you want me to send them. Don't worry, I'll tell them you passed on your messages from your deathbed, not from the other side.

That would scare Millie a lot. What can I say to her?

Take your time. It doesn't have to be long or complicated. I've talked to other men in your position and they normally…

What do they say?

Usually they declare their love, tell them to carry on and remember them and to live. They are always clear that they don't want them to succumb to grief.

That's a hard request, asking your family not to grieve you.

I agree, but it is noble. That doesn't mean forgotten, it means that you are encouraging them to be happy and know that you are at peace. To know that a loved one died at peace must be a huge comfort.

It didn't hurt that much. You would expect agony, wouldn't you, but I've felt worse pain. It stung enough, mind.

I'll tell them whatever you wish, only remember that your words will reside in their hearts always. Your words will impact on how they live their lives.

You think I should tell her to love again? Murph said, very averse to this suggestion. His mood fluctuated from despair to fury; Grey was used to this, the recently deceased often less composed than the long-term dead and usually slightly harder to deal with.

It's not my place to say.

I'm Nathan's daddy.

And you always will be. Nothing will ever change that. Thousands fell, Teddy, and where you'll go there are friends of yours, tougher men than me.

I was unlucky. I never even saw my shooter. It would make no difference if I did; I don't care to know what the kraut looked like. At least…at least I never shot anyone, Grey, I never killed. I died clean in that way. There's no blood on my hands.

That's a good thing to be able to say. I can't say that. It comes easier than you'd think, which disturbs me a bit. I can't be a hundred percent certain it was my bullet, but in my gut I'm sure. By the end of this it'll be routine.

Want to switch places? You can die innocent and I'll bear your guilt in your place.

I can't do it, Grey said, referring to his inability to perform the task.

I'm not surprised by your answer. Millie knew how I felt about her – just tell her it was swift and painless. Call me ungracious if you want, but I'll not give her my blessing to marry again. That's her decision and I'll let her make it herself but I sure as hell am not going to encourage her. Tell her to move out of the city. It's got nothing for her and the bub now. Maybe she could get a flat above a store in a small town or village. I wish I could say something to help you, Grey. I've no information about the Jerries to share – apart from they're good shots, but you probably already know that.

For sure, Grey said, agreeing wholeheartedly with Murph's assessment of their prowess. *All of you who are fallen – we'll never forget you, I swear, and I in particular will not forget you.*

That's lies. Society does not remember the dead. The most I can hope for is to be another faceless name on a memorial plaque and an album full of photographs for Millie and Nathan to look back on with grief and eventually resentment. That's my legacy, he said bleakly. *You actually might remember me – the do-gooder types like you have always got on my nerves, but your inflated consciences make you remember and care. We only talked in passing, Grey, and now I wish I'd made more effort. You put in effort, I thought too much but…*

Take care, friend, Grey said as he heard Teddy Murphy fade away.

While Teddy and most of the other spirits were largely agreeable, not all were so, as demonstrated by an English speaking German who took issue at the counselling attempt by one of his killers.

Taking over our empire isn't enough for you. You want to take over our minds too. We have no peace from our enemies in death?

I'm trying to give you peace. You can move on from this state, Grey said patiently.

If I give you tactical information?

I'd love it if you would, but that has to be your choice. I'm offering to help you regardless.

What are you?

A medium.

You kill and cure. The two don't go together.

Killing comes naturally to very few men…well, that's untrue, there are a significant number who…I digress. Most of us on both sides are soldiers doing their job. If we kill here, in combat, it's not an automatic fail at the pearly gates.

This is my first taste of action and I'll find out real soon whether I can be a soldier and a medium. They're not a natural fit, but I wouldn't say I'm a conventional medium. I'm just an ordinary guy, so much so that I need my gift to enliven my life. Sweet mother of…We'll talk in a minute.

You have a problem?

A legion of problems. Sorry about that, we'll continue. It's a busy day.

How many other dead are you talking with?

Most are quickly helped. They only need a few words of comfort and they find peace. Others might take a few hours or maybe a week. Hardly any remain longer than that.

What's the longest you've known?

In exceptional cases it can go into years.

How many?

I don't think there's a limit. The oldest I've known is from the 11th Century. He's a very troubled soul and that's why he remains. He's not with me now – his problems stem from war and he wants nothing to do with me now for my actions.

That seems severe.

He did bad things in war. Crimes that won't leave him. As much as I swore I'd never do similar he wasn't convinced as he hadn't planned on killing…doing what he did, when he set off. I miss his company but I respect his decision. I'll respect your decision too if you don't wish to talk to me, but I'll try for a while longer before taking my leave, in case you just need time to come to terms with things. You don't have to like me to take my help; plenty don't. I grew thick skin quickly on the spirit plane – I wish I was as hardy in the real world.

So how many have you talked to today?

Triple figures, so far. Some I've only heard a sentence or two from – you, I can hear clearly, others are real faint.

Would it be closer to 100 or 999?

Somewhere in the middle. It's mostly our side.

So why are you spending time talking to me?

Because uniform or allegiance doesn't matter here. I'd counsel friends first, and after that, whoever I can help. Some would view my gift as ungodly, but I am a Christian and I try and follow those tenets.

My faith has helped me through my darkest times, through many battles, the spirit said, seeming to soften towards Grey a little.

And through this last struggle it'll help too. That support is still there for you – you'll see Heaven soon, mate.

Too soon.

We're trying to pack it to the rafters too soon. What must God think of us, what we're doing to each other? It should never have ever come to this. Another guy said earlier that this is the beginning of the end and I hope so because it's a waste, with decent men on both sides blowing each other to bits because of the ambitions of a handful of men…

Another voice broke through the rabble, a voice that combined bitterness and resignation.

I already know I'm dead, Grey, so you don't need to try to soften the blow.

How do you feel about that?

What do you think? I've heard you talk to other voices, voices louder than my own. A lot of them don't handle it well.

It's traumatic for all of you. I hope you haven't had to wait long to talk to me, Grey said, the multitude of voices quietened down to murmurs compared to the clearness of this spirit.

I'm in no rush. You can't help me. You can't offer a hand to the drowning man; you just ensure he's not alone at the end.

It's not the end, friend, it's a new beginning for you.

I've never believed in anything I couldn't touch. I don't fully believe in this.

What's your name?

It doesn't matter anymore. That life's done.

It matters. I'm Grey. What's your name, friend?

Just call me Joe.

Good morning, Joe.

Is it? In your world, Grey, not mine. Strange – I've no senses, but I have a vague fix on your position. To your southeast some Jerries are hiding out in an abandoned village. That's where my body will still be.

If I had any power I'd go there and ensure that your body was flown back to your family. I have no authority to do that, I'm sorry to say. I can promise you that those in charge will try and make sure that all of you receive a Christian burial.

I'm not telling you where my body is to make you go and dig my grave. I'm trying to make sure no one has to dig yours.

I realise that, Joe, and I'm grateful. Sometimes I feel like a leech because you've all been through so much and I'm getting more help from you than I give in return.

You're someone to talk to. I'm not the appreciative or expressive kind, but that means a lot in the darkness. You must wish that we'd all fuck off.

No, I've never wanted that. I'd be dead without your help. I haven't exactly led the fullest of lives so everything that you guys have to say fascinates me.

I'm not going to tell you anything about me, Grey, because you shouldn't be distracted. You're supposed to help me find peace? Well you'll have to win this war first and I intend to help you. That'll be my peace…

The voice of Joe remained with Grey for over two weeks, a focused, strong presence that never asked Grey for anything, instead ensuring his survival and hearing of Grey's life without revealing anything of himself. Grey quickly got the measure of this selfless hero and was initially very upset when this most beneficial spirit left. He soon found himself smiling as he thought of Joe at peace and other soldiers began making requests of messages which he added to his bulging notebook. It was going to take him months to see all of the families who were scattered across the States, Britain, Canada and Oceania, but he would personally visit every one. The thought of how the families would receive him terrified him almost as much as combat.

Grey and Jake Baker sat with their backs against a low wall after a hard day's fighting, mercifully now over. Their unit was scattered around a small village that they had liberated, some of them dealing with German prisoners while others stood guard and others, like Grey and Jake, were ordered by Cloisters to take a break. Grey lit up a cigarette and offered Jake one, Jake declining as he always did.

"Not even after that? I admire you, Jake, I know I couldn't go without," Grey said.

"What do you think Harvey and the others are doing to the prisoners?" Jake said, a little troubled by the thought of what they might do to them.

"I don't think they'll be giving them the kid gloves treatment, but they won't hurt them if they do as instructed." Grey and Jake had both heard of German prisoners being executed by different regiments but Grey had enough faith in his own troop to trust that would not happen.

"Where is everybody? We've liberated this village, so where are the villagers? What do you think they've done with them?"

"Maybe they've been using it tactically and ordered everyone out. We've got places like that back home. Britain does too."

"Or maybe there's some mass grave somewhere."

"I don't think so," Grey said, believing that he would sense that if it were true. "I don't know where they are, Jake, but I do think they're alive – they weren't killed here anyway."

"I haven't even seen a Frenchwoman yet. Not alive," Jake said, remembering some that he had seen and the states they were in.

"We will."

"I'm becoming as bad as Macmurray. I think about sex a lot now," Jake said, feeling dirty because of how much it occupied his thoughts. "I want – I need that comfort that it brings."

"That's why I smoke. That's comfort for me. I never smoked before the war – when it started, I mean – and now my hand feels bare without a cigarette between my fingers. Look, you're not married or engaged so there's nothing wrong with you finding a girl and doing what you fancy."

"There are no girls and I'm not going the way of Hobbs and Neal," Jake said, referring to some salacious gossip (that Grey suspected was true) regarding the close relationship between two of their platoon.

"That's their business," Grey said, non-judgemental of their choices and trying to teach Jake to be equally tolerant. Jake was proving to be a good friend to him, but it disturbed Grey to see the contemptuous glances he shot the two men. Hobbs was timid and cowered at anything, while Neal matched fire with fire and, as one of the toughest in the unit, protected Hobbs where necessary. While Grey had tried to remain Hobbs' friend, Neal seemed to be aggressively possessive and, as Hobbs seemed very happy in Neal's company, Grey backed off.

"It's not right, James," Jake said. He looked at Grey, determined he was right that it was immoral and wanting him to agree.

"I don't know." Grey shrugged and he changed the subject. "So you want a French girl?"

"I'd take German at the minute. I would anyway because, when you think about it, the French ratio of men to women will be pretty close. It's the Germans, along with us lot, who are dying in droves in this war so there'll be plenty of German girls without men. I'm the same as you, I don't hate the Germans and I'd have no problem taking a German girl back with me as a wife if she was the right girl," Jake said, not universally prejudiced.

"No, me neither, only they have been educated – brainwashed – for so many years that I'd find it difficult. You can't expect views that have been ingrained into them for years to vanish overnight."

"They won't all be devout followers."

"A good amount will be, and they can't help it. I know a fair bit about the whole system. A whole generation has been bred for this war. From a young age they have had roles designed for them that they have had to fulfil. If everyone is telling you things as fact, no matter how wrong, you're going to end up believing them as right."

"Do you think girls are that political?"

"If you'd met a girl and you liked her and she was German I would say, go for it. I'm just warning you that there might be problems. It would be better if she was a lot older than you 'cause then she's less likely to be indoctrinated. If she was in her 30's or something..."

Jake shook his head vigorously. He could contemplate taking a German bride home, but not a woman old enough to be his mother. "I feel sorry for them, Grey. A lot of them will get caught in the crossfire."

"Let's worry about that when we get there."

"That day's coming fast. We're on an express train bearing down hard. Time is flying now we've started."

"You think so?" Grey said, very surprised at this perspective. Every day seemed long to Grey now and he felt this was the collective impression.

Jake nodded. "What about you? You seem to keep pretty quiet on the subject of women."

"I thought it would be poor form for the new guy to blow his own trumpet. Truth be told, Jake, there's not much to say. There's only one of my exes I'd be interested in writing to and she's head over heels in love with a war hero officer. I'm not sure I'd want to meet someone new in this crazy environment. It's bad enough worrying about your friends and yourself. Having a lover to worry about would be unimaginable."

"So there's no Iowan girl waiting back on a farm for you?"

"It would come as a big surprise if there was. And we're not all farmers, Jake. I'm from the city; I've hardly ever been on a farm in my life," Grey said, smiling at the cliché. There was most certainly no country girl waiting for him. Grey had tried to have normal relationships with normal girls in the past which never lasted long. His girlfriends liked him at first, but as they grew closer and he revealed more of himself, even without divulging his great secret, they glimpsed the freak and backed away. Maintaining a successful relationship would be akin to a military operation for him as first he would have to find the most broadminded woman alive who also ticked all of the boxes for him and he was pickier than most. With the exception of Daisy he tended to go for high maintenance girls, stunners who quickly lost interest in him when they realised his world didn't revolve around them. If he was unable to be attentive enough before joining up then now the micro-relationships would be even briefer, assuming he could even get close enough to the WAC or the locals in the first place. His head was already in enough turmoil without relationship angst thrown in. Being at war, having a sweetheart to care for, to fight for and to gain strength from would have been a huge boost too, yet Grey knew he just couldn't handle another diversion and would seriously short-change any ladies fool enough to want to entangle themselves with him (fortuitously this list could be written down without ink).

Another soldier slowly came into view, walking towards them with a very leisurely gait, Grey guessing, correctly, that it was Sykes, a 25 year old from their platoon.

"Cheers, don't mind if I do have a butt, Hawkeye, kind of you to offer," Sykes said, slouching down next to Grey who had to dig deep into his pocket to find another cigarette.

"I might need to cadge some off you at some stage, Victor," Grey said.

"That's cool. You're a patient guy, I can tell that and that's fortunate 'cause I'm that much in debt it'll be a while before I even have one pack but when I do I'll share them with you," he said genially.

"I don't understand why you have to play cards for money, especially money you don't have. When Fallon says he'll have you if you don't pay, he's not joking," Jake said, advising him how to live his life to keep him out of trouble.

"He'll get his money, I'm not sweating it about him," Sykes said insouciantly. "What are you two gabbing about anyway?" Sykes could be loud and abrasive, yet Grey liked him, finding many positive qualities in him. He was very sociable, very honest and was very familiar which Grey did not see as a bad thing.

"We're just wondering where all of the women are," Jake said.

"They've fled, haven't they? They know that I've got that much stored up that they can't handle it," Sykes said, grabbing his crotch as he spoke. "They knew me and you were going to fuck them, isn't that right, Jimmy boy?" Sykes said, whacking Grey on the arm, joking with him (or about him).

"Seems as it's just a small country village, I reckon that the Iowan here would stand more chance than you New Yorkers with the locals," Grey said, a little uncomfortable with joking about people who were possibly dead, mainly joking about the cliché of his state.

"That depends on how much they know about international news. If they hear about your lame baseball team they're going to look for winners instead which would see me right," Jake said, bantering with Grey.

"They've got a baseball team now? A lot must have changed in the last few months. You never know, Grey, they might have electricity when you get back!" Sykes said.

"And New York might be a clean, calm place where everyone gets on," Grey countered.

"Who the hell wants that? You go out around the city and you are guaranteed a good night. Right, Jake?" Sykes said, pressing him to agree.

"There's trouble sometimes, but you normally have a good night."

"The trouble's half the fun. Harvey would know what I mean. Ah well, I'll leave you to it. 'The girls would like Iowans better'! Keep on dreaming, bub," he said, chuckling to himself as he walked away.

"What do you think?" Jake said after he had walked some distance away.

"About what?"

"Sykes."

"He's all right; he's funny. When he rips into you it's just in fun. The Iowan jokes don't bother me at all. Pearce is the only one who can get a rise out of me, and I'm trying to learn how to tolerate him."

"His jokes are said in a completely different spirit. Personally, I think Sykes is harmless. Frankie can't stand him. My only problem with him is that he doesn't listen. I've told him on numerous occasions that he's going to get himself into trouble if he keeps on betting with Fallon and even now he doesn't seem to realise how much trouble he's in."

"Maybe the gambling is his comfort to help him through all of this. Even if he loses, maybe he still gets something out of it, it might calm his nerves."

"He doesn't seem to get nerves."

"I know. Lucky bastard."

"So if you haven't got a girl waiting for you on the farm or on the prairie back home then we'll have to find someone for you as well then. After all, your cigarettes aren't going to last forever."

"Good luck," Grey said amusedly. It was hard enough juggling the spirits with his soldierly duties. Throwing a dame into the mix guaranteed disaster.

CHAPTER 4 – DAY 17

Grey considered himself a medium with very limited control and every couple of days there would be an episode, which either showed his complete lack of control, or proved that he had more control than he realised, limiting the episodes. On these occasions the masses of faint voices would all come to the fore at once, bustling like Des Moines on a Saturday night, all competing for his attention, none of them making themselves understood. These episodes deafened and weakened him and thankfully were brief but they were so painful and disorientating that as he sensed one coming he tried in vain to repress it.

It pains me that they left me behind…more names than Old Nick, steer clear of her…her letters were forgettable but when she sang to me my heart swelled like…the sides became blurred. A lover on one side and family on the other. What would you have chosen?…I don't believe the invasion was well planned…'Sit down or there'll be trouble'. A bit late for that warning…if you could tell my mother and father that I don't want a…there's still divisions, lad. Money lives and gets the medals and the commoners die…please prove to them that my death was not accidental. The killer's name is John T…shame you pay scant attention to us, there's important lessons intended…what price upon your head, Charon?…always striving for more, pushing myself beyond…if my wives meet face to face there will be fireworks… The blood stopped…he forced his hands under my skirt…she screamed, just a little bit…where am I…did the shell kill Danno too…her dance would have shamed Salome…you don't have the answers I want – you can't even save yourself…don't drink the water…I was as American as them but that didn't stop them turning me into a trophy for their hunting lodge because of my German ancestry...it took a while for me to realise what they were going to do with the hosepipe…we were split up into two groups…tell them back home that the interviews for working in the munitions factories need to be more stringent…hear me, my brother, your time is running out…I welcomed them into my home…the darkness scared my sister while I…if I had a book it would be more bearable…who do I report to now…clairvoyance was wasted on such as you, with a platitude for every occasion…

Grey collapsed as more voices competed with each other, the strain making him feel like his head would explode. It was not the time for him to be weak, as they were fighting, though fortunately the fighting was mainly confined to the heavy artillery and they had practically finished off a German unit bar a few panzers. He received immediate attention from a medic and the attention forced Grey to sit up on his knees as he stated repeatedly that he was unhurt – there were plenty of other men who were genuinely wounded and needed treatment and there was no medical cure for him. The medic took him at his word eventually, though he kept looking back at him, certain that he'd missed something. Cloisters glared at Grey, a glare that demanded he stand up, and Grey complied, hoping that he could get some rest when the dying battle was over. Fighting the war was proving hard enough for him, but he felt crushed under an avalanche of spirit voices. It had been bad as soon as war was declared and hostilities commenced and he'd imagined that when he started active service it would be no worse. Distance should have made no difference to spirits, yet living at the centre of the storm he found that location did make a difference, a realisation that would perhaps prove useful one day. For now it was too much and he felt overloaded, and at times he resented his visitors and felt guilty for feeling that way – even though he felt his own identity was at risk, he had to keep being a supportive figure to them, a kind voice in the wilderness. There was no other option.

As the others conducted a post-mortem into the morning's conflict, Grey talked to a voice that was clear amidst the maelstrom. His voice had a sharp edge and he quickly revealed himself as a German, Dieter, though he distanced himself from the men that Grey had just fought, calling them the mindless herd.

So many of my people are blind and it infuriates me. They just follow the path set out for them like docile insects. Even the older generation seems to have forgotten that there used to be choices and they don't realise that the dictatorship isn't normal or acceptable. They're like machines, unquestioning, meekly accepting whatever is set out for them. They just shrug their shoulders and say, with a smile, 'I have to change career and do this job now', 'The party knows best.' I learnt quickly, as any man with half a brain would, that just because your regime tells you that you have no choices doesn't make it so. I settled for being mildly disruptive to begin with, laughing out loud during speeches at Hitler Youth meetings and desecrating the Swastika. He laughed for a while and said bitterly, *Only 14 years old and the things they did to me for that.*

It must have felt like an uphill battle, Grey said supportively.

Completely, but I was never going to break. I wanted to openly defy them; I wanted to spit in the faces of the SS. I'm not a Communist and I didn't have any Jewish friends – I'm sympathetic to how they were treated but that's not my issue. My problem with the Nazis is that they wanted to control me, under this guise of a caring Reich where everyone's happy and has a role – could it have been any more obvious that they were creating a slave state? he said agitatedly.

It was pretty blatant. I suppose after the horrors of the last war everyone didn't want to put another generation through that, and let him get away with too much, just to avoid war, Grey said, acting as apologist.

Then why did they even bother with the Versailles Treaty? They took the money, but then they wouldn't enforce the rules. When I saw my 'brave comrades' marching into the Rhineland I was ecstatic, but for different reasons to the others who celebrated it. It was such an audacious breach of the rules that I thought war was inevitable and that he'd be toppled. When they did nothing at that I knew that they never would.

They did eventually, Dieter. Britain and France declared war on Germany, not the other way round, and we've done the same, later than we should have in my opinion.

I was surprised to be honest with you. I thought no one would ever try and stop them. It's better late than never but if the rest of the world had acted sooner and gone to war eight years ago it would have been swifter and the losses would have been less severe. I felt foolish when war wasn't declared then; I'd been so jubilant and convinced it would happen, when, if I'd engaged my brain, I would have seen, as Hitler had, that no one was going to stop the Nazis. The British Prime Minister was weak, the Americans weren't interested, France wouldn't act without support, and Russia had Hitler by another name as their leader. Any idealism I had died around that time.

You're still idealistic, very much so. Dieter seemed like a revolutionary to Grey, a dissident spirit with the energy to change the world and the epitome of angry optimism with enough fire to even take on the Third Reich single-handedly.

An idealist looks to the future with hope, and wants to help create his own, better state. Hitler likely considers himself that – what am I saying likely, of course he does, I know him better than I know myself! he said biliously. *All I am, all I was, was a man who knew what he hated. Hans and Sophie Scholl had political vision – I just wanted to destroy the system. My success was negligible.*

At least you tried.

You understand. Thank you. That is my success, the attempt. I achieved little of practical worth, hamstrung by my unwillingness to kill, which would make you think I was a failure. I've thought that before until I analysed everything. It doesn't matter that I didn't make a dent, it doesn't matter that I won't be remembered like the Scholls. What is important is that I didn't take the easy, straight path. I took the other path, Grey. The other path. Do you understand?

Yeah, I think so.

I don't think you do fully. You're following the straight path.

I think we hold similar views. We're both staunch opponents of Nazism and I agree with you about Stalin. He's untrustworthy and while I don't get many Russian voices, the few I've talked to don't portray him in a good light.

You're an American soldier serving your country in a time of war. That path couldn't be any straighter.

Grey tried to understand what his objection was and couldn't work him out. *Sometimes the straight path is the right path to take. The other path for me would be what? Being a conscientious objector or supporting the Nazis? I won't do either.*

But you're doing what you're programmed to. I'm not telling you to support the Nazis and just for the suggestion I'm tempted to stop talking to you. I'm telling you to use your brain to make a choice.

I'm happy with the one I made and I did make a choice. It was the one that was expected, yes. It was also the choice I wanted to make. To always pick the other path – that's just being contrary. I hope that doesn't sound rude and you were right to go against the grain, but I can't fight against what I believe.

You're an animist. That's…

I'm sorry, I don't know what that means.

It means that you believe in the existence of spirits otherwise you wouldn't be having this conversation with me.

Yes, I do. I call myself a medium.

There is a distinction between an animist and a medium. Mediums require skill, he said scathingly. *You're an animist and that's your first deviation from the straight path and a signpost to which true direction you should take.*

Whatever word we use the result is the same; I hear spirits and I talk with them and I can do that in the army, and I do, sometimes successfully, to help me with things.

You have a skill, but you're not skilled. Develop that and use it against the Nazis. That's your true path.

Again, I can do both.

Can you do both well?

No, I can't do either well, yet. How can you be so certain that that is the right path for me, Dieter?

Instinct. You know it too.

Even if it was, how would I go about it?

Don't ask me, you've got to come up with the rest of the answers for yourself. Keep your eyes open and something will present itself.

Dieter left him shortly afterwards and Grey only considered his advice fleetingly. Life was hard enough without intentionally making it harder through recalcitrance. The next spirit proved a complete contrast, a carefree American.

I know your voice. This is the first time I've ever been aware that I'm having a dream, and it's the first dream I've had without any pictures – I can't see a fucking thing, he said, not taking his situation seriously.

It's no dream I'm afraid. That's the bad news. The good news is that you won't be here long before you find peace.

I swear down I do know your voice. What's your name?

Grey.

You're from Ohio, yeah? the voice said excitedly.

Iowa.

Yeah, same thing, that's what I meant. Potter.

Phil Potter? Grey said. They had barely known each other, having never found time to strike up more than a passing acquaintance, but just like with Teddy Murphy it affected him more, even though he had never clicked with either man in life. It was the reality of passing over that disturbed him, to have known someone, no matter how casually, on both planes of existence. It showed him too vividly that the two worlds were closer to each other than he was comfortable with.

That's me. I'll play the goon and ask all the stupid questions. What are you doing in my dream, Grey, and what have you done with all of the pictures?

If you really believed this was a dream I don't think you'd be asking me questions. I know it's hard, but you have to accept that this isn't a dream.

If it's not a dream then I guess I didn't make it. I didn't really think I was asleep.

I'm sorry, Phil.

Not your fault, Grey. Did you pass away too?

No, not yet, though I do think my time is coming. I'm here because I'm a medium. You're allowed to laugh at that if you want. I don't have the charisma which is associated with the field, but I do have the skills to help you.

My grandmother used to do that. Well, similar stuff. She used to do fortunes from articles of clothing or jewellery, just as a hobby. I'm not convinced she was the full…

Phil, can you hear me? Grey said, surprised by how quickly he lost him. He tried fruitlessly to retrieve him, giving up after half an hour when another voice came to the fore.

Do you talk Deutsch? the male voice said hopefully.

Not a word, I'm afraid. I'm Grey. If English is hard for you to understand we can talk slowly and I can repeat myself as many times as you need. What's your name, friend?

Friend. Danke.

That's thank you, I do know that one.

Ja, thank you. My English not the best, he said, worried that he would struggle to make himself understood.

Mine isn't either, don't worry, Grey said affably. *What is your name please?*

Frederick.

You've got the same name as my cousin. How are you, Frederick?

Sad. I think we lose war.

Hmm. I wish that you were still alive, Frederick, but I don't want your side to win the war.

You American?

Yes, Grey said uneasily, unsure how this conversation would pan out.

No problem with American. You hate Deutschland?

No, just the system, the Nazis.

Then you hate Deutschland.

No, I don't.

Why hate what works? he said, sounding very upset at Grey's criticism. *Hold on. I taught English long, long back.*

There's no rush, we can take as long as you need.

I was born 1921. I know Weimar, I know life before the Nationalsozialistische Deutsche Arbeiterpartei. We all brothers now unt not before.

Yes, the Nazis have galvanised…united your country, at a huge price.

You be Nazi. We…except you?

That's not what I want, Grey said emphatically.

The rejection was enough for Grey to lose contact with Frederick though another German voice instantly took his place, this male voice less accented.

Excuse my countryman. My English is better than his and I'd like to continue the conversation.

Okay, Grey said tentatively, this occurrence quite unusual for him. *Can you wait one moment while I try and get him back and all three of us can talk?*

He's gone. My name's Josef Wittmann, Untersturmfuhrer in the German Army. I'd like to know your first name so that we can have a civilised conversation and I'm interested what rank you are.

Just a private. My first name's James.

You sound young, James, you've no reason to be ashamed of being a private, he said amiably.

I'm not. I'm just learning the ropes at the moment so I wouldn't want any higher rank.

Sensible boy. Sorry, that sounds patronising. You're at war so you're a man now. Knowing your own limitations is more admirable than those who boast they can do far more than they are able and let everyone down. Such modesty isn't always ascribed to Americans.

We're all very different, just as your people aren't all the same. I'm not your usual...don't judge all Americans by me, he said, criticising himself.

I won't. How old are you, James?

18.

I thought so. I was born 12 years before you in 1914 and, like many children of that time, I grew up without a father, when the seeds for this war were sown. Do you know much of German history?

I learn a lot through you guys, but I don't know much about history apart from that. I've never been good at the subject. Was there a leader called Bismarck?

Yes, well done for knowing that, but I mean – it's my fault, history is the wrong word. Do you know much about contemporary German history?

I know about the war and hyperinflation and the rise of Hitler and I've been following events closely for the last eight years.

I imagine the whole world has been. You have reservations about the Third Reich.

Yes, more than reservations, Grey said animatedly. *You can't build an empire on the bodies of your own people.*

I admit that our country uses propaganda to a very large degree. You might be surprised to hear that the Allied governments do too. Not all that you have been told is truth.

Look, Josef, Mr Wittmann – I don't want to argue about Nazism with you. We have very different opinions and let's leave it at that. I want to help you find peace. Had Josef still been alive Grey would have been more interested in debating the issue and trying to teach him where he was wrong and change his opinion. As he was dead Grey saw no need as Josef's views could not extend into action and Grey felt no need to preach to him, preferring just to help him instead.

Perhaps talking this through will be what grants me peace.

What about your family? Tell me about them.

My wife, Paula, already knows how much I love her, as does my daughter, Ilse. I have no messages. We said our farewells and, while I appreciate the thought, I want them left alone.

I can understand that. Do you think it could be your unit? Are you concerned about them? Grey said, looking for what was anchoring his spirit.

Yes, but they'll be in good hands. The thing that I want to talk about is your hatred of Nazism. It will just be a calm discussion, I promise you, he said. He was a fanatical supporter of the Reich, but he believed that staying cool (even when Hitler was denounced) was a better way of converting opponents rather than strong-arm tactics (no longer an option anyhow).

I suppose my main problem would be the death camps. That's inexcusable.

Labour camps, not death camps. That's an example of propaganda. These people are happier together with their own kind.

You can't believe that. What if it was your wife and daughter?

She can trace her parentage back to the days of Bismarck so that would never happen.

If they can callously kill one people then they will be prepared to kill another. Maybe they'll decide in the future that people both in the South of Germany are more subhuman than those in the north.

A German is a German, he said, amused by Grey's flawed logic, which showed a complete lack of understanding of the German people.

What of a Jewish German?

James, the animosity, which is reciprocated by the Jews, is not the heart of National Socialism. They oppose the regime and are enemies and we are fairly merciful towards them, but that's only a small issue and there is much more that must be looked at. Germany has achieved so much under Hitler and has been prosperous – remember that our economy collapsed and millions lost all of their money and many starved just shortly before you were born. The achievements outweigh any negatives. I've seen a people demoralised and struggling to stay afloat turn into a nation where the citizens hold their heads up with pride and our neighbour becomes our friend and our friend becomes our brother. The Fuehrer did not want this war, not with the British or Americans. A peace could be brokered with your side.

Grey had let him speak, objecting to most of what he said, but giving him the courtesy of hearing him out and when Josef was quiet he said, *I don't think it could, not now.*

I think it will happen. I was a year older than you when I joined the 'Nazi' party. Like you, I lacked self-belief until then and it changed me instantly. You would be accepted – your abilities would not be ridiculed either.

I'm an American soldier who hates fascism and racism – I don't want to be a Nazi and they won't want me.

They will. You're an Aryan and…

You don't know that.

I'm fairly sure that you are.

This proves to me how ridiculous the whole system is. You'd accept me as a Nazi, but if I turned round and told you that my mother is Jewish then suddenly I'd be an enemy of the state even though I'm still the same man.

You have a gift – perhaps allowances could be made.

My mother isn't Jewish, but any organisation that would prohibit me from joining on that basis isn't one I want to join.

Are you a proud American?

Yes, Grey said reservedly.

Just 80 years ago your country still practised slavery, 50 years after we abolished the practice.

Black people in America have been treated disgracefully in America by some quarters and there needs to be huge changes still, but it doesn't compare…

All I am saying is that America cannot, and Britain certainly can't either, take the moral high ground with the Fatherland.

At least my country's bad deeds are in the past. Your country is still killing now – I'm sure they don't want to be, I'm sure they're incensed that killing millions is so time-consuming and inconvenient, Grey said bitterly, not directing his anger at Josef.

Your country is killing millions too. You don't mean in the war, do you? You're back to the camps. I understand your revulsion and once I would have shared it. Let me explain.

You can't, Josef, not this.

Let me try. We've been taught – our eyes have been opened about them over the last ten years. Their façade is good, until you look closer and see the baseness underneath.

No, Josef, I don't want to see this side of you. Let's talk about your wife and daughter, Grey said wearily

We will, but first it is my duty to enlighten you…

Over the next hour Grey listened to Josef's extended anti-Semitic monologues, inwardly sighing at the mindless hate and the extent of his brainwashing. Josef seemed a fundamentally decent man to him and Grey considered his moral demise was only partly his fault and largely down to his poor luck at being born in the wrong country at the wrong time. Grey wondered if his own attitudes would have been any different if he had been born in Germany, hoping that he would have had the sense to see through the lies, but unsure – the offer of acceptance would have been hard to resist and he worried that he would have thrived.

Cloisters called the squad together to discuss a forthcoming operation and quickly noticed that Grey was still acting strangely, apparently in a world of his own.

"You fucking look at me when I talk to you, Grey."

"I am paying attention," Grey lied, too distracted by Josef to pay sufficient attention to Cloisters.

"What's the plan then?"

Grey had intended to ask the others for a recap of what to do and, put on the spot, he was forced to admit that he didn't know. "I'm sorry, Sarge, I didn't understand all of it."

"Sorry if I'm boring you," he said sarcastically before bawling, "Get your fucking head out of the clouds." Grey usually got on with his sergeant but over the last week he kept being reprimanded for the same thing and Grey knew he would have to improve his concentration regardless of how many voices were talking to him and irrespective of what contentious things they were saying, though Josef would take some beating. He seemed a pleasant, modest, softly spoken man, with warped, bigoted views.

You're not convinced, are you? It's hard to condense ten years of teaching into one speech.

You're a passionate and charismatic speaker, but the content is not to my tastes. In fact, it makes me feel sick – you don't, you're a separate man from this, Grey said, trying to ignore all that he'd heard and looking for the good in him.

Our views, our beliefs – these are what make us men. It's part of me, James.

It's been drilled into you. I get that.

And it's been drilled into you not to like us, to view us as evil.

It has, and I don't buy into it. I'll fight and kill your soldiers, but I won't hate them.

Josef thought his words over, his statement seemingly contradictory at first listen, and he said, *I can follow that. We'll move on to a different subject because that one does seem to bother you and I don't want to upset you.* His genuine concern aggrieved Grey, who found it unreasonable that he showed compassion for his feelings and none for children and whole families being gassed.

Josef went on to talk about the more palatable side of Nazism at length, routine propaganda that Grey had heard before and listened to again. While Grey was being antisocial with the others in his unit, it did not put Delgado off from approaching him and he filled Grey in on the casualties of the day, leaving one name out.

"Phil Potter died too," Grey said.

Delgado shook his head. "He hasn't, not unless he's died in the last 20 minutes," Delgado said, considering his source to be most reliable. "He's being treated by the medics still."

"I won't be long," Grey said and he tried to wangle his way to see him to check for himself. Grey needed permission to see him as the medics had set up a station that was a mile back from the action.

"You're not pals," Cloisters said, staring hard at him.

"I think he's dead. I want to check that they haven't made a mistake," Grey said. He believed that this had to be the case and he wanted to rectify the mistake immediately before families received damaging misinformation. Potter's family would be given false hope, believing that he was injured, not dead, while another man's family would be wrongly informed that he was missing.

"He's in a bad way, Grey, but he's not dead. I'm not going to let you go and see him if you're going to tell him that he should be," Cloisters said sharply.

"I won't say that."

Cloisters sighed loudly, almost a growl, and controlled his natural instinct, which was to tell Grey to shut up and stop wasting his time. Instead he tried to be patient and he said, "Why do you think the doctors have got it wrong?"

Grey struggled for an answer – it was hard for him when he didn't even know the exact nature of his injuries. "I thought I saw him with his eyes open – he was sprawled on the floor and they were staring, not like – you know how they look when they're gone."

"It must have been someone else. Potter was shot in the leg and he was treated by the medics immediately at the scene. I know that something went wrong when they were treating him – he responded badly to the drugs, or something, but the docs revived him after a little while. Charlie!" Cloisters shouted and one of Potter's friends walked over to them.

"Charlie, tell Grey here that Potter didn't pop his clogs."

"Nah. Looked close to it but. He was worrying them and I think his heart stopped for a few minutes before he came round and he was talking. I wonder if you're the Grey he was talking about," Charlie said, looking at Grey curiously.

Grey gulped anxiously, afraid that his secret was about to come out and he said, "What did he say?"

"Not much, they were taking him away. He said he'd had a strange dream about Grey, which I guess means you."

"He's been dreaming about Potter too. Fuck me, we're going to have a wedding on our hands here. Satisfied?" Cloisters said, feeling that the matter was cleared up.

Grey nodded and looked at them both furtively and made a hasty exit. Phil Potter was going to tell everyone what he was, Grey believing initially that this was the worst possible news. He soon realised how selfish his attitude was and realised that even though he would be completely ostracised and hated, it was still good news as a man who had nearly died had come back from the brink. It was great news for Potter and his family and his friends – his own misery was a minor side effect that was worth paying. Josef was quickly back, continuing his introductory course to the Third Reich, and Grey just listened unresponsively, in no mood to argue, and he let him rant. Eventually Josef stopped the hard sell and asked Grey what was wrong, surprised that he hadn't raised objections at some of his points.

It's going to come out – what I am.

Have you told anyone?

It was a guy like you. He'd died, but they brought him back.

The chances are he won't remember. We're taught that a healthy mind is as vital as a healthy body. The mind has its own defences which can shield us from unpalatable things. If he is able to recall anything, he'll dismiss it as a dream.

I hope you're right. If he sees me again though I know I'll give myself away.

Is it an American soldier?

Yes.

They will likely ship him back home and you won't cross paths again. If he does say anything they'll think he's delirious – no one will believe it. They'll think he's mad, Josef said, assuring Grey that his secret was safe and that his life could continue as normal.

If he says anything I'll have to admit it. I can't let other people think he's mad.

He may well relapse. Whatever happens I doubt you'll meet him again. Your fear of being found out, your misplaced shame, highlight to me why you are on the wrong side. Occultism is accepted in the Reich. You'd be pilloried in the West, not in Germany.

I'm not so sure. A freak is still a freak whatever country you're in.

Surely you don't believe that of yourself.

No, I don't. I'm glad that I have this gift; I'm saying that that is how other people would view me.

If you would just talk to a few important people – I know that there are specific gentlemen you can talk to, and I'm afraid I don't know their names – if you convinced them, then you'd be above reproach. No one would dare call you anything.

I would sooner be condemned than live in an oppressive state without freedom of speech.

Why would you want the right to be abused?

Everyone has to have the right to criticise. If I said some of the things I've said to you about the Nazi regime in a German market square, I'd be executed. How can anyone even dare to get drunk in that climate? You would have to be on guard of what you said always.

Most have no grievances with the party. My friends and I were never big drinkers but when we did we always toasted Hitler and all of our leaders and we remained as reverential regardless of how much we drank – in fact most of us became even more affectionate towards the party after we'd drank a lot, he said, remembering past times fondly.

Josef, I really would like to get back to your wife and daughter, Grey said, worn down by him and the day he was having.

They know, they know. I appreciate the sentiment. You're a fine young man.

Grey found returning the compliment hard after all that Josef had told him and he settled for, *I think you're a good man led astray by a despicable government.*

You've criticised my government again and I don't want you killed for it, I don't resent you for it, he said calmly. This image you have of us as being hateful is not accurate.

Answer me honestly on this score. Pretend you're still alive and I'm standing in the market square in front of your men and I stand up and denounce Hitler and all of the doctrines of Nazism. You don't know that I'm a medium – what would you do?

I'd arrest you, but I wouldn't consider it traitorous because you're not German. I wouldn't push for your execution.

Bear in mind that I would have been very critical of Hitler, maybe crudely so.

James, I know you now, I wouldn't kill you. You're too sensible to do that anyway.

I think you'd kill me. Not now, no, I accept that. But if I was just a stranger mouthing off against everything you revere, I'm certain you would.

Every person on this planet makes allowances for their friends that they wouldn't for strangers. If I returned from the grave like this soldier today and I remembered our dialogues, then even if I found you reciting diatribes in public, I wouldn't kill you, or have you harmed. Such a crime doesn't always mean death – it's usually a beating, and I would ensure that that didn't happen to you. Instead I would take you to these gentlemen where your gift would be respected and where you would learn more about it and accumulate wealth. My introduction would have made things easier for you – they'll be wary of you as an American, but I know you can convince them.

To what end? To help my country lose the war? I know I'll never be an important person in the army, but at least I can respect myself. Money and acclaim don't mean anything if I hate myself in the process.

You wouldn't, you'd feel at home. Your personality and temperament make you better suited to joining my people.

You're all different, just like we are, Grey said. Josef had made him a lot calmer about the Potter situation, but he was tiring him, Grey finding his opinions hard to stomach. Grey was glad when he heard another voice, an Englishwoman, though Josef did not subside and Grey asked him to be patient while he talked to her, Josef accepting the delay most graciously. Grey heard the resentment in Elsie's voice in her second sentence and he suddenly realised she wasn't going to be easy either.

Both of my brothers died in the Great War, as well as my sister's husband, and my mother died from a broken heart. This war should never have been allowed after those terrible years.

That's why everyone was reluctant, because of the Great War.

Reluctant! They've entered into it keenly now. How many lives have been lost? Not just soldiers, civilians too.

I would say a soldier's life is worth as much as a civilian's.

Come, come, you can't honestly think that.

I do, but I understand if you resent soldiers. You think we're the cause of wars.

Not the cause, the tools of war. If you were all brave enough to refuse to fight there wouldn't be a war.

That option isn't available. The Jerries won't do that.

Neither will the British or the Americans, don't just blame the Germans. You just want us all to hate them, don't you, to justify the war? she said, lumping Grey in with her Government's ministers.

I don't hate them, Grey said truthfully.

Look, Grey – I hate what you are, not who you are. I can separate the uniform of oppression from the man. What you all need to do, while you still have souls, is tear off the uniform and return home. If you don't provoke the Germans they'll do the same.

No they won't. Did anyone provoke the Japanese to go to war? he said, growing frustrated with her and not prepared to humour her. He expected more from her than he did from Josef.

Why did the Americans have a base there? Why were their assets frozen? It was a pre-emptive strike. If they hadn't been there they wouldn't have been attacked.

The death toll was high.

It always is in war. That's my point and that's why you have to end it. It's in the hands of the soldiers. Your generals will never end it, they love destruction too much, and the politicians won't stop it because it's good for their careers. You soldiers are the only ones who can stop it.

If both sides would walk away then that would be a possibility. Neither side will though, it's just not realistic, Elsie, he said softly.

Forgive me for having too much faith in human nature, Grey, she said acerbically.

If we did all just walk away what would happen in Germany? The death camps wouldn't close, the oppression wouldn't stop.

Poppycock! You just believe everything they tell you, she said, dismissively.

I'm not an astute person by any means, but I am quite good at seeing through propaganda and I don't swallow the lies. The trouble is, with the Nazis they don't have to lie because the truth is worse than any fiction.

And how do you know that? From the papers? she said snidely.

I know that because I'm a medium, Grey said, snapping a little. *I'm sorry if that sounded cross, it's just I know firsthand what they've gone through.*

Firsthand would mean that you endured it. You know secondhand at best, she said patronisingly, unmoved by his words. *How can violence ever solve any problems?*

Elsie and Josef both talked to him simultaneously, unable to hear each other as Josef resumed the revised tale of the Third Reich while Elsie used statistics effectively in her polemic against the military. He tried to help them find peace but they both made it clear that changing his views would be their peace, Josef trying to make him change sides while Elsie tried to stop him being a warmonger.

A distraction came soon enough for him, one that should have been pleasant. Nearly all of the men were pleased when their mail caught up with them, Grey receiving his letter with a forced smile. He opened it immediately and held it towards him so that no one else could read it.

Dear James,

How are you holding up? Write to tell us where you are and what you've been up to. Keep your head down and you'll make us proud. Your father and I are well. If you need anything write and we'll send you it. Brian has been medically discharged with a shrapnel injury. He seems fine and Geraldine is delighted. Your great aunt Lily has passed away.

Love,

Mother

The letter made Grey angry, not at its content or brevity; he was angry as it meant he had to write a letter back. The last one he'd written was four pages and a monumental effort as he wrote about people they didn't know and didn't care to know about and this would be harder. On a positive note, she made no mention of his change of unit, which suggested that the lame lie he'd given had been swallowed. He could spin a page out about Aunt Lily and Brian– after that he was stuck. He saw Delgado turning page after page contentedly, Jake and Harvey Baker sitting together reading what their mother had written, both laughing at the content (Grey knew from Jake that Mrs Baker was a funny woman), while he folded his letter and put it in his bag, never to read again. It was hard for his parents and he understood that and didn't expect them to articulate their feelings in words – their unemotional letters perfectly summed up their feelings better than they realised.

"You read yours quick, Grey," Delgado said as he put his letter in his bag and began to write a reply (which, despite his close relationship with his parents, he was finding progressively harder and he now made draft copies first).

"I'm a quick reader," Grey lied. "How's everything in Phoenix?"

"It's carrying on without me, to my chagrin. Has Iowa come to a standstill while they wait for their favourite son?"

"Unlikely. You probably do right to use this quiet time to write back to them."

"They've cheered me up today so I want to write while I'm still feeling positive. I still try and describe it all as a jaunt and that's why it takes me so long – if I said what I was really thinking the words would flow like a waterfall and make my folks as miserable as sin. It's not like I'm lying – I prefer to think of it as extreme fabrication. If we see some dead French I describe that as seeing some locals and when we have casualties I describe that as some of the unit deciding to stay behind," he said with black humour. "Are you more straight with your folks?"

"Not really. I'm no good at writing."

"What about your notebook, you're always scribbling in that, and guard it like it's the crown jewels." Two soldiers from a different platoon had made a grab for it one day and Grey had gone wild, retrieving it before it was read but gaining two enemies in the process.

"That's just my journal and that's just for my eyes so it's lame, not like a letter."

"A journal's a useful thing, it'll help you with your post-war memoirs. All of the days are blurring into one for me so I never remember what happened each day. Why don't you look through it and that'll give you some idea what to write?" he said, trying to be helpful.

"I think I'll sleep on it and work on it tomorrow. Do you want me to leave you in peace so that you can come up with something?"

"No, there's no need for that. If you want to stick around I don't mind, pal. You can help me think of a way to sweeten the sound of some of the atrocities." Grey had confided in him that he had left his last unit because they had wrongly believed him unstable, but Delgado had noticed visible signs of manic depression, the depressive cycles much more infrequent than the manic periods (which were not as hyper as most cases he'd read of but a sharp contrast to his low state). Delgado kept an open mind about him (psychiatry was not his field, his diagnosis very much uncertain), but because of the signs of mental fragility he liked to keep an eye on him. They all had good and bad days but Grey's were too extreme as he went from outgoing to introvert. While most of the men in his platoon had worked through their prejudices against him, Delgado remembered that Grey had never been concerned by his ethnicity from the start, something he appreciated and wouldn't forget.

"Isdel, can I ask you a question?" Grey said, deadly serious.

"Shoot."

"When people have been racist towards you in the past have you ever tried to enlighten them, to teach them where they're going wrong?" At first Grey had tried to overlook Josef's prejudices, but after prolonged exposure to them he wanted to help him see the error of his ways, worried that Josef would never find peace while he remained so bigoted.

"Never. I never will. I don't have to justify my existence to anyone," Delgado said forcefully. "One of my friends believes in talking it through with bigots but that's never been my way."

"I don't blame you, don't misunderstand me," Grey said, not wanting to upset him.

"My hackles would be raised if I was having this conversation with most of the others from this unit, but I know you're not racist so don't worry about offending me. As a Christian I do try not to hate the bigots only I'm never going to turn the other cheek. I'm a Christian, not a saint. I'm never going to offer shelter to a KKK member – I don't follow Christ's teachings that literally. I do admire those who have the patience to try and change the attitudes of others, even if it's not something I would ever do. People can change, only it doesn't happen overnight and I'd sooner shake some sense into them, which isn't the way to go about it."

"Has your friend had any success in changing other people's attitudes?"

"Not that I remember. I don't mind talking about this with you, Jimmy, only is there any particular reason for this interest?" Delgado said, feeling that there was more to it.

"I'm just wondering how we change the Germans' attitudes after the war."

"The politicians and diplomats can sort that out. We'll be on a boat going back home then and charities and other sorts of organisations will see them right."

"Are some people unreachable though?"

Delgado nodded vigorously. "Yeah. Don't dwell on the world's ills though. We've all had letters from home and that makes today a good day."

Grey involuntarily grimaced at this, which Delgado noticed and he asked, "Did you get bad news in yours?"

"No. Well, I suppose I did. My great aunt died but she was erm…88, I think. I'd take that," he said glibly. He was putting in a poor performance and would have to appear more cheerful, regardless of how he felt.

"I'd take half that at the moment, at least that way you get the best years," Delgado said, looking down as he started work on his letter. "I'm addressing it to my dad so that he can screen what to tell my mother – which I know right now is damned stupid on my part because my mother is a much stronger character than my father. He thinks the meek will inherit the earth," Delgado said critically. He was closer to his father but he possessed more of his mother's characteristics. His father's endless tolerance was beyond him.

"I hope he's right. It would be nice if that was true."

"You only have to take a look around here to see that it's not. Force wins out."

"Temporarily, then this country and all of Europe and Asia will go back to being free."

Delgado said nothing, smiling at his idealism and naiveté, unwilling to dispute the point as he didn't want to bring him down again, happy for Grey to believe this unrealistic dream.

Grey tried to interact with the others, still conversing with Josef and Elsie but doing a better job of disguising it. Cloisters gestured for him to come over to him while there was no one else around. He was calmer now and said, "You all right today, Grey? You don't seem at the top of your game."

"Ignore me, Sarge, I'm just tired."

"Good, I'm glad that's all it is. You understand that I have to clamp down on you, whatever the reason. If the likes of Pearce see you getting away with anything they'll try and get away with 10 times worse," Cloisters said, letting him know he wasn't as cross with him as he had appeared. "You look a state mind, Grey. If I didn't know differently I'd have thought you'd been on a weeklong bender. Are you getting any sleep?"

"Some. It's the same for everyone though, I'm not making excuses."

"We all handle it differently and whatever your method is, change it. You look wretched and the next time you get leave I'm ordering you to go and get smashed just to get this out of your system. Your parents won't recognise you if you go back like this. There's nothing more to it than tiredness?"

Grey shook his head. "I know I've been distant today. I'll be more sociable for the rest of the day – that might perk me up."

"I'd sooner see you getting under their skin with your jabbering than this."

"I think they'll be glad that this gasbag's had a puncture."

"You're surviving well out there, you're not close to getting a puncture. Keep it together, right?" Cloisters said and Grey knew he was questioning his sanity.

"I'll be more mentally alert in future."

"Good. Hop along then 'cause I've got to see three now who I've really got to clamp down on. You were just the warm up."

"So is everything okay with us? I'm not in trouble now?"

"Not as long as you pay attention next time. You haven't been in trouble yet; this is only a mild reprimand. When you're in trouble I'll be calling you a stupid Iowan farming fucker – you'll know when you're in trouble."

"I must be in trouble with the other fellas a lot 'cause I've heard worse than that off them. With this being unit number two I can promise you from now on you'll only be pulling me to one side for my hunches, not to bawl me out."

Cloisters grinned at this, preferring to see the overkeen soldier desperate to impress over the remote dreamer (and that was the favourable interpretation). Grey's excuses were plausible enough and Cloisters chose to seem to believe them. "My old man always took in the strays. When times were hard he'd drown them..."

Grey tried to make more of an effort with the rest of his platoon, partaking in a leisurely conversation with Jake Baker (who was wistful for home after the letter and his mind kept drifting back there). During a lull in the conversation, with both of them thinking of other things, Grey went down in a heap. Had he been shot in the back of the head? No, it would hurt more, more of a sharp pain rather than the dull ache he felt. He looked behind him and saw Pearce holding his rifle as Jake Baker stood in his way. Grey rubbed his head, feeling an almighty lump – Pearce had brained him good.

"What did you do that for, you idiot?" Jake remonstrated.

"You'll get a whack yourself if you talk to me like that again."

"I'm not scared of you," Jake said convincingly. While Macmurray, who was much tougher than Pearce and outweighed Jake by 70 pounds (and Pearce by almost the same amount), held no fear for Jake and he was unafraid to clash with him and did not want his brother to intervene, the same was not true concerning Pearce. Jake found him intimidating, though he would never let that control his behaviour and he stood up to him. Pearce was a skilled bully and sensed the small amount of fear and worked on it.

"You'd better hope that nothing happens to your brother, because when he's not around to protect you we'll have a serious talk," Pearce said, smiling malevolently.

"You think I'd be giving you any thought at all if my brother was dead!" Jake said, amazed at his arrogance.

"I never said dead. If he gets injured then I'll kick some manners into you, you prissy pissant," he said, inches from Jake's face.

"Jake, leave it," Grey said, struggling to his feet, not wanting Jake to get into a fight over him.

"Cloisters will be kicking some manners into you when I tell him what you did to him," Jake said.

"If he tells on me then I'll tell on you, Grey. You've already been shouted at for drifting off into a coma once today – if I tell him that you're still off on one then you'll get into worse trouble than me," Pearce threatened.

"You think Cloisters will come down harder on daydreaming than assault?" Jake said, shaking his head at him.

"Okay, but you don't tell anyone else about that or I tell Cloisters," Grey said, happy to accept the deal.

"All right," Pearce said, happy that he'd clouted him and got away with it.

"Explain to me why you did that," Jake said. Letting Pearce get away with anything was a mistake in his eyes.

"I'm in enough trouble today so I'll let anything go. If you want to slag off the Keokuks today's the day 'cause I won't respond."

"You can't kick someone when they're down. By that policy I shouldn't run down your team," he quipped.

"You see, Jake, I'm just letting that go. I feel no urge to retaliate by telling you how diabolical your team is," Grey said, acting a little more like the person the others were used to. His head spun, but he managed to put on a better show while still talking issues through with Josef and Elsie.

It's fate that we're talking, Josef said.

I was talking to Frederick too.

And our message is the same. That's a sign.

Josef, you're the loudest person at the moment, but I can hear at least ten more now, one almost as clear as you. I have a lot of visitors and they're all different with completely different messages.

I believe that you're a religious man. You'll know the story of Saul and how he became known as Paul.

I'm not converting, Grey said, getting his gist.

Please free your mind, James. It's too closed. You're different to most other men on this planet and I'm not judging you for that.

That's what your government does!

You can be part of it. I'm not trying to harm or trick you. I'm trying to help you, he said honestly.

I know that you think you are…

Elsie proved equally difficult, and while her message was more palatable, her spiky temperament made communication trying.

We've talked a lot about the war, Elsie, and I'd like to talk about you. Are you married?

And what has my marital status got to do with anything? If I'm not married are my views more easily dismissed? she said indignantly.

Of course not, I just…Is there anyone you'd like me to pass any messages on to?

Yes. I want you to pass on this message to the whole world: the war is wrong.

The war is ugly and brutal. I don't think it's wrong.

So you think something that is ugly and brutal is right?

Not right. Necessary. There is a difference.

Tell that to the widows and orphaned children of the world.

Even those who have lost loved ones in the war generally support the war.

Wake up! Perhaps I'm more outspoken than many, but there are millions out there who think like I do. We haven't all been brainwashed like you.

I haven't been brainwashed. Don't you think that I would be harder to fool than most because of my gift? Elsie, I'd much sooner talk about you than politics. It's a sensitive topic at the best…

You don't understand. Resisting this war has been my life for the past five years. I'm not a part-time protester. Why should we allow the powers that be to do this to us, to turn our sons into butchers? The Bible says 'Thou shalt not kill'. You've broken that commandment and I'm sure it was hard at first – even with all of the conditioning in the world you still know that you're going against nature – but it's getting easier, isn't it? How easy do you want it to get, Grey? Do you want it to be as routine as brushing your teeth in the morning, as forgettable, as insignificant?

As Grey and his platoon set about taking over a large farm, which seemed to go smoothly at first until several snipers halted their progress, Elsie noticed his concentration was completely gone from their conversation and she hollered at him, with disgust, *You're battling now, aren't you? You're going to butcher some poor woman's son. How can you act like such an animal? You hear the dead so you must know the pain that you choose to cause – how can you pretend to be sympathetic to us when you're a ruthless killer? 'I'm sorry that you're dead, Elsie'. How can you express sorrow when you're an advocate for death?*

Things aren't that simple.

You choose to kill. Don't pretend it's not a choice.

It doesn't hurt like it should. I know I should be crying and repentant when I do it and I have become callused to it but I don't revel in it.

Perhaps not yet. That time will come.

Look, Elsie, things are really hectic at the moment. Can we talk later?

No. I want you to justify your atrocities as you commit them.

Grey's platoon managed to shoot three of the four snipers, as well as taking out over a dozen men who came outside, trying too late to use their artillery, and they surrounded the farmhouse and the accompanying buildings. Grey was surprised by how easily it was going, the Germans not usually so easy to catch off guard, though the accuracy of the remaining sniper and the fact that the farm hadn't been cleared yet kept his adrenaline pumping.

While Elsie harangued him, Josef (who was disgusted by the inefficiency of the German soldiers) aided him.

James, I want you to preserve your own life at all costs, that's what's most important. Study my soldiers too, without endangering yourself. You'll see men and boys not unlike yourself, part of a society which you could fit in with and become an integral part of. The German voice you can hear is Karl. He's telling you where the sniper's point is, and where most of his troop are.

That's kind of him. It never ceases to surprise me how selfless all of you are.

We're all trying to save you in different ways. He's trying to save you physically and I'm trying to save you in a different way. I'll tell you regardless, though I hope you will give the ideas that we've discussed today some serious thought.

I can promise you that, Josef, but my personality will have to change severely before I'll become a Nazi.

Fighting in a war is a life-changing experience so there's hope. The sniper's further away than you think, around 1.5km at an angle of 80 degrees from your current position so I hope you haven't moved since he spoke. He's in a foxhole. You took them by surprise. At least half of them were resting in a large barn which should be in sight of you now and which they are unable to leave without running past you.

Thanks.

Grey went to Cloisters and said, after working out which was the correct angle, and pointing to the approximate spot, "He's over there."

"More, Grey. Who?"

"The sniper. He's way back. Look through your binoculars and you'll see. He's on the ground in a foxhole."

Cloisters looked through his binoculars and said, "We came that way. He'd have to be well hidden and it's so far from the farm that I don't buy it. There's no…the son of a bitch. Good job, Grey."

"There's something else, Sarge."

"One second," Cloisters said, running over to two of his finest shooters who quickly dispatched the sniper, something that Grey tried not to share with Elsie but she heard his thoughts and ranted wildly. "Good to see you're awake again, Grey. Any more hunches."

"They're mostly in that barn there. I guess the farmhouse isn't big enough to house them all so some of them had to sleep there."

"It'll be the same as our army, Grey. Even if there were a thousand bedrooms, they'd still have the officers inside and the men outside. How do you know this then?"

"I heard German voices coming from there when we first arrived, quite a few different voices. I would have said something earlier only we were fighting the others and…"

"You're not in trouble so you don't need to make excuses. You can fall asleep during my lectures if you're going to come up with information like this."

"I think the double doors there are the only way in or out. They'll know they're trapped and will probably surrender if we promise them they won't be harmed."

"Get over there," Cloisters said and he silently gestured for all of the soldiers in the immediate vicinity of the barn to move back as he threw a grenade through a shattered small high window, an action that Grey understood but did not approve of, his expression despondent as his unit shot the disorientated Germans who fled the barn.

Josef, I did want them to be captured.

So they're dead? I don't blame you. I am convinced that your hands are clean. I wish I felt the same.

Grey volunteered to help search the house, determined to ensure that any German survivors remained that and became prisoners of war rather than casualties. While the others who had entered the house conducted a slow, sweeping search, Grey ran up the stairs, wanting – needing to be the first to come across their enemy. The others would be too quick to pull the trigger.

As Grey pushed open the door of the third room he checked upstairs, a middle-aged, shirtless German lunged at him with a knife. Grey had not even been holding his weapon and only had time to try to block the blow, using both of his arms to hold his attackers wrists in place, a battle he was losing. His attacker had taken him by surprise and he was robustly built, his strength bringing the knife down closer to Grey's face. A sound that Grey assumed was an explosion ceased the struggle as the German's head was blown off and Grey turned to see Sykes stood in the corridor holding his pistol.

"Nice waltzing there, Hawkeye. I reckon your partner should sit the next one out," Sykes quipped, already walking away from Grey to check the next room where Grey heard another shot. Were they going to kill all of them he thought angrily as he clutched his left ear, his hearing affected by the shot. Or what if it was Sykes, who had just saved his life, that was dead? Grey went to check and saw that Sykes was unhurt and he saw a young German soldier writhing on the floor in agony with blood pouring from his leg.

"He was unarmed so I let him off with that," Sykes said, believing his act to be compassionate. Grey was not convinced. Compared to some of the sights they had seen of German atrocities (the stripped paratroopers hanging from trees with their throats slit had the most impact) it was merciful, but Grey still found it excessive, though he would lodge no complaint. He doubted that he would do so even if Sykes had shot him dead.

A short ladder led to the attic where Grey found a young blonde woman. She stood quivering, her eyes darting as she appeared frantic and Grey spotted that she was holding a knife, a carving knife rather than a military knife though almost as sharp. She was a sight for sore eyes, a way of making up for everything else. She appeared dreamlike to him, resplendent in her thin, translucent nightdress. The whole day had been dire for him until now, this stranger making him elated. Saving her almost justified the deaths, deaths which greatly bothered him as he felt responsible, like a cheat, using his powers to give him an unfair advantage, like shooting a man dead in a duel while his back was turned. It was the underhanded way he had caused their deaths that bothered him most, as he had directly killed and not felt so foul as he did now, the self-loathing fading thanks to this fine woman. Her great beauty was a bonus, though whatever she looked like she would have been a fine sight to him. It was worth storming the tower to rescue the damsel in distress. Saving and liberating her would balance the scales and give him piece of mind, a good deed that had no unsavoury side to it. Playing a small part in liberating Europe also felt like a good deed, but the way they went about it – the only way they could go about it, as, despite Elsie's objections, diplomacy would get them nowhere this time and warfare was the only way – was unwholesome. He raised his hands, trying to convey that he was no threat, a gesture which seemed to have the opposite effect as she held the handle with both hands and thrust the knife into her chest. Grey ran to her and cradled her in his arms. Her eyes flickered then closed and Grey looked down at her beautiful face, feeling like a monster, his stomach churning. He wasn't going to hurt her – he was there to save her. His throat was dry as he shouted the word, "Medics!"

A soldier who Grey only knew very vaguely, Morrison, climbed up into the attic and looked down at the scene, shaking his head. "That's taking it too far," he said soberly.

"No, no, no, no. I didn't do this," Grey said, shaking his head. He saw that Morrison was unconvinced and he said, "It must have been them."

"Is she dead?"

Grey found a weak pulse and lifted her up unsteadily. It was only after he said it that Grey realised how heinous his lie was, but retracting it was too difficult. The explanation sated Morrison and he left and Grey clumsily carried the woman – if that was the right word, girl also applicable – outside and handed her to the medics. He stood away from them as they tried to save her life and focused intently on her. He told Josef of the situation, needing to talk to someone confidentially.

It would be unheard of for even an officer to have a lover with him in the field, in the line of fire, especially if the men were staying in the same building.

That's what I thought, but if she was a local why would she try and kill herself upon sight of me? Grey said, agonised by it.

Your first battle was on the beaches of Normandy so that must have been a complete assault on your senses, almost surreal. My first battle was a lot easier though for me it was still intense, as my initiation. She's just experienced her first battle, without any training or mental preparation. She stabbed herself through shock of that, not because of anything to do with you.

God forgive me, I lied. I said it must have been one of the Germans.

I'm sure that lie would be received well. Don't admit the truth now. It's not as if it was your fault. If she does recover and tells a different story your word should have more sway.

Elsie was also in Grey's ear and she noticed the difference in his voice and pressured him to tell her the full story, only catching fragments.

How can you expect her to differentiate? She saw a soldier, a butcher, a killer – I find it hard to believe that you are so surprised by her reaction.

But I wasn't going to hurt her.

How would your mother react if a man stormed into her house with a gun? You can't expect calmness.

Earlier on I was convinced that I was right and you were wrong. I'm not so sure anymore. This war is fucked up – excuse my language – and I hate what it's doing to me and my fellow man, what it's making of us. I want to walk away, I honestly do, but I want to march forwards more, he said paradoxically, agreeing with her but continuing the fight.

You have to walk away now, surely you can see that, she said softly. They were on the same wavelength now and there was no more need for vituperation, not towards a man who she hoped to convert into a most effective ambassador of her cause.

No. I just have to stay watchful of myself. I won't celebrate this victory with the others because of the deaths.

Every victory is going to be earned through bloodshed...

Delgado stopped Grey as he went to walk past him and gripped him by the shoulders as he examined his face. "Fuck me, are you all right, Grey?"

Grey nodded silently.

“You don’t look it.” Delgado touched Grey’s forehead, performing a cursory examination by running his fingers over his face before saying, “It’s not your blood. Your face is covered though, amigo. I thought you were a demon, your face is that crimson.”

Grey rubbed his head, questioning when he had become so covered. He had felt a warm splash when Sykes blew his attacker’s head off and it was only when Grey looked in a small mirror that he saw how covered he was, his hair congealed in another man’s blood, his face like something out of a horror comic.

“Easy mistake to make,” Grey said dismally.

CHAPTER 5 – THE OTHER PATH

One thing that heartened Grey was the reaction they received from the French as they liberated their towns and villages. Some in his unit were hostile towards the French, viewing them as arrogant and not appreciative enough and it was true that some appeared miserable but Grey felt this was understandable as they had been through a lot. Most of the locals appeared friendly, especially the young ladies who hugged and kissed them. There was no real time for fraternisation usually as time was of the essence and the Nazis defeat took precedence over libido and love and most in the unit accepted this readily without (serious) complaint. Even the ordinary soldiers had learnt what was at stake if they lost, with tales of prisoners being massacred making victory more important than just pride and honour. Victory meant survival for them if they were lucky to see out the war and survival for Europe and for America. They had learnt to prioritise and raging hormones took a back seat for most.

As Grey and the others were mobbed in the small town of Maramont (Macmurray was especially revered with dozens of kisses planted on him to his amusement and Jake Baker's vexation), a young woman forced herself through the townsfolk as she surveyed the soldiers with a clinical gaze. Grey saw her approaching, looking at them intently, and he smiled at her serious countenance, trying to cheer her up as she looked dour at this time of celebration. She was only young, her medium length light brown hair wavy and straggly and she wore a white shirt with upturned collar with a mid-length skirt showing her thin pins. The man's shirt was not the only thing masculine about her, though Grey fancied she could appear attractive with a little effort. As prettier girls kissed him and flirted with him Grey found himself more interested in this other girl and her strange behaviour. She made it through the crowd to the soldiers and scrutinised their faces closer, the right side and ear specifically. As Fallon leaned in to kiss her she pie faced him and turned on her heels and continued her study of the soldiers, specifically those with dark hair. Fallon was spitting feathers at her discourtesy and started spouting off as this girl finally came over to Grey and she espied a cigarette behind his right ear and smiled subtly. Despite seeing how she'd responded to Fallon, Grey still attempted to kiss her cheek. She responded by slapping his face hard. She stared furiously at him and shouted loudly, "Liar! Where have you been, bastard?"

"I'm sorry, I think you've got me mistaken for someone else," Grey said agreeably, trying to pacify her as he felt his stinging cheek. He was not annoyed at the blow and he felt sorry for her, imagining she was a wronged woman whose lover he resembled.

"You are the father of my son. I remember you!" she said aggressively. Many of the other soldiers were guffawing at the scene (most openly, some trying unsuccessfully to repress it) but Cloisters was not amused. Cloisters had seen the commotion from a distance (he had been dealing with another situation, reprimanding Sykes who had responded to a girl's kiss by groping her to her distress) and he waded through the crowd to control this firebrand.

As Grey shook his head and profusely reiterated that it was a case of mistaken identity, the girl leaned closer to him and whispered, barely moving her lips, "We need your help. Come with me if you can." It was said conspiratorially and Grey knew she did not mean that she and the baby needed his help. That was a ruse, a diversion and possible excuse for him to temporarily leave his troop.

"What's going on here?" Cloisters asked Grey and the girl sharply, knowing who he suspected to be at fault, but he wanted to hear what they had to say first before he hollered at her.

"This bastard left me with child and abandoned me with nothing!" she said to Cloisters, sounding aggrieved which Grey now knew to be a damned convincing act. "I've been supporting your son on my own and you owe me," she said, staring into Grey's eyes.

"Nice try, sweetheart, but the dates aren't going to tally. Are you going to pipe down or do you want to make more of a fool of yourself?" Cloisters said firmly to the girl. A middle-aged townsman took greater exception than this to the girl's troublemaking and gave her a hearty shove in the back, sending her sprawling forwards.

"Hey, there's no need for that!" Grey remonstrated and the man walked away from them to shake hands with other soldiers as the girl spat out vitriolic abuse in French in his direction before she turned back to her quarry.

"You haven't seen this girl before, have you, Grey?" Cloisters said. He knew that Grey had never even left America before and doubted this story. Grey seemed too honourable to leave a girl in the lurch like this and he could not picture Grey shacking up with this virago.

"I have met her before in Iowa, but I didn't think there was a child," Grey told his sergeant, trying to lie convincingly, which he found difficult and distasteful. He was not the type to shirk his responsibilities so he feigned ignorance of his fictitious duties to give the story the possibility of authenticity, which Grey felt it currently lacked.

"He's real. Come with me and I'll show you," she said, grabbing Grey's forearm, trying to pull him through the crowd. Cloisters grabbed her arm with only the amount of force necessary to stop her trying to take his soldier away and he looked at Grey.

"If you want to go with her you can, provided you're back in the market square in two hours or you'll be sorry," Cloisters said gruffly. He was being flexible with him and warned him of the rigorous discipline he would face if he did not follow the stipulations.

"Thanks, Sarge," Grey said. He offered his hand, wanting to shake Cloisters' hand for this allowance, which he knew was discretionary but not encouraged, Cloisters sticking his neck out for him.

"20:00 hours, be here," Cloisters said, refusing to shake. He was being indulgent with the boy, and he did not want him thinking him a soft touch and he glowered at him to show him he meant business.

With this permission granted the girl had already made her way through the crowd and she signalled for Grey to follow her. He told Delgado he had unfinished business and that he would see him that night, intriguing Delgado who was too occupied with a bevy of beauties to discuss it (whilst some prejudiced girls were put off by his melanous features, others were drawn to him because of them). "Watch yourself, Jimmy," Delgado shouted down the street, concerned about his innocent friend in this town with a strange companion in looks and deed.

The girl walked briskly with Grey at her side as she moved from the centre of town down side streets, knowing all of the best short cuts to their destination. "I'm Paulette," she said as they walked, giving him a brisk handshake and a fleeting smile.

"I'm Grey. Private James Grey," he said as he bounded along keeping pace with her. She offered no explanation for why she needed him and no apology for the slap or the slur upon his good name. He forgave her for both at once, sensing she had tracked him down for something critically important and he was glad to answer the call. "Is this what I think it is?" he said, not wanting to say exactly what it was he suspected as it would sound too odd if he was wrong and he wanted her to raise the subject first. The subject was something he felt comfortable about in himself, but he was a little ashamed to admit it publicly for fear of being decried as a freak and he wanted her to broach it first.

"I would think so. You've just been recruited into the Pagan Resistance. Our leader told me where to find you and how to tell you apart and he wants to see you," she said, looking at him with admiration, seeing this soldier and his abilities as propitious to the group and their struggles. She was not one for small talk, unlike Grey, and she felt no need to say anything to put him at ease, instead just leading him to her boss. Grey would not go with her silently though and after he got over the shock of her knowledge of him he said,

"You know about me?" He was half-smiling at this, thinking that he could at last open up about this to someone as his secret was already known and he was not being condemned for it. Instead he was actually wanted because of it.

"Yes," she said taciturnly. After ten more minutes of brisk walking she said, "We need to quicken the pace. Tell me if I'm losing you." She ran at full pelt and Grey ran alongside her, as quick as her, but not so aware of the terrain and he stumbled over some areas of the cobbled pavement, using his good sense of balance to stop himself from falling. The town was not especially large, Maramont a sprawling affair, and the house they were heading for was close to the outskirts in an area that was quiet without being remote, a few streets from the countryside. The house that Paulette knocked on five times in quick succession followed by four slow knocks was the largest in its street and larger than any in the row opposite. Grey surmised that the building was once a public house from the architecture and the brackets that once would have housed a sign and now stood bare. There was no immediate answer and Grey stood back to look at the large stone building he had been led to where all of the downstairs curtains were drawn as well as one of the three upstairs windows that were visible from the front.

The door was answered by a brown-haired Frenchman in his late 30's who glanced at Paulette and then scrutinised Grey with his eyes as he gestured them both inside, indicating with a scowl for Grey to get inside quickly before he was spotted. Even at this first glance he assessed Grey as the sort who would be incapable of making himself inconspicuous, subterfuge not appearing to be part of this awed American's repertoire. Grey did not prejudge him at a glance, merely seeing a tall, reasonably dressed man, though he did feel a little unwelcome. Once Grey was inside, standing in a porch area, Paulette left him without a word to go and see what else she could do, her task of delivering him complete. The Frenchman offered a hand, which Grey shook, and he said in English slightly clearer than Paulette,

"Welcome, American. What's your name?" He was slightly more pleasant now but in his gaze there was a little condescension, as he perceived himself to be of superior intelligence and better than this GI. He was a very tall man of average build and his dark brown hair was mid length in a carefully arranged centre parting and he was handsome despite a very prominent nose. He had a moustache and short beard, both meticulously groomed and far tidier than the growth Grey sported last winter before his parents nagging wore him down.

"Private James Grey. I'm a bit taken aback by all of this, but if I can help you please say," Grey said, feeling he had to mention his surprise as he knew it was written all over his face and had been noted.

"I'm sure you can," he said with a smile. "My name is Eric Girard and I am one of the senior members of the group. Our leader will see you soon; for now come with me," he said, taking him through to what had once been the bar where a small group of three women were sitting around an oblong table deep in discussion in French. They were quiet as Eric came through with Grey and they all looked at him in turn, eyes that seemed to weigh him up and stares which Grey found hard to contend with. He smiled genially at each of them, only receiving a smile back from one of them, an elderly Madame in thick glasses and floral dress. The woman who was clearly holding court and the dominant of the three looked at him and then looked away to the other women and began talking again, disregarding him for now at least. She was in her early 40s, dark-haired and of dark complexion and features. Her black eyebrows were set close to her eyes and her features were full – her nose started off narrow and grew to a large tip, her lips were full, her eyes wide and her hair big and her head and body large without being obese. From what Grey could see of her from her seated position, her clothes seemed fairly revealing, especially surprising for her age. The other woman of the three was very thin and her white blouse was buttoned up to her chin. She was in her early 30's and her auburn hair was tied up, creating curls on the top of her head. She stared at Grey the longest and with the most hostility, responding to his smile by narrowing her eyes and fractionally shaking her head. There were plenty of seats at the table but Eric did not offer Grey a seat, instead talking to him standing up by what had been the bar. He offered him a drink, telling him with some affability that they only had soft drinks on offer, regrettably.

"That's all right. I have to be back at my unit by eight o'clock anyhow so I don't want to drink, thanks." Grey told him this deliberately so that he might get to see their leader as soon as possible as time was of the essence. He was unsure he could help them much, his confidence dented fractionally by the disparaging reaction just at the sight of him, but he would try his hardest. "Alcohol turns my legs to lead and I may have to sprint back."

"You might be better leaving your options open. Did you enlist or were you conscripted?"

Grey's mind had momentarily gone blank and he was unsure what exactly each term meant (though he knew they both pertained to how he joined up) and he said, feeling that this Frenchman knew his language better than he, "I volunteered – is that enlisted?"

"Yes, that's enlisted," Eric said with a grin. "That tells me that you want to fight, and wouldn't you rather fight the Germans in the most effective way possible?"

"Of course. So far we're doing quite well, knock on wood," Grey said, proud of his unit and the whole Allied Forces progress in their short time in Northern Europe against a fierce, fanatical enemy.

"Do you think so?" Eric said, making it clear that his opinion differed. He did not wait for an answer and instead looked over at the women who were ignoring them, the swarthy woman diverting them by talking loudly and in a way that denoted importance and demanded attention. Eric told Grey of them, saying of the one who was speaking and leading, "That's Mireille. She's a long term pagan who has fairly strong views about her craft, and everything else," he said, speaking more diplomatically than he wished to.

"The old widow is Margot. She's not usually here. Tonight is a special occasion. The other woman who is ever present is Gervaise. None of them are particularly gifted, but together we are more than the sum of our parts," he said derisively, salvaging his comments from being pure criticism with his last few words. "None of them speak English so I won't bother introducing you to them yet. You won't get to know them properly until we teach you our language."

Grey felt uncomfortable at Eric's words as it became clearer that he was expected to stay with them, which was an impossibility. As he tried to think of a polite way of saying that he could not remain with them (which was proving difficult, Grey already aware that these people were not necessarily going to take no for an answer), Eric started talking again, his commanding manner gaining Grey's undivided attention.

"There are three others in the kitchen who do speak English; only two of them are in the group. Veronique's from the colonies, Guiana, and because of that she brings a different element to the group. Her magic taps into the primitive rather than sophisticated high magic, which can be useful, although she has her own ideas about how we should perform rites which can lead to a little friction. Arnaud is a vessel – spirits pass through him and share their knowledge with him…"

"That's the same as me," Grey said excitedly, smiling at this, happy to find someone else who would truly understand what it was like. "I'd like to go and speak to him."

"Just go through that door over there. Don't expect too much from him and don't be too long because someone else wants to speak with you," Eric said cryptically.

Grey walked through to the large kitchen where he saw three seated figures around a small round table, Veronique instantly identifiable as the only woman of the three. She looked to be in her late 50's and had dark skin and short curly black greying hair and was dressed gaily and she was smoking. The two men seated next to her were younger than her, both looking to be around 30 years old and much more sombre than Veronique, though all were silent.

"Hi, folks. My name's James Grey. Which one of you is Arnaud?" Grey asked, assuming confidence though not fully feeling it.

"That's me," Arnaud said and Grey extended his hand, Arnaud offering a trembling hand which Grey shook, worried by how weak Arnaud's handshake was, Arnaud seeming very ill. The other man (possibly a relation of Arnaud, the two bearing a certain facial resemblance) was robustly built, as was Veronique, while Arnaud was pitifully thin and seemed painfully introverted.

Grey smiled at him, trying to cheer him up, and he said, "I'm pleased to meet you, Arnaud. I understand we have the same gift."

"I wish that was true. You talk to the spirits, but you have control. They take over me. I have no memory of what they say, they force me out of my own skull," Arnaud said, shaking as he tried to prevent what felt like an imminent visitation.

"If you think that he has a gift then you can't have the same ailment," the other man said, snorting indignantly. "He has an affliction, not a gift, and as his brother I should know."

"I haven't met a genuine medium in over 20 years. Have you any messages for me? Anyone wanting to speak to Veronique Del Barrio?" Veronique said with a strong accent, smiling at him though her eyes seemed dangerous, as though they wanted to ensnare him and Grey found himself unable to stop blinking repeatedly.

"Not at present. I can work on it," Grey offered, keen to assist.

Veronique chuckled to herself as she looked at him and she said, "Don't strain yourself, boy. Those that want to speak to me won't pass their messages through you."

"Don't judge me by the exterior. I've talked to a very, very wide variety of people from all walks of life so there's every chance that a message might come through for you." Veronique's comment had seemed dismissive but Grey had not taken offence and remained as eager to assist.

Veronique kept staring at him and she smiled, seemingly approvingly at him, and Grey smiled politely (and uneasily) back and turned his attention back to Arnaud. "You all obviously know what I am. I don't fully understand what your abilities are, Arnaud. What form do their visits take with you?" Grey talked to him with compassion, trying to understand why he viewed his gift as a curse.

"They possess me. They take over me and I'm nothing, I don't even hear what they say, but everyone else does because they are always loud," Arnaud said miserably. Grey noticed that Arnaud's brother rolled his eyes as he spoke, seeming very impatient with his brother.

"I'm sorry. That must be difficult," Grey said sympathetically.

"It is," Arnaud's brother said sharply.

"The American is right. Whether you welcome it or not, it is still a gift," Veronique said to Arnaud. His brother stared at her as though she were insane though she did not return his stare, instead turning her attention back to Grey. She offered her hand to him and as Grey reached across to her she roughly grabbed his hand, twisting it so that it rested palm up on the table. Grey was a little taken aback but could see what she was going to do and raised no objections. Veronique pressed down on his fingers with just enough force to keep his hand secure without hurting him as she began to probe his palm with her free hand.

"I'm not sure I want to know your findings, ma'am, especially if it involves a short lifeline," Grey said jauntily, having a vague knowledge of the practice of palmistry.

Veronique was silent as she closely scrutinised the lines in his hand, lowering her head to examine his palm, engrossed in her task. As she did this Grey offered his other hand to Arnaud's brother and said, "I'm sorry, what was your name?"

"Alain Rousseau, but you won't see much of me. I'm only here because of him; this isn't my scene or crowd. Take my advice, soldier, keep on marching," Alain said, expressing mild disapproval at the group's activities rather than contempt.

"That's the plan," Grey said.

"Plans go awry," Veronique said. "You won't make it back in time."

Grey guessed what she was referring to and he replied decisively, "I will."

Veronique let go of his hand and smiled warmly at him, either liking something about him or amused by him. "If that's what you want, boy, then leave by the back door now or you won't be back to your Dutch sergeant today."

The detail in her prediction (while Cloisters was American, he had revealed that his family were originally from Holland) concerned Grey who was determined to make it back for the deadline, and prompted him to take his leave from them. He told them he was glad to have met them and went back to stand with Eric who seemed more of a central figure of the group.

"Arnaud was not what you were expecting, I imagine."

"It must be tough. I feel for him," Grey said, affected by his plight.

"I share your pity for him. Sometimes power is apportioned randomly."

At that juncture Paulette came into the room, having ran down the stairs with a small black boy on her shoulders. He was young (Grey estimated around seven) and his hair was cut short and he was wearing pyjamas. His eyes showed that he had been crying but as Paulette raced around the room, ducking down as she ran near chandeliers, playing with him, he began to laugh and Grey saw that Paulette looked happy too as she cheered him up, talking to him in French. The boy looked at Grey then looked away, seeming a little timid.

"That boy's more powerful than her," Eric said out of their earshot about Paulette and the boy. "He's called Konah and he's the one who told us about you. He has prophetic abilities without any real control yet. He's young, he can learn," Eric said, more tolerant of the boy's shortcomings than he was of the others. "She has no abilities whatsoever, but she's keen and she does the necessary legwork," he said of Paulette.

"Is the leader in this room?" Grey asked Eric, suspecting Mireille might be as she seemed authoritative enough, but he also wondered if Eric was in charge and about to spring this on him as a surprise.

"No. Georges is upstairs in his bed," Eric said. He shouted to Paulette, asking her something in French and after she shouted back her reply Eric said to Grey, "Go upstairs, he'll see you."

"Whereabouts is he?" Grey asked, not wanting to root around every room to search for him as he felt that that would appear rude.

"You'll find him. He wants to speak to you alone. The stairs are that way," Eric said, pointing to the door Paulette had come through and Grey walked past the women, Gervaise staring at him icily again though this time Mireille acknowledged him with, "Bonjour," and Grey reciprocated as he opened the door which led directly to the stairs

There was a room halfway up the stairs that Grey knocked on and received no answer and he tentatively turned the knob and opened the door. This large bedroom was empty (and therefore not the room he was looking for) but Grey walked inside the bright room and he walked to the window to look out the back to a small courtyard and garden. This room, this whole building, was inviting to him and he could happily have stayed here, abnormally tempted to lie on the soft double bed, but he had a prior duty and a curfew to meet. He exited the room, closing the door behind him and he walked up the rest of the stairs where there was an L shaped corridor offering access to the rest of the rooms, of which there were several as this had once been a resting place for travellers like himself. He knocked on the doors in sequence without opening them and it was only as he tried the last room that he heard a weary voice tell him to come in.

Grey opened the door of the bedroom, which was dark, the curtains drawn, and he saw Georges lying in his bed, covered in several layers of sheets despite the heat, as well as a thick flannelette nightshirt. The old man smiled warmly at Grey and beckoned him with his hand.

"Come closer, my son. You can sit on my bed." Grey smiled at him, Georges the most familiar and welcoming of the whole group and Grey felt relaxed in his presence. He had not expected the leader of this group to be so old, Georges clearly an advanced geriatric with little hair and little strength and he underestimated him a little, albeit unintentionally.

"It's a shame you're not a bit shorter. I'd have given you my clothes. Could have been handy," Georges said, alluding to his imminent death.

"I couldn't take your clothes, sir. What would you wear? This army issue kit isn't as comfortable as it looks," Grey joked.

"I'm not going to be needing my clothes for much longer. Have a look in that cupboard. I have some large shirts that might fit you," Georges said, gesturing towards the larger of his two wardrobes.

"No, no. Thank you for your generosity, but I couldn't possibly. I'm sure you'll want them yourself for a number of years and maybe Eric could have them?" Grey said, declining politely.

"They won't fit him. Paulette will end up wearing them," Georges said, smiling at this notion. He turned sombre and sympathetic as he said, "You're just a boy and you're fighting a war far from home. I've seen this before many times, my friend, and I wish you could be left to the field, the classroom or whatever it is that you wish to do. Alas, that is not to be and you are serving your country, America. What's your name?"

"James Grey," Grey said, not adding the 'Private' this time, realising that these people were not interested in his rank.

"I've never seen your country, James. I'm sure it's wondrous, but I love my own home, ravaged and old as it is. We sum up our homelands, my son," he said, praising Grey as young and fresh and calling himself the currently debilitated France.

"It's a fine country and what I have seen of France is beautiful. It will not be spoilt for long and even all of this war doesn't completely detract from the beauty."

"A compliment for the tricolour is like a compliment to me so thank you. Excuse my manners. I'm Georges Steil," Georges said, offering his hand, which Grey shook, finding it very clammy. "Have they offered you any food or drink?" he said.

"Yes, they have," Grey said, even though he had only been offered a soft beverage. "Unfortunately, sir, I can't stay too long so I declined," Grey said, bringing up what felt like the thorny issue of his departure. He still didn't know why he had been summoned and he did not want to leave them abruptly as he had immediately taken to Georges and wanted to help, but duty called.

"I understand you have to get back to your regiment. This is my regiment here. Probably not as big as yours I'll wager," Georges said. He remained amiable, smiling at him, though he was more serious now.

"No, sir. The Jerries are skilled fighters as we've learned and they have so much territory and troops that we've come as a legion to try and liberate Europe," Grey said idealistically, this being his objective.

"How are you finding the war, James? Do you feel you're making a valid contribution to your regiment or do you feel you could be doing more?" Georges asked this question soberly and very straight-faced.

Grey breathed out at this, which was a tough question to answer honestly, and he admitted, "I have felt at times that I've let people down. My aim is not as good as I would like and I have collapsed in battle before and been a burden. Other times – this will sound arrogant, but on a couple of occasions I think I've done quite well. The good days I have make up for the bad ones so I feel I'm doing okay. Other people might say different."

"Have you utilised your abilities to aid you, James?"

Grey knew what he meant and he said, "At times. The voices are never deceiving – sometimes they are misleading and they are usually a little bit behind so enemy movements differ. The reason I collapsed was that there were too many voices screaming in my head and I couldn't control them. The other soldiers think I have great instincts and I feel a bit of a fraud, but I can't tell them why I know what I do. I'm just glad they don't suspect me of being a spy," Grey said. Talking freely of his abilities felt good, liberating, and he knew he could here without reproach, especially with Georges who seemed very approachable and benevolent.

"They might react kinder to a spy," Georges said, warning him of mankind's intolerance for the occult. "I know of you through my boy Konah and just being in the same room as you I can sense how potent your abilities are. I was once as mighty as you, James, and then I would have been ready to lead the battle charge before I became bedridden and incontinent," he said, exaggerating with a wry grin.

"It must be hard for you to believe now and it's hard for me and I was there – but in my day I was powerful. I grew a little heady from it and as a result I made mistakes and I declined, but I can see you have balance. They say that youth is wasted on the young and I would say power is too, but not in your case – you are a responsible caretaker for your talent. Please stay and have dinner with me – my last supper, my friend," Georges implored, making it hard for him to refuse.

"All right, but I must leave at half seven," Grey relented.

"Excellent," Georges said cheerfully, coughing phlegmatically. He wrote a note in French which he told Grey to take down to Mireille, instructions on what to cook. Grey went straight down and found Mireille was still sat around the table and still controlling the conversation, using strong hand movements to emphasise her points. Grey interrupted her by saying her name.

Mireille turned around to look at him, widening her eyes as she waited for him to speak and he handed her the note. "It's from Georges," he said but she ignored his foreign speech and read the note. After she had read it she stood up and pointed at him, gesturing him to go back upstairs and she pointed to herself and tried to indicate that she would cook and bring the food upstairs. Grey looked at her and smiled politely, unsure what she meant and she repeated the signs another two times (she did this patiently) before Eric said,

"She wants you to go back upstairs and she's going to bring the meal up. How is he?"

"Well…" Grey said, stretching out the word, thinking how to answer this.

"Good," Paulette said, hearing what she took to be Grey's answer. "We need Georges."

Grey went back upstairs, feeling as he walked up the stairs that he should have corrected Paulette concerning her misinterpretation. Georges did not appear well even though he appeared sanguine about his condition and was trying to be sprightly.

"You'll forgive me if I don't dress for dinner," Georges joked upon Grey's return.

"Of course. You'll forgive me if I don't pay for mine I hope. I have nothing on me. When Paulette asked me to come I just came straight with her." Shit, that was something he hadn't thought about – he'd left his kit with Cloisters, which was fine and dandy as Cloisters had told him to, but unfortunately that included his notebook. The need to leave suddenly became more urgent before anyone looked inside...

"No payment necessary. Mireille believes in big portions and thorough cooking so you should enjoy this, but it might make marching hard for a while. Still, better to be bloated than empty," Georges said.

"Very true. Thank you for inviting me to come here because this is the first time I've met anyone with abilities like mine" Grey said, feeling a kinship with him because of this and his openness. "I'm glad to have met you, sir," he said reverently.

"And I you. I've been holding on to meet you ever since my boy told me you were coming. He's not really my boy, of course, but that's how I see him. He's only 9 and he's had a harder life than I have at 79. His parents sold him to unscrupulous traders in West Africa who capitalised on his ability and used to beat him when he made mistakes, as we all do at first. I found him at five and he's been with me ever since and he's come on leaps and bounds in that short time. I regret using him in this organisation, but, unfortunately, we need him and he is probably our best resource," Georges said gloomily.

"Now that you've been liberated maybe things will be better for you all," Grey said optimistically.

"Are we liberated or having a temporary reprieve? The future is never clear. It is normally opaque, and at present it is black. We are on the precipice and a multitude of different things may occur, leaving even the seers uncertain. We can let out a small cheer, however the celebrations and bunting must wait till later. I'm sorry to tell you this because I know all soldiers like to be home by Christmas, but the war is not won," Georges said apologetically.

"I think that's a fair assessment," Grey said, agreeing that the final victory would still take time, "but for your town I believe the war is over."

"Perhaps," Georges said, indulging him though he did not believe this to be true. "Take my shirts from my wardrobe, James." Georges felt Grey was less likely to refuse this request even though they both knew where it was leading.

"But…" Grey did not want to argue, but he literally could not take his clothes. There was no way to explain it to Cloisters.

"Please. I would do it myself only I am no longer able." Grey was unable to say no as Georges was too infirm to do it and he opened the larger wardrobe where a vast array of shirts, mainly white, hung on wooden coat hangers. "Place them on the bed."

Grey did this and Georges sifted through them, putting three to one side and he asked Grey to put the others back. The three that were left were the largest and he told Grey, "Put that next to you, James. That would fit."

Grey did so, standing up with the shirt over him and he acceded, "Yes, I think it would. I could take one, if you are sure, but no more than that."

"Eric will lend you trousers if you ask. There is a pair of mine in there that hang loose on me with a belt and which are turned up. They should be at the bottom," Georges said, trying to persuade him to take more of his clothes.

"I really cannot take any more of your clothes. I do appreciate your hospitality and generosity, but I would be shot by the Jerries as a spy if I have civilian clothes."

"Only if you were caught, James, and I doubt you will be. I have a proposition for you, but I'll make it over dinner," Georges said cryptically.

"Should I give her a hand because I am in a hurry?"

"No, she wouldn't want that. Getting in her way in the kitchen would be almost as dangerous as your recent escapades, James! She won't take long now. Tell me of how you discovered your gift."

Grey sat down on the bed again, putting his arms into the sleeves of the white shirt that did indeed fit (to Georges' delight) and he began to tell the tale he had kept to himself for so long. He spoke of an old reclusive man from his hometown, a hermit as others had disparagingly put it, who had been hounded in his later years and after his death he hounded Grey. Lanfred Hearnus had been his name and he had been very bitter and let Grey know it, his voice persistently haunting Grey who, as only a prepubescent child, was petrified. His parents dismissed his talk as attention seeking at first and eventually took drastic action out of concern, prompting Grey to pretend he had been lying and he learnt to never mention such things again. Lanfred was malicious though never towards Grey and he did not lie, instead giving distorted versions of things that Grey investigated and learnt to be inaccurate. Eventually Grey learnt to control his fear and actually converse properly with Lanfred who was in life and death unbearably lonely and

Grey befriended him which helped him find peace and Lanfred's contented spirit was released.

Grey told Georges of how this profound experience changed him and changed his perspective regarding the human condition and made him more thoughtful of others' feelings (not that he was especially remiss before) and how in time he learnt to control the voices so that he would talk to them when he wanted, a finesse that had evaporated as the war developed and thousands of death screams hit him and shattered all of the control he had built up.

At this point Mireille came upstairs with two plates of roast pork and vegetables with gravy, which she placed on a small side table, Grey moving on to a sitting chair close to his food. Mireille fetched them a bottle of wine and two glasses, uncorking and pouring it for them and after uttering a few words in French to Georges who responded jovially, she kissed him on the lips and left them alone.

"A fine woman," Georges said after she had gone. He began to eat the food she had lovingly prepared; each mouthful was a struggle and Grey ate at his pace too, not wanting to rush him.

"I admire you for running this group. It must have been difficult, especially when you were occupied," Grey said, praising him even though he knew little about the group or what they had achieved.

"Konah is like the son I never had. There would be no future for him in an Aryan world. You will know how the Nazis deal with their racial enemies?"

Grey nodded, his countenance grim, an expression that showed he knew too well, voices relating this traumatic information to him.

"That is why we take the risks and why you and every soldier, why every man and woman fights, for our freedom and right to life irrespective of our differences. The French and the Americans aren't historically the best of friends and neither are France and England or England and America, but this unites us and forges friendships and makes us by throwing huge challenges at us. I am about to throw a huge challenge your way which you will not like," Georges said, pre-warning him.

"Go on," Grey said tentatively.

"In your army unit you are valuable. However, you're young and you are not of the highest rank, correct? That's not a criticism; that's how it works for the young and I believe you would be officer material. The question is, will you live that long? At present I envision you seeing what your comrades should be doing, but unable to make them and hence unable to effect any real change or advantage. You have the insight to make a difference, but you are just a cog in a well run machine."

"My sergeant gives me quite a bit of leeway," Grey said, defending Cloisters and explaining how he could use his abilities for the army's benefit.

"And he should because you can help win the war more than he could, but you cannot ride your luck out here very long. The mortality rate for GI's is high; I know that, as I'm sure the voices in your head will attest to. You're too valuable to lose and you are wasted as a foot soldier," Georges said, trying to make Grey realise his true potential to persuade him to help in a different, more important way.

"We need foot soldiers. We have made real progress and that has been no small feat considering the determination of the Hitler Panzer units," Grey said. He understood that Georges was not belittling the Army or condemning them and his rejoinder was delivered amicably. He was not offended or defensive, but he was letting Georges know what his priorities were and where his duty lay.

"Your army, the Red Army, the British, the Free French – all of your units have shown commendable bravery and yes, every soldier is valuable, but you could do more good in a different arena. Napoleon was one of the greatest leaders of men who ever lived, but put him in a gladiatorial setting and he would not last the distance one suspects. A successful military strategy is to use your resources in the most effective way possible. Those who fight a different war without front lines are no less daring, no less courageous," Georges said, defending his style of warfare vigorously as a thing of honour.

"Of course, sir. I wish you all the best because you will be the unsung heroes, only it's not for me. I signed up for the army – I enlisted in the US Army and I aim to fulfil that obligation," Grey said steadfastly. While he felt bad at disappointing the old man, who he believed was close to death, his heart and head commanded him to rejoin his troops, his friends.

"I understand that what I offer is not to your choosing, but please hear me out. You have the most power and no one else is prepared for the task and they will fold without your assistance. I want you to succeed me as leader. The largest bedroom in the house, the room halfway up the stairs, has been prepared as your room and the others will obey you, especially Paulette, Eric, Veronique and Mireille who will do so without question. Mireille's son is a member of the Communist Resistance and they will assist too whenever they can. I know what I am asking you to do is turning your back on what you promised, and your friends. I know that disloyalty is not part of your nature, but by doing this you will be helping those men more than by staying at their side. You can help make a huge difference here and hopefully end it all sooner. This house will be yours now and after the war and all of my possessions will become yours if you agree. I know your government will punish you if you desert, but they no longer execute deserters, it would just be a small punitive term in a military prison, which I accept is unfair but you would know how much good you had done. If you stayed in France you would likely face no punishment. James – I'm begging you, stay and lead the Pagan Resistance." Grey stayed silent through Georges impassioned monologue, letting the man speak and get his point across which he did effectively.

"What about Eric or Mireille?" Grey said, not wanting the mantle of leadership. He would have been prepared to help the group, if that was possible, but he had to go where he was stationed and they would be moving out soon enough.

"Eric is powerful, and I have seriously considered him. I feel disloyal to the poor boy for my conclusions. I don't trust his judgement enough and even though he is enormously powerful, far more than I am, I believe your ability is of more use, more revealing. Mireille has a lot of good qualities and she can lead; unfortunately, she lacks power. In a coven she has some ability, but the group would be daring and weak which is a suicidal combination. You alone, James Grey, can help us because without you this group disintegrates. I hate to burden you like this – I hate to heap this responsibility down on your shoulders, but I know you can do it," Georges said, staring into his eyes, having a tremendous impact on him, making the hairs on his arms stand up.

"If I'm injured and discharged from the army, I'll be straight back here and I'll do anything," Grey said, trying to appease him with this, wishing desperately that he could do both at once, but he could not.

"Like all good salesmen I cannot accept your first refusal. Indulge an old man a little longer, please. I have more to say."

"I'll listen to you, but I will be remaining a soldier."

"All I ask is for your ears. Maramont is the perfect town for travellers. I can feel that you're like me, James, you want to explore this wondrous world. No postcards or travel books for us, we want to live it, am I right?"

"That sounds good. Truth be told I'd hardly left my home state before all of this, sir," Grey said, moved and honoured by his offer but unable to bend on this, though he heard him out as he continued trying to talk him round.

"And now the bug is in you. Maramont is not a town that embraces strangers, not since the war started. The town has waned from what it was even twelve years ago when it became my home when my travelling bones gave way. Back then I was made welcome in most homes. Old men can get away with eccentricities that young men cannot. At your age I was thrown out by my collar and the seat of my pants of many places that accepted me warts and all in my dotage, but I believe I would have been welcomed in Maramont even in my wayward youth. Maramont in the 1930s was a kind town – many towns are not, unfortunately," he said sadly, grieved that Grey had hard lessons to learn and that people were not always the noble creatures they could be.

"Everyone has been real good to us today and made us welcome so I'd say the town's doing all right in the '40s."

Georges creased up his face, disputing this. "The occupation has changed everybody. None of us will be exactly the same after this. Those of us that survive will change for the better. That's not what this old man hopes, that's what will happen. I saw it after the last war, people embracing life, daring to live with gusto, and Maramont will make up for lost time and become even better than it ever was. This is no ordinary town, James. Can you feel it?"

"I don't think I've been here long enough to know. I think the heartbeat of a town is the people and you all seem real swell."

"Maramont has long been a hub of occult activity. The town is infamous for a massacre of witches that took place in the 12th Century, infamous because of the number of witches and the savagery with which they were killed. This can be your base. See the world, and return here at your leisure. Nearly all of the buildings are historic monuments – this building dates back to the 12th Century, and there are few homes that were built after the 17th Century in the whole town. Even if you never learn the language you have four expert translators in Eric, Paulette, Veronique and Arnaud. I want you to witness the town's rebirth."

"You present a compelling case and if I had a choice I might stay. I have no choice. Desertion is impossible for me. Come what may, I must go forward. I may regret it one day but I'd regret not doing it more. This meeting has brought a lot to the surface for me, sir. I'm used to hiding what I am and it feels good to know there's a place I don't have to do that. I can promise you I'll be back..."

Georges grunted, his body convulsed and he began to make a choking sound. Grey panicked momentarily then checked his airway and saw that Georges was still breathing. With Grey's face close to his, Georges said, "That's all right, friend.

I should have left them better equipped for my death. Good luck in your war." There was no hostility or bitterness in his weak voice at Grey's refusal; instead there was a quiet understanding and consideration.

"I am truly sorry," Grey said, remaining close to him as he heard the weather outside take a turn for the worse. It was getting late now, 25 minutes to eight, and Grey needed to get away but he could not leave this dying man like this. He took his hand in his own and Georges, who was now lying flat on his back, said,

"It's soon. Tell Mireille – tell her to be careful with this bunch. She's at the helm now," Georges said, making an on the spot decision.

"Do you want me to get her?"

"No, no. I don't want them to see me go. You don't have to stay," he said, not wishing to put James Grey through it either, a powerful man who was in some ways still very young and innocent.

"I'm staying. I'm accustomed to death, aren't I? I won't let you die alone, Georges." Cloisters would have his hide for this, but he knew it would all be over soon.

"Would you do an old dying man one favour?" Georges asked desperately.

"If I can I will," Grey said, hoping he was not going to ask him to lead the group again.

"This request does not involve you leaving the army. The boy – he won't be safe here. I'll not let him go to the camps. There is an old friend of mine who lives a few miles from here in an isolated farmhouse. Take the boy to Laura for me, I beg you," Georges said, beseeching him.

"I...okay," Grey said. Even though it meant he would be AWOL for at least several hours he could not refuse this request. Back at the training facility he would have been cleaning latrines indefinitely for this and he didn't know what Cloisters' punishment would be, but whatever it was it was worth it to fulfil Georges dying wish and keep the boy safe.

"There's a pen and paper in the drawer," Georges said, feeling his life ebb away and forcing himself to stay alive until this task was complete. He gave Grey the necessary directions for Laura's home, an idiot's guide to finding her house to ensure he did not get lost. Shortly after he had dictated this Georges smiled and closed his eyes and he lay still. Grey checked his pulse, and as he suspected Georges had crossed over. Grey was practically a stranger here and did not know the full story yet he was certain that a great man had died and that the world would be poorer for his passing, their brief acquaintance having a strong impact upon him. Still wearing Georges' shirt over his army uniform he went downstairs, putting the note in his pocket.

"He's dead," Grey said clumsily in the bar, only Paulette and Eric understanding, their faces showing the three seated women and Konah, who was sitting on Paulette's knee, what had been said. Paulette's eyes were moist, but not as moist as Konah's as the boy cried silently. Eric was sad at the news, yet remained composed and he said in French that he would get everyone a drink. It was now 8:05 and Grey thought of Cloisters and his unit waiting for him, expecting him to turn up any minute. Eric fetched Grey a drink too and when everyone had a drink in their hand (except for Konah) Eric offered a toast to Georges which everyone joined in.

Grey went to stand at the bar so that he could see everyone in the room as he said, "He left me with some instructions. He wants Mireille to run the group. Can one of you tell her that?" he asked Eric and Paulette.

"You're mistaken," Eric said, visibly annoyed at this. "It was understood that I would be leading the group at this time."

"He said that you were very powerful and he greatly appreciates your contribution, but he was quite clear that he wants Mireille to be his successor," Grey said as diplomatically as possible. He did not add that Georges had begged him to be the leader, Eric actually third choice, as he realised that this would be a huge affront to Eric's ego. As Eric grumbled how he was wrong, Paulette told Mireille this news to a look of amazement from Mireille who nodded affirmatively which indicated to Grey that she was happy to take on the role. The elderly widow, Margot, who had been crying, smiled now and kissed Mireille's cheek and Gervaise did the same. Paulette remained sitting on the sidelines near the window and wished her luck as did Eric, begrudgingly, and Grey also wished her luck. He looked into her eyes as she met his stare and she nodded in acknowledgement and smiled.

"He also asked me to do one task for him," Grey said to Paulette and Eric. "He was very concerned about Konah and he asked me to take him away from here to a safe house which I would like to do straight away. I'll help him pack," Grey said. He felt impatient and wanted to urge haste, but he restrained himself, something he was good at.

"He's safe enough here," Paulette said protectively. She knew how much Georges fretted about Konah and she was not prepared to let him be taken away by a virtual stranger without questioning it.

"Georges didn't think so. I've been given directions; I know where I'm going. Could you tell him?" Grey asked Paulette.

"I'm not sure about this. I'm going to ask Mireille," Paulette said as she broke off into French.

"There's no need. I know about it and I say he can take the boy," Eric said, making the decision before Paulette had the chance to fully explain to Mireille.

"Are you sure?" Paulette asked.

"If you had any concerns about him being the enemy you shouldn't have brought him here. He's no Nazi. Let Georges have his dying wish," Eric said sharply.

"All right," Paulette conceded. "I'll get him ready; you wait here," she said to Grey, taking the boy upstairs with her as Eric explained to Mireille, Gervaise and Margot (who didn't take it in) that Grey was taking Konah to safety and more than likely to Georges' old friend, the mysterious Laura. Mireille had no objection to this arrangement, feeling this was no place for a child, and the other two women expressed no opinion.

"Shouldn't someone tell Arnaud and Veronique?" Grey said to Eric, feeling that, whatever the internal politics and friction within the group, they should be notified of the leader's death.

"You're the messenger," Eric said snidely, unable to fully hide his disappointment (and surprise) at Mireille's appointment.

Grey realised that no one else was in any rush to tell them and he went through and tried to break the news gently to them, surmising that it was Georges who linked both Veronique and Arnaud to the group.

"He passed away a few minutes ago," Grey said quietly. "I wish I'd had more time to know him because he seemed a good man."

"He was," Arnaud said sadly. "We knew it was coming," he said, his voice wavering.

"Merde!" Alain said quietly. He had found Georges a strange man but he had proven useful, looking after his brother from time to time when Alain and his family needed some peace.

"Are you leaving or staying then?" Veronique asked.

"Leaving. I wish I could help you all…"

"Wish granted. You said that you wanted to stay so you shall. Are you our new leader?" Veronique asked, prepared to follow him.

"No, Mireille is and I really do have to leave."

Veronique laughed at this news and Arnaud looked puzzled and said, "It's not Eric?"

Grey shook his head. "No, it's Mireille. They're all having a drink through there to toast Georges. Are you coming through?"

"We might as well," Alain said, his brother accompanying him. Veronique stayed firmly seated.

"Are you coming through, ma'am?"

"Non."

Grey sat down across from her and said, "I think if I stayed I'd learn a lot about myself and I know in going I'm missing out on a fantastic opportunity but I have a prior commitment that I have to honour. Georges understood."

"I understand. You're being selfish. You weren't given your powers for your own amusement, you were given them to do something with," Veronique said frankly.

"And I do. I take my gift very, very seriously," he said solemnly.

"Then why do you want to play dress up instead of staying?"

"This isn't 'dress up', ma'am – we're getting killed out there," he said, keeping his cool.

"You might be killed if you stay, under Mireille's leadership. I would rather you were leader, James Grey, then that woman," she said, making her dislike of Mireille evident in how she spoke of her.

"She might do a good job."

"There's more chance of you staying than that. I only came to the group as a friend of Georges'. He was a friend of my third husband, a poor bastard who spent ten years on the island. You think you soldiers have it tough? Ha! Why did you come here if you never intended to help us?"

Grey did not fully understand all that she was saying but he understood that she was giving him a hard time, considering him a deserter (even though that was what he was trying desperately not to be) and he said, "I had – I have every intention of helping you provided I can help you from a distance. I'm still fighting the same enemy when I go back. I don't want to argue, I want to go back to what you first asked me. Who would you like me to try and contact for you?"

"No one. No, contact Georges. I was a true friend to him and you were the one who was granted a final audience with him. We all wanted to be with him at the end and you were the lucky one. After watching that noble man die you can still walk away!" she said, denigrating Grey.

"I...have you never wanted to be in two places at the same time?" Grey said, patiently trying to explain how difficult his position was.

"Let's not talk any more. Your mind is clearly made up, *soldier*," she said pointedly. Grey was starting to rile her as he tried to justify what she saw as indefensible and she bit her tongue out of respect for Georges.

Paulette helped the teary Konah get ready and she accompanied him downstairs with a small rucksack that had his belongings inside. Eric told them they would have to use the back exit and in French he berated Paulette for bringing Grey in through the front; Paulette responded fierily, also in French, that they were liberated and that he was not the leader, a comment he noted but responded to only with a frown. Paulette took Konah through the passage through the bar which led to the large kitchen, the wine cellar and the back door, which she opened for Grey and Konah and she passed Konah his rucksack, observing how small he looked as he stood on the step.

"Be brave, my little freedom fighter," she said in French and she looked up to Grey and said in English, "You be careful too."

"Thanks for bringing me here, Paulette," Grey said sincerely. He had made friends with a sage who had now died, he was in deep shit with his sergeant and possibly facing a court martial, but he was still pleased that he had ventured here with her. It had shown him that he was not alone and not such a freak.

Paulette shut the door swiftly on them as they stood looking at her and she walked back to the bar to see what Mireille's leadership plans were and what was going to happen regarding Georges funeral.

Grey immediately took Konah's bag from him and walked out of the town, taking the boy's hand in his, and into the forest, all of the time looking at his directions. He smiled at Konah who looked a little afraid of him and Grey wished he had some candy or something to give him to relax him and cheer him up. He tried talking to him, asking slowly, "Laura – do you know Laura?"

Konah looked at him blankly and Grey tried saying the same thing in different ways to the same lack of reaction. After they had walked a little while in what looked like the right way, Grey bent down and crouched on his knees and patted his back. Konah knew what this meant and he jumped onto his back and Grey gave him a piggyback over the rough terrain where nettles and bramble bushes were cutting at Grey's thick clothes and certain hills were steep and difficult to climb. Grey pondered over the wisdom of this route, figuring there must have been a better way of reaching this old woman's house but he supposed that possibly Georges wanted them to be unseen and this route was certainly off the beaten track and away from prying eyes. Georges had told him that the house was around five miles away and with Konah still on his back Grey decided to quicken the pace so that he could be back to his unit as soon as possible. He imagined the absolute worst case scenario – of being caught by his own army before he had chance to voluntarily return thereby guaranteeing that all would believe he had deserted and would not believe that he was going to return. The thought of being considered a coward, an accusation that he knew would be being flung around in certain quarters at this moment (from Pearce's lips for one) bothered him greatly. He was not a tremendously proud man but he had some honour and the thought of these accusations being bandied about, sullying his good name, was distressing to him.

Grey remembered as he nearly completed the trek that he had some chewing gum in his pocket and he produced a strip and passed it to Konah. Konah took it eagerly and gripped onto him tighter for a second, a grateful hug. It was a small thing but it was enough to make Grey smile and made him glad that he was fulfilling Georges' dying wish, whatever the personal consequences. If he explained he was helping a kid he felt that Cloisters might understand. It was all a question of what mood Cloisters got into. He had seen Cloisters angered (not directed at him) and in that state there was nothing he could say to pacify him, even helping Cloisters' own children wouldn't be enough to get him off the hook. If Cloisters was in a tolerant mood he might emerge from this debacle with just a severe reprimand as most of Cloisters' gruff holler was just hot air. He hated disobeying his orders and putting Cloisters in this position and knew that whatever punishment his sergeant meted out he would have to accept it without complaint.

Grey was young and very swift and was able to follow directions and found himself approaching a manor with vast fields, fields of beauteous flowers that seemed splendid in the twilight and Grey wondered how splendid they must have looked under the sun. He would not know but Konah would and he felt that Konah would be happy at this isolated home, which Grey also liked, but he preferred the renovated pub as he preferred to be around people. Konah seemed a quiet, timid child and Grey felt this might be the best place for him until the end of the war.

Grey knocked on the door, putting Konah on the ground and instinctively hiding the boy behind his body. The door was opened quickly by a tall woman almost the same height as Grey and around ten years his senior who stared at him impassively. Grey had expected someone a lot older as Georges had said this was his old friend and this attractive woman did not suit the description old. Her long auburn hair was tied in a long plait behind her and her greyish blue eyes worked down to a thin, straight nose that dominated her face, down to thin red lips. She was wearing a soft coloured dress that showed a fraction of cleavage with a cardigan hanging loose over broad shoulders, her frame statuesque. Grey was taken aback at the sight of her, a rare beauty who answered the door coolly confident even though he assumed she was a woman alone here, answering the door to strangers in such a remote, potentially dangerous area. She showed no sign of fear, quite the contrary, looking queenly as though she had no reason to be afraid.

"Hello…are…are you Laura?" Grey stammered, taken aback by her sight and her gaze that surveyed him, taking in the sight of him absolutely. She was so different to his assumptions (he had envisioned a little old benign Frenchwoman, the female equivalent of Georges) and this striking woman threw him momentarily.

"Yes," she replied, her accent seemingly English. "Who exactly are you?" she demanded to know.

"I'm James Grey. Private James Grey of the US Army," he said, adopting no airs of familiarity with her as he realised she would not approve. He offered her his hand, which she glared at and then she looked at his face, as his hand remained outstretched. He kept it lingering there, feeling a fool but giving her the chance to change her mind and she shook it reluctantly. "I apologise for this intrusion at such a late hour upon your estate and thank you for answering. A friend of yours sent me," Grey said, talking respectfully as he was always polite and courteous to a lady and he wanted to please her as he felt from her contumely half smile that he had offended her somehow.

Laura looked at the shirt he was wearing that was stretched tight over his back and shoulders as he had his Army issue jacket and shirt on underneath. She touched the hem of the shirt and said softly, "Georges."

"That's right. Do you know Konah?" Grey said, positioning Konah in front of her and she saw the small, frightened boy that Georges had spoken so fondly of.

"I knew he was there and I know of him from Georges," Laura said cautiously, beginning to see where this was heading and becoming vexed.

"Can we come inside to talk?" Grey asked, able to return her powerful stare even though he could see her brow begin to screw up and her round jaw squared in anger.

"Yes," she sighed, ushering them in, ordering them to the candlelit sitting room where both Grey and Konah stood as Laura took a seat, shaking her head fractionally as she looked at them both. It was Georges she was really annoyed at; dear departed Georges who had sent them here.

"I only met Georges for the first time tonight and I'm afraid I have bad news to tell you," Grey said, not taking the other seat, as he had not been offered it and he did not plan on staying long.

"He's dead. I know already," Laura said, already aware of it and preferring to simply tell him rather than hear him pussyfoot around the fact for her sake. She could handle it and she lay back in her chair, resting her head on the back as she craned her neck upward.

"I was with him when he died and he made a request of me that I came here to fulfil. He seemed to think that you might take in Konah here, for the duration of the war at least," Grey said, telling her as delicately as he could.

"Did he now? I already refused him at his last visit. Ignorant old withered goat," she said angrily, hitting her clenched fist down onto the wood panel of her chair, creating a loud tapping sound.

"Sorry, he didn't say that," Grey said apologetically, feeling he had intruded here and that Georges (who he was not mad at even if she was) had also been trying to impel this young woman to do his wishes as he had persuasively tried to sway Grey to desert and lead his resistance group. He understood that she was just a civilian and he felt that Georges should not have tried to pressure her into doing anything hazardous, but since Konah was here Grey was unsure what to do.

"No, I can imagine he didn't. Is this your last laugh on me, Steil?" she said, looking upward to the ceiling as she spoke.

"He asked me to join his group, which I had to decline because of previous commitments," Grey said, smiling as he held his dog tags, showing his objective and calling, where he should have been. "It was very, very hard to say no to him. He didn't ask you to do this to endanger you or punish you though. He really seemed to care for the boy," he said, sticking up for the late Georges who she seemed to have little time for in her manner.

"Yes, he was a persistent badgering pain who was good at talking people into doing things they didn't want to. That ability went with age though. The gall of him! He didn't forewarn you I'd be like this," she said, knowing that Georges would be aware of how mad she'd be. She missed him and she was sad he was dead, but if he were alive she would have had sharp words for him. While Georges had not asked her to take Konah in, she had been unequivocal that she wanted no involvement with the 'Resistance' group. The thought of that pitiful group traipsing back and forth from her home haphazardly to enquire as to the boy's prophecies enraged her and made her seriously contemplate returning to Scotland (with the boy).

"No, he just told me where you would be. He was very weak and I only saw him for a little over an hour," Grey said, making excuses as to why Georges did not say more.

"Trust me, it was not an accident that he neglected to tell you of how angry I'd be. If he had told you, you would never have come," she said, implying that her wrath was petrifying and insinuating that Grey was not enjoying the visit.

"No, I wouldn't have come if I had known that it wasn't arranged and you'd said no to taking Konah. I would have respected your refusal and left you in peace," he said, giving his reasons why he would have left her alone, fear not one of them. She held court inside this house – she would have held court wherever with her imperious attitude, which was a little overwhelming, but he held her gaze and felt no fear at this glorious woman. He did, however, feel embarrassment at putting her in this unwelcome position and smiled uneasily at her. She did not return his grin and instead for the first time since she had let them in deliberately looked away from him as a statement. She was not amused; this was no game to her.

"But you have come, haven't you?" she replied curtly. "Sit down, you're making shadows form all over the room," she said sharply and Grey obliged, pulling a bewildered Konah onto his lap. Konah was not keen on this woman and hoped the American soldier was not going away.

"I'm sorry. Can you bear with me a few minutes while I try and think of a solution to this pickle? It won't involve you, I promise," Grey said, sighing to himself. He couldn't take him back to the group as he had promised Georges he would take him to safety, but Laura wouldn't have him and Grey had no other friends or contacts in France. Laura's refusal left him in the lurch but he didn't blame her or Georges and instead racked his brain for an answer. Laura stared at him, observing his deep cogitation (which she hoped was exaggerated, for his sake, as he certainly looked stupid as he looked vacantly into space), eager to hear what 'brilliant' ideas such an obviously great mind would produce.

After a few minutes Laura said, "Penny for your thoughts," figuring this was all they would be worth.

"Save your money, ma'am," Grey said, admitting that he was devoid of ideas.

"I don't want anything bad to happen to the child but there are alternative options that would be better for the boy. There are organisations that will look after him – there are a lot of orphans out there and provisions would be made for him. I think he would be better with them than here with me," she said, presenting Grey with an option, prepared to help him work out what to do with the boy.

Grey considered what she said before responding. "That's a good idea and I would agree with it only..." He spoke tentatively, not wanting to offend her and he phrased his declination as delicately as possible. "For any other child that would be perfect, but not for Konah. Georges thinks that there might be people out there who want to get their hands on him so he can't be traceable and he would be if he was with one of these organisations."

"So instead it's better to bring trouble to my door?"

"I didn't say that."

"Did I blame you? You're just the mule who brought him round; I understand that. We both have Georges Steil to thank for this mess," she said angrily, though her anger was confined to Georges.

"When I woke up this morning I thought my only problem was going to be fighting the Jerries," Grey said, rubbing his eyelids, admitting he felt some strain at the situation. "I've fought no one today, but it's been a hard day. Not hard, that's the wrong word – long. I was supposed to be back at my troop at 20:00 hours so I think tomorrow will be more trying." She showed no sign of being interested in him, but his interest in her made him want to talk to her of other things beyond Konah, careful not to sound like he was whining, inflecting his voice so that he remained positive sounding.

"Listen to me, Private Grey. You are now a deserter and I imagine that is Georges' fault. Seems as you are in trouble for doing my idiotic friend a favour, I will help you out. I am prepared to smuggle you and the boy out of the country. I'll get you to the coast and get you passage to England and I'll give you plenty of money so you can find your way to the north of Scotland where I have an estate twice the size of this where you can see out the war and look after this child." She felt she was being generous here and was surprised at his instant reaction.

"That's not going to happen. I will be rejoining my unit and I am not going to be a deserter under any circumstances. At the minute I'm late and that's all I'm going to be, but I'm fighting with my unit," he said vehemently, adamant that he would not see out the war comfortably like this. She had assumed he would do as instructed – there was something about his open face that suggested dimwittedness and his sharp reaction surprised her. "Perhaps it would be a good idea for you to do that."

"I'll live where I want; it's none of your business," she spat back at him at breakneck speed, annoyed by his hostility to her act of good grace.

"You'd be safe there though...I'm sorry, you're right, it's not my business," he said, humbled by her. "Is there...is there any chance I can leave the boy here and the second I am discharged I will come back for him, I swear," he vowed.

She stared at Grey, sensing the genuineness of his words, and Grey, trying to sway her, said, "I'm trying to make this war end as swiftly as possible. It might just be for a few months. I don't have any money on me but I'll pay you for his upkeep retroactively."

"It's not about money – and why should you pay anyway? Do American privates receive a large income, because I doubt that somehow," she said, mocking him a little as she pointed out flaws in his plan.

"If only that were the case," he said, smirking at the suggestion but looking downwards at her feet as he did so after the way she had reacted to his last smile. "If you look after him I'll pay," he said seriously, able to afford this with his salary, which was not that bad.

"Who says you'll survive the war?"

"I'll be careful. I'll have to be. If I die I have a pickup which you can have and should cover quite a lot of food. Living out here a car would be useful and my pride and joy's hardy enough to handle this terrain. I'll sign something now to make it legally binding."

"I'm sure your vehicle would be an immaculate machine," she said, cruelly sarcastic as she saw this boy was not from money. He was well-mannered and not a pauper from the slums, nor American blueblood, decidedly middle of the road. "However, I don't care if it's a plane you're offering." As she spoke she saw the effect her comment about the car had on his eyes which squinted slightly. She'd hurt his feelings.

"If I could take him back to my unit I would, ma'am, but I cannot do that now. The group he came from were mostly – well, they didn't hang onto him for dear life, let's put it that way. I'm an outsider, I don't know the whole story. My old jalopy isn't the best, you're right, but it runs well and it will be worth something, even just as scrap. I wish I had more of value to offer you only I haven't been a working man for long," he said sadly, wishing he had the gift of the gab to convince her. He was quite an effusive talker, but he was not persuasive. Even Fudd would struggle to talk her round and he was no Fudd.

"It's not about money," she reiterated, talking a little softer to him. "It's not your fault. I know who I blame for this. If he wasn't dead I'd make him wish he was," she sighed, shaking her head.

"Can you keep him?" Grey said, suspecting she was about to relent.

"You had better come back soon, Private Grey, or I'll be taking out my anger at Georges on you," she threatened, a dark joke.

"You're not as scary as the Nazis," he said, euphorically relieved, refusing to be scared of her, smiling at her as she tried to play fearsome again.

"Try seeing me when I'm angry and your opinion will change double fast. No wonder I live away from you all. You're all so annoying," she said, half-joking at what she had been talked into.

"Guilty as charged. I am really grateful for this, ma'am, I cannot stress how much because it's not really fair on you, but I don't know what else I can do and I feel responsible for him. If there was another way I wouldn't be burdening you," Grey said seriously, showing how much he thought of her for doing this even though she was averse to the idea.

"Do you want a drink, soldier, to see you on your way back?" she offered, responding to his good manners.

"If it's no trouble," Grey said. "If you tell me where you keep the drink I'll see to it myself and fetch a drink for you and the boy," he said, not wanting to be any bother and trying to do it for Laura so she could keep seated.

"No, I'll fetch you a drink," she said, standing up. "What is the American drink of choice at present?"

"Water or tea would do me, ma'am. Have you any soft drinks for Konah?"

Laura had intended to fetch Grey an alcoholic beverage to see him on his way, but his refusal changed her mind and she was not inclined to twist his arm into it even though she knew he had opted for a non-alcoholic drink out of decorum. She poured him a glass of water and some milk for Konah, which she took back to them; Konah thanked her in French and Grey smiled and said, "Thank you. This is a fine place you have here. I saw your flowers in the field and you'd win prizes for them back in my hometown. I'd just started the gardening trade before I came here so I know the effort that's gone into that and you've reaped the reward with that view. A picture of them would make a dandy postcard."

She arched her eyebrows at this inane statement. "Stop by the tourist shop on the way out."

"Cute. I know when I do return here to pick him up not to fetch you any flowers to say thank you because you certainly don't need any more. I will pay you for this and if any problems do arise – do you know of Georges' group and where they're based?" he said, not wanting to break confidences if she did not know everything.

"I know of his inn and the women and men who aided him," Laura said.

"If it does become impossible for you to keep him, if you could inform them they might be able to accommodate him again. Thanks for the drink," he said, supping up in one large sip, "and for your hospitality. I hope to be back here soon," he said, rising to his feet. He ruffled Konah's hair as Konah remained on the chair looking at him anxiously, imploring him with his eyes not to go.

"I hope that too. I don't require payment, but I expect you back here as soon as peace is declared," she said a little sternly with a fraction of a smile. Her instructions were serious, but her warning was not too foreboding, as she wasn't trying to break this young soldier who was fairly innocuous and unobjectionable. He seemed a pleasant enough man and as he was making a request on behalf of her dead friend, it was hard for her to say no.

"I'll be back as fast as my legs will carry me, which is pretty quick. This shirt – can I leave it here and I'll return for it?"

"It's hardly a good fit, but as you wish. Good luck, Mr Grey."

"Good luck to you, ma'am," Grey said, ushered out of the door by her, leaving his shirt in her hands and leaving feeling better than when he had arrived. There had been some initial antagonism from her, but he left feeling he had fulfilled Georges' dying wish and he felt that Laura was an intriguing woman who he was pleased he had an excuse to return to. He was unsure how she would get on with Konah but he felt sure that she would look after him as she was clearly a capable woman and at heart he felt she was good-natured. Grey had faith in Georges' judgement and he had a good gut feeling (along with other feelings, Laura making an indelible impression on him) about her himself.

Grey ran back at full pelt and became disorientated in the near absolute darkness, eventually finding his way back to town and his punishment. He hoped desperately that his prolonged absence would not be considered desertion, preferring to be thought of as undisciplined rather than yellow. He wished he had opted for an alcoholic drink at Laura's as he realised that returning reeking of booze was some sort of mitigation. He would still face a grilling, but it would not be seen as wilful disobedience.

Grey returned at the rendezvous point at 22:38 hours and he found the market square was full of celebrating Frenchmen and Frenchwomen, but no American soldiers. He asked the townsfolk desperately where the soldiers had gone and they were only able to point him in a general direction. Grey started to wonder if he had made a mistake.

Grey found an English unit in the town late that night and he asked to see their leader who he was led to, the officer merrily drinking in a nearby inn. Grey stood as he told this middle-aged inebriated lieutenant that he had become separated from his unit and he wanted to rejoin them immediately. He was faced with a barrage of questions at this and Grey admitted ruefully that it involved a woman and he had been tardy and missed the time that was arranged for him to return, Grey lying through necessity and claiming he had fallen asleep. He hated to lie, but he could not reveal the truth without endangering Laura and the group he had met, who he imagined liked their business kept private (Laura in particular).

"I don't know where your unit's gone," the lieutenant blasted. "I'm bloody well sure they won't be missing you if this is your idea of serving your country. You need to buck your ideas up. If you were under my command you wouldn't be acting up like this. Still, I'll leave it up to yours to discipline you. Give your details to the sergeant over there and then get your head down because you may as well make the most of your 'holiday' before you go back to your deserved bollocking."

Grey did as he was told though the situation worsened over the next few days. Returning a displaced Yank soldier wasn't top of this unit's priorities and while he was looked after, Grey hated his time with them as it made his desertion seem longer. He was three days late by the time another US unit took him back to his platoon. The sergeant joked when he met them as he pointed at Grey and said, "I believe I have something here that belongs to you."

The American lieutenant, Gibson, looked at Grey, as did Cloisters who said sheepishly to Gibson, "It's the soldier I was telling you about."

"The one you gave dispensation to leave?" Gibson replied, unhappy with Cloisters and Grey and their conduct.

"Yes, sir," Cloisters said, keeping a civil tongue even though he longed to say something different.

Grey was taken back into the unit and he made the same excuses to the assembled force who all stared, seeking an explanation. Delgado smiled at him, the one friendly expression amidst the sea of accusatory gazes. Cloisters put a firm hand on Grey's shoulder blades, gripping him painfully, and said, "Come with me to one side and we'll talk about it," his controlled tone telling Grey that as soon as they were some distance away Cloisters was going to go ballistic on him.

He was right and as soon as Cloisters had led him to a peripheral area, where only a few men were standing point, he launched into a blistering tirade directed with his face inches from Grey's at stentorian volume. Grey had to stand there and take it and as he tried to apologise profusely Cloisters stopped him, shouting that he did not want to hear his bullshit excuses. Cloisters' words made him think and he was pensive at how angry he had made his fairly easygoing sergeant and, worse than that, Cloisters told him that he was very disappointed in him, having expected a lot more from him. This cut Grey to the bone and he tried to speak again only to be silenced again by the irate Cloisters. Finally, Cloisters gave him an opportunity to speak and Grey said, "Sarge – I was never going to desert. I would never abandon my unit or my friends. I swear on my mother's life and in God's name that I was always going to return and the thought of desertion never entered my head. Punish me by stopping my wages or give me the worst jobs, but don't kick me out of this unit, please."

"This ain't three strikes and you're out, Grey. This is one strike and you're out because there are other men's lives at risk here. You're going to have to work fucking hard to earn my trust again. Now fuck off out of my sight," Cloisters said, still enraged but with nothing else he wanted to say to Grey who at least showed remorse. Grey went back to his unit where he found himself the centre of attention upon his return (this was considered by many to be the first time he had done anything of interest) with every other soldier slapping him on the back and calling him a sly dog, the primary clique of Fudd and his friends seeming particularly amused. It was generally assumed that he'd slept with Paulette and Grey let them believe that – he couldn't reveal the truth and part of him didn't want to, aware that this changed their perceptions of him, possibly made them respect him more. He wouldn't elaborate on details when quizzed (he felt ungentlemanly enough letting them believe the lie and would not besmirch Paulette further) and merely said that it was an experience, which the night certainly had been.

Isdel Delgado surprised him by showing little interest in what he had been up to. He seemed concerned initially and asked him how he had been and then walked away from him as others pressed him for details. Jake Baker was very inquisitive and Grey found himself inventing a fictional meeting between himself and Paulette in 1942 in Iowa, a very lame story that led to questions of how and why she returned to France (a sick mother was the best he could come up with). One part of Paulette's lie that he would not go along with was her claim that he fathered her child. He was not the sort of man who would shirk such responsibilities and he did not want to be thought of as that kind of person and instead he implied that Paulette made it up as a ruse to spend a few hours with him. The innuendo made him uncomfortable, but it seemed palatable to the others who believed such a girl would lie to have her desires sated and they told Grey that they were willing to take his place next time.

Pearce, never one to let an opportunity to cause trouble pass by, tried to stir the others to resent Grey by harping on about Grey's cowardice, asking if anyone had any white feathers and stating how he left them in the lurch. His attempt to stir up ill feeling failed as the others were largely unconcerned as they had not been fighting at the time so they did not consider it desertion and they felt that they would likely have done the same as Grey if they had come across an ex-girlfriend. As the others failed to respond to this, Pearce changed tack and settled for trying to make them laugh by making disparaging comments about Paulette ('I didn't see her close up, but I'm sure it was a scarecrow') which was more successful, especially when he started describing the act, mocking Grey's overcurious nature ('This is what passes for my pecker. Do you want to talk about it? How does it make you feel? Can we discuss inserting it? Is that straw up there?'). Pearce ridiculed Grey within earshot, talking loudly to make sure he heard and Grey was forced to ignore him, in no position to afford to be able to get into trouble by fighting. Later that night Grey stood on guard duty, which was his punishment for the immediate future while his superiors decided if further action would be taken. Cloisters told Grey he would perform this duty for two hour stints each night, silencing Grey when he tried to offer to perform the duty all night. Delgado picked this late hour to talk to him about what had really happened.

"I'm glad you're still speaking to me," Grey said, appreciative of Delgado seeking him out while most of the others slept. "Thing is though, don't take this the wrong way, but I should be concentrating on this. The last thing I want is to make another bad impression. Tomorrow we'll talk, yeah?"

"My eyes are peeled too, I'll keep watch with you. This shouldn't take long," Delgado said, accompanying Grey on a sweep around the camp.

"I won't be repeating that anytime soon. Getting displaced...I'm lucky to be back with you guys now, at first they were going to send me further back," Grey said, surveying their surroundings as he spoke.

"That sounds good to me!" Delgado knew Grey was sore about what happened and he said encouragingly, "This'll blow over."

"I doubt Pearce will let it."

"C'mon, who listens to him anyway?"

"If I hadn't missed combat I wouldn't feel so bad. They may not charge me with desertion yet, even though that was never my intention, that was the result."

"It's done. It's pointless putting yourself through the wringer when you've got someone else happy to do that for you. It's my job to whine about things here; you're supposed to be the keen one. Or are you deserting that position too?"

"I'm still keen. Just miserable. You're right, I need to stop dwelling on this. So the rest of the guys don't think like Pearce?"

"Your name took some flak during the battering but now that you're back and we know you came back of your own accord, you're thought of as no worse than before," Delgado answered honestly.

"That doesn't cheer me up!" Grey joked.

"That's not my job. My job is to moan about missed opportunities. Your job is to be that rarest breed, a happy dogface."

"Once I know that there's going to be no consequences for this, I will be."

"This is the punishment. There won't be a court-martial now."

"Lieutenant Gibson said he hadn't decided yet."

"They would have done it already. That's to fuck with your head."

"Mission accomplished."

"Did Paulette fuck with your head too?"

"Hmm. I guess so."

"What's really going on, Jimmy? You aren't a good liar and I can see you're not comfortable with it. You'd never met her before in your life, I could see that when she slapped you. You had no idea who she was." Delgado was reaching out to him, trying to help him here, as he knew there was more to it than Grey was letting on. He had deliberately kept his distance when Grey was talking to the others about her, aware that Grey could not reveal the truth with everyone looking closely at him. No one was close enough to hear them and Grey said,

"You're right, Isdel..." Grey hesitated. "I hate lying, especially to you and Cloisters, but there are some things I can't tell anyone."

"You can tell me, amigo. I was nearly shot earlier today and the way it's looking I won't be lasting long so you've nothing to lose," Delgado said, trying to persuade him to divulge his secret, mainly for Grey's sake as Delgado felt he appeared burdened and wanted to help him.

"I should have been here, shouldn't I? If you had been shot I would have felt responsible," Grey said guiltily.

"Bullshit! Yeah, you would have I think, but you can't think like that. If I get shot I'll blame the Hitler brat who shoots me, or myself for not taking more care, but I'm not going to blame any of you guys, not even Pearce. He's trying to make you feel bad to make himself look good," Delgado said.

"He's not a bad soldier," Grey said, forced to admit this having observed Pearce in battle where his actions were competent and his comments spurred on other men, encouraging them even by insults.

"In some ways he is capable. You're a good soldier too, but you're letting yourself get weighed down here. The number of crippling headaches you have is not normal and I'm guessing that it's stress related. If you want to talk about it I swear it goes no further," Delgado solemnly promised.

"I have talked about it a few days ago, but I would like to tell you too," Grey said, cautious as he spoke for fear of Delgado, who was deeply religious, turning on him. "You're a Christian, Isdel, and so am I," Grey said, showing him his cross. Delgado produced his crucifix and said,

"Hell, without this faith to see me through I would have walked away after the beaches." It was important to Delgado, a prominent part of his life and actions.

"It helps me too, but since I was young – you're going to think I'm crazy," Grey said, shaking his head, very apprehensive about sharing his secret, perspiring heavily as he attempted to tell him, backing out at his first attempt.

"I'm training to be a doctor. I don't use that word indiscriminately. Part of that training also deals with confidentiality so even if you like to dress up in women's panties and call yourself Gertrude, that won't go any further," he said, trying to put Grey at ease with this frivolous comment (Delgado had never seen him so tense) while still making it clear that he was taking him seriously.

"I wish that was it," Grey said weakly, trying to smile, his face screwing up.

"That's just me then. Go on," Delgado said.

"I've heard voices in my head half my life. Spirits have communicated with me and told me things and that's partly why I joined up at my first opportunity, because of this…symphony of voices in my head coming from Europe. There were some American and English and Australian voices too from the Far East and their stories of some of the Japanese cruelty haunted me. Sometimes it's people who've just died and they tell me things which are helping over here – there's no sides in the spirit world, they just tell me to try to help me, and my instincts over here have just been the voices guiding me. Pearce is a better soldier than me, you see," Grey said, revealing his fraud along with his murky secret.

Delgado stared at him, disbelieving his account though he believed that Grey thought it was true, colouring how he responded. "In the heat of battle it's hard to tell what's real. I think you should give yourself more credit."

"I don't just hear those voices in battle. I heard them long before the war. Do you remember I was talking to you of Kaia Yang?"

"Yes. It was at that pub and I remember what you said about her was unclear," Delgado said, seeing where Grey was going with this.

"I knew her in spirit form. She was an educated Chinese young woman who spoke fluent English who was killed in the Boxer Rebellion. She was not at all bitter and she was real swell, a proper lady. I found myself attracted to her spirit, but recently with all of these other voices more desperate than her, her visitations ceased. I get requests sometimes – 'help my child, she's alone in the camp', 'check on my brother in his unit', and I want to help, but there seems so little I can do," Grey said, sighing at how useless he felt at times at these beseeching cries. "Most of the time I can still function but at my last unit I was lucky enough to talk to a brave Australian soldier called Terry and a Polish woman called Katarzyna. Terry was skinned and tortured by the Japanese – what they put him through is more horrific than my worst nightmares and I won't even tell you all of it 'cause it would never leave you. Katarzyna…Katarzyna took months to die. They performed foul medical experiments on her, experiments so painful that she wished that they'd sent her to the gas chambers. My training suffered and I lost all of my friends but I couldn't ignore them."

Delgado felt he knew what was happening here. Grey was a gentle soul and Delgado surmised he was cracking under the strain, which bore no shame, and he tried to think how he could help him without getting him sent to an asylum.

"That girl – Paulette. She came from a group that were using supernatural forces to combat the Nazis and they wanted me to join. I got side-tracked doing something for them and that was why I didn't show up."

"We waited there until 21:00 hours, you know. Cloisters really thought you were going to show."

"I intended to. I feel like shit for getting him in trouble. What I've told you is the truth, Isdel." Grey knew how ridiculous it sounded.

"I would keep that information close to your chest," Delgado advised. "So this girl was a witch?"

"No. I think others were, but she was an ordinary girl."

"You've done the right thing, Jimmy," Delgado said, feeling his crucifix through his shirt. "That group's not for you. However you do it, you've got good instincts and we want you to stay with us. That group – it sounds unholy."

"I don't know. I didn't see any crosses, admittedly, but they're trying to stop the suffering too," Grey said, defending Georges' group's intentions.

"Forget Pearce – for all of the advancements that you have made, and for looking out for the weaker ones like Hobbs and Hill, you are the best damned soldier in this regiment. They might just be damned," Delgado said, trying to stop Grey from being led astray, something that had happened to many of his childhood friends who were drawn into crime and vice though never the occult. He wasn't going to let Grey go down this dark path, not just as a Christian trying to maintain a fellow believer's faith, but as his friend.

Grey felt that Delgado's judgement on the group was unfair and prejudiced, but he was so relieved that his friend had not turned on him over his revelations that he did not press the issue. They talked of other things for the rest of Grey's patrol, Delgado very conversant concerning the Bible. As they fought over the coming days Grey did not bring it up again, but Delgado kept close by his side and noticed him wince at times and he realised that Grey believed he was having a visitation at these times. When Delgado saw this happen he would shout something at Grey – something encouraging, a warning, something trivial, anything to ground him in reality. He wasn't going to let him turn nuts.

Some voices however were forceful and found a way through and could be heard over battle and Delgado could not prevent this. As Grey tried his hardest to fight, he also had to counsel a young English widow who was killed in the blitz and clearly bereft.

I don't understand why we aren't together. My only consolation, my only comfort, was the thought that when I died we would be together again – what's the point of dying if we can't be together?

You can be, Lizzie. You'll be at peace soon…

But what does that mean, James? Does that mean that I cease to exist altogether? Am I just disappearing gradually until there is nothing?

You will cease to exist on this plane, that's all. You'll be together in Heaven.

I'm starting to wonder if he is dead. Maybe that's why I'm still here, to watch over him. You're in the army, is it possible they could be mistaken? she said, hoping that her love had succeeded where she had failed and cheated death.

It depends what they said. Did the letter say missing presumed dead or was it a clear notification of his death?

His ship was sunk and I know it's unlikely, but he could have survived that. Do you think that's possible?

It's possible, Lizzie, but I doubt it. I'm sorry. If you accept his death then you will probably find peace and join him.

Is he in your head? Has he contacted you?

No. Very few do out of all of those who fall.

I was pregnant when the bomb hit. I was due to have the baby in two months time. My baby's gone, hasn't it? There's no chance of meeting up with someone who was never born, she said sadly, resigned to this fact.

Truthfully, I don't know. There's more chance that you'll be reunited with your husband than your child, I would think. I don't know as much as I would like to about all of this. I wish that I had all of the answers.

How much do you know as fact?

Grey pondered this and eventually said, *This realm is more about the senses and intuition rather than facts. You might not have given birth to your child but you have as much right to grieve it as those who lost older children.* Grey sensed that she was trying to force her baby from her mind, as though it were pointless to mourn something that had never existed and he tried to help her.

It's not the same. If I had given birth to it and it had been a boy – I know it was a boy – then I would just be worried about him now, worried about him growing up to serve and die for his country like his father.

Maybe there won't be another war after this one, or at least not on this scale.

I can hear that you're an optimist and so was I, but you know that's not realistic. I hope you are right but I'm unconvinced. How hard is it out there?

You do get used to it. You don't think that you ever will, you think that you'll never dare sleep because there's a moment when you first wake up where you think you're still at home and then you realise where you are and you nearly jump six foot in the air like in a cartoon. I'm not a brave man at all, Lizzie, but even I have learned how to handle it so your husband would have coped admirably I'm sure. He'd be a braver guy than me and if I can cope with it then you can be sure he did. I'm not lying to make you feel better and I'll admit that you never get to the level where you take it all in your stride, but you get to the stage where you can relax between combat.

He used to get terrified. He told me the one time he got leave, the last time we were together. I tried to relate to it, but I couldn't. I held him in my arms and said the right things but I couldn't imagine the naked terror he talked of. All of the bombing in London never really scared me that much – that's why I didn't go to a bunker, I was sure the plane would just pass me by. I never thought for a second that I would be hit.

I know what you're saying. From other voices I know how bad the bombing has been in London through the war and if you went to the bomb shelters every time then you'd probably never sleep. You were just trying to get on with your life as normal. If it was me I would probably use the shelters at first and then get out of the habit of it. Grey felt that it was important that she did not blame herself for her death and while he likely would make the effort to get to the bomb shelter himself, he told a white lie to make her feel better.

There wasn't even one close to me and the route I had to take was notorious for rapes. There were a lot of prostitutes around the area and decent women suffered as a result.

Grey ignored the judgemental tone in her voice, even though he disagreed with her provocative statement, and he said, *That's the trouble with big cities, they can be dangerous places.*

Less dangerous than where you are now. Is it safe for you to talk to me? If I'm affecting your concentration tell me and I'll leave you in peace.

You're not.

I think you would say that even if I was.

I wouldn't, he lied.

Promise me.

I promise.

That's just a promise to make me feel better. I used to do them myself all the time. I should leave you alone. There's…there's one thing I can think of that might be keeping me here, only it's pathetic.

I'm sure it won't be.

Oh, it is. I always knew my Charlie was dead, then when I lingered here I thought that maybe I was wrong. I was right though, he must be dead, no one could be that strong a swimmer, not even him. The only other thing I can think of is Molly. It's not a child or relative, it's just a cat, a thin little moggy that my friends used to call a rat because she was so small. She'd wanted to go out before the bomb hit, so she's probably still alive…I'd feel better if she'd died with me, Lizzie said emotionally.

I'd say there's a good chance your friends would take her in.

They've got dogs and none of them were cat lovers. My husband and baby are dead and I'm going on about a stupid cat, she said, feeling ridiculous.

We had a pet collie and at times I cared about that dog more than I cared for anyone else. It didn't take to me, unfortunately. It was my dad's dog and that was who the dog loved, but I understand how much pets matter, he said, trying to convince her that she was not being silly. Whatever anchored her was a valid reason to her and he would not make light of it and he had certainly heard stranger reasons (a woman consumed by guilt at not returning a library book and a man feeling unfulfilled at not experiencing an unusual sexual fantasy sprang to mind).

*Thank you for your help, but you're in enemy territory, risking your life – my cat's welfare is not more important than your safety. Goodbye, James, I'm not going to cause your death…*she said, deliberately taking her absence from him without finding the peace he was trying to grant her. Grey tried in vain to recall her but she was lost to him.

"You think they'll be wanting volunteers for the firing squad?" Pearce said to his friends as Grey walked by within earshot.

"I was late back by a couple of hours. It only took three days for me to get back here. As desertion goes that's pretty lame. I know I fucked up, Pearce, so you don't need to keep harping on. Like most of your chat, it's real stale now."

"Watch it, deserter. No wonder you were pals with Stafford. Peas in a pod. Back at the base you'd have got away with KP duty. We're in the field now where different rules apply and you intentionally shied away from combat."

"We weren't in the middle of anything at the time..."

"You missed active service and combat."

"Let it go, Pearce. I have to explain myself to other people, not you."

"You may be lucky. 18...that may go in your favour at your court-martial. Or they may want to make an example and shoot you down like the dog that you are."

"As if that's going to happen. I've been allowed to rejoin the unit. That suggests that things aren't as bad as you make out."

"They've got to play it by the protocol. You're not getting away with this scot-free."

"I'm never going to hear the end of this, am I?" Grey said gruffly, mad with himself more than anything as he knew he had given Pearce the perfect ammunition. Whatever Pearce's flaws, he'd never left the others in the lurch; he had always been at his post and had always proven himself an asset in combat. Even Grey saw that Pearce had more of an upside than him in the current environment.

"That depends how long you stay with us. Whether you run again or whether we get to give you the send-off you deserve," Pearce grinned, holding up his rifle and pointing it towards Grey.

Harvey Baker saw this gesture in the distance and bounded over and said loudly, "Aiming a loaded weapon at a comrade – always a good idea, Pearce, what could possibly go wrong?"

Pearce lowered his weapon and said, "A reprieve for now, Grey. Let's see what the brass say."

Delgado passed Cloisters heading back from the latrines as he made his own way there and with no one else around he said, "Have you seen Grey?"

"Don't start," Cloisters said wearily.

"I know he feels like shit so I figured he may be around here. Any chance of easing up on him?"

Cloisters considered this and said, "If it was up to me, yeah. It's out of my hands."

"If you vouched for him Gibson would listen to you. It's not as if he knows him."

"The trouble is I do, and that's why I'm not rushing in to put my neck on the block for him."

"Give him a break. He's got the message now."

"He may get a permanent break. This is his second chance already."

"Mine too."

"Well do yourself a favour and keep your beak out. It should blow over if he keeps his head down. At the minute Gibson's looking into Grey's history in intimate detail. I tell him about the fainting spells and he's out. With any luck something else will distract him and he'll forget about it," Cloisters said, as keen as Delgado to put the incident behind them though the higher-ups involvement hindered that.

"Pearce keeps going on about firing squads..."

"Is that right? I'll put his mind at rest about that. Private Pearce is a good example. Someone took a human mould and filled it up with shit to give us that charming character, but I always know what he'll do next. Grey is a mystery to me. He might be the best sniffer dog in the world one day and the next he's keeling over at nothing with no medical cause."

"We're in a stressful situation. Physical and mental fatigue are not uncommon. Not ideal in combat, granted."

"I don't want to sign the boy's death warrant. If they make the decision to cut him loose it may be for the best."

"Feel free to have the same doubts about me."

"No chance. You're here for the duration."

"Thanks a fucking lot, Sarge. If you're keeping me against my will then you should keep someone who's desperate to stay." Even though Delgado fought Grey's corner he shared Cloisters' concerns. Maybe Grey going home was for the best, for everyone. He was a liability, and combat had created serious mental issues. Watching over him was going to be a full time job.

Over the coming weeks Grey near enough managed to gain Cloisters' tacit forgiveness through several acts of bravery and one specific action that led to a territorial advance. The voices of English speaking German soldiers revealed their comrades hiding place to Grey and Cloisters trusted Grey enough to lead his unit where he suggested. The forcefulness of the suggestion from a man who was anything but, convinced him. After they had captured their enemy Cloisters said to him, "Kept away from the ladies you're quite a good soldier." This was the first positive thing he had said to him since his absence and it relieved Grey. "I guess you can stick around."

INTERLUDE

C'mon. American virgin soldier from Keokuk calling. Keokuk – everyone else I've spoken to lately seems to think it's a funny name. Keokuk – bet ya can't spell it. Somebody bite at this ammo I'm giving you to beat me over the head with please.

I guess this Yank is too vulgar for European tastes. If anybody is listening we're still detached from our troop. If one of you guys out there would talk to me I could work out a path back to them. It's not conditional – I'll help you whether you can help me or not. I'm not the sort of medium who requests a favour for a favour. My palms don't require silver, my brain doesn't require knowledge – actually my brain needs knowledge desperately but that's another story. Even the best spirit can only do so much.

I've worded that badly. When I say the best spirit I don't mean to make it sound like you're genies or emphasise the gulf between the two states. This is what happens guys when I get no response, I ramble. Sheesh. It's quiet times like these I realise how bad my patter is. I make my mouth go all the time in life too, and the material is no better then. That's a defensive action, because when I go quiet that's when suspicions are aroused so I'm forced to chat when I'd like to sit back and relax. Woe is me – if you weren't depressed before I'll have you there soon!

Okay. For the benefit of anyone who might be able to hear me we're still in hiding. There's seven of us. We're from different squads from the same platoon. My good friend Delgado is with me and he's still mad at me. If you came in late you won't know – let's have a recap, there's time. I hope there is anyway. Still, you never know.

Where was I? Genies in a bottle though it's not like that at all. How can silence throw somebody so? You see, for me silence is not the norm. Eight years old, walking home after a game of baseball – we won and the plaudits for that belong to yours truly. James Grey if you're just sitting comfortably now and missed the preamble. I answer to Jimmy or Jim too. Hodge was at the game and had a nightmare. He's never been the athletic kind and only played to make up the numbers 'cause we plagued him until he agreed and then he got ripped to shreds for being useless. Not by me – I've already lost touch with my other school friends but Hodge is a brick. He'll go far – his oversized brain makes up for his inability to catch a ball.

Right. Walking home. Maybe even skipping along. In a tough way of course. It was getting a little dark, dusky say. So when I heard the voice I spun round with a start. There was somebody there when I turned round and I thought it was them until the voice carried on while their lips were firmly pursed. Back then there was lots of confusion, of me mistaking spiritual voices for...earthly voices? Spirit zero was Lanfred, who's long since found peace – he got me through the difficult teething process. Since then silence in this noodle has been a rare commodity. I get the odd block of six hours here and there, or I did before the war. That's enough for me.

I celebrate my ten year anniversary of this gift in four months time. The date is etched in my mind forever, because originally it seemed the blackest of days. The ignorance of youth. It took a good few years before I realised how lucky I am – I could be the star of my own pulp comic! I'm partly serious about that. James Grey, medium-man, righter of wrongs, avenger of innocents! I've worked on building up my physique to fit that profile – move over Doc Savage, your time is up!

Then there's the other side. I may be as smooth as sandpaper, with patter that would dissuade the most ardent believer, anti-charisma. I still have one thing in my favour. I don't care that it sounds sappy, I do care about you guys. I've been brought up in the Church and while I'm a bit wary about the Rev finding out about my power, I reconciled my power and my religion a long time ago. A fair few spirits lose their religion. I get that. My power has increased my faith and as a Christian it's an honour for me to do my small bit to help you guys, to get you to the promised land. I don't just do it to try and tip the scales more in my favour – though if it does then that's good too. Joke. It's the right thing to do. It's cut and dry.

Of course four months is a long, long way away. As things stand four days. Four hours. Four minutes? I'm taking the thought too far there, I believe I have more than four minutes of life left. Throw me a bone.

I'm desperate as hell to cough. There's a German patrol that's just passed our way. I'm amazed they didn't spot us. Hill moved when they were coming past. How they didn't hear him escapes me. They're still close enough we can hear them talking. It's only a small patrol, not that we can mount an attack. We have our weapons, save for Hill, but without ammo they're not much good. Lethal against unarmed men…not that I would use my bayonet against unarmed men. The patrol was armed though so evasion is the better tactic. Fuck pride. Excuse the language, if any ladies or children are listening. Any soldiers out there I think will excuse me when I speak colourfully.

I think they're gone. Lord strike me down if I ever complain about the Army again 'cause I miss being with the unit. We were in intense danger then, yet we stood a chance. On our own, things are going to be tough. I'm safe from a lightning strike folks because I've never complained about the Army. I'm like one of those green kids you see in war films, too young to serve but raring at the bit to go. 'Lemme attem! Lemme attem!' I hold my hands up, that was me. In spirit, I don't think I ever used that phrase, at least not in public. By now you should know why I was so keen, 'cause I'm better informed than most about the Nazis' genocidal global plan. That really is straight out of the pulps; maniacal evil leader with aspirations of global domination and mass extermination, with no redeeming features period, just pure cackling, Ming the Merciless, Fu Manchu evil. No wonder it doesn't feel real. Nope, I'd never complain about the Army because I couldn't live with myself if I didn't contribute something to stopping the greatest threat to civilisation since? You know, I think this is the ultimate. Sure, the Army isn't all sunshine and laughter and breakfast in bed, but it does the job. Mistakes get made because we're human. It's still a fine institution, even after finally accepting me into it. I haven't ruined it entirely yet.

I'd only just got things back on an even keel too before this. I pulled an all-nighter. There was extenuating circumstances. In wartime, in hostile territory, doing what I did – I'm lucky they had me back. Isdel makes out things weren't so bad, but I think it was almost the end of the road for my fledgling army career. Cue mental breakdown. Jeez, I am brittle as fuck! No wonder there's so many question marks about me. Maybe when this is all over I should go to the quacks.

Nah. I know how that plays out. I say about the voices in my head, get a new jacket to wear and doped up to the eyeballs. My brain's mush enough without letting them lobotimize me.

This has happened once before. It lasted five days then. Five long, lonely days. I hate being disconnected from you guys now. A few hours here and there are fine. Any longer and I start my own search party and I can normally find some stragglers to talk to. You ever hear my thoughts and I'm musing over Gene Tierney it might be best to give me a few minutes, but otherwise please approach me. Before, when it happened last. Straight after Pearl Harbor – in fact during it was hectic, when I had the heads-up and couldn't tell anyone. Understand that I didn't know before else I would have warned folk. When it started I…Jeez, that stung. I'm a hypocrite 'cause I like to think all lives have the same worth only when it was Americans dying in their thousands… It hit home for everyone. I strained for weeks after to contact every spirit and I guess overloaded my system. Nothing went pop, it just fell silent. It disturbed me greatly. I'm not exactly filled with confidence about this silence now either. After five days the voices slowly trickled back. I vowed not to push it. I still did though.

I guess I pushed my luck again. I've had a few warnings; I've collapsed a few times before this. Not very Flash Gordon like is it, swooning like a silent film actress – even Dale's tougher than that! I remember one of the multitude of voices, which I'd love to come to the fore because I'd love to hear the full story. 'Be be, antelopes in 1943'. Or Bee bee, Bibi, Bea… I guess you're hearing exactly the same sound guys, so you won't know what I'm on about with the different spellings. Forget the first part; I want to know about these antelopes last year? I'm not taking the piss, I just want to know what you were trying to tell me, pal. The others didn't stick out so much – sorry. I caught one other thread about a guy having more stumps than a wicket. Grim fare. Surviving this war with all of our limbs and our balls intact is harder than any of us thought.

I wish I had been conscious when we became separated. I kinda was and wasn't. We were holding the line. We were relieving another group and I'd had advance warning that this was going to be trouble. Even without the powers it was clear that this was no small scale affair. From all accounts we took one hell of a shelling. The line fell. Macmurray is a definite fatality. Blown apart completely, they say. He has a widow and a baby so that's three lives destroyed in one go. If Joe was still around he'd say that we crumbled but there's some onslaughts that are impossible to repel. Delgado dragged me from the ground and forced me to get my head together, enough to walk anyways. That's a life debt. Pearce and his pal Hartmann were helping their other best bud, Bradshaw who'd been badly wounded. They asked Isdel and me to cover them while they moved him and because I wasn't up to it Pearce blames me for Bradshaw subsequently having his brains blown out. I regret that my mind was too addled to even point at targets but I could have shot anyone so figured it was best not to…his death is on my head as Pearce constantly reminds me. I do feel bad, though I don't accept responsibility. I was a weak link at that moment, not his shooter and there's a hell of a difference.

Even in Keokuk there would be frequent spirit activity. We're not that far from Chicago back home so the Windy City provided the odd dozen grisly homicide. As much as I like the Jimmy Cagney gangster flicks I do think they glamorise crime too much – the reality is brutal. I've heard tales I'd rather not, things that make grown men wince and gave an adolescent nightmares. Back then I questioned whether the powers were worth it. Maybe all those times wishing my gift would go are coming back to haunt me now. If Isdel knew I'd lost my power he'd be ecstatic. That's if he truly believes I have a power to start with. Straight after my collapse, after we got far enough away he had a real go at me. He saw that I'd gone down like I was poleaxed without a single thing hitting me and got agitated about me having an episode at a crucial time, and made out that he was going to make sure I got psychiatric help, for everyone's benefit. The fact I was still out of it for most of his lecture aggravated him further and made him say some things he seems to regret. I've took no offence – I missed most of what he said and I know where he's coming from. He's not worried about me being a liability to the other soldiers, though he may have said words to that effect. He's like me, soft as muck – I know he's worried about my welfare first and foremost.

I've swayed the guys to come back with me to a town we passed through and liberated before. Chances are the Germans have reclaimed it, though even if they have I do have some contacts there. I won't say too much on this score in case this information somehow finds its way out into the public consciousness. For all I know there may be a German medium doing the same as me, with dreaded German efficiency. There's a cheery thought. All I need is some civvies and I can enter the town because without them I can't approach this group. I'd sooner not write my own death sentence but I am damned sure I won't make these guys share my gallows.

There's someone else I'd like to see too, though I can't, the Dale to my Flash. My first impression of her went better than hers of me. She's a character, I've gathered that much. Beautiful too, in an unconventional way. Not my usual type at all, but I think we're on the same wavelength. She's not a medium but I think there is more to her. I'm not in her prayer list yet so I'd like to meet her again and remedy that. I won't be seeing her though. Not until the war's over. She's been pressured into helping whilst this other group are keener. This lady just wants to live her life – I respect that, that's what I'm fighting for. I've still got a mountain to climb there – I can safely say she's not pining for me – but she'll get the full treatment later. I have about a 40% success rate with the ladies, which isn't as bad as it sounds. So what if the relationships don't last a month? At least I can get half of them to agree to go steady, for a little while. Laura…I didn't mean to say her name…Laura's a completely different kettle of fish, a tough nut to crack. She has an aura of mystery about her. Some of that is because I know of her connection to this group, yet even without that there is something about her anyway. An unforgettable character, like a dame in a crime novel. That doesn't do her justice, makes her sound sinister which she isn't. She's got a bark and I don't mind getting bitten, but I think there's a very soft, tender side too. I doubt many men get to see that side, though this man is used to seeing or hearing unusual things and opening closed doors. I can't get her out of my head for some reason. I get like this sometimes. It was the same with Daisy and with Kaia, my spirit paramour. Oh no, none of you guys will approach me now! Let me make it clear I don't make a habit of hitting on spirits. That's not something I'll be repeating, a blot on my medium ethics.

She could leave only she won't. Even now she says she could leave. Well, before the Nazis returned though, you know, I think that still stands now. What's the draw about staying? If you have friends and family or if you're resisting an invader I can understand it or if you're a native – she's not, and she has a home away from these parts in a green and pleasant land not trodden over by jackboots. Yet still she stays here. There's a defiant pride in that – I can't fathom it, but I'm impressed. I'm not sure it achieves anything still. Perhaps it's not meant to.

Isdel's been a pain about heading back. He knows a bit more about my contacts than the others. They think I'm meeting up with an ex. We haven't had a real chance to have a private talk about it which I'm glad of because I think this is the only plan. I know these people will help us. There's nothing else on the table. Of course I'd sooner get back with our troops but where are they? Answers would be appreciated. He's outvoted so he's forced to go along with it. Pearce has even said he likes the plan because it's my neck on the line. I go into town while they stay in hiding. It can only work if I find some other clothes and that's still not working out. We found two bodies the other day – German soldiers, and wearing that uniform would be an even worse idea. I'd either be shot as a spy or killed by a French resistance group. If you can hear me, Elsie, I agree that it's a bad affair when you get so conditioned to seeing such sights that seeing bodies doesn't make you sick to the pit of your stomach. We ate their rations. I don't feel bad about that. I don't feel anything, that's just being practical. Foraging isn't working out so well. I haven't the stomach to kill and cook my own meals anyway so I'm fine dieting for now. It seems like wildlife has been as disturbed by this conflict as us humans. What must the animals think of us? They must think we're nuts and who can blame them? They've either fled or other soldiers have eaten very well here.

We're close to Maramont and it's getting to the stage where I'm thinking of walking to town naked. I can't even wear my shorts as they're army issue and will give me away. If I do this, and it's not my preferred option, it'll have to be in the dead of night when nobody's around. The place where I want to be is on the outskirts. If I get lucky I can sneak around the back without being seen. Most of the people inside are dames, of course. This may work out to my advantage. It would take a cold-hearted woman to turn away a naked soldier in need of aid.

Seven days. That's two longer than the last time this happened. I'm getting worried now guys. I was given this gift and came to treasure it – I can't have it recalled now. Even if it's faulty sometimes I'll keep it thanks. The spirit plane gives off a kind of white noise – I need that sound to sleep. Total silence is difficult. Silence is death, I guess. That's what I feel like now, like I'm in a grave, a silent coffin, dead man walking. I'm not after sympathy and I know I sound melodramatic when I'm still breathing with everything still intact. That's the problem, that something is missing. It's not just that my powers are useful here. Even back home I'd feel the same, like half a man. I know the conflict was bad. I know others have had problems with their hearing since. Plus over a thousand spirits seemed to approach me at once. Still, even if I was mentally wounded by the sudden surge, surely I can heal? If I have to operate at a lower level then that's fine. I can't go from everything to nothing though. Lord, help me, please. Your humble servant, James Grey. Amen.

Chapter 6 – Witch!

Laura stood in front of the Pagan Resistance in the bar of Georges' converted inn and addressed them as a whole as what she had to say concerned them all and she felt that one of them out of the group would do what she wished. She had knocked on the front door, which the young straggly-haired hoyden had answered – she recognised her from Georges' description as Paulette. Paulette had never met her before and she was vigilantly cautious, as she knew she had to be now that they were occupied again. She had asked her in French what she wanted and Laura replied (also in French), "I wish to speak to your group. My name is Laura. I was a good friend of Georges and I think it would be best considering the secrecy of your group if we discussed this further inside."

Laura was pushy and made her point forcefully and Paulette admitted her immediately as it was clear she already knew of them. Laura walked straight through to the bar where two men and two women were present, the women and the standing man staring at her and Paulette for letting her through. The other man sat at the long table at the side of the room, paying more attention to the large meal he was consuming. This was Didier Godet, Mireille's 23 year old son, who was not officially a member of the Pagan Resistance but, as a member of a splinter Communist resistance group, he was keen to help them when his schedule permitted as they were fighting the same enemy and he liked to help his mother. He was dark like her and well built as he had been so well fed by his doting mother when he had lived with her and his features were not dissimilar – dark eyebrows close to his eyes, a broad nose though his black hair was thin, straight and short. Even at the table he wore his dilapidated, warm black coat with a holey white vest and thick trousers and he ate noisily, his mother standing by him with an apron about to dispense more food when Laura had entered. This was Mireille's group now and she vetoed every visitor and she was deciding if this visitor was welcome and she was giving her the once over with her eyes.

Mireille saw that this stranger was clearly a strong, confident woman and she respected that while Gervaise, who was sitting at the bar, saw Laura's poise as arrogance and took an instant dislike to her and gave her a snooty look. Eric (who stood by Gervaise at the bar) stared at her with apprehension, sensing the power in her even if the others, weak and lacking perception, could not.

"She's a friend of Georges," Paulette explained to Mireille, aware that she had to justify why she had let her in so readily without a warning. "She's Laura so seems as she has Konah she already knows about us."

Laura stood at the centre of the room dressed in a long plaid check skirt down to her ankles with a light yellow blouse and her hair hanging loose all the way down to her lower spine. She addressed them, looking at them all in turn with authority and she said, "Yes, I am Laura and I need to speak to you concerning the current arrangement. Georges had not received my permission regarding Konah and it is no longer convenient for me to continue to look after him. I understand he was a member of your group and I would hope you would welcome him back into the fold."

"Have a seat, Laura," Mireille said, staring at her, offering her a chair near her son who was still guzzling, leaving them to sort this out between them. He could help them, like Paulette, with the legwork, physical activity and the risks, but not at this matter of domestic arrangements and child care which did not concern him.

"No, thank you," Laura said, uninterested in the group's hospitality, as she did not want to become embrolled with them, which was what she suspected was the objective. She merely wanted her business sorted out with them so that she could go about her business alone again and have the child off her hands. Keeping him there involved her and she did not want that. He was no real trouble; he was a quiet, well-behaved child, but she wanted to be alone. She could have kept him for a few months or even a few years but she knew if she did not act soon then when this group was inevitably decimated by the Nazis there would be no one to return him to and he would become her responsibility for life, a scenario which would make neither of them happy. She was not heartless concerning him and she intended to do something that would follow Georges and Grey's wishes regarding the boy. "I will help you smuggle him out of the country and one of you to accompany him and whoever does this can stay on my Scottish estate for the duration of the war." She felt this would be a tempting offer to some of them considering they were at risk again and she considered her actions excessively generous and benevolent considering she had no obligation to be either.

"There is no one available to take him as we are all extremely busy with our enemy," Mireille said, responding to this as though it were an affront to her pride. She felt this woman was a pathetic, miserable harridan for being unable to look after a small, near silent, angelic boy as a dear old friend's last wish. Mireille had heard Georges talk of Laura and she had detected much affection in his voice, which she now decided was unmerited.

"I would have thought he would be useful to your group which clearly needs all of the help it can get," Laura responded, matching fire with fire. "Georges held you in high regard but I have heard of you and you will not make any impression against the Germans," she said, assessing their chances of survival, let alone victory, as nil.

"We'll die trying though," Mireille said defiantly with one hand on her hip as Gervaise looked at Mireille with a frown, clearly disagreeing with this sentiment.

Laura realised that this pigheaded woman would perceive that to be a victory and she knew that further discourse would be a waste of time. She did not want to argue with them as they had been friends of her friend and she returned to the matter at hand. "Georges should not have left the boy in my care."

"We are agreed on something," Mireille said. The warfare they were going to lead was not an appropriate place for a child, but she preferred to have him back with them than living with this woman any longer.

At this juncture there was a quiet knock at the back door that Eric heard and he told everyone to be quiet and they all heard it this next time. As Paulette walked around to see who it was, Grey decided he could wait no longer outside at the risk of being seen and he walked through the back door and kitchen and emerged at the entrance to the bar in sight of all in the room.

Lifelines were a rare thing and Grey was grateful that several had presented themselves to him. Entering the town naked in the night, while a passable plan, was never seriously considered – he'd take his chances out in the woods over that. The first ray of hope came with the return of his powers which made him feel like a complete human being again. He learnt that like the previous time this had happened the communication was only stopped one way, with the spirits still able to hear him and thankfully his hearing was now restored. Spirits with senses of his surroundings were uncommon (probably 1 in 10) and he was lucky that he received a spirit with such senses who helped lead him closer to Maramont (and told him that, unfortunately, Maramont had been taken) and into town, yet another soldier who was eager to make sure no more US soldiers followed him to the other side. Grey found the coat himself in the woods – it was saturated and even after Grey shook it down it was still filthy with mud pitted on that would not come out. Regardless, this coat worn over his uniform was enough to disguise him a little in the night, if he was only seen from a distance. He left his pack, helmet and army jacket with the other soldiers as he approached the town where he hoped they could find shelter. This was perhaps the most crucial lifeline, his contacts in Maramont, and Grey knew he was lucky they had not been further from this town or they would have been finished. They had done well to last a week behind enemy lines undetected. Long term they would inevitably have been discovered and then imprisoned or shot but now they stood a chance as survival was possible with help from the partisans. If Georges had still been alive Grey knew they would all have been received with open arms. He hoped the new regime would be so welcoming.

"I'm sorry, but I thought someone might see me if I stayed out there," Grey explained to Paulette and Eric, apologising for barging in without being invited and he looked and saw Laura in the centre of the room. She had turned to look at him and she was smiling, finding him to be very favourable compared to the others in the room.

Gervaise complained in French to Mireille, "He can't stay here. We can't be harbouring American soldiers."

"Paulette, get him a drink," Mireille said, taking an altogether different stance and viewing him as very welcome as she pulled back a chair next to Didier, the same one she had intended for Laura and she smiled at Grey, gesturing for him to sit down. Grey smiled at her and walked across the room, stopping to greet Laura.

"Hello again, ma'am. There's been a setback, but I will return to your home soon to do what I promised. Treat the car well when you get it, I can cope if it goes to a good home."

"You're still alive," Laura said, remembering that she only inherited the car if he died (as if she was ever going to bother trying to claim it).

"It's going to take a long time so the bill's gonna be high."

"Oh well, my gain. You're going in the wrong direction to win, Private Grey. Still, your continued survival is an achievement of sorts," she said, muted praise.

"Are you all right to return to your place by yourself?" Grey asked, concerned for her making the isolated journey as he would have been even if France were free, but he was doubly concerned because of the Nazi presence. "If you would permit me I would like to accompany you, not wearing this military issue, Georges said I could wear his clothes," Grey said, becoming more gentlemanly than normal in her presence. He was not boorish whatever his company, but she ignited something in him that made him amplify his courtesy.

"His clothes on you would look so ill-fitting that the Nazis would shoot without even hearing your attempts at an accent," she said, amusing herself with her comment. "Thank you, but I'll decline," she added, smiling at his sweet intentions. That his companionship endangered rather than protected her did not need to be added.

"That's a shame. I wanted to buy some things from that gift shop. It's good to see you again anyway. You look swell." Saying this felt like speaking out of turn and he walked past her and sat down next to Didier who grunted a greeting and shook his hand.

"What brings you back, Grey?" Eric said in English, knowing this was the only language the American understood.

"My unit was ambushed and seven of us were cut off from our unit and I thought that from here we could contact the army. We were all heading to town only I realised that they'd made it here quicker than us so I've come alone. Sorry I couldn't find a better disguise than this jacket but nobody saw me enter. My comrades are close by and I was hoping to seek refuge here," Grey said, aware what a lot it was he was asking, but hoping the group (who were opposing and fighting the Nazis) would accommodate them.

"You can stay," Eric said, making the decision (which he knew Mireille would agree with, but that was not the point), "but six other Americans and non-pagans is too much of a risk and a strain on us."

"We could do far more damage to them with more members and we could do with more military experience in the group," Paulette pointed out. She felt that more recruits would be advantageous, especially soldiers who would be daring like her and partake in terrorist activity alongside her, making her all in favour.

"We are the Pagan Resistance, Paulette, not the American Resistance or the Communist Resistance," Eric pointed out sharply, a clear dig at what he thought of Mireille's son and his activities, which he felt were incomparable to the purity of the occult rites.

"What difference does it make as long as we destroy them?" Paulette said and she then proceeded to translate to Mireille of Grey's predicament, giving her pause to think. Mireille wanted to say yes, but she had to contend with Gervaise who was shaking her head and refusing vehemently, telling Mireille it was their death warrants. Mireille knew she could ill afford to lose Gervaise from her coven, yet she also wanted Grey's assistance (if not his excess soldiers) and she tried to think of a solution.

"Can't you take them?" Gervaise asked Didier.

Didier curled his top lip and said without thinking the details through, "Yeah. I can sort something out."

Paulette translated to Grey that he and his men would be going with the Communist Resistance and Laura considered this news. The boy Didier – she did not need any abilities to see that he had the foul stench of death upon him, a rancorous odour that was stronger on him than on Georges. The boy would be dead within a short time and Laura knew that if Grey went with him he would face the same fate.

"Merci, merci," Grey said appreciatively to Didier, one of the few French words he knew. Didier did not expect gratitude and paid little attention, planning his next strike against the Germans in his head. Paulette fetched Grey his drink, a beer, which he thanked her for and made short work of.

"If you can take his men, Didier, we'll keep him," Mireille said, thinking of quelling her ranks with another powerful member and with Konah returning too she felt they might become a force to be reckoned with, which was her aim.

"Whatever you want," Didier said, not fussed.

Mireille told Paulette to suggest it to Grey and they were surprised when Grey balked at this. He had to stay with his unit and would not send them off with the Communist Resistance if he were not going too. It was all or nothing and, whilst he appreciated being wanted, it was not going to happen and he made this clear politely but firmly.

A debate in French ensued as Mireille did not want to lose Grey and she tried to convince Gervaise that seven American soldiers around the place would make things easier for her and take the onus off her. Gervaise countered that she was unafraid of hard work and pointed out fervently that she was always there from first thing in the morning to late in the evening, seeking commendation for this, which Mireille duly gave her. Eric sided with Gervaise, telling Mireille that if it was Frenchmen he might reconsider but for Americans, who he said would likely be noisy and indiscreet, it was too hazardous for them, and that if Grey would not stay without them then he was not worth having. Eric questioned Grey's integrity also for not joining the group after his first visit and Gervaise was his ally, nodding at his words. Paulette saw that Mireille was being pressured by them to refuse to help the Americans and she said,

"Georges would have helped them."

"Georges is dead," Eric pointed out, frowning at Paulette. "We're trying to ensure the group doesn't die. I would suggest that we refuse them any help unless Grey helps us. If he refuses then Didier should not help them either," Eric said to Mireille, advising her how to lead.

Mireille did not like this manipulative, devious approach, but she considered it and (as she wanted Grey in her group) she agreed and told Eric to tell Grey so. Eric said to Grey sternly, "We cannot take any risks for you that would get us killed unless you prove yourself to us. We require your assistance in this lodge and if you assist us over the coming months then your men will be safe with the Communist Resistance and if possible returned to your own forces. If you will not assist us then leave now."

"I have other loyalties, Eric. It's not that simple for me," Grey said, weighing up the offer. They were facing capture where they were hiding at and they knew that even if they surrendered they could be shot which made Grey have to contemplate accepting this offer and leaving his unit which would be a wrench but was perhaps in their best interests. This decision weighed heavily on him and

Laura saw that in his furrowed, troubled expression as this group tried to play him, use him for their ends, blackmailing him into something he did not want to do. She did not like this and she intervened.

"You have another option, Private Grey. I would be prepared to take you and your men in," Laura said, surprising everyone. She had come here to tell the Pagan Resistance that she would not look after an innocent child for them as she wanted no involvement and now she was volunteering to harbour seven American soldiers, an act that the Germans would punish her for with far more severity.

"I couldn't ask you…are you sure?" Grey said, instinctively turning down the offer as he did not want to endanger this woman, before he thought of the others and realised he could not refuse.

"Do you believe I'd offer you shelter if I wasn't certain? You can help look after that boy you brought me," she said, making out he was obligated to return to persuade him as she realised that this silly boy was so concerned about her safety that he had misgivings about accepting her help that he so desperately needed. Her house was the obvious choice as sanctuary for them yet she knew he would not have asked her despite his need had she not offered and she respected his consideration.

Grey was speechless with gratitude at first and he said, "Thank you, ma'am. I will accompany you home then after all – or should I come in the dead of night with my men?"

"Come with me now. Have you some clothes for him?" she asked Eric, figuring that his garments would be a reasonable fit on Grey.

"No," Eric said, refusing to be of assistance out of obstinacy as a punishment for Grey not joining them.

"Can I borrow some clothes from you?" Laura asked Didier in French. He was a wider man than Grey and his clothes were scruffy, but the fit would be adequate. Laura explained to Mireille, who had deduced the nature of her offer to Grey, that she was taking the soldiers in but that she would need some clothes to get him to her house and Mireille agreed and she went upstairs and fetched some old trousers and a shirt that Didier did not mind contributing as it was a spare outfit he kept in the inn in case he ever needed a quick change. Grey thanked Mireille and Didier, Mireille smiling at him and wishing him good luck in French and she instructed Paulette to take him down to the basement to change. Grey talked to Paulette as they walked through the kitchen and he promised her that he would try to help the group still even if he were not a member. Paulette asked him to reconsider, telling him that he and his men could stay at her room in a house across town which she swore the concierge hardly ever went inside. Grey thanked her for the offer but knew this idea could not work. He knew how noisy the group would be and, despite all the warnings in the world, no one could make Pearce be quiet and he knew the farmhouse could comfortably accommodate them all and it had the advantage of being isolated. Paulette did not want to lose the added firepower and muscle, comrades like her without mystical ability. In the basement there was a pentagram that disturbed Grey a little and he smiled at Paulette as he took off his jacket, about to get changed. She stared at him and she began to pace the room, looking at him sporadically and Grey realised she wasn't going to leave him alone and he got dressed a little self-consciously when it came to changing trousers but she did not overtly stare as he did so.

"Do I pass as a Frenchman?" Grey said cordially.

"No, but only the Gestapo and the French will be able to tell. The German foot soldiers are stupid," she said, having had her fair share of run-ins with them, exacerbated by her rebellious nature. She did not realise that it was through certain German soldiers' mercy and tolerance of her as a young, mischievous woman who they perceived as no threat that she was still breathing. She did not see the situation that way, perceiving them as invaders who she would repel every step of the way with maximum force and she would take the risks and openly disrespect them at every opportunity.

"I'd better take these with me else if the Germans find them here you could be in trouble," Grey said, referring to his army issue uniform.

"We should expect trouble being a resistance group. Some of our members are treating this more like a recreational group. Not Mireille, she's a good leader, it's some of the others." Paulette let out a sigh of exasperation. "I would be more use in your type of unit."

"You are certainly brave enough, I can tell that. I wouldn't want to cross you after that slap! This group needs you though, I can tell you are invaluable to them," Grey said, flattering her.

"I know and I would never leave them. I still say we should be taking you in," Paulette said angrily, seeing this motion of denying them shelter as a backwards step and not how she wanted the group to progress.

Grey put his uniform into a bag Paulette provided and they rejoined the others, where Laura was waiting. In Grey's absence she had told Mireille and the group that she would keep on looking after Konah for the duration of the American soldiers stay at least but after that it would be up to them to arrange alternative accommodation and Mireille accepted that and begrudgingly praised her for offering to put the Americans up. Laura observed Grey in civilian attire for the first time, the clothes creased and unkempt and they did not suit him and she was unable to repress a small smile at this. Grey asked her the same question he had asked Paulette regarding his appearance and Laura replied that she would tell him outside. Grey said goodbye to the group, looking at them all individually whereas Laura left without a farewell and they exited by the back door, Grey carrying his bag over his shoulder as they made their way to the forest.

"I'm guessing you don't think I look French either," Grey said as they started their long walk.

"You look as French as the Stars and Stripes. You cannot disguise what you are, Private Grey, or not yet anyway. We're going to take a long detour to my abode because there are Germans along our route," she said, talking to him civilly.

"I'll follow you wherever," Grey said happily. "Did you see them on your way?"

"No, I am a woman of some power myself. I know that there are around 30 Germans a few miles from my home on some sort of manoeuvre and to avoid a confrontation I would prefer to walk an extra four miles out of our way," she said, choosing the prudent course of action.

"That sounds better than my ability. It sounds like you have a radar which is more up to date than my frequency," Grey said, praising her and pointing out the shortcomings of his talent.

"You have some power though. The boy was clouding things before as were that group, but now I am alone with you I can sense it," she said, surprised at the power that emanated from him.

"No, I'm just a novice who doesn't know what he's doing. I didn't know you had power actually until just now, but it fits. It suits you," Grey said, complimenting her, not acting startled by it, as though it were unlikely, like she had as she realised about his gifts.

"Power is innate, Mr Grey. You have power and in time you will learn skill. Power cannot be learnt if you see the distinction."

Grey thought this over and grasped her point and said, "I guess we're both pretty lucky being born with our abilities."

"There are drawbacks to it, but yes, I would agree. Your challenge is to survive to learn skill in this environment. For all of the friends your power might grant you there are also enemies and I am talking powerful enemies here too. The Pagan Resistance are raising their heads above the parapets and they are such an inept unit that basic soldiers could annihilate them. My advice to you is to keep a low profile and learn about yourself quietly. That's the rules under my house too – your soldiers have to be reasonably quiet and I don't want to be shouting orders at them all the time so that is your responsibility. I'll continue to look after the boy, that was just a joke, but you control the men."

"I will do. They'll treat you with courtesy. They're mostly a good bunch of guys."

"They all have to behave. I mean it, Private Grey. I don't let many people into any of my homes and I expect a reasonable standard of behaviour. I can tolerate some levity, but in moderation." Her home would not become a dosshouse.

"Trust me, I am, and they will be, so grateful that there won't be any misbehaviour," he promised solemnly.

"I hope not."

Laura led Grey back to her house, making it there in good time, her walking speed brisk though she was never out of breath and she showed him around her house, showing him the upstairs bedrooms of which there were five in total. She did not show him her bedroom which remained locked but he saw the others, all furnished and three of which were fairly large. The upstairs toilet and bathroom were very plush and downstairs Grey saw there was a Spartan toilet and sink and a large library which consisted mainly of books about the supernatural, some of the manuscripts appearing to be very old. There was also a large room which Laura used for storage so that the rest of her house did not look cluttered which consisted of antique furniture which had seen better days. There were also the rooms that Grey had seen on his previous visit, the large sitting room and the kitchen, and there was a basement that she briefly showed him, a large dark room where she kept her wine and there was a table and chairs. They went back to the sitting room where she instructed him to sit in preparation for hearing the ground rules.

"Firstly, you don't have to wait for permission to sit down. Seeing as you are going to be residing here for an undetermined length of time you should make yourself at home. I feel I can say that to you as I feel you would treat your own home with respect. Instil that thought into your fellow soldiers because I would not like to see them lying across my chairs or sitting on my tables. The library is off limits to them at all times. They are going to be bored here and I do not mind them reading some of my novels to amuse themselves, but none of my specialist text. You may read the books in there. The upstairs bathroom and toilet is for my convenience and not to be used at any time. The downstairs toilet is for your usage and the sink is sufficient to bathe under. I will permit you to use the upstairs bathroom and toilet, but I do not want a procession of soldiers using it so it's up to you which you use. If I ever instruct you all to go down to the cellar you have to make them go down immediately and make them remain silent until I come down and tell you the coast is clear, however long that takes. I don't mind providing food for you, but I will only cook for myself so you will have to organise that between yourselves. They can go outside in the garden whenever they wish unless I instruct them to come in. I believe that covers my house rules," she said seriously, these conditions needing to be accepted before she would aid him in bringing his men back to her home. She'd encountered too many soldiers and heard many stories over the years, her experience dictating how she received them as even a small group of seven would run riot if she let them.

"We'll happily follow them. What time do you normally go to bed because then I'll make them be quiet – especially quiet after then?" Grey said, trying to show her how considerate they would be.

"Late. That's not a great concern of mine. If it were seven like you I would be happier. Still, I have said yes now. Shall we go and get them?"

"I'd like to, yes," Grey said. He was very worried about them as it had been several hours since he left them. "You might shock yourself and like them," he said hopefully. "If you can get on with me then getting on with most of them should be a cinch."

"I wouldn't say that's been established yet," Laura said dryly.

With Laura's aid in guiding him to where was safe and which routes were not, Grey came close to his men at which stage Laura said to him, "They're nearby. Go to them and bring them back to the house. I'll return now and if you come back the way we came you will be safe. The divisions are far away and going further as we speak. I'll see you back at the house."

"Okay. Thanks a lot for this, Lau...ma'am," Grey said, correcting himself, aware he was becoming too familiar.

"If you're going to be living with me, Mr Grey, you'll have to decide what to call me," she said, mocking his indecision regarding her name. "You can address me as Miss Laura."

"Uh...thanks, Miss Laura," Grey said, feeling his cheeks go red as he addressed her by this title, which made him feel like a dick. She would have permitted him to call her Laura but his hesitation amused her and made her playful.

Grey found the men where he had left them, Delgado patting him on the back as he returned, though the others, while glad to see him alive, were less welcoming. When they had arrived at Maramont some of the group had wanted to head to town with Grey in case it had not been occupied yet. Grey was adamant that they stuck with the original plan with him going in alone and assured them that Maramont had fallen. None of them had heard or seen any enemy activity for a few days and they had covered the distance in good time and doubted his claims and wanted the group to stay together, accompanying him. He had refused, insisting that he had to go alone, and a heated argument had developed which ended with Grey begging them to trust his intuition, and they eventually relented and let him go by himself, figuring that a never-ending argument would give the Germans time to arrive. Pearce had started getting into their heads, insinuating there was something off about Grey's contacts, implying he was a double agent, pointing out his previous successes with his hunches as proof that he had contacts on the other side and that this was why they couldn't meet his contacts. There were holes in Pearce's theory which most noted though the seeds of doubt were planted.

Grey smiled and said, "Good news, fellas – we've got somewhere safe to stay. Follow me."

As he walked with them he faced a barrage of questions, their tempers calmed down when they heard that the town was occupied and his fears were justified, and he told them they would be staying at an Englishwoman's farmhouse, prompting salacious questions from some quarters about her. Grey responded poorly to this and he said seriously, "You can't say that sort of thing to her. She's a respectable lady who won't tolerate any guff and she shouldn't have to because she's doing us a huge favour."

He was offended for her and the others realised it. Strapulos, a Greek American soldier, joked, "Suave Grey scores again when he's AWOL."

"It's not like that," Grey said. "She wants us to behave or we're all out so please just..." Grey stopped short of saying what he intended. They meant no harm and he was overreacting. "And as for being a suave lady-killer – I sure wish that myth was true," he said, making light of himself in good humour.

When they arrived back at the house Laura was already present and Grey let himself and his men in, asking them to be quiet and he led them to the kitchen where Laura had set the dining table which had a small meal and wine set out for seven and she stood at the head of the table and looked at the men who were entering her house. Grey wondered how she could have got back in time to do all of this and he was extremely grateful and he said so.

"Thank you for this, 'Miss Laura'." He said this with gratitude, but he said her name pointedly with amusement. It had been a joke when she said it (he now assumed), which he was prepared to keep up.

"I imagine you are all hungry," she said with an air of indifference as she looked at the men who had spread around the table, still standing, all coming closer to get a good look at her. Grey introduced them to her in turn starting with Isdel Delgado who was next to him and working round to the others in turn. Dwight Hill, Ray Pearce, Nikos Strapulos, David Winters and Glenn Hartmann completed the roll call. Laura was unimpressed with them at first sight as even in this attempt to be gracious there was something prurient in their glances, concupiscent looks, and Hartmann, a bald, bloated fellow, even dared lewdly wink at her. She ignored this and looked at Grey, the one of the group she could tolerate and who she held accountable for the group's actions and she said, "Would you like to sit down to eat?"

"Would we ever! Thank you," Grey said and he did not need to tell the others who were already taking their places and tucking in, Pearce and Hartmann both draining the wine first. Grey was the last one standing and he said, "Aren't you joining us?"

There were only seven places and he surmised in her stance that she did not want to eat with them. He wanted her to, he wanted to somehow make her like these men and talk to them, but he could sense now that it would be difficult.

"I have already eaten, Mr Grey. You know the layout of the house and you can show them all to their rooms. I am going to the library." Before she had chance to walk away Delgado said,

"We are very grateful for this." She seemed very cold and aloof and Delgado wanted her to know that her actions were appreciated even if that did not make her any more friendly. She was doing them a favour and he wanted to acknowledge that.

"Yeah, we are," Strapulos said seriously. "Stick around and we'll tell you how we got here." To leave now felt like antisocial behaviour to Strapulos and he wanted to get to know her so that they would feel welcome here.

"I have my own business to take care of," she said coolly. "There is some more wine in the cupboard. Grey, you can handle this, can't you?" she said, walking away, leaving him in charge and as concierge.

"Of course. If I don't see you later on, good night, 'Miss Laura'." He let her leave without an argument even though he felt the same as Strapulos and felt that a dinner together would have been the best way to talk to her and the men and break the ice. After she had closed the door to the kitchen and gone to the library, Pearce said loudly,

"What a frosty bitch! She's built like a Panzer, Grey, what's the appeal there?" Hartmann and Hill laughed at this and Grey said,

"If you feel that way don't eat her food, don't accept her hospitality. Without her help we'd be fucked." He swore so infrequently that his angry words had impact.

"No, you want to be fucked is the truth Grey. That behemoth will rattle your bones and make you 4F so you can get sent home, you yellow bastard." Pearce's words made some of the others laugh until he talked of Grey's cowardice which the others considered to be offensive. That was one thing that no soldier seemed able to laugh off.

"If I am a coward why was I so far forward?" Grey said, unable to ignore the insult, referring to his position near the front before he blacked out.

"You were probably trying to give yourself up," was Pearce's instant retort, to Grey's exasperation.

"You fucking idiot," Delgado said crossly. "Can you not remember what happened two minutes ago, that he risked going into the town in his army issue even though he guessed that the Nazis were back? This guy's helped us out when we've really needed him," he said, putting a supportive arm around Grey's back, trying to pacify him too as he could tell Grey was ready to go ballistic on him. "Try and be grateful, all right."

"She cooks good, don't she?" Hill said, the food even better than they were served in the army canteens.

"She does," Grey said, calmed down by what had been Delgado's attempt at conciliation which was admirable as he knew how little Delgado thought of Pearce but he still kept a level head. He had to as well, no matter what was said. His anger completely dissipated when he thought of Pearce's friend, Bradshaw;

even though he knew rationally that his death was not on his hands, he felt a little guilty and understood Pearce's resentment towards him and tried to be understanding.

"He's let us down when we've needed him too. It was me who got us out of the mess," Pearce said, correcting Delgado. "I was the one who spurred you on to not surrender and led us away from the Jerries." He spoke arrogantly, wanting all of the credit.

"You played your part, Pearce, but we all did it together," Grey said, trying to pacify as he stood up and took one of two bottles that were inside the cupboard. Each of their glasses were empty and he walked around filling each one up and when he was done he sat down and raised his glass. "Here's to us for surviving that and I think we should toast the rest of our unit wherever they are."

The rest of them agreed with this toast and said cheers as they raised their glasses and Grey added, "And to Laura and her hospitality." Pearce grumbled and would not toast to this and while the others did toast to her, they did so in muted fashion.

"Grey, there's another bottle in there. Crack that one open too, make it a proper celebration," Winters said bossily. Grey complied reluctantly, saying,

"We shouldn't finish it off though, guys. We don't want to get drunk on our first night here." That would create a terrible impression and he already felt that Laura was less than impressed.

"Give your head a shake, Grey. There's seven of us and one and a half bottles of wine. We're not going to get plastered on that. Well, most of us won't anyway," Pearce said, looking to Hill disparagingly, making Hartmann and Strapulos laugh.

"I wouldn't get drunk on that!" Hill said incredulously, laughing with them as they laughed at him.

"You're pissed on one glass, you little fuck," Pearce said. "I'll bet you couldn't walk steady around the room now."

Hill stood up, responding to the challenge eagerly like a child and Winters covered his eyes with his hand, fatigued with Hill's childish behaviour and not wishing to see this display. Hill walked round the table twice, asking each of them if he was wobbling. Delgado reassured him, a little tiredly, as he said, "You're not, Dwight, don't worry about it," and Grey said words to the same effect. Hill sat back down and said,

"They say I'm all right for more."

"Grey can't see straight at the minute because of big, bad Bessie, and Delgado..." Pearce let out a laugh of derision as if there were so many reasons as to why he would be wrong that he did not wish to begin.

"We can finish the wine if you behave, Pearce, otherwise I put it back," Grey said strictly. "Us seven might be together for a while so we should try to get along."

"We fight the same enemy, Grey, but we are never going to be buddies," Pearce said, closing the door on that possibility.

"I gathered that the first day we met and I can't say I've lost any sleep over it, but we have got to get on while we're here. This lady is endangering her life in putting us up here without reward and she deserves some courtesy." Grey's words made all of them think and after a subdued drink Grey showed them upstairs to the bedrooms. He remembered that she had said that they could use the four rooms – the fifth was locked as it was hers and he suddenly wondered where Konah was sleeping. The boy had seemed sorry to see him go and he wanted to see him to show him he had meant his promise that he would return (even if Konah had not understood it). Pearce and Hartmann insisted they were having the first bedroom they entered which had two large single beds and they were assertive about this, Hartmann probing his clenched fist with an open hand as he asked if anyone objected. Grey disapproved of this tone but he left it, as there were enough rooms for all of them even if it meant that some of them would have to share double beds. Strapulos and Winters chose to share as neither wanted to share with Hill, whose personal hygiene was commented upon, and Grey offered Hill the single room, choosing to bunk with Delgado which suited him too. Grey realised as he sat on the bed that he had not shown them where the toilet was and he knocked on all of their doors and told them to follow him downstairs to the toilet.

"There's one up here," Hartmann said having already used it. He pushed the door open and they all saw the ornate bathroom with a large round tub with a short toilet, nearly down to the floor. The room was pink and orange and commodious – a 'tart's boudoir' Pearce piped in with, but that was not how it looked to Grey. The tiles and the decorations on them, images of men and women, naked but not explicit, were elevated above pornography by their sheer quality, artful rather than sexual images (though certainly unorthodox). There was nothing crude or bawdy about the room and Grey felt it exuded class rather than crassness.

"No, we can't use this one," Grey said. "This is just for Laura. There's a bathroom downstairs for us."

"Fuck that. If I need a shit in the middle of the night I'm coming here," Pearce said.

"You've been in the army for nearly a year and it's built you up to be such a tough soldier that you can't face going downstairs to use the shitter. Cloisters will be pleased to have you in the unit if that's your attitude," Delgado said dismissively, feeling he had let Pearce get away with too much downstairs.

"Cloisters is an ass and so are you," Pearce said, confrontational in voice and his stare.

"Cloisters is a good sergeant," Grey said loyally, "and you are the only one acting like an ass." He was trying to keep the peace, but Pearce was too provocative and he could not help but say this.

"Fuck off. This is all bullshit, and don't call me an ass again, chicken," Pearce said, walking back to his bedroom followed by Hartmann.

"You can't use this bathroom again though. Don't you want to see where the other one is?" Grey said after them.

"Whatever. I'll find it," Hartmann said, apathetic at this, and Grey knew he had no intention of doing so. Winters murmured discontent, implying he thought Laura a whiner about such a minor thing but he was willing to comply with the instructions as were Strapulos, Hill and Delgado and he showed them to the plain toilet and wash basin and poured them out one more glass of wine each as a reward for listening to him. Grey stayed in the kitchen as the others went to bed, bar Delgado who sat down with him around the table, talking of how lucky they felt to dodge all of those bullets and of the three that were felled. Grey had one of them in his head now but he did not tell Delgado who didn't need to know this disturbing fact. Delgado addressed Grey's earlier collapse, telling him that he stood by his earlier words and thought it would be best for Grey if he left the army and helped the war effort in a different way, but he promised he would not tell on him. Delgado made his case powerfully without criticising Grey, who took it as well intended advice and did not feel under assault, Delgado praising him for the most part, his only issue being the blackouts. Grey thanked him for his concern and promised that he would try to control it, not the answer Delgado was looking for but he let Grey change the subject.

"Do you want to go to bed, buddy?" Grey asked as it drew late, feeling he was keeping him up.

"You want to speak to her, don't you?" Delgado said perceptively, wanting to talk more of her with Grey. Grey had revealed a little of the characters of the group he had briefly met – mainly Georges, Paulette, Arnaud (one of several who had been missing from the tavern) and Eric, but not Laura. Delgado wanted to know more of her partly because she was their landlady and held their fate in her hands, but also because he wanted to know what his friend felt for her. He was certain Grey felt something for her based on how he had acted around her but he wanted to know the full story, as he could not help but worry about this mentally fragile GI

"I do, pal. I have to. She's something special, ain't she?" he said, smiling broadly as he admitted that he felt something for her, a large amount of affection and desire.

"The jury's out for me, Jimmy, because I don't know anything about her bar the fact that she's letting us stay here, which I am grateful for. What do you know about her? You don't know her through that group, do you?" he said, suspecting the worst.

"No," Grey lied unconvincingly. "I don't know much either, but I like her. The girls in the dance hall were nice, but she's not like them, is she?" Grey said, her unattainable, exotic lilt exalting her in his smitten mind.

"No, she isn't like them," Delgado said, acceding this point. "I'll leave you to it then, Jimmy, but be careful, all right?" he said, fixing his eyes on his friend as he stood up, instructing rather than advising him.

"I will be. Thanks," he said, grateful that Delgado cared, though he was determined to follow his own inclinations.

Grey took a deep breath after Delgado had gone and he walked to the library door, which he knocked on lightly. Laura came to the door, saw him standing there and noticed that he was a little apprehensive as he smiled and he said, "They've all gone to bed now. I was just wondering if you wanted me to make you anything? Tea, coffee, something to eat?"

"I'm fine. Do you want to come in?" she asked. Her tone was civil and inviting, a sharp contrast to how she had appeared with the others before.

Grey nodded keenly and she moved aside and Grey entered her library as she shut the door behind him. Lit by a small gas lamp in the darkness with the moon also visible through the large bay windows the room looked even more impressive. The large room, which was Laura's library and private study, had a big, sturdy table with a comfortable chair and three immensely tall and wide bookshelves dominated the walls. The bookshelves were made of carved wood and next to the windowsill there was a large seat where a huge wooden chess set lay. The thick red velvet curtains hung loose and Laura, seeing how curious Grey was, left him for a moment and she returned with a chair from the dining room which she placed next to the table.

"Have a seat, Mr Grey," she said and Grey smiled at her, shaking his head.

"No thank you, ma'am. May I look at your literature?"

"Yes, you can use this room anytime. Some of the books here might interest you."

"You must have hundreds," he said, impressed at this selection which was even vaster than his father's at home. He had thought his father a voracious reader, but Laura's collection was something else. As he inspected one bookcase that was full of English classics from the last century, he turned to Laura and said, "We are all extremely grateful for this. I am personally indebted to you. I didn't want my men to go with the Communist Resistance without me."

"That road leads to death," she said, assured of this. "Personally I am not interested in your men in the slightest, but they can remain at this sanctuary until such a time as it is safe for them to depart. I seek out company that I crave and this company that is thrust on me I will tolerate, but little else." Her disdain was reserved for his fellow soldiers and not for Grey.

"They are largely good men. There's one I am not friends with, but…"

"That would be Pearce," she said accurately.

"Yeah, but how…?"

"You are an open book," she said with a satisfied smile.

"Just as well I'm not trying to fight my war in the field of espionage," he said good-humouredly and he added, finishing what he had been trying to say, "Even Pearce at heart has good points and we are fighting the same foe, only he's better at it than me, not that that's saying much. This country will be liberated again and you will live as a free woman."

"I already do," she said, seeing little difference in who held the whip hand of the people. Either way she was unaffected.

"You think? The Nazis would not let you do certain things," he said, trying to convince her that his noble fight would somehow benefit her.

"You are at war with the Nazis. I am not," she said, laying down her neutrality for him to see.

"That is probably the wisest course of action for you to take. Helping us is already doing more than enough for the war effort," he said, expressing approval.

"I am not helping you because you are Allied soldiers. I am helping you because you had no one else and you have to stay alive to fulfil your obligations," she said, making out that this was the prime reason.

"Where is Konah?"

"Around. I'll take you to him later. There is no point the others knowing he is here," she said, determined to keep the boy's existence a clandestine affair.

"They wouldn't tell," Grey said, vouching for them.

"Under torture you would be surprised who people will turn on," she said, clearly thinking of specifics.

"I am not an especially brave man, but I would never tell on Konah or you throughout any torture," Grey vowed, staring at her intently.

"I believe that," she said, nodding gently. "You seem an honourable, dependable chap. As I say, Mr Grey, I can tolerate you and for your sake I'll accept the other waifs and strays, but keep them out of my business and I will stay out of your military business."

"Can I ask you a question?"

"You can ask, yes," she said, making no promises that she would answer him.

"Why didn't you leave the country when the Nazis advanced? You have money and a house in Scotland and you aren't French, you're English. I know it's not my business – if I'm out of line I'm sure you'll tell me double-quick. I'm interested as I think many others who had a lot less than you would still have fled."

Laura sat down in her comfortable chair and Grey sat down on the hard-backed chair she had fetched for him, looking at her as she thought over what he had said. "To understand that you would have to know a lot more about me and I don't think you're ready for all of that. It's late and I don't want to give you nightmares," she said, adding this to unsettle him a little. He did not flinch, able to stare at her as she smiled with a hint of malevolence.

"I bet a year of my wages that your story would beat any of these books in here," he said seriously as he stared into her eyes, flattering her. "I love my country, 'Miss Laura', but I'm just from Keokuk in Iowa. The small time that I've been here I've had a brief insight into a different world with a rich vein of stories and lives that I know so little about. Georges seemed a great man and I would have loved to have known more of him, of all of you."

"Such stories are very routine after a while. You would be better reading one of the books up there," she said, feeling that the silly boy had a romanticised view of what such a life was really like.

"Any suggestions?" he said, open to her influence. "This is a long shot. I don't suppose you've got any Amazing Stories, Fantastic Adventures or Unknown?"

"Are they trashy mags with alien girls in leotards on the front?"

"Ah, you have heard of them!" Grey grinned. "On occasion, yes. To be fair it's a competitive market and they have to draw our gaze somehow with the tried and tested failsafe. A lot of the serialised stuff came from novels. My dad chucked most of my collection out a couple of years back because he says pulp rots the brain."

Laura tried not to take the bait though found herself unable to resist teasing him. "You do make a strong case for the prosecution."

Grey shook his head, pretending to take umbrage and said, "You literary snobs stick together. I've amassed a bigger collection since I started working which I'm hoping survives further spring cleaning. That's why the war has to be won quickly, Laura, to preserve my pulp collection – sorry, 'Miss Laura'," he said, making a show of correcting himself. It was excessively formal, almost like a supplication or flashback to an earlier time and custom, but to please her he did it with a grin, letting her know that he was in on her joke. His earlier embarrassment when she had suggested this moniker was now gone, replaced with amused tame playfulness.

"That's better, Grey," she said, talking down to him as though he were lowly staff who had forgotten his place, jocular abuse. "It's probably as good a reason as any," Laura said, partly serious.

"As I say, back home I used to love anything science fiction or adventurous. Your tastes are probably more mature than that."

"Naturally," she said with a smirk as she stood up followed by Grey and she walked to the second bookcase that he had not looked at. This was her section on books by world authors as well as history books and she found alphabetically placed in the French section Jules Verne.

"I've heard of him," Grey said as she pulled out a book, picking one of his more famous ones that she felt would suit him. He looked at the copy of *From the Earth to the Moon* and expressed approval as he glanced at her. "Can I take it out of here to read or is it just in here?"

"No, you can read it in your room or whatever. I have two other Jules Verne books in English so tell me when you get through that and you can move on to the next if you like him. I feel you will," she said, assessing his tastes.

"Thank you for this. Do you mind if I take one more book for my good friend Isdel? Anything of your choice that you wouldn't mind him borrowing."

"Only for him though. I don't want them all doing it because those like Pearce will not respect my property. What would he want?"

Grey exhaled hard at this as he thought of his tastes. "I feel like I should know," he said, scratching his head. "Probably something not military. I would think he'd like something more sedate as an escape. Actually I do know. If you have any medical reference books that would be great."

"Science, whether aliens or biology, isn't my sphere. I do have a book about anatomy."

"Excellent. He's training to be a doctor so I'd like to try and help him keep up to speed."

As Laura located her book on anatomy Grey said, "Obviously I've heard of Verne though I've never got round to reading him. Visiting his homeland seems as good a time as any to read his work. What's the heroine like in mine? Is she a dark-haired beauty?"

"I've never read it," Laura said curtly, putting an end to any more comments like that for the night.

Grey stayed up with Laura for another hour, holding onto the two books as if he was about to leave but he stayed where he was. He told her of his adventures since he had seen her last, colouring the accounts to keep it as blithe as possible, covering the consequences upon his return to the subsequent battles and general performance of the two factions. He spoke of the adrenaline of war to her, telling her to tell him to shut up if he was boring her (which she did straight-faced before she told him to carry on) and he spoke a little of the voices that had failed him a few days ago.

"It was like having armour removed from me. I felt like the others – I am like them, but I have an unfair advantage and I felt stripped without it and very vulnerable and alone. The courage of those men upstairs to do it without any powers, you know?" he said, pointing upwards and shaking his head, so in admiration of their bravery that it was impossible to express in words.

"I disagree. To most of them, when they started at least, death would have been unimaginable. The young male generally believes himself to be impervious. You, however, have had such a link to death that you knew how possible it was, but you've stepped forwards, foolishly perhaps, but certainly bravely. Why do you think your power failed you?" she asked, trying to help him. His company had been most welcome over the last hour and she was prepared to help him better his abilities. He was still subtly flirting with her, though it seemed unconscious and she let him get away with it.

"I wish I knew. It could be overkill. I have relied on it a lot. It was active on the beaches, loud and clear, and after I saw so many die I thought that without my guiding voices I could be next so I've strained to use it, trying to hear muffled faint voices that probably aren't even intended for me. Maybe I've abused it, I don't know." Delgado was a good confidant but he could not talk to him in-depth on matters like this. He had tried once and made him uncomfortable whereas Laura was perfectly relaxed on the topic and very understanding and compassionate. He wished she had been like this with the others.

"Think of your abilities in another sense, James, as muscle. If a muscle is not used it atrophies away. If a muscle is overused it can ache and be painful, but overuse is better than not using it at all and in likelihood will make you stronger. Hartmann might be the most muscular out of all of you and thinks he's a big man, but you are the most powerful," she said, complimenting him, flattering him because it was true and to assuage his doubts. He was mostly a modest man and she thought it would be healthy for him to develop a mild ego.

"I'm not sure and even if I am the most powerful man, I'm not the most powerful person here, am I?" he said knowingly, looking her way.

"Certainly not," she said quickly. "You might not even be second. There is Konah remember? Come on," she said and she led him downstairs, both of them in good spirits now. She was mischievously cheeky – he had been tempted to say so to her but he refrained for now, playing her game and amused at her remarks which at times were so blatant that they left him nonplussed. There was no available quip for some of her comments. She led him down the stairs to her wine cellar, which was a well stocked affair, bottles stocked in holes in a large cupboard, enough to last her till the next summer. At the bottom of the cellar there was a large wall but no doors or other exit bar the stairs and Grey wondered where Konah was. Laura probed the wall with her hands, said a few faint words in a strange tongue, and James Grey watched in wonder as the wall stretched towards her creating a narrow passageway large enough to walk down. She gestured for Grey to follow her and through a small corridor they came to a small room where Konah was sitting unhappily on his soft bed. There was a toilet in one corner, a supply of food in another corner as well as several children's books in French and there were air vents but no windows and he had a phosphorescent light glowing above him, a magical light as there was no other explanation for it.

"Behold the most powerful male in this house," she said to Grey who had already crouched down to Konah's level. The poor boy was miserable and Grey reached over to him and hugged him and the boy hugged him tightly back. This subterranean cell was no place for him and Grey disapproved of such treatment strongly and he asked him how he was, forgetting about the language barrier for a second. Even without a verbal response Konah's face had told him all that he needed to know, as did the desperation in his embrace.

"Laura, I don't think this is the place for him," Grey said pensively, his tone sombre.

"No, I agree, but he has been supplanted from his bed by your arrival. He is getting used to down here; he is quite adaptable and as soon as you all go he will come back up to his bedroom," Laura said, intractable on this matter. Konah's residency had to stay private – that was what Georges would have wanted and it was in the boy's long-term interests even if he was unhappy in these temporary conditions.

"He's only a kid. They won't say anything to anyone, I swear. Hill will kip in with me and Isdel, and the kid can have his room back, can't he?" Grey said imploringly.

"No," she said emphatically. "You can come down and see him, but Konah remains secret. He understands and so should you. He's young and malleable and certain people would like to manipulate him into working for them. This is for his own protection."

"I'll protect him," Grey said. "He can share with me and I'll look after him."

"Until you get back to your unit and leave me with the problems," she complained. "Besides, you cannot even control your own abilities so you should not fret about his. Getting yourself in order should be your priority."

"Part of my ability involves counselling those in distress. I can't turn away from the unhappy and I don't want to. It seems cruel to leave him here buried alive."

"I can get him out at any time," Laura said, failing to see the problem. "Spend time with him and you'll make him feel better. Okay?"

"Okay," Grey agreed, settling for this. He felt bad as Laura told him she was tired and he kissed Konah's hair as he tore himself away from him and moved back as Laura sealed the wall shut. The image haunted Grey but not Laura who told him she was off for a bath and bade him good night. He spoke politely to her, bidding her the same, and he stayed down in the cellar touching the sealed wall beyond where a little boy was silently crying his eyes out. He also thought of Laura, of her power – what was he compared to her? His powers were more like a party trick; hers were a miracle visible to the naked eye. She was a cool woman but talking to her – there was something inside of her that he wanted to reach. She was not the good woman Delgado talked of meeting, but he felt there was something intrinsically good about her despite some of what she said and alluded to.

Grey went to his bed where he saw Delgado was already in bed. He had left the light on waiting for Grey and Grey wished he had been asleep, as he was not prepared for an inquisition. He desperately wanted to tell him of the poor little boy behind the wall, of Laura and his tangled feelings, but he could not. To try and reach her he had to keep her secrets; he had to prove himself to her.

"Long time no see," Delgado said, stirring and raising himself up, "Do you want to talk, buddy?"

Grey hesitated, nodded and said regretfully, "Yeah, real bad, but I can't. One day I might. I've got a book for you," he said, changing the subject and throwing him his book that he caught.

"Thanks," Delgado said, flicking through the pages. "I guess that means you got into the library."

Grey nodded. "It's her private study really, but she was good about it. She's a special lady, Isdel. I can't say more than that."

"Don't worry about it. I'm here if you want to talk," he said, rolling over to sleep. He could see Grey was troubled over something, but he left it up to him to bring up.

The next day Grey was up early and he saw Laura standing outside her bathroom in a long grey dressing gown, her hair looking frizzy and dishevelled and she glared at him as she hammered on the door again impatiently. Grey was back in his army issue uniform and he said to her, "Is somebody in?"

The question was moronic and she said sarcastically, "No, I'm just standing here to pass the time."

Grey banged on the door as hard as he could. "Who's in there?" he shouted. The door opened and Hartmann wandered out in his underwear, scratching his groin.

"What the fuck's the matter with you? There's another bathroom downstairs you know," he said to Grey. Looking at Laura he said, "Good morning, darling," and sauntered back to his bedroom.

"I apologise for that," Grey said, holding his hands up. "I did tell them last night. Have you got a lock I can fit and only you have the key?"

"It shouldn't need to have an external lock. And whoever tried my doorknob in the middle of the night – well next time I'll leave it unlocked and give them a shock," she said, irate at the liberties these soldiers were taking. She was unused to sharing her house and not fond of it at all.

"It wasn't me, I swear," Grey said, desperate that she not believe this of him and he was equally mad at whoever attempted it. "I'll ask who it was and…I'll deal with them."

"I know it wasn't you, I am a good judge of character. Bad start to the day though, Grey," she said, walking into the bathroom and locking the door behind her. "You disgusting bastard," she said loudly and Grey asked her if she wanted a hand with whatever she had discovered. She shouted at him to go away and he went downstairs where Winters was sitting at the dining table with Pearce, waiting for breakfast.

"What's she cooking us for breakfast then, loverboy?" Pearce said mordaciously.

"She's not and don't talk about her or to her like that ever," Grey said fiercely, feeling he had to put his foot down with them. Laura deserved courtesy and respect because of what she was doing for them and her gender played a part in Grey's thought processes too. "We cook all of our own meals from now on."

"Fucking hell, she's not good for much, is she?" Pearce said, trying to make Winters laugh. He was not the easiest audience, though he seemed slightly amused.

Pearce did not know when to stop and Grey lunged at him, clutching him by his collar as he stared into his eyes as Pearce tried to push him off. "Did you try and get in her room in the middle of the night?"

"I did more than try, boy," Pearce said with a contorted sneer, finding it impossible to grin while Grey had hold of him.

"Outside now," Grey said and he dragged him out to the back garden with Winters walking after them. Grey pushed Pearce away from him, keen for this to be a fair fight, and said, "You're going to start acting better around here."

"Go fuck yourself," Pearce said and he charged at him breathlessly, swinging his right hand back and aiming at Grey's face. Pearce telegraphed the blow which made it easy for Grey to dodge with his superior speed and reflexes and he inflamed Pearce's temper further by cockily smirking at him, mocking his failed strike. Grey missed with his own right hook but before Pearce could gloat about this or capitalise on his miss, Grey's left fist had already made an impression on his kisser. This first blow caused Pearce to taste his own blood and increased his anger and desperation to pound Grey into the ground and rub his face in the muck that was scattered around Laura's farm. Unfortunately Grey wasn't giving him the opportunity and while Pearce did catch Grey with a good shot above his eye, which cut him open, Grey was all over him like a rash as Hill and Strapulos heard the commotion and came outside to watch. Strapulos told them to pack it in and Winters told him to stay out of it or risk getting smacked off them and he watched as Grey forced Pearce's head down and kneed him in the face, this action finally grounding Pearce. This was not enough for Grey and he began kicking his body and at this point Strapulos tried to pull him away. Grey knew he had gone too far as Pearce huddled up his body, making it as small as possible, and he relented, backing away. From the bathroom window Laura had watched this spectacle with a towel wrapped around herself, unnoticed by the combatants and the other spectators. Grey tried to help Pearce up, seemingly penitent of what he had just done but Pearce shrugged him off violently, spewing vitriolic words at him, seemingly having learnt nothing from what had just transpired. Laura knew that Grey was not violent by nature and she imagined that what she had said had set him off to act violently as he tried to chivalrously defend her honour. He was a silly boy and she was slightly impressed by this.

The blood from the cut above Grey's left eye continued to pour down and his nose was bloodied too though his gut hurt more as the few blows that Pearce had landed had been very firm, neither combatant coming out of the fight unscathed. Grey stood in the kitchen and watched as Winters and Strapulos tended to Pearce. Hill tried to help and was told to fuck off and he backed away slightly but kept adding unwanted hints of how to stop the bleeding and swelling that was affecting Pearce's face. Winters kept silent as he mopped up the bleeding, neglecting to mention that it had been he who had tried to enter Laura's room in the dead of night. She was an aloof bitch, but, having the opportunity, he had decided to try his luck. Pearce was too quick to accept blame to cause trouble and Winters let him have it, as did Grey.

Hartmann and Delgado came down together, and Pearce shouted for Hartmann to come over to him. Hartmann asked him what hit him and when he said that it was Grey he was very surprised. Delgado was equally surprised and asked Grey what had come over him.

"He's got no respect," Grey said weakly, aware that he was stating the obvious and wondering now if he had gone too far. Pearce whined to Hartmann, expecting him to do something about it, but he would not as it was not his concern. Grey had beaten Pearce one on one – Hartmann would do nothing about that, to Pearce's chagrin.

Laura gave them a few more minutes to sort themselves out before coming down to see what state they were in and entering the kitchen she looked at them all. "Dear me, boys, you're not on the battlefield now. No more sanguineous displays please." She walked through them to prepare herself a breakfast and her good cheer was noticed by all and prompted a renewed attempt by them at trying to converse with her. Strapulos asked her what sanguineous meant, stressing that he wasn't ignorant and informing her that because his parents were Greek and he spoke two languages, he couldn't be expected to know every word in both tongues. Hartmann asked her what she was cooking and she answered both civilly, but without humanity, Grey sensing a world of difference between how she talked to them and how she had addressed him the previous night. The others talking to her and her responding – now it made him jealous and he tried to curb that. It was best for everyone if she could get on with them all, though already he felt territorial towards her and would fight again if any proved to be competition. Delgado thanked her for the book, prompting Hill to ask about books, wondering if he was given one.

Grey said, "I'll sort you out with one when we get back to camp. Miss Laura – do you want to relax in the study and I'll fetch you through your breakfast," he said, trying to be helpful and keep her separate.

"No, I've no time to be sitting around. I have animals to feed, things to do," she said, declining, retaining control of the situation.

"Do you want any help?" Delgado asked, beating Grey to the question he was bursting to ask.

She considered this and said firmly, "No." She finished making her breakfast in silence, ate it at the table and left them to go and run her farm.

"She's one cold fish, isn't she?" Strapulos said, amazed at her discourtesy. There were several things going on in the kitchen, that much was true, but he and Delgado had been prepared to help her without anything else attached and they were all rebuffed and dismissed as nothing.

"Do you want me to kiss your ass, Miss Laura?" Pearce said, mocking Grey who he saw as fawning, who glared at him after he said it.

"I fucking would, I tell you," Hartmann said lustily. "There's something there, Grey," he said, praising his taste and planning to prise her from him. "She's a big girl, there's no denying that, but I'm a big enough man to handle her. She must have money as well living here. You lot go fight the war, I'll keep her satisfied here," he said to favourable response bar from Grey and Delgado who was standing at his side.

"Come on, Harty, you can do better than that. It's a fucking man; it's not Laura, it's Larry. Look closely at her skirt and you'll see there's a pair hanging there. That's why she doesn't want us walking into her bathroom, she's scared we'll find her standing up taking a piss. A scarecrow and a queen – I'm going to run a book on who or what your next conquest will be, Grey, you pervert. The animals won't sleep soundly tonight," Pearce said.

"Call me a pigfucker if you want as long as you leave Laura out of it. I know you're no gentleman but she's a lady and that lady is keeping us alive," Grey said, trying to keep his composure under intense provocation.

"You are a pigfucker for shoving it up Big Larry. Then again, all this 'Miss Laura' carryon – you must have been the one pushed over a table by the limey."

"Give it a rest, Pearce," Delgado said and Pearce quietened down as he plotted his revenge. Delgado ended up making breakfast for them all, eggs and oats. After breakfast as the troops spread around the house Grey went outside to find

Laura who was feeding the pigs. Unlike many farmers she did not keep an early feeding schedule and she fed the animals either early or midmorning, depending, and they ate the swill and grub ravenously. Laura saw him stand by her side as she did this and she saw his nose looked sore and spotted a scar on his forehead and she looked away at her animals. Grey did not speak at first as he stood at her side before he ventured to say,

"Do you want a hand? I'm bored, I want to help."

"Your fists are not your best weapon, Grey. You shouldn't fight like that really," she advised.

"I don't see how I can use internal voices to beat him though."

"Come back to the library tonight and we can discuss that. The third bookshelf holds the answers to that," she said, looking at him, smiling slightly as she examined him. He let her scrutinise him, looking at her placidly as she took in his features.

"What do you think I'm good for?" he said, deliberately setting himself up for a pratfall at the end of her sharp tongue as he asked how he could assist.

"More than brawls," she said, surprising him as he anticipated a put-down and instead received what was at heart a compliment even if it was critical of what he had done. "The hens need some grain. I'll show you where it is." They fed the hens together; Grey tried milking the cows with messy results and after this he volunteered to muck out whatever animals needed doing.

"Hartmann," she replied instantly before letting him do the farm animals for her seems as he was so desperate to help.

"Do you ever use your powers to help with this?" he asked as she watched him shovel out the pig excrement.

"No," she replied, shaking her head. "It goes back to what I was saying about muscles. The body has to stay active too."

"I know, but there's no man around here – apart from now – so you would normally..."

"Shovel shit? Yes, every day, and I have no problem with it. I am not proud. I was born in a barn, Grey, I have no fancy airs and graces." She was haughty and down to earth, an unnatural combination which confused all.

"That sounds like chapter one of the real book I was after. After we're done I'll go and start my book. Isdel's not taken his eyes off his. I'll wash my hands first of course," he said, assuring her that her book would not be tainted.

She was not sure of what he was talking about at first and looked at him quizzically before realisation struck and she smiled at him, almost laughing. "Oh, that story. No, I think you have to tell me more of yours first. Yours will be shorter, I can guarantee that," she said happily.

"It will. It's at a good stage at the moment," he said, looking into her eyes tenderly, making her look away.

"What – being up to your knees in pig shit is a highlight?" she said, making light of his feelings, those eyes that were like an animal's, trying to get under her skin, asking her for something she wouldn't give. It was like a cute puppy trying to ravish her leg; it was endearing, but unwelcome.

"Yeah," he replied, nodding vigorously, "I'm not proud either."

After Grey had finished he went to change into the clothes he had borrowed from Didier and washed his clothing. He had covered himself in helping her;

something she never did and she showed him her washing line at the back of the house. The others were not bothered about washing their uniforms – they were not plastered with shit and, importantly, they did not want to be shot as spies but Grey knew he was safe in these civilian clothes as he knew Laura could warn him of any advances. The mood was light – her mood was light, and Grey asked her if he could put off reading his book for now and could see Konah instead. Laura agreed, leading him down to the cellar, opening up the walls and then she said she couldn't stay but she would be back for him in an hour. Grey thanked her and sat with Konah on his bed, the boy jumping onto his lap needily and both trembled as the wall closed, trapping them, and Grey understood the boy's panic. It felt like being buried alive and he disguised and then dismissed his fear. Laura would return – he knew that and he had asked for this. The strange phosphorescent light with no clear origin glowed and Grey picked up one of the books Konah had in his cell to entertain him. It was written in French and Grey was wary of trying to speak the language, acutely aware that his pronunciation would be atrocious, but he still gave it a shot, stumbling over the words. Konah did not care and he sat engrossed, glad of this small attention and act of kindness and after Grey had been reading for a while Konah would say words back to him with the correct sound. Grey smiled at him and tried to say it his way and still got it wrong, making Konah laugh a little. Grey shook his head and chuckled and put two fingers to his own head and uttered gobbledygook from his mouth, rolling his tongue as he spew out a strange collection of sounds as he acknowledged he was rubbish at this. He started to read again and now Konah was very quick to correct him, finding it amusing, and as a result the story (whatever it was about) progressed very slowly. Laura returned after a little less than an hour and Konah's laughter instantly stopped and Grey hugged him and promised he would see him later. He was like a limpet and would not let him go but Grey knew it was time and left, Laura sealing the wall behind him. Grey began to wonder if his group's shelter was worth this boy's entombing. If the Germans didn't kill them their treatment in a POW camp would be better than Konah's current living conditions.

That night the soldiers were again early to bed and Grey went to see Laura in the library and challenged her to a game of chess. She beat him quickly, Grey giving scant consideration or planning to his moves and she told him to join her at the third bookcase. He stood next to her and saw a large collection of books, many archaic looking and in poor condition, the binding worn and many were foreign texts.

"This is my collection of witchery," Laura said, comfortable with the word. "This is as extensive a collection as you'll find and should prove to be a gainful utility to you. I don't know the full extent of your abilities and the answers might lie here." She was trying to help him and talking seriously.

"These books – they look rare and valuable. I wouldn't want to ruin them," Grey said, judging himself as unintentionally careless.

"I trust you, Grey, otherwise you wouldn't be in here. I think you need to study more about this." She handed him three thin books, one written in Old English and hard for him to decipher as he sat at the table. Originally she had addressed him as Mr Grey or Private Grey but now that he lived with her, more often than not it was just Grey. The way she used it sounded familiar and he liked it. He kept up calling her Miss Laura unless they were talking of important matters at which point she became just Laura, which, in the midst of a serious discussion, she would not address.

He read ardently, trying to understand but what he read seemed in no way relevant to him, talk of spells, curses, blessings and rites. It grew late, Laura standing and sometimes pacing around him as he read, like a teacher monitoring a pupil and Grey eventually closed the book he was reading and rubbed his eyes.

"Do I get a tea break, 'Miss Laura'?" he asked pertly. "If I do, what would you like?"

"We can leave it for tonight. Any comments about what you've read?" she asked curiously.

He was flummoxed as to what to say and exhaled loudly before saying, "Jules Verne is easier to read. These books are heavy stuff. Is there any…about me? About people with powers like mine?" If there were he would be enthralled by them over these books of magic.

"Not specifically, no, because none of us are identical. We are blessed or afflicted in different ways. Tomorrow I'll have a look over them all and see what I can find," Laura said, accepting that, while he might have the application for study, he did not have the interpretative skills to decipher relevant information and the books would remain text to him, merely words on paper. She would have to bring it alive for him.

"Are you sure you don't mind? You're doing so much for us, Laura, that I think you should let us cook your meals instead of cooking your own," he said insistently.

"No thank you, I like things as they are," she said politely, but firmly. Whenever Grey felt like he was making any progress with her she turned unapproachable again, but he would not be dissuaded.

"All right, but let me cook for you sometime." He stood up and made her a cup of tea and one for himself which he brought back to the library and he began to talk of himself, recalling as he had to Georges about his first visitation and the effect it had on him. He held her attention well when he talked like this and he even mentioned Kaia Yang and his infantile crush. He recalled how he had spruced himself up and prepared a candlelit meal for two, a gesture that Kaia Yang appreciated even though she could not partake in it and Grey ended up throwing her food away untouched. He presented this as an act of stupidity, and she sensed real sorrow amid the self-deprecating tale.

"Silly, ain't it?" he said, smiling as he berated himself, shaking his head. "Falling in love with a spirit – there's no future in that, is there?"

"Read more of my books. There might be," Laura said optimistically, the future being open with far more possibilities than he currently realised. If he wanted this young Chinese woman she would be prepared to help him in this as it would rid him of his crush on her. She was prepared to accept him as a friend – she liked him and his company, but not enough for anything more.

"No, she's gone now, she's at peace," Grey said, that door closed, that infatuation ended. "I grieved for her when she went, but you've felt real loss of late. How are you bearing up without Georges?" he asked sympathetically.

"Fine," she responded instantly. Grey had been so open with her so quickly – she was more guarded and she opted not to tell him of her relationship with Georges, their brief spell as lovers. It would give him unproductive ideas and make him believe that her sex was attainable. She did not want to hurt him and wished there were another woman around to attract his eye, the soldier merely wanting female companionship and affection, an understandable, commonplace desire

"You're not still cross with him, are you? I believe that he did care deeply for you," Grey said softly, hoping that her anger towards her old friend had dissipated. He felt this would be healthier for her and felt Georges would not be at peace if she hated him.

"No, I'm not cross with him," she said truthfully, a small admission.

Grey wanted to see Konah before he went to bed, joking to Laura that he could do with a pass to spare her the chore of opening the walls for him every time, acknowledging his importunity. As she opened the walls she said, "I don't think you'll ever be able to do this, Grey. Your abilities – I don't think they will ever manifest themselves as physical forces. That makes you no less powerful though," she said encouragingly, regarding him as a protégé who she wanted to help develop.

"But it does mean that you're going to harass me perpetually," she whined, glaring at him. He caught the glare and smiled slyly at her. There was affection there in her glance and it warmed his heart.

"Consider it the burden of power and knowledge," he joked.

Grey showed Konah four issues of Yank magazine, guessing correctly that he would enjoy the comic strips. While he was a regular reader and savoured the magazines, he was happy to give them away, as he could buy more soon enough and the pinups did not have the same appeal as before. After spending a little time with Konah, Grey went up to bed where he found a note stuck to his door, a message from Pearce who had done what he suggested earlier.

GREY TO HAVE SEX <u>NEXT</u> WITH ?
Animal 2-1   Harty $2
Woman over 70 4-1   Strap $1
Man over 70 3-1
Young woman 100-1   Greaser $10
Delgado EVENS
Hitler/SS 40-1
Prossie 25-1   Hill $1
Corpse 2-1

Grey tore it down, a little cross with all of them at first (bar Winters, who had not placed a bet because he knew Pearce would never pay out), not so much because of what they had bet on but because he did not want Laura to know of it. As soon as he realised that she had likely not seen the note he calmed down (though he still waited a few minutes to go into his room, determined that not even Delgado see how uptight it had made him).

For the next fortnight things ran smoothly. Every morning Grey would help around the farm, learning how to keep his clothes as clean as possible as he did this under Laura's watchful eye. She had assisted him at first until he told her to make the most of him while they were staying with her and made a chauvinist crack about it being man's work. It was jocular and she knew it but after that she had no problem standing back and letting him do as much hard work as he wished as she watched intently, offering some advice, mildly disparaging comments at times, but he responded to these with light quips, becoming bolder in word and deed. As they walked to a further field one day he tried to hold her hand.

"You've been stroking the cows, Grey, please!" she said, wringing out her hand in apparent disgust. It was an act for she was not disgusted though she wished him to believe so.

"If I hadn't been?" he asked, gravely serious, his eyes squinting as he asked this crucial question.

"If you hadn't been stroking the animals you wouldn't be you," she said, sidestepping the question, commenting on his kindly nature. Her words were not necessarily complimentary and she walked at a distance from him.

He had almost finished his book now, and had acquired another book for Delgado who was a far more voracious reader than he and had finished reading the book Grey borrowed *From the Earth to the Moon* and was now reading one of his childhood favourites again, *The Three Musketeers* (also a favourite of Grey's) with the anatomy book returned to Laura. Delgado had appreciated his friend's gesture in wanting to help him study but anatomy was not an area where he needed his knowledge refreshing. Grey persevered with the arcane books despite feeling like he was making no progress. Laura did not pester him to read them but he tried some afternoons as she sat in with him researching other books, trying to aid him. He was levelheaded and a good man – precisely the right sort of person to have been blessed with power and she wanted to maximise that potential for his sake. She needed no allies, but he needed a hand and he was inoffensive enough that she wanted to aid him. He could not comprehend some concepts she talked of; she saw the cogs in his brain trying desperately hard and she did not lose patience with him (but she pretended to often). Grey would often tap on his head during these sessions, knocking on wood, and she copied this infrequently when she felt he was being extraordinarily dense, her touch ethereal.

"It's just a hollow sound in there," he said, admitting he felt he was being slow.

"No, it's not empty in there. I know you will be able to get this." Grey touched where she had lightly prodded him, not as one clutching a wound, but as one prizing a love bite. The gentleness of her touch was what affected him. Her tongue could be cutting but she had tapped him as though she were touching a baby, hardly copying the loud sounds he made himself on his thick skull.

The other soldiers were mostly behaving themselves, entertained with regular afternoon poker sessions. As long as they were well fed (at the expense of some of Laura's livestock) and living in relative comfort they were reasonably satisfied. Delgado and Winters wanted to know when they were going to try and rejoin their unit and Grey just said soon, in no rush to leave. Winters stated that he felt cowardly hiding when they should be fighting and Delgado said that he wanted to return to action as soon as possible. Delgado was persuasive, making Grey consider his plans and why he was here. The voices in his head were not silent; the carnage was not over even if for them it had paused. Laura told him the truth – that they were surrounded by an influx of German troops and that it was a long way back to their lines and Grey relayed this information to the others, promising them that at the first opportunity they would leave. The rule about Laura's bathroom had been ignored but Grey had found a solution, transplanting a lock from a barn to her bathroom door under her supervision, ceasing that problem.

While Laura could get on with Grey she remained distant with the others and when Grey made an effort to integrate them (while he liked having her to himself he recognised that some of the others were uneasy and that it would be healthier if everyone felt as comfortable as he did in Laura's house), running his suggestion past her first before trying it, Laura told him not to include her in any activities with them. It wasn't that she had an aversion to them; she was merely indifferent and she expressed this. "Did you think that we'd all become firm friends and that I'd be up on the table singing Lilli Marlene?" she asked.

"I would never have thought to ask, but seems as you've brought it up that would be awesome. I'm so new to the army that I've never seen an army show so that strikes a nerve, being deprived of entertainment, so if you will do that for me that would make up for it," he said pertly. "Just one verse and one chorus, I won't push my luck."

Laura shook her head as though she found him incorrigible, an act as she could easily take his mild ribbing, used to much worse from her late husband and select friends. "I'll refrain from performing somehow as I wouldn't want to take the sheen off the first army show you do see, which would seem bland by comparison."

"I'll risk it."

"Who is it you all like – Betty Grable is it?"

"I prefer Gene Tierney."

"I don't know who that is. Maybe Gene then will come and sing for you. Look forward to that. I cannot sing for toffee, James, is the honest truth."

"You know I'd think differently. You'd sound good to me."

"I've heard of…something being blind, but never deaf!" Laura said, unable to say the word love. She could give him a lot of things: lodgings, food, even her friendship. Love wasn't on the table and his subtle advances were gaining him no ground, Grey testing the water which Laura instantly made choppy to dissuade him. She was growing closer to him but only as a friend, and as his flirting was restrained and respectful she could tolerate it, and was a little flattered by it. A sleazy lothario trying it on with her might have annoyed her (or maybe not, Laura sometimes acting on a whim); an earnest, decent young man who genuinely adored her trying to gain her affections wasn't ignoble, though it saddened her a little as the poor bugger was doomed to failure.

Grey bit the bullet and decided to try his hand. He was an optimist and he knew he would never forgive himself if he didn't try, even if the desired outcome was unlikely. Better to regret on his deathbed that she turned him down than regret that he had never tried. He sat Laura down late at night when everyone was in bed and told her he needed to talk and began.

"I had every intention of making this speech when I left here. It seemed fairer to put my cards on the table then, if I haven't already. It's no secret how I feel about you."

"James, you don't need to…"

"I do need to. Life's too short to wait. Waiting wastes what we could have now, a perfect month or two together. I know you don't love me like I do you – that's okay. If you feel any affection towards me, which I'm sure that you do, that's a base to work on."

"My affection for you is not romantic."

"But there is affection? That's something," Grey said, grinning at her, taking this to mean much more than it did.

"It is, but I stress, I have no romantic inclinations towards you."

"I accept that and I won't push the issue. All I ask is that you keep an open mind, allow me hope, because I can see us together. Let me keep working on you and I think a breakthrough might happen that'll surprise you as much as me. We both know miracles happen."

"You say miracle, I say spell. Lift the veil, James. What you think I am is not what I really am."

"I know you're a witch. It takes more than that to make me run to the hills."

"Forbidden fruit is always tempting. Also inadvisable. It's not going to happen."

"I know that prophecy isn't one of your abilities."

"It doesn't need to be. Subject closed," she said firmly.

"Okay," Grey said letting the matter go for the moment, remaining hopeful that time would be his ally.

As Hartmann's birthday approached he and Pearce decided to have a premature celebration. They sneaked down to the wine cellar to partake in a session and they grabbed four bottles each and prepared to go back upstairs to their room. Laura came downstairs and caught them in the basement with their hands full, having come down to release Grey who was speaking French (without understanding more than a few words of it) to Konah in his hidden room.

"One bottle will suffice for tea tonight," she said, raising a finger, feeling that even this was extreme benevolence on her part. "Put the others back," she said humourlessly.

Pearce stared at her hard, ignoring her command. He had never craved her, he had barely talked to her during his stay, but he knew that Hartmann wanted her. "It's his birthday Friday so we thought we'd celebrate. You're welcome to join us." His offer was lascivious as he anticipated watching his friend fuck her.

"Well, you are not welcome to my wine without my permission and you can have water tonight, the whole lot of you because of you two," she said sternly, disliking his tone and him in general. She would give Grey some wine over their late night talk but the others would do without for a while because of this.

"Fuck off. We're requisitioning these bottles," Pearce said, as if saying a word that was often used by the army transformed the theft into a legitimate act.

Spurred on by Pearce's smugness as he said this, Hartmann chimed in with, "I'll be expecting a birthday kiss, love."

"And he's not talking about on the lips," Pearce added crudely.

"Put the bottles down and get out of my sight now," she said threateningly as she stared at both of them. Pearce looked at Hartmann and gave him a subtle look that signalled something before putting down his bottles as Hartmann followed suit.

Pearce advanced towards Laura who held her ground as he said, "You're not very friendly, Laura. Might be time for you to learn. Grey won't help you; he can't beat Harty. How'd you want her, mate, on her knees?" Pearce asked Hartmann who was unsure what to say. Pearce was going a bit too far with her and while the thought of taking her appealed he wanted it to be consensual. Bullying was one thing, rape another. He grappled with temptation and morality.

As he made up his mind Pearce decided to help him by deciding to thrust her to the floor in readiness. At the least she would be stripped to her underwear, a lesson for her haughtiness and to teach Grey whose pride would be dented by this treatment of his woman and Pearce would end up running the house. He felt blameless, believing that she had provoked the situation by needlessly stopping them from taking her wine, which she had an abundant supply of.

The second Pearce tried to touch her she pushed him with her right arm and he was propelled across the room, a distance of over four metres. After hitting the wall he slid to the floor and Hartmann looked on in amazement. He looked at Laura, a woman he had desired who now became something else, something freakish, a woman who had hurt his buddy. He charged at her and she held up her arm and he was forced back to the far wall too. There was a big difference between the two incidents. She had not physically touched Hartmann. Pearce observed this and it confirmed to him that there was some other force at play here, a gust of hurricane force wind seeming to force them into the wall. He felt weak but he was determined to get out and he tried to rouse Hartmann who was groggy. Laura smiled at Pearce and he forced his friend's arm over his shoulder and struggled to lift the beefy soldier past Laura, Hartmann murmuring weakly as he saw her and Pearce somehow managed to get him up the stairs.

Strapulos saw Pearce and Hartmann as they walked through the hall and he helped Pearce carry him and they took him to the kitchen where they put him in a chair and Hartmann slumped forwards across the table. Delgado was in the kitchen, trying to teach Hill how to play chess (which was frustrating as he kept trying to turn it into checkers). The game ended abruptly as Delgado asked, "What on earth's happened to him?"

"That bitch," Pearce said, irate and emotional with anger and fear. Delgado went to Hartmann and saw a huge lump at the back of his head where he had struck the wall and he tried to talk to Hartmann, asking him who he was and holding up his fingers and asking how many he was holding up as he moved Hartmann's head, forcing Hartmann to look at him. Hartmann answered correctly on both counts but Delgado could see he was dazed, and suggested they put him to bed with someone monitoring him. Hill volunteered, wanting to help, and after he had been placed in bed with a cold towel at the back of his head, the rest of them went into Winters and Strapulos' room where Winters was reading and Delgado asked Pearce exactly what happened.

"Grey's not here. Shall I find him first?" Strapulos asked Pearce and Delgado as he could tell this was a serious matter and felt that it concerned all of them.

"No," Delgado said firmly with a shake of the head, surprising them as they thought he would have answered differently. "Go on, Pearce, what happened?"

Pearce remained standing as did Delgado whilst Winters and Strapulos sat on their beds and Pearce took a deep breath, trying to calm himself as he spoke. "She's a fucking witch. She hurled me and him across the room," he said, feeling his aching chest and he lifted up his shirt, showing an almighty red mark, an impression of Laura's hand. His back was equally sore, but there was little to see as he displayed this.

"She's a well-made, sturdy-looking woman. Those shoulders are wide. It doesn't mean she's a witch," Strapulos said reasonably while Delgado mused over the matter gravely.

"Harty's 300 pounds at least and she hurled him – no, she didn't!" Pearce said excitedly with extravagant hand gestures as he realised he was misinforming them. "She never touched him and he flew into the wall."

"Bullshit," Winters said, looking at him with disdain, this practical joke pathetic. He stood up and went to see Hartmann who he was sure he would find feigning an injury. He returned realising he was mistaken.

Strapulos looked at Delgado and said, "You don't believe this shit, do you?" They were both committed Christians of different denominations; Delgado a Roman Catholic and Strapulos Greek Orthodox and Strapulos felt that Delgado, being a Christian, could not believe this lie. Delgado's grim countenance which seemed to be questioning and working something out internally suggested otherwise and indicated that he was at least giving Pearce's words some credence.

"What exactly happened?" Delgado asked Pearce sharply. He knew that the two men in question could be difficult and provocative and he had to know the full story before he talked to Grey and Laura about it.

Pearce told them about the bottles and how Laura had tried to stop them and they wouldn't listen to her, omitting the sexual references. Delgado believed there was some truth in his story and it troubled him, making him think of Grey's talk of the Pagan Resistance. The charge of witch would have seemed ridiculous in regard to most people – in Laura's case he did not find it that hard to believe.

Laura casually replaced the bottles in their correct holes and she walked to the wall, opening it a little later than she promised. Konah had appreciated the extra time and Grey had not noticed, finally reaching the end of a small book he had been reading him. Grey kissed his hair as he said goodbye and as Laura closed the wall again he said cheerily, "I could live to be a hundred and I'll still never learn that language."

"The more languages you learn the more power you have. Think about that. If you spoke German now…" she said, leaving the statement hanging and Grey knew her meaning and realised she was correct. She led him to the library where she played him at chess, leaving study for later, indulging him in a few relaxing games. She was not angry with him and did not speak of what had transpired. If it had happened the first day of their stay then the haranguing rebuke he would have suffered would have left him quivering. Now she was more inclined to punish the guilty.

Laura joined the men for dinner, which Delgado made, and she sat at the head of the table, looking at the soldiers who all looked at her differently bar one, Grey, who sat at her right side. Pearce sat as far from her as possible and he saw, as the others did, that she relished this fear she now inspired in some of them, smiling at the tips of her mouth, an evil, contemptuous smile. Grey had no idea that anything was going on and he asked the others where Hartmann was.

"He's not feeling too good," Delgado said to Grey, glancing at Laura momentarily as a statement. She returned the stare, impassive and indifferent. The conversation was very uncomfortable and Grey soon noticed the negative atmosphere, the sense of foreboding. He tried but he could not lift it, getting next to nothing back from his fellow soldiers, Delgado making the excuse that they were all a bit gloomy as they felt it was time they made an effort to return to their unit. After dinner Laura decided to go for a walk, and Grey stood up quickly, offering to accompany her.

"Stay here, I believe they want to talk to you," Laura said, walking out with a certain amount of attitude as she imagined what was to follow. Grey's reaction was up to him and she left him to make his own mind up without firstly offering her side.

As soon as she had gone Delgado said, "We do need to talk, James, she's right there. Let's go upstairs." He wanted to talk privately and he wanted to help his friend and he wanted answers himself.

"This concerns all of us. She's a witch or demon, Grey, do you know that?" Pearce said.

"Fuck you, what do you know?" Grey said with vitriol, advancing towards him. Delgado intercepted Grey and managed to lead him to the stairs, Grey looking back at Pearce, ready to beat him up again. When they got to the bedroom they shared Delgado closed the door behind him and asked Grey to sit down. Grey did so edgily, initially resistant at his friend's attempts to relax him. Delgado talked smoothly but Grey could foresee that something was coming.

"Do you know Laura through that resistance group?" Delgado asked, feeling that Grey had lied to him previously.

Grey hesitated, feeling his friend's eyes bore into him and he could not lie to him a second time.

"Yeah. She's not a member, she just knew a member," Grey said, abashed at his lie being seen through and wishing he had told him more now.

"Is she a witch?"

More hesitation followed as Grey looked upwards and around the room. "I don't know if that's the word. She has power like me." Laura used the term when talking of herself but to use it about her seemed misleading and conjured up foul, malignant visions.

"Okay," Delgado said, forcing a partial smile as appreciation for his friend's honesty. "Follow me."

Grey followed him to Hartmann's room where Hartmann was lying flat out, rambling on about nonsense, vaguely aware of them. Delgado pointed to the lump on the back of his head that had been caused by Laura who put him in such a state.

"How did this happen?" Grey asked Delgado, filled with concern for this man who he did not always get on with. Delgado's eyes stared at Grey's as he conveyed his answer without words.

"No," Grey said, shaking his head animatedly. "Don't pin this on her just because she's different. He causes trouble and you know it," Grey said, speaking out of character as he condemned Hartmann.

"He's not at the moment, is he? He will be all right but he might not have been. Look, Jimmy, you've got power, yeah, but you cannot move people by thought. She did – she slammed him and Pearce into a wall. While I don't know the rights and wrongs of what happened beforehand I do know that she has done wrong here," Delgado said firmly, judging her and trying to turn Grey from her. Grey had an added sense – possibly – but he was not the same as Laura as far as Delgado was concerned.

"I'll talk to Pearce and find out what happened," Grey said, trying to salvage the situation and keep everybody happy with the exception of Pearce and Hartmann if they had misbehaved. If they had erred against her Grey considered this a fitting punishment. Tears began to roll down Hartmann's cheeks as he talked of his mother and Grey began to soften, unsure what was right or wrong, seeing him so pitiful.

"We both know Pearce is trouble, but that's not the point here, James. If she's a witch then I'm not staying and the others largely feel the same. Once he's up and about we should leave here – all of us," Delgado said, having no intention of leaving Grey behind. To him that would feel worse than leaving him in the Nazis clutches and he would drag him out if necessary with the others support.

"The Jerries are all around us. I know this from the voices in my head and she knows it too. She has like a radar warning her when strangers are coming." Leaving was not an option yet.

"She's done a lot for us and in spite of this I'll thank her again when we leave and be courteous but it's time to go anyway. This has just made up my mind sooner. All of our families are suffering at the moment thinking us dead and they need to know we're still fighting fit. Don't you want to get to Paris?" he said, trying to appeal to Grey's sense of adventure, the side of him that talked of exploring the world.

"It's not safe to go. I want to fight too, but we will not get through the enemy lines," Grey said forcefully. "Yes, I care for her and I am enjoying staying here, but I am driven to fight first, only we can't yet. Maybe we can in a way," Grey said, realising that they had to do something instead of waiting for the Allies to reach their position again.

"What, the Communist Resistance? I'm game," Delgado said keenly, nodding his head once in approval. It was better than staying here where he feared for the soul of James Grey.

"No, I'm not allowed to join them and I won't see any of you go off with them if I'm forbidden," he said protectively, needing to be able to watch out for them. "The Pagan Resistance wanted my help. I think it's time I did something for them." Grey realised that love had clouded his resolve a little and duty called again.

"No," Delgado said angrily and he punched Grey at the top of his arm. Grey rubbed the affected area and looked at him with a furrowed brow yet he did not fight back and Delgado said, "You're flesh and blood like us. You can be hurt and killed. You're special, not because of any of this, because of who you are inside. Your gift doesn't make you unholy, but walking down this road – James, I'm scared for you," Delgado said powerfully. Delgado had a healthy appreciation of life and considered few things worse than death but he preferred the thought of dying rather than consorting with demons and engaging in Faustian pacts. It disturbed him that Grey didn't seem able to realise that he was risking damnation.

"I'm scared of the Nazis. I'm scared of the Panzers, the Luftwaffe and the intensity of some of the young German units. I'm not scared of her or the Pagan Resistance group. For me this is the perfect adventure I've talked of – in my dreams I'm braver but I can put on a half decent front. She's helping me, Isdel, and I'm sorry if I haven't been there for you so much, pal, because I value your friendship big time, but I'm in love. She discourages me, she says I should find a pretty young French girl but I don't want that. She's got a great chess board – I'm going to ask her if you can come in and have a game tonight." He wanted Delgado to spend a little time with her to show him that she was not the monster that his upbringing demanded he consider her.

Delgado was unresponsive to this and he stayed with Hartmann as Grey went downstairs and he headed outside for a walk. It was slowly growing dark and after a short walk he saw her coming closer, her eyes fixed on him. He was on her side whatever, but he needed to talk of this.

"What did they do to you?" Grey asked, showing her at once that he knew she had been provoked. She was pleased at this response, his concern for her noticeable as he walked close to her, clearly wanting to lend her a protective arm.

"Nothing. They tried to raid from my wine cellar, I forbade them and then they became threatening. They insinuated they were going to force me to perform oral sex on them," she said, revealing what had truly happened with candour, completely unaffected by what had happened.

"I'm sorry," he said sincerely, his eyes moist that this had happened to her. Pearce and Hartmann could go and hang for all he cared at present. He was reflective for a moment before saying, "The others all want to leave now. Maybe we should. It would be best for you."

"The Germans are everywhere. That's not an option," she said, advising him to be prudent.

"This should not have happened to you in your own home after all you've done for us," he said, shaking his head, unable to get past this. She wouldn't want them there now – she didn't before really and now he felt it would be wrong to stay. They had abused her hospitality and her personally.

"I utterly agree, but it will not happen again. They are petrified of me now. If I wanted you to leave you'd know, trust me," she said, smiling at him, showing him she had no problem. He did not ask her for a game of chess against Delgado after learning this and he instead spent the night lavishing attention on her in the library. His attention was as harmless as it came, completely non-sexual as he totally curbed his flirtation after what had happened earlier as he did not want her to lump him in with those two brutes. He was not like that. As a result he was deadly serious and she teased him relentlessly, trying to lighten his mood, ultimately succeeding. Before he went to bed he flung open the door to Pearce and Hartmann's room and stared at them. He saw they were both terrified as the door opened, anxiety in their face even when they saw it was just him. His anger subsided and he merely said,

"Stay away from her."

Their behaviour had been seriously off, only now he found it hard to be so hateful of them and he walked to his bedroom where Delgado was sitting on the bed still in his uniform. He had not even wanted to lie down in bed for fear of drifting off to sleep, which he could not do, as he had to have a prolonged talk with Grey. Grey shut the door, sat on the other side of the bed and said,

"After all that happened I had to talk it out with her, but she says you can play chess with me tomorrow. I don't think she's going to be around but she says that if I'm around you can use the library." She heard him talk of Isdel this, Isdel that and when he asked her about playing him at chess once she showed him she had no problem with this by giving him permission to come in every day.

"We'll stay tomorrow and after that we're going. Everyone agrees." Strapulos and Hill were unsure, but the others had swayed them.

"In the First World War they used to order the troops to march out of the trenches straight into enemy fire and landmines to certain death. Us leaving now would be the equivalent. I can help fight the Nazis in civilian clothes, but you lot can't leave here in your army uniform."

"I'm not exactly going to blend in as a local whatever I wear," Delgado said, smiling as he pointed out that his dark skin hue would automatically raise the Germans' suspicions. "I have a story I want to tell you. Have you heard of Homer's Odyssey?"

Grey shook his head, sure he would hate the story's meaning. He tried to be open-minded so as not to be a hypocrite. "No, 'fraid not."

"There's a Greek myth – a whole series about a great leader called Odysseus who was one of the military leaders responsible for the fall of Troy. He lived far away from Troy and after a long war he was desperate to return to his wife and son so he set sail, only his travels were not short. The war was more like the prelude to his real struggles and adventures. A giant Cyclops – that's a one-eyed monster – sea beasts, whirlpools – this mighty adventurer faced them all and then some. On one island Odysseus' men went aboard and found a beautiful woman, the only inhabitant of this island though there were lots of animals, and she kindly invited them to dine with her. Her name was Circe and she was an enchantress and she turned the men into pigs. Odysseus cleverly managed to win her heart and she reversed the spell and eventually he got home, but my point is this – we are men, soldiers, and we live in the real world and she does not operate by our rules, our morality. I'm a Christian and I'm proud of it, and what she is – I'm sorry to tell you this because I know you like her, but it offends me," he said, clutching his exposed crucifix.

"Laura is not Circe," Grey said defensively without being aggressive.

"That's who she brings to mind for me. Me and the others would risk a whirlpool or try and beat a beast – and Nazi Germany is a good analogy for that – but we can't beat Circe. Her rules are different, we don't know what to do with her and our best course of action is to stay away."

"I'm tired. I'll speak to you tomorrow, yeah," Grey said, unwilling to hear any more of it.

"Fine, but you will hear more of this tomorrow. Kiss goodbye to her because we're not staying."

That would be desertion Grey realised as he tossed and turned in the night. If he let them leave and he stayed, that was abandonment even though they would be the ones going.

The next morning after he had performed his farmyard chores he showed Delgado around the library as Laura left him to it, going upstairs to her bedroom for some privacy. Delgado made straight for the bookcase all about witchcraft and while he was careful of the books, respectful of others property, he could not help but give the material his unadulterated contempt and disapproval. Grey told him not to worry about it and challenged him to a game and Delgado sat facing him across the table.

"If I beat you, you're coming with us. Deal?" Delgado proposed.

"That's not fair. You taught me how to play."

"You've beaten me before."

"I'll bet I don't now. No deal," Grey said, making the first move without further discussion.

"I don't plan on walking around on all fours and sprouting trotters," Delgado said, making his first move.

"Somehow I don't think she has that planned," Grey said, countering. Delgado's comment was jocund in delivery but at the root of it was serious…prejudice and Grey addressed this.

"You were great when I told you about me. I'm a Christian too, Isdel, and I thought at times that I was sinful because of my gift, but she makes out that it's a blessing and I feel that way too. You never condemned me and I don't feel you should condemn her either, especially considering you know very little about her. She acted in self-defence and without her abilities she would have been gravely wronged yesterday." He was trying to make Delgado think and he accomplished this.

"Perhaps and I would have helped her out had I known, but…she doesn't need our help or want it. We're not welcome here, which is fine, it's her home and up to her."

"What if she was a Muslim or a Jew? Would you not stay with her then because she's not a Christian?"

"That's completely different. I would have no issue at all with that. Cloisters is Jewish."

"I didn't know that," Grey said, unaware of this and surprised, though it made no difference to him.

"Yeah. It surprised me when he told me – he's not Jewish by birth, his wife is and he's a convert. He's still of the Jewish faith. I am not discriminative against anyone. I know what you're getting at and that's a little sly, James, trying to play that card with me," he said with an undertone of disapproval and surprise that Grey would be so wily. That he had talked with Cloisters about his Catholic upbringing in an attempt to change his views weakened his argument and was left unsaid.

"All I am trying to say, in my own clunky way, is that if you want to hate her, hate her for who she is, not what she is," Grey said, a little chastened by Delgado's comment, but still arguing his case.

"She's kept all of us bar you at a distance so all I can do is judge her on the glimpses I've had and the stories I've heard. Check."

Grey looked at the board and did not have a clue what he was doing, his concentration screwed. "You win, I concede. But not about her. Laura has a lot of good in her."

"I'll bet if I look through those books I'll find spells to hurt people, to tear them asunder," Delgado said confidently, certain that he was right. "People can believe what they want to believe – that's partly why both of us are fighting, but I don't believe in invoking dark forces and hurting others. That craving for personal power is something else I would be prepared to fight." His eyes were wide, his jaw determined and his views obstinately fixed.

"If you think she's a demon then so am I. You have to cast us both down to the darkness," Grey said, challenging his friend. Delgado was being inconsistent in Grey's view.

"There's no need for that. I reckon you're going to find your own way there," Delgado said gravely and he walked out on him. Grey was a little shook up by his words and he went to see Laura who came downstairs (Grey had still never seen the inside of her bedroom) and they talked. He talked of his appreciation of her efforts again and told her odds and ends of his past. He did not talk of leaving but he knew now that he was and in his voice she could tell something was troubling him but he did not bring it to the surface, intending to tell her that night. He later pulled Delgado to one side and said,

"I think we're making a huge mistake, but I guess I'll get shot with the rest of you." There was no eagerness in his voice but his word was trustworthy and Delgado smiled and patted him on the back.

"What I said before – I didn't mean that," Delgado said, wanting him to know he did not feel that way, apologetic now.

"That's okay. I think I was trying to bring your being Mexican into it and I'm sorry about that. I haven't told her I'm going yet so don't say anything to the others."

"My lips are sealed. This time next month it'll be Paris and we can see if it's changed since Dumas' day," Delgado said zestfully, trying to gee up his friend. Grey would be down at leaving her but he could deal with that and help him through it and Delgado wanted this nipped in the bud before Grey fell too far.

Mid-evening Laura interrupted the men as they were finishing off an extra bottle of wine she had graciously provided around the table and she said with urgency, "You need to get down to the cellar now with your belongings." They all looked at her, unused to seeing her so animated and Grey stood up first and said,

"They're close, aren't they? I'm not leaving you to face them alone." His protective male pride endangered rather than saved her and she replied quickly, witheringly,

"Get down to the cellar now." She raised her voice as she stared at him and he led the way as the others followed him with Laura at the rear. Strapulos heard something outside and there was an unmistakable hammering at the front door.

"We'll fight them," Winters said, stoic as ever.

"I'm glad you believe you can take on 34 armed men. However, I don't agree," Laura said, her tone mordacious as she touched the walls as they looked at her incredulously, all bar Grey.

"It's okay, guys," he said softly, trying to calm the others as she did this, which he knew would unnerve them. They all took it superficially well as the wall opened and Grey urged them to walk down the narrow passage to the young boy who looked at them all, surprised by all of the people. Strapulos went first followed by Delgado, Hill, Winters, Pearce and Hartmann who was very apprehensive and had to be hurried along. Grey went last and said to Laura, raising his eyebrows, "Don't worry about us. Don't take the fall for us either. Just be careful, please." He was imploring her.

"You keep them quiet and I'll be careful," she said seriously and Grey squeezed in with the others as the walls closed behind them. Konah seemed perfectly relaxed (to Grey's surprise), more so than the others. Grey asked them all to be quiet and told them that everything would be all right.

"I've got to get out of here," Hartmann said, feeling claustrophobic.

"Calm down," Grey said, having to hold onto him to keep him quiet, Hartmann embracing him as he looked up at the bright light above them. They could all hear multiple footsteps above them.

"Well, they won't find us in here," Strapulos said darkly, gallows humour in disbelief at what he had just witnessed.

Upstairs Laura was making the German unit at home having opened the door to them and inviting them in. The sergeant talked English, a man around 30 with good manners who shook her hand and asked her if he could look around her premises. She was most agreeable and offered to cook a small something for them, which they gratefully accepted. As the soldiers looked around upstairs and down in the cellar Laura cooked quietly, seemingly carefree as the soldiers returned from upstairs and talked to their sergeant in German. Laura understood, but pretended not to as they talked of the two rooms being locked. The sergeant asked her about them and she explained that she always kept her bedroom and bathroom locked and she handed them the keys at once. Another soldier mentioned that some of the beds looked to have been slept in and when she was questioned about this she said that friends of hers had stayed over the previous night. She seemed so open to them that the sergeant was not suspicious of her and he ate next to her in her lounge as his soldiers piled around her table.

"Sorry for the intrusion," the sergeant said as he ate, "We've only just become aware of this estate and this is just a precautionary search. I have to ask you about your business here."

"There's nothing complicated to it. I run a farm, Herr Weller."

"By yourself?"

"A lot of people seem to respond that way. Especially men," she said with a smile. "Yes, I manage it by myself."

"What are you doing in France?"

"You mean because I'm English. I have lived here since before the war. I am not very impressed with my home country – it has a dangerous leaning towards the left. When war broke out I was in no hurry to return home," she lied convincingly.

"My grandmother was English," he revealed openly. "Our two peoples are very similar. We shouldn't be fighting."

"Britain declared war. You merely responded," she said, charming him and putting his mind at rest. She proved most accommodating and welcoming, answering his questions with a positive attitude and seemed ideologically concordant. He kissed her hand as he left and when his troop were many kilometres away she went down to the basement and opened up the walls. The soldiers rushed out, having spent over two hours in cramped conditions and they stretched out their legs and breathed deeply. Some of them had worried that she would not let them out and they breathed a sigh of relief, even more determined to leave her den now. Grey went straight to her, looked her square in the eye and said,

"You okay, Laura?"

With a tender glance and subtle nod she answered him.

"Everyone can go back to what they were doing now," Laura said loudly as she walked back to the wall, ready to close it again.

"What about the kid?" Delgado said loudly, aggrieved and a little outraged at the thought of her trapping him back in there. Laura turned to stare at him and Grey interceded,

"There's no point now, Laura. They know." He spoke reasonably and Laura hesitated, realising that sealing him up now served no purpose.

"Fine. You can sort out where he sleeps; I'm going back to the library." She did not say this in pique but spoke levelly, leaving Grey to handle it, as she knew he was capable of arranging something. After she had gone Grey explained to the others that Laura was hiding the boy to protect him as the Germans were after him (a line which only convinced Hill with the others agreeing that the boy had to be removed from her clutches when they left). Hill was exhilarated and gushing about the power Laura had just demonstrated which made his subsequent behaviour stranger and Grey gained greater insight about why he had been cast out of his original unit. It seemed logical to Grey and the others that Konah should have Hill's bed – Hill took the suggestion as a personal affront and was indignant with Grey as he was the first to suggest this. Despite everyone else for once agreeing Hill was initially adamant that he wouldn't move and that they couldn't make him before reluctantly conceding defeat after a lengthy heated argument. While Pearce was still unquestionably the bad seed of the whole unit, he was far more political than Hill who came across as very selfish in trying to deprive a kid of having his own bed because he believed he was rightfully entitled to it as he had it first (Grey was quick to tell him that by this rationale he had to vacate the room as Konah was there before him).

Grey collected some fresh bed linen and after giving Hill time to move his things he led Konah back to his old room where he changed the sheets for him and put his few clothes in the cupboard for him. Konah blocked his nose as Grey picked up Hill's old sheets, a gesture that transcended the language barrier and made Grey chuckle. "I'm sharing with him now, buddy. Here you go," he said, opening the window.

"Merci."

Grey took Hill's sheets downstairs to wash later and collected some more sheets. Considering she lived alone and was a very solitary person Grey found Laura was exceptionally well supplied and commented on this as he passed her which garnered the response, "Not as well supplied as before you came. So how are you doing it? Who's sleeping where I mean?"

"Konah's back in his own room. He already looks happier," Grey said, very moved by this.

Laura had already deduced that Grey would likely be the one to forfeit his own bed – which was ridiculous as the lot of them were only there because of him – and she said, "There's a settee in the spare room. Take the sheet off it and dust it down and it'd be better than the floor."

"All the stuff in that room looks valuable so I'll pass, thanks. Me, Isdel and Hill are sharing the bed on a rota basis. One night out of three on the floor's fine – way better than sleeping outdoors, in foxholes."

Laura left him to it and Grey found Delgado in their bedroom. As Grey put the blankets and pillow down in the corner of the room he said, "Sorry about adding another roommate without consulting you. I figured you wouldn't mind – cheaper rent with a three way split," Grey joked, trying to defuse the tension as when he entered the room Delgado gave him a black look.

"We'll have to manage." Delgado was not overjoyed about sharing with Hill though he accepted that it was necessary as the others wouldn't put up with him and Konah deserved to have his own room. "I think I might swap with you – the floor might be better. I may have to have a word with him about his hygiene."

"If you do, say something to all of us then he won't take it as a personal slight. I don't want to see psycho Hill unleashed again! Where did that come from?" Grey said, amused after the fact by Hill's outburst.

"To be fair he had just seen a close-up demonstration of witchcraft so any strange behaviour he exhibited is understandable."

"She put her own neck on the line for us. That's the bottom line. I can appreciate you're even more keen to leave and I'm not backing out, I swear, but we can't go now. Surely after tonight you can see that?"

"The others still want to go – bar Hill, he thinks it's cool that we've got her on our side. He thinks she's Phantom Lady now. I think we have to wait a little longer," Delgado said, taking his point. It was the realisation that he had to stay longer with this witch that affected his mood and he tried not to take it out on Grey, even though he had led them all here. Their refuge was a witches den and, regrettably, for pragmatic reasons, they had to remain a while longer, which proved even harder after her latest action which proved beyond any doubt that Laura was a practising witch. Worst of all, it proved that she had ungodly ability. Grey could not sell this as a positive thing no matter how he tried.

Konah was visibly happier now and several of the soldiers played with him indoors before heading to bed. Grey had his regular late night chat with Laura where she told him all about the visit and Weller and almost apologised for her tone with him earlier without uttering the word sorry. He was not leaving her now and he was glad.

Konah woke up Grey in the middle of the night, tugging on his arm, and Grey led him downstairs to try and have a talk with him and find out what was wrong. He could see Konah had been crying and he sat him down at the kitchen table and made a snack for the both of them and poured Konah a drink out and sat next to him. Laura had a dictionary that translated English to French and Grey tried putting it into practice, trying to tell Konah that everything would be all right. Konah understood this and shook his head. Konah said a few words which Grey had trouble translating and he had to keep asking for Konah to repeat himself. Fortunately Grey had learnt how to apologise in French, which he did every time he made this poor child repeat his woe, though Konah didn't seem to mind, remaining patient. Eventually Grey offered the book to Konah who pointed to the right pages and Grey saw that he wanted to go home.

"Soon, pal, I promise," Grey said before looking for a translation. After Konah had finished eating Grey asked him to wait for him while he fetched some paper and a couple of pencils and he handed them to Konah. Grey said Paulette's name to him and tried to demonstrate with signs that if Konah drew a picture for her he could give it to her. Konah started drawing at once, with a slight smile on his features as he began. While he did this Grey took an atlas from Laura's library and pointed to Iowa (Keokuk was not listed, annoyingly) and he pointed to this to Konah, trying to relate that this was his home. Konah looked at the map and shook his head and continued with his drawing, which he tried to hide from Grey's view. When he was done he showed it to Grey proudly. Konah had drawn Paulette, who was just about recognisable, largely due to the masculine attire. The standard was perhaps a little poorer than would be expected for his age but the important thing was that he was smiling. Grey found some crayons for him to colour in his picture and Konah put her in bright colours with a beaming smile, which was how he usually saw her. He wrote a little note at the bottom and handed it to Grey. As Grey tried to translate the message Konah shut the book and insistently said no.

"Okay," Grey said, and he etched randomly, depicting a menagerie of animals with legs of varying thickness. Konah opted for another full length portrait and drew Grey in his army uniform, with shapes around him in the form of ghosts and mouths and eyes, surrounding him entirely.

"You've made him too handsome. You're right about the spirits," Grey said before adding, "Merci, merci," as he shook Konah's hand, accepting the gift. He tried drawing Konah and representing his gift pictorially to show that he understood, stalling as he struggled to think of a way of drawing the future, settling for drawing Konah with a big thought bubble in which he drew robots and flying saucers. Konah looked at the picture and puffed his cheeks out, laughing at how fat Grey had made him look. Grey laughed with him before reaching for the dictionary again and he pointed to the thought bubble and asked Konah if it was hard. Konah nodded and the expression on his face changed as his eyes reflected unknown sadness. Grey took his hand in his and promised him again that everything would be okay, crossing his heart to signify his promise was guaranteed.

While Konah's pictures of Grey and Paulette were flattering his third drawing was a caricature as he drew a hook-nosed witch with pointed hat and broomstick, obviously meaning Laura. Grey chuckled a little, (unintentionally and he quickly stopped himself as he saw this made Konah angry as he was deadly serious) and tried to downplay Konah's fears by using the dictionary to explain that Konah, Laura and himself were all the same, all gifted. Konah refuted this, repeating the word mal in a sentence Grey couldn't quite decipher. It seemed Grey was the only one who appreciated their landlady.

Even though he no longer had to leave after a few days, Grey (who had been stirred up by Delgado's talk of duty) realised he had to do something for the war effort. Dressed in Didier's tatty clothes he asked Laura if the coast was clear in the early evening as darkness approached.

"Fairly," she said apprehensively. "Why?"

"Georges asked me to help his group and I refused him because of my duty to the American Army. I don't have that excuse at the moment and I feel I have to try and do something for them." He felt like Georges' group was being brave and bold, taking risks, while he was nestling down contentedly. It wasn't right and he aimed for both – he could help the Pagan Resistance while still living with Laura and the other soldiers.

"You owe them nothing. They refused to help you when you needed their help."

"Well, they did offer to help me only it was too conditional and you stepped into the breach for us," he said, smiling broadly at her. "The thing about being a soldier is you help people whether they appreciate it or not even if they wouldn't do the same for you."

"I thought being a soldier meant following orders. Stay here until you can get back to your troops, then become a soldier again. Until then just remain as my farm hand." Her manner was overweening as she urged him to stay and he was tempted, but he resisted.

"I'm not going to live with them, I'm just going to ask them how I can help. They might just send me back," Grey said, unsure of what to expect and not wanting her to worry about him.

"They won't, they'll use you somehow," she said with certainty, the word 'use' deliberately accentuated.

"If I don't come back is it all right for the others to stay until Allied forces are near? They'll take Konah back with them too," he said, pleading with her for this.

"If Allied forces come near. This war can go either way, Grey," she said, reminding him that nothing was certain. "Your best course of action would be honing your gifts. Still, I can see your mind is made up and I am not going to stand in your way," she said coolly, taking her leave from him. If he would not be reasoned with and wanted to die that was his choice.

Grey called after her, "Laura, I... thank you," he said with heartfelt gratitude and she turned to look at him. Her expression gave away nothing and she left the room and he was certain that he had annoyed her. That was unfortunate but she knew why he was there, as he had talked in detail of his feelings and his desire to win the war. Spending time in her company was heavenly but he had prior obligations that he had neglected for too long. He told Delgado where he was going and faced similar objections, Grey telling him that he had to go alone as he was the only one the group would deal with and there was only one civilian outfit they possessed. He surprised Delgado by telling him in jest that he and Laura were agreed on something for once as she also thought him stupid for wanting to go.

"It's not stupid to go. It's stupid to go alone," Delgado corrected him.

"If I don't come back can you take Konah back to safety?"

Delgado agreed and told him to be careful and Grey was on his way, stumbling around in the darkness, trying to be as stealthy as possible. Through the fields and hills he did not see or hear a soul, but as he arrived close to the outskirts of town he was even more cautious. Hiding in some overgrowth he saw two German soldiers walking the perimeter of the town, talking to each other loudly while watching vigilantly. Grey waited until they had walked well out of sight and he made a run for it, knocking on the back door of the tavern loudly. Around the back he felt out of sight but he saw there was light emanating from inside and he wanted them to respond quickly just in case.

Paulette shouted through the door in French, asking who was there. Grey recognised her voice and he replied quietly, "It's me, Grey."

As soon as he said this she unlocked the door straight away and smiled at him. He had come back to aid the cause. Grey smiled at her and she gestured for him to come inside and she locked the door behind him. She was wearing tight pinstriped trousers with a loose blouse and her attitude seemed as militant as before. She instructed him to go through and looked at him curiously as he unbuttoned his shirt and picked out a sheet of paper he had tucked under his clothes. "This is from Konah. I'm sure he'd appreciate a note back."

Paulette looked at the picture and after reading the note she asked, "Do you know what he wrote?"

"I don't know what it means. He wanted it to be private."

"Just give him a hug from me. I'm bad with letters," Paulette said awkwardly and once Grey left her she tore up the picture and burnt it in the hearth. As much as she loved Konah she could not leave Maramont now and she did not want the others to know he warned of severe danger for fear that their resistance would become even milder and cautious.

Grey walked through to the converted bar where he saw three people were present, all sitting around the table. They all glanced at Grey then looked back to each other, resuming their conversation in French. Grey recognised the three as Mireille, the new leader, with her son Didier, whose clothes he had indefinitely borrowed, along with Eric. On the table Grey could see several explosives along with pagan artefacts but he did not presume to try to join in the conversation and he stood patiently. Paulette saw that he was being ignored and offered him a drink, which Grey declined, telling her he had come to offer his services if there was anything he could do for them.

"We're doing something tonight. Didier and me are anyway. We're planting explosives around the town if you want to help," Paulette said, including him as she felt the others should. Eric glared across at them and put his forefinger to his lips, gesturing for them to be quiet as they talked. They talked and planned for another five minutes after which time Didier pocketed the explosives and the artefacts, leaving a little under half for Paulette to take which she did at once, fitting them into her deep trouser pockets which she then buttoned closed. Mireille and Eric walked to Grey now, Mireille smiling warmly at him and extending a hand, which he shook, Eric doing the same.

"I've come to offer my services," Grey reiterated. "Can I be of any assistance? Should I help Paulette and Didier?" he said keenly.

Eric relayed this to Mireille and they talked over the matter in French. It seemed a waste to use Grey for donkey-work but they were unsure as to what he could do. Eric asked him what he could do to help them.

Grey stumbled over this question, rubbing his rough chin as he considered how he could be of assistance to them. He knew that Eric was talking in a magical sense and Grey suddenly felt that there was little he could do. Laura would have been indispensable to them with her powers but he was not Laura and his power was not the least bit showy. There were voices in his head currently offering him assistance and advice but they were French voices and no good to him. "I could plant the explosives," Grey said, feeling that was all he was good for.

Georges had talked of this American as their saviour and Eric now found that laughable as he stood there humbled, a basic, next to useless, Yank. Yes, there was power there, but no comprehension of it and Eric saw it as a waste and advised Mireille that they may as well use him for this. She agreed and Mireille produced more explosives and more of the artefacts, which were foreign to him. Along with the three explosive blocks he was given three coral necklaces and three small vials of a pink liquid. Eric explained to him, talking slowly and patronisingly, that he was to place the explosives within the coral circle, douse them in the liquid, and then leave them.

"Why not just light them?" Grey asked.

"Do you know what the liquid is for or the relevance of the circle?" Eric asked him, talking down to him, knowing this American would not understand.

"No, I don't, but if we're at the targets we might as well just..." Grey responded rapidly with some fire in his voice as he felt that Eric was being unfair. He was here to help and while he did not demand gratitude, he did not expect derision.

Eric interrupted him mid-flow and said, "Just do as we ask or don't help us at all." Since Mireille had taken over as leader Eric had superficially accepted the status quo but he was so involved in helping her and dispensing orders that she sometimes wanted him to cease but it was hard to tell him as she needed his help and power. The problem was she knew that he was alienating members of the group. Gervaise had complained privately to her of his treatment of her, and Margot, after a rollicking, now attended even more sporadically. Paulette gave lip back and stood watching Eric as he laid into Grey, wondering what his game was. Eric was worse with Didier around, utterly urbane to him and Mireille and rude to everyone else, expecting too much.

"I'll help," Grey said, stuffing his pockets, "but I would like to know what I'm doing."

Mireille said something to him, which Paulette rushed to translate before Eric put a poisoned slant on her words. "Do you want any dinner before you go? She's happy that you've come."

"I had a big meal before I came, thanks," Grey said, looking at Mireille and Paulette translated for her. It was not time to strike yet and Didier went upstairs for a lie down and Mireille and Paulette talked as they did the washing up in the kitchen. Eric offered Grey a seat around the table, which Grey accepted but he was not genial with Eric now, still a little offended by his cavalier attitude. Grey could take criticism well, he could handle being the butt of jokes or ordered around, but Eric had talked to him as though he were shit. He did not have the right to do that or any reason to and as Grey had come here to help he found the attitude unacceptable.

Surprised by Grey's stony countenance, perceiving him as the type to tolerate anything, Eric changed tack and said surreptitiously so that no one else could hear, "The group's falling apart. I know I'm being tough – I have to be because I'm trying to keep it together. The second we were occupied again their resolve went."

This explanation satisfied Grey who replied, "It might be better to support them with kindness. I know a kick up the backside can work well too, but sometimes all it does is give your troops a sore fanny and hurts your own foot in the process." Pushing them was not the way and Grey saw that and tried to persuade Eric to change his philosophy.

"They're sloppy and lackadaisical. Compared to the efficiency of the Germans they're just lambs to the slaughter," he said, showing a certain respect for some aspects of the Reich.

"The Germans have spread themselves too thinly. They're fighting too many wars at once. So are we, unfortunately," Grey said, thinking of the war in the Pacific and poor unfortunate voices that he understood painfully well that drove him to fight. He was talking to Eric like a friend now, forgiving him for the earlier slights now that he understood where Eric was coming from and he said openly, "Do you ever think about what this world will be like at the end of it all?"

"More of the same," Eric said without giving the matter much consideration. "What – do you think there's going to be some huge change – that we're all going to be struck by an epiphany and vow never to do this to each other again? That won't happen," Eric said cynically.

"This war has already proved longer than The Great War and even though a corner has been turned, there may still be years to go. I never thought it would last this long when war was declared. I haven't been here long, I'm not complaining, but for you guys this must feel endless," Grey said, a touch morose as he anticipated the night's events and in the mood for talking such matters over.

"France and England were involved in a series of wars known as the Hundred Years' War," Eric said, trying to put it into perspective for Grey who seemed to have no sense of scale. He was too affected by events – maybe that was what Georges was responding to and why he wanted him in the fold, because of their similarities.

Paulette presented Grey with his counterfeit identity papers, telling him that they had been intended for him for a long time. The documentation looked convincing to him (though, having never seen any other identity papers, he was not a good judge) and his alias was Luc Steil, Paulette explaining that had he stayed as planned after Georges' death, he would have been passed off as his estranged son. Grey felt honoured by this, his proud reaction at his sham identity baffling Paulette.

Much later Grey accompanied Didier and Paulette as they left the tavern; Mireille kissed her son goodbye and Eric sternly warned Grey and Paulette not to lead anyone back to them. They skulked in the shadows, Didier leading the way as Paulette whispered to Grey of the plan. Didier was going to hit the town hall, which was being used as a headquarters for prominent Nazis in the town, unfortunately not major enough, to Paulette's regret, as she and Didier liked to hunt big game. He was also set to take out some other targets but Paulette did not tell Grey of this as she spoke of what they were to do as she and Grey were going somewhere different. She told him that they were leaving town to go to a makeshift barracks at a country manor, which also had a small tank regiment that they were going to blow sky high. She was ebullient as she talked of this, going into the lion's den exciting her and she played with her pistol as she spoke, twirling it around under her coat. There were only two pistols, Didier having the other and he had only brought two with him (he had not expected Grey to accompany them). Didier wondered as to the point of Grey's presence as Paulette was capable of the task on her own, though he respected the American for taking the risk alongside them and he was uncritical.

Making it through the town was surprisingly easy and they dodged two patrols by diving into back alleys, Grey's and Didier's eyes and ears sound. They neared Didier's first target, which to Grey seemed like an ordinary cottage. It was semidetached and at the side of the house (which led only to a road) Didier placed the explosives in the circle, and doused the liquid over it and then grabbed a clump of grass and twigs from a nearby lawn and covered over his handiwork, making it seem to blend into the environment. He did this all at lightning speed and told Grey helpfully that that was how to do it, partly boastful without being overbearingly so. Paulette translated this and she wished Didier good luck as he went his own way. She did not bother to tell Grey the story behind this attack, of the informer and his equally repellent wife (who pleasured numerous Nazis) who lived there, albeit not for much longer. A few minutes later they heard a gunshot from the direction Didier had ran in and Grey stopped walking and looked around. He started to walk towards where Didier had gone and Paulette grabbed his arm to stop him.

"That's the risk we all take. He's probably fine. Either way it doesn't matter. We have to perform our task," she said coolly. It was a shame if he was dead but Paulette was committed to her task and she would grieve later. Grey was still drawn to check if he was all right (despite several military spirits trying to toughen him up, he remained more concerned about people over missions) and Paulette pulled at his arm, badgering him and he followed her. She was older than he was yet spending time with her Grey found her to be more youthful, seemingly enjoying herself with a joy for her task as she set out to re-secure liberty for France. She walked close to him, creating the illusion of lovers if they were espied, entwining arms, which he permitted though he made no efforts to get closer to her. He found her to be at her most open as they made their way across and out of the town together, Paulette surprisingly talkative. She whispered of previous heroic acts she had done and in tandem with whom. She talked of another girl who she clearly admired greatly, Cecile, who had worked at her side before she was caught and taken to Paris for questioning where she had died without revealing anything.

"We found Cecile through Konah as well. Georges thought she was going to be the final piece in the puzzle to make the group unbeatable and that pressure weighed down on her a lot. She was only my age and so clever and brave. She could – I don't really understand all of this stuff, she could see people's auras; she said there was a whole rainbow of colours. That was useful on our missions at first because she could tell if someone was evil at a glance. I thought she was amazing, only she lost faith in herself because people who she thought had good auras were doing bad things."

Paulette was so absorbed in her stories that Grey felt she was not being quite alert enough and he dragged her into a garden suddenly as he saw a jeep approach. He had been rough with her through necessity, as they had to move fast or they would have been seen, and he apologised and she said, staring at him quizzically, "For what?"

She understood the need for swift action perfectly well and found his apology unnecessary and she felt it showed he had little experience as a field operative. Didier had shoved her into walls, into marshland and even over a bridge once to evade detection and had never apologised and she never expected it. The law of the jungle demanded such actions and it was not really the place for niceties and manners. Inquests into forays happened later at Mireille's (as Paulette now considered the pub to be Mireille's).

Grey observed that it was a strange sort of barracks, this tall private building which was clearly visible from some distance as they crawled through fields to enter it from the rear. Most of the building was in darkness bar the lower level and Paulette was the first to spot soldiers patrolling the grounds on sentry duty. As they waited they gathered that there were two groups of two soldiers making a circuit of the grounds and Grey asked Paulette if he could use her pistol. His aim had improved and he was willing to chance it, as there was no way they could reach their targets while these soldiers blocked their progress. There were at least 30 tanks here but they were too far away to hide behind.

"I could do some damage in one of them," Paulette observed gleefully.

"Yeah, but how are we going to do some damage to them?" Grey asked. She would not give him her gun, insisting that if they shot the soldiers then their explosives would be found and the whole operation ruined.

"We can wait another 20 minutes and if they haven't moved away by then, you can shoot them. Are you a good shot?" Paulette checked her watch before she spoke, timing of the utmost importance.

"I'll have to be," Grey said. He was much improved but shooting four soldiers with only six shots was a challenge and he would have to move closer and lose his cover of darkness and grass to stand a chance of striking all four.

Two jeeps arrived at the front of the building (Grey and Paulette could not see the front but they heard them pull up) and the soldiers went together to investigate this. Paulette was running to the building before Grey had chance to say they should strike and she told him to do the tanks as she hurriedly placed her explosives in the circles and covered them with the liquid. She did this three times around the back of the building and she looked for potential coverings, pulling out roots of flowers, weeds and grass clumps and trying to arrange them naturally. She had given Grey the easier task and he tried not to look at these majestic machines that had been aiming at him weeks previously as he copied what he had seen Didier demonstrate, scattering his explosives so that hopefully they would take out every tank. He was able to just about hide them under the tanks and when he was done he looked across at Paulette who was still trying to cover up her third bomb. Grey ran to her, checking that it was safe on all sides and he panicked as he heard German voices becoming louder. She was done but Grey knew they could not run back across the field – it was too long and flat, they would be spotted, and instead he led her to the side, hoping against hope that the other patrol was not coming from this side. They hurdled over the fence to another field and they ran looking behind them, having to take a detour to return to town, Paulette advising him to run.

"Gervaise!" Mireille said, greeting her like a sister as she stood on the back doorstep, Mireille hugging her tightly. Gervaise walked straight through to the bar after the embrace and took off her thick coat, still having many layers on underneath. The fire was raging and the table was pulled into the middle of the room with Eric sitting at it.

"We didn't expect to see you so late," he said, a mild reproach for her non-attendance earlier. Mireille heard this and disapproved. She knew that Gervaise had not come earlier because of Eric and she was grateful that she had second thoughts and had come to help at this late hour.

"Take no notice. Thanks for coming. We're doing it in five minutes," Mireille said, anxious and excited. "Time for a brandy if you want."

"I wouldn't say no," Gervaise said, taking a seat and staring at Eric who returned her hostile glare, making Gervaise look across to Mireille.

"It's not the time for you to be out on the streets," Mireille said. Gervaise was a respectable woman who was married to a bookkeeper who was working in Germany as part of an enforced labour group and she was quite sanctimonious in her views on others. She did not consider herself a witch – she considered herself spiritually blessed and her desire for piety restricted her access to her innate ability. She was too strait-laced to ever give vent to her potential.

As Mireille poured her out a drink, Eric said quietly to Gervaise, trying to cultivate her as an ally also, "The American's back, can you believe? I wanted rid of him, but she wouldn't have it."

"Oh, we don't need him!" Gervaise said, having no time for Grey. Firstly, they were a French group and the English/Americans with their bomber planes were as much a threat as the Germans (this sense of national pride was one of the reasons why she silently opposed Veronique's membership). Secondly, with some exceptions and even though their leader had been a man, Gervaise considered them to be a women's group. Women had this power more often and Gervaise found herself more comfortable in the company of women, able to open up more. Men didn't understand – she had never even talked to her husband of her extra senses (and had no desire to, preferring to keep him separate from her craft). Georges had been a venerable old man who everybody liked while Arnaud was practically handicapped and utterly harmless. Eric (who had annoyed her previously, but who she was warming to again with thoughts of his superiority to Grey) was tolerable. Grey was not, he was not her type of person and with his status – that of enemy of the Nazis – she did not want to be involved in harbouring him. He wasn't worth it. It was bad enough Didier being involved (a non-pagan and Communist to boot), but as he was the son of her good friend Mireille she let that one go without discussion. Grey was another matter.

"He hasn't got a clue. I'll bet he screws up our plans," Eric said, telling her what she wanted to hear. He fell quiet as Mireille came back within earshot and after Gervaise had consumed her brandy Mireille sat away from both of them at the table and they all held hands in a circle. Mireille made them chant as they all closed their eyes and she spoke of fire and flames. Mireille was adept at ceremony and while her words did contribute to their spell, many of her best lines were extraneous and had no impact or spiritual power. It took ten minutes of chanting and solid will from all three before they heard something. The explosion was quiet, but the fact that they heard it from so far away made them all cheer.

They heard another a few seconds later and while the barracks were too far away to hear explosions from, they felt sure that building had gone up too. All three felt drained afterwards and Gervaise asked if she could stay the night, Mireille telling her she did not have to ask and she led her to her room.

"She's one of our best members," Eric said to Mireille when she returned downstairs, expressing approval of Gervaise for joining them and making the spell easier.

"They're all good members," Mireille said. "Paulette would do anything, us three have proved our worth tonight and many other times over. Didier's been a huge help and Margot – if you're nice to her she'll come more often to strengthen us further. Sometimes Arnaud comes out with some useful information. And Grey's come back even though he didn't have to and we didn't give him much reason to want to. We've got to start being more appreciative of what we've got," she said pointedly.

"They need discipline," Eric said, making out that his hard-line approach was intended to help her.

"They're not in the army. They're volunteering to help us, risking their lives. Hollering at them is not the way Georges ruled and it's not my way either. Don't misunderstand me, if necessary I'll come down on them hard, but at present I'm thankful for everything they've done." She was laying down the law, letting Eric know explicitly that she was in charge and that she was displeased with his manner towards other members of the group. She accepted that he was a senior member, while letting him know that she held the reins. She could be forceful herself if the situation arose but it had not yet and he was disciplining for the sake of it, as a show.

"We were liberated and we let the Nazis come back in. We were doing something wrong," Eric said, justifying his stance.

"We didn't have Konah to warn us," she said, purporting that it would not have happened if the child prophet had still been with them. She believed this even though his visions were erratic and he only shared them with those he trusted.

"No, but there are six of us – five and a half, I won't count Margot as a proper member. Three – Paulette's not either despite her keenness and Arnaud can't be counted either. Us three should have been enough and we weren't. I'm sorry, Mireille, but I have to say it – you've fucked up." She had been reprimanding him and thinking about it, it riled him, to be talked to like that by a woman who was not in his league, a common dark woman of Romany stock doubtless. He was unable to repress his bitterness and told her what he really thought of her leadership.

"And what would you have done differently, Eric, if Georges had seen fit to entrust you with his group? How would you have stopped the invasion of thousands of men?" she said, her eyes aflame. She was a woman of strong passions and questioned so she had been provoked. She had tried to be reasonable with him, but if he was going to behave like a petulant child then that was how she would treat the jealous bastard. "My best way would have been working with Grey's soldiers and showing him we were his friends only you wouldn't go for that. You want to be the leader of a group then that's fine, but not this one because I actually care about these people. Get your own."

To be spoken to by her in such a manner was too much, her acrimonious delivery, her severe stance as she stood with hate-filled eyes. It was over in Eric's head now. Despite the late hour and the sound of activity, Nazis patrolling trying to catch the terrorists who'd perpetrated these acts, Eric walked out with his head held high. Mireille did not call him back; she did not worry about him out in the streets. Her son risked his life every night – Eric Girard could take his chances as far as she was concerned.

The multiple explosions from the country manor and the tanks outside it, coupled with the explosions across town from the informer's house, the Town Hall and one mysterious location that Didier wouldn't reveal, rocked Grey and Paulette as they sneaked through the heart of the city. The populace was awakened by the commotion and Paulette changed destination, leading Grey down a darkened back alley route leading to the four-storey tenement she called home. She could not use the front door now – it was much too late and she shimmied up the drainpipe to her window on the third floor which she had intentionally left open. Grey fretted as he saw her clinging onto the loose drainpipe, which was barely able to take her weight, but Paulette was calm and made it inside safely. She then came downstairs to the front door, which she unlocked, and she rushed Grey up to her room just in time as she heard other doors on her corridor open as hers closed. Voices were raised and people were asking each other what had happened. Paulette heard them all and was unable to repress a slight giggle as she looked at Grey, hearing these people who assumed their town had been bombed by the British. Their town had been bombed in a way but they had no idea that one of the bombers was so close to them and this amused her. She left Grey for a moment and after taking off her shoes and coat she walked out into the corridor and questioned her neighbours as to what had just transpired, a long discussion ensuing, some praising the British, some slating them. Grey realised she was just doing the same as Laura had, putting on a show to maintain appearances, but he felt that Laura did so with less glee whereas Paulette was exhilarated and excited. Grey was proud of the little that he had done tonight in supporting the war effort, though he still felt a little grief at the lives he had taken, German voices beseeching him in their native tongue.

Grey was unable to relax fully in the small cluttered room where Paulette rarely spent her time and when she did it was just to sleep, not to tidy. Her bed lay flat on the floor, the legs having collapsed long ago and Grey sat on the base thinking of Laura, Isdel and the others back at her farmhouse which he juxtaposed with the country manor he had assisted Paulette in destroying. Now that he had helped he wanted to go back to them and return another day to help the Pagan Resistance, not that he had felt like he had made much of a contribution anyway. What could he do? He heard voices and he treasured this gift now for he could aid these poor souls, console them and help them find peace, but Eric's words had made him feel inadequate.

Paulette stayed with her neighbours, looking out of a window on the landing, able to see flames burning far away and the Nazis running around like scurrying ants. When the show was over she returned to her room in a euphoric state of jubilation. Grey sprung to his feet upon her return and she flung her arms around the back of his neck. "Well done," she exclaimed, on a high.

"What exactly happened? How did they blow up without us lighting the fuse and how come the explosions were so huge?"

"The Pagan Resistance. While we were out planting the seeds, they were at the pub lighting the match. It was set to blow everywhere at one o'clock and that's what happened," she said, letting go of him and standing up as she removed her trousers, making herself comfortable and ready for bed. She gestured for Grey to move off the bed and he did so and she shook off the bedcover which was encrusted with food and lice and she took off her blouse as Grey looked away from her, unable to resist looking peripherally. She was unashamed as she removed her underwear, climbing under the covers naked and she continued, "It gives us time to escape before the impact, but we can't have too long else they might find the bombs."

"Any chance we can recruit you for the US Army? You're brave enough and capable enough for combat," Grey said, praising her.

"I'm doing my bit with my group, Grey. You joining me?" she asked and he assumed she meant in the group.

"Yeah, when I can because I'm with another group too," he said, a group he longed to get back to.

"I'm not talking about that, that's done for today. You can't leave now so you may as well join me." Grey got her meaning now and he looked down at her, her breasts uncovered as she gazed at him seductively. She had not contrived to make this happen and she did not especially desire James Grey but he had stood shoulder to shoulder with her tonight and proved his mettle to her. Now that they were alone, thrown together, a man and a woman, it felt natural to her and she encouraged him. She climbed out of bed and put her arms around him and kissed his neck above his round-necked vest top, kissing him hard. It was a severe love bite for she was thinking of Grey being seen leaving her quarters and this would make it clear to the other residents as to why he had been there and what they had been doing. He knew that would leave a mark and that Laura would see it and he tried to pull away as she kept a tight grip on him.

"There's someone else," Grey said, trying to be tactful as he tried to resist, beginning to feel tempted as her naked body rubbed against the length of him. This was only the second time he had been invited into a girl's bedroom; on the first occasion he had discovered, frustratingly, that Verity Holdsworth's reputation was unfounded as she set ground rules that made the visit a waste of time. Paulette was a different character entirely, and while she did not fit the profile of the perfect woman, he wished she had been around making the same moves in Keokuk.

"Of course," she said casually. "She'll never know," Paulette purred in his ear. It was only sex, that was all she wanted and the other two men who she had served with and led back here had no qualms about saying yes, both actually initiating it.

"She might. And I would," Grey said, realising this was important, and he prised her hands from him as gently as possible. Instantly he knew he should not have done so as it made it look like he was desperate to disentangle himself from her, making the rejection even worse. "This is the first time I wish I'd never met her, because I'm going to regret missing out on this." There was some truth in his words, for while he doubted he could ever love Paulette, she proved very alluring and Grey re-evaluated his opinion of her upon seeing her naked.

"It's up to you," she said, slighted by his rejection and unable to hide it.

"After the explosions we've caused tonight I could only disappoint," Grey said light-heartedly, trying to make a joke of himself to reduce her embarrassment.

"I don't care. You might as well still share the bed."

There was nowhere else for him to sleep and he agreed to this, keeping his trousers on as he tried to sleep. Paulette slept easily and Grey looked at her lying next to him, a desirable, naked woman who he had turned down because of his unrequited love for Laura even though he knew nothing would ever come of it. Even so, because of the slenderest of threads of possibility he refused a sure thing. Damn it, why couldn't she be the hideous scarecrow Pearce made her out to be to make it easier? Despite her lack of womanly curves she had a great ass he wanted to caress...He was still erect just thinking of what had happened and what he had turned down, something that was not exactly an everyday occurrence for him. His virginity was not a burning issue that he needed to remove like some though it was something he kept quiet and there was life in his loins now. The opportunity had passed and he knew that if he woke her and asked her to reconsider that even begging wouldn't work now that her pride had been dented. He'd done the right thing – sleeping with her would kill outright any slim chance he had with Laura but it was going to be a long night.

After Grey had gone out and the other men and Konah had gone to bed, Delgado knocked on the library door where he suspected Laura was situated. She opened the door and looked at his serious countenance and said, "Yes?"

"We need to talk or rather I need to talk to you," Delgado said gravely.

"About that idiot Grey? Come inside," Laura said. She was annoyed with Grey for the risk he was taking. She could sense in the air that sorcery was afoot tonight, death was looming somewhere. If it was Grey who entered the spirit world she felt it was a waste.

Delgado walked inside and refused the seat she offered him. She stared at him with a supercilious expression of mild offence and she sat with her legs crossed, her long plaid skirt down to her sandals and her long hair cascading down her back in a long thick ponytail. Laura was dressed down in a white woollen cardigan and vest top, but Delgado knew Grey would still find her irresistible like this. That was the problem.

"We knew what you were before the Jerries visit, but now it is something that has to be addressed. I believe you to be a witch, Laura," he said, a trenchant denouncement.

"Have I ever claimed otherwise?" she countered. Her voice was calm though her manner was abrupt and cruel.

"As a Christian I find it unwelcome to associate with your kind. Your lifestyle is repellent to my ideals, but I accept that your business is not my concern. Grey is my concern though," he said protectively.

"He's a grown man who can do what he wishes, Delgado. Tonight demonstrates that," she said, remaining softly spoken even though she was antagonised by his condemnation of her.

"All I'm asking of you is to discourage him from thinking of you in that way. You must know how he feels towards you and you must agree that it would never work."

"I do not have to agree to anything, however, I will admit that the notion of Grey and I as a couple is risible. Do you want me to break his heart?" she asked, staring at him to find out exactly what he expected from her. Was she supposed to tell Grey he was a fool, which she had said many times, but this time mean it and trample on his feelings, stamp on that doe-eyed, soft-hearted idiot just to placate Isdel Delgado?

"If you end it now it would be best for everyone," Delgado said coolly, anticipating Grey's anguish but he was confident it was for the best. "We won't be here much longer and while I appreciate what you have done for us, I hate what you're doing to him."

"Do tell, what exactly am I doing to him?" she said, fascinated by this and showing contemptuous amusement with a small peal of laughter.

"You're opening up doors that should remain closed. He's a simple guy, down to earth and pure, but that won't last around you. Have you read the Odyssey?"

"Oh dear," she said, putting a hand to her head wearily in the face of this bore. "Which one do I represent then? Circe, Calypso or Scylla?"

"Circe. She's the darker of the two enchantresses," Delgado said, releasing his hostility as he was honest with her. "You do seem to have a dark side."

"It would be fitting after the amount of my livestock you've consumed to turn you all into swine and in some cases not much of a transformation." She spoke with dark humour, but Delgado did not flinch at this threat. "Grey could not be less like Odysseus."

"Exactly. If he were the world-weary warrior I would stand back and let him make his own mistakes, but he's not. He's not a pagan yet and I don't want him to be." Delgado spoke strongly, standing up to her in spite of her demonstrations of power.

"I opened up my house to men, not my heart. You're all lodgers who are only here until you can return back to your unit and then back to your country, well away from me. You think you understand things and you don't. Fortunately, I am not of a mind to teach you," she said, dismissive of him, gesturing for him to leave with a regal wave of her hand.

"My parents have taught me everything I needed to know, thank you," he said, though his thanks were not in the least bit sincere. He left her, neither of them having raised their voice, but it had been a very ugly scene, a declaration of judgement on his part and more disrespect from her, of him, of mankind and of James Grey, the fool who loved her.

CHAPTER 7 – DEMON!

"Hello, Major," Inge said as she flounced into Major Klaus Von Strauss' office. Her words followed the necessary decorum as did her salute which he acknowledged (but did not reciprocate) from his chair, but she was playful too, unable to resist a little coquettish smile. Strauss ordered the private who escorted Inge in to leave them alone and Inge walked briskly to her lover's desk, leaning down to kiss him. He was cold, acquiescing to the kiss and opening his mouth as she kissed him passionately, without being very responsive. He knew how to play her and knew this would turn her on more and, regardless, now was not the time for such things. Business came before pleasure, which he would orchestrate on both counts, and making her wait drove her mad and made it better.

"Have a seat," he said, pointing to the chair opposite his desk which she trudged to. Being so close to him she wanted him there and then and being kept at arm's length like this frustrated and aroused her. "I did not summon you for that. Tonight I will ravish you and make you scream, but until then you will have to be strong." His words teased her and she anticipated the session he had in mind, hearing the masterful domination in his voice.

"For you I will be, Klaus," she said dreamily.

"I called you because of a little matter that has cropped up," he said seriously, standing up and handing her a small black iron pentagram and a vial of a strange pink powder. Inge took them from him as he stood at her side, monitoring her face for a reaction.

"Dear me, I haven't seen any of this for decades. May I keep it, darling?" she said, amused by the vial, a curio.

"Of course, my love," he said tenderly, bending down to be level with her face. "We found these artefacts on a young woman two hours ago along with some explosives. She refuses to speak and I wanted to be sure that this was a supernatural matter."

"I'm not sure it classifies as that, Klaus. This powder has been used for centuries by ignorant would-be witches and it is a tool of the trade, but it has more to do with ceremony than power," she said, dismissive of the object that she wished to keep. "And as for that – this is a very amateurish witch," she said, almost laughing as she looked at the pentagram. Strauss smiled at her, correct in his assessment that she would be able to help him in this matter.

"Perhaps, but I cannot disregard this completely because of the explosives. The young woman has displayed much courage under interrogation," he said, displaying admiration for his captive. Inge sensed this and it immediately maddened her.

"Has she? Have you tried to extract anything from her?" Inge said, her meaning contentious due to her jealousy. She trusted Klaus, but she was jealous by nature and possessive.

"No, I don't sully my hands with that unless it's an imperative matter. I haven't had them go too far with her yet because I knew that you would be able to persuade her to talk."

"Oh, I guarantee that I can," Inge said keenly, wanting to inflict some pain on this woman merely because her lover had shown slight approval at her strength.

Strauss leant towards her and passionately kissed Inge, wrapping his hands tightly around her throat, holding her down as he reddened through the forcefulness of his ardour, rough, exactly how she liked it. He pulled away leaving her gasping and smiling and he offered his hand, assisting her in standing as he led her to the prisoner, his guards saluting him as he passed with this beautiful woman at his side. Inge was beautiful and, made up as she was, decidedly carnal, a woman of the flesh and they all envied the Major tacitly, many wanting to be him, a fine role model for these young Germans. This blonde bombshell demonstrated what they were fighting for better than the images of homely mothers, an Aryan Goddess. The girl they held in custody was ethnically sound, but she lacked any qualities that Inge possessed. She was a thin brunette without any real curves, Inge possessing her share, and her hair was straggly, a dull brown whereas Inge's, although shorter, was coifed immaculately, straight at the front with a little curl at the back. Inge positively pouted at all times with her full red lips and large blue eyes and their prisoner was plain, her face free from make-up and drawn, and features incomparable to this uber-woman. Despite her position and inferiority their captive showed little fear and frowned at them and all of these factors made beating her easy, especially after she laughed at their first blow and mocked them.

Inge walked in alone to the room where Paulette was housed; Paulette slouched against the wall in the unfurnished cell. She was not too badly hurt by the Nazis weak shots at her and she suspected they had been holding back. That was idiotic she felt, as she would not show them any consideration were their roles reversed. They were enemies and that was how she liked it, the battle lines clearly drawn.

"Stand up straight, girl," Inge ordered in flawless French and upon sight of her she now felt she had nothing to fear in the way of rivalry having seen the girl who clearly cared naught for how she looked. There was potential there, Inge was able to accept that, but it was buried underneath the girl's hostile countenance and earthy living. Klaus would have to have been on a sub for months with only men for company to even consider this wretch and this heartened Inge. Even so, she determined to be cruel to the girl as she wanted to impress her man and she was not leaving without all of the information this girl possessed.

Paulette complied, standing up tall, but she did not lose her hostile look or show any fear as Inge advanced towards her. Inge put her forefinger under her chin, raising it sharply, and Paulette turned her head away, loathing this inspection. Inge slapped her and the blow knocked Paulette down and she clasped her cheek as she lay on the floor. She had always been a tomboy and she had fought with boys and men always, and in all of that time she had never been punched that hard and the blow had just been a slap, effortlessly delivered. This overdressed, painted mannequin was too slightly built to possess that amount of strength Paulette felt and she realised she was in trouble. Inge stood on Paulette's other hand, keeping it cemented to the floor, moving it absolutely impossible, and Inge pulled her hair hard, making her gasp.

"I understand why you couldn't bear me gazing at you because you aren't much to look at. Still, I'm sure you could develop into something sufficient to catch a Frenchman if you tell me what I want to hear. Otherwise after I'm finished the boys in the death camps would turn their noses up at you." Inge talked sadistically as she pulled her hair so hard that Paulette felt agony in her neck which felt close to breaking and she actually willed for her hair to be pulled out to stop the pain. Inge had grabbed too much for that to happen. She would not spill her guts though, not to any inquisitor and especially not to this bitch who mocked her people and made light of the death camps. However, Paulette did want to live and she tried to talk her way out of it.

"What do you want to know?" she asked, pretending she was willing to be co-operative.

Inge kicked Paulette's back hard and Paulette once again felt the tremendous power and strength that this woman possessed. This was the competition, the Nazis' witch, and to Paulette's regret she was 20 times more powerful than they were. She was out of their league and she feared for her group, especially for Mireille and Konah, as Paulette knew that this woman could (and likely would) tear them apart.

"Don't play games with me," Inge said impatiently. "You know what I want to hear and you are going to tell me. What state you are in at the end of it is up to you," she said menacingly.

"You want to know about the explosives," Paulette surmised. "I made them," she said, gasping in pain. She would implicate no one else.

"That sounds plausible, but I can sense you're lying," Inge said and she smiled as she kicked her back again. "And as for the pentagram and potion – they're not yours. You have no power, not even the faintest trace!" Inge said, dismissive of her, talking down to her. She was perceptive enough to know intuitively that this girl had nothing of the arts in her. "You are going to talk to me, girl, and soon, or else your life ends in this room at my hands."

Strauss ordered one of his men to check in on Inge every hour and after the third hour he ordered a soldier to request for Inge to join him in his office. She was annoyed to leave the job incomplete, especially as she felt she was making progress. The girl was talking now, naming her co-conspirators – it was all bullshit to throw her off the track and Inge knew so; listening to her heartbeat revealing the girl was lying but the truth would rise to the surface soon. The girl had passed her pain threshold over an hour ago and was practically hers. Inge lifted her up by her hair, threw her against the wall, creating a dent, and Inge took her leave from her and went to see Strauss. She remained immaculate, not a hair out of place and her make-up looking as though it had been freshly applied, but she was no longer smiling as she was left alone with her lover.

"She's not going to talk, Inge," Strauss said calmly, having taken a measure of the girl and finding her resolution and fortitude admirable. She was the sort he wanted on his side and he had decided on a new strategy.

"She will talk and soon. She's interfering with our time together so I am going to get everything out of her: her allies, her plans, her first lover," Inge said, incensed at Paulette and determined to break her down to nothing. She felt she had something to prove and she wanted to show her man that she could help him as he so rarely asked for her aid and she would not fail him. It was also a matter of pride – she was the Inge and this little creature was shit on her heel and would not defeat her. There were no prurient thoughts in her mind for once – she was focused on besting her prisoner, instilled with a work ethic for possibly the first time in her hedonistic life.

"If you go much further you'll kill her and that goes against my plans. Alive, we can use her to lead us back to her friends. Is she in any condition to escape?"

"She'll be lucky to crawl at the minute," Inge said showing a slight satisfaction at the damage she had inflicted, tempered by the shameful fact that it had induced nothing from her lips.

"We'll give her a little time to recover then. She might be brave, but she's small fry. You know how good a fisherman I am – well I often throw the small ones back because I want the big fish," he said with a slight smile, feeling in control.

"Or you could say she's the worm on the end of your hook," Inge said, sitting on his desk and looking down at him with a grin, hearing in his voice that he had something planned for his enemies.

"Precisely. We can reel her back in later when I have her masters. You go back home, slip into something more revealing and I'll be back in at least two hours."

"Klaus," she said, stretching his name out, pronouncing it slowly in disappointment. "That is not going to give us any time together."

"I told you before it would happen. Do I ever break my word?" he said firmly.

"No," she admitted, "but I am going to wait here with you. You might still need my help. She is insignificant, but we don't know who she works for yet." She had tremendous faith in Klaus as he had proven that strategically he was a brilliant military mind, daring and at times ruthless, but she knew that if there was supernatural forces at work then all of those fine qualities might count for nothing.

"That is up to you. I am going to go and talk to our prisoner now. You can join me if you wish."

"Oh, yes!" Inge said keenly, a little turned on by this.

Strauss found Paulette lying face down, her body outstretched in her cell, her blood covering parts of the floor and walls. Inge smiled at him as he admired her handiwork, "There is a place for you in the Gestapo yet," he whispered in German before shifting to French as he lifted Paulette's head up to look in her glazed eyes.

"So you will not co-operate? Your choice but if you will not respond to this gentle line of questioning we will have to send you to the Fatherland for processing." He let go of her and led Inge out of the room, Inge following him, eagerly asking him if he meant what he said about the Gestapo which, coming from him, she perceived to be a compliment. He did not respond at all until they were in private back in his office where he still did not answer her question, instead telling her of his plans for the prisoner. She nodded in approval and offered to help him as he completed some paperwork so that he would be home soon but he refused coolly.

"I'll be glad when this war's over," Inge said, moaning but only slightly as there was affection behind her complaint which was that she did not see enough of him.

"We all will, but I will still be busy with the Reich after we crush the British and Americans. Remember, after France is re-secured I am going to Russia to halt their progress. To win the world is going to take us realistically around another five years and after that we cannot relax. We have to stay firm and alert to ensure the peace remains and that means I am going to be based in Russia for many years. The Reich is my life and my duty, but you know I love you and you will have the best of everything at my side." He was unapologetic regarding what she seemed to view as a dereliction of duty towards her and he vindicated himself without raising his voice, understanding she was a creature of highs and lows and loving her for it whilst he remained calm and level, stoic, except in the bedroom where he valued what a prize he held.

"Moscow would be nice," she said enthusiastically, remembering past happy times in that city in another age. She understood what he was like and would have it no other way in reality.

"That is what I'm aiming for," he said ambitiously. He was more of a realist than a dreamer, but at quiet respites during his busy day, he would envision the future and smile. "When we next go to Paris go out and buy three fur coats, Czaritza." This compliment and generosity lifted her spirits and made her desperate to get home to be ravished, but she was good and kept quiet as he did his work, sitting away from him in a corner and softly singing snatches of modern songs she had performed in Berlin and Danish songs from her girlhood. The years had been kind to her and she endeavoured to ensure the future held more of the same.

Paulette was hoisted up in the middle of the night by two of the soldiers who had beaten her and she was dragged along the corridor leading to the exit where she knew her journey would begin, her death march. She would be there frighteningly soon, Germany closer than she wished. Another prisoner was dragged down the corridor and was made to stand next to her, a swarthy male a few years her senior who had also been beaten, his left eye closed through swelling and his nose appearing askew and broken. Their guards let go of them, keeping them penned in a corner as they talked to the driver and two soldiers who had arrived with him who were set to transport this pair of miscreants. Paulette was just about able to stand on her own by leaning into the wall and her fellow prisoner asked her compassionately if she was all right.

She nodded vigorously and said with steely grit, "They can't break me. They can take me to their shitty country, but they can't make me talk. How are you holding up?"

"Better than you I think. You might be going there – I'm not," he averred, equally determined.

After a brief talk the guards exchanged prisoners and as the driver entered his van the two guards took a prisoner each by the arm roughly and opened up the back of the van to load them in. The male prisoner suddenly resisted, punching his guard and making a run for it. Paulette's guard pushed her to the ground, ordering her to stay where she was, and both guards ran after him. Weak as she was, Paulette saw this was her chance and she seized it, struggling to her feet and trying to run but only able to limp along, looking behind her as she did so. She saw in the distance, as she tried to fuse with shadow, her fellow prisoner dragged back along, bloodied and marked as both troops had hold of him, manhandling and beating him and they shouted, raising the alarm, and more soldiers emerged from the Major's headquarters, the converted police station. The chase was on now and Paulette knew she had to be quick or she was dead and she forced herself to quicken her pace.

The prisoner was dragged inside where Strauss was present and he patted him on the back and ordered him to take a seat, having played his part and taken a few hard knocks in the process to ensure realism and credibility. Strauss ordered his immediate subordinate, Looste, to have word sent to his manor at once when the girl's destination was discovered and to not act further without his permission. The trap was set and he returned home with two guards and Inge.

For the first mile Paulette was followed and she knew it and she trawled along the town to lose him and felt great satisfaction when she did so even in her slowed down, injured state. What she did not realise was that this was deliberate and that Strauss had sent an ordinary soldier behind her, aware that he would be clunky and conspicuous. As an escaped prisoner she would expect to be chased, possibly realising that her escape might have been orchestrated and Strauss let her know that she was being pursued, but gave his soldier orders to lose sight of her after an allotted amount of time as it was no use if he actually retrieved her. There was another soldier on her tail that she was never aware of, a stealthy, tactical man with years of covert operations experience and tracking her was one of his easiest assignments.

Paulette had no keys to the tavern and she stumbled around the back where she knocked repeatedly. Eventually there was a response, Mireille coming down in a dressing gown along with her son Didier who had dressed completely in readiness for who was outside and he opened the door with a knife concealed at the back of his trousers for protection. He saw it was a bloodied and battered Paulette and he reached out to her, helping her inside, wrapping her arm over his shoulder as he led her to a chair. Mireille saw her and kept exclaiming various curses in shock as she followed Didier and Paulette. "Don't put her down there, Didi. Take her to bed and I'll sort her out."

Didier followed his mother's instructions, carrying Paulette upstairs to one of the spare bedrooms where he placed her on the bed, told her to be brave, and asked his mother if she needed any more help. "You go to sleep, son," she said, able to handle it from here and she undressed Paulette once he had gone and she was astounded at her injuries. She was a purple and black mass of bruising and bleeding. Whoever had done this Mireille condemned as inhuman and she said so to Paulette who was feeling the full effect of her injuries and was subdued.

"She was," Paulette said, the words an effort as talking made her whole body ache, especially her chest.

"She? A woman did this! What with?" Mireille said, the ferocity of the assault making her assume that the attacker had been a man and likely a group of men.

"Her bare hands. The Nazis have a witch of their own, Mireille, and she's one tough bitch. I'm sorry, they took the explosives," Paulette said shamefaced, feeling that she had let her down.

"That doesn't matter," Mireille said, trying to comfort her, looking for a place to touch her supportively but not finding anywhere that did not look sore. "They might have a witch, but we are a group and she has declared war on us with this act. She'll pay," Mireille promised.

"We might need help. Grey, his men and Laura could prove useful," Paulette suggested. Mireille knew how brave this girl was and how keen she was to take on superior opponents and now she was advocating swelling their number before tackling this woman. This proved to Mireille that this was going to be a test to her leadership and the group as a whole. She welcomed Paulette's suggestion for she was not so arrogant as to believe that her group was invincible as they currently stood. She had wanted to help the American soldiers originally, dissuaded by Gervaise and Eric who she could ill afford to lose and she knew Didier would persuade his Communist group to aid her in this struggle. Laura was another matter – she would not beg her and if Paulette wanted her assistance then either she or Grey would have to ask her to join them in this fight. She tended to Paulette throughout the early hours of the morning, seeing to her wounds as best as she could and left her when she drifted off to sleep, kissing her forehead. She did not care how powerful the German witch was – there would be payback for this.

Strauss was woken at four in the morning with the information he requested concerning his prisoner's movements; Inge was aggrieved at the intrusion even though he had insisted upon being informed at once. It was not the entry into her boudoir by one of Klaus' most trusted guards that annoyed her – she was unashamed of her nakedness and made no attempt to cover her exposed breasts – it was the timing as they had only just got to sleep, Klaus living up to his promise, and now she wanted rest for both of them. Strauss dressed at once as he learnt the details of where she had gone, down to the convoluted route she had taken and her final destination, a closed down tavern.

"Who owns it?" Strauss asked his guard as he readied himself, "Who resides there?"

"As yet we don't know. Do you want me to send the messenger back out to find out?"

"At once. We need to discover whom she has gone to before we act and we must be quick before they flee. I never let any of my catches escape forever," he said, talking to the guard and Inge, a resumption of an earlier conversation.

By midmorning Strauss was encamped in his office, hearing all of the details of the tavern with Inge at his side (she joined him hours after he arrived, after 10) as it was reported that the owner who bought and closed it down years ago was Georges Steil. Inge stood at Strauss' side as the messenger reported the news to him and she repeated the name like a mantra. After she had said it twice and gained her lover's attention and silenced the messenger she said,

"I know that name. Georges Steil. I've got it," she said, struck by realisation and gleeful that she could help on this score.

Klaus held up his hand to her, gesturing for her to be quiet. He very much wanted to know but not in front of anyone as he wanted the information to be just between the two of them if it entailed anything occult. He heard out his messenger who reported that Georges had died recently (Inge grinned at this) and that the girl they had captured was called Paulette Lefevre and she often stayed there. He told them there were said to be a handful of others, but as yet they only had the name of one other person who frequented there, an unpopular housewife called Gervaise Sores whose name was given up by a fellow townswoman who detested her. The messenger had little more information and he was sent away and Strauss asked Inge to tell him all that she knew.

"He was powerful, Klaus, it's good he's dead," she said positively. "I never knew him. In his youth he had power before he experimented with a spell so risky even I would hesitate and he was reduced after that, but he still had the knowledge if not the gift."

"So their leader is dead? If that's the case I'll send a unit around later today to bring them all in. The place is being monitored now and as soon as we have a few in residence I will disband their little group." He was almost ready to act, just wanting to make a few more enquiries that were being carried out as he spoke.

"No, don't," Inge said forcefully. This garnered his attention and she explained as he scrutinised her with his eyes as she questioned his decision. "There is a little more to this than just that. Georges was the lover in his youth of an old…acquaintance of mine. She was called Flora the last time I knew her. She picks different names for different eras so she might be called something different now. She has power, Klaus," Inge said, gravely serious. As such soberness was unlike her, Strauss knew this was of the utmost importance.

"So she could be the leader?"

"It's unlikely. It would not be in character, but don't strike yet just in case."

Strauss contemplated it and said. "To hell with her. Later today I'm sending a unit and I'm going with them and I'm bringing them in whether she's there or not." He would not be beaten by anyone, even by a powerful witch, and the Reich would crush her if she opposed them like they would anyone. There were no exceptions and there was no room for fear as boldness had won them all that they currently held.

"No, you have other matters that you have to deal with, earthly matters. This is my realm. Leave it with me and I will infiltrate and destroy this group for you. I can do this, you know I can," she said, trying to sway him.

"I would appreciate your help," he said, accepting her abilities and superior knowledge on this matter. "However, we will work together on this." He was not having her going off half-cocked and arrogant and blowing his operation and risking herself foolishly. He would call the shots.

"Agreed," she said as she started to plan things for herself. She would follow his instructions up to a point, but he had no real idea of how this subculture worked as, despite being her lover, he was not drawn to the occult per se and unlike many of her past partners she could not impress him this way with her abilities. He was a man of the physical world and she occupied the physical and spiritual and in the spiritual she was his superior and would do what she had to to win. The tactics required to beat men would not work here; it was a different arena and she began to formulate her own battle plan.

James Grey decided not to return to the Pagan Resistance for a little while to give the furore time to die down, as even escaping from Paulette's the morning after the attack had been awkward. An elderly man had seen him emerge from her room, his love bite visible, and the old man grinned at him and Grey grunted in response, unable to risk trying to speak a word of the language. He wandered the streets as a Frenchman, past scores of German soldiers as he tried to present himself as a normal man going about his routine business. He was not stopped fortuitously for he knew if he was then that was the end of him. On his travels he walked past Georges' tavern – he did not knock or go inside to give them a progress report, figuring the best he could do with the current heat was stay away from them and go back to his hiding hole, his refuge. He was careful as he approached, cautious of being followed – he would bring no trouble to Laura's door or at least no more than he already had. When he was satisfied that the coast was clear he ran back to her home where he found her feeding the hens. He said to her, out of breath, leaning on the fence, "They haven't been any trouble while I've been gone?"

"No, they've laid five eggs," she said facetiously, knowing full well who he meant.

"Gee, things have changed," he smiled warmly, playing along with her. "Do you want to know what happened?" He was consciously covering over his hickey with his hand; this mark, which to many would be a trophy, was a nuisance to him as he hid it like an unfaithful husband.

"Yes, but tell me in the study. You go and get changed or whatever, see your men and we'll lunch in there and you can tell me all about it." She was interested and when he did relay the story later he did so with such gusto that she almost felt like she was there. He knew she would not tell and he told her everything, Laura interested as to how they had made such powerful explosions (she had been aware of them when they happened, waking her up).

Delgado was also interested in talking to him privately, though the subject matter was not to Grey's liking, another lecture about Laura.

"You could never have an equal relationship with her."

"She's quite a bit older than me and has a lot to teach me and my ego can cope with that. I don't care how bossy she is as long as I can have her."

"That's doomed to failure. You don't care how your relationship is or how she treats you as long as you're together? That's unhealthy."

"Is there such a thing as a standard relationship? I know this much. All of the 'normal' relationships I had back home which followed all of the right protocol were lifeless compared to this. She's sweeter to me than those girls were."

"Who're your ex's, the Gorgons?"

"No, they were nice girls, who spotted something in me that I'm not ashamed of but which was enough to repel them."

"And that's why you won't be repelled by her, because you know what it feels like?" Delgado said, trying to understand why his friend was attracted to Laura.

"There's nothing repellent about her," he said protectively.

"Maybe you think this is what you want now, but what about when you get older? What happens if you cheat on a woman like that?" Delgado said, trying to make Grey appreciate how dangerous Laura was.

"I would be faithful."

"Everyone thinks that at first. Maybe an even bigger monster will blow into town and knock you off your feet."

"Not funny."

"I'm not trying to be." The topic was closed, Delgado realising that his criticism could push Grey towards her even more and giving up for the moment. He couldn't induce an epiphany in him; it would come in due course naturally, hopefully while his soul was still intact.

That afternoon as Grey and Laura talked in her study his collar fell loose and she saw his hickey for the first time and she commented at once.

"Is that why you stopped out all night, Private Grey?" she said, smiling wickedly at him as she teased him.

Grey saw where her eyes were fixed and he felt caught out and, innocent as he was, he felt there was no way he could make her believe the truth in the face of this evidence. Nevertheless he tried and he said earnestly, "She kissed me but I wasn't interested and it stopped there."

"Why? Soldiers should live for today and if she'd do that for you I believe she would do more," Laura said. She was not criticising him and was instead actively encouraging him to sow his wild oats.

"I like her, but she's not my type," Grey said, not naming the girl but as he had said that he stayed at Paulette's Laura knew who he meant. His heartfelt look at Laura as he said this made it clear that there was another he cared for though it remained unspoken as his bolder attempts to romance her had met with mild rebuffs.

A short while later Grey, sensing an undercurrent from the previous night when he left her, asked, "Are you cross with me for helping the group?" She did not seem to be now that he was back, but he wanted to make sure and clear up any ill feeling.

"No. I would not have done so in your place, but it was your decision to make." She said this calmly for, while she felt him foolish, she understood that he had to follow the voices that drove him, both spiritual and his own.

"Voila," Grey said proudly as he presented Laura with *From the Earth to the Moon* as she sat in the library eating a sandwich, awaiting her regular evening visit which had become a secret pleasure. He sat opposite her and said, "In a couple of months I'll be saying whole sentences. I've just finished reading that now. Thank you."

"Verdict?" Laura asked, guessing that he hadn't enjoyed it that much as she knew he would have been effusive and far more animated if he had.

Grey grimaced for a second and said, "Verne is highly respected. There's stuff I liked but you know me, I like the pulp stuff best from writers considered trash. The sort of lowbrow stuff I like I'm not going to find in your refined library," Grey said, denigrating himself in jest.

"Giving you a grown-up book probably was a folly," Laura joked. She racked her brain to think of which books she could give him which would appeal more. She gathered his father genuinely resented his love of frothy and frivolous fare while Laura found this aspect of him appealing. She had been forced to devote her life to learning to survive and found an interest in academia as she often associated with intellectuals and their tastes rubbed off on her. That Grey's tastes seemed juvenile was right as he was still very young and she was overjoyed that he could still enjoy such things and hadn't let his powers overwhelm him and turn him morose and deadly serious. Laura stood up and looked at her English classics bookshelf for inspiration.

"It would appear so. By the time it got to the good stuff where I wanted to know what happened next it ended! It was enjoyable, don't get me wrong. Anything that keeps my mind off other things equals a home run. I can just get away with Wells, if I'm in the mood. Burroughs is always a winner. Conan Doyle too. Conan the Barbarian's even better."

"You've lost me there. So Conan's a character?" Laura said, turning to look at him and she saw that Grey was looking down at her table, focusing on her half eaten sandwich. "You can finish that off if you like."

"Hmm? No, no, you're okay. I'm here returning gifts, not scavenging your food even if it does look delicious," Grey said, turning his gaze back to Laura. She realised he hadn't been paying her sandwich any thought – he was dealing with a difficult spirit. "Conan's a character, yeah, but I'd be mighty surprised if you found him in there."

"Well, so would I, but I think the book's possible," Laura joked.

"That's optimistic."

"How do you feel about Conan Doyle's Holmes series?" Laura said, seeing a possibility.

"I've read them all quite recently. My dad has the full works. There's a pulp series that I think you might like. It follows a female lead in olde worlde France, Jirel of Joiry, a tough lady who dabbles in the occult and takes no prisoners."

"I definitely haven't got that."

"Neither have I anymore."

"Your father shouldn't touch any of your belongings now you're a man," Laura said disapprovingly.

"I was 16, he thought he was doing me a favour," Grey said, weakly defending his father's actions.

"If you must read puerile tat that's your prerogative and nothing to do with him."

"Thanks, I think. I guess they are a bit goofy. Mediums, sorceresses, prophets – they feature all that hokum. Real farfetched stuff."

"That French lady one doesn't sound so bad. We could do with her riding into town and getting rid of Germans and certain Americans."

"Am I on that list?"

"Pencilled in so a reprieve is possible. Pearce is written in the thickest ink. Which Wells didn't you like?"

Grey remained seated and he said, staring into her eyes, "Sit down, Laura. The story I want isn't up there. Chapter one of the Laura Spencer story would be enough to make me settle down for the night." He spoke persuasively, pushing his luck with a goofy, genial grin as he tried to sway her. She knew all about him – all about his power and inner friends, all about his small town Americana life, from childhood to manhood and his experiences in the army. He told her fresh stories of his past daily, but she knew the crux and she had for a while. James Grey was an open book and he was engaging and disarming and she decided to impart a little information.

"Why start at the beginning, James? You can ask me any question you like and I am sure you will want to know something other than who my parents were." She was giving him an opportunity to discover what he really wanted to know and his question was highly personal as he wanted to know of her feelings of the heart.

"I am interested in your parents, in everything about you, but that's not my question. My question is, who has been the love of your life?"

Laura had expected the question would be in this vein and she was prepared for it. "John McKinley," she answered without hesitation.

Grey felt worried by this, hearing a rhythm in her voice as she cooed his name. This rival had him beaten hands down. "Who was he?" he said, seemingly unfazed, guessing correctly that he was deceased.

"My husband. I think you realise that I am long-lived, shall we say? This was many years ago – the 18th Century – and he is the only man I have ever married. I own an estate in Scotland – I have talked of it with you before, I wanted you to go there if you recall."

Grey nodded vigorously, showing that he had taken in all that she had said and remembered her making this offer.

"At the time that was my only landholding, though I had other assets, and I spent a good deal of my time there. It is a much larger area than here and I decided to employ staff, a housekeeper and a gardener and I wanted to extend my property so I hired some labourers. He was their leader who dealt with me and my first impression of him was not very favourable. He was not what would be defined as an intellectual nor was he was particularly attractive, past his prime at 52. I found the work unsatisfactory and I demanded they start again and he stood up to me. He wasn't rude, but he put his side forward well, explaining how they had worked themselves into the ground to finish the job to my exacting schedule and he volunteered to correct the areas I didn't like on his Sundays as long as I paid his men and him the agreed sum. The work wasn't terrible and they were obviously so desperate for the money that I agreed to this."

As Laura paused for a moment Grey said, "Can I ask you something? Why didn't you build it yourself, with your abilities I mean?"

"Witchcraft is very vulnerable to witchcraft. It would be like living in a house of straw in a land of wolves so I paid some men to make my renovations out of brick. Anyway, I didn't pay him for working on the Sundays because he was just fixing his mess and he worked long hours for months trying to fix it to look how I wanted. He won the other servants over, they felt sorry for him and he would tell me I was a cruel woman as I kept him to his word though it was clear he didn't mean it. After nine months he was done and in that time he had rebuilt it entirely to my liking but he still came round the next Sunday to see 'his baby'. He joked that he didn't know what to do with himself on his day of rest now and he said he was going to risk putting his head in the lion's jaws again – he asked me if I wanted any other work doing. We had grown to enjoy tormenting each other and there was something about his spirit that appealed to me. He could be earthy and crude and he was uneducated – he was just a simple, happy man and in his own way he was charming. In all of our 18 years together he called me every name under the sun, but he never spoke a word in anger to me, he just libelled me in play and received 10 times worse back. When I told him I was a witch he just said that he'd have to watch his step and he offered to take back some choice words and to learn the art of grovelling. I milked this for all it was worth, obviously, and a few months later he asked me to marry him and I accepted. He had a small cottage in the nearby village and I moved there with him, living the rustic life, which I enjoyed, as he carried on working to support me. That was his choice; he could have been a kept man. When he died I returned back to my manor and I had a long period of mourning for the old bastard." There was affection in her voice as she said this, speaking very candidly to Grey who had earned her trust.

"It sounds like you loved each other very much," he observed, realising that winning her heart was not impossible for it had been done before, but he also accepted that he had a long way to go, a steep mountain to climb. "I'm sure they would have been the best two decades of his life," he said, complimenting her and acknowledging how lucky he felt this McKinley had been.

"Without doubt," she said with a supercilious grin. She did not mind Grey knowing of her past for she did like him, but he would not have her and that was why she encouraged him to go with unsuitable girls like Paulette. Grey picked himself back up though and persevered, spending time with her and a week later as he prepared to go and help the Pagan Resistance again, she did not quarrel with him, instead talking pleasantly to him in the study.

"You can go without argument now, I won't pressure you. It would please Georges – that is how I look at it. He was my lover too. Did he tell you that?" she said candidly.

Grey shook his head. "No, he just said that you were a friend. I could tell he thought fondly of you, I didn't..."

"In his youth I hasten to add. Now there was power, James! We were only together a little time, a few years, but it was a powerful union. He liked to show off his powers in a travelling act – an awful travelling act, but his effects were powerful enough to compensate for his corny spiel. He wanted the world to be full of magicians and he wanted to teach everyone how to access that part of themselves, believing that such power resided in all, a falsehood. He coveted too much power too quickly and he was undone and broken. The shine went from him then and all I reminded him of were his past glories that he could never recapture. It would have been akin to a fish trapped in a puddle by the shore forced to watch the big fish swimming around freely as he thrashed about helplessly, close to that majesty but forever removed. Perhaps I can explain it better than that. Men can live with goddesses in blissful harmony. Former gods cannot do the same because jealousy would pollute the love. Don't worry, the same holds true for women and gods as you will discover. We stayed in touch and in his later life we did spend a lot of time together." She talked of him fondly, her critical reflections not representative of her feelings.

"He's left a legacy though. His group remain that and they thought a lot of him," Grey said. "He had good taste too." This statement was a little too clear but he said it without shame.

"Remember though, Grey. If Paulette offers again, don't say no. You've no reason to hold back." Laura pushed him away with her words into the arms of another woman.

"Yes I do. I don't love her. Would you if you didn't love somebody?" he said seriously.

"Not now, but at your age, yes. I have been led to believe that it's impossible for men to refuse. Perhaps not all men. Good luck," she said and she shook his hand and turned back to her bookcase.

Lotte Wirsing climbed down from the train onto the platform, very apprehensive about what awaited and what was expected of her. As promised in the letter, there was a young German soldier, a boy even younger than her youngest son, waiting for her to pick her up. Lotte spotted him looking in completely the wrong direction, approaching other women and asking them nervously if they were Frau Wirsing. Lotte smiled at seeing this, at seeing his embarrassment at his own greenness, and she immediately liked him and thought of her own two boys who were in the service and then thought of her third, her husband, also serving the Fatherland. They were all fighting on the Russian Front and she longed that just one of them was fighting on the Western Front so that she could spend some time with them, preferably one of her sons. She loved her husband dearly, but he had joined up to look after his boys and it would cut harder into her heart to bury her boys. Reinald was mature and ready for death if his time was up and while she would never love again, they had discussed his death the night before he went away and he had said that if he was the only Wirsing to die, then that was an acceptable price of war. Their goodbye had been final and he had made it clear that his mission was sending her boys back to her whatever it took. War between men was cruel, but between boys it was a cardinal sin and she agreed with him on this point, touched by his selflessness.

She introduced herself to this poor, incompetent boy who appealed to the mother in her and she smiled generously at him, pretending she had not noticed his indiscretions. She thanked him kindly as he took her two medium-sized suitcases and she did the talking as he led her to his Kubelwagen, telling him trivialities of her trip which made him perk up. During the journey she inquired as to where he was from (Düsseldorf) and upon hearing this she told him of how her sister lived there and she relaxed him thoroughly and he was almost sorry when he arrived at the manor on the outskirts of town where she was going to stay. Lotte told him she was fine from here and would take her own bags in and she was so insistent on this that he left her on the doorstep as she good-naturedly shooed him away. She did not want the poor boy in this web.

After he had driven away Lotte knocked on the door and before she had finished knocking, Inge was there, clad only in her long pink silk dressing gown and she smiled triumphantly at seeing her ally. Lotte looked haggard to her, her straight medium length light brown hair making her face appear long and her brown eyes appeared heavy and her eyebrows too high on her face. She was thinner than Inge had ever seen her before, and this made her appear in the best shape she had been in since her youth with the exception of her dried out, tired face. Lotte smiled back at her and they both hugged. Inge noticed the bags as they embraced and asked why her escort had not brought them in. Lotte sensed he would be severely reprimanded for this and she said, "I wanted to see you alone and after seeing you he wouldn't want to go, would he? You look radiant," she said, distracting her from her ire with compliments, appealing to her vanity. It worked and it was also true for Lotte had never seen a more attractive woman than Inge who had so intimidated her 25 years ago at their first meeting. She had wanted to be like her, something that had never happened and something she learnt quickly enough was the last thing she desired as she matured fast and embraced her humanity and lover over this dark power. Like a drug, she had been unable to completely give it up and she had practised in moderation to refine her gifts, but her life with her husband and sons was her priority and of her family only Reinald knew of her powers.

"I'll fetch them in for you and show you to your room then," Inge said, lifting the heavy bags with ease and skipping up the stairs followed by Lotte who felt a fleeting flash of envy at her figure and vitality. To be like that must be fun she mused, but then she thought of the jealousy, the admirers, the maintenance and, most importantly, the price. Imperfect as she was, Lotte was happy with her lot and she knew that she had far more than Inge did in her family and a man who loved her irrespective of looks. Therefore she also had more to lose and she surmised this was the purpose of her summons. Inge wanted her help in some affair and would perhaps offer a reward if she did so – such was her way, buying people rather than cultivating friendships. Lotte commented on the fine house and asked her how she was finding France, harmless small talk. Inge was responsive as she showed Lotte her huge bedroom with adjoining bathroom and toilet. The four-poster king-sized bed was the biggest Lotte had ever seen and she sat down on it at once. It was quite a contrast to the well worn mattress she was used to in her small, cosy cottage in Munich that she had slept on last night and was sad to leave behind. However, she knew she could not ignore this summons and she tried to make the best of it, waiting for Inge to reveal what she wanted from her.

"I'll let you unpack, dear, and then you must tell me all about your boys. I'll bet they are doing their country proud, especially that Peter. He seemed a real character." Inge left her to it, telling her to have a bath too if she wished, as there was no hurry. Lotte decided to take her advice and she settled into the hot water and tried to relax. Peter was doing his country proud all right but that was what troubled her and Reinald so, but she could not confide in Inge about that. He was still only 19, but he had possessed the bloodlust for his enemy for years, instilled into him by his instructors in the Hitler Youth, by his teachers, by everyone around him it seemed, bar his parents.

Lotte dried herself and changed into a fresh blouse and long skirt, her clothes plain and drab compared to Inge's as Inge was now wearing a black slinky dress that revealed her cleavage and full thighs, more of a late evening dress than early evening sitting at home attire. Inge patted the space next to her on the settee and Lotte sat close to her and was forced to recount all about the last three years to Inge who looked enraptured even if Lotte felt that was not the case. Her eyes widened as though in curiosity and Lotte knew it was all building up to a request. She tempered her words about her family, making out that they were all proud German citizens, happy to fight for their country without question and total believers in all of the Nazi ideologies. Peter was the only one who had been sucked into the hate. Their eldest son, Jan, at 22 had lived more years before Nazi rule and proved harder to brainwash. At first he had come out with the same lines as Peter but working together she and her husband had questioned him about the things he was saying, careful not to blame him as they accepted he was not at fault and they had helped him see other sides. Some indoctrination had succeeded on him but some of his parents' beliefs had filtered through too. Reinald was as against the Nazis as they came, a member of the Communist party when she met him before he settled into domesticity but certain left-wing politics remained in him and he silently loathed the new regime. His firebrand spirit of youth had left him and with a family to consider he posed no opposition to the Nazis and was now their tool, but for his own reasons.

After hearing Lotte out patiently (she had genuinely been interested as she needed to find out as much as she could to bribe her with), Inge gave details of her continued relationship with Klaus Von Strauss who she was very proud to say was now a Major who would be a leading eminent figure in the expanding Reich. Lotte expressed admiration and commended Inge and her man on their successes and asked her how the Western campaign was going with the Americans now involved.

"Quite well. My Major can handle the soldiers and drive them to the shores, but there's a different kind of enemy who are very close at hand. There's a coven in the neighbouring town who are trying to disrupt our advancements," Inge said, getting to the point.

"Don't they realise negative spells always rebound?" Lotte said for this was her credo and the only spells she would use were benevolent, mild actions.

"They don't seem to think very far ahead. Unfortunately, a woman I have had run-ins with before seems to be on their side. She's no pushover either," Inge admitted frankly.

"For either side to use sorcery in this to me is utterly wrong. Yes, I have tried protection spells on my family, but never anything aggressive because..." Lotte had trouble articulating why it was wrong, why she found it fundamentally unacceptable. Spells were used to help individuals, but to use sorcery to change the course of history was too great a responsibility and an abuse of their powers.

"I know – but they started it, Lotte, and I aim to finish it. I aim to destroy this resistance group and I called you because if she is helping them then I will need your aid to best her. Would you mind assisting me? If you did I'm sure something could be arranged concerning your boys," Inge said, offering them safety for her aid.

"What do you want me to do?" Lotte said. She would do whatever was necessary with this bait. She knew she was being used and she did not care for it suited her purposes.

When Grey arrived at the pub and saw Paulette he was moved by the state that she was in. She had refused to stay bedridden and she sat with Mireille, Gervaise, Margot and Eric around the table. Mireille had brought Margot back to the fold by boasting of their huge success in their night of bombing which had taken 47 lives, 45 of which were German along with the informer and his wife. Mireille had also told Margot that Eric would not harass her again and this had changed her mind and Mireille was most persuasive, going to her house and not leaving until Margot came with her. Margot liked to help out, but only occasionally – she had health problems and looking after her house was sometimes more than enough for her but Mireille wanted a strong alliance and was insistent. Some of Eric's points had been true for they had not done enough to stop the

German's returning to their town. More militant action was needed, as was revenge for Paulette. Eric had returned a few days later and neither he nor Mireille talked of their quarrel and both talked agreeably, Mireille quick to ask his opinion and Eric asking her permission before proposing ideas. Things seemed healthier in the group; Grey was unaware of any of this and was solely focused on Paulette's face, the left side of which was bruised black. He went to her, asking her what happened and she relayed the tale of how her intended act of heroism/terrorism had been foiled and how a superhuman, demonic bitch had tortured her. She knew her name, one of the soldiers saying it thinking they were out of earshot and even though they had spoken in German she had picked this bit up and could also tell they were talking lustily, dreaming of being with her.

"None of us have heard of her, unfortunately," Eric said, turning to talk to Grey without any of his usual condescension.

"No, I haven't either," Grey said, thinking that he might know somebody who did. "Is there any plans against her or for activity tonight?" He was there to help but no one seemed to be directing him. At least in the army he always knew what he was supposed to be doing, the rigid organisation preferable to roaming around uncertainly. The other soldiers back at Laura's were becoming excessively restless now and were starting to argue amongst themselves chronically. Hartmann had fought with Pearce, blaming him for the trouble with Laura and he had switched beds with Strapulos who was keen on the move, irritated with Winters whose incessant moans about rejoining their unit were driving him nuts. He agreed with him and told him so but Winters would not stop repeating the same stock phrases about it and he could take no more. Hill was the only one who was happy (bar Grey) and he liked Laura more now that he had seen her power even though they did not converse, though he seemed to believe that they did, talking of her as a close friend. While she was not friendly towards Hill, he was one of the soldiers she was most polite to, along with Strapulos and Winters, Laura finding these three inoffensive.

"Didier's not here, but I'll go with you," Paulette said, refusing to give up the struggle even for a day. Mireille guessed what she was saying and shook her head, telling her she was staying put. Margot agreed animatedly as she peered down her spectacles at Paulette, calling her pet names as she told her she should be in bed. Eric made a suggestion to Mireille who quickly nodded, keen to be approachable with him, and she told Eric to ask Grey. Eric was not usually a risk taker when it came to terrorism as he considered that beneath him but he was prepared to risk himself in dealing with merchants and he asked Grey if he would accompany him in the morning on an errand. After agreeing to this Grey was rewarded with a hearty meal big enough for three which Mireille imposed upon him, insisting he finish his plate and she made a bed up for him though not in the room Georges had tried to give him (that room was Didier's now that Mireille ran the house).

Before they went to bed they heard the back door open and they all looked at Grey apprehensively. He was the one who would get them shot and they expected him to hide but as no one told him to he remained seated. They all breathed a sigh of relief when they saw it was Didier Godet, accompanied by some members of his Communist group. Mireille hugged her son and immediately began cooking for him and his friends. Gervaise assisted her as it was preferable to sitting and talking with Communists. Eric felt the same aversion to a greater degree and after greeting them he excused himself and went to bed. Didier and his friends crowded around the table that Grey was using and attempted to talk to him, though the majority gave up quickly due to the language barrier. This did not put off the oldest of his group, Lilian Demont, a 29 year old radical Communist with impressive credentials (he had been a Communist long before the war broke out and had visited Russia many times), who began using his very limited English to try and communicate with him. Grey believed that he was trying to tell him that he had a sister in New York, but he was by no means sure of this.

The other two people who Didier had brought were far more interested in Paulette and each other than in trying to bridge the language barrier with Grey. Fabian Beauvoir and Sandrine Lassarde were lovers who would never have got together were it not for the war, Fabian's family being of wealth and repute, Sandrine's family on a par with the Godets. They had met through Didier, Sandrine one of his cast-offs, a dark-haired stunning beauty who had entranced Fabian from his first sighting of her. The attraction had been mutual, Sandrine attracted by his charm and his curly golden locks, and with all the chaos going on around them Fabian's parents tolerated the relationship. Didier had brought his comrades around to see Paulette, all of them wanting to see for themselves what state she was in. Didier had something of an open mind regarding the occult because of his mother while his friends were more cynical and they quizzed Paulette as to what had happened. Paulette was touched by Fabian's concerned expression as she had had a crush on him for a long time though she knew she stood no chance next to the beautiful Sandrine, owner of the straightest and shiniest hair in all of France and model good looks. She could contain her jealousy enough to be friendly with Sandrine (she couldn't blame her for going out with him), Paulette friendly with the whole group as she admired their guts. Sandrine sat on Fabian's lap, twiddling his curls around her fingers as their meals were served while Grey was still being pestered by Lilian, who was being friendly but was too determined to get his words across; Grey asked Paulette for help, which did not materialise as she was too distracted to translate. It was only after the group left (bar Didier who stayed, his mother running a bath for him) that Paulette told Grey what it had all been about, just the two of them left downstairs.

"They found it hard to believe that a woman did this to me. Didier had told them it was bad and they wanted to see how bad. When I left the room with Sandrine I showed her in the cellar. I tried to tell them it wasn't a normal woman."

"It is hard to believe that it was a woman. And you say she wasn't even built like a truck?"

"What? Non, non, very petite. You don't have to go tomorrow, I'll do it," Paulette said determinedly.

"I want to help. If she'd bashed me like she had you I would be taking it easy and that's what you have to do."

"Georges always used to call me his little Valkyrie or sometimes an Amazon. I don't need to rest," she said, taking pride in the strong comparisons.

"Perhaps not, but you will arouse suspicion looking like that. You can hardly walk, Paulette – let me have a turn to do something," he said, making out she was hogging all of the work.

"Just this once," she said.

"What happened to Arnaud and Veronique?" Grey asked. Arnaud and Veronique had been the two members of the group who interested him most (after Georges) at his first meeting and he wondered why he had not seen them since his first visit.

"She left before we'd even buried Georges," Paulette said with disgust, directed at Veronique for deserting them. "Arnaud's still here. He spends most of the day in bed."

"Do you think I could see him? I'd like to," Grey said keenly.

"Yes. Take a pen and paper with you. We always write down what he says and it's likely he'll be having one when you go up."

"So they're not letting up?"

"The opposite. He's lucky to sit through a meal without it happening. It's the room on the left before Georges'."

Grey thanked her and went upstairs immediately and he knocked on the door and received no answer. He could hear Arnaud's voice mumbling something and he opened the door and saw Arnaud lying on his side on top of his bed, talking frenziedly and he seemed to be fitting, his arms and legs huddled up and shaking violently. Grey could see in Arnaud's expression that he was not conscious and that he was receiving a visitation and he went to him, holding his hand. Arnaud ranted in French for several minutes before he suddenly quietened and his body went limp.

"Arnaud – it's Grey. You're okay."

Arnaud's face showed signs that he understood though he did not open his eyes, needing time to compose himself before he could talk. His face and body were covered in sweat, the smell very strong in the small, stuffy room.

"Sometimes if I have a bad…bad isn't the right word, if I have a difficult…trying time with a spirit, I need time to sort myself out before talking to anyone so just forget I'm here and we can talk when you're ready," Grey said.

"I don't know if it was bad or not," Arnaud said tiredly. "Did you write it down?" This was important to Arnaud – if he had to suffer the visitation, he hoped something useful had come from it.

"No. It was in French. Should I have got someone else?"

Arnaud shook his head, his eyes still remaining firmly closed. Grey excused himself, saying he would be back in a minute and he returned with a glass of water which he offered to Arnaud who opened his eyes and took it from him.

"Do you see why I don't welcome my 'gift' now?" Arnaud said, shaking as he spoke, drinking in hurried fashion. He looked drained and even unhealthier than before but Grey was glad to see him.

Grey nodded and said, trying to elevate Arnaud's spirits, "I've been reading up a bit on people with abilities like you and me and some of them only have their powers for a limited time. It might not always be this way for you, Arnaud."

"It will. It's 20 years and counting since it first started and it's worse now than ever. I thought nothing would be worse than the Spanish Civil War – I was possessed daily then, but this war it's a dozen times a day. My brother told me the record was 37 times in a day," Arnaud said, depressed by his wretchedness. He forced himself to move, sitting up and drawing his knees to his body to give Grey space to sit down and gesturing for him to do so.

"That's horrific but it won't always be this way. I'm the same, the war has increased my contact with spirits and when it ends it'll go down to what it was. Were you frequently visited in peacetime?"

"No, maybe every couple of days. That sounds like nothing, I know. It's not knowing when it'll happen – you can't do anything. You daren't go anywhere just in case. I'm 27 years old and I've never worked in my life because of this. My brother has a wife and two young sons to support and all I am is a burden to him."

"No, you're his brother. There might be tensions sometimes but that's just families. If he didn't want to help you, he wouldn't, so he must care," Grey said optimistically (knowing little of the facts but observant enough to notice how weary Alain had looked the one time they met).

"I don't think so. People often do things they don't want to just because it's expected of them. I am tremendously grateful to my brother for all that he's done for me and I would have starved on the streets long ago without his help. He gets frustrated though," Arnaud said, lifting his shirt up to reveal multiple black and purple bruises on his emaciated chest.

"That's...he shouldn't be doing that," Grey said, picking his words carefully. He did not want to overly condemn Alain as he was Arnaud's brother and while he was clearly in the wrong, it was a unique, difficult situation, the circumstances tempering him from being more critical.

"He works for twelve hours and comes home and hears me shouting some message while he's trying to sleep, waking up the whole family, scaring the children. It's rare he does it; most of the time he's patient," Arnaud said, justifying his brother's actions, feeling disloyal for revealing the secret.

"I'm sure Alain is a decent man, but even doing it once is too much."

"It's not like I feel it. Not until after, anyway."

"You aren't doing anything wrong. You do know that, don't you?" Grey said, trying to help Arnaud accept his powers as he did the same. Grey stayed up through the night talking with Arnaud, trying to raise his self-esteem and make him look forward to the future. Grey's sympathetic ear proved useful to Arnaud who opened up to him, revealing how his father and his teachers used to try and beat the demon out of him and how his mother used the church to perform innumerable exorcisms on him. As he revealed more of his life, including how he lost his only girlfriend (who only stuck around as long as she did because she was a nurse and believed he was suffering from a variation of Gilles de la Tourette syndrome) due to a very ill-timed episode, Grey began to realise the full extent of his suffering and he acknowledged that Arnaud was much more unfortunate than he was. At first Grey had believed that their abilities were analogous, both dealing with spirits, and now he realised how much luckier he was than Arnaud. Grey viewed his abilities as a precious gift and he saw there was no way Arnaud's abilities could be described so. It was a hijacking, and Grey offered to help Arnaud banish future invaders.

"I would like that, only I need to keep having them for now to be of any benefit to anyone. My body's in no shape to fight and neither is my mind so this is about the only way I can help. If it helps the group then I'll put up with sharing my body with legions."

"That's noble of you, only you have to think of yourself first. I end up friends with most of the spirits I talk to, but I don't know if I would be so welcoming if they invaded my body like they do with you. It's your body, Arnaud, and your life."

"I can't do anything about it so I might as well accept it."

"So what happened with Veronique? I was hoping to see her again because the last time I saw her it ended on a sour note."

"She left because of Mireille. I like Mireille, I think everyone else does. Veronique didn't. She said she was going back home – I don't know how she would manage that in the current climate but it wouldn't surprise me if she did," Arnaud said, admiring Veronique. "She liked you. She said that she tried to badger you to stay and she wouldn't have done that if she didn't like you. She's from French Guiana – that's where she's trying to get back to!"

"Eric told me. Is that in Africa?"

"South America."

"Jeez, she'll never manage that. Or maybe she will; I don't know her abilities. I hope she does. She was saying something to me I didn't understand about her husband having it harder than soldiers by being on an island," Grey said, hoping that Arnaud could enlighten him.

"Devil's Island. Have you heard of it?"

"Yeah, there's been movies and I have heard…it's meant to be really tough over there, I know that much."

"She liked it over there though I'm not so sure about her husbands. The first one was guillotined and the third one was in the prison there a long time, then he had to stay on for the same number of years in the colony as a 'free' man. He was Georges' best friend. Georges talked to me about him a lot and so did Veronique sometimes. He was no threat to anyone but he was a chronic drug addict and for that they gave him ten years imprisonment and permanent exile. He was called Auguste – I can't remember the surname. Georges was a true friend to Auguste. He visited him twice a year even though he had to bribe guards to do so. Georges was too modest to admit it but I think he kept him alive. When Auguste had completed his sentence in the prison he had to remain in Guiana and Georges stayed with him for the whole six years until he died."

"That's true friendship."

"I used to be able to listen to Georges tell me about his life for hours. They have piranhas and crocodiles and these ants that can strip flesh down to the bone. It would stop me attempting to escape."

"You know, I reckon I might give that place a miss. I would have liked to have heard more of Georges' stories."

"He had one for every occasion," Arnaud said fondly, happier talking about other people rather than his wretched self. That was why he liked Georges and Veronique, for they took him under their wing and regaled him with long stories from their complex lives. Whether Georges' tall tales, which included talking his way out of a cannibal tribe's pot and befriending a man beast, were true or false, he had loved hearing them and these had been his happiest times, when the group was full of life and enthusiasm. While Mireille was kind to him things were not the same as the group began to merge with the Communists and became far more violent. Grey was right to be wistful for the group he sighted briefly, for they were changing for the worse. Veronique was condemned for going home yet

Arnaud understood her decision and appreciated that he was the only one she said goodbye to. "The Guiana stories were amongst the best."

"You can never go wrong with killer ants in a story. That sounds better than most of my pulp books back home," Grey enthused. "If I get to his age I hope I have as many tales to tell."

"I'd settle for getting to 79 without a single story to tell," Arnaud said darkly. "I'd have more chance of reaching that age on the island."

"That's bleak. You've got the Yanks here now, Arnaud. We're in the home stretch, pal," Grey said jauntily, trying to buoy Arnaud's spirits.

The next morning Grey set off with Eric through the town to the train station, talking at a murmur. Grey found Eric very quiet as he was anticipating what was to come instead of focusing on the present. As they boarded their train and found a carriage unoccupied with Nazis and where the other passengers sat far away, he took in the sights, seeing France as a civilian or so it felt and he had to remind himself that was not the case. He walked past the Germans unopposed, but that did not mean peace had been declared; it just meant that for a day he was pretending to be someone else. Part of him wanted to enjoy this sojourn, this relaxed feeling, but he knew they were on a mission and that he should not be as calm as he was as he would be shot for this if caught. Even worse than that, the group would be jeopardised and his fellow soldiers at Laura's would be without him. Laura would manage fine without him, but he felt he would be letting her down after his promises and he focused and turned deadly serious and he asked Eric about their mission and the man they would be dealing with. Eric possessed little knowledge regarding the merchant and imparted the little he knew to his interested companion whose politeness and deferential manner massaged his ego. Rouen was a name in underground circles; he was not a practitioner of the occult, just a renowned supplier of items that were notoriously hard to get hold of though no one knew who his sources were. The man was new to the scene, turning up in 1935 in Western Europe (though Grey considered this to make him an old hand, nigh on ten years) and there were both positive and negative stories circulating concerning him which Eric put down to satisfied and disgruntled customers.

"You can't please everybody, I guess," Grey chipped in, choosing to believe the best of this man whose goods they needed (though for what he did not know).

Eric continued telling of how he had met Rouen once and found him to be very unassuming, something of a letdown after the build up, but he vouched for the quality of his goods if not the man who remained an unknown quantity.

"I'm glad I'm not doing this alone, Eric, for a dozen reasons. I'd never get past the Jerries for starters, but even if I did I'd be clueless about what artefacts do what. The sort of magic that you lot can do – it isn't in me," Grey said, shaking his head, denigrating himself and considering the group and Laura as far more knowledgeable and capable than he. He wanted to help but he knew he was a disappointment to the pagan group; that was etched in their faces as they realised he was no saviour, just a man with a minor, impractical talent. He felt that he was only useful in a grunt capacity and it depressed him.

"No, but your powers are not dependent on any outside factors. Like Konah you are self-sufficient," Eric said, praising him. He thought very little of Grey who

Georges had wrongly perceived as messianic, but as Grey showed him respect he returned the favour. As long as Grey remained deferential they would get on fine.

"I am happy with my gifts and wouldn't swap them. I just wish I could do something momentous and stop this whole war in a second," Grey said, explaining his frustration.

"No creature in history could do that. Not warlock, scientist or general."

"What about God? Do you believe?"

"Non," Eric said sharply, uninterested in talking further on that topic. A small group of German soldiers boarded at the next station and Eric instructed Grey to pretend to be asleep. Grey complied and Eric said a few words to the Germans who were civil to him, but were more interested in talking to each other in German, French hard for them to understand.

Grey and Eric were quiet as they departed the train and slowly wandered around the coastal town, the rendezvous not for two hours, which gave them plenty of time to check out the current state of the town. Although they already knew that the town was occupied they were still surprised by how many German soldiers were milling around, some on guard duty and some acting as though they were on leave. Grey's face ached from the fixed sullen expression he was pulling, but he maintained it, talking with his mouth nearly closed to avoid others hearing him or reading the English words from his lips. He was surprised by how calm he was even though he knew his cover could be blown at any second. He assumed it was his link to the other side that relaxed him as he knew that death wasn't as bleak or as final as many believed. Laura, Isdel, Konah and the others were what he was concerned about rather than his own life. After Eric had walked Grey in the vicinity of the small cottage Rouen used, he took him to a small hotel café where he treated him to lunch. Eric left him momentarily to relieve himself, at which point an elderly Frenchman with a pipe leaned behind to talk to Grey who grunted at his words. Unfortunately the stranger was not put off by this and kept talking at him rapidly, looking into his eyes and Grey knew that soon he would detect something was wrong if his face showed no signs of comprehension of his words which sounded as though they were becoming derisory before the words inflected to sound upbeat and the man seemed to smile cryptically. Eric returned to his seat and, hearing some of this, he salvaged the situation by making out that Grey was a retard, which he considered a very palatable explanation. Eric felt more than capable of handling this affair himself, but he had a minor, nagging doubt about Rouen and Grey's presence reassured him though he'd never admit it. Nevertheless, he found himself getting on well with him; Grey's geniality and inanely personable nature made the day pass pleasantly enough. Eric was elitist when it came to choosing friends, his artistic set largely removed by the Nazis, but Grey made a good temporary friend, utterly disposable. Eric enjoyed that this was his mission and Grey was his underling and he left Grey's status unspoken as it was enough knowing that he had authority without flaunting it. The whole group should have been his and all decisions his to make, but for the day he determined what happened.

Grey's inquisitive nature moved the quiet conversation along as he asked Eric what he had done before the war and Eric proudly told him that he had been the curator of a military museum on the Belgian border before war had driven him back. Eric talked at length on the topic and of his bohemian, intellectual pack and their dispersal and demise and his new start. He was evasive on the topic of his current income, referring to a fortunate acquisition in his youth that facilitated his current leisure.

"Will you go back to that job and life after the war?" Grey asked, his interest genuine as always; his calling ensured that he was always hearing stories and it was fortunate that he possessed an enormous fascination with human lives and feelings.

"Some soldier who's fought for a day and spent the war in comfortable confinement will take my job, a man with no soul or finesse," Eric said, coming across as very cynical and critical.

"I wouldn't think so. Your people will want everything to return to normal, as it was I would imagine. Myself, I have no idea what I'll do after the war."

"You'll be fine, your country will take care of you. You'll be a hero. All of the jobs will be filled by soldiers."

"I wonder. Surely the men who've stayed and have learned the trade are keeping things going on the home front and will keep their positions and there'll just be odds and ends left for us. I was working as a gardener. I hadn't been doing it long and I wouldn't feel right taking that job off the man who's replaced me. I think peacetime might be hard, but compared to this it'll be bliss," Grey said. He knew there would be different challenges after the war, but he felt these would mainly be economic and he remained positive. At present the thought of scraping a living by hard, unsatisfactory graft felt like heaven compared to war.

"For the soldiers, yes."

"Did you ever think about joining the Free French?" Grey asked, detecting Eric's anti-soldier stance and trying to determine why he felt so. He felt personally under attack a little, but he did not get angry as he understood that some people from all nations hated soldiers and he could understand some objections without agreeing with them. Grey hoped that if he had been alive during the Great War that he would have had the courage to be a conscientious objector as that war seemed needless to him, unlike the current struggle.

"I'm no coward, Grey," Eric said angrily, defensive at this question.

"I wasn't suggesting that. We're taking a risk here and I would never criticise anyone who did feel scared, and your actions, your…desire to lead the Pagan Resistance leaves me in no doubt of your valour. You…I could be wrong, but you seem to think soldiers have it easier than civilians. You're entitled to your opinion, but remember we were civilians before the war and I would say it's harder in the army."

"You were not a civilian in an occupied country," Eric pointed out forcibly.

"Fair point."

"You all receive the glory after the war, while we unsung heroes receive nothing." Eric was very self-important and the thought of these parades riled him.

"I am not acting for personal glory. In my head I'd love to be the guy who saves the day, the matinee idol, but I know I make a damned poor hero. To make a difference anonymously would be more than enough for me. To take Hitler out and for no one to ever know it was me would be satisfying – it would probably be better not to be known if you achieved that because they adore him as much as we hate him."

"You believe that killing Hitler would stop the war?"

"The European war, yeah. I have talked to English speaking Germans and they agree that he is enormously important. One of them talked of him as his god. In the States we love our President, I'd jump in front of him if a sniper was around and I think everyone would, but in Germany they are even more…the soldiers have to sign their lives away to Hitler, their hearts and minds are bound to him." The whole Nazism regime and ceremony sickened Grey, but he hated few Nazis, finding it easier to hate the system than the practitioners.

"And you haven't had to sign your life to the United States army and your President?"

"I enlisted and swore to serve my country, but it's not the same. I'm more tied to my country – and only if I believe it's acting in the right – than I am to the President. If Hitler dies it's over, and I would take no joy in killing him, but I would feel joy at what it would mean."

"You would want the parade, Grey. Or do you not covet the adoration of your peers, of women?" Eric said, smiling at Grey but trying to find vice in him.

"I get that anyway, in my dreams," he added quickly, modestly. "Recognition from others would feel great, but personal satisfaction's better. I imagine anyway."

"You asked me why I didn't join the Free French. My specialised area is witchcraft, which I can use aggressively or defensively. You've never seen what I'm capable of, but hand me a rifle and my power is wasted. I would have fought gladly, but it was pointless because England and your nation did nothing as Germany flaunted the Versailles treaty and became, in plain sight of the watching world, the formidable fighting machine which has crushed Europe."

"Not Britain," Grey said, quick to point out that Germany was not as powerful as he claimed.

"Britain only remains free because of its island status and now because of your country's late interference."

"I wanted the States to be involved earlier. Opinion was fairly divided I admit up until Pearl Harbor, which changed everything. We're fully committed now and we're facing huge losses, but we're not giving up because that's not our way," Grey said, proudly patriotic in response to what sounded like attacks on America and Britain.

"I know and we are grateful, but it's results that count, James. Not much has been achieved yet," Eric said, modulating his criticism which he knew had come across as too scathing.

"That's fair comment, but they say Rome wasn't built in a day and Europe can't be reclaimed in one either," Grey said levelly, the argument returning to healthy debate. "Maybe with the things we buy today that might change. What exactly will these items do?"

"All resistance groups operate similarly. Sabotage is the form of our resistance and these artefacts should maximise our damage. You won't be needed for that side of things."

"I can be there though if you want. If numbers help."

"Let's get the goods first. Let's make a move."

As Grey followed Eric to the cottage in the centre of the town they were both surprised by the sudden lack of visible patrols, almost as though the town was unoccupied. They remained cautious as Eric let himself into Rouen's home, the routine all guests of this man adopted. He preferred intrusions to guests loitering at his doors arousing suspicion and Grey followed Eric inside then insisted upon taking the lead as they walked from the hall to the darkened front room. Grey was a soldier and Eric was a civilian and he felt that it was appropriate that he take the fall if it was a trap. Rouen was seated and gazed at them and smiled genially at them both. He was a balding middle-aged man with stooping shoulders and a large midriff and he paid particular attention to Grey. Eric began talking, reminding Rouen of their previous meeting and he asked to see his merchandise. Rouen meandered, talking of prices and risks before showing him anything and during this hesitation Grey's body began to shake as voices trickled to the fore of his consciousness, growing into a crescendo of incomprehensible protesting voices that nearly caused him to double up in pain. Occasional words of English were thrown in with the foreign dialect though they were unhelpful, anodyne words, but Grey understood the essence of what they were screaming at him. He ran at Rouen and lifted him off his feet and pinned him firmly against the wall by his lapels.

"You killed them," Grey said, staring at him wild-eyed, certain that this man had committed the most heinous of acts. Rouen protested to Eric and Eric tried to pull Grey off him, wondering what had brought on this uncharacteristic turn.

"This is our contact, Grey, control yourself," Eric said, clutching Grey's throat to try to prise him off.

"He's not what he seems. He's caused agony," Grey said, keeping a firm hold as the voices kept up their fervent laments and he heard the genuine anguish in their voices.

"His past isn't our concern. Let go of him," Eric said, still trying to force him to relinquish his hold and using more force to try to accomplish this, but Grey wasn't flinching at his best efforts, disturbingly focused on Rouen alone.

"Not yet. Get me some rope, flex, anything," Grey commanded. Eric reluctantly searched and found some rope remarkably easily with which Grey bound Rouen's hands tightly as Rouen continued to protest, more vocal now that he was bound and Eric asked Grey where he was going with this.

"I don't know, but I'll need your help. Tell him I know what he is."

"You've already jeopardised this operation. We should just find the stock and leave. You can do what you want, but I'm leaving soon," Eric said as he went upstairs to ransack Rouen's property. They were making a dangerous enemy here, but Grey had already done too much irreversible damage and, as they were now enemies, Eric sought out Rouen's treasure. He would have Grey carry most of the items, make Grey be the conspicuous one, and if they got back successfully they could do some damage. Or maybe not. Eric thought of taking some items back to Mireille to prove the mission was successful and retaining the rest and setting himself up in time as the next Rouen with his booty.

As Eric searched frantically upstairs, Grey's eyes remained trained on Rouen who kept protesting indignantly, yet Grey remained convinced that he was correct without understanding the languages (mainly German, though there were other undetermined European languages mingling) of his informants. Grey's anger made his visage fairly intimidating, but Rouen was clearly not scared in the slightest. Despite the language barrier Grey told him what he thought of him, breathless through repulsion, with his face inches from this sadistic man.

"You've had others in this position; don't deny it because I know. You've tortured them to death, but I won't let you forget them. I'll be their mouthpiece at your trial and you'll be lawfully executed for all that you've done." Rouen stared at him impassively. Grey strongly suspected that Rouen understood him, but he was giving nothing away.

Eric searched meticulously yet found surprisingly little. He found enough to fill his rucksack and hid small items in his pockets and against his body, but Eric had intended to seize the opportunity to change direction and there was insufficient magical material for him to change course. Grey went upstairs to check up on him and he saw Eric rooting through Rouen's things and he could tell how frustrated he was.

"There's something there," Grey said, espying a necklace on the patterned carpet that Eric had missed when he emptied a box. Grey picked it up and said, "I know you need the rest, but I'd like to keep this one thing."

"As you wish," Eric said, ready to concede one necklace as he already had seven down his trousers. The voices remained frantic in Grey's head, giving him a sense of still present danger and he warned Eric that they should leave, Grey checking that Rouen was still securely bound and he glared at him as they departed. There was still no sign of any soldiers as they left the cottage but Grey kept looking back and he saw two soldiers try to sneak into Rouen's cottage unseen. Grey told Eric to run and they both ran at full pelt, Eric losing a couple of artefacts along the way. As soon as they noticed a German unit in the distance they went back to walking pace so as not to arouse suspicion and they were fortunate to find a waiting train at the station which they boarded just in time. Grey knew there would be soldiers coming after them and as the train pulled away he felt that they had been very lucky. The train was packed and Grey closed his eyes and pretended to sleep as his hand caressed the necklace in his pocket, an old, worn down relic from another age with a brass pendant in the shape of a half moon. It was not the best present in the world, but it was a gesture.

Mireille was pleased with what they brought back, Eric giving her nearly everything, and the group began to use some of the materials. Grey offered to help in the spell and was told his help was unnecessary. He felt impotent again and did the washing up to make himself useful, unable to leave because of a build up of soldiers in the surrounding streets. It wasn't until it grew very late that the patrols left the area and Grey left, promising to return soon (though he doubted they wanted him back). Laura had gone to bed and even though she sensed his return she did not come down to greet him. Grey went to bed and saw Delgado and Hill top and tails in the bed and he slept down on the floor feeling dejected on more than one count.

Inge entertained Lotte over the afternoon and early evening and reminded Lotte of what a vibrant creature she was, her finer qualities almost compensating for her huge character flaws. Inge was opinionated and delivered her bitchy gossip with verve – 'If he was really King Heinrich, why would he settle for being an underling? He'd want to be the leader – he was quite an agreeable monarch, I found, but he was no one's stooge'. 'She's nothing special. The Berlin Olympics were so meticulously organised and chronicling the incredible story of our Fuehrer – those two subjects are so great that it would be impossible to make a bad film about them.' 'Their kind only copies us to be fashionable and upset the English establishment. I respect the English who oppose us more than those silly bitches. The 'suicide' attempt was only to try to impress Hitler. Anyone who means it carries it out.'

While Lotte didn't agree with everything that Inge said, she kept her enthralled and it brought to mind calmer times when she had been a spectator of Inge in her prime, accompanying her, almost like a shadow, as she dazzled Berlin's nightlife. Inge's patronage had opened many doors for her and as a shy teenager she found Inge a comforting person to be around, Lotte knowing she was safe while in her company. Her mentor's dark side, which was still present back then, was never exhibited towards her and in her youth Lotte judged Inge only by how she treated her, not how she treated others.

Strauss did not return home until after nine and he was weary upon his return and gave a minimal greeting to Lotte who felt awkward, like an intruder. This was not her home and she made her excuses and retired to bed, stressing that she had undertaken a long journey. Inge stood up and kissed her good night and she went to greet her lover properly with a kiss. He held her at arm's length and said, "Does she have to stay here?"

"She's a small-town girl from Bavaria. She doesn't know anyone here, she's never left the Fatherland in all of her life and she's agreed to help me," Inge said, hoping this would cheer him up.

"I like you to myself in our home," he explained. "I'll arrange for her to be placed nearby – somewhere nice and secure, I promise."

"All right," Inge acquiesced. She had talked to Strauss about Lotte coming to aid her but he seemed to have lost interest in the pagan element of his opponents as he was so focused on the numbers of Allied soldiers he had to fend off and had no time or inclination to deal with this trifling matter. Directionless Inge was now far too involved and craved their destruction so much that he wished he had just had that French girl shot instead of opening up the sorry affair. He knew what Inge was, but that was not what had attracted him to her and he did not want a coven forming in his house – he had been raised a Catholic and one witch in his life was enough. With Inge promising she would let him evict her guest without quarrel, he kissed her, trying to demonstrate why it was better they kept the house to themselves. He was tired, but he was an Aryan, physically tough and enduring, and he would show her the advantages of that tonight.

The next day as Strauss prepared to set about his duties, Inge said to him from their bed, "Could you perhaps requisition a house for Lotte by herself? She won't be alone and she'll need the space for her guests."

"More witches?" Strauss said, wishing he had never suggested going into battle with the Pagan Resistance on their terms. He knew he should have dealt with them as he would any other terrorist group. That option still remained and if Inge did not sort the problem quickly he would assemble a death squad to exterminate every person inside the tavern.

She heard the disapproval in his voice and said, "No, darling, she needs the space for her family. Her husband and two sons are all fighting on the Russian front and I was hoping you could request a transfer for them," she said, her voice demulcent as she tried to sweet talk him.

"That's out of the question," he said peremptorily. "We need every able-bodied man over there and I am not going to make things any harder for those remaining or any easier for her family just because of what she is. They have a duty. Impossible," he said, grumpy at the suggestion.

"They could still perform their duty on the Western Front. Trust me, Lotte can do far more good for your cause than three soldiers," Inge said forcibly, trying to make him understand her world.

"That is untrue. Three soldiers of the Reich have more to offer than her," Strauss said, puffing out his chest, feeling an inflated pride as he spoke of his unshakeable faith in the power of the Empire and its agents, from the Majors to the lowest rank.

"How about one then?" Inge said, trying to compromise and to show Lotte her word was true.

He grumbled for a moment and said before leaving, "I will give the matter some consideration when I have time." He left cranky and Inge shook her head after he left at his stubbornness. It was a strength of his which she usually admired, but today she saw that it could also be a weakness.

Grey talked of Inge to Laura as he performed her farmyard duties for her. Laura's face froze at the mention of her name and she asked Grey for the full story with some urgency. He told of how she had attacked Paulette and the sorry state she was in and Laura said to Grey, "I didn't complain when you went there, however, now I insist that you stay out of it. Fight the German army as a soldier, but do not fight her. I can get you all back to your unit with a little effort which is what all of your men want desperately." Laura was adamant about this, deadly serious as she planned their immediate evacuation.

"No, I don't want you to do that for us. You've done enough," he said, unwilling to risk her or desert her if there was trouble coming.

"You have no clue as to what you are facing. Stop that," she said and Grey stopped cultivating the ground and followed Laura as she walked around the perimeter of her fields.

"Inge is around my age, Grey. She would claim to be younger, I would like to think of myself as older, but our ages are comparable. We were both born in the Dark Ages."

Grey exhaled loudly and widened his eyes as he looked at her, "That's before the Middle Ages, right? That's way back, yeah?" He was merely surprised and staggered, not appalled.

"Yeah," she said, mimicking him, widening her eyes. "You can hear her chapter one – legions of men have over the years, she is not particular as to her bedfellows. Inge is a Dane – technically a Jute, consider that a Dane – and her tribe were a cult back in her mother country, mighty yet passive. They tampered with dark forces a little like Georges did, but they did it en masse and they pulled it off. The age-old enemy of witches – mankind and intolerant religion – dealt with the cult by massacring them, all bar one who escaped, screaming into the night. They hunted her down like the dog she is, and she used her feminine wiles and found refuge for a price she was willing to pay. That survival instinct has preserved her well but that is not what has kept her alive as she is also a very capricious creature, reckless at times, pragmatism only one facet of her nature. What has kept her alive is power. When her group died she absorbed their power and once she realised this, Inge was truly born. The woman has been everywhere, meeting everybody in her quest for power, wealth and satiety. She was a pack animal in her promiscuous tribe – perhaps that is why she feeds off the attentions of others, I don't know or care. I have met her twice; the first time we fought and she grievously injured me. That was in England shortly after the Conquest. She was fucking a Norman of some note and she decided to clean up his land for him in Wessex. We sensed what the other was upon sight and she went for me as I was performing a reading for some customers and I responded. 17 villagers died in the backlash of our battle and she walked away and we took it as a draw, but she hurt me. The next time we met was much later, in 1821 in London. She was dressed like a whore, the fashions suiting her much better than those from antiquity, and we passed in the high street and circled the other. We were both alone and I was poised to strike until she apologised, telling the story of her Norman lover who had made her do his bidding and she treated me to lunch where we discussed our lives. She had been the courtesan of a French officer who had died at Waterloo and she had ventured to the land of the victors and she talked as though I was an old friend who she had done no harm to. I was polite through prudence and I learnt as much as I could and we parted on pleasant terms. If she's with the Nazis, which is in character – she fucks warlords with a perverse pleasure – then you cannot fight her. She would crush you without breaking a sweat." Laura was trying to help Grey, trying to help him understand what he faced which was annihilation if he opposed her directly.

"If this is her, then they need my help more than ever," Grey said, feeling that maybe he could be of use somehow. "I'm meeting them in three days time, but not to fight her, just to talk and maybe a few more bombs." Grey did not know what he would be doing when he rejoined the group, though he assumed it would not be action against Inge yet.

"Fine, but do not act against her or whoever her lover is. I am serious about this, Grey, this is conditional to your stopping here," Laura said, refusing to be dragged into the fight.

"Fine, I agree to that. I wouldn't mind having a crack at beating her seems as she hurt you," he admitted, feeling protective of this powerhouse of a woman, "but I won't."

"Don't. Don't even joke, Grey, just don't," she said soberly, glaring at him.

Grey waited until the evening when the other soldiers were in bed to tell her of his and Eric's mission and of Rouen. He had put it off till late as he had spent a lot of time with the other soldiers, especially Delgado and he had told him the story three times, Delgado requesting to hear it again. The dark world that Grey was drawn into was abhorrent to Delgado and he wanted to know as much of it as possible with the intention of having such 'organisations' closely monitored by the Church. That was a matter for after the war (which took priority) though he would not see Grey get into trouble as he intended to drag him out of that world when the opportunity arose. Grey had also hesitated to talk of Rouen to Laura because he wanted to give her the present he had stolen for her at night, which he hoped might make it seem more romantic. He talked of Rouen first over wine, gravely serious as he talked of the voices who he knew had been damaged by Rouen.

"Your intuition is correct. Rouen is a Nazi operative who delves in pagan matters, though he is no true pagan. I have never met him, but he is notorious. There is a female operative with a similar agenda in London called Delta," Laura said, confirming Grey's instincts were correct and giving him a warning regarding the only other agent of this kind that she was aware of.

"I'm glad you've said that. There and then I knew it as fact, but the voices have subsided now – I know he's a Nazi, but I was starting to doubt the level of his activities but I know it's bad," Grey said, having allowed doubt to enter his mind after the event. Rouen was bad, but the fact remained that Grey didn't know what the voices were trying to tell him and Laura's usage of the word notorious made him feel that he had acted fairly.

"He's a killer who extracts confessions. I don't know any more than that, James, but I think that is enough to draw your own conclusions from and you were right."

"It's like darts, Laura. You throw enough at the board and you'll get 180 eventually," Grey said, making fun of himself and his nescience, but he was smiling and felt better than he had the previous night. He told her of how the confrontation ended and of how Eric took the necessary items (he described them to her as best he could as no one ever told him what they were for) and how he had kept one. He produced it from his pocket and laid it on the table. He had tried cleaning it at length; still the brass remained looking weathered. "I've already got enough necklaces," Grey said. "I want you to have it."

Laura saw the affection in his eyes and she inwardly sighed. "It's a nice thought, James, only I have no use for an infertility chain."

"What? Is it bad? I'm sorry, Laura, I thought…" Grey said, chastened by this and looking downcast, rubbing his chin as he realised that his present was a thing of darkness, the last thing he intended.

"Calm down, I know that you did not know what it meant. I would teach you, but there is no point as it is not relevant to your talents. This was a much requested item in its day – not everyone wants children so this is early contraception basically, when used in conjunction with a minor spell. Just for the history of the item I would be happy to keep it," she said, accepting the gift, explaining why she would never wear it. She didn't want any children (and highly doubted that it would even be possible for her to be a mother now) and would have worn it if he would not assume anything from it, but she knew he would delude himself with romantic fantasies about what her wearing his gift represented.

"I was always bad at this, giving presents." Grey went on to tell her of some of his terrible childhood buys for his parents and friends, which amused her because of who he was. Grey's inquisitiveness should have made him acutely aware of what presents his family and friends would want, but somehow he still messed up. The conversation was very relaxed and fun and as they both tidied up, readying themselves for bed, Grey went back to this conversation, saying. "I have learned now from that look of disbelief on everyone's faces when they open up my gifts so I'll get you what you want when I come back for Konah. I'm sure I can find a fox for the henhouse somewhere," he said, playing with her.

"Thank you for the present. That was a nice thought. You can bring back a fox and I won't say a thing but do not bring Inge back here," she said staidly.

"I would never endanger..."

"I'm tired, Grey, and I don't wish to discuss this. You aren't fighting Inge, end of story," she said, flouncing out of the room, her hubris at an overwhelming high as she laid down the law to him.

Lotte was re-housed in a cottage near a barracks and Strauss assigned a guard to remain with her. Lotte enjoyed his company and the humbleness of the house suited her better than the mansion that Inge resided in. The house was a mess, clearly hastily departed, and Lotte enjoyed trigging up the house, enjoying having something to occupy herself with. She found photographs in a drawer of the French family who must have once resided in the house and it shamed her as she knew she was trespassing, but she pacified herself with thoughts of her own family. Inge had promised her she would return them to her and this thought governed her actions, this reward worth any price. Her correspondence was forwarded to her and she was relieved to receive her regular letter from her husband who wrote to her by far the most with his progress reports. She took the letter to her bedroom and read it privately. It was over four pages long and his letters were always lengthy as he told her what he could of their mission and of the boys. He served with Jan and kept an eagle eye on him whilst he kept in touch with Peter through other soldiers, asking them to pass on messages to his unit who were stationed in a region many miles away. She saw the war through his eyes, envisioning the vastness he spoke of and the resiliency of the Russian people he wrote of. He harboured no hatred for them and he made that clear, though he admitted that they fatigued him and the others and he wished they would be beaten. He was one of the elders in his unit and he spoke of what the younger ones joked about him and she knew this would be well meant banter and that her husband would be keeping spirits buoyant, the father figure to more than just Jan. He wrote for Jan too, Jan losing several fingers through frostbite the previous year, Jan's message brief but significant as he spoke of how much he missed her – he was poor at articulating his feelings but she still cherished his words. She was spared the details of exactly how harrowing it was over there, but she had heard reports, rumours and accounts of the injured who had returned. Even though it was icily cold over there, she knew they were in hell.

Lotte had possessed the potential in her youth to become one of the greatest, most proficient witches in eternity, until she had lapsed and embraced different paths over her destiny. Now and for the next few months, or years if necessary, she was going to re-educate herself and maximise that innate potential. Inge came around that afternoon, escorted by her driver who waited outside. Inge kissed Lotte and got down to business and Lotte began a Tarot reading. Inge smiled at the cards (they were very familiar to her and reminded her of days long gone) and Lotte interpreted the cards slowly, using her insight to see more than was revealed, the cards just a push in the right direction. The Runes were no longer to her liking as they were too linked to Nazism now and she turned instead to this practice.

"There are men involved," Lotte said coolly, trying to decipher the exact meaning.

"That sounds like a promising start!" Inge said excitedly. "Is Klaus one of them?"
Lotte shook her head. "Two male strangers. Natives, either French or possibly Belgian. Dark features and connected to each other. They don't like each other," Lotte said, looking for the meaning in what she was discovering and how Inge could use it. Inge was impatient by nature, but she was patient with Lotte, not pushing her for explanations, letting it flow in her own time.

"The older man has power – some power and potential. Perfidy, perfidy. His friends are his foes. He hates them. Eric," Lotte said, straining for this. "Eric Girard."

Lotte stopped for a moment, holding her head and she resumed, dealing more cards to help her. The meaning of the additional cards denoted sacrifice. "He wants the other man to die. He is a man of violence, a soldier – no, a resistance fighter. This act will bind him to you," Lotte said, looking into Inge's eyes.

"What do I get out of this?" Inge said, looking to how this grudge between two men would be advantageous to her.

Lotte had to struggle for an answer and the cards gave it to her. "The dissolution of the group opposing Klaus – two groups, the physical and pagan."

"Ooh, that'll do me. I'll have to meet this Eric quick smart," Inge said, beaming at this news which would impress her lover and make his task easier. Ten townsfolk had been shot as reprisals for the bombing, and Strauss had made it clear he was still dissatisfied and wanted vengeance and the culprits shot at once.

That day Delgado (who had set a date three weeks in advance as a definite leaving date) talked with Grey some more of 'Circe'. Perhaps she wasn't damned he accepted, relenting slightly. Redemption was available for all and he realised he could not condemn her so without making some attempt to save her and he talked to Grey of his own Christianity. Delgado was a committed Christian and while Grey professed to be the same and was certainly charitable, Delgado had his doubts about this. Yes, Grey thought he was a good Christian and wore the cross, but Delgado had plenty of devout friends and family and he knew Grey was not that committed. He did not say this explicitly to Grey, instead saying tactfully that he did not feel that Christianity ruled his life. The decisions he made and people he associated with were contrary to a Christian life.

"I would agree with that," Grey admitted, "but I do still believe."

"That's cool, I was just saying," Delgado said, stressing that he had no problem with him. "I imagine she'll bite my head off, but I am going to try with her."

Grey accepted this and left Delgado free to attempt to convert her. Grey cared for Laura whatever she was, but the thought of her becoming a Christian was appealing. She could remain a pagan too as far as he was concerned if the two were compatible. Laura heard Delgado out before shooing him away, his sanctimonious claptrap unwelcome. He could worship the dead if he wished but she would not waste her time. She was disrespectful of his religion, feeling that he was disrespecting her and Delgado walked out feeling that he had at least tried. Missionaries and preachers would fail with her he felt and he had given it his best shot. He clutched his crucifix as he left, the 'jewellery' of his 'profiteering' church and he smiled inwardly to himself. Whatever tricks she could pull, whatever forces she could summon, here was real power in his hand. Power, wisdom and something else of importance – grace. He had refused to be provoked by her this time, using his Lord as his template. Serenity was the best reaction against her.

Eric Girard lived on the top floor of a townhouse where he had several rooms that were all well furnished. By no means a wealthy man, he got by without struggling though no one seemed to know exactly how he generated his income. With his late 30's approaching he felt that he had not done enough with his life, his long-term relationship washed up and his power, his glory, now seemingly insignificant compared to this woman Paulette described. Still, he consoled himself with the knowledge that even if he were as powerful as Inge the group would still heed stupid fucking Mireille over him. Nobody had taken more pride in the lodge than he, yet Georges had passed him over. No, it was worse than that; he had shafted him, fucked him over as badly as his unfaithful lover. Georges knew he had not joined his group back in '41 and risked his life all these years to be an underling to...vermin. Mireille and her family were the utter dregs of society and Georges appointed her as his superior. She wasn't even an original member of the group. Georges had brought (and also bought) Konah in especially for the formation of the group and his old friend Veronique Del Barrio, along with a resident who Georges had been friendly with for years who claimed to have some power, dotty old Margot Roy. This original group was nothing special yet they had been happier times when Eric felt he had some input. His fellow lodge members were geriatrics and a child, yet those were the days when they made more of a difference, largely thanks to his power. Georges needed him then and regularly praised him, fluffing his ego; Eric now realised this was all lip service. If he had truly recognised his power then he wouldn't have put her in charge. Even Arnaud had joined the group before her, before she came to their door selling charms and Georges invited her inside...Veronique had the right idea, getting out of town before their new leader led them to destruction. Veronique was a prickly character yet she knew her place and had no aspirations of leadership, accepting her role, and even she couldn't stomach following orders from Mireille Godet.

Going back had been a humiliation, but he had stomached it, biding his time for something – but for what? He looked in the bathroom mirror as he returned from doing his shopping. His brown eyes looked tired, his beard unkempt. Something had to change.

"Buy anything for me?" Inge said as she walked through from his bedroom, surprising him and he turned around with a jolt, trapped by her in his small bathroom as she stood with her hands high on the doorway. She looked beautiful to him, well-groomed and styled in a light black fur coat with a thin knee-length dress visible underneath, a dress that shined and also showed the wealth that this woman possessed. He knew who she was and that was his main concern, fearing he was next to befall what Paulette had endured, maybe worse for he was far more of a threat.

"Relax, Eric," Inge said with a smile, showing her polished white teeth, aware that he knew who she was. "I'm not here to hurt you. I'm your fairy godmother, here to offer you a dream."

Inge moved her arm and gestured for him to follow her through to the sitting room where he copied her example and sat down. Inge lit up a long cigarette as she waited. Eric was very hesitant around her despite her assurances. "I'm a Nazi, Eric. Unofficially, but the Nazis progression through Europe coincides with my goals so I aim to see their goals come to pass. Unfortunately, some people in this small town are standing in my way. Resistance groups are a nuisance and I swat nuisances like flies."

Eric was silent. She obviously knew he was involved and he had to wait until she revealed what she had planned.

"I have no desire to hurt you, but Rouen wants to eviscerate you and your American friend. He checked his inventory after you left and you took a lot, didn't you, Eric? Good for you I say because once you've mildly vexed someone like Rouen the end result will be the same so if you're going to be hung for a sheep, you might as well take the whole flock. Admirable," she mused, seemingly impressed.

"Unfortunately, your actions were also suicidal as Rouen's past form shows that disembowelling is a speciality of his. I find him distasteful because he is workmanlike; there is no flair to him. I have known some inquisitors who were visionaries, artists, and those men I admire, but Rouen is simply efficient. He lacks your power, Eric, but he has the contacts and that is why he'll beat you. If you chose to work with me, however, I could deal with Rouen with a click of my fingers," she said, flirting with Eric as she made this offer, alluding to her power girlishly.

He did not answer, still very unsure of her plans and apprehensive of speaking in case he offended her.

"France is quite fortunate really, being allowed to have its own government still, don't you feel?" Inge said.

She was not out to get him he suddenly realised from her offer and this knowledge relaxed him and he spoke, not quite confidently but giving it his best shot. "The Vichy government has some merits and many elements of Nazism are a good direction."

"Exactly. It is vilified by those who don't understand, narrow-minded individuals who have no place in respectable society."

"Like the Communists," Eric said. His lover had left him for a pretentious Communist artist and this had augmented an already substantial aversion.

"You don't like the Communists?" Inge inquired.

"I don't want them running this country. That would be my worst case scenario," Eric said, staring at her more and more. Her outward beauty coupled with the immense power that radiated from her made for a remarkable woman.

"Is there anything I could do to help you ensure this does not happen? If you knew the address of any Communist members or groups I could deal with them, confidentially, naturally."

Eric contemplated this. He hated Didier having his feet under Georges' table, strutting around shirtless; he hated his ideals, his very presence in the home he had hoped to inherit. He hated Mireille equally and turning him in seemed a perfect revenge on both of them. "I know where a group convenes and I would be most willing to share that information with you," he said keenly.

"I think this calls for a toast." Eric dug out some wine and poured two glasses and Inge sat forward close to him and said, holding up her glass, "Let's toast to the dissolution of undesirable groups and to the formation of fresh alliances." She spoke enticingly, promising him the world if he followed her wishes. Eric relaxed and sat back, assessing his future. This was a new possibility, a very welcome one, and changing allegiances came easily for he was staying true to himself.

Laura had begun to talk of herself to Grey and now that she had started she felt no desire to consciously hold back. He did not judge her, he was a good listener and he wanted to know very much – all of these things persuaded her to tell him more. She told him chapter one over a late supper that Grey cooked and which they ate alone in the kitchen. She told of how she was born in a barn, her home for her first seven years as she grew up in abject poverty in Northumbria. She was born nameless from an act of violence which her mother detested her for and on her seventh birthday her mother burnt down the barn that had been her home and flung her in a lake to drown as she left her to seek a life in pastures new with no past. Grey's eyes were moist for portions of the story while Laura was indifferent to the events that shaped her. Somehow she had made it back to land and peregrinated across the region, scavenging for food, killing small animals when desperation took hold and hiding from other humans. She enjoyed this adventurous life which only lasted for two years. An old woman came across her, the archetypal old crone, and she took her in and her initiation into witchcraft began. She quickly overshadowed the woman and by the time of her first menstrual cycle the old crone was dead and before she died she spoke in riddles, telling her that she had taken her place now.

"I wish I'd never pushed you for it all of the time now. That sounds harrowing," Grey said, wiping his eyes.

"It was different times, James, a different world. It was much, much harder and crueller than the present and, accordingly, the people were harder and more resilient," she said, perfectly composed. Grey was not quite crying but close to it and he cleared his throat as he stood up and walked from her to the sink to compose himself.

"It sounds like you've known happiness since though," Grey said, consoling himself with this thought and no longer jealous of her other lovers now.

"Of course. I think you misunderstand. I would live no other life than the one I have enjoyed," she said with a large smile. She was not morose or melancholy – far from it. Such optimism befitted him more and he realised that there was still so much that he did not understand about her.

"More wine, Grey?" she asked, prepared to fetch another bottle from the cellar.

"No thanks, ma'am. I'll end up getting drunk and doing something stupid like crying," he said, his voice clear and his eyes dry now. "The hardships you've gone through and what you've achieved show tremendous strength of character. You know I'm no sage, Laura, but through the spirits I know how many people sink into bitterness over their problems and there's none of that in you. There's probably not enough paper in the world to write your story," he said, admitting he was awed and fascinated by her.

"There is, but not enough people who would want to read it. Inge's however – even I would read that tale of debauchery, if I could find the time to finish such an epic tome," Laura said with a smile.

"You've got one reader here, 'Miss Laura'." It had been a while since he addressed her so and he did so to show his continued, unabated respect for her.

"Thank you, Mr Grey. I don't think Inge's book would be to your tastes," she said, complimenting him on his refinement over that creature.

"For that book to sell I think it would have to be pictorial," he quipped.

"Of her nothing would surprise me," Laura said, laughing lightly at the thought. Nonetheless, Inge's appearance on the scene was a serious matter and she was pleased she had his assurance that he would not act against her. Even the bombings were tempting fate but she accepted this as long as he didn't go deliberately against her. That would be minnow against shark, not even an entertaining contest. Even under her expert tutelage, under which he had improved greatly and even if his powers were not increased his understanding of the occult was, she doubted he could beat Inge. Could she?

Chapter 8 – The Stand

Yves Cremont was an ordinary French citizen. He had served his country during the Great War and he had cultivated and restored damaged land and made a success of his farm, which was a few miles out of town and which provided for himself, his wife and his two daughters. He had not acted to repel the Nazi invaders – he was too old and too portly now and he left action to the young, but as a patriot he supported those who did act. He aided Didier Godet's sprig of the Communist Resistance from time to time and they used a barn of his to hold meetings, one of a number of places they used. Only four of the six strong group were there: Didier Godet, Fabian Beauvoir, Lilian Demont and Sandrine Lassarde. There was no official leader as such but Didier was the most fervent and clamorous and, like his mother in her group, took the lead and made many decisions. Lilian was the most militantly communist, the oldest of the group at 29 with a private life away from the illicit activities and he had a lot of influence on their actions, but everyone was listened to. Sabotage and violence were their main interests and they discussed this as Fabian checked their weaponry that they kept stored here. It was growing to be an impressive arsenal, mainly the enemy's stolen guns, grenades – even Nazi knives, and they enjoyed using their foes implements against them.

Lilian brought up the topic of the informant and his wife whose funerals were being held the next day. Didier was proud of his actions and maintained so and Fabian and Sandrine, a young couple who fought and loved together, fighting for their future, supported him. Lilian agreed that Didier had done the right thing and commended him and he questioned how a person could turn their back on their country and countrymen, something that was anathema to him with his fierce commitment to his cause.

"I don't know but it's hardly an isolated case. After this war is over there needs to be a full investigation into it all and we need to look at their documentation and round up every single collaborator. They have no place in our new Republic," Didier said, planning on taking lives even after the cease-fire.

"I was thinking a similar thought myself. You have no place in our new Empire," a female voice said confidently in flawless French, as Inge appeared, smiling devilishly as she entered the barn. She was dressed in one of her least favourite dresses which was still a fancy number, beyond most workers' salaries, and she scanned the four faces in the room. The older one with weathered ugly features and short brown hair – he was not the one. The young man with extremely curly shoulder-length blond hair which reminded her of the fops of yesteryear – he was not her main target. The young woman with dark brown hair with a dazzling sheen, her natural glamour shining through and having an incendiary effect on Inge – not her either. The young man with the straight fine short black hair and determined eyes, this surly rogue who she assumed would be a terrorist in peacetime just the same – this was Didier Godet whom she had discussed in-depth with her new friend Eric.

Fabian went to grab her, aiming to pull her into the room fully so that they could question her and ensure she did not escape while they decided what to do with her. She gripped his hands as he made his attempt for her and she crushed the fingers in both hands and pushed him to the floor, Fabian shrieking in pain as he fell. Sandrine grabbed a weapon after seeing this, picking up a Luger, and she fired at close range at Inge's head. Inge clutched her forehead and said, aggrieved at this, "You little bitch. You've bruised me."

Inge advanced at an astonished Sandrine who had no comprehension of what had transpired. Inge lifted her off the ground by her neck and she held out her free right hand, the fingers pointed sharply, talon-like, and she thrust them into the young woman's torso, dragging through flesh, from her breasts down to her guts. She dropped her in a heap and as she turned to face the others, Didier lit a short fuse and threw a small stick at her, which blew up in her face. The impact made Didier fall to the ground as he was close by and some shrapnel hit him but he grinned as Inge shrieked in pain, covering her eyes. Lilian grabbed a machine gun as Inge staggered around and he fired at her, making her move backwards as she groaned as each bullet struck her neck and her exposed forehead. She had been complacent coming here alone, believing she could handle this group with no trouble. Didier reached up for a blade, which he threw at her throat with speed and force. It did not cut her, but she felt it and she reached down for what had hit her and she looked through her fingers. Her eyes stung, but she could still see and picking up the knife she ran at Lilian, ignoring the bullets that hurt her the closer she got. Examples had to be made and she was feeling particularly sadistic after what they had dared do to her and after scalping him with the blade she cut his head off. Didier struggled to his feet and kept shooting her in the back and eventually he jumped on her back in desperation as she began slicing into Lilian's neck but he was too late and she used his friend's head to beat him off with. After knocking Didier off her she beat him to the ground with the head and kept up the assault until she felt he was incapacitated.

"Don't worry, boys," she said, still keeping hold of the severed head as she looked at Didier who was lying flat out, concussed and mumbling incoherently, and at Fabian who was crying in grief over his lover and friend and a little for himself at what awaited him. "You don't have to die yet, and if you're lucky you won't die at my hands. You're coming back with me for questioning."

Yves Cremont had heard the gunfire and the explosions and he felt compelled to see what had happened on his land. His wife and daughters urged him not to go outside, but he had to know, partly out of curiosity and, more importantly, he had to try and keep his family safe. He stood at the entrance to the barn looking at the bloodied remains of two people, at headstrong, proud Didier lying prone and Fabian whimpering and a woman towering over them, revelling in the scene. She saw him and as he spluttered something, trying to construct a sentence, which felt difficult in his shock, she walked slowly to him and punched his gut, her fist emerging out of his back. She had to raise her leg and push it into his chest to retrieve her fist and forearm, after which she wiped her lower arm on some hay. That would teach him to harbour enemies of the state. She did not care for the circumstances, and the man's corpulence and smell (she smelt animals on him) and undesirability made killing him very easy for her. Sullying her hands so was unpleasant and she would have to lock the bathroom door for a long time tonight to arrange her toilet. That was for farmers to dirty their hands, not her, and she had no admiration for such an occupation. There was no glory in it, just filth and tedium.

Inge had a driver waiting and she dragged her prisoners roughly to him and she stayed with them in the back as they were driven to the old police station where Didier had been before for brawling in his youth. It was Fabian's first time and he wished that Didier were fully conscious to help calm him down. They were the same age (23) but Fabian had led a more sheltered life, his parents respectable and well off. The Godets were poor though Didier's mother worked and worked hard, but as a single mother who dabbled in the occult and was straight-talking, calling a spade a spade, Fabian as a result had been told not to play with Didier. They had become true friends in their late teens and Didier had introduced Fabian to Sandrine, an impoverished, clever girl who he now knew after her death was the love of his life.

Grey had arranged to meet the Pagan Resistance late at night and managed to squeeze in a lesson with Laura before going. Laura noticed how tense he was and wondered why he was putting himself through it. Georges had been a gentleman but the rest of them were not at all appreciative and not worth the effort. She knew his mind was made up and she understood his motivations and did not try to discourage him, instead praising him – the night would be hard enough for him without her stressing him out further.

"You've learnt a lot lately. Your knowledge of the occult is much improved so we can call it a night," Laura said, taking the book he had been reading and putting it back on the shelf. "Do you want one glass of wine – a mild one – or would you rather not touch anything?"

"I'll definitely have one glass, thanks," Grey said keenly. "Dutch courage is needed now 'cause I'm going to have to go real soon."

"I'll get you a glass but I think you have all of the courage you need without it."

"I wish that was true. I'm actually not so bad with this group because as far as I know I won't be actively fighting anyone. It's active service in the army that makes this burst out of my chest," he said, thudding his chest by the heart. "Being at war doesn't prove how brave you are. It proves to yourself how scared you are, especially when you see men around you bearing up well while you feel like you're going to soil yourself. I've managed to stop myself from using my drawers as a latrine up to now, but one thing I find hard to stop is my voice going. When we're in extreme danger the words tend to come out quick, which is fine, but the notes go up and down. It wouldn't be so bad if it just went down – that's sort of manly I suppose – but it goes right up too, as high-pitched as a bird. People are being brave and stoic around me and they must think I'm trying to be like Curly from the Stooges, putting on a comedy voice." Grey was being honest, but was also trying to amuse Laura and he was succeeding, Laura putting her hand to her face as she laughed at his words. He gave her a couple of examples of how he wanted his words to come across and then how they came out which had her laughing out loud.

"Stay quiet then, James," she said, wiping her eyes.

"A good solution, but with the insight of the spirits I can't. They're telling me things and I have to relay the information quickly. You don't ever imagine that you'll be as scared as you are. The worst of it is when you know you're vastly outnumbered and that your opponents may well choose not to take you prisoner and just kill you instead. My mind wants to fight because they have to be stopped, but every fibre of my body wants to run the other way instead of advancing towards them."

"Yes, but your mind is far more powerful than your body. I would act differently however. I know society views men who don't fight in wars harshly, but I honestly believe that you should stop. You are not guaranteed to survive this war. You would still be doing your bit by counselling the fallen. You don't need to actually fight to make your contribution."

"My power doesn't give me a free pass not to do anything."

"Nor does it make you obliged to assist. As I say, you can assist without putting your body on the line. Helping the spirits is your most valuable contribution – that's where you're irreplaceable, not as a front line soldier. They're ten a penny."

Grey exhaled deeply at this contentious statement. "You underestimate them. It looks like we'll have to agree to differ. It's even harder than it sounds though, being a soldier, for this amateur anyhow. The medium part of it is easier than fighting, by a huge margin. There's no fear there."

"Exactly, James. There's no fear because that's your area of expertise."

"The bottom line is that I can't expect others to endanger themselves if I'm not prepared to. Plus I couldn't deal with the shame of being considered a coward."

"But why care what this society thinks? Running away isn't cowardice; it's intelligence."

"I would never be able to face anyone after the war. And even if I did fool everyone, I would never be able to face myself."

"A sense of shame would be easier to live with than a disability. I know you don't agree with that, I'm just saying what I would do if I were you. You have a tremendous amount of potential, James, and it might go to waste. Due to the long length of my life I am an authority on this subject and I can promise you that your sacrifice won't make a damn bit of difference. Young men on this continent have long been bred like livestock purely for the killing fields. This isn't even your land; it doesn't have to be your fight. Keokuk's safe, we both know that. Wars are won in blood and even the victorious nation has to sacrifice multitudes of their own young men. Everyone loses."

"I know, and that's why I'm against most wars."

"And yet you will still fight. I commend you on your bravery, however, your fear is justified. The rules of war are always forgotten in several cases. What is happening in the camps is heinous enough, but you know from the spirits that atrocities have been inflicted upon soldiers as well as civilians. The last war had the Crucified Soldier to go down in folklore – do you want to go down in legend as the tortured figure from this war?" she said, warning him of the very real dangers he faced.

"I've already imagined the worst things in the dead of night, especially since I've started working with the Pagan Resistance. I just have to believe, like every soldier, that it won't happen to me."

"Oh, yes, you can't live thinking that it will be you because it is just a lottery. Mess with Inge though and your chances increase dramatically," Laura said, reminding him of his promise.

There was much activity in the town as Grey kept his rendezvous with the Pagan Resistance, knocking on the back door of the tavern as he tried to blend in as he saw the French stream towards the centre of the town, paying him no heed and much commotion could be heard in that direction. Paulette answered the door with a grave expression and bade him to come in where she told him what had happened. Didier's group had been destroyed and two of them killed in bloody fashion and now at nine o'clock the remainder of the group were to be shot in the town square as a warning. Paulette was the only one in the house, Mireille already in position at her own Golgotha with Gervaise and Eric, watching and waiting. Paulette had wanted to join them too but Mireille had told her to stay in case she was recognised by the soldiers she had escaped from. Paulette knew better than to argue with her as she saw her choking back tears at the sad news and prepared herself for her son's execution.

Grey shook his head at this terrible news and covered his mouth with one hand as he looked into space searching for the right words. It was terrible, but what could they do? He faced death, as all soldiers did, but to be killed in your hometown, in front of your friends and family, shot down like an animal – that was unbelievably cruel for everyone. Grey was unable to stay in the tavern, needing to see what would happen next, and he wanted to pay Arnaud a quick visit first in case he didn't see him later and he asked Paulette if he was in his room.

"He's gone. I guess you wouldn't know. After our successful night of bombing, the bastards have woken up to the fact that we're a threat. Not the group, they're not that clever, us, the townspeople. There's been some shootings and they've took around 200 men to work as forced labour – Poland we think. Poor Arnaud was one of them."

"Shit!" Grey exclaimed, unable to prevent swearing in front of a lady at this news. "Excuse me, sorry. It's just I doubt he'll be able to cope."

"I agree with you. His brother was taken too so that might help him," Paulette said optimistically, though she suspected Arnaud was effectively dead.

"Let's hope so," Grey said, unsure if his presence would be helpful or make a bad situation worse.

Grey felt even more depressed as he went to the town square, blending in quite well with the throng and he made it there in time to see the spectacle that had brought so many there, more than had greeted him and his unit when they had liberated them. That felt like a different time – he was with the army then, under Cloisters' command, and it was the first time he met Laura. In the darkness of this occupied town the atmosphere was different to that day, spectral, and the voice of Sandrine called on Grey, a wailing lamentation which he was unable to understand.

There was a strong German presence, many visibly armed, and even Major Klaus Von Strauss was in attendance with his entourage, scrutinising the crowd which was already over 500 strong and Grey walked past him from a distance as he tried to join the others. He recognised that Strauss was someone important from his uniform and the way soldiers were running around following his orders and obsequiously saluting. Grey melded into the crowd as the prisoners were led out from a truck and stood against a high wall with their hands tied behind their backs. There were three prisoners in total, Didier and Fabian the two who appeared worse for wear, both rocking to and fro as they tried to stand still and their faces showed that they had been brutally beaten. The other prisoner was one of the two remaining members of the resistance who had been rounded up, a 15 year old boy, Jean-Marc Pascal. His mother had tried to hide him in vain and had been arrested herself, her fate as yet undecided. Didier's 20 year old friend, Hugo Tremaint, remained at large, wilier than Jean-Marc and able to evade capture. After hours of torture at Inge's hand and under threat of worse, Fabian had talked, revealing all that he knew. He regretted it afterwards and Didier, who had also suffered but remained stolidly silent, turned from him as Fabian tried to make his peace. He was a traitor in Didier's eyes who had needlessly signed Jean-Marc and possibly Hugo's death warrants and he was finished with him and he ignored his desperate pleas for forgiveness.

Didier instead looked into the crowd where at the front, as near as the damned Nazis would allow, he saw his mother standing with Gervaise and Eric. Mireille was unaware of anyone being around her as she looked at the battered state he was in and the worse treatment he was facing imminently. He barely opened his mouth and made no sound as he subtly mouthed the name 'Inge' in her direction. Mireille nodded in recognition, showing she understood him, and she repressed her tears as her son stood bravely showing no traces of fear. His eyes were no longer trained on her and she saw where his eyes were looking. Odette Piena.

Odette was a diminutive girl, a little over 5ft tall, and the biggest part of her was, without question, her swollen belly which housed Didier's child, the bump making the hem of her dress rise higher than was respectable. She was just 17 and had been a pretty, carefree thing before her accident – she was still pretty but her new circumstances changed her mood as her future became uncertain, changed more by this new state of her body then by any of the wartime activity which she kept out of. She was no Communist, no political, just a pretty girl who Didier had seduced and whose future now looked bleak. She kept fiddling with her bobbed ash blonde hair, which curled inwards, and she cried silently as her parents stood with her, her father shaking his head vigorously. He was unable to stop himself from having a go at his daughter about her lover, telling her that it served her right and him too. The Pienas were common too, but not as common as the Godets and they saw this union as beneath their daughter and they had only tolerated the liaison because she was pregnant and ruined.

"We're not bringing up this bastard for you, my girl. It's hard enough managing with your sister's three. You'll have to find somewhere else to live," Mr Piena said coldly now that it was clear that Didier Godet would not be taking care of his responsibilities. Odette's sister, Francoise, lived at home too with her three children but she was older and had been respectably widowed in 1940, her husband killed while fighting the enemy. Odette was a different matter and as she had not heeded their numerous warnings, her mother accepting that she was having sex and urging her to use contraception, then that was it.

Odette looked through teary eyes at her mother who said, "We can't afford it and we haven't got room. I'm sorry." While she was apologetic, she was as final as her husband.

Odette looked at Didier with regret now, regret for everything and regret for what would happen to him. Mireille walked over to her and the Pienas retreated back further into the crowd whilst Mireille put a protective arm around the girl she believed would have one day became her daughter-in-law. Grey stood alone, Eric eventually coming over to him as the time approached.

"You're taking your chances being here," Eric said, surprised by his presence.

"I heard and I had to come," Grey said, explaining how he had been compelled to watch this, which was his way of paying his respects.

"This is revenge for our explosions. After this I think we should not pursue that approach," Eric said, having reasons for discouraging violent resistance.

Strauss ordered the peasants to be quiet and spoke in substandard French to the townspeople, telling them that this was the price for resistance and that they should not think of these men as martyrs for that was not the truth. Instead he talked of the 10 who had been killed for the explosions whose deaths were not on the hands of the Germans who were retaliating, but instead were the fault of these men who had harmed the otherwise smooth relations between the Germans and the French. Some agreed with his words and felt that the terrorist groups were the everyday people's worst enemy while most felt otherwise as they saw young men and a young boy who they had known for years and witnessed grow up, stand against a wall as rifles were pointed at them. Strauss gave the order; Fabian still pleaded with Didier at the last, and they seemed to dance in a hail of bullets before they all fell to the floor. Strauss ordered the bodies to be taken away by his men, stating that the men did not deserve decent burials and this crushed Mireille who collapsed, beating the ground with both fists as she shouted loudly. To be denied even the body destroyed her and Odette knelt beside her as Gervaise quietly went back to the tavern and the crowd dispersed, talking amongst themselves, the hush dissipating. It was back to normality now for nearly everyone.

Grey went back to the tavern too and eventually Eric returned as did Mireille and Odette, Gervaise arriving back before all of them. She and Paulette were making teas all round and they both hovered around Mireille when she came in, asking what they could do to help. Odette knew what the group was and instantly felt out of place, but she had nowhere else to go and Mireille had insisted she return with her as the only part of him she had left – the baby. Odette was calmer than Mireille and while she was sad at losing a lover, her future with Didier had been uncertain and their relationship had been rocky. She grieved for him, but she was not as inconsolable as Mireille who kept violently bursting into tears, stopping, then resuming again. No one could say anything to placate her and she shrugged off attempts by Gervaise to hug her.

"Inge!" Mireille said suddenly and aggressively as she recalled Didier's message. "That's what we're going to do. We're going to kill her." She spoke so agitatedly that Grey asked for a translation and Paulette obliged him.

"I'm not sure that's going to be that easy," Grey said. He felt like it was the wrong time to say anything discouraging but he could not let them go off half-cocked after what he had learnt of Inge. He disclosed what he could without mentioning Laura and her involvement, merely saying that he knew how long-lived she was and of her great power. Eric asked him how he knew this and Grey lied, claiming to know of her through the warnings of spirits. Lying was better than betraying Laura's confidence.

"I don't care how powerful she is!" Mireille fumed when Paulette translated this. "I'll rip her eyes out. Her long life ends now!" Even Paulette was more prudent then this and looked to Grey seriously as she told him what Mireille had just said. Of them all (as far as they knew) Paulette was the only one who had ever met Inge and that one meeting had frightened her. She would still fight, but there needed to be a plan, as Paulette knew she would be very difficult to beat and she felt that of them all Grey understood this best.

Grey made his exit before midnight (as did Gervaise and Eric) and he traipsed back to Laura's. Again he had been no use and three young men were dead now and Mireille's heart was broken and Odette's child would grow up without a father. He grieved for all three men, but part of him was unable to stop from contemplating a selfish, self-obsessed plaint which he had no business thinking. Who would mourn him so?

As Grey and the other soldiers sat down for breakfast Laura rushed in and said, "Keep them quiet, Grey, someone's coming."

"Jerries?" Delgado asked, this news affecting all at the table as thoughts ran through their heads – did they face imminent capture and possible execution or, equally daunting, did they have to hide in that tomb again?

"I said someone," Laura said frostily though she was not particularly cross with Delgado. She was annoyed at facing another intrusion, her quiet life already affected enough by these soldiers (who were outstaying their welcome, but she begrudgingly accepted that the climate was not safe for them to leave). The soldiers, Konah, Herr Weller and his troop – her house was becoming a social club against her wishes. "It's just a girl, but I don't want her knowing that you're here. You can stay here and eat your breakfast," she said as she noticed Pearce and Strapulos rising to their feet. "She won't be coming past me."

"We'll be silent," Grey promised.

"You! Good luck in attempting that," she said, teasing him.

"Hey, this mouth won't open again until you come back through," he said, pretending to take umbrage at her insinuating that he was a chatterbox.

"I'm sure your men will be delighted to hear that," she said, smirking as she went to the door to deal with her approaching visitor.

"'Your men'," Pearce said quietly, taking offence at this. "As if we'd take orders from a little piss-ant like you."

Grey looked at him angrily and put a finger to his closed mouth, trying to tell Pearce to shut his mouth. Grey was the only one who remained silent, the others whispering amongst themselves. Delgado did not bother talking to Grey, aware that he would want to remain silent so that he could boast to Laura when she came back through, like the lovesick teenager that he was.

Laura opened the front door and stared at the girl on the bicycle who pedalled unsteadily towards her. She didn't look like a spy, but Laura's long life had taught her that appearances could be deceptive. Who would have thought that Inge could floor heavyweight boxers with one half-hearted slap or that James Grey could provide a link to another plane of existence? While they were mostly sacks of meat, occasionally these human bodies could house surprises and, accordingly, Laura was cautious, even of this teenage girl. She was a thin girl, around 5ft 7 with strawberry blonde long hair and she approached Laura very anxiously, climbing off her bicycle and walking with it to the door. Laura stood, arms folded, staring at her (she noticed that this unnerved the girl, and she did not care as unsettling visitors made a return visit less likely) and she said abruptly, in French, "Is there something I can do for you?"

She replied, also in French, "I'm sorry to intrude, but I didn't dare ride into town. Didier said if anything happened my father was supposed to take his…er, his…things to the pub. He mentioned that you were with the group too and there were no checkpoints between us. Then I thought they might impose one with all the troubles. I thought that…eh…perhaps I could…"

"What is it?" Laura said, the girl's nerves and grief (she sensed that strongly) making her almost incoherent so Laura removed the blanket from the bicycle basket to see what she was transporting. The basket was filled to capacity with grenades, Nazi knives and small pistols plus handwritten documents; the first was a hit list and the second was a list of addresses along with several maps.

"We haven't kept anything. I know it doesn't seem much, but we haven't hung onto a thing, I swear. H…h…he went to other places. Lilian might have kept a lot of their weapons at his house and there is more under my clothes. May I come inside to…"

She was gibbering and Laura cut her off. "I assume you're talking of Didier Godet and I assume you are aware that he was executed for possessing items like these which you are trying to offload on me. You have been gravely misinformed about me because I am not involved with the Resistance in any capacity and if I take these items from you it will only be to dispose of them." Laura was unhappy about doing this but the girl was young and scared and would face possible execution if found with this small arsenal, a fate Laura could save her from. This girl was no suicidal resistance fighter, she was just a scared civilian who found herself in possession of a dead man's tools and was now terrified, and with good reason. Even though it meant personal involvement (to a small degree), Laura invited her in, escorting her to the library where she told her to hand over everything that she had.

"I wanted to throw them away too, but my mother said that the group might punish us," the girl said as she produced explosives from her person. She was a little calmer now that she knew Laura would be taking the items from her.

"Your only worry should be the Germans," Laura said, surprised by how much she had hid upon her person, much more than had been in the basket.

"Aren't you terrified too? At least I have my mother and my sister," the girl said, believing that Laura lived alone, a situation which she would find impossible under occupied conditions, anticipating rape, torture and death, yet Laura seemed imperturbable.

The girl's concern for her made Laura feel selfish momentarily for thinking of turning her away. She quickly reassured herself that she was not selfish as she had no duty towards the girl and was already doing more than her fair share by looking after the **eight** visitors encamped in her house.

GERMAINE! GERMAINE! GERMAINE!

The voice screamed so loudly in Grey's head that he felt like his brain was about to haemorrhage. He tried to mask his pain, resting his elbows on the table and placing both palms on his forehead, covering his face with his arms, but this action brought more attention to him, all looking at him quizzically bar Pearce. Pearce was already occupied, standing with his ear to the door and had mouthed to the others that the girl had entered the house.

"You can break your vow of silence and speak, Jimmy. We won't tell her and it doesn't count if you're in pain," Delgado said sympathetically. He saw it for what it was, another 'episode', and he wasn't going to let Grey suffer it silently.

"Just a migraine. I'll be fine in a minute," he said unconvincingly.

"Mighty sudden migraine. She'll have done something to him," Hartmann said, believing Laura to be capable of anything.

GERMAINE the voice repeated with urgency.

I hear you, I hear you, please don't shout. Is this a warning or are you saying a name?

Germaine is there; I can sense my little girl. Grey could hear that the disembodied voice spoke English with a French accent. *She's safe, thank God, she's safe.* Grey could hear the relief in his voice at this realisation.

Is that who's here? Your daughter?

Where's here? I want to talk to Germaine NOW!

Grey winced at this and fell forward, Delgado forcibly pushing his arms down so that he could see him. "A headache doesn't make you deaf, James. I said it's your turn." Grey looked down and saw that the others (bar Pearce, still by the door) had started to play cards.

"All right. What are we playing?" he said tiredly.

I SAID NOW!

"Sorry, I can't play," Grey said, realising it would be impossible to have his mind on two things, the spirit too forceful and he needed him more.

"Tough, we're playing doubles and you're on my team. Have a minute to look at your cards. We're playing poker," Delgado said.

Grey used the minute to pretend he was looking at his cards (anything could have been in front of his eyes and he would have been oblivious) as he tried to talk to the spirit.

I won't let her leave without talking to her, but I need to have something to say to her first. My name is James Grey. What is…

I don't care about you. I want Germaine.

She won't hear you. I'm your link to her and I'll relay any messages for you, but talk to me first. Stay calm, nobody can hurt you now.

They're all still in danger.

Who are they? Tell me about yourself.

If you insist but then you go and talk to her. Yves Cremont, 48 year old farmer with a loving wife and two fine daughters, Germaine, 14, and Carol, 12. She killed me – not long ago I think.

Who – was it your wife? It was a personal question to ask, but Grey's years of experience of talking to spirits had taught him that many fell victim to those nearest to them.

HOW DARE YOU SAY THAT! The force of the furious voice in his skull would have made him stagger were he standing and it took tremendous effort to mask the pain from his features.

"Just forfeit the game and have us four play," Winters said and Grey caught this (though he was aware that other things had been said which he had not heard) and played his cards randomly.

It was a demon – demoness, whichever.

I believe you because I know that there is a…woman of dark power around these parts. I'll go and talk to Germaine for you. Grey knew that Laura would not be pleased (and he understood her objections), but he had to see their visitor and he stood up and attempted to move Pearce.

"What the fuck you doing?" Pearce said quietly. "You open that door and she'll hear you."

"I know," Grey said, forcing him aside and closing the door behind him. The girl was visible to him, Laura ushering her out of the door, Grey only able to see her back as the door was about to close. He called her name loudly, making both women turn around sharply.

"What are you doing?" Laura said to him, enraged at his behaviour. Of all of the soldiers he had been the one she had expected to behave and now he had exposed her, standing in his US Army attire, as being a partisan.

"I have to speak to her, Laura." The voice in his skull was going mental, echoing her name again and again (though thankfully not as loudly as before).

"There she is and the damage is done, so talk," Laura said, storming out of the house. Why did she just not go back to Scotland for the duration of the war, she wondered.

The girl looked at him fearfully, biting her bottom lip as he gazed at her. "You are Germaine, aren't you?" he said, wanting to be certain.

She nodded. "But I haven't done anything wrong."

"Don't be afraid of me. I…this is going to sound mad. You should sit down for this."

"I would but I have to get back. Mother…sh…she'll get worried," she said, backing away from him slowly.

Stay, Mimi, Daddy needs you.

Grey saw that she had picked up her bicycle and he quoted her father verbatim to stop her before she cycled off. His words made an immediate impact and she dropped her bicycle and stared at him, looking for some trace of her father and quickly finding none.

"He's with me, your father Yves. I hear things in my head, spirits call out to me, and your father is with me now and is desperate to speak with you. He hasn't said much to me yet, but I can feel how much he loves you and he's frantically worried about you. Even if you think I am a lunatic, please hear me out because I think he might have an important warning for you."

Don't speak to her boy. Just say these words exactly, Yves said crankily.

"He has things that he wants to say to you and I'm just going to say them so remember that it is him speaking. Please sit down, Germaine."

Germaine re-entered the house warily and allowed Grey to lead her into the library where she sat down by the table as Grey sat near her.

If you had cycled away this oaf wouldn't have caught you. You haven't fallen off your bike since you were six when you tried to ride it around the pigsty.

As Grey relayed these words Germaine clutched her mouth in shock and took a sudden sharp intake of air.

You didn't cry even then. Such a happy child, cycling around like a blur, making me and your mother dizzy. I don't want you to cry now either.

"How can I not with you gone and gone like that. Papa, what happened to you?" she said, absolutely convinced of Grey's authenticity now. She cried inconsolably and Grey offered his hand across the table (which she accepted), Grey trying to make her feel better.

A demoness. I'm sure you think soldier-boy is fabricating here because I am not the kind of man to believe in anything fanciful like that, but that's what she was. Did you view my body?

Germaine answered by nodding tearfully, but Yves was unaware of this and asked Grey what she was doing. He was evidently able to hear her (and detect her presence), but he could not see her and Grey described her state to Yves. *She nodded – she's very upset, poor girl, but you're right to talk to her as I can see that this means a lot to her.*

I don't want your interpretations, go back to being the middleman, Yves said authoritatively, only wanting facts from Grey (who he resented, having a dislike for most foreigners and jealous of Grey for being alive while he was not) and not opinion. Grey did not mind helping him even if it was unappreciated, though he felt that Yves' attitude was unnecessary and counterproductive as other mediums could possibly be put off helping him by his aggression.

I wish you hadn't seen that. Truthfully, it didn't hurt much. She put her hand through me and all I felt was shock, not pain.

"At least…at least you're here with me now, Papa," Germaine said, clutching Grey's hand tighter, talking and looking at him as though he were her father. It made Grey uneasy, but he took a back seat, allowing Yves to converse with his daughter without making any contributions himself, simply his mouthpiece.

Not just now, always. On your wedding day, when you have children. I am going to constantly watch over you and there won't be a fiercer guardian angel out there, vetoing which men you can see to make sure you end up with a man who'll treat you like you deserve. Grey felt that Yves was making promises he couldn't keep – it was very rare for spirits to linger around for that long, but he made the speech regardless.

"They'll never match up to you."

Of course not. I know you're still scared, Germaine, but I promise you this war won't last forever. You will be free before you're a woman – I know it. Until the war ends you are going to have to help your mother run the farm and afterwards contact my good-for-nothing brother and tell him it was my dying wish that he help you out. What he's doing in Marseilles will keep for a while. Let him know that I was insistent that he helped – he won't dare refuse me, even in death, and then let him stay for three harvests. Do not let him stay in the house; he is not getting his feet under the table. The barn will do, give him free lodgings and food and he can't complain at that – your mother should be able to keep him in his place. Get through three years with him, then you should be back on your feet and you'll be able to hire help – I don't expect you to take care of all of this, tell your mother to sort it out.

"What else, Father?" Germaine asked desperately, Yves' messages drying up and already she was scared that she was losing him again.

"He's gone quiet. He hasn't gone yet, I can get him back," Grey said, sensing his presence still.

"Please do it."

"He needs time to rest – it's hard for him too. Thank you for believing me. My own parents don't believe that I have this power, and you do, so thank you for that." This was a significant event for Grey, the first time he had passed messages on from the other side, and her credence was a great relief.

"They're his words – you couldn't make them up. Was he in pain? Was he lying to make me feel better?"

"I feel you'll know more about it than me, Germaine. I'm merely the vessel; it's you who he wants to talk to. What happened to your father is extremely unusual. When you die, which will not be for many years yet, you will go straight to Heaven. Those that don't, that exist on the spirit plane, tend to be those with unfinished business; perhaps they are unable to accept their death so it is often those who died suddenly. As soon as they accept it, they can then move on to Heaven, which is where you'll see him again. What he was saying about your wedding – few spirits stay on the spirit plane that long, they come to terms with their condition pretty quickly ordinarily, but I think he means he'll be there in essence." Grey was trying to allay her fears, as he did not want her to believe that she would also become a spirit without a body.

"Can't he stay? Can't you make him stay?"

"I don't think I could if I wanted to and we have to think what's best for your dad. He seems a very strong character and I think he would want to stay with you forever, but he deserves peace after what happened to him."

"I think he could cope, you know, he is strong. If he wants to watch over us, why not? Please," she pleaded.

"I don't have the power. I hear voices and that's about all I can do. I can make them come to the fore if they're faint, and I will with your father again soon, but I can't make him stay. Why don't you think about what you want to say to him?"

"How can I say goodbye to him? What do you say?" She felt that words could never do justice to her feelings.

"I can help you there. The spirits never know either, it's common not to know how to say the final goodbye and I always tell them to keep it simple. It's not the time for any grievances – in your case I can see that's not an issue. Your case is very unique because your father can hear you – often the only voice they can hear is mine, so your father will hear the emotion in your voice, as important as the words."

Germaine took his words in, flopping her head down on the table, putting pressure on her cheek and temple as she stared into space.

"Do you wish I'd let you leave without telling you?" Grey asked, unsure if he had done her any favours, his question conveying sympathy and apology.

She tried to shake her head, the motion hardly visible as she remained with her cheek to the cold wood of the table as she tried to make sense of the impossible.

Suddenly she sprung up and said, "Please come home with me. You must talk to my mother and sister, please," she begged.

"I'm an American soldier. If I was found in your house the three of you could be killed for that and I know your father wouldn't want me endangering you like that and I don't want to do that either."

"I passed no soldiers on my way here, I didn't see anyone. We're only two miles away and it's not a populated route. What if I brought them here?"

"No, this is Laura's house. If I'm going to see them then it will have to be at your...make it in the barn, then if we do get spotted you can claim that you just found me in there and were going to turn me in."

"The barn was where...we don't like to go in there," Germaine said, her voice wavering as she thought of it.

"Sorry," Grey said, realising this was where they had found the body. "Have you any other outside buildings?"

"There is my father's tool shed. We wouldn't turn you in," she vowed solemnly.

"I know, but if we are discovered let me take the blame for it. They might just put me in a prisoner of war camp and I know that civilians aren't that lucky."

"So you will come back with me?" she said, smiling through her tears at this.

"Only if you're absolutely sure that's what you want," Grey said, still harbouring reservations about doing so, not so much for the risk he was taking (he took the same risk when he contacted the Pagan Resistance), but because of the danger he felt he was putting the Cremonts in.

"Please, Monsieur, yes."

"Wait here. I have some civvies upstairs that I can change into, then we'll go. Are you certain, Germaine?" Grey said, wanting to renege on what he had just said.

She nodded resolutely and as she seemed to be certain that she wanted this, Grey went upstairs and changed swiftly. Delgado came up as he was getting ready, demanding to know what was going on.

"If you think you're going anywhere you've got to get past me first and I want answers," Delgado said, blocking the door. "Why the hell do that? We wanted to stay concealed, Laura wanted us to remain concealed and you went against everyone's wishes. Why?"

"It's just a young girl and her father had a message for her. She's no threat. I understand if you're all mad at me, but she doesn't know that there's any other soldiers here."

"Under torture she'd say where she saw you. If you think you have a message you could have given it after the war. You should have put it in the notebook with the others," he said through gritted teeth.

"She was in the next room and her dad was desperate for her," Grey explained.

"How is she now after what you've told her? Better or worse?" Delgado said, seeing Grey's claims as potentially damaging.

"She believes me. She's very upset, but her dad only died a few days ago so that's natural. Any repercussions for this will fall on my head alone."

"This is one of the stupidest things you've ever done," Delgado said, leaving him to it. Grey could tell he was disappointed in him, but his duty lay with Yves and Germaine for now as their need was greatest at present and he would make amends to Laura, Delgado and the others later.

Grey saw Laura as he walked out across the field and she called his name (just his surname, shouted malevolently) and he told Germaine to wait for him as he went to speak to her alone.

"I thought you were going to stay silent," Laura snapped at Grey.

"I did. Yves Cremont didn't."

"Oh, he can speak of his own volition, can he? Are you just a dummy that he projects his voice through?" Laura said sarcastically.

"No." Grey thought about what she had said and replied, "Maybe that's exactly what I am. Yeah, that's a fair comparison."

"Well your show's nearly over because once you're shot by firing squad – after a couple of days of torture at the Nazis' hands – your ventriloquists won't be able to do much with you. Such idiocy! You are a bloody dummy. Why the hell do you have to go back with her?" Laura said, irate with him.

"He wants to say goodbye to both of his daughters and his wife. I have to take that risk for him. Look…if it was your John, how would you feel? Wouldn't you want to speak to him, to say goodbye?"

"You've never spoken to him and I doubt you ever will. Fine, if you want to use things I've told you in confidence against me, then just go," she said dispassionately, washing her hands of him. She didn't want him to face such risks, but she would not stand in his way.

"I wasn't saying it like that. I wouldn't. I'm not trying to be hurtful. Laura, and I am certainly not criticising him or you. I am just trying to say that when these spirits ask me to do something, it is so important to them that – providing it's possible and not immoral – I have to do it, to give them peace. These messages are so important, that's why I've got them all jotted down in my notebook"

"I understand that, but you aren't trying to return to America to give those messages at breakneck speed because you know, rationally, that you have to wait. Give his family his message when it is safe, after the war if necessary, if your side is victorious."

"He's with me now, he can talk directly to them. If I wait weeks, even days, then they won't get the chance to have a conversation with him."

"Do what you want," she said sourly, walking away from him.

Germaine led the way to her family's farm, talking quietly in case there was anyone hiding in bushes or behind trees. She kept expressing her gratitude which Grey assured her was unnecessary, but she would not desist from doing so.

"The spirits help me as much as I help them so I don't mind doing what they wish. Their knowledge has kept me alive over here," Grey said, making out it was a reciprocal arrangement, but she did not fall for this (though there was truth in it), believing this soldier to be most magnanimous. He didn't have to help her and would get nothing from it yet he still exposed himself to the risks and offered to accept the punishment if discovered.

"Is my father back yet?"

"I'll work on getting him back when we reach your farm." Sometimes Grey used spirits to get from one point to another as they could be useful in picking up nearby troops but Yves would not be useful in that role. He was too fixated on his family to help Grey effectively and more likely to be a distraction as Grey attempted to determine for himself if they were alone.

"I still don't know what to say."

"That you love him is enough. Tell him that you'll make him proud. I think your father will do a lot of the talking anyway," Grey said, feeling that the forthright Yves would control the conversation.

"Probably," she said, smiling slightly at this. "He doesn't mean it when he called you an oaf – he's like that with boys, but..."

"Don't worry about it, it's cool. I'm in the army, I get called a lot worse than that," Grey said, taking no issue with Yves' words and not requiring an explanation.

"He's only teasing," Germaine said. Grey was not entirely convinced of this, but it didn't matter as even resentful spirits still helped him and, likewise, he helped all spirits.

Germaine had Grey wait in the tool shed as she went to fetch her mother and sister. She did not attempt to explain the situation to them, merely saying that she had handed the weapons over and that someone had returned with her who needed to speak to them. Mrs Cremont was unhappy with her for bringing a stranger home and wanted to see him alone but Germaine managed to convince her that they all had to see him. Mrs Cremont, a tall woman of slim build with light brown hair tied up in a bun, stared at Grey with unconcealed hostility as he stood on her property. They had handed the weapons back, they had lost Yves – what else did this group want from them? She stood protectively in front of her youngest daughter, Carol, a sturdily built girl who looked to be the older of the two girls.

Grey exhaled deeply, feeling nervous as he began. "I know of your loss, Mrs Cremont, Carol. Yves was a good man who loved you very much."

"Don't pretend to know him!" Mrs Cremont snapped. "He didn't help any foreigners!" This man did not know her husband to venture any opinion of him. Her words seemed strange as from her accent she also sounded like a foreigner here, seemingly English, possibly Cornish?

"He's on our side, he's American," Germaine said. "Please hear him out, Mother."

Mrs Cremont listened to her daughter and stared at Grey wide-eyed, indicating that he could continue, while making her aversion obvious.

"I never knew him in life, no. I don't know if you've ever heard of mediums or spiritualists but that is what I am."

"They've lost their father. I've lost my husband and we have to try and run this farm while the Germans come and take from us. We don't need you coming here and upsetting us, putting our lives at risk," she snapped. "I'm sorry if you've nowhere else to go, but you can't stay here," she said, relenting slightly before her anger reasserted itself. "No, I'm not sorry. You aren't welcome here so leave and never mention my husband again."

"I'm not here for shelter. I'm here for Yves. He will speak through me," Grey said, attempting to contact him. It was going badly, but it had with Germaine until he had spoken her father's words. He searched for Yves, the search fruitless for several minutes, Mrs Cremont shouting at him to leave, Germaine asking her to be patient.

Keep your voice down, Claire. It's enough to wake the dead. I know my strong daughters can cope with your shouting – I'm not so sure about this fragile soldier.

Germaine smiled gleefully, aware that her father was back from Grey's words. He looked at Claire as he delivered Yves' dialogue, her face turning blank, revealing nothing.

I know that making you believe this will be hard because nothing would have convinced me. Ask me anything, anything, and my answer might help convince you.

"How dare you! Get out of here now!" Mrs Cremont said, offended at this mockery and she gave full vent to her anger, pounding Grey's head with her fists, striking down upon him. He covered his face instinctively, but made no other moves to protect himself.

The midwife told us Carol wouldn't survive the night. We didn't believe it, we took her to the doctor and he…

"You've spied on us to find out this," Mrs Cremont said, striking him harder as Germaine tried to stop her, trying in vain to hold her back.

"Mother, please, I want to hear what father has to say."

"Your father's dead! How dare you put your sister through this?" Mrs Cremont said, turning to Germaine and slapping her cheek, making her cry before she turned back to Grey and pounded him afresh.

"Please listen to me, Mrs Cremont, I only want to pass on your husband's final message for you and then I'll leave," Grey said, starting to stagger from the onslaught. Mrs Cremont tried to scratch him, finding unprotected skin at his forehead and she tried to pull his short hair. He knew he could stop her from hitting him without hurting her, but he resisted doing so, letting her revel in the (understandable) anger, hoping it would pass soon. She left the shed suddenly, leaving her two daughters with Grey who lowered his hands to his sides and looked at them both and he told Yves that he could continue.

Carol, don't be scared. You're your father's daughter, much tougher than your mother and your big sister. Until your uncle comes to stay I'm going to put you in honorary charge of the animals while your mother and sister do the crops. When your uncle does come you can still be in charge – tell him what to do, keep him right. Both of you – if any Americans or English or even your countrymen, make any offers for this farm, you turn them down flat! This will be your fortune, girls, manage this farm right and you can set yourself up for life. You'll get men who'll tell you that women can't run a farm and who'll 'volunteer' to help you if you let them have a share of the profits – do not believe them. Hire farm hands as and when required; best stay with young lads to start with as you can pay them less and…

"Make him stop, Germaine!" Carol shouted in French to her sister, unable to cope with what sounded like her father's words. It unnerved her as he was too convincing, Grey copying the inflections in Yves' voice.

"I don't want him to. We can run the farm, Papa, don't worry," Germaine promised. "Talk to him, Carol, it might be your only chance."

Before she had a chance to speak, Mrs Cremont returned with a carving knife. She stared at Grey, her eyes moist and sad as she said, "Leave. I don't know how you know what you do, but I can't handle this so just go."

"Mrs Cremont, I apologise for any distress I've caused you or your daughters," Grey said sincerely. "If you want me to leave I will."

You can't go yet, Yves protested.

I have no choice, she's got a knife. You can tell me everything that you want to say to them and I'll write it down and they will receive it after the war, I promise.

She won't use a knife on you. Go on, talk.

I think she will and that's not the only thing. I'm upsetting her too much and I have to consider her feelings as well as yours. Germaine has handled it brilliantly, but your wife and Carol need time. My presence is damaging to them.

Stay. Please stay even if you don't talk to them just so I can be near to them, he pleaded, accepting that he had no power.

"Go," she insisted, beginning to cry.

"Again, I'm sorry," Grey said contritely as he walked past them out of the shed. Germaine tried to follow, Mrs Cremont grabbing her arm, preventing her from doing so though Germaine did manage to reach the door and could see Grey walking away. He shook his head, upset at how it had gone – he hadn't soothed a family's grief, he'd added to it immeasurably.

"Papa, please don't go!" Germaine shouted, crying as her mother restrained her. It was a sad sight to Grey's eyes and he wondered if he should have let her leave without saying a thing to her, like his friends and Laura wanted. Had his actions helped anyone?

That cannot be the last memory they hold of me, Yves said sadly.

It isn't. Only Germaine fully believed. Your wife and Carol will think of me as a madman. I'm sorry, Yves, I was inconsiderate.

I don't blame you, Grey, I pushed you into it. How could she not believe it was me?

For some it's too incredible to believe even if they're given details which no one else could know. Don't despair, Yves, the situation is still raw. After the war I can approach them to try again – if they reject my approach then I will just have to back off.

Will that be too late for me? Already I can't hear you as well as I could, you're all getting fainter.

Tell me everything you want to say and I'll write it down. I have a notebook, which I use for this.

Thank you. That's an expression I've never been good at saying if you can't tell, especially not to foreigners. The voice was different now, melancholic and kinder, but Grey was not surprised, as he had learnt long ago through his gift that most people had many different sides to them.

No problem, Yves, no problem at all. As soon as I get back we'll get straight on with it.

Grey lived up to his word and went straight up to his room and filled seven pages with messages from Yves to his family, individual messages for all three as Yves found his way to the root of his feelings and he did not mention the farm once. He had obsessed enough about that in life and he wanted his family to know that they were what was important to him. Being the proud owner of the best maintained farm in France was not his legacy – Germaine and Carol were that. His message to his wife revealed that she was English and that they met during the Great War when she had been a field nurse and he took great pride in persuading her to break one of the fundamental rules of her training, luring her away from her vocation. Grey even managed to persuade him to soften towards his brother and there was a short message for him too, part reprimand, but mostly a way of saying goodbye and making peace. His voice petered out and he was gone just as Delgado entered the room. With Yves gone Grey could return his attention to his friends and he said, "You were right in what you were thinking before. I did more damage than good."

"More messages?" Delgado said disapprovingly, noticing the notebook.

"Yep, a long one too. I want to say to you and the others and Laura – I am a fuckup. I should have listened to you. I made the wrong decision."

"So you're saying you won't do the same again?" Delgado said, prepared to let it go if he'd learnt his lesson.

"After the war I'll pass on the messages, but the families don't need to know that the words were passed on after death. The absolute truth will scare them too much I reckon."

"What happened to your face?" Delgado said as he looked at him more closely, several scratches visible on his forehead as well as a huge lump above his right eye.

"I upset a grieving woman – it could have and maybe should have been a lot worse. My approach was appalling," Grey said, berating his technique.

"Hold still, those cuts are bleeding," Delgado said, returning with a wet flannel and he proceeded to mop him up. "If it had been me and you'd been telling me you'd talked to my dead relative – I can understand her reaction, Jimmy."

"I can too. Have you seen Laura since I've been out?"

"Yes. Basically, your name is shit here with everyone, especially with her. I could square it with the others for you – bar Pearce, but that's no great loss. You'll have to talk to Laura yourself – again, that's no great loss either."

"She's harboured us when others wouldn't. I'll go and see her now if we're cool?"

"Go on. My guess is you'll take longer to clean up once she's through with you," Delgado said and Grey was unsure if it was a joke. He passed Winters and Strapulos as he looked for Laura, who made disapproving comments about his wandering which he accepted, telling them that he knew he'd messed up.

"Other people's lives are at risk here, Grey. You keep going off and having these little adventures without giving a thought to us. That's bad enough, but you're the one who tells us to respect Laura and you're the one who is putting her life at risk," Strapulos said. They had talked about Grey as a group and had come to negative conclusions about him in his absence and even the easygoing members of the group had been convinced by Pearce's diatribe and risen to anger. Grey had led them to the witch and had some form of relationship with her, which he kept secret from them. He also kept the details of his excursions secret, but expressly forbade them from wandering off, different rules applying for him. Pearce felt that there was no reason for Grey to keep these matters private and had convinced the others that he was involved in something sinister and while Delgado shook his head at this, he was not vocal in his objections, too wound up himself by Grey to defend him.

Grey apologised (not that it had any effect) and continued to search for Laura. He found her in the basement with the weapons and documents Germaine had given her, which she was examining closely.

"Still alive I see, though clearly the message was unwelcome," Laura said coolly, "The Germans will mark you worse than that. Inge could likely cause those marks just by blowing on you."

"Sorry. I thought I was doing the right thing."

"Who's to say you weren't? Right and wrong are not the issue here. It is more a case of safe and dangerous behaviour and your actions were dangerous. To pass on a dead man's message you were willing to risk becoming a dead man, as well as risking his family, your men and me."

"No. I would never endanger anyone else's welfare. How…how is this different to me going to the tavern?" She seemed prepared to tolerate him going to help the Pagan Resistance (provided he did not oppose Inge), but she appeared very disappointed by his actions today.

"I know of them through Georges and, while I do not trust them as I did him, at least I know who they are. You presented yourself to that girl without a clue as to who she was or her allegiances."

"Through her father I knew," he protested. If he had held any doubt as to the girl's motivations he would not have risked them and he wanted Laura to know this.

"No, you trusted instinct over facts." She was aloof with him and turned away from him and looked at the maps.

"I wonder where that's meant to be," Grey said, looking over her shoulder at the map. "I did nothing when they shot Didier and his friends. There was nothing I could do…"

"I'm surprised you didn't dive in front of the bullets," she interrupted, poking fun at his suicidal notion of helping others recklessly.

"I wasn't tempted to do that, trust me," Grey said, having felt enormous fear as the soldiers had pointed their weapons at the men. "His child will have no father now. Poor Mireille is devastated while I – the guy who Georges thought could lead the Resistance – just stood idly by as they were shot. When Yves – the spirit – asked me for help I was pleased because it was something I could do. Only it was a bad move that upset everyone." He was unsure if his failure to help the Communists had influenced his decision (he likely would have spoken to Germaine anyhow), but he felt that it might have been a subconscious factor and presenting it in this way made it more palatable to Laura.

"Their deaths are not on your conscience. Never mind, it's done," she said, forgiving him. It was in his nature to help and while it riled her in this instance, it was not a detestable trait. "Though I will be locking you in the hidden room if you keep it up," she said mock angrily.

"I'll go back to being a farm hand instead of a bad medium," he said smoothly, relaxed again now that he knew he was forgiven.

"You're not a bad medium. Not everyone will want to know and trying to convince those with closed minds is a waste of time and a very boring task," she said, speaking from experience. Grey sat next to her and they rooted through the items together, Grey coming to the hit list.

"Do you think this is contact names from the organisation?" he asked.

She shook her head. "No, it's a list of those that the group want dead. The ones that are underlined are to be tortured before death," Laura said. Nearly every name was underlined on the long list, which had a majority of feminine sounding names.

"It's bad enough to kill someone, but to torture someone to death?" Grey said disapprovingly.

"Don't blame me, it's not my list."

"No, I wasn't. I just...why oppose the Nazis if you want to act like them?" he said, failing to understand their mentality. "These names sound more French than German."

"They are. This is a list of collaborators. Some of these girls have probably just slept with Germans – perhaps they're in love with a German," Laura said non-judgementally.

"I don't mind handing the weapons over to Mireille, but not this list," Grey said.

"Why don't I just lock you in the room now?" Laura said, raising her voice fractionally, feeling he never learnt. "I'm destroying everything and I will not discuss the matter. The girl gave them to me to destroy and that's what I'm doing." Grey saw that she was not to be argued with (and doubt crept into his mind as he thought of the weapons being used on harmless civilians, wrongly considered enemies) and he said,

"Can I help you with that?"

"No. I think we'll probably argue if we spend too much time together today so you go away and I'll see you for your lesson tonight," she said. Grey was glad that they were still speaking and did not push it.

Somehow Delgado managed to pacify the other men (bar one) and Grey was forgiven though the incident would clearly not be soon forgotten. A visit the next morning from Germaine did not help, especially when Laura insisted the soldiers and Konah had to hide in the cellar (though thankfully not in the secret room) whilst allowing Grey to stay to see the visitor. Germaine already knew that Grey was there so there was nothing to gain from concealing him from her and Laura expected that she would want to speak with him. She answered the door and Germaine asked for the American soldier, having forgotten his name in all of the drama. Laura invited her in and left Grey with her in the kitchen while she went about her chores. They sat around the table, Grey asking her if she wanted anything to eat and drink, Germaine politely refusing. She asked tentatively, "Is Papa still with you?"

Grey shook his head sadly. "I'm sorry, no. That means he's at peace now, Germaine."

"Good," she said, wiping her eyes, stopping herself from crying, "I didn't think he would be after yesterday." She was unable to hide her disappointment.

"I blame myself for that. I handled it poorly. How are your mother and your sister?"

"In denial. Mama knows it was him, but she won't accept it. She doesn't know I'm here. I had to come though. Carol's scared by it all – I don't think she heard enough to convince her."

"Perhaps you should convince them that I was lying. I've heard these voices since I was a child and my own parents wouldn't believe it – I was sent to an asylum for three months when I was nine," he revealed openly, exposing himself to try and help her and her family. "I pretended that the voices stopped because that was easier for my parents than the truth. You know the truth and I hope that grants you some peace, Germaine, I hope that I haven't wronged you, but I think it's in their best interests to believe me a liar. The truth hurt them too much."

Yves dominated Germaine's thoughts and she ignored his advice and said, "What did he say? Please tell me everything."

"He left messages for you all – I vowed I'd pass them on, but I don't feel that I can, not to your mother and sister. I'd feel like I was hounding them," he said guiltily. He was reneging on his word to Yves but Yves was at peace now whilst his family had already been troubled enough by Grey.

"I'll pass them on, you don't have to. I'm so sorry about my mother. She is not violent."

"I know. Her reaction was automatic, not conscious, and I owe her the apology. I took the messages from your father to give him peace of mind – I had no real intention of passing them on to any of you. I could have maybe talked to his brother because I could have made out he gave me the message when he was still alive so as not to unsettle him."

"He left a message for Tristan? Papa…they weren't close," she said, stopping herself from saying that her father hated his brother (though she believed this to be the case).

"It's not as affectionate as the messages for you three. Seems as you are here – do you want to see the message he left for you?" he said hesitantly. It was another judgement call and he was unsure if this was the right thing to do.

"Yes! Did you write it down?"

"It's his exact words. He wanted to do it in French. He wanted to talk to you in French too, but I'm afraid I couldn't do that. He wanted me to copy the sounds, but I couldn't do it," he said apologetically. She didn't care about the apology, just wanting to read her father's final message for her and her eager eyes bored into Grey and he got the hint and fetched the thick notebook downstairs. She was crying silently when he returned, with a wide grin on her features, longing to see what her father had in store for her. Grey turned to the two pages just for her, a declaration of her father's feelings for her from her birth up to now. She read quietly and reread it when she was done, turning the page in the vain hope that there was more.

"That's for Carol," Grey said. She said nothing and kept on reading, Grey allowing her to read Yves' parting words for the whole family.

"He did let up on Tristan a bit," she croaked, her voice affected by her tears and strong emotion.

"He was his brother."

"Tristan wasn't a good brother. We used to have a farm in the South of France – my grandparents that is – and while my father fought the Germans, Tristan went to North Africa and behaved like a roué. Papa was doing his duty to his country, but his parents were too old to run a farm themselves and it was ruined. That farm was much bigger than the one we live on now and Papa never forgave

Tristan for losing us that." She did not sound personally angry with her uncle, but she sought to justify her father's enmity.

"In the end I think he did. I think Tristan was such a big disappointment to him because he loved him so much, that was why he expected more from him."

Germaine noticed that the messages from her father were near the end of the notebook and she asked, "Is this full of messages from the dead? This is not your diary?"

"It's not a diary, no. The spirits have far more interesting things to say then I," Grey replied, though the truth was that his life had become most interesting of late but he downplayed this self-deprecatingly.

Germaine would not dare to read someone's personal diary, but as this was not his diary she turned to the front and began reading. Grey did not like this and he stared at her, his expression unguarded and showing his displeasure as he said, "The rest of it is private, Germaine." These dead men's messages were not to be read or known by anyone other than the people they were intended for and were certainly not for a child's prying eyes.

"I won't tell anyone," she said, too transfixed by his journal to look up at him. She compared her father's message to the messages these soldiers had given their loved ones and she was crying by the third page as she learnt of children being orphaned, of young widowed brides along with soldiers little older than her saying goodbye to their parents.

"How would you feel if someone else read the message your father left you? Pass it to me," he said gently, no longer annoyed as he saw how affected she was by the words (which touched him but never made him cry).

She ignored his order, wanting to know every story, needing to read every word. He was not prepared to prise it from her and instead watched her reactions. He could read his writing upside down and he noticed that the tales of fathers felled in war especially got to her, regardless of which side they had fought on. It took her a long time to finish, at which point she turned back to the messages her father had left and she said, "You've passed this message on now. Can I take it out of your notebook?"

Grey nodded and said, "But don't show it to your mother and sister." She ripped it out carefully and handed him his notebook back at long last. She wiped her eyes, which were very moist, and she sighed repeatedly, only just able to talk.

"You're right, those messages were private," she said, feeling like she had peered into their very souls. "I meant no disrespect."

"I know. Sorry if I sounded crotchety about it."

"It's your book. Curiosity got the better of me. There's so many. Is there always someone in your head with you?" she said, fascinated as to how his gift worked.

"No. I think there could be if I worked at it. Since the war started it has been a lot busier in there because of the increase in sudden deaths. I shouldn't be telling you this, you should be at home playing games." She was a child, ill equipped to deal with what he was telling her (though she was the one who was enquiring into it).

"We have been occupied for four years by the Nazis. My childhood ended a long time ago. I should be at home helping, but I want to know more about this first," she said resolutely. She knew that she was not tough, but she still wanted to know every facet of this spirit world, disturbing as it was.

"Germaine, you have your father's message. He loved you and he's at peace now. Why probe further?" Grey said. Laura and Georges had helped him realise that the occult was not necessarily bad, but he still felt it was unsuitable for a girl of 14 to research. For Konah, who was younger than Germaine, it was different as it was relevant to him as he had the gift and Grey wished that he had had some mentors around him when he had been growing up to tell him that his abilities did not make him bad.

She shrugged, looking for an answer. "Because I'll never have this chance again and I'll wonder. My mama won't let me leave the house after this and you won't be staying here forever. Please," she implored, reaching across the table for his hand.

Against his better judgement he relented, pulling his hand away and scratching the back of his neck as he said, "It's never scary. Some of them banter with me, and hold different opinions to me, but they're always helpful."

"How did it start?"

Germaine wanted the full story and he more or less gave it to her. He told her of Lanfred Hearnus and how he had helped him find peace and mistakenly believed that his release would be the end of it before the multitude of voices began. She wanted to know of every spirit and Grey had to rack his brain to think (he could remember most of them, but she wanted them sequentially), reminding himself of them in the process, intentionally omitting several. Laura came in to see if the girl was ready to leave (she had been there for nearly two hours and the men were, understandably, getting impatient) and she heard Grey talking of the legion of spirits that had visited his head and she took a seat, interested in this topic herself and he hadn't talked of every spirit he'd ever known with her. Grey looked at her, unsure if she was trying to hint that she wanted the girl to leave and she said,

"Continue. Tall tales have always interested me." She pretended not to believe because of Germaine's presence and Grey understood this and continued.

He told of his contacts with spirits up to the present day but edited his life story carefully so as to not mention the Pagan Resistance or the details of how he had come to stay at Laura's. When he was finished Germaine said, "How can I learn to do what you do?"

"I don't think it's something you can learn and if it is, it's not something I can teach. These spirits can never harm you, they can never contact you directly, so don't have nightmares," Grey said reassuringly.

"I think you're lucky," Germaine said, envying him his gift. "Thank you for telling me all of that," she said gratefully.

"You were right, you are mature enough to know." He thought of telling her that, when she was older, there were ways for her to enter into the occult, but he resisted. That would not be what Yves would want and probably not the best option for Germaine.

"Incidentally, I have some books by Hans Christian Andersen and the Brothers Grimm that you might like to borrow if you enjoyed those stories," Laura said to Germaine.

"It's real, you know," Germaine said seriously. She sensed that Grey was used to disbelief and mockery, reading between the lines of his life story, more sadness than he realised seeping out, and she stuck up for him.

Grey was not offended, aware that Laura was pretending not to believe him merely to preserve her own secrets and he said, "Remember what we said about your mother and sister. If people don't want to believe then it's best not to try and convince them."

"Well, I believe you, James," she said kindly. "Whatever happens to me I promise that I will never tell on either of you," she said to them both.

"Thank you," Grey said, holding her to her word. If there were only himself to consider he would advise her to tell on him if she were in danger but with Laura and the others welfare at stake he needed her vow to be binding.

"I doubt that you will have any more trouble," Laura said supportively to her. "I destroyed all of those things you brought me. If you stay on your farm you should be fine."

"I hope so," Germaine said and she stood up, aware that it was time she left.

Grey walked with her to the door and said, "I know things still look bleak with the Jerries regaining territory, and the awful loss that you've suffered, but things will get better, Germaine. After the war I don't mind coming back and working on your farm for one harvest if that helps you," he said generously. He would attempt to fix things with her mother and sister by claiming the war had driven him temporarily mad. He wanted to do this as an attempt to rectify things with Yves and his family (though he had no intentions of doing so for long as he had important messages to deliver). His motivations were not entirely selfless as he made the offer largely because of his feelings for Laura. Helping the Cremonts keep their farm running was a goal of his and it would mean that he could remain close to Laura without crowding her and even if she moved back to Scotland he could offer to be her caretaker in her absence and score brownie points and keep the connection.

"It would definitely help. Papa might think that Tristan will do as he's told, but I don't. I'll make sure my mother doesn't act like a psychopath again."

"She didn't," Grey said, shaking his head, having no problems with her mother.

"She did, but that wasn't her. You won't have to sleep in the barn either."

"The barn will be fine, the last few months I've stayed at worse so a barn sounds great!" he said jovially. "Take care, Germaine."

"You too, James," she said, hugging him tightly on the doorstep, Grey reciprocating.

"The rakish James Grey acquires another admirer!" Laura said teasingly as Grey returned to the kitchen.

"She's a child," Grey said dismissively. He had turned down a naked, fully-grown woman because of his love for Laura, so a 14 year old girl (off limits anyway) stood no chance of enticing him. "She's grieving her father, that's all that was about."

"She was very quick to defend you and is very pretty. You could do worse, James," she said, quick to palm him off on someone else again.

"It would be unethical," he said, shaking his head at the idea.

"She's 14 and you're 18. What's wrong with that?" Laura said, seeing no problem with such a union.

"She's too young."

"A four year gap is nothing. Still, it's your affair," she said, still teasing him. "You must think something of her to tell her so much of your life. I'm jealous, James, you hadn't told me all of that."

"I've told you much more than I told her," Grey said, hurt at the joke as he'd revealed so much more of himself to Laura. "One thing I did tell her, which I've never told you because I never wanted you to know, was about my stay in an asylum. I only told her that I stayed there for three months when I was nine. I care more about you than her so I'll tell you more about it. My parents put me there to fix their lunatic child and it worked because after that I never mentioned about the voices in my head. Those voices were the only things that kept me sane during my stay in there. The other patients were adults – those poor souls were unhinged and terrified me. I had shock therapy, mild experimental surgery – my parents changed their mind about a lobotomy as I was being prepared for the operation. Some of the staff beat me, which I'm not complaining about because I heard far worse things happen to the female patients. It's long ago, Laura, and I'm over it now, I'm not bitter because life's too short," he said, smiling though he had been morose as he relayed the story of his time inside.

"I'm sorry," Laura said.

"I wasn't telling you that to try and make you feel sorry for me. It could have been a lot worse. I'd better make it clear that the lobotomy was cancelled in case you're wondering," he added, poking fun at himself. "My point is that you know me better than she does, probably better than anyone, and you deserve to know more about me more than she does."

"I was only jesting. You didn't have to tell me that. I can understand that you would want to keep that secret."

"I do and I have up until now. A few other people know that I was institutionalised, but no one knows about what they did to me in there."

"I can be a little cruel – I think you'll attest to that, but that won't end up as a taunt or witty put-down," Laura said earnestly.

"I know that. Where's Isdel and the others? Are they still in the cellar?"

"Yes, and they might also give you a hard time," she warned, feeling that it was unwarranted.

"They have been down there a long time while I've been up here. How long has it been?"

"Over three hours. You don't have to explain yourself to them. Just go in the library if you want and I'll deal with them," she offered.

"No, I should see them, but thank you," he said, appreciative of the gesture.

"What the hell have you been doing all that time?" Pearce demanded to know as they assembled in Winters' and Hartmann's bedroom, all bar Winters who had chronic diarrhoea which he had somehow repressed up to now and was now attached to the bowl.

"Just talking. It was the same girl from yesterday. She won't be back," Grey promised.

"Will the SS be coming instead?" Strapulos said.

"Not because of her, no," Grey replied, certain that she would stick to her promise. Germaine understood how important it was that he delivered those messages and Grey felt she would endure personal suffering rather than betray him.

"I think we should all teach him a lesson," Pearce said to nods from Strapulos and (to Grey's surprise) Hill and Delgado. Hartmann was staying out of it, sitting quietly on his bed with Konah.

"If you want I'll stay down there for the same amount of time, all day if that's what you want," Grey said, trying to appease them.

"At least you'd still know what was going on. We didn't know," Strapulos said angrily. "It feels like you're not in our unit."

"I reckon we should ask for him not to be if we ever get back," Pearce said.

"No, him spending the next couple of hours in the cellar should do," Delgado said. Grey had acted up (again) but Delgado knew that expulsion from the unit would hurt him too much (though might be enough to actually teach him a lesson).

"A good kicking wouldn't do him any harm either," Pearce added.

"He kicked your ass last time. Come on, we had to be in the cellar for hours so that should be what he has to do," Delgado said, appealing to the others.

"Why couldn't we be upstairs? Why did we have to miss out again?" Hill asked Grey, hurt by this.

Grey was unable to provide a satisfactory explanation and said, "Take your best shots." It seemed easier just to let them hit him then to try to explain what had happened. Pearce took him at his word and swung his arm back, Delgado preventing him from connecting by charging him and sending him crashing onto Winters' bed.

"Beating him up isn't going to solve this, Pearce," Strapulos said, walking out of the room.

"This is Grey's business. Why don't we just stay out of it?" Hartmann suggested. He knew (as they all did) that Grey was involved in something underhanded, which he was trying to keep them out of. Hartmann wanted to be kept out of it and didn't understand why the others were so angry.

"Come on, Harty," Pearce said, brushing himself down where Delgado had touched him, Delgado backing off and standing by Grey, "This fucking cocksucker's gambling with all our lives and he won't tell us why. I'll tell the brass what you've been up to, don't worry," Pearce said, threatening Grey.

"What do you think brass will do when I tell them what you tried to do to Laura?" Delgado said, negating that threat.

"They don't believe greasers," Pearce spat out.

"I apologise completely to everyone bar Pearce – you're vermin," Grey said with disgust.

"Well done, Pearce. I was pissed off with him before but you've restored my anger back to its rightful target," Delgado said, his voice guttural as he contained himself.

"Yeah, your spick parents for bringing your spick ass into this world," Pearce responded. Grey had to hold Delgado in place now, restraining his arms as he tried to advance on an unfazed Pearce who laughed at him.

"Don't blame me," Hartmann said. "Don't mention me to brass."

"No one is going to get reported to anyone," Grey said. "They'd never believe it all."

Grey delved into Laura's thin record collection and put a record on during their usual private time at night and asked her to dance with him. Laura refused and he applied some pressure.

"Take pity on me. I need the practice real bad. You're already my teacher in many things so this may as well be one more," he said with a modicum of charm, enough to make her reluctantly get out of her seat. She knew he had endured a hard day (much of it self-inflicted) and she indulged him again. Somebody had to spoil him and his parents had fucked him over almost as bad as her mother had her. She now understood why Grey's father threw out his pulp collection, fearful that such outlandish tales could lead him off the straight and narrow. She was pleased to see that his confidence was growing and he led adequately, capable of slow dancing though anything complex or quick was beyond him, with a few moves going awry.

"You're doing well," she commented, avoiding his eyes for the most part as they danced as he largely focused on her.

"A good partner hides many cracks."

"I'm not a good partner," Laura admitted, chuckling lightly as she knew her limitations. She could dance magnificently, but not like this. Traditional dancing was too stifling.

"What exactly is the Danse Macabre?" Grey asked, figuring she'd know.

"Dancing with women like me probably covers that."

"Wanna show me?"

Laura's expression creased up as she quickly dismissed the idea. "Best stick to this. You'll find more use for this kind of dancing."

Grey tried quickening the pace and soon they were making so many missteps that the pair of them began laughing and Grey misjudged the signals and leaned in for a kiss. The kiss was brief as Laura quickly pulled away from him and sat down leaving him standing crestfallen.

"I'll take that as a compliment, James, but I don't know how you've misread the signals so. I've always made it plain that I'm only offering friendship…"

"Which I appreciate. I admit I would like more, but I shouldn't have done that. It was the moment. I erred. Dance with me some more, I promise I won't repeat that," he vowed solemnly, a little regretful.

"I can't risk getting slobbered over again."

"I won't break the rules again. I'll let you steal the next kiss."

Laura looked across at him dubiously and Grey smiled and said, "Or not." He held out his hand and said, "One more dance."

Laura stood up and took her position, and as they entwined hands and began again she said, "This is our last dance because it makes you too frisky. Unless I can get my hands on some bromide."

"It'd take more than that. I didn't mean anything by it. No, I did, I mean – you don't want to go over this."

"Concentrate on the steps. Neither of us are good at this so practice for when you can dance with a girl who is right for you." His ardour grew more fervent, while she liked him more and more, though the kiss had not awakened anything, no spark present. She had not allowed there to be, pulling away as soon as his lips locked on hers. The fault was hers for agreeing to the dance initially. Slow dancing, their bodies entwined with his arm wrapped around her waist, hers around his shoulder – this was not intended for platonic friends but for lovers and she should have taken the hard-line stance and ignored the puppy dog eyes. He apologised several more times that evening, enough to redeem himself for the faux pas and she didn't hold it against him. She knew that to certain men she was irresistible.

After learning what had happened to Yves Cremont coupled with his dejection at what had happened to Didier and his group, Grey consciously tried to communicate with the dead, those left destroyed in Inge's wake. He found this hard as he was trying to select the spirits that visited him, a process that was tremendously hard compared to talking to the random voices that frequented his skull. He needed peace and quiet for this and he waited till all were in bed and he sat at the kitchen table and concentrated. He had no luck the first night though he did encounter some interesting people. The next night the voice of an upper class Englishwoman came to him effortlessly.

My woe is absolute, undiminished even after so much time. I am bereft. I lost my husband and life and both to the same woman of whom I believe you require information. Your summons beckoned me.

Grey was surprised as he had not even begun to try hard that evening and he replied, *Forgive me for the intrusion. You have had dealings with Inge?*

To my eternal regret, yes. William and I were happy. He was an admiral and…

When? Sorry to interrupt.

William and I were wed in 1840. She came on the scene six years later. His previous mistresses had been discreet and I could tolerate that, but Inge was brazen and attended functions with him, she met William's friends and some of mine. I had grown used to being supplanted in the bedroom, but she wanted to take over many of the other better aspects of wifely duties. I was disgraced.

Sometimes people can destroy others through insensitivity. I can feel your sadness and I'm sure your husband would have acted differently if he had…

No, he wouldn't. Inge was not merely a receptacle for his lust. He loved her and she commanded his attention. I was nothing to him; I was merely a reminder of an earlier folly.

I'm sorry.

Why? You haven't experienced heartbreak yet, your voice is too balanced. If you take up the cross of love beware. Your name is?

Grey. James Grey.

I am Aveline, James. Aveline the abandoned. You're not English, are you?

American, but I regard the English as cousins. Nowadays we do, our nations are friendly.

I'm glad that everything is so cordial in your age. How is this possible? Has that viper Inge gone to darkest Africa?

Sadly, no. She's in France, as am I, and me and my friends are opposing her plans of conquest. I know something of her past, and I would like to find out more.

Have you met her?

Not yet, no.

Control yourself when you do. She bewitches men, makes them love her and that'll be the ruin of you. She'll have led William to ruin, mark my words.

She has committed cruel acts which would make it impossible for me to love her.

I like your words. Make sure you live up to them. I tried to beat her too. I let the affair continue for two years, even letting my husband ship me to my father's house when he wanted Inge to visit our home. I spoke with her; I went to her sordid boudoir and demanded that she leave William alone. She laughed at me and removed her clothes – she is a continental – and she denigrated me. That William wanted such a jade sickened me, but I would not give up on him. I enlisted my father's help and he sought out a man of low breeding, a criminal who specialised in eliminating such as Inge by offering bribes and dispensing violence when necessary to persuade drabs and undesirables to move on. His body was found in a street near her home and because he had been beaten to death I didn't suspect her – the underclass often provoke trouble and have more enemies than the reputable. Inge dared to visit me at my home while William was on manoeuvres and I protested at her intrusion and she began pounding me, beating and throwing me around every room of my house and telling me that my husband was hers now. Death has never scared me, James, but the knowledge that she took my place and had William and my home to herself – I refuse to rest until she has paid.

How do you know she hasn't?

You have told me that the slattern is still breathing and even if you had not, I would know intuitively if anything had happened. I've talked to many mediums over the years and you aren't the only ones with fine senses.

You can't let this hate dominate your thoughts. Surely tranquillity appeals more?

Tranquillity can wait. Vengeance can not. I'm vaguely aware that William died, but he is not my concern anymore. She is and will be until she is decimated. Her body is rigid so I would suggest heavy weaponry, possibly cannons.

I oppose her, but I do not intend to kill her unless it's absolutely necessary.

Go after her with that attitude and you may as well drink poison now, James, because let me assure you it is vitally important that you kill her. She will kill again if you do not and you will be to blame and I can tell that you don't want that on your conscience.

Grey promised nothing of the sort as he had not determined to kill Inge yet and would not make such a decision lightly. Instead he said, *I will keep you informed, Aveline. If you tell me more of your life I will try to research what happened to William.*

William died and knowing that is enough. I grieve for my marriage, not for my husband. I am elusive, you will not contact me again, but I will know whether you win or lose. Good luck, James Grey, and heed these words – reserve your mercy for the deserving.

Shortly after Aveline's departure Grey managed to trace another past adversary of Inge with only a little more effort.

How do, guv'nor. You want my 'elp? a cockney female asked chirpily, her cheerful voice a complete contrast to Aveline.

Yep, if you don't mind. I'm James Grey and I need to know everything that you can tell me concerning Inge if you know her.

Yeah, I know 'er. Well, knew of 'er and met 'er at the end. I was a lady of the night, Jim, and I always swore down that I knew the face of the man who'd kill me when my time was up. I 'ad a vision of 'im every night, I always swore that I'd never go with a man like that and then she comes and makes a liar of me. I always 'ad to be different to the crowd so it figures I get killed by a doxy, a bloody supernatural one too!

You sound very…well-balanced considering what befell you.

Old news, darlin'. Death came with the job. 'Alf of the time they'd blurt then whack you over the 'ead or throttle you. I've got thick skin or I 'ad before I became this spirit. My body is used up and I like this, I feel free.

You could truly be free. I could help release your spirit from being trapped in this state.

What, to send me to 'eaven or 'ell. Some of us like being in the middle, love. Sometimes when you free people you're really 'arming them. Once you've got a few more years under your belt you'll see what I mean. I'm Long Lou, how'd you do?

I'm well thanks.

They're my old business lines, Jim, not an invitation. I'm out of business now.

Lou…

Long Lou. I had legs to make an 'orse proud – only two mind, but what the gentlemen loved I only 'ad one of. Once a group of gentlemen paid for me to 'entertain' an 'orse. I'll bet that's shocked you, Jim. She enjoyed telling him this, Grey hearing the relish with which she spoke.

I try to never judge anyone, not even the men who paid you to do this – it must have been dangerous – act.

There's ways of fitting things in. You sound like a sweet kid; I'd 'ave taught you a few things for free.

I'm at war at the moment, Long Lou. Anything like that has to wait till later.

Normally war means we're rolling in it. Soldiers like a bit of the old in out.

I hear legions of the dead in my head. You're cheerful and I'm glad, but most of them are heartbroken and I have to try and console them and promise them their families will be safe when for all I know they won't be or their children might already be dead in the camps. Not a turn on.

Turn on? Oh, I see what you mean. Sorry, what was it you wanted to know about Inge? She is obsessed with sex so why…what do you want to know, love? she asked, unsure of what he wanted to know and unsure how she could help, but keen and willing.

My friends and a woman I care about are in danger because of her. What do you know about her?

She's a legend. They said she was old and had doctors make 'er look young and some even said she was ancient, 'undreds of years old. I laughed 'eartily at that one, but the joke was on me in the end. Us prostitutes used to know 'er because all of our men used to talk of 'er, wanting us to look like 'er, act like 'er. Only the toffs that is, our neighbours and friends 'ad never 'eard of 'er. She 'ad blonde hair, little thing next to me, and she 'eld parties – I was never invited, but others were in London where things 'appened that I won't repeat.

Please do, it might help. I might blush, but at least you won't see it, Grey said warmly, trying to persuade her to share everything no matter how crude or trivial.

Inge danced for the men – she had many friends of the gentry and after she teased them she 'ad the girls finish them off. Inge was quick to point out that she was no prostitute, but she was as good as. At least I've always admitted what I am and if the world don't like it it can kiss my pale white arse. The guests would pay Inge lots of bees for these parties, but during the orgy she normally took 'er Lord to her private room. 'Er Lord was a bit of a bastard but 'e paid well and 'e liked me – they all did back then. Inge 'eard about it and came round to my lodgings asking me if I wanted to come to one of her parties and asking me about 'er Lord. She was trying to stay calm, but I could see she was spitting mad, but I couldn't take 'er seriously. Don't get me wrong, I'm not fearless. My pimp made me lose three babies with 'is beatings and the third one was brought on by a glare 'e gave me 'cause 'e terrified me, but Inge? No. She wanted to be a toff, but she was a whore, she was mixed up and I told 'er I'd come, but only if I got to fuck 'er Lord. Wicked thing to say I know, but life's too short to mince your words and it amused me. 'Er punch didn't. She punched me in the chest and I reckon she ripped my 'eart out. The party would have been boring anyway…

"Please, sir. Please don't have me shot. I'll do anything. I know I'm just an idiotic French peasant girl, but please, sir," she said, unbuttoning her striped blouse, taken, like the rest of her outfit, from a French girl who had been shot.

More games. The war, the occupation, the Reich – these things obsessed Klaus Von Strauss. He had turned his back on his (once substantial) faith because it was not part of the Nazi doctrine. Even before the war most of his time had been given to the party as well as his funds – he was born wealthy and had become poorer through his involvement with the party prior to the war. He could exchange formal pleasantries with anyone and his job often required that, but he only made friends with other Nazi officers or ministers. His rise had been gradual and he was glad of this, happy to prove himself at every step of the way. How he handled his affairs now was crucial and he knew it, welcoming the pressure. The Allies were near and Strauss knew that another advance could be imminent. The French, who he governed, also knew how close the Allies were, making the likelihood of an uprising greater. He knew that there were resistance groups out there and that they would strike again, his brain constantly assessing the situation and prudently considering all of his options. His superiors did not tolerate failure and Strauss would not either as it conflicted with his big plans, his destiny. He would not die like his father who might well have been a successful businessman but was also a vapid and corpulent individual. True greatness did not lie in money, it lay in power and the respect of one's peers and Strauss' stock was rising all of the time.

He had given of himself to the Reich, changing his personality when required, but he had one thing for himself that had nothing to do with Nazism. Inge was the one separate thing in his life, a dalliance that most of his friends and senior officers had supported in the initial stages of the romance, with crude (and sometimes heartfelt) encouragement. As it became more than just a fling the encouragement ceased and Strauss became aware that Inge was not considered suitable as his permanent partner. The disapproval was largely kept tacit, only his closest friends voicing their concerns. He was not prohibited from having her (it would have been a very difficult dilemma for him if a ban had been imposed), but it was made clear that he could not show her off at the homes of respectable people. This arrangement worked well as the tame dinner parties with the boring and invariably plain wives had bored Inge and she preferred going to the more risqué events and mingling with the officers' mistresses. Because all of Strauss' friends were friendly to her when they met at exclusive nightclubs and at occult parties (strangely most of Strauss' friends were more interested in this scene than he), she had no idea that she was considered persona non grata.

"Get on the bed and take all of your clothes off," Strauss commanded, Inge doing as she was told. Even though she was supposed to be playing a frightened prisoner, she could not resist making her strip provocative for him, smiling inappropriately as she did so, though Strauss only acknowledged this by looking even sterner. She sat on the bed clutching her knees to her body, covering her breasts and deliberately fully exposing her vagina to his eyes. He walked over to her slowly, taking his time as he examined her, his gloved hand running over a shoulder, the base of her spine, brushing through her pubic hair. He grabbed her ankles and pulled her legs straight in a sudden gesture and spun her round quickly so that she lay fully on the bed, a show of strength on his part as she was heading for the floor, but he manoeuvred her deftly. Strauss heard her gasp in pleasure at this and saw her laugh a little as she closed her eyes and he smiled at her as she lay with her eyes shut, his smile replaced by a frown as soon as she opened her eyes again.

Supporting himself with his arms, Strauss lay atop Inge on the bed and looked down at her face and said, "You want us here, don't you?" It was no question, it was said as fact.

She nodded. "Even though I'm a bad French girl who would never deserve a Major like you, yes."

"We're doing you a favour, aren't we? We protect you from the English and the Americans."

"You do," Inge said, saying whatever he wanted to hear. The role-playing was his idea, but she was enjoying it just as much as he, though she was keener to skip to the event.

"You need us. If I spare you how would you show your gratitude to me?" he said, unbuttoning his jacket. Inge hoped desperately that this meant he was about to undress (with him it was not guaranteed, Strauss teaching her that it was not just women who could tease sexually) and she felt almost unable to speak. His sculpted perfection proved as appealing now as it ever had, the extra years merely making him more distinguished, and Inge envisioned he would still be breathtakingly handsome when he hit 50, though that was 7 long years away yet.

"I would do anything. I would lick your feet, swallow your piss..."

He lifted her up from under her thigh and smacked her bottom with all of his might. She smiled at this and this once her smile was infectious and he kissed her open-mouthed before he pulled away and got back in character. "Never swear in front of an officer."

"I'm sorry, sir. You should ravish me for that," she suggested lustily.

He said officially, no passion evident in his voice, "Beg for an invasion."

"Please invade me," she said, using the right mixture of allure and innocence.

He remained motionless atop her, seemingly impassive, aloof even. "The term invasion is inappropriate because the offer is benevolent. An occupation is mutually beneficial – I gain a warm, soft territory, space of my own to explore at length – you gain a hard protector, a firm hand and body that can tend to any areas that need attention with care or with force." His voice remained very formal, as though he was discussing a proposal with a subordinate.

"With force," she said animatedly, "Enter me with force." She licked her top lip and looked at him for a reaction – she could feel him bulging against her while his expression remained indifferent. The sang-froid front didn't fool her a bit but it did turn her on.

"All in good time. I want you to honour Germany first," he said as he slowly began to undress.

Some promises were impossible to keep. Didier Godet, Yves Cremont, Fabian, Lilian, Sandrine, the boy who was shot (whose name escaped him and he felt bad about that), Aveline, Long Lou – Inge played a direct role in all of their deaths. Grey had to act against her. He changed into the raggedy clothes he had borrowed from Didier who was now just another victim of the Reich and this imbued the clothes with some significance to Grey. Didier had died because he had continually fought the great German war machine; his commitment and bravery had sealed his fate. To die like that was commendable and Grey (despite his anxiety) was prepared to face the same fate and hoped that if his time ever came that he would be as composed facing public execution. Ever since he had entered France he had been acutely aware of the danger, but now it was amplified, this Inge woman adding a new complexion to matters. He had only been able to communicate with two spirits who knew her after hours of straining in vain for more and Aveline and Long Lou's tales of what she inflicted on them were noted and Grey heeded their warning, but did not let it stop him from acting. Through them he had some knowledge of her, Laura also giving him much information and he knew she would crush the Pagan Resistance if he did not aid them. Just getting to the tavern during this period of intense occupation was difficult but he had done so before and he would do so again.

Delgado came into the bedroom that they shared as Grey was putting his boots on and he guessed where he was going, Grey sharing much of his concerns and ramblings from his brain with him. Sharing the room with him also meant that he heard Grey's nightmares and he heard him speaking as much in his sleep as Winters did while awake. "Fitting in with the natives again, Jimmy?" he said, suspecting he knew what was going on, making a joke of it.

"Apparently I can't because I look too red, white and blue, but I am trying, yeah. I need to talk to you, Isdel," Grey said seriously and Delgado sat down in readiness. "I have to go and help the group – they're not going to make it otherwise and I think I can help. If I survive I'll be back and if not – if you don't argue with her, I think Laura will let you all stay until it's over." Grey felt bad as he felt like he was deserting them – he was, but he intended to return if he lived through the confrontation that was coming. He had no idea how to beat Inge, but he was going to try. He suspected that he would fail and was saying his goodbyes just in case.

"We can't stay here without you, pal. We don't want to stay here forever either. If you're acting against them, we'll come with you and help you now," Delgado said, showing his total support.

"No, this isn't a normal battle. And I know how you feel about all of this supernatural side of things and I don't blame you, buddy, because all that I've learned has freaked me out. I feel guns and strength won't help in this fight. I'm not sure I can do anything, but if I don't – they asked for my help and I know they are hanging on by a thread."

"Look, Jimmy, you need to sit down and think this through. You want to go in there alone and fight what you've described as a demon. So you can hear voices in your head – how the fuck is that going to help you against her? You want to fight the Nazis then do it with us as the damned fine soldier that you are. We need to get back to our unit and away from all of this and your place is with us." Delgado was firm in making his point and while he was no longer dismissive of these powers – Laura had changed all of their minds – he was still appalled at such powers which he considered to be dark and ungodly. He did not view Grey as such and he believed that Grey's powers were purer than the others, but he felt that if Grey meddled with the others and delved further in this world that this purity about him would vanish and he was trying to save his friend twofold, body and soul.

"I know and I'm torn up over this…but I'm going. Good luck in your degree – I know you'll breeze through it. You've helped me though this war a lot and if I can, I'll be back to see through the tour of Germany with you."

"If I can't talk you out of it I guess I'm just going to have to wish you luck," Isdel said, standing up and shaking his hand before Grey went downstairs and knocked on the library door where Laura (or Circe as Delgado would say) was sitting deep in study.

"Come in," she shouted and she looked up as she saw Grey in civilian garb, such as it was, and she instantly knew what this meant. He was going to endanger himself yet again, but looking at his face she felt that this time was different.

"Please don't be cross with me. I am going to fight Inge, but I can explain."

"No, no, no," she said shaking her head. "You are responsible for these men here. You cannot go gallivanting off playing the hero like in some boys adventure comic you've read while you have an obligation here." She pointed her finger at him, talking down to him as she tried to make him bend to her will. Grey was used to her now and he was not intimidated or chastened by this and he walked closer to her and stood by her side.

"I remember what you said about Inge and I'm not disobeying your house rules…"

"I said that you can't fight her and you're going to fight her. What an impeccable memory you possess! No wonder you need that notebook."

"No, you said that I couldn't lead her back to you and I would never do that. That's why I'm leaving. I have to fight her, Laura, I have to try and beat her. From what I've learned of her my gut tells me that they're in her sights so I'm going to help them and if we beat her I'll be back. If there's any doubt then I won't return as I won't endanger you."

"How will you beat her? You're powerful, James, but your power won't help you against her. I could go to any pub and find a dozen men who could beat you individually while Inge could beat the same dozen men collectively."

"When provoked I'm a decent slugger but I'm not going to take her on in a boxing match. We'll use weapons and guile."

"Guile?" Laura gasped incredulously.

Grey nodded. "Guile. What you said about if I spoke many languages got me thinking. It doesn't matter if I speak the language or not as long as someone else understands it and Eric speaks five languages. Yves wanted me to speak to his family in French, just copying his sounds, and I wouldn't. I made out to him I wouldn't do it because I would make the words sound wrong, but I don't think that was it. I wanted control; I wanted to know exactly what messages I was conveying. If someone else can understand the spirits who speak foreign languages then we can still use the information and have two way conversations with them. It might be slower and I won't know what's been said until afterwards, but that doesn't matter." Acting as just the middleman, a mouthpiece for the spirits to convey their messages to the group and for the group to communicate their words to the spirit world was not something that would tax or stimulate him, but was perhaps the best way he could help the group.

"I can accept that that might grant you more information though it means that you are giving up a lot of power to them..."

"Only with the ones who don't speak English. I'll talk to the English speaking spirits myself as normal."

"And perhaps make enemies of the others. If it's you who's passing the messages on then it's you who they'll blame if that group agitate them and they likely will offend many. Do you believe that because they're dead that they have no power?"

"They don't seem to."

"You've never offended any. Benevolent mediums tend to fare better than the more unscrupulous of your kind. I've never told you of Mad Anniela, Eyeless Enid or Mercer the Uncanny, three of the more interesting mediums who were once widely talked about as cautionary examples. Besides, you have other reasons not to leave. If you feel so strongly that you must go then I would be prepared to let your rabble stay but they won't listen to me. If they decide they want to leave then they will, even if I tell them that it's unsafe. 'Evil Mab is telling us not to go because she wants to cook us tonight! Hold up your crosses to her and we might be able to evade her accursed clutches!'" Laura said, mocking Delgado and the others for their (justifiable) apprehension and distrust.

"I've told Isdel that I might not be coming back. You two aren't ever going to be friends, I know that. I still think he'll listen to your advice about when it's safe to leave. Isdel will control them; they'll be no real trouble. They'll behave – obviously not perfectly, but they'll be good. Less trouble than me."

"I know. You're right, you are the disobedient one. You intend to leave for good because you don't want to lead Inge back to me? She might still make the connection. Let's pretend that your side wins the war and the Germans are defeated – you'd still be doomed because she's survived the collapse of other empires she was closely aligned to. She'll survive this war too, as will I. You could too, if you wanted to." Laura was frustrated with him rather than angry as she realised that he was determined not to drag her into his suicide.

"I do want to survive. Everyone does, but I have to do my duty even though I would much rather stay with you. I appreciate everything you've done for us – for me," he said earnestly, acknowledging that he knew her benevolence was performed as a favour to him. "I have to do this because it's right to me at least. Georges' group are not strong enough to deal with Inge and I cannot turn my back on them in need. I joined up to pacify the voices in my head, the suffering souls who wanted their loved ones saved as they themselves were not, but that was not the only reason I enlisted. I believe in this war, God help me, I do. I can kill my enemy because I believe we are in the right and I have to do this even if it means betraying my country and leaving the US Army. My goals are the same as theirs, only I can help this once in a different way. I wish you had never been dragged into this, Laura, but I am glad to have met you. You know what I think of you – you think I have a stupid crush on you, you believe that it's just an infatuation. I don't have your experience, but I know myself, I know my heart. I don't flatter myself to believe anything else regarding you; I just wanted to express that to you in case this is our last goodbye."

Laura sat quietly, stunned by his little monologue. He had talked quickly, not giving her an opening to respond. Such ardent passion in him regarding his actions – and her. This idiot was going to get himself killed because he had to, a kamikaze instinct in his brain ordered him to embrace danger. She mused on the superiority of the female who this tendency seemed to be less dominant in (with the exception of some of those cows from that fucking group). Female nobility and bravery took on other forms; Grey's bludgeoning, no-brainer approach seemed to be an impractical statement, a display of courage and balls, but nothing else as neither would avail him well without a plan.

"I'll bet you're never going to visit my country now after meeting me," he smiled affably. "I hope I haven't ruined all Americans for you."

"No, just the pigheaded idiots," she said, standing up, saying her words contemptuously to his face and then sighing. "Wait until I get my coat."

"No, don't," he frowned, disapproving of what she proposed. She had already done more than she really wished to for them and he understood her resentment and he wanted her to remain out of it. He was driven to assist – it was his nature, not hers and he only wanted her to do what she felt comfortable with.

"Don't argue, Grey, I'm not in the mood," she said fiercely.

"Then don't come. I don't want you to."

"It's a free countr…" Laura paused, realising she was incorrect which blackened her mood further and she continued angrily, "I can go where I want to."

This unexpected development made Grey consider postponing or dropping the idea altogether. He didn't want Laura risking herself further than she already had, especially not for something which she didn't believe in. Unfortunately she was so stubborn that making her see sense was going to be virtually impossible. Laura did not bother to change her clothes, remaining in her striped long black skirt and black tunic and she put on a grey overcoat and walked out and Grey said tentatively,

"This is going to be dangerous, Laura. I really would prefer to do this alone. I didn't want Isdel's help and I would…"

"Shut…up," she said deliberately slow, each word enunciated with so much anger as to make him reconsider saying anything more. They walked in silence, Grey unable to try and persuade her to turn back without risking a more violent paroxysm. Laura led the way, using her abilities to choose the best path, which involved descending steep banks and walking crouched down to avoid low branches at one stage; this was the quickest route though best suited to foxes or hounds or children rather than robustly built adults. She walked quicker than he had seen her do so before and it was a reminder of his training and he was glad he was physically fit else he would have been lagging behind. After a mile he ventured to speak again and said gratefully,

"Thank you." He said no more – now was not the time for superfluous platitudes or for being diffuse.

She considered his words and said, in a calmer mood now, "I would quarrel with you about this course of action, only what would be the point? You'll never learn and you can't help yourself so I have to." She talked down to him, but he could tell he was forgiven and he felt better for it. She did not disguise her affection as well as she thought from him.

"And your help means the world to me. I have thought about where I would be if you weren't here. I would probably be in a prisoner of war camp or shot. At this moment you're thinking they sound good scenarios. Your behaviour towards us has been exemplary and I am serious when I ask you to come back to my country. I have to return this hospitality and while you may find my living standards not exactly on a par with yours, I'll still make sure you have a good time and show you everything there is to see. I've never seen any of the sights myself, truth be told, so we could discover the Statue, the Grand Canyon, Mount Rushmore and Hollywood together. I promise I'll only do what you want and not annoy you over there," he said jokingly, referring to his actions now which had riled her.

"Why make promises you cannot possibly keep?" she said, pretending that he was insufferable. "Try to survive the war first then you can make plans for touring your homeland with a sweet young girl. The places you speak of could not interest me less." Her frankness was a little cold because she was still slightly mad. Hollywood and the like would enthral Inge, but she was not Inge.

"Tough crowd." He thought for a moment and said, "I would still like to take you to those places, but how about Salem too? As a practising witch does that hold any interest?"

"That's better," she said, flashing him a toothy smile as he slowly learnt. She was not an impressionable teenage girl – the sort this young GI should have been trying to seduce, and it would take different things to reach her. Talking of her occupation and reason for being was a start.

"What about the Indian reservations? A lot of them were massacred over the last few centuries, but they believed in spirits and…aw shucks, I don't know properly about them, I admit it, but that might be interesting?" he said, trying to add another potential place she might want to visit, admitting as he started talking under her watchful gaze that he knew little about it. It was just an attempt to win her over so that she would visit him.

"That would actually be very interesting," she said genuinely, reassuring him with a smile that this suggestion, which he seemed to give up on midway through, was a good one. "You see, Grey, I am a homebody. Always was, always will be and I have never left Europe. It took me a long time to cross the channel and I have never longed to go any further. Columbus' discovery of the New World came as no surprise to me as I was aware of these other states long before him, but I would have preferred it if these explorers had left well enough alone. The vying for power among my kind has at times been a bloody affair – Inge and I survived so long because up to now we never involved ourselves with war. We left that to the men. It has always been survival of the shrewdest. The opening up of the passage to America presented us with many of our rivals for there were of the indigenous peoples of North and South America many with power to spare. These were rivals to me and I had no desire to step onto their turf and many of those who did didn't reach this century. They could beat my kind, but your kind – the great white invaders, conquistadors and immigrants – involved another battle that they could not win. That power has now largely died out and I would like to travel to their points of worship now that their day is done." She was interested in the topic and happy to share this with him, informing him of part of his country's history that he did not know about.

"Wow. I had no idea about any of that," he enthused, amazed at this knowledge that she imparted.

"You wouldn't because there is a secret history running parallel with the history books which very few are privileged to know. During the conflict between the Red Indians and the Europeans I was not in your country, but if I had been should I have intervened? Should I have assisted the natives in ridding their land of the whites and massacred your forefathers?" The question was not rhetorical and Grey, who as yet had not grasped her point, but did not feel that he was being needled, replied,

"There's two sides to it. I mean, they've had a rough deal from us, but they've done stuff as well – or maybe that's just the Westerns making me think that," he said, questioning his beliefs. "I don't know," he said, giving the matter serious thought and coming up with no answers.

"Live as long as I have and you learn, fast, that it is better to be a witness to history than a part of it. What will happen will happen and I have no desire to pick sides in matters that do not concern me. You can never know what would have happened so it is best to assume that everything happens for the best, part of a grand design. Could I defeat the Nazis if I tried? No, they're too powerful now, but because of you I am intervening for the first time ever in a war and even if we succeed we might be dooming history to a worse outcome," she said, trying to make him fathom the enormity of what they were doing. She resented him for impelling her to act – even though he had not wanted her assistance, because of his decision to fight she was forced to assist him. She was particular about who she was friends with and she vowed to be even more discerning after this but because the friendship had already developed she aided him. Grey was an idiot like Georges, but like Georges he was also her friend.

"I know what people think about me. Jimmy Grey, he's a soft touch. You can screw him over, bust his balls, push the envelope pretty far before you get any reaction. What people don't realise is that the things I hear – not exclusive to the death camps but that's a major part at the moment – the things I hear, and the fact that I keep my composure, makes me hard as nails. And I don't want to be,

Laura, this isn't some machismo thing. What's happening – I can call it obscene, horrific, yet it doesn't convey it. I know what I hear, my link, doesn't convey it truly to me. If I ever have the misfortune to see the reality…I'm always going to hear sad stories, that's the drill, I'm a medium, but what I can't stomach is that this carries on. It's all that is yet to come. If that can be avoided, I have to try."

"Look, such outrages should provoke a reaction from men and women and make them stand and act against such atrocities. However, this has happened many times before in history – read *Red Rubber* when we return home if you want a relatively recent example. Granted, the colossal scale of the genocide this time is particularly egregious. I am questioning our involvement as mystics. This is an affair of men and therefore does not really concern us," she said, unmoved.

"Yes, we have powers, but we're still human. You and even Inge are too, long-lived, but still members of the human race," he said reducing her, bringing her down to his level. He admired and thought reverently of her, but now he was almost slapping her down, forcing her to look at these crimes from the ordinary perspective as he insinuated for all her power that was all she was. She felt insulted, especially because he had said it as fact and confidently stared at her, into the heart of her being, aiming for some breakthrough.

"Me and Inge are not the same as you. You're diversions to us – toys who parade around in your uniforms with your puffed out chests and your metal weapons that are supposed to inspire fear and do in your fellow insects, but compared to us you're nothing and that is how we view you. Temporary, disposable flesh, nothing more, nothing less," she said, contumelious in tone as she laughed at him anew, at his precious humanity that she was not a part of as she proudly grouped herself with Inge. If Grey had known what the word misanthropic meant he would not have considered her such (though Delgado would), but now she appeared so, for the first time.

"Okay, you are greater than us, Laura, when it comes to power," he said holding his hands up, conceding this point before he added, "but that doesn't make you any better. We love, we care, we help – that's why we're here now, to liberate these peoples and end this oppression and I think we can be proud of that," he said patriotically, but also defending the integrity and worth of the human race (which he still viewed her an extraordinary member of).

"And the attack on Pearl Harbor had nothing to do with it?" she sneered as a counter.

"Yes, it did, but some Americans were fighting before then and we have been supportive of Britain in other ways. As I say, I am sorry for dragging you into this because I know you don't want to help. I can go it alone the rest of the way if you want to get back." He was apologetic, not for what he had said to her about her condition, but rather for involving her in matters that went against her wishes.

"Don't tempt me. I'm far too curious as to what you have planned to go back now," she said in mordacious fashion, almost willing him in a fit of pique to do badly.

"I am sorry if I've offended you, but what happens will affect everyone everywhere, even you. We're all connected. You are separate in many ways, not just location, and you are unbelievably special and to these smitten eyes breathtakingly beautiful," he said, flattering her, trying to undo some of the previous damage without being disingenuous as he believed it all, "but you live in this world. We all share the planet and if some people have groups who they won't share the planet with – who they won't tolerate – then that becomes a problem for all of us. There have been purges on witches in the past, Laura," he said, reminding her she was not necessarily safe.

"Oh well, tell me, which is the pro-witch faction?" she said sarcastically, widening her eyes. "Either way I don't mind as past witch hunts have worked out favourably for me. Last time around it dealt with the competition and the impostors."

"I'm not sure if there is a pro-witch faction," he said, ignoring her glee concerning the deaths of her rivals, "I do know that the Axis are the group that believe in mass extermination and refuse their people basic freedoms such as freedom of speech or democracy. I won't lie and say that you'd be welcomed with open arms if you declared that you were a witch in the States because that's not true as we are a very Christian people. I think I can say that you would not be prosecuted or oppressed for it, you would not be killed on a whim by the government," he said idealistically.

"You have a lot of faith in your country, Grey," she said, hearing him out and speaking levelly. "It could benefit from men like you in charge – it would collapse in a day, but it would be an honourable collapse," she said, both criticising and praising him. He lacked knowledge of how things really were, his naiveté and idealism extraordinary considering his gifts which she felt should have made him wise to mankind's true nature and more cynical. His boldness at arguing with her about what she was had ruffled her, but his courtesy since had slightly pacified her, as had his clear belief in what he was saying. He was not making points to be contentious as he was not like that and he normally preferred to try and get on with everyone in an affable manner. He spoke out because he believed so passionately in what he was saying and there was something admirable in that. Of course for his insult she might choose to let him fall flat on his face, but she would help him get up.

Paulette opened up the back door for them and she smiled when she saw that Grey (who she expected it to be) had not come alone. This Laura, Georges' friend, was needed now and Paulette welcomed them inside. Mireille had been hell-bent on revenge and had ordered Paulette to plant six bombs the previous night at great personal risk. Paulette did not mind this, but what annoyed her was that after she had endangered herself the group had failed. The combined circle had failed to ignite any of the bombs and the mission as a result was an abject failure with the Nazis having their hands on their valuable explosives. Paulette had done her part and in future she would be tempted just to light the fuses herself after this debacle. Mireille had been irate – the circle was large with herself, Eric, Gervaise, Margot and a press-ganged Odette, but it just hadn't gelled. Odette blamed herself and said they should try without her as it wasn't her thing – she had no interest in the craft and the lessons that Mireille were inflicting on her were most unwelcome. Didier had understood nothing about it and Mireille didn't seem to care that her own son did not practice his heritage and Odette tried to tactfully point this out. Mireille snapped at her, claiming that it was different for men who lacked the innate ability and she shouted that as Odette was carrying her blood she should be imbued with some ability. Odette rolled her eyes as she looked away from this madwoman and she pretended to listen as Mireille resumed class, but in truth she paid little attention, merely saying yes or no at intervals to feign interest and pacify her. Eric had stared at Mireille quizzically regarding her comment about men lacking the gift, her reason for expecting nothing from Didier. The comment disregarded himself, Grey, Arnaud and, strangest of all, Georges who she had been most fond of, and he inwardly seethed at her conceit. The truth of it was that her comments were not meant critically and she was still overcome with grief, alienating Odette in the process, judging the slovenly girl who used her pregnancy as an excuse to get out of tasks as unsuitable for her beloved son. She bullied Margot, insisting she attend every meeting which meant she barely left the tavern, unable to refuse Mireille after her tragic loss even though she longed to get home and spend some relaxing time by herself playing solo card games.

Gervaise did not need to be pressed into coming, glad to be there for her friend, though she was unhappy about one matter, the Communist they were harbouring in the cellar, though she voiced no objections; Mireille was not to be reasoned with on the matter. As the last surviving member of her son's group Mireille treated Hugo Tremaint like her own (he was close to her son's age, only two years younger and looked loosely similar to him), her nurturing of the Communist justifying to Eric his course of actions. He realised why she had no time for male mystics; she was too busy fawning over male resistance fighters, fatuous, boorish men who violence came too easily to. Having Hugo staying at the tavern was like having Didier back, all of the best food lavished on him. He was less of a nuisance and did generally stay in the cellar but Eric found him an arrogant shit, smiling in his direction cockily – Eric knew he'd clearly been the butt of some joke at some time. Hugo also showed contempt subtly for Odette, in body language rather than with words, and this just made Mireille like him more, Hugo also seeing her for what she was, unworthy of Didier. Hugo's contempt was based on an affair they had had while she was seeing Didier, Hugo judging her harshly for her betrayal, refusing to admit that he was also in the wrong even when Odette pointed out his hypocrisy. She was considered the sinner by many just for being pregnant out of wedlock by her boyfriend of two years – what would the town think of her if it was known that the paternity of her child was in question? It wasn't Hugo, the timing wrong, but there were two others who were the potential father, one of them a German soldier. She knew how insane Mireille would be if she knew there was any doubt and wisely discussed it with no one. Didier was equally unfaithful and she felt no guilt, but she hoped that the baby looked like him or she knew questions would be asked, and if Mireille had her way a stake prepared for her.

Mireille looked up from the table as Grey entered, greeting everyone with reverent nods accompanied by Laura who Mireille glared at. She felt aggressive, pugnacious even, and this conceited Englishwoman was a most suitable receptacle for her anger and Mireille sneered at her. Laura remained standing at Grey's side and she looked down at this mercurial woman who had recently been bereaved. Her hostile countenance made it hard for Laura to be sympathetic towards her and she looked back at her unfazed.

While Laura and Mireille were locked in a lengthy stare, Mireille glowering all the more as she felt that Laura's eyes taunted her, Odette looked at Grey. The

American had greeted her and she smiled back at him – he seemed almost as much of a pariah in the group as she herself was. She heard them talk about him disparagingly (she was so insignificant that they talked freely with her around, ignoring her as though she were invisible) – something about being a lowly one-hander (whatever that meant). The sympathetic glances he had aimed in her direction on the night of Didier's execution lingered in her mind as she weighed up possibilities and she had asked Paulette what she thought of him. Paulette had been equally scathing, calling him an empty book, still slighted by his rejection of her. When Odette mentioned him again Paulette had softened and said he seemed a decent man, but Odette trusted her first words more, which suited her. He was less than striking (vaguely handsome at best and Odette always strived for better than above average) and not her usual type though his nationality made him appealing. America sounded damned tempting at present, but she would wait until she had given birth before making her move. He was obviously fairly broadminded to associate with such a group and if he was as naïve as was made out then she felt she could persuade him to take on another man's child with a little effort. The language barrier was a hurdle but actions undoubtedly spoke louder than words in the sexual arena. In return for the American life she would be a dutiful wife…

Her brief reverie was disturbed by the woman at his side, a woman who looked old enough to be his mother, and who he looked at affectionately, a churlish hag. Odette knew that she was much more attractive than the other woman yet it would not be enough, for she would not be to his peculiar tastes. There would be no escape from Maramont for her.

Grey broke the tense silence and said, meaning for his words to be translated by Paulette or Eric to Mireille,

"We've come to help you as best we can against Inge." Laura translated this for him, pointing out to Mireille that the words were his, not her own.

"We don't need your help," Mireille snapped at Laura. "He's little use, but at least he tries, but you! I can beat her without your help." She spoke proudly, refusing assistance for the sake of a statement.

"She would have to be at her lowest and you would have to be at your zenith and even then you would struggle for a draw," Laura responded superciliously.

"Get back under your rock, bitch. Hide away from it all in your country home, close your eyes to the youth of this world being slaughtered. Georges must have been senile to think anything of you. I'm not a man and I am not impressed by you," Mireille said, goading Laura into a quarrel with this tirade which entertained the others, bar Grey who did not understand the words but the tone of her invective and Mireille's exaggerated facial contortions spoke volumes. He turned to Paulette and said,

"Tell her we have come here to help against Inge and if she doesn't want our help we'll do something by ourselves." He spoke angrily, angry at seeing Laura (who had not even wanted to help) treated so discourteously for no valid reason.

"Don't," Paulette said, wanting them all to work together and she translated for Mireille and pleaded with her herself. Laura smiled, appearing to be amused by Mireille's outburst at her and after a pause she spoke.

"You're doomed. This whole group is doomed under your leadership. Your son died and you're angry and want blood. That is understandable, yet you fail to comprehend how hard it is to draw Inge's blood. You seem to seek some sort of brawl with her, or in her absence me – you would win neither. Anger is a primal force, which used correctly can be a deadly weapon and used improperly is blunter than mercy. Your victory is dependent on understanding your foe, not in physically besting her. The Nazis are dominant here; physically they are superior so look away from that sphere. You are the Pagan Resistance group – live up to it and live up to Georges' belief in you. I criticised you all to him, I told him you were nothing and he wouldn't accept that. What do you say now, Georges?" she said looking upwards. Her words made everyone bar Odette (incurious) and Grey (linguistically challenged) stop and think, even Mireille musing over what she had said. She found her an irritating bitch, but her words provoked a response.

"And you have a solution?" This was a challenge; Mireille was asking her if she could do better.

"A simple one. Inge is too powerful so we don't take the fight to her. She knows she can win, otherwise she wouldn't have presented herself. She's an exhibitionist, but she's not a fool. However, if she's siding with the Germans then there can only be one reason for that. She must have a lover in the army, probably of high rank. Drive him and the other Nazis away and she'll follow." Laura held court now, looking at the other pagans as she dispensed this advice and direction that they desperately needed.

"We want rid of them, of course, but we can't just magic them away," Eric said, grinning at her foolhardy suggestion.

"You're not much of a witch then, are you?" Laura said straight-faced, disputing his talents the best way of dealing with his impudence. "We need some more chairs for the table," she said to Paulette who promptly fetched two more chairs, Mireille, Gervaise, Eric and Margot already seated.

Laura told Grey to sit down as she sat next to him and she explained that they were going to attempt a difficult spell to try to drive back the Nazis. He was thankful of the explanation and he was keen to assist and enthused so, and Laura gained Mireille's consent to lead the spell. Laura clutched Grey's and Gervaise's hands tightly as all around the table held hands as Paulette watched and Odette gave Paulette a wary look directed at the witches and she left the group to have a rest in her bedroom. Laura chanted in tongues and then French and English and she instructed the others to chant a short mantra as she spoke over them. The table began to shake, the effects of the power visible, and Eric panicked as he did not want the spell to be successful and he worked against it. Laura sensed a hostile presence interfering with the spell and she broke her holds and said to Eric, "That's not helpful."

They all opened their eyes and looked at Laura, then at Eric who she was staring coolly at. They had no idea what she was referring to and Eric said, "What?" like a wronged innocent.

"Our powers don't blend," she said as means of an explanation and grounds for dismissing him from the circle. She was not giving him the benefit of the doubt for she suspected his attempts at sabotaging the spell were deliberate, but to save a quarrel she gave this innocuous reason. "Please leave the circle." It was not a request; it was an autocratic edict.

Eric protested vociferously, looking to his leader and inveighing against this interloper. Mireille considered his words, but she overcame her dislike for the woman and backed up Laura. "We'll try her way for now," Mireille said. At the first sign of failure she would have fresh words for Laura.

Eric stood up in a strop, glaring at Laura as he walked away and he stood with Paulette as Grey moved his chair around to cover the gap left by Eric, able to easily reach Laura and Margot. Laura found Margot no great help either, but she was no hindrance, trying in her dotty, small-scale way. Gervaise and Mireille were both very helpful in this task as was Grey – he had come a long way in the short time she had spent with him and she sensed as they performed the spell that there was more there. He was trying the hardest, his face furrowed in concentration making him look silly and Laura smiled at this, keeping her eyes open as the others closed their eyes as told to. It was a long, complicated spell, which triggered minor phenomena – ornaments falling from shelves, spoons revolving, but nothing overly dramatic though Paulette was excited by it, watching with a fascinated smile. Eric watched with palpable disapproval at Laura's apparent success, which seemed effortless on her part even if the other four showed signs of strain. This bitch, who they had all assumed would play no part in the conflict, was meddling with his plans. His future lay under Vichy rule, under a conquered, swastika and eagle emblazoned world. Liberation was now a thing of dread to him, a return to dull, and insignificant normality.

Once the spell was complete Laura let go of the others' hands and looked at them as they all looked fit to collapse and would have were they not seated. Mireille ordered Paulette to fetch them all drinks, which they swigged back desperately, all bar Laura who was a picture of cool stillness. Grey was not and he downed the whisky at once and Paulette fetched them all refills. With the task complete Laura suggested making a move to Grey. Paulette delayed them at the back door, quizzing Laura as to what exactly would happen as a result of their spell.

"Hopefully liberation," Laura said, promising nothing. The spell was successful, but there were other factors, variables that always had to be considered. She did not reveal the specifics of her spell, which seemed more grandiose left secret. No witch could control an entire army and she acted creatively, trying to control two men. Not two men at the top of the hierarchy – they would be protected and her spell would leave a trail which would be discovered. Instead she settled for two men in the middle, a German and an American, both with enough power and influence to affect a small pocket of France. Making one pawn go forward while she made his opposite number move back ensured that their troops moved with them.

Shortly after Grey and Laura left, Eric made his excuses, saying that if he wasn't needed he might as well go home. He did not disguise his bitterness and instead exaggerated it so that his exit did not appear unusual or suspicious.

As Grey walked with Laura through the fields leading to her home he said appreciatively, "That's another one I owe you, if you're keeping score."

"I am, in a notebook thicker than yours," she replied.

"After this we're comrades too. I'm your brother in arms now."

"Wonderful," Laura said sarcastically, ignoring his geniality, as he seemed to think this was a good thing.

"I do understand you know. You must see us destroying each other with cruelty and hate and want no involvement in that. I can understand and I'm not judging you. However, even God intervenes sometimes," Grey said. He did not expect her to be radiantly happy for he knew she was averse to intervention, but he was trying to make her see that she had done a good thing.

"Please, no. I've helped you tonight, spare me the sermon," Laura said desperately, conveying how tiresome and boring she would find such dialogue.

"No, I'm not. Priests or preachers give sermons and I'm not either of them, am I? I'm not at a pulpit, looking down at anyone, Laura. What do I know about religion when I haven't lived for even a minute compared to you and some of the ancient voices in my noodle?" This was said gently and self-deprecating as he tried to express himself. "I'm not saying even I believe everything in The Bible 100 per cent, or even understand a lot of the Old Testament but I like what it stands for, for what Jesus stands for. I think the message and spirit is the point, not the…" He struggled for words, but his meaning had got across to Laura who was interested in this line of thought.

"Yes, I accept some allegories are effective and I find the Bible a fascinating read and as an allegory I could enjoy it. As a historical document, no. These books of literature convert people, which is fine, but then they feel that they have to convert others – that is my problem with religion, Grey. I think it breeds intolerance and tribalism – those who will not join up are vilified and seen as the enemy." She spoke calmly, her words a polemic, but not aggressively so.

"That's not the ideal. That's not the spirit."

"No, I accept that, but men will take words of peace and use them to wage war." Relenting a little from this mass generalisation she said, "Every one of you is different, I accept that, and some of you do achieve grace, but not through praying twice daily."

"I apologise, Laura. I know that Isdel has talked to you of religion and I have a little too, when you have your own reasons for not believing and it is your choice. It makes us no better," Grey said tolerantly. He regretted his small attempts at converting her, accepting now that her beliefs and all people's beliefs were their affair and no business of others, however well intentioned.

"And no worse either. Speaking as one who has been demonised for my lifestyle I am not going to condemn you for your beliefs and I say stay true to them, Grey. You haven't pressured me – if you had I would have let you know," she said, fiercely, but playful.

"Well I won't at all in future, comrade. I have a good feeling about how things went in there and however things do turn out, I'm forever indebted to you for helping me and them. I might be being presumptuous but I think you might get your tour of the States soon because I think the war is winding down," he said optimistically.

"That's the difference between us. You call this *the* war while to me it's just *a* war."

"Don't you think that this war will go down in history as the most significant? Seriously?"

"It'll have to last a lot longer. To become the most important war ever it has to supplant the lengthy and extensive Roman military campaigns, the Crusades – the Napoleonic Wars were a major event at the time."

"But were they to you? The Napoleonic Wars, I mean," Grey said, trying to find out if she had ever let events touch her.

"I was around during all of the Crusades too. The English Civil War in Britain – a king was executed and the monarchy was abolished, for goodness sake!"

"For real?"

"I suppose you were probably taught American history at school. Yes, England had no monarch for a number of years. Regrettably it was only a short-term arrangement. There were two Lord Protector Cromwells instead," she said, teaching him without patronising him.

"Is that Oliver Cromwell? I've heard of him, though I've never known what he was supposed to have done."

"That's right. In my youth whenever war was declared I felt a little anxious. Perhaps if I was a man and I thought I would be made to fight it would be different. Having said that, no one could make me fight now no matter what my sex. My experience has taught me that war is constant. There is always strife somewhere."

"And there's always foolish idiots who speak out of turn and make their benefactress uncomfortable. What I said before, Laura – I do care about you, but I won't bring it up again until I leave. I've been inappropriate enough."

"I am flattered by your crush, only..."

Grey interrupted her before she dismissed his feelings for her as insignificant. "It's not a crush. I've had crushes before – this is completely squashed to oblivion. It's not the powers – that first day I was bowled over."

"I know it's not the powers – although you have to admit they are spectacular," she added, overweening and egotistical to relieve the tension. Telling a love struck admirer that he stood no chance was a hard thing to do when he looked at her so earnestly and she cared for his feelings.

"Show-stopping. Georges should have worked them into his routine if he wanted a hit. You'd blow Broadway away," he said with a huge grin as he nodded, his words a mixture of effusive charm and flummery, blandishments intended to make her happy.

He cut the crap and said, "You are my ideal woman, Laura. You've – I'm going to have to be careful how I express this – you're not the woman I dreamed I'd want, but that's because nobody could imagine you. I don't want to talk with you about it yet though, it's not fair," he said, delaying the talk that had to come. It would be easier for her to reject him when he was leaving if that was her wish, and he would pull out all of the stops then.

"Fine. Students don't make passes at their teachers anyway and I want to draw out that potential I sensed tonight. I don't think you're aware of what you can become – you're never going to be an all-rounder like Georges or myself, but in the field of clairvoyance you can be a prominent figure. I can guarantee you a lengthy 'session' tonight," she said, flirting with him a little to show she wasn't annoyed though he knew that he still did not possess her heart. Nevertheless, progress had been made (she would not have acted against the Nazis so if she did not care for him) and Grey hoped that he had at least another month with her to try and make her care more for him.

Lotte had sent her guard round to Inge's and Inge had come at her summons and she was being briefed as Eric arrived. Lotte disliked him when Inge had brought him round twice previously as part of her new coven yet she knew she had to deal with him. They had talked amicably at their first meeting but then he had come round alone without Inge and he had gloated to Lotte about the downfall of the Communist Resistance and the emotional breakdown Mireille was heading for. As a mother with sons in danger constantly she could not celebrate another mother's loss and to see him so jubilant about the effect it was having on his former friend sickened her. She masked her disgust but she was no longer so courteous to him, their relationship merely functional. She told him as he came through the door about the spell that had just been cast, sensing the energy in the air and he told her about it, looking at Inge most of the time as he spoke.

"So what's happened exactly," Inge asked Eric who seemed to know the specifics of the spell whereas Lotte just knew they faced upheaval and a problem.

"They've performed a powerful spell. I tried to sabotage it, only she was onto me and barred me from the circle. They're trying to drive us back," he said, including himself with the Nazis.

"They haven't the power for that," Inge said with a haughty laugh. The impudence of such an insignificant group, trying a spell of that magnitude, amused her.

"They succeeded," Lotte said. She didn't need to hear what Eric had to say; bad tidings were in the wind.

"They were helped by that Laura, Georges' friend," Eric said, explaining how it had been carried out. Eric had described Laura to Inge already and she felt sure that it was her old acquaintance.

"Why would she get involved? We'd leave her alone if she kept herself to herself – which is what she's always done," Inge said, confused by this sudden change in behaviour. After her first clash with 'Laura' (or whatever she called herself) she had talked to others of her and discovered things. She was an isolationist with small plans who restricted herself to minor affairs, powerful, but not worth tangling with as she posed no threat left unchecked and not worth befriending as she would not assist in disputes. Inge had not kept her involvement with the Reich a secret and she felt that Laura must have known of her connections and still performed this spell. To Inge this was a declaration of war between the two of them.

"It's because of the American soldier. He wanted to help beat you, but he's too weak so he got her involved," Eric said. Inge looked to Lotte to confirm this and Lotte shrugged, uncertain as to the veracity of Eric's words. She had made a reading of two men again, two foreigners from a far off new land, one who would be Inge's enemy and one who would be her ally, but it was unclear.

"He's going to die then," Inge said with fire in her eyes at the trouble this American had wreaked.

"We should discuss this later. I think it would be a good idea if we attempted to counter their spell with one of our own," Lotte said, thinking of damage limitation.

"Good thinking, Lotte," Inge said and she threw several cups and saucers from Lotte's table and Lotte and Eric sat around it as Inge did the same. Lotte took the lead in this spell, having more of a spiritual knowledge than the far older Inge did and all three gave it their all. Involved in this coven in the act of casting, Eric felt the true scale of their power for the first time. They were giants; they would be dominant.

The spell only took ten minutes after which Lotte wiped her flushed face with her hands and exhaled deeply. Inge looked at her and said eagerly, licking her lips, "Has that driven them back?"

Lotte shook her head. "Probably not. Our spell might cancel theirs out, but they acted first and unethically, I hasten to add."

"Then let's do it again to drive them further back," Inge said with a child's mania and limited comprehension.

"It wouldn't work. We can't create fresh soldiers. It's like chess. They have made their move and we have made ours, but if we try to change our move then the original manoeuvre won't happen. We're moving men around, imbuing them with direction and drive, but that energy is inherent and once we stop moving them they are in grave danger because the fatigue will hit them, like a puppet whose strings are cut," Lotte said staidly. To influence and control others through subtle guiding was fundamentally wrong to her and she felt the consequences on both sides could prove catastrophic and many of the losses would be on pagan heads from both groups. The stakes had been raised, but Lotte stayed in the game for her promised prize. Inge kept promising her that one of her sons would return soon, but there was still no sign of either of them.

"So you think Laura's fucking a GI?" Inge asked Eric, returning to this over Lotte's heavy talk of morality and cause and effects, preferring salacious gossip.

"I don't know. He's an idiot, a real imbecile, but he seems to have drawn her to the group because she certainly dislikes the rest of us. She's more powerful than Georges ever was," Eric said.

"You never saw him in his prime. Neither did I, but it is said that he was something briefly, promising for a day before his meridian quickly ended. Not many can maintain it at the top for long," Inge said arrogantly, vaingloriously applying lipstick in a hand mirror as she thought about departing and returning to the manor where her lover would be returning shortly. "Is he handsome?"

"No!" Eric said, laughing at the notion. He was uncultured and untidy with an incongruous face in Eric's opinion.

"Big? Small?"

"Average," Eric replied. "He's not as tall as me."

Inge smiled at Eric, sensing that he wanted approbation, a brief, disingenuous smile and she said, "Describe his appearance."

"There's little to say. He's a soldier so his hair's cut short – his hair is a dull brown, the colour of dishwater. He's got brown beady eyes and looks like a fool."

"Have you seen him naked?"

"No, but I doubt he's anything special there. The Americans are all talk," Eric said disparagingly, mocking Grey for his own amusement. Lotte was unimpressed with Eric's critical tongue and while fate had pitted her as Grey's enemy she had no hatred or disrespect for him as she sensed he was the adversary from the cards. Inge was equally unsatisfied for she felt that Eric's description of Grey was prejudiced and she wanted the truth or at least a woman's perspective. Eric's blanket condemnation was not helping her understand what Laura might see in him.

CHAPTER 9 – MASSACRE

Grey scrutinised his face as he shaved at the sink in the downstairs restroom. He was nothing special by any means and had certainly never had to beat the ladies off with a stick, but he felt he was handsome enough that Laura wouldn't refuse him on those grounds. The others shaved less regularly than him – bar Hartmann none of the others considered Laura a dame and saw no reason to make any effort with their personal grooming for her benefit. Grey did not imagine that Georges would have been devilishly handsome in his youth, but he had a glint in his eye while McKinley was old when he and Laura became lovers and according to her looked older than his years yet she still loved him deeply. Even though he knew appearance wasn't much of a factor for her he still had to try to appeal to her because unlike those two lucky gentlemen he wasn't in possession of her heart.

There was a loud knock at the door and Grey said, "I'm nearly done. Can you hold on a minute?"

Several loud knocks followed this and Grey put his razor down in the sink and opened the door, intending to finish shaving after. He looked around the corridor and stepped out of the room and saw Laura approaching, smiling at his asymmetrical appearance as he had only shaved the right side of his face and neck, with the left still lathered. She noted his quizzical glance and she said, "I sense Konah ran off – I have that effect on him."

"He doesn't know you well enough yet," Grey postulated.

"Or knows me best of all," she said, darkly humorous.

"He'll come round. Do you know which way he went?"

"Down the cellar. I could perform a spell to stop stubble growth, if you fancy."

"Thanks all the same, but it's no hardship. My daily cuts are barely into double figures now, so there's no need."

"It would only be temporary. It could retard the growth for less than a year, then normal function would resume."

"What would it entail?" Grey said, less than eager but curious, sensing she was keen to do this for him.

Winters came along at this juncture and said to Grey, "Are you finished or what?"

"Go on, I'll finish off later," Grey said, intent on continuing his conversation. While he was no expert on women or body language, he felt that the fact that Laura kept looking down at his bare chest was a good thing.

"It would be virtually painless," Laura continued when Winters had locked the door.

"Virtually?" Grey said, pretending to be appalled.

"Minor, infinitesimal amounts. I would just place my hands on the areas and kill the hairs at the root. I haven't done it for 300 years but I haven't lost the knack."

"Wrong time frame for John…" Grey said, instantly assuming it was him before correcting himself.

"He let himself go to seed as soon as he left his mother's home. In his line of work and lowly place in the social caste it didn't matter. For a soldier I think it could be helpful. I won't even charge you."

"I couldn't take any more charity from you, so sorry, I regretfully pass."

"Not even pain, that's the wrong word. Momentary discomfort. I've done it myself on my legs."

"I thought you hadn't done it for 300 years?"

"I haven't. I did them before then, around 1530. I made that permanent."

"It might start a dangerous precedent. You might want to practice all of your other spells on me."

Winters emerged from the bathroom, and while he tried to adopt a neutral expression as he passed them he did not succeed. The door was not so thick that he could not hear them and he found their conversation utterly nonsensical.

"Well, James, are you doing it yourself or shall I spare you the chore for a while?" Laura teased.

"You see a bit more clay that you have to work with and you get ideas. A small part of me is tempted but a year is too long. I'm game if it's for a week."

"Best get back to your razor than, James. The nature of the spell means it has to last longer than that. Come and see me in the library when you're done and I'll go through a small selection of the myriad of spells that are possible – descriptively, not demonstratively," Laura said, finding his reactions to such things amusing, reminding her of how she herself had been astounded by the things her mentor showed her. His eyes had already been opened by his own abilities and more knowledge would help him further.

"I'm going to check on Konah first then I'll be right there. Can we focus on the good spells first?"

"I suppose I can talk about other practitioners' arsenals before getting to my own."

Grey grinned as he finished off shaving, thinking of Laura. If there was such a thing as playful malevolence she'd cornered the market, though she did it amusingly. She was always so quick to remind him she was no saint, which did not deter him one iota as his feelings for her were by no means saintly. Grey dried his face quickly and threw his shirt on and buttoned it as he descended the cellar steps. He couldn't see Konah and was about to turn around and look for him upstairs when he felt something pressed into his back. He turned and saw Konah, dressed in someone's uniform, pointing a rifle at him, Konah ran around him to place the rifle into his lower back again. Grey could not help smiling at Konah in the ill-fitting outfit, playing soldier, and as Grey knew there was no live ammunition in the house he played along, putting his hands up.

"You got me, partner. Is this your base?"

Konah reacted angrily, incensed that Grey was not taking him seriously and he shouted the same phrase at him repeatedly as he jabbed the rifle end into Grey's back sharply several times and Grey turned and took it from him, using as little force as possible though Konah fought back fiercely, desperate to retain it. Grey took it away from him and said calmly, "Sorry, mate, but these aren't toys." The penny dropped and he said, "Are you trying to tell me something?"

Grey was about to fetch the dictionary to try and surmount the language barrier between them when Laura appeared at the top of the stairs, alerted by Konah's shouting. Konah ran past her and Laura opted to come down to Grey and she commented, "What's he playing at now?"

Grey knew that Laura could easily find out what Konah was trying to relay to him. The process would distress Konah and the meaning seemed pretty self-explanatory in any case. There was a bullet somewhere with his name on it, heading for his spine. If Laura did find out about that she would become even more vocal in her objections to him rejoining the fight and that was not an option. "He wanted to play soldiers and I was wary of him handling a real rifle. I was heavy-handed – that's why he reacted as he did. My fault."

"You're right, he shouldn't be handling weapons at his age. Neither should you, by the by..."

Konah's predictions weren't set in stone; he was sure he'd heard someone describe them as erratic. All he could do was take care and try to make sure he was always facing trouble head-on. Despite the temptation he wouldn't quiz Konah any more about it. If it was inevitable there was nothing he could do about it and knowing the specifics would make it worse. Perhaps it was just a child playing games, trying to keep him there so he would not be alone with Laura again.

Lotte accepted her letter gratefully when it arrived, thanking the young German soldier who brought it for her and she gave him a small tip as she went to her kitchen table to read it. Several days had passed since they had performed the spell around the table and already the reverberations were being felt with action centring on the region once more. Everything was up for grabs and Lotte felt trepidation at the potential pitfalls and the overwhelming losses that would be felt on both sides. Already there had been so much death though she had no involvement in the skirmishes that had already occurred. In this coming clash she was, unfortunately, a factor.

The letter was from Reinald (she knew that neat handwriting anywhere) and she used a letter opener to tear the envelope and she read the contents

My dearest Lotte,

I write this with a heavy heart, a letter I wish I never had to pen, and I regret bitterly what has happened and that I am unable to break the news to you in person. Our son has been taken from us. Jan died yesterday. I'll share the details of how when we are next together if you want to hear them, but I will tell you that it was swift. He did not appear to suffer – that is what everyone has been repeating to me as they try to aid me. I know it is little consolation. I failed him as I failed you in my promise for which I beg your forgiveness. It is obscene that I should live when he is gone, a good young man in his prime, our firstborn. I live for you and Peter now and for Jan's memory. I wish I could be there for you now Lotte. I wish I had taken that job in Switzerland now and kept our boys away from all of this. I have erred and I will never forgive myself but we have to think of Peter. He may seem tough but we have to stay strong for him because he needs us still.

I know that all seems lost and you may feel disconsolate. Don't. You are a wonderful mother and our boy worshipped you. I knew that before this war but during these years together in combat he has talked of you so lovingly and we became even closer. Time and distance put everything into perspective. One day we will all think of Jan and smile, even laugh, and I know he would want us to. One day we may even forgive the Russians for what they have taken from us. Today and every day we remain a family, separated by distance and death but never love…

The letter continued over five pages and Lotte wept as she read it all. She wept for her son, her dear sweet son. She wept for Reinald who she knew was distraught and now alone, feeling guilt even though he was blameless. She wept for herself and she looked through a small photo album she had with her. In her lugubrious state her tears stained the covers, but she paid no attention, too absorbed by the pictures. She looked at a picture of father and son together in uniform. There was no similarity – Jan was weak-chinned with short thick brown hair and a perpetually anxious smile, Reinald was strong-jawed like their youngest son and his thin brown hair was receding back a little every day and he grinned confidently though his forehead had more worry lines than enough. She looked at a picture of Peter, Peter who had been so impatient after his father and brother left, Lotte unable to assuage his restlessness. Peter had bright blond hair and his father's confidence and he had a physique that paid testament to the effort he put into his exercise regimen which he saw as devotion to the Reich, becoming as strong as he could be. He wanted to be a perfect Aryan – there were endless pictures of him winning trophies and awards in his Hitler Youth group with his 'proud' parents. If that was what he wanted – she had to be more supportive now.

The front door opened and Inge stuck her head in and walked through to the kitchen, poking her head around the door with a playful expression and smile. "I've got a naughty boy here, Lotte," she said and she dragged an American soldier in by his ear. He winced in pain, yet made no attempt to escape. He was wan and bore a sergeant's stripes, appearing to be in his early 40's and he seemed vaguely familiar to Lotte. His features were haggard for his age, his dark hair receding further than her husband's and the skin around his eyes loose and dark. He was taller than Inge but had to stoop to her level because of her grip and did so compliantly.

Inge noticed Lotte was tearful and saw that she was looking at old photos of her family. She thought that Lotte was just being sentimental and tried to cheer her up by getting her 'pet' to demean himself for her, his debasement a spectacle they could both enjoy. "He's good at shoe-shining, this soldier. Clean Lotte's shoes for her." Inge released him and at her command he knelt down and began licking Lotte's shoes. Lotte recoiled and tried to push him away, horrified by this, but he would not stop until Lotte stood up and moved away from him.

"Relax, Lotte, I know you wouldn't want him to go any higher. I know that's private territory and I wouldn't let him anyway," Inge said, enjoying denying him and making him suffer. "Do mine instead," Inge said and he obliged as Inge looked at sorrowful Lotte who stood at her side.

"Jan's dead," Lotte said, breaking down after she said this for the first time.

"Oh no," Inge said sadly. She booted her lapdog off her, kicking him and he ended up across the room as Inge hugged and tried to console Lotte. Her sympathy was genuine and her support helped Lotte and she cried on her slender shoulder, finding strength in this hard woman.

"I'll talk to Klaus again tonight. I'll get you Peter and Reinald back," Inge promised, breaking off the hug to look at her as she clasped her hands in her own.

"Please do. That's all I want, my family back," Lotte said emotionally. Her family was already torn asunder but having her husband and son back would give her something to rebuild on. If either of these two died she knew she would find it very hard to continue now – if both died there was no hope.

"You'll have it, I promise you. You've helped me. That reading about the foreigners which you said might be two Americans or an Australian. It's another American and there he is," Inge said, pointing at the sergeant who looked a state, struggling to get to his feet, winded by the kick.

"That's hmm…" Lotte recognised him and struggled for the name.

"Colin Irwin," Inge said, smiling smugly as she said the name. "My toy from 20 years ago. He was young then, of course – he hasn't aged well, has he?" Inge said with a disparaging laugh.

Lotte was in no mood to see anyone else's humiliation and she answered merely with, "How do you think we should use him to help us?" He would help, that was guaranteed, for Inge owned him body and soul and Lotte knew that now that she recalled who he was.

"He's my tool against Laura. My American against hers. Eric said that Laura wouldn't directly attack me because she's scared of fighting me again." The last part was Inge's interpretation and not what Eric or Laura had said. "That suits me. Irwin can kill Grey for me and Laura can heed the lesson."

"I'm not sure where Grey is at the moment," Lotte said, unable to help her find him.

"That's fine. Eric can bring him to us on some pretext, or rather to Irwin. You want to kill him for me, don't you?" Inge said, talking down to Irwin as though he were an animal.

"It would be an honour," Irwin said, bowing subserviently.

"I think we'd better leave Lotte for now, my pet. Take care," Inge said considerately before she gripped Irwin tightly by the hand and dragged him off. Lotte was glad to see them go though she did feel that Inge had been nice to her. She had treated him disgracefully, but that was not Lotte's concern at present and it was not her place to intercede.

She knew the history, a story of Inge's wrath, motivation for her never to cross her ally. At present she had no reason to betray her for Inge promised her what she desired most. She felt that Colin Irwin must have wished he had behaved better towards her, or at least acted with more discretion. He had been a Mongol Warlord – the name escaped her, but with Inge installed at his side he had triumphed many times over. She had loved him and aided him mightily and they had been unstoppable. His libido raged as much as hers but, unfortunately, he was not as exclusive as she was and she found him with a dead rival chieftain's daughter. She incinerated the girl and battered him before taking her dread vengeance, a bloody death that was left undisclosed. She loved him, she loved him still, but he had humiliated her. His life was forfeit but the remnants of her affection prompted her to bring him back. By the time he was reborn she had found other lovers and the reason for his rebirth was obviated. He was surfeit to requirements, but in other lovers' monogamy, better men than he, she felt intense, immoderate anger at his betrayal. He became a living embodiment of her anger, a warning to her subsequent lovers for fidelity. She could draw him to her and she destroyed him again and again, her toy to amuse herself with, the remains of a once dominant man. She revelled in bringing him low, scraping the last vestiges of his pride away and that had long perished now. Lotte had met him in Berlin where for five years Inge had kept him in her service before discarding him when she laid eyes on Strauss. She had felt him near the previous night and she had summoned him, such was her hold on him. He no longer even craved independence and felt lost without her orders. He now lived solely to do her bidding and preferred harsh treatment at her hands to being without her.

That night, after depositing Irwin in a safe but squalid residence, Inge went to the police station to speak to Klaus. He was very busy and asked her impatiently what it was, telling her before she spoke that he would rather speak to her at home. He felt harried and he knew things were on a knife's edge and he wanted to give his full attention to the Allied soldiers who were too close and he knew they were ill prepared for a large attacking force. They would fight to the finish but he knew they might just be slowing their progress rather than stopping them, just like on the Russian front. Love and sex had to remain on the back burner.

"I need to speak to you about Lotte's family again. Her eldest son died and she's devastated. Can't you please have her husband and other son transferred? I'll make it worth your while," she said suggestively.

"Inge!" He raised his voice then modulated it and gestured for her to sit down on his lap. She did so and he said more reasonably, "If I transferred them I wouldn't be doing them any favours. The war is not won on this front either. There are many battles and intelligence suggests that there will be one imminently. I intend to win and we are preparing for an onslaught, but… we have all given our all and whatever happens we will have cause to be proud for what we have achieved and we will not surrender, down to the last man we will fight. The women do not fight; this is not Russia. I want you back in Berlin, Ingelise," he said determinedly.

She had never heard him speak of defeat as a possibility, which he now did. The resolute boldness remained, but his certainty had faded. "They might advance, but it will only be temporary," Inge said, trying to lift him with this news which she felt certain of because of their counter-spell.

"Go and look after the townhouse. If you want to help me, help the people of Berlin."

"I can't leave you, my love," she said, wrapping her arms around his neck needily.

"I only summoned you because I believed it was safe here. That is no longer the case. Rouen and Delta are dead. This indicates to me that you are not safe. When things improve I will recall you." He spoke with finality – as far as he was concerned she was heading back to Berlin.

"No," she said, blatantly defying him for the first time in their relationship. Tears welled in her eyes as she did this and he stared at her coldly and prised her arms from him and pushed her from his lap. He went to leave the room and she ran to stop him. "Please, Klaus, I can't leave you now," she said desperately.

"If you go on a train tonight then I will organise those two transfers. Otherwise, no." He felt he was bending here and being accommodating.

"Tomorrow?" she said, instantly agreeing to go on those conditions, and just wanting one more night with him, a sudden licentious smile breaking through the tears.

"Tonight," he said firmly, knowing full well that time was of the essence. She nodded and he kissed her, stroking her back. "We'll get another chance. It'll spur me on to finish them quickly."

"You don't need spurring on," she observed. He was so committed to the party, a devotion that evoked jealousy, but also touched her and seemed noble. She understood Lotte's desperation for her men to live for she shared the anxiety and would act to ensure Major Klaus Von Strauss lived and prospered.

Laura offered Grey a glass of her finest wine as they sat together late at night, as usual the last two up. He told her to save it until the end of the war, a comment which she ignored as she returned with her best wine which she poured out for both of them.

"Everything will become more readily available after the war so enjoy it now," she said as she sipped from her glass.

"From what I hear things might still be hard in Britain. I'm not just saying that to try to persuade you to visit my fine country, a good few British people have said words to that effect," he said as he swirled the wine around in his mouth, unsure if he liked the taste.

"I expect some items will be in short supply for the general public. Do you really think I won't be able to get what I want?" she said, as cocksure as ever.

"I'm sure you'll be able to; it'll be easier still in the States. Thanks for this wine."

"You don't like it, do you?" she observed.

He shook his head. "It's too rich for me. I'll finish the glass though."

"No you won't," she said, pouring his glass into hers. "Go down and fetch one that you like."

"If I can find one that is. I dread to think how big the tab is going to be when we leave," he said, very grateful to her for how much she had provided for them.

"You will be indentured to me for this life and the next."

"I can think of worse fates," Grey said. What she threatened him with didn't sound so bad as it would mean he'd keep seeing her. He returned with one of her cheaper bottles, which he poured for himself as he sat back down.

"Are you preparing the tab now? You sense it too, don't you?" Grey said. She offered him what she considered her finest wine for a reason, because she knew, as he did, that Allied forces were near and they were prevailing. It was what Grey wanted more than anything, even though the price was high. He would have to leave Laura before he was ready, before he had achieved his heart's desire.

She nodded. "They're close, but so are a large unit of Germans. I'll tell you when you have safe passage. I wouldn't bother telling the others yet."

"I'll wait till you say," Grey said, in no rush to leave, and a little melancholic.

"Chin up. You believe in this war and your side – this might be a little premature, but I believe they are winning."

"You're right," he said, forcing himself to be cheerful. "I'm glad I got to finish off your garden."

"Estate, if you don't mind," Laura said grandiosely, deliberately talking in the manner of one of Grey's former customers he had told her about.

"Of course, I was your estator, not gardener. I wanted to do a better job than I did but you know, obviously I couldn't go into town for supplies." Grey had asked her two weeks previous which areas of land were not hallowed ground which he could try and spruce up for her as one way of saying thanks and to showcase his gardening skills to her. Grey had enlisted Konah's help in this to try and cheer him up as he was particularly glum of late and a spot of gardening had the desired effect (Grey knew what was coming when he let him man the hose but it was worth it to see him laugh and Konah was almost hysterical with laughter when Grey chased him with the hose), though Grey enjoyed the work even more.

"Why not, you've treat this place like a hotel and come and gone as you've pleased?" Laura joked. "I'm happy with the result. I won't make you do it again like poor old McKinley had to. Because I know you're leaving I can admit I'm impressed. You have versatile talents."

"I might get scared of you like the others if you start acting too nice!"

"Don't worry, there's no danger of that."

"I've enjoyed getting my hands dirty. I didn't realise how much I've missed it."

"I noticed. You can stay on as my gardener if you want."

"Another time."

"Alas, this is a one-time offer."

"What would you do if I did say yes?" Grey said, smiling at her. They both knew he wouldn't and were playing with each other, both very comfortable with each other now.

"Go over the new ground rules, as appropriate between employer and permanent staff. The offer is genuine."

"You'd probably have more regulations than the army."

"Definitely. One can't have staff exceeding the boundaries."

"That would be most improper," Grey said, copying the cut glass accent Laura had taken on. Returning to his own accent he said, "If there's no chance of impropriety that makes my decision easier. The gardening will have to wait because we have a trip to look forward to. It's my turn to play host."

"When did this become concrete? A possible trip, James," Laura pointed out.

They stayed up talking until they had both finished their bottles at which point Laura made Grey an unexpected offer. He had told her of how Hill liked to practice football in his sleep, kicking out violently every hour or so, and as they slept top and tail Delgado or himself (whichever had drawn the short straw that night and shared with him) were usually woken a couple of times by a kick to the head or throat, or if they were lucky just their chest or back. Delgado was more cross about it than Grey (Delgado was grumpy whenever he first woke up and being kicked awake tested his patience to its limits) though Grey was glad it was his turn for sleeping on the floor, which he said, in passing, he was going to do, glad of the wine as he said it would get him to sleep quickly.

"You don't have to sleep on the floor. There's a double bed in my bedroom which I'll let you share, as a friend," she emphasised.

"Are you sure you don't mind?" he said, taken aback by the offer.

"You're not going to be here much longer so I think I can put up with your snoring for one night. It'll be their turn for the floor the next two nights and I sincerely doubt you'll be here beyond that. This is purely platonic – misjudge the signals tonight and you'll be drinking bromide through a straw," she joked, aware that Grey wouldn't push the issue now until he went.

"Best behaviour tonight, I promise. Even I have too much class to try and take advantage of your generosity," Grey said solemnly. At the time it had seemed so right to kiss her and ever since he'd regretted it. It had cast him in the role of predator, as a wolf rather than a potential beau, as he falsely believed that it had shaken Laura up.

Delgado opened the door of his room as Grey and Laura stood by the door to hers, Grey acknowledging him with a look before looking away from him. Laura saw that Delgado was shooting daggers at them and after unlocking the door she ushered Grey in and stood by her door, refraining from entering for a moment. "Pray for him," she said melodramatically, smiling terrifyingly.

"I will," Delgado said severely and he went into his room.

Delgado had spoiled the moment a little for Grey, but he quickly dispelled him from his mind as he looked at the interior of Laura's bedroom for the first time. It wasn't painted black or red, there were no gargoyles, no pentagrams – all of the imagery that the others had invented when talking about what lay in her room was absent. It was an ordinary room; it was large, painted white and was very tidy. There was a thin bookcase by Laura's large bed, which Grey looked at and he noticed that the manuscripts housed here looked prehistoric and he did not touch them.

"Is this what you expected?" she said exuberantly.

"It's got a bed so it passes muster with me. It's nice," he said truthfully, though it was plainer than he anticipated.

"My bedroom in Scotland is painted black with the constellations on the ceiling – my astrologer friend loved that. This room is a deliberate contrast to that."

"That room sounds good too. I know that you practice witchcraft, Laura, and if this room had been representative of that, it wouldn't have bothered me in the slightest. At least I know I won't get kicked tonight."

"You're certainly safe tonight. I've been told that I'm a very passive sleeper. If I'm completely immobile and don't seem to be breathing pay no attention," she said casually, trying to pass off something very unusual as routine.

"I'm glad you've warned me of that otherwise I'd have given myself a heart attack thinking you were..." He didn't want to complete the sentence and didn't need to, saying enough to please her.

"I want to get changed now so you should go to the bathroom. What do you sleep in? You don't sleep naked, do you?" Laura said, doubting this, but also not permitting it – she was inviting him in as a friend only.

"No," Grey said, shaking his head. "When it's hot like this just my shorts. Is that okay or do you want me to leave my undershirt and pants on? I mean my trousers," he said quickly.

"I know; I'm inured to your bastardized English now. It's not necessary for you to wear your trousers or your vest as long as you keep your shorts on," she said and Grey left her for ten minutes and knocked on her door, waiting for her to call him in before re-entering.

When Laura had told him she had wanted to get changed Grey had imagined she would change into a nightdress, or maybe pyjamas. He had not expected her to have changed into what she was wearing: his army jacket with nothing underneath, her torso bare and her cleavage fully exposed, the jacket buttoned only at the bottom, Laura also wearing a spare pair of his shorts (Grey had assumed someone else had stolen them as a prank yesterday and had not expected her to be the culprit). She saw he was pleasantly surprised, knocked for six at seeing her like this, and she led him by the hand to a chair and sat him down as she stood on the bed facing him and sang Lilli Marlene for him. Even a treat like this had to have a little sting so she fulfilled his request and sang the song he asked for, in perfect German. He was captivated regardless.

After Laura had finished, ending by stretching out the final note for as long as she was able, she jumped off the bed and said, "You experienced something more exclusive than an army show there, so if the stars can't be bothered to come out and perform for you, at least you've had one performance."

"Bravo, Laura. I'd love an encore because that was great, but I'm so grateful you did that for me I'm not going to ask for anything more," Grey said, grinning broadly as he clapped.

"What I just did goes with you to your grave. Don't tell anyone I did that. I have a dark veneer to protect," she said. She had a strange feeling in her gut that Grey wasn't going to survive the war and gave a little more of herself than she ordinarily would because of this. Acting like a fool was worth it in this instance.

"That's all it is, a veneer," Grey said, more convinced than ever of the good that resided in her.

"You didn't know me way back when, thankfully. I told you I couldn't sing."

"And I said you'd sound good to me and you sure did."

"Come back safe and you might get the English version." Laura took a long black nightdress from her wardrobe and said, "You can get changed now and get into bed. I'm going to the bathroom."

"You don't have to. I'll go so you can change," Grey said, determined that no one else see her like that, even if it would disprove Pearce's contention that she was unattractive once and for all. The army uniform had never looked so good.

"I have to go, quite literally. Don't worry about protecting my modesty, James, I do intend to wear my dressing gown."

"Okay."

Laura returned in her long nightdress and dressing gown with his clothes and a glass of water and found Grey sitting on her bed in his shorts.

"Seems as I'll be back in the army soon enough I've adopted the mindset of a private again, which means I need instructions for the simplest of things, hence me sitting here. So 'Sarge' – which side do you want me?" he said jocularly.

Laura put his jacket and shorts down and smiled at him and said, "The left. I put my water on the table." As Grey moved under the covers Laura took off her dressing gown and lit several incense candles which were positioned around the perimeter of the room. He watched her intently, her sleeveless nightdress covering most of her body, down to her ankles, covering the shapely legs which he had now seen in all of their glory. The long life she had lived had not taken its toll on her soft and supple body. His own body was in good shape mainly due to his training prior to joining the army and he felt no embarrassment at Laura seeing him stripped down, perhaps hoping to impress her a little, though he suspected that even if he had the body of a god she would be no more interested. The sight of her half-dressed, or even in her nightdress, blew him away, while she barely looked at his body as he sat up in bed. "Your sergeant actively puts you in danger while I try, in vain, to talk you out of danger so that job's no use to me. Not that any danger exists worse than that which you're in now!" she said archly, playing up to her stereotype, talking of herself as a supervillain.

"The Pagan Resistance gals – nice as they are – scare me more than you, Laura."

"That's fair comment, I can hear where you're coming from there," Laura agreed, lighting the last of the 13 candles and walking around the bed and climbing into her side. Grey lay back and instantly felt a huge difference in comfort between her bed and those in the guest rooms. The black sheets were thick and he instantly felt warm under them, her pillows soft and luxurious and he felt ready for sleep, but he resisted.

"This is better than sleeping on the floor. Thank you," he said, wishing desperately that he could make a move on her, or that she would seduce him, settling for being her bedmate if not her lover. Paulette had aroused him when they had shared a room but it was nothing compared to how he felt with Laura, even though she was mostly covered.

"This way I'm guaranteed a helper in the sty in the small hours. Sorry, I don't think I told you that there were conditions," she said sharply

"After a night on this bed I'll be able to lift the pigs around if you want. What's in the mattress?"

"A good magician never reveals her tricks. Actually I just brought the bed in a shop in Brussels," she admitted. "Not everything is down to witchcraft."

"Your survival isn't. It got you eternal life but you've known, or have known of, a lot of other witches in that time who haven't made it. You've got the power, but your survival through trying times is down to you. I'm having enough trouble surviving one war and you've survived hundreds and all of the Inquisitions. Makes me seem like a dope for not following your advice more now that I think about it."

"There's no need for a simile, and hundreds of wars is a slight exaggeration."

"I'm still going to ask you for some tips before I go back."

"The first and most important tip would be don't go back but we've done this argument to death and we've both made ourselves clear, Private. Give yourself a bit of credit though. You say you're having enough trouble surviving this war, yet I didn't notice any sign of injury on your body, and I dare say you would have told me anyway."

"I'm probably saving up my injuries for the big one, a shell in the face."

"Or maybe my good fortune will rub off on you. At least you can tell all of them that you slept with me now and you truly can, I don't give a damn what they think."

"I can't do that."

"Delgado thinks we're sleeping together now. You'll be believed and it'll help your reputation – in some quarters, others will think you need purification."

"My reputation isn't that of a man about town, but if the only way I'll get that tag is by besmirching you, then I'll stay as I am."

"You're far too honourable to survive as long as I have. That's why you're sharing this bed, because I know I can trust you. I've shared my bed with female friends and eunuchs before and you're not that different."

"One difference springs to mind," Grey said, unsure what to make of the comparison, but not pointing out the difference as he felt it would be inappropriate to do so. If she only expressed an interest he could show her the difference and talk as much as he wanted about it, but as she made it clear that sex was prohibited, he kept quiet. "They were eunuchs before they went to bed with you?" he said, expressing fake concern.

"I think so," she said, feigning uncertainty. "You can sleep soundly, they were, and they did it to themselves. That's why I don't have many friends, because my judgement is criminally poor and I always pick the oddest people around."

"A good survival technique. It keeps other people away, because the masses are always scared of what's different – that would be the same throughout history, right?"

"I wish it was. They're scared individually and then they all get together and find courage in a mob. How are you finding the candles?"

"They're very strong. I'm not complaining though, I can't leave this bed for the floor now."

"Don't worry, I won't throw you out of the bed now. Not until four in the morning anyway when you're going mucking out. What do you prefer: being shook, me shouting in your ear or a bucket of water over you?"

"If you could gently touch my arm and say my name quietly – was that an option?"

"It can be. Shall we say eight, then they can all see you come out of here?"

"I don't want that, Laura. I don't want them running you down."

"More than usual, you mean. I'm already a demon to them so I don't mind being a harlot too. If you really don't want them to know then I'll wake you about seven. I don't suppose Delgado will tell the others. He'll be lecturing you interminably tomorrow," she warned.

"Again, after sleeping in this bed I'll be ready for even that. Really, it's just a normal bed from a shop?"

"Yes. It wasn't cheap though. If I did decide to go to America, and that's a big if, I'd help you find a good bed."

"And we could always do this to save money, if you don't mind."

"It was my suggestion and you know I don't suggest things if I'm not prepared to do them. I will want to go to sleep soon though and that's your cue to be quiet when I say so."

"How is that different to in the daytime?" he said, making fun of her dominating persona.

"Your choices again are water, shaking or shouting."

"Point taken, I will be silent. You don't mean now?"

"No, I'm not tired yet – and that's where you come in," she jested.

"So that's my function. Do you want more about my school years or the trips every summer to Uncle Frank's?"

"Please don't," she said, laughing in mock despair. "I should be able to fall asleep naturally. You're the first person to share a bed with me since Georges. Pleasant dreams, James," she said tenderly, turning on her side away from him.

"This is appreciated, Laura. I'm so grateful that I can fit in one story about Uncle Frank before you go to sleep. It was the last summer before the war..."

"No, no, no. Sleep, sleep, sleep, sleep," she said, folding her pillow over her exposed ear.

"It can wait then. Thank you for giving me this moment – this is kindness. It means a lot to me now and it'll mean more when I'm back with my unit," he said gratefully.

"You treasure strange things. Wallowing in pigshit, and trying to sleep while a witch talks about eunuchs and threatens you with various annoying ways to wake you up – that all sounds unpleasant to me. I just didn't want you to sleep on the floor. If it makes you happy, then great, but good night."

"Good night."

Screaming resounded in the Cremonts farm. Yves Cremont's two young daughters, Germaine and Carol, screamed as they saw their mother being kicked around the kitchen by Inge and they clung to one another for support. Their mother was coughing up blood as Inge did this, while Inge called her a treacherous bitch (Inge viewed any who opposed the Nazis as traitors) whose husband got what he deserved, Inge pretending to be irate with her, her anger a performance. She was not cross at all, this was just to scare the family and it worked magnificently, especially as they had discovered the three grotesquely disfigured bodies in the barn and were already hypersensitive, fit to snap. The trauma and the loss had been hard enough to deal with as a family and then Grey's visit had created discordance between the three of them, making their lives difficult enough without Inge's unwelcome visit (which succeeded in instantly uniting them).

"Please leave her alone," Germaine wailed, pleading for mercy. She felt sure this was the beast her father and James Grey had warned her about and she was terrified.

"Shut up," Inge said, staring at her. "I'm requisitioning this farm now and you all have to be quiet or you die. Talk again and I tear your mother's head off." Germaine fell silent, appearing to laugh as her jaw quivered in hysteria. Inge dragged their mother by her hair, which was now dishevelled, hanging loose instead of in a bun as it had been, and she flung her down the cellar steps. Mrs Cremont managed to grab the banister midway down, but her momentum meant that she found herself falling still and she landed at the bottom. She tried to get up to go to her girls who had been pushed towards the stairs by Inge and they descended quickly before they were pushed down also.

"This is my farm now," Inge said to the three of them, "and you live down here until I leave. If you scream I will come down and kill you all." There was only one way out of the large cellar and Inge would leave that locked at all times. No one could know she was here bar Eric and Lotte, as Klaus had to believe that she had gone back to Berlin. She boarded the train under surveillance, exiting before the train departed, unnoticed by the guards. She had unfinished business and was not going to abandon her lover to the Allies and the Pagan Resistance. That was her fight.

As Inge climbed the stairs Mrs Cremont mumbled to her, "Please, Madame – we have no food." She was scared to speak, but for the sake of her daughters she risked another assault.

Inge said nothing and several minutes later she opened the door to the cellar stairs and smiled down at them all. She had gone outside and made a noose from rope and snared a pig, which she now presented at the top of the stairs, and she gave it an almighty push. Mrs Cremont was still lying on the floor and she had too little time to move out of the way as the pig rolled down the stairs towards her, almost breaking the wooden steps with its sheer weight. Carol tried to drag her away before she was struck while Germaine found herself taking a step backwards. Inge closed the door and she did not see the collision and she assumed they would get out of the way in time and make use of the pig and she locked the door. The large sow crushed Mrs Cremont, and Carol quickly died from the blow she took, leaving Germaine alone in the darkness, too afraid to scream. The pig was slowly dying and in its death throes made a hideous noise and Germaine covered its dirty mouth with both hands, so petrified of Inge coming down if she heard any sound. Blocking its mouth did not seem to dim the sounds and she hit it to silence it until finally it was still. She then began to cry, shedding a torrent of tears. She was alone now with no family to speak of and a bleak future, but she did not wish for death. Despite it all she wanted to live.

With Inge safely on her way back to Berlin Major Von Strauss could concentrate on the task at hand again. In retrospect he should never have had her by his side while the war was not yet won though he could never regret any time he spent in her company. As things currently stood he was unsure whether they would ever meet again. Ever since the war began he had been in constant danger, and now that danger seemed strongest as decisions were made that made no tactical sense to him, decisions that could only signify the beginning of the end.

These incomprehensible instructions had to be carried out and he gathered his men to hear his speech from their woodland base a few miles outside Maramont.

"I'll be as brief as possible because time is pressing. We will be withdrawing from our current position immediately. A decision has been made – a decision I don't personally agree with, that we should be operating a more defensive campaign. Orders are orders and we must follow these instructions."

"Sir, how far back are they sending us?" Jaeger asked. Jaeger was one of his best soldiers and Strauss knew that this rankled with him almost as much as it did with him.

"I queried the order when I received it, but my superior was clear. I appreciate that you're all disappointed. This particular area has attempted to be problematic, and while their resistance has been crushed and there have been reprisals, I am not satisfied. This is our final night here. I suggest we make this the final night of Maramont. Tonight, while the majority of us start heading back, I need volunteers to form an intervention group to implement a scorched earth policy there."

Dozens of hands went up at once and Strauss continued, "I want every male over the age of 16 killed. Any women who prove to be a nuisance join them. If they look at you the wrong way that's sufficient reason – in this instance you will face no reprimand. Gentlemen, tonight you have a free pass to do anything you wish without recourse. This is no ordinary town. Beyond the terrorists here, there is something grotesquely corrupt at this town's black heart. Burn every house to the ground and stake the heart."

As Strauss's subordinates picked the best 40 men from the volunteers (Strauss knew he needed volunteers for this task, refusing to force his men to do this, noting that some were unwilling and thinking no less of them for it) he talked quietly with Looste. "Make it clear that everyone, man, woman and child dies at that tavern."

Looste nodded. "There's a manor a few miles out of town where an Englishwoman lives. Do you want that destroyed too?" Looste had only become aware of this information recently and had not brought it up until now as Strauss had vetoed the topic of the Pagan Resistance shortly after first talking of it.

"Do you know her name?"

"Laura Spencer."

"Raze it to the ground and have her decapitated." If they could not stay as conquerors they would leave as destroyers.

The Pienas lived on the outskirts of town, thankfully at the opposite end of town from the tavern which decreased the chances of running into their wayward daughter, Odette. They heard a commotion outside, raised voices yet again and a few anguished cries and looked at each other fleetingly before Mr Piena looked back down at his paper while Mrs Piena continued knitting. Odette was out of their lives yet Mrs Piena still found herself knitting baby clothes. "It doesn't bear thinking about," Mr Piena said, refusing to discuss the matter more than that.

The Pienas other daughter, Francoise Mathieu, was more curious than her parents. Carrying her five year old son she drew back the curtain and looked onto the street and saw a small group of German soldiers running about with purpose, with a handful carrying flamethrowers ominously as she saw a handful of her neighbours standing outside, disconsolate.

"Come away from the window," Mr Piena said. "Don't draw attention to us and they'll pass by."

"There's something terribly wrong," Francoise said, letting the curtain fall back into place. "They're up to something."

Francoise had two other children, a boy of eight and a girl of seven who were playing on the floor with cars. The boy, Etienne, said, "What are they doing now?" his words combining anger, as he knew he was supposed to hate the German soldiers who killed his father four years ago, and fascination.

"Your father's right. It's best not to think about it," Mrs Piena said, that option removed from them all as their front door was booted in and three soldiers marched in. Mr Piena dropped his paper in shock and was shot through the brain before he had chance to speak, his mouth hanging open, the sentence he prepared never to be spoken. Mrs Piena screamed loudly and was shot three times in the head and neck. Francoise turned her back on the soldiers, trying to shield her son as best she could from the bullet she anticipated heading her direction. She gestured for her two oldest to come to her and they clung to her body, with Etienne staring intently at the soldier who had killed his grandparents who eyeballed him back threateningly. There was a brief, tense exchange between two of the soldiers before Francoise was forcibly dragged from the house and her children shepherded out with her as the house was set ablaze by a flamethrower. She was left to stand in the street where three of her female neighbours were stood, all looking dazed, as they looked along the street, at the homes ablaze and the progress that the troops were making, as more lives were destroyed.

"Animals!" Anne Breton shouted, finding her tongue. She stood next to Francoise and had just seen her husband of 52 years bayoneted in front of her, a man who at 83 was still worth a hundred of these boy soldiers. Her insult did not go unpunished as several rounds were fired in her direction, one grazing Francoise's arm. She tried calming her youngest as he started to cry loudly, determined that her children would live unlike her poor parents and the Bretons and seemingly every other adult male in cursed Maramont. She hoped they would spare Odette, though she knew that some of these men were capable of killing pregnant women.

Grey withdrew from a conversation he was having with Delgado and entered the library where Laura was sitting looking out of the window. Grey closed the door behind him and leaned on the table for support, stunned as he said under his breath, "They're killing everybody?"

Laura turned and looked up at him sorrowfully and said, "I thought you might sense it too."

"It's a massacre."

"This is why spells are inappropriate in these matters. Yes, they're leaving, but they're destroying everything before they leave," she said, philosophical on the matter. What she found sad about it was that he knew about it too – she had hoped his senses would fail him this once though she knew there was no chance of that. He was too good a medium by far, and his knowledge was what was going to cause the problem and likely his death.

"This wasn't supposed to happen. They were supposed to withdraw."

"They will, once they've fulfilled their objective. This is a routine practice in war."

"Not here. They usually practice this on the Russian front. We…not we, you were railroaded into helping…I caused this."

"They were killing townsfolk before you came, James. An Allied victory would mean they'd have had to withdraw eventually."

Grey shook his head. "It's not common practice here. This is retaliation. I have to go and stop them."

"An Allied force is tantalisingly close. Wait."

Grey shook his head. "I have to go now. Every minute I wait another life is lost. I'm going to ask the others if they'll come – I'd best say bye now. This is all on my head, not yours," he said, totally deflated.

"Go and speak to them and see me before you go. I have weapons."

Grey looked at her quizzically and she said, "You'll see."

Grey gathered the men in his bedroom and told them about the massacre, pretending he'd heard about it on the wireless.

"She doesn't have a wireless," Winters said.

"Must be something the lovebirds share," Pearce said querulously.

"Don't start, Pearce, I'm not in the mood," Grey said emotionally. "I have weapons, if you'll come with me. The odds aren't great."

"Without ammo they're impossible," Strapulos said cogently.

"If we had ammo would you be willing?"

Pearce refused to go with him at first until he learnt that the others were all willing which would leave him alone with Laura, bar the brat. This changed his mind.

Grey ran downstairs and joined Laura in the library again. He saw an arsenal of weapons on the table and he knew where she'd acquired them. "I thought you destroyed them. I'm glad you didn't," he said, picking up a pistol. This small collection could make the difference, with over 20 grenades, at least 100 rounds of ammo, 3 pistols and 5 knives.

"Dishonesty is the least of my flaws," Laura responded. She had planned on giving him the weapons stash when he finally rejoined Allied forces – until then it proved easier to pretend they were destroyed so that he did not ask for weapons when he joined the Pagan Resistance on manoeuvres. "Criminal judgement is my biggest failing, picking you for a friend. A strong Allied force is coming. If you wait you'll survive. I know you won't wait."

"This is my fault."

"You don't know that conclusively," Laura said. "Good intentions don't always pan out, but don't beat yourself up about it. They need little reason to kill."

"I have to try and make amends."

"The people of Maramont are historically strong and proud. They'd rather die free than live enslaved, even if that means a large number of them won't be around to enjoy their freedom."

"The way they're killing it sounds like none of them will be left."

"I can't help you. I've already broken the habit of a lifetime by intervening once and as demonstrated, that doesn't always go according to plan. I didn't predict this; this isn't some lesson to teach you that intervention is wrong. I genuinely thought…we English have a habit of underestimating the Nazis."

"You played your part to perfection. Now it's time for soldiers to finish the job."

"You're not even going to bother changing into civilian garb?"

"The men are coming with me and I stand with them. If I die tonight I'm proud to die an American soldier. Wearing the uniform makes me no braver though – either outfit equals death tonight, if captured. This is a very dangerous night, Laura, and I don't like deserting my post here," he said dolefully, looking deep into her eyes, the dreaded puppy dog look that was starting to strike some unwelcome chord. He was walking into the gates of hell, and doing so fearfully, yet his greatest concern was for her. Why couldn't his powers have failed him for one night? If she'd have felt the shockwaves sooner she could have made him sleep through it. Unfortunately he knew about it almost at once and it was too late to perform well-intentioned spells on him.

"I didn't know I had my own guard, like the King," she joked, trying to diffuse the atmosphere.

"I'm happy to wear the funny hat, if you you want me to."

"Come back with your head on your shoulders, then we'll talk. I wish you well, but I can't be involved."

"And I would never want you to be. I didn't before. I believe that what we did was still successful," he said, trying to convince himself.

"I do too. Whatever happens, it ends over the next day or two, one way or the other."

Eric Girard heard the commotion and looked out of the window and saw bedlam. The city was ablaze and scores of people were running from the flames. Had the Allies reached them already, turning Maramont into a war zone again? He put a dressing gown over his pyjamas and walked out into the street. A man who was vaguely known to him ran past him, pausing for a moment to say, "Run, you idiot, they're slaughtering everyone."

Eric saw German troops on the horizon, advancing from the direction where the fires blazed. Surely they would pass over his house? Even if they did Eric knew how this would be viewed, though he knew that the chances of them doing so were very remote. One soldier had the effrontery to fire at him, and Eric was forced to slow the bullet as it approached, stopping the momentum totally so that the bullet fell to the ground inches from him. The scene was so mad that if anyone witnessed what he had done they would not be surprised. Eric could not chance his luck further and he was forced to run with the crowd, abandoning his home and his valued possessions. He had already changed allegiances once and as he ran, hunted like a dog in his nightclothes, he weighed up his options anew.

Mireille peered through the window before unlocking the door, relieved to see that the person hammering at her back door was James Grey dressed in his army uniform. He had explained to the others that he had to warn his friends in town and would try and meet up with them after, prompting criticism from Pearce, comments about meeting his scarecrow lover again to try and shelter from the storm. Grey was completely out of breath after running the whole way at full pelt.

Mireille was relieved that Gervaise and Eric were both at their own homes as she knew how they would react to this reckless gesture if they had been there. Mireille might have agreed with them once but ever since Didier's death she had no inclination to play it safe and any enemy of her enemy was a firm friend who she would readily sacrifice herself for. She gestured for him to enter after a brief hello and she called Paulette to come down to translate for them, pouring a drink for him as they waited. Grey didn't have time to wait and he took two Lugers from his backpack (Hill had needed the third, his rifle abandoned during his last battle) and pointed to the door. Mireille didn't understand and Grey pointed to the stairs and Mireille accompanied him upstairs where Grey called out Paulette's name, unsure which room she occupied.

"Coming," she called from Arnaud's old room. Grey misheard her and caught her in a state of undress again, just topless this time as she pulled a blouse overhead.

"Sorry," Grey mumbled. "Time is of the essence. The Jerries are destroying the town and killing every man they find and a fair few women too. I have two Lugers if you want them – she'll kill me for this, but you could stay with Laura 'till this is all over."

"Give me the Luger," Paulette said keenly, a bloodlust coming over her. Mireille stood in the doorway and asked Paulette for a translation which Paulette delivered quickly and they headed downstairs. Mireille went down to the basement where Hugo Tremaint was still hiding out, sleeping in a hidden anteroom (Georges gave Laura the idea, though the room in the tavern was even smaller and was opened by a switch rather than through magic), and she roused him and returned upstairs where she saw Grey downing a pint glass of water.

"I have to go. You know where Laura lives though, yeah?" Grey said, having done what he set out to. They needed to be warned as they were most at risk.

"I think so," Paulette said, posing with the gun, pointing at imaginary targets. "Grey – save some for me."

"There's plenty to go round," Grey said grimly as he left, hoping he could rejoin his men who were hopefully approaching town now.

Hugo slept in his clothes and after putting his shoes and jacket on he joined the women upstairs. After Didier's capture and execution and Paulette's capture, the Pagan Resistance were without weapons, as was the one surviving member of the Communist Resistance. Hugo picked up the other Luger and said, "Where's the ammo?"

"We have to make our bullets count," Paulette said.

"There are weapons well hidden at the Cremont's farm – give me the ammo from that gun, Paulette and I'll go out now and start picking them off," Hugo suggested. "Or I could rush back there now and arm us for victory. There's a ton of ammo there."

Paulette approved of this idea and looked to Mireille who strongly considered it before shaking her head. Her heart said yes, but her head was just about in control, only because she was leader and had to act responsibly. "That would mean leaving the town and we should be here for what happens."

"I can be there and back in under two hours," Hugo said.

"No. The Germans know it was used by your group and could be watching it still. You might miss the action if you left. They'll be leaving soon and we'll be helping them on their way."

"I want to fight them more than you do but we can't do much with 12 bullets," Hugo said, challenging her decision more than he would any of the senior members of his old group. While he did not consider himself a member of Mireille's group he did feel indebted to her and would not leave to get the ammunition without her approval.

"Sorry, Hugo, but I can't give you the bullets because there's six German soldiers waiting to receive them from me," Paulette said breathlessly and an argument commenced as Mireille also wanted a weapon. Hugo claimed to be proficient with handguns (untrue but Mireille was predisposed to let him have one of the guns) and claimed one while Paulette pleaded her case for the other, praising Mireille but telling her she didn't have her experience in the field. Mireille liked the feel of the metal in her hand and liked the idea of revenge even better.

"Please, Mireille, I've used guns before, maybe more than him," Paulette said, earning her a black look from Hugo who wasn't giving his weapon up.

"He's under sentence of death – he needs a weapon."

"Okay, but can't I have the other? You're a great leader and a powerful witch but this is my field."

"I want to shoot one of them and then you can have it," Mireille said, a compromise which suited them both, though Mireille immediately went back on it as she thought of her grandchild. "I'm sorry to disappoint you, Paulette, but I have a much more important mission for you. You could kill every German here, I know that, and I entrust you with something greater. Hurry Odette to Laura's home. Konah will be delighted to see you again. Keep them safe until this is over."

Paulette sighed and handed the gun over to Mireille, begrudgingly accepting her assignment. "Be careful, Mireille. When you first use them they can be tricky."

"I won't flinch," Mireille said with certainty. "Another time you'll get your chance, I promise."

By the time Paulette had roused Odette from her bed and ventured downstairs, Mireille and Hugo were gone and Paulette envied them. She joined the group for action and had to play nursemaid instead while adrenaline coursed through her veins. Odette was reluctant to start the trek and Paulette lied to her about the distance, promising her they'd be there within 20 minutes. Paulette put Odette's arm around her shoulder as she tried to hurry her along, taking her weight as she marched her quickly despite the pain she still felt from the assault.

"Slow down a bit!" Odette protested after a few minutes.

"I would carry you if I could but I can't because of what that demon put me through. If we're slow now the soldiers will put us through worse. I'm not going to be raped or killed by them and neither are you."

"Are we nearly there yet?"

"At least halfway," Paulette lied.

Eric had run away from one German troop straight into another. This squad seemed less trigger-happy, forcing Eric to join a 20 strong group of men on a forced march. Eric had no choice but to copy the other prisoners, marching with his hands on his head as their captors surrounded them, though he knew where this was headed. This was simply a tidier form of liquidation, to be performed out of town presumably. The grand vision that he, Georges, and even Mireille had for the Pagan Resistance was coming true – indirectly they had brought genocide to Maramont. They had made such an impression that it was to now be blotted from the map, wiped off the face of the earth. Saving himself now would prove hard and would require using his powers beyond any level he had attempted previously.

Of all of the people to play saviour James Grey was the least expected. One of the soldiers at the front hit the ground and looking down the street, facing them head-on he saw Grey fire again, striking another German who also hit the ground though remained conscious unlike the first victim who seemed a fatality. Grey quickly took cover at the side of a house as a dozen shots were fired in his direction, yet while they fired at Grey, pinning him down, shots rained from another direction, striking another man down. One of the prisoners, a fool or a hero or both, seized the dead soldier's weapon and managed to blow one German's head off before he was shot in the neck. Half of the prisoners snapped at this and some fought back while others ran to nearby side streets, Eric included, as the Germans began to retreat. Grey was able to move forward from his position in the chaos and Eric saw three other American soldiers advance with him. Eric did not recognise Grey – from a distance with his helmet on it could have been almost anyone, but Grey had seen Eric and he progressed to his alley and gave him a few words of encouragement while he reloaded.

"We've got this in hand now, Eric. Once we pin them back a bit more make a move." Grey could not offer Laura's home as a sanctuary to Eric simply because it was too late now, with the battle in full swing with the possibility of Eric being followed.

"Are there only seven of you?" Eric asked as Grey stood by the corner of the street, waiting for the right moment to show himself and strike again.

"There's not many of them either. If I go down that street there can I circle round them?"

"Probably."

"That's good enough for me," Grey said, signalling to Delgado who was in a parallel side street that he intended to try and strike at their rear while the others progressed with the frontal assault. As Grey ran from his position Eric made a move too, away from the conflict, to try and find a safe place for the night and to gather his thoughts. Having his life saved by a man whom he was conspiring to kill whilst his own allies left him to rot fucked with his head. Eric had never harboured a grudge against Grey and he had always been troubled by Inge's plans to kill him, for while Grey was a fool, he was harmless and, unlike the Communists, didn't deserve what she proposed.

The victims of the death squad had been informative enough to lead Grey to action; one of the death squad who spoke pidgin English proved even more useful and Grey now knew conclusively the extent of the genocide that they planned. Unbelievably, the spirit was able to rationalise his actions. Grey hid his disgust and tried to be non-judgemental and gleaned as much information as possible. There were 40 of them in total with two squads of 18 and one small group of 4 on a separate mission which Ulrich knew nothing about. Ulrich's squad killed the Frenchmen wherever they found them whilst the other squad (presumably the squad Grey was now facing) opted to round up small numbers and kill them out of town before setting fire to the corpses. While there would be much death tonight, Grey knew that even if they had not come to help, the Germans would still have failed their objective. Sending 40 men to massacre and despoil a small village would have been feasible, but for a medium sized town a much larger squad was needed. Already at least 10 of the 40 soldiers were dead, some like Ulrich, killed by the French townsfolk they underestimated, and their weapons armed another enemy.

Grey found weapons pointed at him as he turned the corner leading back to the action and discovered that there was already action at the rear of the German offensive. A small group of four men and one woman were armed and between them and the American soldiers the Germans were surrounded. Grey was quickly recognised as an American and the guns returned to their correct targets and Grey fired alongside them. The woman risked running across the street to him, firing as she did so, and she said, "How many of you are there?"

"7, including me. There's only 30 Germans involved in this. The rest have fled."

"There's less than 30."

"There's another squad doing the same. Let's talk later," Grey said, taking another shot, hitting his quarry again, a clean kill if there was such a thing. All of the training and advice was paying off as he became a sharpshooter.

The final three Germans surrendered and the Americans and the French closed in on them with the French reaching them first, with Grey rushing alongside them, trying to ensure that they didn't succumb to wrath.

"They're our prisoners. They'll pay for this, I promise you," Grey said as the prisoners hands were bound tightly behind their backs by the group Grey had just briefly fought with.

The woman stood by the most unimposing member of the group and she said, "I'm Mimi Levre. This is Blanc, our leader. Our resistance group has been operating for years working with your people. When it comes to matters like this, we decide what happens."

Pearce and the other soldiers came onto the scene and Pearce saw Grey conversing with a pretty Frenchwoman – better looking than the scarecrow or witch with curly blonde hair and he said, "You're a sorry excuse for a soldier. You abandoned your post again for a skirt."

"Shove it, Pearce. Ask Blanc what he intends to do with them, Mimi. Please," Grey said, realising his manner was brusque.

Mimi spoke in French to their leader and then told Grey, "Blanc understands you have to follow the Geneva Convention. We do not. They were not."

Grey shook his head. "We didn't help for them to be slaughtered. In battle's different. While we delay here there's another squad killing at a quicker pace than this one were. Ask him to hold fire on making any decisions until we've defeated them."

Mimi translated for them and Blanc and Grey were able to come to an agreement with the three soldiers guarded by one Resistance member, a barrel-chested man called Minsa, while the soldiers and the other Resistance members followed Grey who claimed to have seen where the other group were headed. As they marched Strapulos nudged Delgado and said quietly, "He'll kill them as soon as we go."

Delgado nodded and said, "Without a shadow of a doubt. He doesn't know that and it's best we keep him in the dark."

At the front Mimi was quizzing Grey for Blanc. Somehow they knew of his visits to the tavern and expressed disapproval and considered the other resistance groups as inferior and stated that he should have tried contacting them instead.

"All they have done is make life harder. They believe any action is better than no action. Idiots," Mimi said resentfully.

"They've made an impact," Grey said, trying to be diplomatic, unwilling to get into an argument as he needed to convince these people to hand the prisoners over to him, yet unable to agree with their harsh assessment of the Pagan and Communist Resistance.

"Because of them more of our people have been killed and shipped off to labour camps. Small victories are meaningless. We strive for higher aims – cracking codes, damaging supply lines, working in conjunction with our international counterparts and military intelligence," Mimi said dismissively.

"He ain't the leader. You can talk to all of us," Pearce said as he walked alongside Mimi.

Mimi looked at him with contempt and said, "He has all of the information," and she turned from him pointedly.

"He gets it by funny means. He's not quite right in the head," Pearce said.

"Just like you can't get on with all of the Resistance groups, I can't get on with every US soldier," Grey explained. "This battle might be tougher. I'm not sure you should come all of the way."

"I've taken more risks in this war than you know, far more than that bitch, Paulette. I'm as good a shot as you and I don't worry about taking prisoners," Mimi said. Grey saw a great deal of Paulette in Mimi, deducing that this was why they didn't get on as they were too alike.

Laura opened the door and looked down at Odette's bleeding legs, slashed to ribbons from the journey she'd undertaken while Paulette, sensibly wearing trousers, was fine.

"I apologise, Laura. I know you don't like to be involved," Paulette said as she supported Odette.

Laura ushered them inside, and said softly, "You're right, but these are extenuating circumstances. Have a seat. Grey invite you by any chance?"

"Yes. He said you'd kill him for it."

"I doubt I'll need to. I don't mind, Paulette." Laura went to the foot of the stairs and shifted to French as she told Konah to come downstairs. She looked at Odette's bleeding legs and said, "It's hard finding your way here in the dark. I'll get some bandages."

"Let's hope the Nazis can't find their way here at all. I'd actually like them to, to deal with them myself, but Mireille ordered me to come here," Paulette groused.

"I think I've been quite friendly! I've given you a warmer welcome than Grey received," Laura joked, pretending to take offence.

"No, I don't mean anything. I wanted to fight them," Paulette explained.

"You may yet get your chance," Laura said. Konah appeared and his face lit up as did Paulette's and she opened her arms and he ran at her. "I thought that might change your mind. You didn't see that coming, Konah, did you?"

"Might have," he muttered.

"Are you being good for Laura?" Paulette asked.

"He's been fine. The men however…"

"You like Grey, though, don't you?" Paulette said, assuming she was joking.

"For some unknown reason, yes," Laura admitted. With all that the Pagan Resistance knew that she had done for him lying about this seemed pointless. Also with Grey currently in grave danger she was concerned about him and couldn't bring herself to deny her affection for him.

"It's obvious he loves you," Odette said knowingly.

"Now I never said I loved him. Let's make that clear."

"Does he know that you don't?" Odette asked, intrigued by their relationship which seemed more interesting than her own humdrum existence. If Laura didn't want him there was still hope of a potential passport for her and escape to a new life.

"That topic's closed," Laura said, protective of him. "There are bigger things going on tonight. Did you get out before they came to your street?"

Paulette nodded. "Is it as bad as James says? Are they killing everyone?"

"Every man, yes. They're sore losers. They know they're on the ropes so they try and show they've still got power by killing unarmed civilians."

"They'll find we're not all unarmed. Oh, I wish I was there," Paulette said yearningly.

"You don't value being alive?" Laura asked.

"I do, but I'll risk myself to take them down. I know this is a horrible night because a lot of us won't survive it but this is what we've needed since they came back – to have to fight for our lives, because too many are too damned complacent, accepting the Nazis in power, when we should have repelled them every second of every day."

"People want to survive. If not for Georges I would be in Ravensbeck in Scotland, just outside of a small village that will never be bombed unless the bombers go dramatically off course..."

"They are imbeciles, that's possible," Paulette said.

"I stayed here for Georges, to rescue him if necessary. Now it's hard for even me to leave, but I am safe here still."

"At least you have the choice of leaving," Odette said. "What you said about them killing every man. You just mean the young ones?"

"Every man. James was contacted by an 82 year old man."

Odette's eyes twinkled as tears formed. "My father's 49. Do you think..."

Odette trailed off and Laura offered her some hope, stating, "Allied forces are close by and some American soldiers are already there and as Paulette says, the townspeople will rise up themselves when they see it's do or die. James' powers can be used lethally."

"He's too soft to do so," Paulette observed.

"If I had my way he wouldn't be fighting only no one ever heeds my advice. He's not ruthless, but he is tough and can make a difference."

"In body, yes, but not in mind," Paulette said. "I have no problem with him but I'd sooner have Hugo or Didier in my corner."

"Which proves you don't like a safety net," Laura said.

"You don't like him being criticised," Odette noted.

"Not unless it's coming from my lips, no. Are you worried about your father?"

Odette nodded. "They live on the edge of town. He won't get involved so he should be all right."

"That's why people do need to rise up, otherwise everyone's doomed," Paulette said.

"I have no idea how you've survived this long," Laura said to Paulette, a parting shot as she left the room to fetch bandages. Laura knew that Paulette had been one of Georges' favourites, and she had always found her polite and respectful, though now she found herself antagonised a little by her, over her comments about Grey, even though she was speaking the truth. He could risk his life in battle, march to certain death, yet when it came to certain hard decisions, morally murky choices, he was not cut from the same cloth as Laura or Paulette and Laura viewed this as to his credit, not something he should be censured for.

"I'll do it if you like," Paulette said agreeably when Laura returned.

"You've got Konah on your lap, I'll bandage her," Laura said, making an effort to be friendly with her. Paulette's comments had not been that contentious or even particularly critical – she was being hypersensitive, and she had to nip that in the bud. As a grown man he had to stand on his own two feet and fight his own battles without her rushing in taking umbrage at imagined slights. He'd fight for her honour, but he loved her while she…what a headfuck. "My goodness, have you crawled here, Odette?"

"I couldn't see a thing. The bushes didn't look thorny," Odette said, whimpering as Laura cleaned her cuts.

"The perils of living at the back of beyond. Konah, why don't you show Paulette around the house?"

Konah was glad to get away from Laura and he took Paulette by the hand and led her upstairs. As soon as they were gone Odette said cautiously, "So are you and Grey a couple?"

"That topic is prohibited, remember? Are you interested?"

Odette looked down to her bump and said, "No man is going to be interested in me any time soon."

"Under normal circumstances single mothers face prejudice. These are not normal times we live in. Many other women are in exactly the same position as you, without your good looks to fall back on. You'll be fine," Laura said reassuringly.

Odette forced a smile which quickly drooped. "Do you want a girl or a boy?" Laura asked as she continued bandaging her legs.

"Anything but twins."

"I wouldn't worry about it. Millions of people bring up kids so it can't be that hard. And we're done," Laura said, standing up and moving to her chair. She sensed that only four of them were coming to her house, aware of four men approaching – four men with Teutonic blood. They were still a long way off, possibly not heading her way, though it affected her composure. Odette asked her how long she'd lived there and Laura ignored her question and led her to bed. Paulette closed the door to Konah's room, shutting him in, and she smiled at Laura and Odette.

Once Laura had put Odette to bed Paulette whispered, "I need a word with you."

Laura gestured to the stairs and Paulette ran down followed by Laura. "Konah's just told me that four Germans are coming here to burn the house and…behead you."

Laura looked at her curiously, surprised at the beheading aspect. "How could he see that? That could never happen."

"He says that's their plan. He said you'd kill them. I thought you should be warned so you can arm yourself ready."

"Go and join Konah. I'll handle this," Laura said wearily.

"I said I wanted to get rid of them. I'll help."

"That's not part of the prophecy, so go."

"Konah says there are many futures. In this one I can be present."

"There is only one future. There are myriad possibilities, but only one actuality. As a prophet Konah should be seeing the actuality, otherwise he's no more prophet than you or I," Laura said, washing her hands of Odette's blood and iodine at the kitchen sink. Beheading? Could they know she was a witch?

"I want to fight. Georges called me an Amazon, a Valkyrie, a..."

"Maenad?" Laura offered snidely.

"What's that?"

"You don't know all of your mythological references then. Excuse my ill temper, Paulette, but I never wanted any part in this war and now I've learnt I have to kill again, something I haven't done for a long time."

"I can kill them without compunction, if you have weapons," Paulette offered.

"I can kill without compunction too. They're coming to kill me so I have no qualms about this. It's still tiresome. And they're almost here," Laura sighed.

"Are they?"

"You were there when I performed the spell. You know I have power. I haven't the time to quarrel with you. Come outside if you wish but know I can't guarantee your safety, or be sensible and leave me to it. I am in no danger."

Laura opened her front door and walked a few metres from the house to try and deal with them away from the property. They trampled her flowers as they made their way closer, the flamethrower operative catching her eye as he pointed his weapon at her garden threateningly. Paulette irritated Laura by appearing behind her, loitering in the doorway, observing the four men who paused as they surveyed the scene, standing some distance from Laura.

"Go inside," Laura said to Paulette without turning to look at her.

Paulette ignored her, shouting at the soldiers, "You must be proud of yourselves, targeting women."

"They don't understand," Laura said, shifting to German so that she could converse with them. "I'm sure I already know your purpose here but I'll do you the courtesy of giving you one last opportunity to salvage the situation."

The self-appointed leader of the small squad showed amusement in her words and the authoritative delivery, scoffing and looking at his comrades. "Are you the Englishwoman?"

"You're not exactly natives here yourselves. Yes, I am," she said, challenging him with a stare as to what he was going to do about it.

The soldier pulled a short sword from his pack and gave his men the order to fire. Two of the group fired, while the flame trooper waited his order, conserving his fuel as much as possible. Both of their guns backfired as they attempted to shoot Laura and Paulette, injuring one man's hand grievously. He fell to the ground and was attended to by the other shooter.

"Hard luck," Laura said. "I heard German manufacturing was highly efficient. Take that as a portent and leave my property now!"

The leader commanded the flame trooper to fire and as he fired he found his feet growing heavy. His flame died out without reaching her and as he examined his weapon the ground below him turned to quicksand. He noticed his colleagues sinking too, as confused as he was with only one making any sound, a low, guttural cry. Within ten seconds he was buried six foot deep and sinking further as the earth formed a seal above him...

Paulette stepped forward and said calmly, "How far down did you send them?"

"Not quite to the earth's core. At least 50ft, maybe more."

"I wish you'd been with us from the start. I know you've always been on our side, you just like peace," Paulette said with admiration.

"What I just did had nothing to do with their nationalities. They came here to murder me and that outcome is what awaits anyone who threatens me. Don't tell Grey about it."

"I wouldn't dare. You're not one to trifle with."

"Truer words have never been said. He wouldn't understand. He believes in the Geneva Convention and other idealistic fare while I believe in survival," Laura said, using her power to restore the flowers above them to how they had looked, as it was the sort of thing her gardener would notice. She turned on her heel and walked back to the kitchen and poured herself a glass of water which she quickly finished and she poured herself another and sat down as Paulette sat watching her.

"You seem stressed," Paulette commented.

Laura grimaced as she considered her words and replied, "Not really."

"She was complaining when I rushed her, when she got cut up, but it's best that I did. They weren't that far behind us."

"They came a different path. I told you I didn't want an audience."

"You told me it was dangerous. I don't desert my comrades."

"Do me a favour, Paulette. All being well, the war should be over for you now. Don't be one of these people who can't adjust or who remember it as a golden age. Think about what you're going to do next now that you're free. Let it end, yes?"

"Once the war's over."

"Once they're out of France. You're not a soldier; you're not going to be forcing them back to Berlin."

"We might still perform spells to help them on their way. When they're dust, then we celebrate and move on." Konah came downstairs and looked accusingly at Laura for a moment before he bounded back onto Paulette's lap. "It came true, little mate. She did well. Why don't you tell us how Grey's doing?"

Konah shrugged. "I can't see everything. He doesn't listen anyway," he said moodily.

"He doesn't speak French, Konah, so that might pose a problem," Laura said.

Konah withdrew and started playing with Paulette's hair as he turned away from Laura. Paulette said to Laura, "He did well with the soldiers. He didn't tell me the method, but he knew they were no contest for you."

"Can you see anything then, Konah?" Laura asked.

"Can I have a snack?" Konah asked Paulette.

"I'd have thought so, once you answer the question," Paulette said softly.

"Grey lives…through this. After that I can see six different futures, four dead, two alive."

"So what does he have to do to make sure one of the two alive happen?" Laura said, masking her feelings.

"Dodge bullets."

"Good answer. What would you like to eat?" Laura said, grateful for his honesty. A 1 in 3 chance of survival was not encouraging but it was pointless telling him about it. His mind was already made up even if every possibility equalled death.

Lotte sat in the darkness as she heard the destruction continue. Hearing it was bearable – sensing it was worse, feeling that pain. All she had done all day was read and reread her latest letters, the last she'd receive for a while with content that upset her in both letters.

At least Horst was safe. Horst had guarded her since she first arrived in her new home and had been the perfect sentry. It had taken her time to make him relax as she acted as his surrogate mother and doted on him. She still never found a way past that stoic front but she managed to get him to open up about his home life, about his little two year old girl, an angelic little girl he showed her pictures of. He wasn't her servant and she made that clear, though he took his responsibility to keep her safe like some royal decree. It amazed Lotte that they weren't winning the war anymore as they surely had the best, most committed soldiers.

Horst had been ordered to take Lotte to the train station and put her on the next eastbound train with an allowance to see her the rest of the way home. Lotte accepted this instruction when Horst relayed it, until he told her that Inge had already left. Lotte knew this was not true, and if Inge remained then she had to also. Horst had not expected Lotte to refuse and he informed her that Maramont was not a safe place for her anymore and that he himself was leaving. Lotte had tried to explain to him that she was a special agent and that she could do her job behind enemy lines (even though the thought of this scared her) and she saw that she was bewildering the poor boy (although a giant of a man he was only 21 and she still viewed him as a child). He viewed her refusal to leave as a personal failure and sat disconsolate as she tried to persuade him to return to his troop. His work was done.

Horst left eventually, his departure gloomy. She did not tell Horst what she had foreseen for him. In three months time he would lose his left leg, an injury which would see him reunited with his family, a happy ending of sorts. She fretted for the pain he would experience, yet thought his family lucky – to have Peter or Reinald home such an injury would be a price worth paying. He had told her that he would have to inform Von Strauss that he had failed and Lotte foresaw that he did exactly that and was sharply rebuked for his failure – that was regrettable and made her feel bad. She was the one who had defied the order, not him, though perhaps she would pay the bigger price. Lotte's prophecy answered fewer questions than she liked and she could not see what the night had in store for her. Would they pass over her house, if they got that far, or was she now doomed to die at her own countrymen's hands?

As they ran through the town people reacted in two ways – half ran the other way while half joined them. Blanc was known to many and known as a rational man and if he thought it was time to make a public stand then that meant they stood a chance or there was no other way. They ran into five more members of the Resistance on their travels, all armed as they approached the more aggressive platoon. The progress of this platoon was impeded by their eagerness to have fun with attractive French girls who cowered too much to fight back. Even adopting this approach they still fancied that they'd take more scalps than the other group which wasted time marching men to their deaths when they could be easily killed where they were found, whether on their sofa, in bed or hiding in a cupboard like one coward who begged for his life and pissed himself when discovered.

Grey trusted his powers to lead him in the right direction though the smoke gave the game away, the flames only visible as they drew closer. Over 40 houses blazed, all in the same area, and Blanc asked Mimi to convey his thanks to Grey, who had led them on the right path before the smoke was apparent.

"No problem. Now things get tricky," Grey said, slowing down his pace at the front, advising them to approach with caution as they drew very near to the enemy force. Blanc and Mimi and the others marched past him fearlessly and Grey caught up with them and said, "Slow down, guys, they're very close now. Take cover and we'll work our way forward."

Mimi quickly translated between Grey and Blanc, passing on Blanc's message. "We can hear our people screaming. We end this now." Blanc employed tactics, ordering his followers to surround them like before, remaining in the frontal assault with Grey and the other soldiers and two dozen men and a few women. Despite his gung-ho statement he heeded Grey's caution, though still wanted to move things along as quickly as possible.

Over 25 spirits bombarded Grey's brain which felt close to meltdown: this was the centre of the storm. Only two spoke English and they were largely drowned out by the others. It was time to ignore the pounding in his head and trust his soldierly instincts. In that case he was doomed, Grey thought, amidst the maelstrom. As Grey surveyed the scene, looking for the best way to approach without exposing themselves, two of Blanc's best men were already ahead of him followed by Pearce and Strapulos. Focus, man! He was a good tracker, yet now, prior to the battle, his brain was letting him down and Grey knew that if he couldn't get his brain to settle he was going to collapse soon. Delgado noticed his swaying stance and came away from the injured man he had been patching up and put a hand on his shoulder and said, "Sit this one out. I could do with a hand."

The combined force was strong enough now that Delgado felt able to concentrate on saving lives rather than taking them. The middle-aged man he was tending to had been shot in the lower abdomen yet remained conscious and calm, even as Delgado examined his wound. Delgado had noticed that Grey had gone from being a boon to a liability, again, and he tried removing him from the fray. "Soon," Grey promised.

Delgado didn't have time to argue with him and he returned to his patient. Hill, Winters and Hartmann had all progressed past him now, as had most of Blanc's impromptu army and Grey heard the sound of gunfire as the enemy was engaged. This spurred Grey to action and he ran around the corner alongside Blanc and Mimi as two Germans began lobbing grenades at their force, while four others employed precision shooting. The grenades turned the street to a shrapnel strewn hazard and as Grey looked through the smoke at the scene ahead of him a stream of bullets were fired in his direction. Grey was spared, and Mimi was merely grazed by a bullet which slashed her right cheek while Blanc was directly hit in the right thigh and he slowly went to ground. He tried to fight the pain and remain standing yet proved unable and Grey and Mimi quickly dragged him to the side of a nearby house as another round of grenades were thrown, accompanied by maniacal laughter. The other platoon had at least tried to portray a façade of a civilised troop carrying out orders. These men they now faced were nihilists who would destroy everything and everyone, which presented a different fight completely.

Mireille scowled as she looked up at the three Germans hanging from the lampposts. She had heard a fracas and she had run towards it, a few paces behind Hugo, only to find she'd arrived too late. A small group had assembled around the bodies and looking around she saw a burly man ten years her senior, Minsa, admiring his handiwork.

"I see you've come out of the woodwork, Tremaint. It's safe now, your death sentence is revoked. Unless you try and force your Communist shit down our throats," Minsa chuckled. "We didn't shed any tears over your group's demise, but you're entitled to help, if you want."

"Where are they? Are there any left?" Mireille asked desperately, needing to kill. One life would do, to balance the scales.

Minsa shrugged. "One of the Americans said there was only a few left and my group should be finished with them by now."

"Then how can we help?" Mireille said.

"You just missed me hanging these three by five minutes. The short one there took forever, swinging around, kicking about – you missed his death by seconds. They're staying up there for a few days. We've got some others loaded in a van. If you want, Tremaint, you can come and help me bury them."

"They don't deserve to be buried. Leave them out for the birds," Mireille said bitterly.

Minsa chuckled again and said, looking at Hugo, "They're not getting sermons or coffins. One mass grave is all we need. You can piss on them as well if you like, 'cause I will be."

"Fine, I'll come with you," Mireille offered.

Minsa shook his head. "I'm not taking any women."

"You have women in your group!" Mireille protested.

"Only two, and you're not Mimi or Rachel." The identities of the members of each Resistance groups had been secret for the most part when the town was originally occupied, and details were revealed when the Germans originally withdrew, before they returned en masse.

"I've bitten my tongue while you've talked of the Communist scum deserving to be shot like animals, even though my son was one of those killed, because tonight isn't about our differences, it's about destroying them, and I need to play a part in it," Mireille said passionately.

"She's okay. I vouch for her," Hugo said.

"Your word doesn't exactly reassure me. Get in the van then. You'll have to get in the back with the bodies."

"I'd have it no other way," Mireille said gleefully, trampling the corpses as she climbed inside. Her son's body was taken from her; now these carcasses' dumping place would be unknown to their parents forever more too.

Hugo joined her in the back, along with another two male volunteers, and Hugo kicked the bodies to one side as he tried to create some space for them to sit down. Kicking them only moved them so far and after he made a small space he pointed to the area and said, "Mireille, you don't have to touch them. Have a seat."

Mireille smiled at his courtesy and did as he asked. She'd kept him alive, despite the tacit opposition from her group and she considered that one of the group's shining achievements. The spell had rebounded on them, though it was worth it to bring things to a head, but saving Hugo was all down to her. He could return to his room across town and back to his roguish lifestyle – that was what she wanted for him. The bourgeoisie and stuffed shirts about town viewed him as expendable, while she saw him as the salt of the earth, as imperfect as all young men were, yet in that imperfection humanity was revealed.

Hugo piled the bodies to one side so that they could all sit down without touching the corpses. Minsa stood at the back of the van and said, "She can come in the front. Marcel doesn't mind sitting in the back."

Mireille shook her head and said, "I have things to do here." She crawled to the nearest body and began stripping the clothes off the German soldier. She saw that her actions had gained their attention and she explained, "We bury the bodies first and then you're invited to a bonfire at the back of the tavern where all of their belongings go up in smoke. These men came here to slaughter us – we make sure they can never be identified."

One of the men in the back noted, "Listen to Madame Guillotine here!"

"What's your purpose here then?" Hugo said defensively, taking offence and pointing out his hypocrisy.

"Stop squabbling or I can find any number of volunteers to take your places," Minsa said before slamming the van doors shut. He had another man drive as he sat alongside him, preoccupied with how Blanc and the others were doing. Hopefully the rest of their 30 strong group would converge on the scene of the next battle, where he would rather have been instead of handling waste disposal.

Grey returned alone and Laura saw in his expression that the night had taken its toll. Konah was asleep on Paulette's lap while Odette was in bed, taking the double that Winters and Hartmann shared. Laura stood up and walked to him and said, "Do you want a drink or snack?"

"I'll just grab some water, thanks. I'm okay, I'm not even scratched."

"Not physically," Laura said, noting his sombre expression. Her impulse was to put a consolatory hand on his shoulder yet she refrained, puzzled by her growing tenderness for the man. Half of the time she wanted to touch him purely to wring his neck while increasingly at other times she imagined touching him in completely different scenarios. She had caught herself fretting for him and even felt nauseous.

"How's Maramont?" Paulette asked, lifting Konah up and placing him on the chair so she could talk to Grey at the dining table where she took a seat, as did Laura as Grey poured himself a glass of water at the sink.

Turning to see he had two avid listeners Grey said, "Do you two want a drink?"

Paulette shook her head and said, "Is Maramont still standing?"

Grey sat down and nodded as he drank. "They've burnt down a lot of houses. Some will be salvageable. When the fire crew came they shot them…They killed about 70 men and around 10 women. It would have been more but the worse group of the two…I don't know, people lose their heads, their souls. They started raping the women, which slowed the slaughter down. Strapulos didn't make it."

"That's unfortunate," Laura said. While they had not been close she held no ill feeling towards him – on reflection he was probably the least annoying of the whole squad, Grey included.

"The others are staying in town to help. I'll rejoin them tomorrow. I wanted to come back because there was a group of four Nazis unaccounted for. I didn't think they'd come here, but I wanted to be sure."

"And you've run all the way," Laura said, listening to his heavy breathing. "I think you should get some rest, James."

"If you stay tonight, Paulette, I'll walk back with you tomorrow," Grey said.

"Fine. Odette's in bed so I have to stop the night anyway. Is the tavern still standing?"

"They never got that far. I saw Eric. They were going to lead him out of town to shoot him. We managed to stop that from happening."

"Good. Did you see Mireille or Hugo?"

"I didn't see Mireille. I don't know what Hugo looks like."

After Paulette carried Konah to bed and joined him, Laura asked, "Does it always take this much out of you?"

"That's the running; I'm not as fit as I used to be. There was a different Resistance group and they killed three prisoners. They strung them up from the lampposts. I don't know why that haunts me more than the slaughter and rapes they committed. They even volunteered for the death squad. That should negate all sympathy."

"And it would, from most people. Your big, soppy heart is not suited for a soldier. It goes against your nature, yet still you put yourself on the line. I admire you and deride you for it in equal measure."

"Paulette and Odette came here because I made the offer. I know I should have consulted you first."

"Yes, but don't worry about it," Laura said, waving her hands out, showing the trivial matter was not an issue. "I know we have enough beds but I still want you to share mine tonight. This is the last night and I think I need to keep an eye on you."

"I'm okay."

"You're functioning. You're not okay. Why you volunteer for something that traumatises you is beyond me. Go to bed, James, I'll follow you up."

"I'm not as bad as I appear. Losing Strapulos is a blow 'cause our forces are so close that I was sure we'd rejoin our platoon together. We've lost men before, I'll get by. Tonight was hard and my mind is very active still, dealing with the fallout. Not many of them speak English so they're getting agitated and louder. It's nothing I'm not used to."

"I'll translate for you and we'll shift them quickly."

"It'll take all night. You should hit the sack. You've done so much for me that I don't want to keep you up all night doing this."

"We can do it in bed." Grey's eyebrows darted up at this and Laura quickly said, "That's better. Come on then, soldier, let's try and tidy up your brain."

Grey left the room for a moment and returned sans boots, socks and his shirt. Laura looked him up and down quizzically, her eyes drawn to his sweaty vest, and Grey said, "I stink. I've put my boots by the porch, out of the way."

"I didn't want to offend you, but yes, you do."

Grey sat down again and said, "It's not like you to hold back. I didn't think you'd mind me taking my shirt off too. We don't wear so many clothes on the track and I've been running like…I've been running…" He trailed off melancholically. He'd busted his guts to get to town (and to get back) and even so he'd still been too late for so many. The sight of the people killed in their homes, ordinary families trying to get on with their lives in trying circumstances…

"Breaking speed records, I think," Laura joked, trying to perk him back up. "I'll run you a bath."

"I'll clean myself up at the sink, you're all right."

"You're sharing my bed again so you have to be fragrant. That's the rules." In retrospect Laura regretted imposing such idiotic, petty rules regarding her bathroom – what did it really matter who used it? She had lived in the times before sewers when the streets stank of human excrement and she was suddenly too hoity-toity to let seven men use her bathroom? Six of them may have been unwanted guests but they were guests all the same. She had always allowed him to use it, though he rarely did as she had the key and he never asked, preferring to use the same facilities as the others. This last night he would get the full run of the premises.

"Maybe you should run it now before I completely pollute your house."

"That's where I'm going," Laura said, pulling her blouse over her nose as she left the room. When she returned downstairs she noticed Grey was lost in thought, sat staring deep into space. "Those pesky spirits again, eh?"

"Blighters, they are. I'm only saying that 'cause I know they can't understand me. Wanna swap? I'll do your spells, you get the spirits," Grey said light-heartedly.

"You'd have to stop wearing your cross and truly damn your soul," Laura said melodramatically.

"Best not then. I treasure my gift, you know that, but nights like this," Grey said, putting two fingers to his temple and pretending to fire. "It's not as bad as all that. It goes with the territory. At times of mass deaths mediums are kept busy – they're our peak trading hours."

"You've done well keeping your sanity the last five years. It's worse closer though, isn't it? Proximity, I mean, so Keokuk was moderate," Laura said.

"You've been paying attention. I'm impressed."

"If you'd like I could wash that uniform now and if it's not dry in time you've got a spare."

Grey shook his head. "I'm not asking anymore of you now. You've helped me enough."

"Washing clothes isn't that taxing."

"It won't be dry in time and it'll make my pack heavier, but thanks all the same."

"I could make it be dry as a bone in two minutes and show off a harmless spell in the process."

Grey smiled at her and said, "Show me when I come back. Yow! A German one now, and the German language can be sharp sounding and this guy is loud and frantic. Drill sergeant loud. Aargh. Listen to me, whining like a...ah...baby. I'm going to get some air and give you a bit of peace before you end up sharing my headache."

Grey left by the front door and hunkered down by the wall and lit up. He had managed to scrounge a butt from a grateful civilian (they offered and he never refused cigarettes) and as the smoke hit his lungs he instantly felt a little better. Laura joined him and sat down next to him, dirtying her skirt, and she observed, "I thought you wanted some air in your lungs, not smoke. Surely you saw enough of that."

Grey nodded. "It takes more than that to put me off. I'm an inveterate smoker at 18 years old. When I have more money I'll get even worse. I was 40 a day in Keokuk. I could go triple that here, if I had the supplies."

"It's bad for you. This isn't a retaliatory sermon. Do what makes you happy; just be aware that tobacco is harmful."

Grey shrugged. "I believe you, but I can't be deterred. Wanna draw?"

"I just told you it was harmful so you're effectively offering me poison," Laura said stony-faced before she smiled and said, "The answer's yes."

Laura only took a few draws as she knew he needed the cigarette more than she did. She looked at where his eyes homed in on, the burial ground. With his cigarette back in his mouth Grey walked over and examined the ground.

"Paulette and Odette trampled it. Leave it," Laura instructed.

"I don't know how they've managed that. The soil is completely uneven. Can you generate a bit of light and I can do my best now?"

Laura shook her head. "It's hardly a good time to create a beacon with Maramont still in chaos. I'm not bothered. I didn't even have a go at them."

Grey spluttered at this and sat back down next to Laura and said, "You ladies always stick together. If me or the guys had trampled your garden like that we'd have been hung, drawn and quartered!"

"Obviously that has crossed my mind, with all that you've done wrong since you've been here, but it's too messy. The kraut still giving you grief?"

"It's even worse out here. Have you got any spells to make this cigarette last longer?" Grey grinned as his lifeblood ebbed away.

"You're an addict."

Grey nodded. "It's been hard going without."

"I can't think of anything offhand. I could light them for you without matches."

"That's one good thing about going back. I'll be able to get supplies again. It doesn't make up for the big downside."

"I'm a big downside, am I? I know I'm not exactly svelte, but big downside?" Laura said, pretending to take umbrage.

"It's a colossal, gargantuan downside," Grey said and Laura whacked his arm playfully. "Leaving you – there's not a word big enough to describe that."

"You'll manage."

"I'll have to, but I don't want to. In an ideal world..." Grey stopped speaking as he grimaced in pain.

"I didn't hit you that hard. We'd best make a start on getting shot of them otherwise you'll end up passing out in your bath and miss out on the end of this glorious war. Hit me with it. Tell me what the spirits are saying."

"We can do it inside in the warm."

"You're still overheated and I barely feel the cold. It would be quicker if I tell you what to say back without translating but this is your arena and I feel strongly that you should know what you're saying so I'll tell you what they're saying to you and if you tell me how you want to reply I'll tell you how to say it."

"Let's do it the quick way. I trust you. You don't need to translate. You're not going to make enemies for me."

"Not deliberately, but I don't have your gentle touch. I'd tell them to get over it which isn't your way." A 2 in 3 chance he'd be dead – if he wasn't going to survive she'd regret not taking this opportunity. Yet if she did give in (to herself, not to him) then she'd have mixed feelings about his fate and she couldn't put herself in the predicament where she willed Konah's grim prediction to come true. For all that she scolded him about keeping his romantic attentions under control, if he broke her rules and acted licentiously she'd reward him at this moment. Once she would not have vacillated so. She would have succumbed to her desire. They were both willing; what was the harm? Instead she acted pragmatically, considering the future and the repercussions for him. Not that inviting him to share her bed was pragmatic, such actions liable to confuse him more than she herself was, her messages mixed. She debated joining him while he bathed, 'platonically', and repressed suggesting that he needed supervising to ensure he didn't pass out.

"Sometimes it's hard to let go. They still have hope and that's a powerful thing," Grey said, speaking from personal experience as he looked into her eyes, obviously referring to their 'relationship'.

"I doubt even you'd be an optimist in their disembodied shoes. It's time to give up, surely? Oh, there are ways back, but they're not easy or advisable. Is Adolf subsiding yet?"

"Nothing I can't handle. I'm 'hard as nails' Jimmy Grey, remember? This is our last night together for a while so I'm savouring it and a small headache's no big deal. Saying that I vote we help him first."

"In this one matter alone," Laura stressed, "you're the boss, so give me his quotes."

Laura was not surprised to learn that this German was one of her victims. She was thankful he did not speak English or she would have been revealed. She lied to Grey about what he was saying and managed to make him depart by threatening him with worse, though Grey did not realise that he was passing on a threat as he tried to aid him. It worked and he left Grey alone and Grey instantly felt relief as his head ceased throbbing at such a high intensity.

"Thank you, Laura. The jackhammer effect is gone. Let's do the rest later. I'd best go up before the bathroom floods. You're welcome to join me."

Laura was more tempted by this than Grey realised yet outwardly she gave no sign of this. Instead she gave him the opposite impression, arching her eyebrows superciliously and Grey said, "Worth a try. If you're not gonna join me where's your rubber ducky?"

"Strangely, I don't have a 'rubber ducky'. We reach a certain age and find better toys to play with at bathtime," Laura said suggestively.

"You're in a funny mood tonight." Laura felt exposed by this comment as he noticed that she was acting queerly. "That's a good thing," Grey said, trying to reassure her that she was helping him. The boundaries were coming down as they grew increasingly intimate. Pointing this out seemed unwise as she reinstalled walls and turned suddenly remote, withdrawing into herself, copying him and going into a trance.

Laura almost recoiled as Grey stood over her and put a hand on her shoulder. She looked up at him and he said, "In the morning, when I can see what I'm doing, I'll do something with the flowers before I go, my final act as your gardener."

"Too late, you already turned down that post. I like it like that," she said curtly. "The customer is always right, as your stories demonstrated."

"True. I guess it's your land."

"Another time, James. Make sure you're scrupulously clean before you come to my bed."

"Yes, ma'am."

Laura stayed where she was, hoping that the cool air might bring her to her senses before she did something foolish. Grey was able to control his ardour; on what was probably their final night together Laura found her lust was harder to manage. He was a doomed romantic fool and with their time ebbing away that grew appealing. Decision time loomed.

Paulette and Konah were the first to rise, closely followed by Laura who made a breakfast for them. Paulette had heard both Grey and Laura enter her bedroom and had heard them talk through most of the night, though had been unable to overhear the nature of their conversation. She wanted to ask Laura about her relationship though respected Laura's refusal to discuss it and had to hope she brought it up. Laura sat down after dispensing two plates of fried eggs and porridge and said to Paulette, "When he takes you back don't mention about those four soldiers."

"I promised you I wouldn't, though I still say you should be proud."

"I'm neither proud nor ashamed. I did what was necessary. James Grey operates with a different moral compass to us. He would start thinking about Christian burials and it would lead to arguments."

"I won't tell anyone, if you prefer, though I know Mireille would be impressed. One day I think the two of you will become good friends."

"I'm curious as to what you base that assumption on."

"You share the same enemies and the same goals."

"We don't. We share some of the same friends."

"Is he better now?"

"He's never going to find war easy. That's the nature of the man. Nevertheless he is more than capable of doing what he has to do, which is fortunate because by the end of the week he should be back with his unit fighting again."

"With the Nazis gone I can take Konah back."

Laura shook her head. "This may be another false dawn. He'd be happier with you but let's see what happens."

Grey bounded down the stairs, in a much better mood after talking with Laura through the night and he said to Laura, "You didn't wake me."

"You can't rely on me now you're leaving."

"I'd better go and feed the animals now."

"Already done. Sit down and feed yourself instead," Laura instructed.

Grey did as commanded and said to Paulette, "This is how she always talks to me."

"It's better than he deserves," Laura said as she made Grey's breakfast. "He's broken every rule I've imposed here. If he behaved in the army like he does here he'd be straight in the glasshouse."

"What's that?" Paulette asked the couple (which they had to be, even if they both denied it).

"It's where the bad soldiers go. Going AWOL for seven weeks might qualify me for a stint."

"The fact you've been behind enemy lines should spare you that fate," Laura said. "You don't have that excuse anymore. They've gone, again."

"This time it'll be for good," Grey promised. "Germany is starting to exhaust its supplies of manpower while in the States we haven't even scratched the surface – there's millions more who can come over, if required."

"The thought of millions more Americans coming over here is the stuff of nightmares so just win the war quickly, please, James," Laura joked.

"For you, it'll be my pleasure. Do you want to wake Odette, Paulette, and then when I've had one last gourmet meal we'd best make tracks?"

"Do you mean leave?" Paulette said.

"Yep. I probably worded it badly – I'd go and wake her myself but it's best I don't, you know? She doesn't know me that well..."

"I envy her," Laura quipped.

"Brutal, ain't she?" Grey mugged, looking for sympathy from Paulette.

"I wouldn't dare comment," Paulette said pointedly, standing up and leaving the table.

"Huh?" Grey said once Paulette had left. "Have I missed something? On second thoughts I don't want to know your answer to that. Can we have a private word before I do go?"

"Okay," Laura acquiesced, dreading the talk, and the departure a little. Grey kept talking while her mind drifted and she was glad when Paulette and Odette came downstairs. Odette had no appetite and refused breakfast and Grey felt all eyes on him as he tucked into his meal. All eyes bar Laura's – she withdrew to the library, telling him stiltedly to pop in before he left.

Grey went upstairs to Laura's bedroom and put his jacket and backpack on. He sat down on Laura's bed and rubbed his eyes. He was the guy who never got the girl, or got the girl because she wanted to get closer to his friend. Now he had to find the words to win Laura around. If he couldn't enchant inexperienced teenage girls why did he think he stood a chance with Laura Spencer? There was a connection though – even she couldn't deny that.

Grey employed Paulette to act as translator as he said goodbye to Konah. He had tried to be there for him, like a big brother or uncle, yet he knew he'd been remiss. He had been around Konah's age when his gift had revealed itself and would have loved to have had an avuncular figure in the same position reassuring him that his difference made him special, not abnormal. Konah was a quiet boy who didn't push himself forward, not that dissimilar to Grey in his youth though he at least had his sports which got him positive attention. Because of Konah's low profile he had been easy to sideline as Grey's attention gravitated elsewhere – even now, during their farewell, Grey was thinking of Laura and how he was going to word things to persuade her to give their romance a chance. His intentions had been good and he seemed to have helped Konah a little in their brief time together but given the chance to do things again he would spend more time with him. Now that Paulette was around as far as Konah was concerned nobody else existed, akin to how Grey knew he behaved with Laura.

"This is it, buddy. The last of the smelly Americans is leaving. Keep watering the garden for me. You can keep the Yank magazines – now that you've defaced the pinups you might as well!"

Paulette translated Grey's words and Konah gave a short, subdued response. He sat on Paulette's lap, yearning to be close to her as he had already seen her leaving in his mind's eye. Paulette said to Grey, "He doesn't like goodbyes. Don't expect him to say much. He did tell me last night that he likes you. Thank you for coming in with him when he's had nightmares." Paulette had regularly shared a bed with Konah when he had lived at the tavern and knew he didn't like sleeping alone as he scared easily.

"Hey, they were some of the best nights' sleep I had. It beat sleeping on the floor. I didn't share with him often 'cause it wasn't giving him much room but when he used to come and wake me crying I tried my best to comfort him. I hate the language barrier, 'cause he's a great kid and I wish we could have had proper conversations so tell him I'm going to learn his lingo so that when the Boche are done for I'll come back to Maramont and have a proper chat, about our powers and stuff."

Paulette condensed Grey's words for Konah, translating the essence. Konah mentioned about Grey's low odds of survival again and Paulette said to Grey, "He thinks there might be a medal in your future."

Grey chuckled and said, "Metal, maybe. Tell him I'll make things quick so he can go home soon. Does he know when…nah, forget it." Grey reached into his pocket and produced a strip of chewing gum which made Konah's eyes light up. "This is from one of the other soldiers – an unlikely source, in truth, though they all liked Konah."

Grey crouched down to pass Konah the candy (given to him by Hartmann expressly for Konah) and he saw that Konah's eyes were moist. His body was twisted towards Paulette and Grey could not hug him without embracing Paulette too so he offered his hand instead and said, "Shake, little man?"

Konah shook his hand limply and turned fully towards Paulette. "Leave him to me," Paulette said. Grey wasn't fully happy with how this goodbye went and now came the hardest goodbye of all.

"It's still safe," Laura said as Grey entered the library. "Once you return to the fighting obviously that changes." She was not trying to persuade him to stay. He was welcome to stay for the duration of the war and if his side lost she would escort him out of the country but she made no offers to him. She understood him better now and she realised that he would fight the war until it was over or he was.

"Yeah, you're right, but a man can't hide in a safe haven forever even if part of him would like to. I guess it's time to go – I'm running out of stories and I don't think you'll want to hear the same ones twice."

"Hell no. Once was pushing it. Don't take any crazy risks just for the sake of better stories, just play it safe and make some up."

"This exit feels sudden even though we've been here nearly two months. I have enjoyed your company tremendously and I've learned a lot. The voices from Inge's past that talked of her atrocities – it was your training that helped me sift through the spirits to find the relevant ones even if they didn't help us much." He blamed himself for Inge's victims availing them naught, feeling that he must have asked the wrong questions.

"They did because they helped reveal how psychopathic she is and what she is prepared to do on a capricious whim. Anything that provides knowledge is helpful – maybe not today, but someday."

"With her on the rampage have you thought about leaving too? You could return to your home in Scotland," Grey said, thinking of her welfare.

"I had a house built for me here during the Napoleonic Wars. While I don't enjoy strife, at times I choose to be at the periphery of it, observing it. I suppose you'd call it a ringside seat. I still use my Scottish residence – I alternate according to mood, but things are constantly changing here, not for me, for others. There is a potential new world beginning, James, and I want to witness what transpires next. I will be fine but I have to remain amidst the maelstrom until it comes to a head." Grey found it hard to understand her logic. It was pointless her being so close to the action seems as she did not intervene (bar helping him after pressure) and she preferred to look away yet deliberately lived close to the carnage. She purported to be unaffected by what happened yet was living on the mainland because of the war, proving that it did influence her behaviour.

"I don't like the new world they propose and I don't think you do either. I like your talk of the past, I like being able to vote for a politician, I like liberty – I like all of the progress that you must have witnessed in your lifetime regarding human rights. Things weren't perfect – my rose-coloured glasses aren't that clouded, but I like the old world better than what they want to replace it with. Diversity is what this planet is about and you have opened my eyes up to that because I thought I was broadminded before and you have erased all of my prejudices, so thank you for that. We can choose to be what we want to be in my world and I don't mind fighting for that." He had been deadly serious, rousing himself with jingoistic talk before he smirked at the end, acknowledging he had been ranting but he was still an idealist and stood by his words.

"Well put. Don't fight for Uncle Sam. Fight for James Grey," Laura said, advising him to live and act for himself, as that was where his only duty lay. She stood up and walked to her world literature bookcase. She handed him Homer's Odyssey, telling him he could read all about her in that, poking fun at her own dark image and giving him something to remember her by.

"Thanks, Laura, I will. He doesn't call you that name anymore, he calls you Calypso now. I gather that's better."

"Fractionally, though that depends on your perspective. I'm not certain you'll like it – it is quite a hard read – but I think you should read it just to understand his references." Laura sat down again looking at him, the atmosphere uneasy. Both smiled and Laura felt that it was strained. This was a pivotal moment for both of them and it completely hung on how she reacted and she still hadn't decided how she was going to handle the situation.

"I'll like it," Grey said, looking at her seriously. Even if it was the worst book he had ever read he would like it simply because of who it was from.

"I would give you a different sort of book to research only under the circumstances that would likely cause you to be ridiculed and possibly worse. Instead we'll cancel school for now and you should go home after the war and write to me and we'll arrange for you to have a holiday sometime to further your education. If the Nazis do manage to turn it around and beat you, and I very much doubt that they will, then you can return here and I'll gladly take you back to safety."

"It was much easier to leave my parents than this," Grey said, longing to stay with her.

"I wouldn't tell them that," Laura said, feeling sorry for him. He thought it was true love and leaving was a wrench for him, Grey having admitted to her previously that there had been no previous lovers or serious girlfriends. She was his first love and his feelings were so strong that they were not dampened by the (fairly obvious) fact that they were not reciprocated, or at least not to his level. Bizarrely he seemed far more confident than she did. Laura was aware that she was acting skittish and couldn't control it – her indecision caused the problem, proving that it was best he left now before something irreversible happened. There had been a brief moment of madness last night as he was deep in slumber, enjoying the sleep of the righteous, of the innocent. She had conjured a luminous light and gazed down upon him and entertained carnal thoughts. He was the most handsome man who'd slept alongside her, edging out Georges by a whisker. Clothes did him a disservice, his athletic frame concealed by them...she had controlled herself and fortuitously he did not stir, saving her from having to concoct a lame excuse as to why she was studying him.

"I don't tell them much nowadays. You know me a lot better than they do, whether you want to or not."

"How do you walk with all of those appliances on? You must all waddle," Laura said with a good-natured smile. She did not want to talk seriously, but he would not be discouraged.

"I love you, Laura. It doesn't sound smooth coming from my lips, does it? I'm not exactly Cary Grant, I know that. I haven't done anything to warrant that, to deserve you, but I want you very much. The thought of leaving you cuts me up but I'll be strong because I'm coming back."

He took a deep breath and started again. "I don't expect you to feel anything back. I love you regardless. You've put a spell on me, Laura, and I don't want it to ever be removed. Whatever happens I want us to be friends and after this war I insist that you let me take you across the States to repay your hospitality, all my shout. No strings, I'll be a perfect gentleman, I promise. If you turn me down then, when I come back, I'll accept it for good and I'll still want to take you back to the US because whatever happens I want you in my life, if not as my wife then as a friend."

Laura didn't agree to this sincere and heartfelt supplication and instead smiled kindly at him.

"Take care," she said, "and we'll see what comes to pass." She decided to give the poor bugger hope as he was going off to risk his life, and because an outright no could remove the offer from the table before she'd made her mind up. He would meet more women on his travels, as his army liberated other towns, or his powers would see him helping some young lovely. He dismissed his own allure, genuinely unaware of his appealing qualities, but his admirers would see the pure heart and would not dillydally with Sir Galahad as she had. By giving Grey hope she knew he would not get involved with anyone else – it was a little unfair, slapping a reserved sign on him, but by the end of the war she would decide whether to become involved or set him straight and free his heart for another.

"I know I said you'd steal the next kiss, but could you indulge the returning soldier with one more favour?"

Laura tutted and stood up and put her hands on his upper arms and kissed him open-mouthed. Grey responded, wrapping his arms around her waist, pressing close to her. Laura broke away and wiped her lips and said, "I'm going soft in my old age."

"I can't say the…" Grey trailed off, deciding it was best not to finish the sentence, inappropriate even. She wasn't his lover, not yet, and didn't need that much information. "That's me instilled with enough vigour to take on any enemy."

"Bar one," Laura said, taking her seat again.

"You've improved one soldier's morale very much these last few months. If I've pushed my luck too far I apologise."

"You have on many things but you've always been respectful. Go now before I decide I won't let you." While she spoke darkly they both knew her meaning, which was that she wanted to keep him safe.

"It doesn't work with me any more when you try and sound ominous."

"You see the good in everyone, James. In one sense it's a gift, in another a failing. I'm going to have to push you out of the door, aren't I?" she said, shaking her head as he remained rooted to the spot.

"If I don't make it…"

"No talk like that. C'mon, time gentlemen please," Laura said, pointing to the door. "You have ten seconds or you'll see out the war here."

"I guess you really don't like goodbyes," Grey chuckled, though still he remained.

"Not protracted ones. We'll meet again, et cetera. Good luck."

"You're the best. This time has been the best…"

"Three seconds left. Don't test me. It's because I like you that I may keep you here, which your conscience won't allow while millions suffer, remember?"

"Okay," Grey nodded. "I faltered slightly there. I was always going, it's just damned hard. Right. See you soon," Grey said, forcing himself to head out. He paused as he realised she was not following.

"Keep going," Laura shouted through. "Do a good job and you might see me by Christmas."

Grey raised a clenched fist in triumph as he left. He'd made further progress with her. There was more Grey could have said to her and as they walked away he wondered if he should have said more of his feelings. He felt at the time that he had made his point sufficiently and now he felt that he should have extolled her virtues more and articulated why he cared for her so. That was hard but he felt he should have attempted it. He had thought about her feelings and had not wanted to make her uncomfortable. That was a mistake. He was leaving and if she disliked what he had to say then there was no problem as he would not be there to bother her again until his return.

Laura breathed a sigh of relief as she heard the door close. While the kiss had not produced fireworks, with her feelings fluctuating it had triggered something that she wanted to remain dormant. If he'd stayed for another week there was every danger that she would have relented and ended up fucking him. She didn't want the relationship that he wanted; he wanted a life partner and friend, while all she wanted was a friend and occasional lover. If he wasn't so besotted she would already have slept with him, if it would mean as little to him as it would to her. She liked him a lot – a damned lot, but sex and friendship would not go together in this instance. It was better to keep the friendship alive and then maybe in 20 years time she could consider offering him more. Trust him to leave her with a parting gift, an addled brain. They weren't even compatible so why the hell had he infested her brain and her fantasies?

"If those four soldiers do turn up in town they'll be ripped to shreds quickly so don't worry about that," Grey said, leading the way through the woods as Paulette and Odette followed.

"I'm not worried," Paulette said.

"We met up with another Resistance group, led by a guy called Blanc," Grey said. Blanc had impressed him, showing courage through the night as he refused to let his wound stop him and he had used a rifle as a stick to move around and had only allowed Delgado to treat him once all of the second platoon were killed. He seemed a friendly figure; he didn't shout, didn't get mad and epitomised good leadership.

"Before I joined the Pagan Resistance I tried joining Blanc's group. You would think they'd want as many people as possible. I was told my help was not wanted," Paulette said bitterly.

"Their loss," Grey said supportively.

"A stupid whore I used to fight with in school is in that group. She'll have told him not to let me join. I hate her, but I could have put my hate to one side to work with her to get rid of the Germans."

"I think I met her. Mimi, blonde curly hair, down to her shoulders."

"What did you think?"

Grey shrugged. "I don't have a strong opinion. Obviously I know how brave you are and what you're capable of so I know they made a mistake refusing you but it hasn't stopped you making a contribution. That night we did the raids you led the way and I just got by on your coattails."

Odette groaned as the terrain worsened and she stopped walking as she looked for a good path through the bushes. "There must be a better way than this," she complained to Paulette.

"There's a road if you want to walk an extra two miles," Paulette said. She knew that Odette would not want to walk even an extra metre and hoped that would stop her whingeing.

"What's up?" Grey asked Paulette.

"She doesn't like the route."

"I can carry her if she wants."

"She'll want you to, but I wouldn't bother. It's not that bad now that we can see where we're going."

"Make the offer. She is pregnant."

Paulette translated Grey's words and Odette immediately walked to Grey, in position for her lift. She wrapped her arms around his neck as he scooped her up. Even with the bump she was light enough that Grey's speed was hardly affected.

"I doubt you'd move so quick carrying Laura," Paulette said. Grey's expression soured at this comment but he always found himself unable to argue with women and he didn't verbally respond. Paulette meant no harm by the comment, admiring Laura immensely, and she said, "I'm not criticising her, I like her. You two are very quick to be insulted if someone says something about you."

"We're good friends."

"Who share a bed."

"So did we."

Paulette smiled and said, "Fine."

"Tell him he's very strong," Odette instructed Paulette.

"Even with your baby you don't weigh much more than a child," Paulette said. Men were supposed to be able to carry women, especially if the women were a foot shorter than them and Paulette didn't think it merited praise or any comment.

"Still tell him."

"Yes. Odette says you're very strong," Paulette said to Grey.

"My pack weighs more than her. Merci, merci," Grey said to Odette who smiled at him.

Odette looked to Paulette and said, "I should have studied English."

"It doesn't take that long to learn. I only started after we were invaded."

"Why learn it then?"

"I knew we would be working with the English so learning the language would make that easier. As it's turned out, with our war over, I've only needed it to talk to him."

"Ask him if he's staying."

"He's not. He's said goodbye to Laura because he's leaving with the other soldiers."

"Shouldn't they stay to make sure the Germans don't come back?"

"We don't need them for that."

"Ask him if my house was targeted."

Paulette sighed and tried to explain to Grey which part of town the Pienas lived in. Grey didn't know the town that well and it took Paulette two attempts to describe directions from the market square to Odette's family home.

"Don't tell her this, because I might be wrong, but I think that part of town was where they…let's just see," Grey said grimly.

"What did he say?" Odette said frantically, picking up negative vibes. She patted Grey's shoulder, making him stop and she jumped down to her feet. She didn't want to be carried anymore.

"He doesn't know," Paulette said.

"Let's just get there quick," Odette said, marching forwards.

Paulette smiled as they arrived back in town and she could see with her own eyes that the tavern was still standing. "You coming in for a drink?" she asked Grey.

"I'd best not. I should join back up with the men. There's plenty to do."

"Maybe they've encountered those four soldiers?" Paulette said queerly. She intended to keep Laura's secret but was doing so poorly, raising Grey's hackles.

"Are you trying to tell me something?"

"I don't understand. My English isn't so good."

"It's always seemed great to me. I guess this is goodbye then."

"Until next time."

"No, no, they're not getting a toehold here again, cross my heart," Grey said, making the gesture as Paulette walked away from him. Grey saw what had drawn her eye: there was a body at the end of the street crouched by a lamppost. He had seen it earlier and had wanted to shield the women from it, imagining that the figure was a dead German displayed in some form of revenge. Grey saw the figure move as Paulette approached him and on closer inspection Grey saw it was a shaven-headed woman bound to the lamppost with her clothes torn to tatters, barely keeping her decent. Grey followed Paulette as Odette trudged behind them. Paulette spat at her and Grey bundled Paulette away from her crossly.

"Don't do that," he said sternly.

"I missed all of the action. That's nothing compared to what she deserves."

"Do you know her?"

"I know why this has been done," Paulette said. Two men walked towards Grey and Paulette and one offered Paulette assistance, which she refused, telling him she had the matter in hand as Grey let go of her, shielding the young woman from her.

"So do I, and it stinks." Grey bent down to look at the scared and tired young woman and took out his knife and cut her free.

"I wouldn't do that," Paulette advised. Grey ignored her and she found herself playing peacemaker, lying to the two men (both of whom she recognised as bad sorts who would think nothing of cutting Grey up) that the US Army was taking her away to punish her further. Unlike Paulette, Odette did recognise the girl, Delphine Brun, one of three people who knew that she had slept with a German soldier and she exchanged a guilty glance with her. The two men left them to it after first calling Delphine several derogatory names. Paulette shook her head at Grey and said, "That was reckless."

"I don't walk by things like this. I'm not judging anyone, Paulette – I haven't been through what you folk have. If this was for informing then I can understand it, but if it's for..."

"They said what it was for. She fucked a German."

"The ultimate crime!" Grey said facetiously.

"You are not serious, yet your words are true. You don't betray your own country on your back."

"Love doesn't work like that..."

"Love!" Paulette scoffed. "How are you going to cope if you get to the death camps? You're not tough enough."

"I know. It's still going to take time so I'll try and get tougher. I don't want to ever be hardened enough to leave somebody in distress like this – I would have untied the Jerries too."

Paulette flailed her arms out in exasperation. "What? Oh, goodbye, Grey," she stomped off back to the tavern, followed by Odette. Odette wanted to check that her parents' home was still standing but couldn't walk through the town with Grey and Delphine in case Delphine spoke about their mutual activities – morally her crime would be considered worse, for while Delphine and her boyfriend were in love, Odette bunked up with her partner instantly, their three date liaison purely carnal. As Grey wrapped his arm around Delphine chivalrously and helped her through the streets Odette knew that Delphine would not be planning ways to persuade him to take her back to America – she was strictly a one man woman looking to escape to Germany.

Grey was caught off-guard by two Canadian soldiers. While he beamed in delight at seeing them, relieved that Maramont now had protection and seeing this as the first step in rejoining his unit, they were sullen-faced with him and ordered him to hand over his rifle.

"We're on the same side. I'm American," Grey said, bewildered by their stance.

"Then you should understand English. Hand your weapon over."

Grey hesitated and found a rifle pointed at him leaving him no choice. Grey and the woman were marched through the town, passing a dozen Canadian soldiers on the way before Grey encountered the remaining American soldiers sitting at an outdoor café.

"Do you recognise this man?" the more forthright of the Canadians asked the group.

"We've never seen him before in our lives," Delgado said pokerfaced, which the others agreed with.

"I thought so," the Canadian said, gripping Grey's collar. "Come with us."

"It's a rib," Grey said. "How come you lot are sitting here with your feet up?"

"The bodies have been disposed of, Grey. It took us all night. We're entitled to some rest and wine after that if that's okay with you," Pearce said mercurially.

"We know him, he's one of us," Delgado admitted.

The Canadian let go of Grey and handed his rifle back to him and said surlily, "If you didn't associate with collaborators we wouldn't get the wrong idea."

Grey shrugged off the misunderstanding saying, "No harm done. Can you tell your superior officer I'd like a word?" Grey saw in his eyes that he thought he was going to complain about his treatment and Grey explained, "I need to talk about her, please."

The Canadians walked away without promising anything and Delgado jumped from his seat and fetched a chair from a nearby table and shouted to the waiter. Grey grabbed another chair and led the woman down to the seat next to his. "They're giving us free food and drink," Delgado said.

"Champion. That includes wine, I guess," Grey said, looking at their glasses.

"This is France," Hartmann said.

"Free food won't extend to her. What are you doing with her, Grey?" Pearce said disgustedly.

"She was tied to a lamppost like a dog. Look at her belly – she's obviously pregnant."

"Gee, I wonder who the father is? A Nazi, you think?" Pearce said goofily.

"Probably a German, not necessarily a Nazi," Grey said.

"Quit splitting hairs. So where have you been this time, Grey?" Pearce said.

"I told Isdel where I was going. There was one squad unaccounted for so I had to check that Laura was safe."

"Like that witch had anything to fear," Pearce said, sneering at him.

"I've never known anyone think with their dick as much as you, Grey," Winters said, his tone ambiguous, the statement possibly a compliment.

"I had to go and say goodbye to her too. Whatever you all think of her, she's done all right by us."

"So did they show up and terrorise her?" Pearce said.

"I'm glad to disappoint you. No, they didn't. What's going on?" Grey said, talking to Delgado.

"We've managed to acquire a casket for Strap. He'll be shipped home."

"Good, that's important..."

"Don't pretend you're involved!" Pearce said furiously.

"Fucking...just shut the fuck up, Pearce. I left after the battle. Quit trying to shift blame. Nikos is dead and I'm as sad as any of you and you use it as an excuse for your hatemongering. I've had to leave Laura behind, and maybe I'll never see her again, and I want to show my gratitude real bad, but I probably won't get the chance, so just don't get in my fucking face, right?" Grey erupted.

"You're pissed about leaving her, nothing else," Pearce observed.

"Yeah, this war's just a backdrop to my romance."

"Tell us something we don't fucking know. After the night we've had you waltz off and come back with another stray."

"Another stray? Who was the first stray? Laura wasn't the stray in her own house, you brain-dead moron," Grey snapped.

"Shut him up, Delgado, or I'm going to fucking knock him out, God's honest truth," Pearce said, even more irate than Grey.

"Last night was tough," Delgado said smoothly, trying to pacify Grey. For all that he hated Pearce, the fact remained that during the difficult night Pearce had worked hard and had personally dug 15 graves while Grey had been absent and Delgado considered cleaning up the mess (and the mess here was horrific) as important as participating in the action. "The Canadians have only been here a few hours and we only sat down ourselves 20 minutes ago."

"The food's good," Hill chirped up.

"Is this the garcon?" Grey asked, noting what looked like a waiter approach.

"He's the owner," Winters said. "We saved his café and his life so we can have as much wine as we want."

The owner smiled at Grey and stood with his notebook ready as he hovered by him, speaking enough pidgin English to ask him what he wanted. His eyes kept wandering to Delphine who did not belong at the table with the town's saviours. Grey gave him his order and the owner returned immediately with some wine before heading back to the kitchen.

"Get that down you," Delgado said and Grey duly obliged. The townspeople had been coming over to the table and shaking their hands and kissing them and that changed with Grey and Delphine's arrivals as they started attracting suspicious glances.

"Get rid of her, Grey," Winters said. "It makes us look stupid, dining with a German's whore."

"When I get chance to speak to an officer she'll go," Grey said levelly.

"Come on then," Pearce said.

"What?"

"What lie are you going to spin?" Pearce said.

"I'll tell them she's given me shelter and ask them to keep her safe."

Delgado rubbed his eyes and said, "You should have left her where she was. If they were going to kill her they would have already. They wanted their revenge on her and they've had it. Bringing her here – I don't see the wisdom in it but I'll let you sort it. It's celebration time."

"For five of us. Why don't you take her to that table over there?" Pearce said, pointing to a free table.

"I'd sooner break bread with her than you," Grey said biliously.

"It's your neck that wants fucking breaking. I'm out of here," Pearce said, finishing his glass and standing up.

"They wanted us to stay here," Delgado said.

"I cannot sit with him, else I'll be digging another grave. You coming Harty? There's a pub round the corner. The rest of you are welcome to join us, but not him or her."

Hartmann agreed and Delgado said, "It might be best if you do go until you both calm down." Winters and Hill remained at the table, both hungry and tired, and Delgado and Winters both sighed as they saw Grey halve his food with the woman, a gesture that was noted by the townspeople and the owner who inwardly seethed at providing food for her (although she wouldn't touch the food, possessing no appetite).

"Tell me about last night. I'd have been no use to anyone if I had been here 'cause I'd have been thinking about Laura, but how bad was it?" Grey said as he tucked in.

"Grim as grim gets," Delgado said. "You saw the bodies. They weren't many coffins at hand, so we filled them first and then had to settle for sacks. There were a lot of burnt bodies in the destroyed houses. I got to put my medical training to some use. Two of the rape victims were badly hurt. Objects were used. I've done my best; the proper medics are dealing with them now."

"That blonde was sweet," Hill said, envying Delgado for getting to examine her.

"All right, Dwight, knock it off," Delgado said, losing patience with him, finding it hard to believe anyone could be so thick as to think examining rape victims was a perk of his profession.

"And while you're dealing with that I just slept in her bed again. I get why you're pissed," Grey said, a little rueful.

"You slept in her bed?" Delgado quizzed.

"Nothing happened. Maybe I have been the shits throughout all this but Maramont's done now. I'm going to have no more distractions so I'll be more reliable from this point forth. You don't look convinced, guys. Cross my heart."

"I find that gesture from you a bit unconvincing," Delgado said. "Shake on it instead. That from this day forward, until your dishonourable discharge, you're going to concentrate on the job at hand."

Grey shook Delgado's hand as Winters said dryly, "Too many discharges is his problem. He just can't keep it in his pants."

"Now that we've left you can tell us, did you fuck Laura?" Hill asked, the question crude yet delivered innocently.

"Not to my knowledge, no, but I'm sure when we get back with our boys the story will say that I did. Nope, it was all above board, unfortunately."

"Pull the other one," Winters said.

"You're a cynic, Winters."

"You wanted to speak to an officer," a booming voice said behind Grey and he turned and saw a Canadian captain standing there. He hadn't expected to see such a high rank and Grey cleared his throat and stood up and saluted. Hill copied Grey while Delgado and Winters saluted while seated, continuing their meal. "At ease, sit down."

Grey sat down and offered the captain a seat; Delgado moved his plate and glass to Pearce's seat which he took so that the captain could sit next to Grey. "Yes sir, I wanted to speak to you about this lady here."

"Uh huh?"

Grey exhaled and said, "Well, I don't know her that well, but she has given me shelter for one night, and a change of clothes – they're in my pack, I can show you them. That made walking through the town easier when we were behind enemy lines. I don't know...I don't know what else she's been up to – she probably did sleep with a German, but she helped me so I want to help her now."

"What's your name?"

"Grey."

"Are you the father?"

"No. If it makes it easier to get her out of this you can consider that answer yes," Grey offered.

"Just tell me the truth, don't worry about that," the captain said reasonably. "All right, I'll see that she's not further harmed."

"Thank you, sir." Grey offered his hand and he shook it.

"You three okay?" the captain asked the other soldiers who he had briefly acquainted himself with earlier.

"We're fine. You should eat here yourself, sir," Delgado said.

"I might. The other two around?"

"They're not far. I know where they are," Delgado said.

"Probably doing what this miscreant's been up to, eh? Don't answer that, I'd sooner not know."

The captain stood up and ushered Delphine to her feet. Delphine understood that Grey had not led her to trouble – she knew that he was trying to help her and was facing some repercussions for it and as she stood up she put her hand to her chest and said to Grey, "Delphine Brun. Vous?"

She could do nothing suitable to show her appreciation now, but at some point in the future she could write to him and thank him properly if she knew his name.

Grey understood and put his hand to his chest and said, "James Grey. Bonne...anyone know what good luck is?"

The captain gestured for one of his men to take Delphine to the side as he said to Grey, "She knows that you're looking out for her." He then bent down and whispered in Grey's ear, "And I don't believe any of that hogwash you've told me, but I don't like seeing that sort of thing either so I'll help her out, son. You've got to learn to lie better than that in the army."

When he walked away Winters said, "You're lucky Pearce wasn't here, or he'd have blown that bullshit story to pieces."

"He knew I was lying and he's still going to help so result. Right, I can relax now. More wine anyone? One more glass and I'll be pissed so let's make a day of it, yeah?"

"You've only drunk two glasses," Winters frowned.

"I'm a lightweight. I'm a smoker, not a drinker." Grey's words were for effect – he wouldn't really be drunk, though it wouldn't take that much more, yet Winters took everything literally.

"Keeping you out of trouble sober is hard enough," Delgado quipped.

"Am in the doghouse for life here?" Grey joked back.

"You managed to tear yourself away, which I didn't think you'd manage, so I'm prepared to wipe the slate clean, but no more fuckups, right? You're aging me before my time. The tour begins again, buddy," Delgado said pouring fresh drinks for everyone.

"What do you think, men? Should we let these reprobates join us again?" Cloisters said, studying the six soldiers who he had given up as lost to them.

"We've had a nightmare," Hartmann said, still troubled by what had happened at Laura's home. Cloisters talked to them away from the others and Hartmann began recounting the tall tale to an incredulous Cloisters.

"She wasn't like that at all," Grey said defensively as Pearce demonized Laura too.

"So she was a tough broad?" Cloisters said, failing to understand why they were all so fired up about her (and not in the understandable lustful way).

"She didn't just lift us up. She moved the walls," Pearce said.

"What do you mean?" Cloisters said, screwing up his face.

"She parted the walls," Delgado said and Cloisters (despite being a cynic) was inclined to believe him.

"She had powers," Hill said with a goofy smile of admiration, imagining having superpowers himself.

"No, she didn't, there was a switch," Winters said. It had appeared to him at the time as though she had done it supernaturally but that was illogical and he was now convinced that there was a reasonable explanation.

"I'd keep this to yourself else they'll be talking asylums or they'll think you've made all this up to cover up for something worse," Cloisters said, shaking his head in disbelief.

"Grey was fucking her, Sarge," Pearce said, trying to get him in trouble.

"Good for Grey. I don't know what's being happening to all of you, but playtimes over. Do you understand me?"

They all nodded and said they understood and he left them to it, telling them to stick close to him in future. Their story was a worry to him as it was too implausible to believe, but he didn't believe they would all lie to him and he walked away to deal with easier problems. The sight of Fanelli by himself disturbed Grey, Fanelli cutting a tragic, forlorn figure and Grey could tell from his countenance that something terrible had befallen him. He quickly learnt of Jake

Baker's death, which struck him sharply because he had not felt it. He talked with Delgado of this, feeling acute guilt for being unable to talk to his spirit.

"Look, Jimmy, you can't talk to them all – I'd rather you didn't talk to any, but I can tell you do. You were pals with him when he was alive – isn't that enough?" Delgado said, not quite understanding Grey's mindset (though attempting to).

"I just thought I'd know," Grey said sadly.

"Let's save omnipotence for God and get on with fighting this war," Delgado said forcefully. He respected Grey, but he would not give his views credence here as his guilt was misplaced and he would not allow it.

Grey learnt why Harvey Baker was missing from Cloisters and he was relieved to hear that he was still alive though had lost most of his left leg. He talked of Jake's death with Cloisters, needing to talk it through, disturbed by it, yet needing to know all of the intimate details.

"How did Harvey take it?" Grey asked Cloisters.

"Gutted of course, but he got on with it. Harvey's tough, he bounced back. He was joking when his leg came off," Cloisters said, possessing much admiration for Harvey Baker.

"On the surface he's tough, but he and Jake were..."

"On the surface is all that matters here. Stop digging, kid," Cloisters said sternly.

There was a new sergeant in command of the second squad of the platoon and Grey congratulated Sergeant 'Fudd' Rhodes.

"How are you finding your stripes?"

"Piece of piss. I wasn't looking for the job. When Wilson snuffed it Cloisters put me forward to the lieutenant. You guys coming back has messed things up though! We might need to have a third squad again to fit you all in. Still as awkward as you ever were."

"As long as we stay in the same platoon. I didn't expect things to have changed so much."

Fudd nodded and said, "The RTC seems a long time ago."

"It must affect you more than most. You got on with everyone."

"Bar one. Now that you've fought do you understand what I meant about Stafford? We have to be in this together."

"I understood before. I'd still do the same."

"Stay in Cloisters' squad, will ya?"

"That's the plan."

"I'm pleased to hear it. Damned shame about Jake Baker."

Grey nodded in agreement. "I wish Harvey were here so I could pass on my condolences."

"Harvey's a bigger loss to the unit than his brother. If I had any say they wouldn't be sending 18 year olds."

"He was mature enough."

"It's too young for active service. You should still be back home training yourself."

"All the training in the world doesn't prepare you for combat. It's trial by fire, and I haven't been burnt yet."

"I don't want any in my squad. I'd feel I'd have to protect them too much, more than the others. Jake died under my command – I'm not writing another letter like that for a youngster," Fudd said, recalling bitterly how hard that had been, the sense of responsibility for his death still burdening him. "Poor Jake prob'ly never got to taste pussy. That's not right."

"I wouldn't be sure. Jake was too much of a gentleman to brag about such things but he was no different to the rest of us," Grey said, recalling Jake alluding to having some experience.

Fudd was unconvinced and thought Grey was lying to try and enhance his dead friend's reputation. Irrespective, Jake Baker was by no means worldly-wise and was dead too damned soon. "We all know you're awash with it. The boys used to look to me for tips on how to charm the broads into bed 'til you came along. Did you have a good time with this Laura?"

Grey nodded. "Not how you think. Not yet."

"Getting slow, aren't you?"

"Some women are worth waiting for, though it's hard to be patient. I make my play once this is over."

"Why the hell did you wait if you had six weeks?"

"If you knew her you'd realise that the progress I've made with her in seven weeks is a major miracle," Grey said, correcting him as to the timescale as he remembered every day.

"I'm not being funny with you, but that sounds like an opportunity missed."

"It gives me the best incentive possible to make sure I stay in one piece to go back and see whether I can scoop a prize bigger than Europe or if I was chasing rainbows. This isn't like sweeping a teenage girl off her feet – this is punching way above my weight."

"I heard she was older. I may rib you about that but it can work."

"That's the hope. I could never quite match you in the chat stakes before and now I'm absolutely no threat to your title 'cause that's where my head's at."

"Don't let it get in the way of your job. If she's already wavering she's going to make her mind up quick if you head back with half your face missing."

"I know I'll be all right. I didn't before, but I do now. I guess I'm definitely staying in the A squad then."

"Barring unforeseen amalgamations, yep. You're gone hook, line and sinker," Fudd chuckled, amused by Grey's extreme infatuation. He knew that Grey would remain a good soldier even if the war was not at the forefront of his mind anymore, providing a backdrop to his romance. It was pointless telling him to be cautious and to concentrate – Cloisters would have already said that and it would go in one ear and out the other. Fudd and Grey were both happy with the platoon restructure – Cloisters picked the problem cases for himself, Pearce and Grey, along with Delgado and Fudd took Winters and Hill, who had shown signs of improvement. Hartmann requested a transfer to a different unit, which was ultimately granted.

On the day of Grey's return to his unit he heard one of the clearest voices he had ever encountered, its clarity and volume (loud, but bearable) momentarily startling him.

A repeat performance, James.

I'm sorry?

An American in France fighting in a great war. That's my story too. I hope yours has a better ending.

What war did you fight in?

The Great War. By the time yours is done you might have to rename my war.

We won't. I think any war is hard and pushes people to their limits but yours sounds harder to bear than the one we're fighting. The worst thing about our war is our enemy, or the leaders at any rate. Combat is hard but it's not trench warfare – that must have been very difficult.

At first, but we got used to it. Only one man from our unit went crazy which is more impressive than it sounds if you knew the amount that did go nuts. If you've got your pals with you even hell becomes habitable.

What's your name, buddy?

Del Hoon from Detroit. You'd have adjusted to the trenches, James. The hardest bit was when you were sent back and had a break from them because you had to get used to it all over again. I was in the hospital three times with minor injuries and each time going back felt like it was the first time in the trenches. I can't imagine France without them – I don't want to imagine France without them, he said, strangely sentimental and attached to the foul craters.

What I've read of your war makes me think that conditions have improved. The officers treat us better now – I'm guessing here, Del, for all I know you might have been an officer, Grey said, realising he was being presumptuous and chiding himself.

Not fucking likely, pal! I was the same as you, James. I was a year older than you when I was shot in the throat. It was a slow death, unfortunately.

I'm sorry.

Them's the breaks. It's okay, it doesn't hurt now. I saw others die worse, thankfully not my close buddies. I died before my friends. They were with me and that helped. It's easier being the one who goes than the one who's left behind though we were a big group so I wasn't leaving them in the lurch. Even though I didn't want to leave them, I still felt like a deserter, the lowest of the low. When I was alive I was glad that they shot deserters because I was staying to fight and I had no time for the cowards who abandoned the rest of us. Since then I've found that my feelings have softened towards them – I can't blame anyone for wanting to hang onto life. When I got back all I intended to do was to go back to working in the factory, marry my childhood sweetheart and just live an ordinary life. That simple life would have satisfied me then, but now I know how precious life is and if I had another chance I would strive for more, to make the most of every moment and opportunity.

You're right, that's how life should be lived.

And that's how you must live your life. Leave regrets to the dead and live. Don't let the gloomy souls who haunt you bring you down.

You don't sound angry, Del, so I'm wondering why – I'll explain what I'm trying to say. Spirits like yourself often only remain on the spirit plane for a short time unless…

Unless they can't find peace and until they do, etc. etc. I've heard you for a while, James, I know your patter and you're good at it. Not like *some of those power hungry monsters who call themselves mediums. Some of them seek to use us and if we don't do as they ask they threaten to send us to hell or reincarnate us as worms.*

I would never do that – I can't bring people back anyway, but even if I could I would never threaten any of you, Grey said, appalled at this misuse of power.

I know that, that's why I've chosen you to talk to. That and because you're the first fellow American I've come across – an English spinster was getting through to me during a séance and I blanked her. Harmless old duck, but I had nothing to say to her. You can't tell someone like that what it's really like, can you?

You can be as frank as you like with me. I'm genuinely honoured that you have chosen to talk to me. Was there something that you really wanted to do or do you have a general feeling of unfinished business? I won't bore you by going over the way things work as you already know, so you'll know that your continued presence is unusual.

But not unique. That admiral's wife, Aveline – she goes back a lot further than me.

You heard that?

Every angry word. Bitterness is keeping her around. That's not the case with me – I hope it's not anyhow.

You don't sound bitter, Del, trust me. I have a friend who's a spirit, Linus. He's been with me about three years but he won't see me through the war which I understand because he had a hard time at war in the crusades so I know that spirits can remain around for a long time, over 800 years in his case. I won't discuss his problems because that would be breaching…do you know them already? Grey asked. Del had overheard his talk with Aveline and Grey was checking if he had knowledge of all of his discussions on the spirit plane.

No. It was only when you reached out to try and find spirits who knew Inge – and I can't help you on that score, I'm afraid – that I became aware of you. I don't know much about my existence but I sense that you were putting yourself out on a limb there. That could have been a mistake because if it brought you to my attention, then what else has spotted you?

All of the spirits – sometimes I don't like calling you that because it takes away from what you are, makes it sound like you're not human and you are…

We're not. We were, but we're not now.

All of you guys have been great to me, benevolent. The thing with Linus is that he's been around for centuries because he has unfinished business that he has to resolve. If you think long and hard, what is there that you feel might be keeping you around?

I'll try and think, James, only my husband didn't shack up with a demon mistress, Del said, jokingly referring to Aveline.

We can rule that reason out then, Grey said cordially. He was uncomfortable with the joke because Aveline's pain was not funny but he knew that no malice was intended and he made no issue of it.

I waited till now to contact you because I know that you're back with your unit now. The one reason that I'm glad I went to fight is not because of the French or the Belgians; it's because of the friends I made, brothers that meant more to me than flesh and blood.

I'll be honest and show you my pettiness here. I envy you for that. I'm glad you had good friends, Del, don't get me wrong, I just wish I could achieve that myself.

The reason for that is because you're not always with them, are you? Your mind has to go elsewhere. If you'd been in my unit and I'd tried talking to you and I'd seen that your mind wasn't even in the conversation then I'd walk away from you. If you'd told me the truth then I'd probably have ridiculed you and kept a further distance from you because what you are is hard for the living to accept. Some of them must like you though; you seem a good man.

I have one true friend who knows everything. I have some other friends but not like how you put it, not like brothers.

That's a shame yet while we're with you I doubt that'll change.

Then I'll have to stay unpopular because I'm not turning my back on any of you guys, Grey said resolutely.

Look it at as their loss because you're worth having as a friend. In your war is there as much camaraderie and banter? I'm guessing there is.

Yeah, there's some funny guys out here. My friend in my first unit was hilarious, used to have me cracking up.

Sounds like Baska. He could make you laugh at the bleakest of times. I hope he made it.

That's something I can do for you. I'll find out if he did survive the war.

If you don't mind there are a lot of others I'd like to know about too. A dozen at least.

Not a problem. It might take me some time, but I'll find out.

I know you can't do anything now. You'll make it through this war, in one piece too. I wish I could be there serving with you boys. I'd make sure you were included.

Grey greatly appreciated the sentiment and he said, *Thank you. Maybe we've come to know your war by a misleading name but there were certainly some great men fighting in it.*

There were some damned great men, no doubt. To know what happened to them – that would mean the world to me, maybe that's what I've been waiting for. Don't worry, I know lots of details about them. I can remember four exact addresses and one partial. Even if you can just find one of the gang he'll be able to tell you what happened to the rest. The thought of being reunited with his old friends (albeit by a third party) preoccupied him and he was silent for a moment as he contemplated it before he spoke again, adding patriotically, *At least we won.*

We'll win this one too.

Of course. We're winners and that'll never change. I want to help the cause so I am going to try and help you.

Thanks, Del. If I do survive the war it won't be so much down to me but to my comrades, alive and…

Dead. I'm fine with it, James. I know some aren't, but I've had a lot of time to adjust.

True. That's a long time to be alone though so any time you want to talk, I'm here. You can give me some tips on how to win friends, he joked, Grey not as concerned now as he had been once about his fellow soldiers' opinions of him. Laura's opinion of him mattered more now.

Shutting us out is the only guaranteed way. Besides, you've made one here if you want one. It'll be hard for us to go out drinking together but we can talk at least.

This is a good day then, Del. I'm back in my unit and I've made another friend I know I can trust.

Grey decided to try to reach Fanelli who clearly needed some help and he approached him, asking him how he felt.

"I never liked you, Grey, and what – you think because my friends have died off that I'm gonna confide in you? Shove your sympathy up your ass!"

"You don't have to like me, Frank, but…"

"Call me Fanelli!" His friends could address him by his first name, not Grey.

"I'm not going to have a go at you, I just think you should talk to someone and probably not me. The padre might be the way to go."

"A sensible suggestion for you."

Later that day Fanelli tracked down Grey and apologised, fairly rueful but still detached.

"No apology necessary."

"I shouldn't talk to you like shit when you're trying to help. Let me make it clear that I don't want your help. Your way of talking things through isn't my way."

"I don't think it's my way either. Have you seen how lame I am at it?" Grey joked self-deprecatingly. "Sorry, go on," Grey said, sensing that, despite Fanelli's insistence that he didn't want to talk, something was forthcoming.

Fanelli looked into space, not quite ready, and Grey said, "They'll fit Harvey with a false limb. Knowing him – not as well as you do, but I have a measure of the man – he'll be back here if they let him."

Fanelli lit another cigarette and surprised Grey by saying, "So what exactly have you been up to?" Grey hoped that mentioning his close friend Harvey would elicit some response, this seeming to be his best shot at reaching him, but Fanelli wouldn't touch this topic and instead, for the first time, expressed an interest in Grey instead and asked him a question, his interest seemingly genuine though certainly not intense. Grey answered him, trying to be as straightforward as he could as he realised this man wouldn't like cryptic talk.

After Grey had finished speaking, stretching out the tale to last a little over five minutes, Fanelli said, "So this Laura is the witch they're talking about?"

"No…yes, they mean her, but it's not how it's been presented," Grey said, only slightly defensive, protective of her reputation.

Fanelli said no more on the subject and walked away. To Grey's surprise, from that day on Fanelli began talking to him. He never talked of anything remotely personal, opting for general talk of the war, short comments which Grey keenly pounced on and expanded, sometimes going too far causing Fanelli to involuntarily grimace and walk away, but Grey soon learnt when to shut up. Fanelli remained distant and did not talk to the padre, but he now accepted Grey's company occasionally, Grey still trying to help him and realising that the best way was simply to be a quiet friend to him. Fanelli's friends were not up for discussion and Grey did not pry as he now knew that lengthy baseball discussions (Fanelli was a fan, though not a fanatic, knowledgeable of the game and players and wistful for the sport now that he was deprived of it) were more beneficial to Fanelli than talking of his lamented comrades.

A few days after returning, the padre (after talking to Delgado and some of the others) requested to talk to Grey. He had been informed of Grey's infatuation with what the others called a 'fallen' woman of dark power and he wanted to address this with him.

"You're shivering, son, are you all right?" the padre asked as he readied Grey for their talk.

"It's just a cold thanks, Father," Grey said, wiping his nose with the underside of his fingers. "With the amount of layers of clothing I've got on I'm amazed I could catch cold, but that's all it is thanks."

"The cold always finds a way in, doesn't it, and with the weather as it's been the Jerries will be wondering if they've wandered across to the wrong front," the padre said, both men equally genial initially though Grey suspected something was up, sure that his 'romance' with Laura had been mentioned. There was no romance, just an infatuation on his part, but he knew the other five surviving soldiers who had stayed at the farm believed that more had gone on than in actuality did, just one kiss (Grey only counted the mutual kiss, the earlier stolen kiss a mistake) the extent of 'their' passion.

"Are you a religious man, James?" the padre asked, holding onto Grey's arm as he spoke. Grey consciously tried not to shiver (he knew the padre thought he was nervous of him), but was unable to stop his whole body trembling, his natural state the last few days. He was apprehensive but this was not connected to his trembling.

"Yes, Father, I am. Not…not as devout as some, but I believe."

"Some of the things you've seen and still have to see – I can understand men losing faith, I truly can, and I would not blame any one of them. This war has made me question my faith in man, at what mankind can do to itself, but men like you have helped me keep my faith. Do not lose faith in mankind, James, because, as abhorrent as man's actions can be, these atrocities do not represent us or even the perpetrators. Some soldiers have lost their faith in God, which I understand, but I feel they are being unfair and misunderstand. The atrocities – do you know what I am referring to?" the padre said, checking that Grey was on the same page. Grey's grim nod showed that he knew all too well.

"God did not allow these things to happen. God gives us freewill to choose what we do…" The padre continued his sermon and Grey listened attentively, waiting his turn to speak though in truth he had little to say. He enjoyed talking to Delgado about religion where they both discoursed freely, but he could not debate with a chaplain.

"Some of your friends are worried about you, James. Whatever you tell me goes no further," the padre said, moving his grip to Grey's shoulder and staring him in the eye as he said, "Tell me about Laura."

Grey was flustered by this question momentarily. He felt himself turn flushed, and he regained his composure and said, "She is the woman I love, Father." Laura was no demon, no representative of the devil; she was a witch, but she was not evil and whilst he would not advertise her witchcraft to the padre, he was keen to demonstrate that he was not ashamed of her (even though partially he was, though he felt guilty over that).

"The others have talked of her and mentioned witchery. Do you know anything about that, son?" The padre was trying to comfort Grey and assure him that he was in no trouble whilst simultaneously making it clear that he was in dark waters, implying that it was imperative he accepted this offer of amnesty.

Grey looked downwards, away from the chaplain whose eyes bored into his. "She's special," he offered.

"Hill referred to her powers as miracles. That isn't true, James, and I think you know that."

"She's a good woman, Father," Grey said, surprising himself with the sharpness of his tone for which he immediately apologised humbly.

The padre ignored his apology, refusing to leave the pressing issue. "The other men all dispute that she is good and that she is a woman. I am not condemning this woman, James, even though I believe in the sincerity of the men's claims. I am not trying to take away the woman who may or may not be your great love. But if the men are correct about what she is then I cannot allow you to throw your life away." This last line was said authoritatively and impacted on Grey who felt slightly afraid. "I am going to recommend that the church investigate her and, despite the seeming aptness of the phrase, I don't mean a witch hunt."

Grey protested vociferously now. "Father, this continent has seen enough persecution and suffering without us adding to it!"

"If she was deemed to be a witch there would be no punishment meted out, just offers of acceptance back into the fold then none would object to your romance and if she is judged not to be a witch, then your union would have our blessing and our profuse apologies. It would only be if she was proven to be a witch and remained unrepentant that we would stop your relationship."

Grey wanted to ask him how he would stop their 'relationship', but he disliked confrontation and did not want to argue with a chaplain. He understood that the padre thought he was acting in his best interests but Grey's mind was already made up about Laura. He wanted her, he needed her and whether she liked it or not – he loved her. He understood why the others were afraid of Laura for she was different but if she was a demon then so was he as he was not normal either and Grey was in no doubt that he was not demonic which cleared Laura also. She was more human than others thought, more human than she herself was willing to admit.

The padre kept lecturing Grey who had the good grace to not contradict or quarrel with him though the padre knew that his words had had no impression on the private who he would be keeping in his prayers for some time. If the others claims, particularly Delgado's, were correct then the padre felt Grey would be better off falling in combat rather than jeopardising his soul by involving himself further with the 'woman'.

CHAPTER 10 – MASSACRE II

Grey felt more comfortable upon his return to his unit than he had before and not just because he had grown in confidence. Just in the two months he and the others had been separated from their unit it had changed greatly with many new faces which no longer made him the newcomer and helped him integrate. Grey remained highly sociable but as before he was occupied with spirit visitors and now he also spent a lot of time thinking about Laura, and his fellow soldiers preferred him quieter, the toned down version more palatable than the intrusive do-gooder they were used to. Pearce tried to sabotage Grey's improved status by telling the others that Grey had been fucking a witch, Pearce telling them that he'd even seen her fuck him with her broomstick (bristle end first), but his comments failed to even raise a titter. His stories could have worked as tongue-in-cheek humour, but he tried to present his tall tales as fact, and even his loyal cohorts wouldn't play along with him, believing that he was trying to make fools out of them.

Grey still found time to forge new friendships, befriending an outsider, an 18-year-old replacement soldier (as he was considered by the others) called Wes Autry. He was intelligent but too tense and found simple instructions hard to follow even though he tried, and he always said the wrong thing to the other soldiers (who were hypersensitive with him, very quick to find fault with everything he did). Grey tried to give him tips, finding him near impossible to teach (even with constant repetition it didn't seem to get through to him, or if it did, he would forget it by the next day), but he persevered with him. Cloisters knew how poor a soldier Autry was and regularly harassed him, bawling at him more than the others, trying to shame him into improving. At first he had been patient with him until he realised just how incompetent he was and the only reason he hadn't kicked him out of the unit was because he could tell he was trying to do his best. Grey felt that Autry's problem was that he was trying too hard and he tried to relax him, with limited success. Grey tried to talk the others into going easier on him and learnt how tenuous his own improved position was in the process ('You're fucking lucky we're talking to you, part-timer'). Delgado and an older soldier, a very religious and charitable man called Lol Shaw, were the only ones who promised him they'd try and help Autry out. Grey thought of Autry surviving the war and how he would remember it – friendless, disregarded and unappreciated, alone amongst masses that bonded like brothers as he stood on the sidelines, and Grey wanted to make sure that the war improved for Autry so that he might remember some parts fondly, some good memories to soften the trauma of the other moments, the things everyone would remember and didn't want to.

As Grey tried to help out a new friend in the physical world, he also tried to help a new friend on the spiritual plane. Del Hoon was not always present but each day he and Grey would talk sporadically, Del sharing bits of his past as Grey told him of the present and how things were different.

They should have preserved at least some of the trenches. They owed us that.

It would serve as a good reminder, to try and prevent future conflicts. The cold, hard truth of it is that there's money in land.

I get that and I'm not saying that Gettysburg should have been untouched – the Great War should be remembered. Maybe if it hadn't been forgotten this war that's killing off your generation wouldn't be happening now.

The two wars are connected. This war goes back to – you remember I told you about Versailles?

So they think they were shafted? So what do they think we'll do to them after this one with all of the fucking war crimes they've been committing? Del found himself becoming annoyed with the Germans, for daring to believe that they were hard done by after being responsible for the war that cost him his life, along with millions of others.

Their mentality is that they won't lose so it's not an issue.

They lost last time and they'll lose again. They can't beat us, Del said, cocksure of this.

Their progress has halted. They're certainly not finished yet. I think we'll have them beat within two years, definitely. I've no idea about Japan.

I don't even get why it concerns them. I think that's where our forces should be instead of in Europe – Europe can wait, they're the ones who had the audacity to attack us on our own soil. Del found some of what Grey told him very hard to stomach and it aggrieved him greatly (he considered his homeland hallowed ground, untouchable) though he did not blame the messenger, glad that Grey was telling him everything.

I understand what you're saying, but I'd rather stay and fight in Europe first. We have troops over there too and the British and the other Allied forces are there.

You weren't kidding about this war being more global.

America is still one of the safest places to be and there's been no fighting on the mainland, Del.

Good. So why would you rather be in Europe, James? Is it because of Laura?

No. I wanted to be sent to Europe from the start, before I met her, though she's a reason why I want to stay. The Nazi regime has to be brought down for what it's done to its own and other peoples. The Japanese regime might not need to be overthrown – that's trickier political stuff. Here I know what I'm fighting for.

Maybe I shouldn't, but at the moment I hate both nations.

You're not alone, but that's something we all have to look out for. We start hating them and viewing them all the same and we might end up doing the same as some of them have, maybe worse.

I respect you for your compassion but I don't see how you can be so forgiving while you're fighting in a war. Surely all of the ordeals and hardship that the Jerries are putting you through enrages you?

I get mad sometimes and I have felt momentary contempt for the enemy; it's something I try and control. Without these powers I'd probably be more hateful and believe more of the propaganda, but I've learned that there's no such thing as a bad nation. There are good and bad people from every nation – the problem is that the bad Jerries are the ones who run the country.

If I was alive I'd be going on a rampage against them, God's honest truth. If I'd lived would they have let me fight, because I'd have wanted to?

How old would you have been? I don't think they would, not unless you were a high rank. It's our turn anyway, Del, no one should have to fight in two wars.

I'd pretend I was younger then, just so I could fight. I'm enraged, Jimmy, and the thing is I know that I've calmed down tenfold since becoming a spirit so if I were alive I'd be blowing a gasket now. I'd be berserk. I'll calm myself down. I was going to help you out with this Autry kid, Del said, having become distracted by Grey's details of the conflict.

The situation is improving. Isdel's helping with him, even though there's a good few people he wants to catch up with, so I'm very grateful for that. Have I mentioned Lol? He's a brick; he's got a heart of gold. He suffers from a bad stutter and he looks out for those who need it just by being there rather than chatting away incessantly. That's my forte.

Hey, I'm glad it is. If you haven't noticed I'm not exactly quiet myself. Encourage this Autry to talk more. Yeah, some'll get pissed off with him for that, but he'll make more friends that way than by being silent.

They're not interested in what he has to say. If he says that a battle was tough then they'll say it was nothing and that he should have been at Normandy. If he says that he didn't think it was too bad then they say that any battle's easy as a spectator, ripping into him. He can't win.

If he learned how to be a great soldier he'd win their respect.

I agree, only his confidence is so dented by their hostility that I can't see him improving. I hope I'm wrong.

You can't fight for him. It's up to him to prove himself.

Me too. I haven't fought in a while, Del, and I know from other voices that we've got a fight coming soon.

Autry's still a civilian. That's the problem. You're a soldier and you'll be fine. If I asked you to slaughter some for me you wouldn't approve, would you?

No, but I have to try and win so you might get your wish. You can't win a war peacefully, unfortunately.

It had been a long time since Grey had fought a battle and lived as a soldier and he found readjusting easy and he fought even better now. He was starting to be able to control the voices in his head, banish the ones that were irrelevant (until later at least) and screen each voice separately, however many legion called him. This way he heard fellow Americans, Canadians, British, New Zealanders, fallen allies whose information was helpful, alerting him of enemy positions and artillery. He had no free rein, but Cloisters gave him a little slack to move around and Grey used it well, shouting out instructions to his fellow soldiers who trusted his impeccable judgement. There was little chance for respite, but during a rare interval Cloisters went to sit next to Grey on a short wall and offered him a smoke, which Grey accepted.

"So what is all this about and you and this broad? Are you trying to fuck your way all over France?" Cloisters manner was jocular as he teased him with a nudge.

"No, Sarge, it's not like that. She's English anyway."

"She's still a woman and that's what counts. Tell me about her," Cloisters said with interest, losing the prurient edge from his voice. The others talked of her as a demon and he wanted to know what Grey thought as Grey was the only one who thought of her as a woman. He had noticed that Grey was different, meditative, and while he was still friendly it was crystal clear that his mind was elsewhere. He remained a good soldier and he was more effective in battle than before, but when the fighting stopped his mind wandered.

"She's called Laura and she's special. The others didn't like her, but I did and when it's over I want to go back to her," Grey said wistfully.

"What's all this witch talk? Is that just bullshit?"

Grey hesitated, looking away from him as he smoked before saying, "She's unique." He would not expand further on this side of things.

"Look, Grey – Sheila's parents didn't welcome me with open arms. They expected a well-to-do Jewish gentleman and they got a Dutch boy from the Bronx instead. We don't care; we've made it work. What does this Laura think of you?"

"I think she likes me, but I'm not sure how much," Grey said. He was hopeful still that there was a chance she would change her mind and give him a try and being apart from her he pined and pinned his hopes on the narrow possibility. "I'm not giving up yet," Grey said resolutely.

"That's the spirit. Ignore them lot – if you want her you go for it," Cloisters said, offering his sincere advice.

Another American sergeant came over with some men and introduced himself to Cloisters, outstretching his arm. His men loitered behind him and Cloisters could tell at first sight that they were not an efficient unit. He said nothing of it for he had problems with his own at times, but they looked a shambles and the smiling sergeant didn't seem to care.

"Sergeant Irwin," he said as Cloisters shook his hand. "We've come to help you."

"You sure? I've heard nothing about that," Cloisters said, normally on top of what was going down. He accepted his word and said, "Cloisters. There's no action at the minute so do you wanna have a talk about what to do?" Irwin nodded keenly, leaving his men standing still as Cloisters took him on a tour, Cloisters looking back before leaving and saying,

"Good shooting there, Grey." His aim had improved substantially now and it had to be acknowledged.

Irwin looked back at Grey. This was the one – he could sense it now, the one he had to kill to please Inge. Serving her was his life and already he was planning his demise. He had traced his unit, now he had traced the man, who sat smiling at them as they departed. He would not be smiling long Irwin determined.

Irwin's squad didn't respect or trust him and they apprised Cloisters' troop as to what he was like. They fabricated because the truth didn't sound that sinister though there was something inscrutably wrong about him that they couldn't put into words, a gut feeling inherent in them all. Pearce told them if they found their harmless looking sergeant sinister it was as well they hadn't been with them over the last few months and tales were told which the other troop believed, inclined towards believing such notions because of their creepy sergeant who, regrettably, was their immediate commander.

Cloisters and Irwin talked at length, the experiences of war always providing plenty to talk about. The conversation bored Irwin, but he talked tactics with him for a while before bringing up the subject that interested him.

"I could do with a marksman for a mission I've got planned. Could I borrow him?" Irwin asked casually.

"Who?" Cloisters asked. It had been almost an hour since they had walked away from Grey; Irwin was so fixated on him that he had thought that Cloisters would know who he meant at once.

"The one you said was a good shot. Grey, was it?" Irwin said, careful to conceal his desperation, aware that he'd already messed up.

"Grey? The kid ain't no marksman. He's come a long way, but you don't want him. Tell me a bit more about it, if you can, and I'll find someone."

"He'll do. For the mission I don't need the shooter to be perfect."

Cloisters looked at him quizzically, narrowing his eyes and frowning a little. "Do you want a marksman or not? If you do then we can sort that out, only it won't be Grey. I'd never send him on a special mission."

"Why not?"

"Jeez, why the interest in him? He's only just come back after a stint out so he'd be too rusty anyway. He's a fine soldier, a likeable enough kid and that's all I can say about him. He's not going to win outposts for you – actually he might 'cause he has for us but that's just his instincts. He has an outstanding awareness of enemy positions but he can't beat them for you."

"Leading us to them would be good enough. I wouldn't expect him to do all of the work."

"Grey's tracking methods are simply him saying 'They're over there!' It's like sticking pins in a map at random. Yeah, he's always been right up to now but I would prefer to put my faith in an experienced tracker who can tell me why he believes the enemy are there. Grey can't, it's pure gut."

"My gut tells me that he's the one I need."

"Irwin, what's up with you? He's got hardly any experience – he fainted a couple of times in combat when he first started out. I wouldn't feel comfortable lending him out to you because I don't feel he's up to difficult missions."

"I'm prepared to take that risk. Please."

"Grey's my soldier and I'm not prepared to take that risk with his life. I've got things to sort out so I'll have to leave you to it. You should get some rest, Irwin," Cloisters said, letting Irwin know that he thought his behaviour was strange. He had concealed his desperation well at first but as Cloisters kept refusing him he began to feel ill and asked with more urgency, prompting Cloisters to view him as unhinged. He was prepared to suppliantly beg to get his hands on Grey, but it wouldn't work and he knew it. Instead he went to Grey.

It was hard for Irwin to find a private place to talk with Grey, a small copse the best place he could find. Grey went along with him willingly (Irwin said that he needed his help and Grey was not leaving his troop, as they were not on the move), eager to be of assistance. Irwin had suggested walking further away but Grey would not leave the area he was restricted to without Cloisters' approval, which meant (unfortunately for Irwin) that there was still a perimeter of soldiers around them. This made it harder for Irwin to kill him and get away with it, but the option remained and he had his blade at the ready.

Irwin was silent as they reached the copse and after a while Grey said, "How can I help you, sir?"

Irwin did not answer him, instead lighting up a cigarette and offering Grey one, which he accepted gratefully. He remained silent, sitting on a tree stump as Grey stood by his side. Grey felt a little uneasy, Sergeant Irwin a very hard person to read and an enigma to him. Delgado had gestured for him not to go when Irwin had approached him, completely unsurprised when Grey ignored his advice and Grey understood why Delgado had subtly shook his head and wondered if he was right and made sure that he stood facing Irwin.

"Sorry to rush you, but I will have to go back to the others soon," Grey said. "I would like to help you. Whatever the problem is, I'm listening."

"Are you having déjà vu yet? You said similar things to the Pagan Resistance," Irwin said calmly.

Grey spluttered at this, trying to respond with a denial before changing his mind and saying, "How do you know about that?"

"I knew Georges. I've seen the others since you left and they told me about you. A clairvoyant soldier must be useful."

"I always say medium. A good medium soldier would be…good, I guess. I'm average – that's why I like the word medium," Grey said, already over his surprise and talking to him affably.

"Medium, clairvoyant, spiritualist – the name doesn't matter. All that matters is that you have the gift."

"Wow. I thought I'd left that all behind for now," Grey said excitedly. "Did you know Veronique and the others? I'm just wondering what happened to her," Grey said, hoping that she did manage to return home.

"She'll be fine. How did you find your stay at Laura's?" he asked ambiguously.

"Fine. It was good…I mean, I wanted to be fighting and doing my duty only we couldn't get back," Grey said, not wanting him to believe that he had deliberately stayed longer than necessary because of his feelings for Laura.

"I'll bet you're already in deeper than you thought possible. My men talk about visiting Paris, the Moulin Rouge and suchlike without understanding that there are greater sorts of women out there. I can see in your face that she already consumes you. You know it's dangerous and you're already over the edge, you'd sooner risk falling than turning back to dull safety. Don't think that you'll ever possess her; she possesses you. You'll drown in her and she'll barely notice."

Grey looked at him strangely, confounded by his odd words and unable to mask his surprise. "She was our landlady," was all he could offer in response.

"I understand the other five with you hated her."

"There was six and they didn't. Look, we've all got pictures of different pinups because we've all got different tastes so you know…" Grey said, struggling to explain. "Even though you knew Georges, who I really wish I'd spent more time with, I still can't talk that much with you about her. No disrespect, sir, but I wouldn't even tell General Eisenhower about her."

"Your choice, Grey. I don't understand you though because there is no secret. I know what she is and how long she's lived…"

"Not everything Georges told you is necessarily true. Father O'Haire is conducting an investigation about her and because of that I would rather not go into details, but I do want to talk to you about the others and what they're up to. How long ago did you see them?"

"Four days ago," Irwin lied, having never met Georges or the Pagan Resistance, Inge having told him as much information as she could about his target and his allies.

"Do you have any abilities, Sergeant?"

Irwin shook his head. "My wife did, that was how I met Georges before the war. She was the same as you, though she called herself a clairvoyant, and that's how I know how useful you can be. I want you to be transferred to my section, Grey."

"Now I've got déjà vu. Thank you for offering me this; I appreciate it, but I hate difficult decisions," Grey said, rubbing his chin as he considered the proposal. Grey was happy in his unit but because Irwin knew something of the occult world, Grey felt that he might give him a freer role when required and listen to his suggestions regarding enemy positions. His abilities (which were more refined than before) made him the ideal scout and he felt Irwin would let him utilise his powers to the army's advantage.

"How is this difficult? You turned Georges down because you didn't want to leave the army. This way you remain an active soldier who gets to use his powers to help end this war quicker. How can you possibly refuse?"

"I need time to think about this."

"We won't be stationed with your unit forever. Sleep on it and get back to me."

"I will do. Thank you, sir," Grey said, shaking his hand and returning to the others while Irwin remained where he was. He had wanted to kill him as they spoke, but had repressed the urge. She instructed him to kill him, only Irwin wanted to do better than that to make his goddess proud of him. He wanted to present her with his head as a trophy. As he was the lover of Inge's rival, Irwin considered cutting off his genitals too, another trophy that Inge would approve of. Perhaps his heart too – his whole carcass. Killing Grey was easy; it was transporting the body to Inge that would prove difficult, though as soon as he was in his unit it would become a lot easier.

Grey was unsure what to do, finding himself leaning towards accepting Irwin's offer. He was happier in his present unit than he imagined he would be with Irwin but his happiness was unimportant, victory was what mattered. He decided to ask Cloisters if a transfer was possible, just to test the waters, and he was surprised by his fierce response.

"What do you think this is? You've been AWOL for a day fucking that spitfire, you've spent two months shacked up with your lover and now you're turning round and asking for a transfer. This is your second unit, Grey; the first didn't want you 'cause they thought you were insane. Now I don't think that, I think you're a good soldier, but you've got to realise this isn't like home where you can pick and choose what jobs you do. If Irwin could give me a good reason why he needs you then I'd let you go without a murmur, only neither of you seem to be able to explain why I should authorise this."

"I didn't say I wanted a transfer, Sarge." Cloisters' words revealed that Irwin had already talked to him about a transfer and Grey wished that Irwin had told him this

"What about your friends? What about Delgado and what will Autry do without you?"

"If I did go they'd manage."

"Until one of you gives me a better reason, I'm putting my foot down. You're staying with us, Grey. I'll do you a favour and not tell the others that you're desperate to leave us if you do me a favour and forget all about this nonsense. Irwin makes me look like George Patton. You're not stupid; you must be able to see that his squad is shoddier than ours. His interest in you is not kosher. Do you hear me or do you want me to spell it out?"

"I get what you're saying and it's not like that. I'm not that way inclined and I don't believe he is either."

"That's about the only explanation for it in my eyes. Be thankful I'm not authorising it 'cause while you might think it's all innocent, I know it's not."

Grey did not let Cloisters' adamant refusal put him off, convinced that Irwin would have an idea how to force the move through if he decided he was leaving. It was a big decision because Grey now felt that if he did push for the transfer that he would be leaving under a cloud, on bad terms with Cloisters for one, and maybe more. He apprised Delgado of the situation, trying to make him understand at least. He told him more, of how Irwin was acquainted with Georges and the Pagan Resistance and why he had to change units, to fulfil Georges' request. Delgado proved less understanding than Cloisters.

"You knew this Georges for what – two hours? Because a dead man who you barely knew would want you to leave our company – because of that you're going to leave. My grandfather despised Americans and would turn in his grave if he knew I was fighting for the United States. He'd probably root for the Jerries, but just because he wouldn't want me to fight doesn't mean I'm going to down my weapons. Respect other peoples' views but make your own decisions. I know I'm telling you not to go but I don't expect you to just do as I say, I'm just trying to make you realise what you're doing so that you can make an informed decision." Grey's extraordinarily poor judgement riled him to anger and he tried to control it.

"Okay. Pretend you'd qualified as a doctor and then you were given a choice as to how you could serve, as a soldier or in the Medical Corps. You'd take the Medical Corps because you'd want to go where you could make the most difference."

"Yeah, but joining that wouldn't endanger my soul."

"Irwin's squad isn't comprised of devil worshippers. It's just ordinary guys like us."

"Why leave now when you're fitting in well? I remember you when you first joined our unit. You were desperate to be accepted and you've achieved that, only I don't think it means anything to you now. Our opinions aren't that important anymore. You want to be accepted by the devil worshippers and the occultists, not by us soldiers. You're not going to get me to say I approve of this because I don't."

"That's a shame, because I would like your approval, but I don't need it."

"Then there's no obstacle for you, James. Good luck," Delgado said, shaking him by the hand briskly then talking quietly in his ear, "You do know that if you go to hell, it's a one way trip. If you don't like it there's no plane or ship to get you out of there."

"Then I'll have to trust that that is not my destination. I just want to end this hell as quickly as possible. There's no sin in that."

"So the end justifies the means?"

"You make it sound like I'm going to sacrifice babies at a Black Mass. I'll be doing the same as I'm doing here, only he'll give me more freedom and trust my word without needing proof. I'm not a devil worshipper and I don't have evil intentions. You know that."

"What I know, James, is that I thought when we got back with our unit that all of this occult business would go away. There's enough to be dealing with here without that to contend with. You are what you are and I think your gift is for real and I have no problem with you being a spiritualist, but I'd prefer it if you were just a soldier for now. Like you say, I want to be a doctor, Hill wants to be a farmer…who else can I pick? Sykes wants to be a barkeeper. We've all got other things that we want to do, but we have to put them to one side, even if it's what we've dreamed about our whole fucking lives, because we have to get on with this war."

"I can do both."

"What does that mean? More trances, collapsing again, crippling headaches? That's the formula for a perfect soldier," Delgado said sarcastically.

"That happens whether I embrace it or not."

"You've said your control's better and I've seen that for myself. I'm certain that you're capable of fighting but if you decide that you're going to 'specialise' in spirits and just concentrate on that, you might take a backwards step. I've been thinking about a move myself. I was considering seeing if I could join the artillery so that I could make a difference because after those months away I don't feel I've done much to help the cause so I can comprehend what you're saying about wanting to do more. What put me off was leaving the unit. I've never gone out of my way to make friends here, but when I thought seriously about leaving, I realised I couldn't do it. There are some bozos in this unit, but there are some decent men too. Even the resident Iowan is bearable."

"That's debatable. I'm sorry, Isdel. I've been thinking of Laura a lot, that's why I didn't realise you were thinking of a move."

"There's no way you could have known. If I'm pissed off I'm completely transparent, but if I'm weighing up my options I'm a closed book. I figured it would give me something to write to my parents about because after staying at that house for two months my material is thin. My aim's good with the mortar so I thought it could be worth having a try with the big guns. If I'd decided to do it I would have told you first."

"I wouldn't have stood in your way. We'd have missed you, but the war is going to be so short that it would've been okay," Grey said, crossing his fingers on both hands and looking upwards as he spoke. Delgado looked at the contradiction, a

Christian up to his neck with occultists, looking upward to his Creator. His comment was largely frivolous but Delgado felt that his friend did still have the faith.

"No point changing unit then, not if there's only a matter of months," Delgado said, playing along with him.

"I was thinking weeks. All right. I'm going to have to raise my game so that I can become corporal in this unit and work my way up from there." Duty to his friends had won out over duty to the masses, Delgado talking Grey around, even though he had been set on the move.

"You've only got weeks to make general so you're going to have to concentrate out there," Delgado said, extending his hand and shaking Grey's hand vigorously (after some of the things that had been said he made the gesture to show there was no bad blood) and patting him on the shoulder before letting go of him. "Sorry about the Satanist slurs."

"That's why I'm staying, fear. I daren't switch units 'cause I know you'll burn me at the stake if I try it," Grey replied amiably. "You said that some of your mother's family were from Spain. Were they involved in the Spanish Inquisition by any chance?" Grey said, laughing as he said this.

"Yeah, just for relaxation, of course," Delgado replied, laughing with him. "I have this strange feeling that you might not have fared so well at trial then, amigo."

"What makes you say that?" Grey said, laughing out loud heartily, his laughter interrupted by the sight of Sergeant Irwin watching him at a distance. Grey acknowledged him, instantly sobered up by the glare he was giving him, while Delgado did not attempt to stop laughing.

"Sergeant," Grey said, wishing that Delgado would stop laughing, for once not finding laughter infectious.

"Private," Irwin growled in reply, clasping his knife tightly, before he walked away.

Grey dreaded telling Irwin his decision the next day and decided to get it out of the way, going to him early in the morning, just out of earshot of Irwin's men.

"I trust you've considered this fully and haven't been influenced by any other parties," Irwin said coldly before Grey gave him his answer.

"No one else has affected my decision," he lied. "I wish I could have duplicates made of me so that I could be in five places at the same time," he said, a frothy comment that did nothing to change Irwin's sullen countenance.

"That's ridiculous," he replied humourlessly.

"I'm sorry," Grey said, though Irwin's reaction convinced Grey that he had made the right decision.

Grey was glad to see Delgado come bounding over to him, an excuse to take his leave from Irwin.

"Grey. Come here, now," Delgado shouted, still a distance away from him.

"Thank you for the offer anyway, sir," Grey said, offering his hand and Irwin presented his to Grey though Grey was the only one of the two who made any effort as they shook. As he sprinted to Delgado he asked, "What's up?"

"Come with me," Delgado said, putting his arm around his shoulder and roughly steering him well away from Irwin. "Cloisters is dead."

"Fuck. Has there been any fighting?" Grey said, convinced that there hadn't.

"His throat was slit in the night as he slept. They'll want to talk to you – they're talking to everyone – but you shouldn't say that you wanted a transfer and he refused you."

"So it was one of us?"

"It's got to have been. They've been talking to Pearce for half an hour and he's likely to try and throw some shit your way. They only talked to me for five minutes so they might think it was Pearce."

"I don't. I can't see any of us doing it. Have they talked to Wes yet?" Grey said, worried that he might be a suspect because of his poor relationship with Cloisters.

"Yeah, and they spent less time with him than they did with me. They're not fools. He might have got reprimanded thrice daily but that's not much of a motive so you don't have to worry about him."

"Good. Damn it, I liked the Sarge and the last conversation we had was an argument," Grey said, cross with himself.

"Don't mention that. You got kicked out of your last unit because they thought you were insane. If they do some digging they'll find that out and if they put that together with you having an argument with him then they might come to the wrong conclusion," Delgado said, trying to protect him from false charges. He gave him a quick warning on what sort of questions they might ask, telling him what they asked him and coaching him as to how he should reply. The investigators had over 300 men to talk to and by the time they got to Grey he had grown very anxious and he was relieved at how smoothly it went (they only asked him four simple questions: had he seen anything; where had he been; did Cloisters have any enemies and was there anything else he could tell them).

A replacement sergeant was quickly assigned (one of Delgado's closest acquaintances, a taciturn but brilliant soldier, Melvin) and life carried on as normal, though the manner of Cloisters' death cast a pall over the platoon. Their lieutenant, a private man called Gibson, for once became more involved with the men, offering to listen to their grievances and concerns, filling Cloisters' role temporarily and helping Melvin adjust to his new position. A strange man called Irwin, a sergeant in another unit, had begged him for Cloisters' position, the oddness of the man making his refusal very easy. Melvin had only been a corporal two weeks before his unexpected promotion but Gibson had confidence in him and preferred to teach him rather than have to work closely with Irwin, whose platoon, thankfully, parted company with theirs. For once Autry felt involved with his platoon as the murder had everyone talking, the topic cropping up again as they sat down to eat their dinner.

"Seriously, Wes, don't worry. This is abnormal, soldiers don't normally get killed by their own," Grey said, assuring him that he didn't have to watch his back amongst his comrades, Autry admitting that he hadn't slept since the murder.

"He's right. Accidents can happen with bombers sometimes but what happened with Cloisters is unheard of," Delgado said. "If you let it stop you from sleeping then you won't be able to deal with the Jerries who are the ones you should be worried about."

"But the killer hasn't been caught," Autry said, unable to understand how they could be so calm when the murderer was likely still amongst them.

"There are people working on it," Grey said, making a concerted effort to contact Cloisters whenever he had chance, his attempts fruitless though he persevered. He looked into space, trying again, his eyes looking vacantly at Pearce who took it as an accusation.

"Fuck off, Grey. I'm sick of telling all of you that it had nothing to do with me. I've said that I'd kill half of you in anger, it doesn't mean a thing," Pearce said, wishing that he had never said, after being severely censured by Cloisters, that he'd slit his throat.

"What? I never said anything. I know you didn't do it," Grey said, believing this act to be beyond Pearce.

"Somebody did though. If you kill yourself you go for the wrists, not the throat, and you'd go clean across. You wouldn't carve huge chunks out," Sykes said. "Cloisters had a voice like a foghorn so they've been clever there by cutting out his voice box. Some thought's gone into that, which completely rules out Pearce. If it was him he'd have been caught anyway – he'd still have the blood under his fingernails now."

"Fuck off, Sykes," Pearce grunted, unable to take being the butt of a joke.

"I'm defending you, you stupid son of a bitch."

"Bullshit. I wish I'd seen you get the shit get kicked out of you by Fallon and his gang," Pearce said, trying to wind him up.

"He's going to do it again next month if I don't pay up so you'll get your chance, Pissy Pearce," Sykes said, remaining unruffled despite Pearce's attempts to annoy him and the threat, which he did not worry about – if it happened, it happened. "At least you'll get to see my fight again. I'm gutted I didn't see 'Grappler' Grey take you out."

"It wasn't a fair fight. He had assistance," Pearce protested.

"Who from, storyteller? Snow White and the dwarfs or are you sticking with the witch?" Sykes said, mocking him.

"Let's not argue," Grey intervened, not wanting Laura to be mentioned again. "Our fight got broken up – there wasn't really a winner." This comment pleased Pearce who let the matter lie and they returned to the topic of Cloisters' death. Autry had turned pale at the added details Sykes had given as Grey and his friends had been shielding him from the full details of what had befallen Cloisters. Grey turned even paler than Autry when he saw Irwin again, minus his stripes. He approached Grey and the others and extended his hand to Grey, shaking Grey's hand very powerfully this time.

"It's good to see you again, Serg…it's good to see you, I'm just a bit surprised," Grey said uneasily.

"What are you doing here?" Pearce demanded to know, also noticing the difference in uniform and, therefore, rank.

"I've transferred over," Irwin said, answering the question but looking solely at Grey, keeping hold of his hand.

"One of your fuckers killed our sergeant and I'm the one getting the heat for it," Pearce whined.

"That seems a strange thing to do, transfer from a different unit and accept being demoted from sergeant to private," Delgado said, staring intently at Irwin. He had considered him initially as a potential suspect for Cloisters' murder but without any evidence he had kept an open mind. His reappearance aroused his suspicions anew.

"You're right, it was one of my unit. His uncle's a bigwig at the Pentagon and they're going to let him off with a warning. I wanted him out of my squad and a court-martial and I got their backs up so they did this to me. I started off as a private, I can be one again," Irwin lied, fairly convincingly.

"What do you mean, they're not going to do anything to him? Tell us what he's called and we'll sort it out," Sykes said. He had not been close to Cloisters, but he was not prepared to let his murderer escape punishment.

"Max Hartley," Irwin replied, picking one of the soldiers from his old unit at random.

"How do you know this for sure?" Delgado asked.

"His story didn't add up and some of the others incriminated him," Irwin said, improvising.

Grey felt that he needed to talk to Irwin privately and led him away from the others. After they had gone Delgado turned to Autry and said quietly, "Wes, you know what I said before about you needing to sleep? Ignore me, you were right. Stay awake," he warned.

"You wouldn't come to me so I came to you," Irwin said matter-of-factly. It had not been easy convincing Lieutenant Gibson to let him join his unit, his lies eventually securing him a place. He told Gibson of how he had been an exemplary soldier until he had come across James Grey, who he believed was his estranged son, his story told well and convincing Gibson. He begged Gibson to give him the chance to get to know the son he had never had a chance to meet, raised by another man who Grey believed was his father. Gibson decided to grant him his request for two reasons; out of compassion after hearing his heartfelt plea and also to improve Irwin's unit, Irwin clearly unfit for any form of leadership and Gibson felt that whoever replaced him would do a better job.

"But you've damaged your career in the process. It wasn't worth it, Colin. I appreciate it only you can't give me any leeway to do things now because you're the same as me. Is there any chance they'll reinstate you?" As far as Grey could see, Irwin's actions served no purpose.

"No."

Irwin looked at Grey blankly, with nothing to say to him and Grey looked back at him, scrutinising him in an attempt to understand him. There was no point to the transfer and Grey had no idea what Irwin was thinking.

"Did that man kill Cloisters?"

"I don't know. I had to provide some explanation as to why I was here."

"Colin, they won't just let it rest! They'll do something about it," Grey said angrily in frustration. "You can't let an innocent man be blamed for it."

"He died two days ago so there's nothing they can do to him," Irwin said, lying again just to placate Grey. Grey was still unhappy at a stranger's good name being slandered, but as there could be no real repercussions for a dead man, he let it go. Irwin had messed up his life and because he seemed to have done it just to be close to him, Grey felt an obligation to him and offered to introduce him properly to everyone. Irwin was uninterested in meeting the others and made this clear.

"You'll be serving with them now until the end. It's easier to fight with friends." Irwin was unresponsive and Grey asked, "Is everything all right? You don't seem…How do you feel?" Irwin seemed detached from everything and Grey tried to reach out to him, to help him.

"Fine." Everything he said and did increased Grey's feeling of malaise and when Irwin began following him everywhere (including whenever he needed the toilet), Grey found himself questioning Irwin's motives, thinking terrible things of him fleetingly before chiding himself and trying to befriend him again. Grey had succeeded in befriending quiet men, like Lol Shaw and Frankie Fanelli (up to a point), but Irwin was unfathomable to him and their conversations were always awkward and completely one-sided. Delgado's suspicions about Irwin grew daily but he was unable to share them with Grey because of his continual presence – whenever he tried to talk to Grey somewhere private, Irwin followed, a habit that quickly made him a laughing stock, though being mocked by the others didn't bother Irwin at all.

"I never had you down in the book as going with a 40 year old man, Grey," Pearce shouted over as Grey walked around the camp, followed by his 'shadow'. "At least this time you're the one wearing the pants, not like it was with big Larry."

"There's enemies nearby, Pearce. Focus on that," Grey said tersely.

Irwin's lies got him into trouble after a little while, Gibson asking him why he'd told the other soldiers the identity of a man he suspected of killing Cloisters. Irwin denied saying anything of the sort and Gibson stormed away from him, wanting nothing to do with the man. The newly appointed sergeant, Melvin, was concerned about him as a liability and told Delgado, in confidence, Irwin's tale of being Grey's father, a story that Melvin doubted.

"He's not and there's an easy way to prove that. Grey's mother is called Shirley. If she was meant to be his lover he'd be able to tell you that," Delgado said, doing what he could to get rid of Irwin, who refused to answer the question when Melvin put it to him, claiming it was none of his business. Melvin took his refusal to answer as proof that he had lied again and he tried to think of a valid reason to have him discharged. His habit of telling tall tales wasn't sufficient and would just lead to him telling more lies to cover his tracks and Melvin watched him closely, looking for mistakes, any minor infractions he could discipline him for and make a record of. As he watched him more closely he noticed that even Grey, one of the more tolerant soldiers, was perturbed by him and from Irwin's clear obsession with him, Melvin felt that his unease was justified. Melvin ordered Irwin away from Grey (he was very reluctant to go and had to be shouted at five times) and Melvin told Grey he could get rid of him in an instant if he would say that Irwin had made a move on him, a claim that everyone would believe.

"That's not true though, Sarge, so I can't say that," Grey said, unwilling to lie. Irwin's presence unnerved him and while his life would prove easier without him around, he did not want to make things any harder for him, mindful that Irwin had wanted to help him even if he was no longer capable, his mind seemingly addled. "I'm not bothered by him."

"If you won't help me get shot of him then that's just as well," he snapped before sighing and saying, as calmly as he could manage, "If anything does happen with him, come and talk to me immediately."

"I will, but I'll be fine. He's no threat."

Two days later battle ensued again as they assisted a larger group who were trying to take over the remnants of an abandoned town, decimated by ground battles and air strikes. They remained for several days without making much progress, the artillery involved in the action more than the foot soldiers, though they had to be ever ready for combat and ready to move when the German artillery attacked. Grey's squad took over a tenement house, a gloomy and dank building but it was still shelter and would offer them some protection.

Irwin decided that he would have to seize the chance while it remained as he was fully aware that the new sergeant was trying to get rid of him and he was concerned that he would eventually succeed. He had been desperate to present Inge with a trophy, but she had not requested any keepsake and he realised he would have to settle for the kill (perhaps he could chop off a toe, no one would notice that). He knew he could kill Grey at any opportunity; the challenge arose in killing him and getting away with it and he looked for opportunities in combat, growing frustrated as no orders to advance were given. Grey shared the frustration, having some knowledge of the positions of various units in the town and wanting to progress, but because of snipers they were all kept on a tight leash, only going outside when ordered. Grey was desperate to be sent out in a recon party (most of the others were at some stage, even Autry), but Melvin never picked him or Irwin, ignoring Grey when he volunteered, telling him he'd get his turn, with no intention of ever sending him. Grey questioned Delgado at length when he returned from a short expedition, listening attentively and after he had finished he asked him if he had any idea why Melvin wouldn't send him.

"He's freaked out by Irwin and that's rubbing off on you, because you won't do all that you can to get rid of him."

"I'm not going to lie to get rid of him. He doesn't deserve that."

"And Cloisters didn't deserve to get his throat cut while he slept."

"We don't know that it was him."

"I know and that's why I'm not saying that to anyone else. You're not missing out anyway, Jimmy, don't worry about it," Delgado said. Unlike Melvin he was not cross with Grey, understanding that he would remain tolerant of Irwin whatever happened or whatever was said and while Delgado still wanted rid of Irwin, feeling more strongly about it than Melvin, he did not expect Grey to lie about it to make it happen.

"It's like you said about feeling you needed to do something after being inactive for so long – well I'm feeling that."

Delgado smiled broadly and said, "Now do you get what it was like for us at Laura's? You had other things going on and while my kin would obviously flay you for that, it made you feel that you were making a contribution. At the moment it's like a siege and once it's over you'll be fighting again. We've been out there patrolling and we're telling you everything that happens so it's not like you're missing out – you've probably got a better idea than us on the lay of the land," he said, referring to Grey's abilities (and positively so).

"If I've got all of the positions correct, then it's ours for the taking," Grey said, not fully sure if the map he held in his head (thanks to many of the fallen) was up-to-date enough to be of any benefit.

"Do you want me to have a word with Melvin for you?" Delgado offered.
"Yep, if you don't mind."

Grey turned to Del for advice regarding Irwin, thinking he would be a useful sounding board (it was hard for him to talk to anyone else about it as Irwin rarely gave him the chance and he could talk frankly with Del as whatever they discussed was guaranteed to be confidential). Grey described the whole situation to Del (who was profoundly interested in all of those around Grey now that he was actively serving again) and he was a little put out by his frivolous response.

You're a lucky guy 'cause you've got something I never had – a shield. Use him as armour; let him take any bullets earmarked for you. He's not your friend – he's some sort of lurching freak who sounds like he wants to skin or stuff you.

That's harsh, Del.

Come on. You don't criticise anyone, even when you should. You would probably say Jack the Ripper led an unorthodox life rather than calling him a bastard like I would.

If I had known any of the victims or seen the bodies I would call him a bastard but as I didn't, then I'd try and understand him. Even if someone does seem evil I don't think it does any good to just turn away and give up on them because of that. My philosophy is that you have to look for the good in everyone, even when you don't feel like it and would sooner give up on them. I have communicated with a lot of murderers over the years because they have trouble finding peace and while I hate what they've done, I find there's a lot more to them than one mistake. The second I undergo any real suffering I'll probably change my tune quick smart and say hang 'em all, Grey said, though he hoped this would not be the case.

When I was a kid they had a shrunken head at the museum and I thought it was the greatest thing I'd ever seen – we all did. That's how he looks at you, like a curiosity, and maybe true mediums are rarer than hen's teeth, but why are you such a novelty to him if his wife was one too?

Perhaps…perhaps my abilities bring back the memory of her, Grey said weakly, not even believing it himself.

He's a loony. You're smart, but you're too easily conned. Trust Delgado's instincts on this one.

On most things I would, however, he's too prejudiced when it comes to matters like this. He was never going to like Colin after I told him he was involved with the group.

He'll hate him for that reason and he'll also hate him 'cause you're his friend and Irwin's hounding you. I consider you my friend now and I hate him for the same reason. It's my job to hound you, not his. Tell Irwin to back off and bark it if you have to – I'll script you, if you want, with words that'll guarantee you peace, Del offered.

Thanks, but I don't really mind him following me around. I was just letting off a bit of steam, take no notice of what I was saying. If a small thing like that makes him happy then it makes me a small man if I make a fuss, Grey said, backtracking.

You're too concerned with other people's feelings, at the expense of your own. Even if you won't admit it to me, admit to yourself that he's making you miserable. You need to cut loose, pal. If I was alive I'd be dragging you out round the bars just to ply you with drink, 'cause that's what you need, Jimmy.

The next time I get chance to have a heavy drinking session I will. I wasn't going to do it at Laura's. Would you have got blotto at the house of a girl you were trying to impress? Grey said rhetorically, feeling that no one would.

No, but they never had wine cellars or their own homes. You're on to a winner there, Del quipped.

Fingers crossed.

Badger her and you will be. She's already proved that she cares by taking you and your friends in. I think it's not just Irwin who's bringing you down. I think we're at fault too. Your problem is that you see how life ends, not just 'cause of this war either. You don't hear the happy stories of old granddads who died in their sleep after a long and full life; you get the young soldiers, the murder victims, the tragic deaths. Just from what I've heard over the last month I can see how it must be dispiriting for you but their deaths and mine are not on your head and not worth brooding over. Even when you joke you're still very serious and you don't have to be. You can have fun and a laugh without being disrespectful to us. Don't keep one foot on the ground, ready to play confidant to us – don't worry about any of that. Tell me the funniest death you've ever heard.

The question was not to Grey's liking, but, not wanting to appear humourless he replied, *That'll be mine. I'm sure I'll go out in a farcical manner.*

Come on, I want a real death. At the time when you were talking to them it wasn't funny I'm sure, but looking back on it you can find it amusing – I want you to tell me about a death like that. It doesn't mean that you're glad that they're dead – if you say it's me then I'll be cool with that, Del said, trying to make him lighten up.

I know which death other people would find funny but I would feel like a traitor to him if I told you.

Has he found peace?

Yeah.

Then why not tell me? You don't find it funny, fine, but share the story with me.

I can't, Del. I'm sorry. Admit it, you wouldn't want to come for a drink with me, Grey said, feeling that Del had a dynamism that he lacked (but which he would do without if it meant making light of others' pain).

Del was quiet for a while before he said, *You're wrong, I would. You're not me, and if I had your gift I would handle it differently, a little less solemnly, because that would help me cope with it. Perhaps your approach is the only one that works and mine could see me locked up in a bedlam.*

Been there already, Del.

Honestly? Del said, surprised by this.

As a kid. It was my parents' decision to put me there, I wasn't mad. Don't know about now mind.

Tough break. I am not criticising you one iota, Jimmy, understand that, Del said emphatically. *I am damn grateful to you, just to have a decent guy to chat to after a long time of silence is a blessing. If it was me I'd make light of everything for my own benefit, but it's better for all of the spirits that it's you. All I'm saying is put yourself first. We're like a virus in your head. If you can live with that virus, then great, and if you can't, get it treated. You're approachable and accommodating and we reap the benefit of that and wouldn't change you.*

It's ten years and counting since this all started. I'll note your suggestions because I'm not saying I've got it perfected but I have to stay reverent to you all – that's not flexible.

Fair enough. I'm going to guess what this ridiculous death is, mind. That doesn't count as you breaking a confidence. Del found that he thought more of him for not telling him the details of this poor unfortunate's death, believing Grey to be a better man than he while Grey thought that Del was the more interesting out of the two of them.

Okay, Del, I'm not such a killjoy that I won't go along with that, Grey said, aware that Del would never guess how Thomas Wall met his end, though Grey was able to laugh at his suggestions (though he gave nothing away, not even Thomas' name and would not tell Del when he was close). Grey was glad that the subject had been changed from Irwin, Del's suspicions about him just making Grey more sympathetic to Irwin as it seemed that everyone was against him. There was the possibility that everyone was right, perhaps even a high probability, but as his only friend (though their relationship was a strange friendship) Grey would not turn away from him, ignoring everyone else's advice.

The matter was taken out of Grey's hands. Melvin acquiesced to Delgado's request and arranged for Grey to be able to go out on patrols – in Fudd's squad. Grey took the news that he was transferred badly and gathered his things and trudged to the adjacent building where Fudd and his men were situated.

"I thought you weren't having any more 18 year olds under your command?" Grey said to Fudd.

"Extenuating circumstances, Casanova. Between us me and Melvin came up with this solution. You'll have to raise your game now you're with the A squad."

"I'll think about it."

Fudd shook his head and said with a grimace, "Fucking teenagers."

"So what's the score? I know Melvin's down on me about one thing – is that why I've been moved?"

"We both feel this move is in your best interests. The lieutenant has imposed Irwin upon Melvin so this is our way of separating you."

"Irwin's not a problem."

"Yeah yeah yeah. I know your spiel. You want to think the best of him. Remember, we already know how bad your judgement is. You stuck by Stafford when you shouldn't and we saw you were doing the same with Irwin so we're moving you without asking you because we know you won't play ball. You're still in the same platoon. It could be worse."

"You can't still be mad with Eric, surely?" Grey said disapprovingly.

"We're not all saints. Irwin most definitely is not. Focus on your girl – that predator's bad news."

"Irwin isn't homosexual. He was married."

"Who says? I wouldn't believe a word that came out of his mouth. See, there's no harm in being naïve but being pigshit stupid is another matter, and you're starting to lean more in that direction."

"I'd sooner be naïve than cynical and distrustful of my comrades."

"Cynics live longer out here. Pull your head in, Grey. You're here and you're staying here – it's not up for discussion."

"I'm going to have to accept it but I'd prefer to be transferred back."

"Two words, and the first one's tough. Earn your own stripes and you can start making decisions. You'll still see plenty of Delgado and Autry," Fudd said, understanding why Grey was displeased at the minor upheaval.

Grey exhaled and said, "I don't mean to give you a headache. I liked how things were is all. This is better than going to another platoon. I want your word that that won't be proposed."

"What's that?"

"That you won't ask for me to be sent to another unit, or a different platoon."

"That depends on you," Fudd bluffed. He saw that Grey looked concerned at this and he took pity on him and admitted, "No, we won't let Irwin force you out of your own platoon. You came in late but you're an old hand next to him. Next to many nowadays."

"It's not always the ones who you'd think either, who make it or don't."

"No," Fudd said, remembering his two best friends, cut down during the first month of fighting, one before he even reached the beach. "I'll see that you make it to 20. After that you're on your own."

"By then I'll be back at Maramont."

"You'll be Laura's problem then, not mine. I can't wait."

"Me neither. As long as you don't keep me cooped up like Melvin has I'll keep my grousing to a minimum."

"Boys, we have a volunteer to head out with me today! We'll give it an hour then we head out."

Grey nodded. "I've been going stir crazy so I don't care if the town's overrun, I want to get out there."

Before heading out Fudd found time to have a private chat with Grey, who quickly settled in, making the best of the situation.

"The first day you walked into the barracks I pegged you as a bit of a gasbag…"

Grey spluttered at this and said, "Glass houses…"

"Nothing wrong with that, being a good talker. I said to my pals that out of the three of you you were the best part of the deal. Couldn't work out why you were kicked out of your unit. The others thought it was you were too nosey and put some noses out of joint. Now we know how troublesome you are. Breaking our code by talking to Stafford, going AWOL fucking an ex for half the night and morning before deserting for a lengthy stretch trying to seduce an old crone, and now refusing to heed your senior officer's advice about a bad seed who's as lustful as you but for dick rather than pussy. You're having an eventful war, Grey, and none of that's got anything to do with the fighting," Fudd said amusedly.

"My old life was pretty dull. It seemed okay at the time but now…" Grey struggled to complete the sentence as it was impossible for him to convey how much his horizons had broadened and how much more alive he felt. "I'd sooner this whole conflict never happened, but as it has I'm overjoyed that I got to come out here. It was touch and go at one stage, when they kicked me out of my first unit and if I hadn't come it would have been the absolute ruin of me."

"You'd have been envious but you'd have been okay. One of my mates has been stopped from coming and he was pissed at first but he's learned to live with it."

"I wouldn't have coped. Well, I guess I'd have had to, but I'd try and find another way of getting here first."

"You're showing your age there. There's no other way of getting over. That's a schoolboy's fantasy. So what's the appeal for you?" Fudd said. Of the platoon he was the one who had to be the most optimistic to buoy the others' spirits, but he did not share Grey's enthusiasm for the experience. "The women?" he joked.

Grey grinned and said, "Mostly, yeah. Even on my worst days when I can't do anything right it still feels like I'm making a small difference. Sitting on my backside in Keokuk doesn't end the war any quicker, but my being here, even if I'm being sloppy, is something."

"You're on your way to becoming a good soldier. Not there yet though, don't let my praise go to your head."

"I won't end this with medals, Fudd, but that doesn't matter. It's not about that. It's about stopping something that's wrong. If I can play a small part in that then I can walk away happy even if I don't get the girl. If I get the girl too, then this smile is never going to leave my face."

"Woman. A girl's a dame under the age of 18. Your Laura's no girl. You've never said exactly how old she is."

"At least 10 years older."

"Than who, you or Gibson? She's more in my age bracket."

"Your patter might struggle on Laura."

"I'll let you believe that. Shame you haven't got a picture of her."

Grey nodded. "I didn't think to ask. An oversight, for sure."

"It makes a difference, something to hold. I think you'll get her, and my gut's never wrong. It's almost as good as your senses."

"Here's hoping."

Fudd took Grey and two other men, Fallon and Eccleshall with him and split into two teams. Fallon had been there from the start and was one of Fudd's closest friends and he trusted him to look after the new blood as Eccleshall had only been with them for a few weeks, though seemed a natural. Fudd stuck with Grey and allowed Grey to lead them as he told them where enemy troops were positioned, leading to a short firefight that left three German soldiers dead.

Once the fighting was done Fudd said, "How the hell did you know that they were there?"

"Does it matter as long as I get results?"

"I've been out with you and I'd like to think I've been eagle-eyed too and I had no idea they were there. Spill."

"It's less about eyes and more about ears. I have exceptional hearing."

"You must. I know you used to play tracker for Cloisters too but that was from three streets away!" Fudd said, impressed by Grey's instinct. Grey did not feel inclined to share the truth with him, particularly because this was another instance where using his powers didn't sit that well with him. They'd escaped without a scratch because they'd caught them unaware because of his power –

was that unethical combat? Thinking of the greater good and the bigger picture didn't help in the moment.

Irwin had been using the toilet when Grey had been transferred out of the squad and he had spied on Grey's new base from an upstairs window since. He saw Grey leave with three other men and after a minutes delay he left the building without authorisation. Delgado had noticed he was stalking Grey by staring, practically unblinkingly, at his new home and he followed him to the door and shouted out tetchily, "Where are you going, Irwin?"

"My business, Spaniard," Irwin replied disdainfully without looking back.

The comment was strange even for him and Delgado was torn between following him and reporting his movements to Melvin. He rushed to Melvin and said, "Ring up Fudd next door, see if Grey's on patrol."

"Why?"

"Irwin's just left the building."

"The sooner I get rid of him the better," Melvin grumbled. "Has he gone there?"

Delgado shook his head. "He went straight out into the town, with purpose."

Melvin rang the building and started a lengthy conversation which Delgado told him to wrap up as time was of the essence. When Melvin was finished he said, "Calm down. His desertion's a good thing."

"Is Grey on patrol?"

"He is, but he's with Fudd who'll deal with Irwin."

"We should go out there."

"No. Irwin's abandoned his post. The longer he's away the better as it makes it easier to get shot of him."

"I believe that man is capable of anything," Delgado said ominously.

Melvin shook his head. "He's not capable of anything, that's the problem. I don't know how he ever got to be sergeant."

"Is it all right for me to go out there?"

"I've got to put my foot down here, Isdel. The whole saga's been a fucking mess so I'm not going to send more people randomly out there. None of us need the distraction."

"That's not Grey's fault, and he's the one who might suffer."

"I've bigger problems. End of discussion."

Time was running out. Inge was never the most patient of souls and he had kept her waiting long enough. There had been half opportunities he neglected to take and now Grey was in a different squad – soon it would be a different company and he would fail in his task. Once he would have seized half chances. Hazy memories remained of an earlier time, of how different he had been. The men grumbled about the harshness of war – in his head there were flashes of true brutality, of close range combat with bloodier weapons than guns. Back then, as inconceivable as it now seemed, he appeared to have the whip hand over Inge. He commanded, she obeyed unquestioning…

Even now he still loved her. Regaining her love was paramount and executing her rival's lover was the first step to achieving that. He had killed before to entertain her and he recalled how excited that had made her, at a time when he benefited from her pleasure. Even if things could never be as they were, he would put a smile on her face again. He had to – other flashes of his past displayed violent images that troubled him, of acts done to him when she was not smiling.

He thought of past victims, of faces that meant something even if most of the circumstances were long lost in the ether. He had killed men of substance, warriors with sinews of steel. That he had proved so ineffectual against a nonentity like James Grey shamed him further and he resolved to act immediately and show that there was something of the former life still in him. He had never shied away from getting his hands dirty and killing Cloisters had revived the bloodlust in him and he would kill Grey for his own pleasure as much as Inge's. The dull life he had been forced to return to when she tired of him had been saved by the outbreak of war and he enlisted and found that long dead dormant instincts were revived. He hadn't completely forgotten how to lead men into battle, and a small measure of military tactics emerged again. Even as a shadow of his former self he was able to make an impression on his superiors, until she came back into his life and unravelled him again.

Irwin approached his target casually, ignoring the other man with him who was full of hot air, a true nobody who would join his long list of victims if he stood in the way of his quarry.

"What the fuck are you doing?" Fudd said furiously, conscious not to shout.

"Patrolling," Irwin said listlessly.

"By yourself?"

"Delgado is with me. We split up."

"Go find him," Fudd ordered.

Irwin did not move, his eyes remaining trained on Grey.

"Am I not making myself clear? My words are what should be interesting you here, Private, not my soldier."

Grey could no longer defend Irwin, not when he stared at him in a clear state of psychosis in No Man's Land. "I'll take him back inside, Sarge," he said apologetically.

"We're all going back in. I'm calling this patrol off. Wait here while I get Fallon and Eccleshall," Fudd said, evidently incandescent with rage, mostly directed towards Irwin though Grey felt he blamed him a little too. It was time for Colin Irwin to go home and get some rest to grieve for his wife properly, or fix whatever the problem was.

As soon as there was just the two of them Grey turned to face him, keeping his hand firmly on the trigger of his rifle. Irwin was surprised by Grey's good instincts and wondered if he would prove more difficult to kill than he had thought. Fortunately for Irwin, Grey was soon distracted.

I've found peace at last, James, a familiar voice said sadly.

Arnaud? Is…is that you? Grey said, hoping that it was some other unfortunate Frenchman and not him. As soon as Grey had heard that Arnaud Rousseau had been sent as conscripted labour he felt that his chances of survival were slim and he had prayed for him every night. Arnaud had led a hellish life and Grey wanted him to have a bright future to compensate for his past, a future that was now denied to him.

It is. I won't talk to you for long. I know what it's like to have your head invaded and I promise I'll keep it brief. I just wanted to say goodbye.

Arnaud, I don't mind. You're welcome – there's that little going on in my brain that there's room for more, he joked, though he was very sad and not really in the mood for joking, forcing himself for Arnaud's sake.

That's kind of you to say but I know the truth. My mind is clearer now that I'm dead. The stolen moments are gone and my mind is my own. We must have been born under unlucky stars, James, because we were cursed to lead shared lives. There's too many out there for you to handle – do you ever get a moment's peace?"

They're not always with me – not at the forefront. I can draw them closer and sometimes I choose not to if I'm tired – and I hate myself for that but it's true. I would rather share my life with too many than have the reverse, being alone. That's harder.

I'm used to unnatural company too and I know that I prefer being alone. Bad company is worse than no company.

It's natural for me now, Grey said, inured to his condition. *If they ever all went I'd find that hard.*

You can learn to love what destroys you. You see some of the townswomen flirting with the German soldiers, making the most of a terrible situation. Everybody wants to be alone sometimes and have space to think.

The thing is I'm not some happily married father of five with a demanding job and dozens of friends and family members that I have to fit into my life. I have the time for them and often when I've been down they've lifted me. It took a lot of time and some special cases before I became so accepting. Life is all about sharing other peoples' lives and in some ways I'm luckier because I get to know them better than I ever would if they were alive. We all have our defences to keep others out and they tend not to. There was a huge bonus to his powers – they gave him hope with Laura. Without his gift he would have hardly garnered a glance from her and because of them he had her attention and a measure of respect. While he felt that she would have still taken him in even if he had no powers, he felt that his abilities made her more inclined to be friendly towards him. Laura did not judge (he believed optimistically) but grouped people on certain criteria and as a medium he was raised a strata.

You look to the positive, but at the end of the day it's intrusive and a burden.

It can be. It can also be a blessing. What happened, Arnaud?

The Germans are crueller in Poland than they are in France. On the first day…

What the hell is he doing with that rifle? Grey thought as he looked at Irwin who was pointing it at his chest. Grey forced it down and said, "I'm rattled enough with the thought of snipers blowing my head off, so please be careful with that, Colin. Everything's going to be sorted, I promise."

…Alain broke my jaw so that no one would hear me ranting and passed my fits off as epilepsy.

I'm sorry, Arnaud, I didn't catch all of that. A minor incident distracted me there.

I can go. I can try and talk to you when it's more convenient, Arnaud said, not at all put out.

No, no, we'll talk now. Please carry on.

I thought that if I kept on having fits they'd send me to a concentration camp. I never thought that…they never even gave me a chance. Three guards, all big men, beat me to a bloody pulp at the end of the first day – they'd never even seen the fits, that was just because I hadn't worked hard enough. I tried my hardest and then they expected me to work harder after they beat me so bad that I could barely stand up. By the third day, after they'd seen me have two fits – Alain had already broken my jaw by then, an injury that was never treated – well, I thought when they dragged me off I was going to a camp. I was terrified because we all know what happens in the camps and I was praying that they were just going to beat me again instead of boarding me on a train. They didn't take me to a train station – I wasn't worth all that procedure. Instead they shoved me into a ditch. I was praying for a visitation when they pointed the gun at me just so I wouldn't feel it.

I hope bastards like that don't survive the war, Grey said judgementally.

Don't be bitter about what happened to me. I might have lost my life but it wasn't much of a life anyway. I was never going to die a hero's death.

You opposed the Nazis – in my opinion that counts, Grey said, trying to raise Arnaud's low self-esteem. *I won't give you the full spiel, Arnaud, because you know the drill. Are there any messages you want me to pass on to your brother or the group or anyone else, maybe that nurse you told me about?*

Just wish the group good luck for me. Are you seeing them soon?

No, probably not, but when I do I will pass the message on. I'm back in the army now. Your town's liberated by the way, Grey said, glad that there was some good news to tell him.

Excellent. Do you think it will last this time?

Yes, I do. We're making good progress. I'm sorry that it's too late for you.

It's not your fault, James. It's better that I died than my brother, Arnaud said, believing this to be true. *If you're back fighting again all I can say is take care. Getting shot is agony, much worse than I thought it would be. Be very, very careful out there.*

I've seen other men's reactions, I can see that it must be excruc…

Grey's attention was split and Irwin seized the opportunity to fire his rifle into Grey's back at point blank range, in the middle of his lower spine. Grey hit the ground at once and quickly became a bloody mess and Irwin smirked over him. Grey could not even look up and he lay prostrate on his chest, his cheek turned into some debris that cut him. The voices were out of control now in his head – they were all trying to help him, shouting at him to get up and shoot him else he would be dead, but it was just a cacophony, the chorus too loud.

Irwin believed, mistakenly, that because there was no one else in sight, that no one else could see him, forgetting that the town was full of snipers on both sides. An American soldier from another unit had seen Irwin fire the shot at Grey, a completely unprovoked attack, and he saw Irwin lower his rifle to the back of Grey's head to finish him off. The sniper took aim and fired at Irwin's head. He missed, but his shot made Irwin turn around and he shot again, firing two rounds into his chest. Irwin was dead but it took over 15 minutes before Grey was moved to relative safety (by Fudd, Fallon and Eccleshall) and 20 minutes before he received medical attention.

Delgado went to him as soon as he heard and saw that it looked bleak for him. Delgado clasped his hand tightly, making sure not to get in the way of the medics, trying to keep him awake by talking to him as he saw Grey's eyes glaze over.

With his free hand Grey tugged at his cross, which he did not have the strength to remove, and he said to Delgado, "Give this to Laura." His words were sepulchral and weak and Delgado nodded and promised that he would, taking the cross. From what Delgado could see it was clear that his spine was shot to shit. He would not walk again and there would be gross damage to his internal organs – that was his best case scenario if they had got to him quicker. Because of how long he had lain in that state it was fairly obvious that he was going to die.

Delgado went to Melvin and told him about Grey's condition and about the request.

"I could get there and back in three days. If he's got that long he'd want to see her," Delgado said, pleading Grey's case. Grey was dying and even though Delgado disliked the misanthropic witch, he knew how infatuated Grey was and wanted to do this for his dying friend. It was not a seal of approval from Delgado, simply a parting gift.

"I'll have to ask Gibson," Melvin said, very surprised by how accommodating Gibson was to the request, even providing Delgado with a motorcycle as well as five days authorised leave. Gibson heard a report of the double shooting and how Irwin was killed for shooting Grey and he instantly believed it to be true. Because he had authorised the transfer, despite some reservations, he felt partly responsible for Grey's injuries (as did Fudd who cursed himself for leaving Grey with Irwin and urged him to recover, reminding him he wasn't writing another letter). Irwin's death did not concern him at all. He spurred on Delgado to be quick, not because of the length of leave being a problem, but because of Grey. He didn't have five days; he would be lucky to last the night.

The terror subsided to a level where she could think almost coherently. The beast was still above her, a beast that had killed her father, her mother and her sister. Would she live to see them decompose in front of her, or would the demon come down to slaughter her too? She was starving and thirstier than she had ever been, but she was alive and she didn't want to die. She had a bleak future without a family, any happy endings that she had ever read about or seen in movies now denied to her, but life continued regardless of one's circumstances and she had to go on existing. They would want her to live, not blaming the coward who had not assisted her little sister in moving their mother, a simple act that would have saved them, something she would always hate herself for. She had no one left to live for and she wondered what was stopping her from committing suicide. Was it fear of inflicting pain on herself, Germaine never able to understand the soldiers and resistance fighters, how they could cope calmly with the thought of danger and pain? Was it fear of returning as a spirit, suicide the sort of unnatural death that could cause her to appear to a medium like James? No matter how bad life got, however joyless, it had to be endured – had she really absorbed that creed from her fortitudinous parents?

Back to the web Delgado thought as he rode at full pelt. He was stopped twice and showed his pass granting him special dispensation and when he explained that it was an errand of mercy he was granted passage but the next unit were more bureaucratic and asked around before finally giving him clearance to proceed. He thought he had left this world behind him, the world of witches, but he was back at her door knocking loudly as he panted for breath (he had had to run the last two miles, the terrain likely to damage his bike), leaning on her woodwork. Laura detected him coming and had already placed Konah in the hidden room in the cellar, which she saw was an unnecessary precaution as she saw Delgado standing in front of her. She was surprised to see him and invited him in coolly. He followed her through to the sitting room and flopped onto a chair without her permission as she sat facing him.

"To what do I owe the honour of this visit? Have you come to learn more of my craft or are you here to invite me to church," she said superciliously. Grey was not here now and she could talk to Delgado how she liked.

"Neither. You know what I think of what you are and I can't change someone who doesn't want to be a child of the light," he said, equally cold and fearless of her.

"I doubt you could convert someone who did!" she said, ridiculing him.

"I'm not here to trade insults with you. I'm here because of the one person who we both care about. I'm here for Jimmy's sake and I'll swallow my pride and beg you to come with me."

"What about Grey?" Laura said, losing her attitude as she looked at him, her countenance serious as she took in the gravity of the situation. For Delgado to come here indicated that it had to be serious.

"He was shot in the back last night. He's not going to make it. He gave me this to give to you," Delgado said, handing her the cross.

Laura took it in her hand and said, "Did he say why? He knows I don't want this. Give it back to him," Laura said, distant and uncaring again.

"He wasn't exactly up to expositions. He's probably dead now – I'm hoping that's not the case. They'll let you see him if you want to, but we've got to be quick." Delgado spoke aggressively, her indifference annoying him. He knew Grey would walk hot coals for her and he felt that Grey was already risking perdition for her and she talked like this of him, as though he were nothing.

Laura began to fidget as she considered his words. She hated feeling rushed and she didn't know what to do. She liked Grey and she was upset but she had warned him before he went that he would be in danger and he had accepted that risk. He had certainly learnt a hard lesson now. It felt unfair but that was the way of the world and these tragedies occurred every day somewhere. Her mind was still clouded about how she really felt about him – in an unpleasant way this made her life easier, made up her mind for her. At least it got her out of the American trip. She felt like laughing at this thought which she didn't really mean and she wished she could tell Grey it. No, that transmigratory expedition was as dead as he would be and she would stay on her farm in peace after returning Konah to the Pagan Resistance. The Nazis were gone and she felt they wouldn't be back and without Grey returning to attempt to prick her conscience she would not have him. He was a harmless child but she did not want him and he was not her responsibility. With both Georges and Grey dead that promise was now void – she'd completed her obligation (not that it was her duty in any event) as it was now safe for him to return to Paulette and the others, where he would be happier.

"I'm busy here. I'll send a wreath – send me the details and I'll pay for a lavish funeral," Laura said, feeling this was reasonable, fidgeting as she spoke.

"You cold-hearted bitch. I'm going to try and see him myself before he dies," Delgado said, shaking his head angrily and in disbelief at her as he marched away. He did not take the cross back as Grey had wanted her to have it and he had fulfilled his wish, even if she did not deserve it.

Laura walked to the door and watched him run off. No quips or insults had sprung to mind to return his slight and she understood his pain for they had seemed to be close friends. She paced around her rooms downstairs. Soon she would have her solitude again, but not here. She didn't want to live here now. Georges was dead, the war was as good as over, in these parts at least, and she would return to Scotland. She felt an urge to be away and to visit McKinley's grave. That would help and she thought of that silly old sod who she loved so much and she began to perk up. She would sell her livestock for a tidy profit for she knew that food was scarce.

The old world order that Grey spoke of felt secure to her so it was fitting that she returned to her residence for peacetime, France her home for war. The Nazis new Reich had been a heartbeat away from becoming universal reality, but now it was atrophying, losing ground in different territories and in spirit. They prized their indomitable power, but that was proven to not be the case. Laura thought of a story from one of Grey's favourite books, of the Tower of Babel. The achievements of men would always pale into insignificance compared to other powers and it didn't matter how they strove, they would always be dwarfed. The achievement for the Nazis was achieving all that they did and the achievement for the Allies was stopping them. Move; counter move, a constant game in session. Men like Grey stopped them and she knew it was not because of powers – it was because of spirit. She was not a soldier or a warrior, but she saw that there was something to respect there, Grey's 'death' hitting home.

Silence reigned as she entered her study and she hated it. She went to release Konah and made him a light tea and she returned to the library. It would not be like this in Scotland, it would be better. Her own company was sufficient, it always had been. Companions, friends and lovers were all transitory; solitude was the norm for her. She was unable to fully convince herself and she was unable to concentrate on the book she was trying to read. An ex-lover and good friend in Georges had died. She had barely felt his loss because of Grey, who in a sense took his place, but now he was gone too and it was like a double blow, a void that she could not just shrug off. If he wasn't dead he would be an invalid, discharged from the army and she would let him recover on her estate in Scotland. She considered him a friend and even though she felt his wounds were partly self-inflicted, she decided to have a try at saving him. She confused Konah, locking him away again as she made her way, following her instincts to lead her to him.

There was a makeshift hospital several miles back from the front and Laura made her way there. She had no passes but through smooth talk of her plight she made her way to the hospital and she asked to see him. As she walked through the hospital Laura hoped that she was the only one for whom the rancorous smell of death was overwhelming – that had to be her powers, that couldn't be the natural odour? She passed two doctors and a nurse trying fruitlessly to revive a patient whose heart gave out as Laura entered the ward (completely unrelated to her presence though Laura knew several people who would blame her) as his friend in the next bed, who was missing parts from three limbs, his left arm the only limb completely intact, shouted at his friend to fight, and then at the medics treating him, ordering them to save him. Laura's eyes were drawn to the scene, Laura seeing that the dying man (she could sense there was no hope), unlike his friend, seemed completely intact, no wounds visible. Perhaps he just didn't want it as much…that was unfair as she knew nothing about him, about any of them bar one. So many of them were missing limbs, and there were horrific sights just walking down the ward, sights that made her wonder what year it was – the calendars said 1944 but it might as well have been 1855 or 1066. She was a sturdy character and the sights were disturbing even to her, with her past. Laura wondered how a soft-hearted person would cope in such an environment. The nurse showed her Grey, laid flat on his back which Laura assumed would be the worst position for him. It was, but he was more comfortable like this and the doctors had done all that they could. He looked wan, hoary and prematurely old and he didn't see her at first, the drugs he had been given for pain relief dulling his senses. When he did see her approach his side he made an effort to raise himself in his bed as he smiled, a huge joyful grin. She smiled back at him as she tried to hold him in place, telling him to stay on his back.

"There's not much left of it to lay back on," he said weakly, letting her know it was okay to joke about it. He knew he was dead and he was not scared for he felt he would join his friends in his head. They were sad for him and encouraged him to try and live (Del tried to spur him on to recover by telling him that there was a wine cellar waiting for him to raid it), but he told them it was over. He had grown pluckier and liked tough fights but he told his spirit friends hyperbolically that even the mighty Grey was beaten.

"I heard. Speaking of which, I have a bone to pick with you," she said, her pun deliberate as she held out her hand which had his curled up cross inside. "This is becoming a habit with you, Grey. You keep giving me things I don't want. First the boy and then this." She fastened it back around his neck and said, inches from his face,

"The kisses though – they were tolerable." After saying this she kissed him, Grey surprised but palpably eager, opening his mouth, his tongue lolling to the side lifelessly. Laura had to kiss him as he was passive throughout, trying yet too weak and his mouth tasted as though it was in a state of decomposition, like there was a nest of insects inside.

The kiss meant little to her and she saw it as an act of charity to a friend who needed it in his defeated, moribund state. There was no self-pity in him, but she pitied him upon sight of him and had been touched by his plight. He would misinterpret it – she expected no different, but that could be a problem for another day. For now she was satisfied with making him feel better. She made her joke about the cancellation of the trip, expressing relief, and Grey shook his head, telling her she had to go now and that he had forced Delgado to promise to tour all of Europe in his stead. He drifted to sleep mid-sentence and Laura performed a basic spell to keep him unconscious as he would not want to be awake for this. Laura questioned the reasoning behind putting him bang in the middle of a busy ward – they knew he was dying so surely a private room would have made more sense, for the morale of the others around him more than anything else. Plus it would have made her next task easier as she would have preferred privacy for her spell. Ideally she would have turned him onto his front, opened up the whole area and patched him up but instead she had to reach under his sheets and under him and perform the 'operation' blind. It required intense concentration, her task not an easy one. That was fine – she was no ordinary healer and she was not prepared to give up on this lost cause. A British nurse interrupted her midway through and (spotting that Laura was touching his spine) asked her to leave, as her patient needed his rest. She would let relatives stay with the dying until the end (though that was rare, most of the relatives a channel or continent away), but upon seeing that Laura was touching him, gripping him where he was mortally injured, she would make no allowances for such a woman. She knew that relatives and lovers could be transfixed with the injuries only this was too much and detrimental to him, even though she knew in his condition he wouldn't feel anything.

"He's not having a rest, he's dying so leave me be," Laura said autocratically, commanding the nurse stricter than any doctor or matron ever had. She backed off, intimidated by her, but she had a duty to her patient and she tried to attract a doctor's attention. The doctor said he would deal with her after he checked on his other patients, paying the nurse lip service as they were talking at cross purposes. Had he known Laura was touching Grey's wound he would have had her frogmarched from the building immediately but when Nurse Rhodes told him that she was touching Grey under the covers he misinterpreted what she meant and while he couldn't publicly condone such actions he instead turned a blind eye to it.

After 40 minutes Laura broke the hold and wiped her brow though there was no sweat on it. Grey was still very ill and would need a lot of care but he would not die from this gunshot wound. His spine was now restored and his shredded guts had been restored to their correct shape though he remained very ill, partly because Laura had chosen to ignore some internal injuries. His recovery would be gradual, to ensure that he never had to participate in this war again. Laura walked over to the nurse and said, "I have had some medical training and I just wanted to check his injuries for myself. I was wrong – he won't die. You should check him." She spoke authoritatively though this time without her bite and as soon as she was gone the nurse intended to check on him anyway. Despite his serious injuries he always smiled at her and made no fuss whatever she had to do to him, irrespective of pain. She liked him and felt his visitor was unworthy of him.

Delgado entered and saw Laura milling around, Laura almost ready to leave, her healing hands clasped together and held up below her chin. Delgado gestured for her to walk with him to a quiet corner where he said, "Thanks for coming. I guess I was wrong about what I said."

"An apology will suffice," Laura said, turning the screw. It was hard enough for him to say what he had and she pressured him for more as entertainment as she watched the nurse checking Grey in the distance.

"I am sorry," he said slowly, looking into her eyes. "I hope you enjoyed that moment as I doubt I'll ever be saying that again." These words contradicted the apology.

"If I turned you to a swine you might. But I forgot, I've graduated, haven't I? It's Calypso now," Laura said, playing with him, smiling severely.

"Yeah, but it's subject to change," he said, staring back at her stony-faced before he said, "But after you coming here I think you won't go down any further than that. Was he awake when you came in?"

"Barely. What was he doing? That wound was close range. Was he that close to the Germans?"

"He has been before. A German didn't shoot him though. He was shot by an American, and not by accident." This strange occurrence shocked Delgado and he relayed it to Laura who had turned up and deserved to know.

"What?" Laura spluttered. "Was it Pearce?" she said, thunderous with rage if that was the case.

Delgado shook his head. "It wasn't anyone from our unit. It was a sergeant from a different company who was practically a stranger to us. He was connected to your mob, one of Georges' friends. He's dead now anyway."

"Good," Laura said, musing this over. "Do me a favour, Delgado. Look after him for me. He'll live; the doctors don't know that yet and neither does he, but he'll live. I have something I have to take care of." She spoke through gritted teeth and this and her grim countenance conveyed her anger to Delgado who knew it was not directed his way.

"He's not going to make it, Laura," Delgado said.

"As a Christian you know all about signs and wonders. Have a little faith," Laura said as she walked off. The military hospital was no place for her now. She had done her part and she was glad that she had gone to see him. She couldn't let him die and seeing him had touched her and surprised her. Seeing him bloodied and doomed made her appreciate him more and want to maintain the friendship. She had done her good deed for the day and now it was time for her bad deed…

Lotte still felt embarrassed as she thought of what had happened that morning. The small house she had been residing in during her time in France assisting Inge had been empty when she arrived but there had been pictures of the previous, rightful occupants. With most of France liberated they had returned and found her inside. The woman had bawled at her and got in her face threateningly and the man had shouted at her, pointing to the door. She had dashed around, trying to gather her essential items hurriedly and the woman had lit a fire in the meantime and began to throw Lotte's possessions onto it as Lotte protested in German that she was leaving. As the photo album was thrown in the hearth Lotte lost heart and stood still, watching her beloved photos frazzle and burn. She had more at her home but they were far away like her husband and son. After seeing this she left at once with just the clothes on her back as the Frenchwoman cackled in triumph, Lotte walking away with one solitary tear rolling down her cheek. The tide had turned, but she was pleased it was not down to her or witchcraft, the two groups negating each other. That was the only positive aspect of her country's impending defeat and ruin. All the sins of the Nazis, which she accepted were myriad, would be revisited on the German people. Peter lived to be a Nazi – after their dissolution and ruin how would he survive? Hard times loomed, impossibly even harder than they had already faced.

Her country was going to hell, perhaps a justifiable punishment for putting so many other peoples through hell though she thought not, but she could have coped with her country's destruction if she gained what she wanted. She, Reinald and Peter could go to Switzerland now; it wasn't too late and she could live like that. Unfortunately that was not to be. Inge had fulfilled her promise, to no avail. Lotte had received two letters (which she was extremely fortunate to receive, both arriving the day of the German withdrawal before the lines of communication were cut), one from Reinald and one from Peter, comprised of the same message though wildly different in style. Peter was furious with her for trying to organise his transfer to an 'easier' front against more 'civilised' enemies. He refused point-blank and, evidently, his superiors hadn't insisted – Lotte imagined they would have admired his fierce refusal and wanted to retain him. Peter stated that he was already with his family and encouraged her to try to get his father moved to the Western Front instead though he put it nastily, referring to his age in insulting terms that were not jocular.

Reinald was apologetic in his letter as he tried to justify why he had not taken the opportunity to return to her side. It was where he longed to be, he reiterated that over and over, but he had a duty. Not to the Nazis and their hate machine (he alluded to that carefully) and not to his country though he did worry what state the conquerors would leave his homeland in. He was not even there because of Peter who he tried to see often but even the one time their two units had worked together Peter had stayed away from him, chiding his father for breaking off from his position by a fraction. The reason he had to stay was because of the other men in his unit. He viewed many of them like sons and he could not leave while they remained. They were young and he wanted them to have his place before him, but he did not ask Lotte to arrange this. Instead he told her not to arrange anything. He guessed that Lotte had been granted this for doing something in return and he advised her to stay safe and only do whatever she believed in. He and Peter would return if they could and while she had given them the chance, now it was in their hands. His words made her think and in her confusion she had wept, everything appearing ruined.

She had nowhere to go bar one place where she knew Inge was secretly staying. She found it difficult to walk through the town, a German stranger in a liberated French town, and she kept her head down, trying to avoid the stares of passers-by, using her senses to lead her to Inge. Walking through a field to the farmhouse Lotte's presence created a ruckus amongst the animals, notably amongst the pigs which almost knocked her over as they occupied the same field as the cows, the sheep and the hens as the farm lapsed into disorder. Lotte knocked repeatedly and after a while Inge shouted for her to enter and Lotte let herself in. She found the farmhouse in a dreadful state, Inge making no effort to tidy up after the scuffle and she was sitting on a soft chair in the lounge painting her toenails.

"Hi, Lotte," she said cheerfully. "I know it's a mess, but I'm not going to be here long and those bitches can tidy it when I go. It's bloody freezing, mind," she said, warning her of the biting cold which had to be bad if she could feel it.

Lotte had a flash and sat down on the floor ready to do a card reading when she remembered that her cards were back at the house that the French couple had reclaimed. "Did something violent happen here?" Lotte enquired, troubled by something in the air.

"It was in the barn where I killed them," Inge said casually.

"No, in here. Below here. There's death," Lotte said, putting her hands to her temples to soothe the throbbing.

"That's just the pig. I threw it down to feed the farmer's family. What do you think – red or pink?" Inge said, stretching out her toes near Lotte's face, showing them off. She distrusted Lotte's tastes when it came to style and what men preferred, but she talked to her as a friend and viewed her as such though not as kin.

"It's not animals. I can't feel animals' deaths," Lotte said. To ease her mind Inge led her down to the cellar where they saw Germaine crying and quivering in the corner and her dead sister and mother and the dead pig.

"I can't believe they didn't move out of the way. What would you do if you saw a pig rolling towards you?" Inge said, making out it was an accident and blaming the victims for their own deaths.

Lotte did not answer and she instead walked towards the girl. Germaine bit her bottom lip to stop herself crying out loud, to block any noise, and Lotte put her arms around her. Inge's way was not her way. The girl was scared and shaking and Lotte spoke soothingly, concentrating on calming sounds rather than words. Lotte had to practically carry her upstairs and Inge followed them, looking back at her handiwork. It was unfortunate though hardly lamentable, but she knew Lotte, with her mothering instinct, needed this and allowed her to try to nurture the girl. Lotte sat her down next to her and stroked her hair and put her head next to the girl's, whose eyes squinted at the light after so long in darkness. Her tears would not cease and Lotte began to cry with her. If it had been James or Laura or any of the townsfolk who had rescued her Germaine would have embraced them and cried on their shoulder, something she would not do with this woman. She seemed kind enough, and Germaine felt that she might protect her from Inge, but it was obvious the two were friends and it stopped her from turning to her.

"Shall we let her have a go?" Inge said to Lotte, then in French, "Do you want to paint your nails?"

Germaine shook her head vigorously, scared that this would be a cruel game in which she would end up hurt. She felt safer than before staying close to Lotte and she was sticking by her until her chance for escape came. Would her trembling legs even be able to get her out of the front door before the demon caught her, escaping requiring nerves she doubted she possessed?

"By the way, Lotte, you know that reading you gave the other day? It came true. Irwin's dead, I felt it. I think he did what I demanded. If he didn't he'll pay for it next life."

"And if he did?" Lotte asked, questioning whether there would be any reward. She had no fondness for the man, but his endless fate and suffering at Inge's heels seemed cruel, too cruel for anyone. There had to be a time when Inge allowed him to live again, if he was able to without her now as he seemed completely dependent on her whims. The suffering, the torture and the hatred had to stop sometime. She would not intervene for him, but she hoped that Inge would eventually tire of abusing him.

"Then my pet gets a treat," Inge said. Nothing would change, his fate recurring like Prometheus.

Konah was sent upstairs when Laura returned home and she shut the door to her basement and began a primal spell, the sort that she was much requested to do in her youth, the heyday for witches and sorcery. Spells of death and curses were popular then and after making the circle Laura removed her blouse and undershirt and stood in her long skirt with her breasts exposed and her lengthy hair hanging loose and she began the dance. She had no name, no image in her head for the man, but that did not matter for she knew there was a man. Inge never acted alone, Inge never slept alone, but she would soon, for a short while at least. It was tit for tat. Inge had hurt her male friend and now she would hurt her more intimate male friend, the nameless, faceless Nazi. Inge had initiated this feud, Grey's injuries reeking of her influence, and Laura was paying her back for that and for her attack on her at their first meeting. It was the unstoppable force hitting the immovable object, a clash of titans back then, and now there were no rules and others could be used to gain vengeance. Vulpine, heinous deeds were the order of the day on all sides.

The curses spewed from Laura's lips as she spun round giddily, her arms outstretched. She reached for her liquids and began to strip further until she was naked and she began daubing herself as she crouched on the floor. Her face contorted and her often sarcastic, sneering smile was replaced by a smile of pure hatred – the emotion needed to make this work. She picked up her clothes and walked to her bathroom and had a long soak. Inge deserved this lesson and she closed her eyes as she luxuriated and she felt very self-satisfied.

Major Klaus Von Strauss suspected it was over when he sent Inge away. It was spelt out to him now. He remained in a tank near the rear as the battle continued, the Allied soldiers proving to be better fighters than their propaganda machine would have them believe. The Nazis had been kings for a few years and even if all were lost they would fight as though everything was still possible. They had a triumphant spirit and optimism; they remained valiant and stoic. History would reveal them as heroes and inspire another revanchist revival that would not fail.

He mused over what Inge would do without him. She never talked of her past lovers but he knew he was not the first for he knew exactly what sort of a woman she was. She would mourn and do so spectacularly. Then she would pick herself up, regroup and move on as he would. She was attracted to the ceremonies of the Reich, the glamour and decadence and some of the excesses that he only skirted with, and which others embraced with abandon. She swore loyalty but he knew that was paper thin and that without him she would grow bored with it and she would be no long-term advocate or preacher of their ideologies. It was possible that during the coming renaissance she would stand in their way. That was how Inge was, easy to read and (for him) more loveable because of it.

Strauss ordered his unit to advance as he noticed them retreating. That was unacceptable and he ordered the driver of his tank to move to the forefront to set an example. No withdrawal and no surrender. His mind knew they were lost but his heart disagreed and he was satisfied as he saw his enemies swatted like flies, blown away by his tank. To beat them, the mighty Aryans, they would have to suffer incalculable losses and lose their nation's generation of young men as they were.

Fate favours the brave he thought, his creed since boyhood. It had gained him power and prestige and Inge. He did not care if it killed him now for he would die with honour and would not go down easily, or so he thought until his tank ceased to function, leaving him a sitting duck…

The scream from the farmhouse could be heard for nearly half a mile. Eric had turned up and was discussing the next plan of action with Inge as Lotte kept stroking Germaine's back and arms, trying very hard to console her and seeking solace herself. Germaine welled up again at the scream and Lotte clutched her to her bosom protectively as Eric blocked his ears. The windows smashed, the animals were disturbed and Inge cried, torrents of tears streaming down her cheeks. Eric and Lotte had both heard of wailing banshees and after Inge's ululant cry the image sprung to mind to both of them. When Eric felt his hearing return he said, "What on earth's the matter?"

"He's dead," she said, tears cascading down onto her corselette, Inge lounging around and not going out so not bothering to dress fully. She made a pitiful sound as she covered her face as she felt that painful moment. She didn't feel the pain or know exactly what happened, she just knew suddenly that Klaus Von Strauss was dead. She was utterly alone again; she even craved her lapdog Irwin. Strauss had understood her, introduced her to fascinating people and a way of life that she adored. He was the perfect lover and companion, he provided everything that she needed and she even gave up the stage for him, breaking the hearts of half of Berlin (covering both genders). Her world had come crumbling down, all possibilities ruined now. The future held nothing now and she wished that she had died with him or even better that she had died with her tribe and never experienced the poisoned chalice of love. All it meant to her was loss, again and again. They always died, usually bloody, and she was left with nothing. Immortality was a curse and love was the form that this curse took, as insidious as they came. She looked at plain old Lotte and envied her for what she had. She wanted no ordinary husband or family herself, but she saw someone who had achieved her heart's desire, something she only managed herself for a fraction of an interminably long life.

Lotte nodded. "Do you have the cards?" she asked. "There was something in the air – I don't know if it was natural." Lotte was trying to help her and as soon as she said this she wished that she had not for she knew people would now bear the brunt of Inge's vengeance.

"You're right. That's the only way they'd ever beat my Major," Inge said loyally, even prouder of him, perversely so, now that he was deceased.

"The group won't have even convened yet," Eric said truthfully. He had no loyalty towards Mireille's group, and simply told Inge the truth, sensing that it was in his best interests to play it straight with her. Eric had found himself at another crossroads following the massacre and contemplated changing allegiances again. If he had total freedom of choice he would have picked the Allies side. They were winning now and a free France was what he had always wanted – that was the whole point of the Pagan Resistance, before the motivations became diluted. He felt no affinity to them anymore and would soon cease all contact. Unfortunately Eric knew that he had no real choice. The Germans were gone, but Inge remained, deadlier than ever.

"Somebody has though, haven't they, Lotte? Not that group, they couldn't wipe their arses without help. I know who it is all right," Inge said animatedly. "We're going out," she ordered.

"I have to stay with her," Lotte said, still holding onto Germaine.

"Lock her under the stairs or I'll kill her," Inge said, staring at Lotte, showing she meant it and Lotte tried to do as commanded, trying to guide Germaine to the stairs. Lotte intended to leave the door unlocked so the girl could make her escape but Germaine was rigid with shock and Lotte's gentle and more forceful attempts at moving her had no effect.

"Please. Eric, can you tell her that she has to go in the cellar and that she'll be fine?" Lotte pleaded, desperate to get the girl away from Inge. Before Eric had a chance to say anything Inge grabbed Germaine by a bony arm (how long had she kept her locked down there?) and dragged her across the floor, Germaine silent as Lotte begged Inge to let go of her.

"Don't push me or I will kill her," Inge said, lifting Germaine up by the scruff of her neck, positioning her at the top of the cellar steps where she was somehow able to stand unassisted. Inge was not inclined to be gentle and she had been very merciful to the girl just to pacify Lotte. Lotte was still whining at her ('that's good, Inge, we'll leave her there and go and do what you want, just leave her alone'), while the girl was silent, looking intently into space, her head making occasional violent jerking movements. Inge would have left her where she was if Lotte had been silent instead of agitating her and instead Inge gave the girl some serious thought for the first time. This was no innocent child who deserved her mercy as Lotte suggested. This was a partisan's daughter and probably involved with the resistance herself, either as a member, accomplice or lover and she deserved her father's fate. As Inge prepared to swing her fist through her body, Germaine's swaying frame fell down the stairs, rolling to the bottom where she landed on the sow. Inge descended a few steps before changing her mind and getting back to the matter at hand – if the girl wasn't dead she would be injured and would soon starve in the cellar anyhow.

Inge headed outside with Eric while Lotte put her shoes on, using the opportunity to run across the room and unlock the cellar door, rushing around as she knew if she took too long to join them that they'd guess what she'd done. With any luck while they were gone the poor girl would seize her chance and escape (if she was able). Lotte knew that Inge was unhinged now and that anything could happen and she dreaded the night, her stomach churning at what lay ahead and she felt sick.

Germaine found that the pig made a surprisingly soft landing for her at the bottom of the stairs. Perhaps the pig could warn James of what had happened to her. She imagined five pages of his notebook filled with the word Oink over and over, the pig's message to its piglets, and she began to laugh hysterically. She imagined James Grey bending down to the piglets in the sty, putting a protective arm around them as he delivered the news, his clothes covered in mud and pig shit. It would cheer them up – perhaps he could visit her skeleton when he came to do this. That would be nice. Her decomposing mother gave her a sour look and her laughter ceased.

Laura packed a suitcase quickly with a few changes of attire, some money and a few books. She talked kindly to Konah as she opened up the cellar walls again and she told him that she had to go away for a while and that when she came back she would return him to Mireille, Paulette and the others. This promise cheered him up and she left him with around two weeks supply of food and drink and the light remained glowing above his bed. After sealing him in Laura went to see to the animals, giving them all excessive amounts of food, which they would not touch at this late hour (bar a few greedy hens). Laura knew they would overeat and not make the food last as long as it was supposed to but there was nothing else she could do. There was a chance that Inge would realise her involvement in her lover's death and she would seek vengeance. Laura was not running from the fight for she knew that if Inge was out to get her that she would find her eventually. Laura was leaving because she feared that Inge might avenge her lover by finishing off Grey who was helpless to stop her – though that would be the case even if he were at 100 per cent. She wanted to see his surprise when he found out that he was going to live and the thought of his reaction excited her. Analysing the situation in retrospect Laura realised that the English nurse who touched Grey, examining him and looking at him with doting eyes – that had annoyed her. She seemed a pleasant girl, pretty with brown curls and perfect for Grey, the sort she had pushed him to find. She wasn't so sure now. He was only a child, that was how she always perceived him, but he had acted with bravery and had the courage of his convictions and languished in agony and nearly died for them. If that didn't complete the rites of passage into manhood, what did? Was he mature? Yes and no, mainly yes. He was her friend anyhow and she knew she valued him now.

She thought as she left how close she had come to remaining home when Delgado had come to tell her of Grey. She knew now how huge a mistake that would have been and she hoped he did not know of that. He would be dead now otherwise and that would have been a waste of potential and a waste of a good man. Also she would have missed out on what she anticipated would be the most moronic tour ever given which she suspected he would compensate for with pep and enthusiasm over knowledge. If nothing else she would probably fill a whole bookcase with American works. She had saved a friend, not a bedfellow. Even her finest spells couldn't help out on that score for the foreseeable future, his entire lower half a dead loss for some time, which gave her time to weigh up her options. She had wanted him the night of the massacre. The soldier returning from the battle, sweaty, troubled, spending his last night with her before heading into the abyss – on a primal level it struck a chord. The wounded soldier triggered dormant nurturing instincts in her, completely separate from lust. His injuries made her grow more attached to him though proved a backwards step to their slim potential for romance.

"Eric. Grab a seat, we're going to try to reveal collaborators in the town," Mireille said chirpily as she sat around the table with the Ouija board at the centre. Gervaise and Margot sat with her as Paulette sat on a stool at the old bar next to Odette who kept whispering her complaints to her. Mireille was still grieving for Didier but she was more composed after the apparent success of the spell in liberating their town, an action which she dedicated to Didier though she did not claim the glory, begrudgingly accepting that Laura had been a great help. Freedom offered a chance for rebirth and the child in Odette's stomach was her hope. Unfortunately, she disliked the unborn baby's lazy mother who had turned Didier's old room into a tip and was proving quarrelsome. Odette felt picked on by Mireille's cavilling and she had told her not to enter her bedroom if it bothered her. Mireille made Odette do a lot of housework because she found her so slovenly and after the first few days Odette rebelled passive-aggressively, claiming to have cramps whenever she was told to do anything and giving Mireille the evil eye whenever she criticised her. Mireille would say to the others within Odette's earshot that she would be working after she had the baby and no mistake and Odette confided and bitched to Paulette who had no helpful advice as she saw both sides.

Mireille made few concessions for Odette despite her grief over her parents deaths – Mireille had lost both parents when she was younger than Odette and she told her to pull herself together whenever she cried, assuring her that it hurt far worse to bury a child than a parent. Francoise and her children had left the town to live with her late husband's parents in Bordeaux and she had promised she would arrange lodgings for her too, either with her in-laws or they would find a small place together. Francoise's father-in-law was even more fastidious than their departed father, which was why Odette couldn't just arrive on their doorstep, but Francoise promised to talk him round or she'd move out. Once this escape route was sorted out she would leave Maramont forever, never to see the town or Mireille Godet again. As awkward as Francoise's father-in-law was, nothing could compare to Mireille, the ultimate mother-in-law from hell.

Eric had entered by the front doors as he always did (they all did now that they were liberated again). Another figure entered followed by a third who looked down, clearly not wanting to be there. That was Lotte but Inge stepped forward boldly to examine the group. Paulette nearly fell off her stool in shock at seeing her and Inge stared at her and smiled broadly. Paulette's facial scars had faded but her body was still a mess and she would never forget that day. She searched around for a weapon and found nothing substantial and she resorted to throwing a glass at Inge who raised her hand, the glass smashing into her fist without causing any damage.

"What the hell's going on?" Mireille demanded to know, looking to Paulette and Eric for an explanation. She looked at Inge and remembered the physical description that Paulette had given and she saw Paulette whose face remained hard but whose legs were buckling as she stood looking at this woman. This was

Inge, the animal whose name her son had mouthed before he and two other young men were shot publicly by firing squad.

"You're Inge, aren't you, you bitch?" Mireille said, standing up and looking at her with her mouth open as she advanced towards her. Inge was going to kill her, but not yet and she moved across the room and grabbed Odette, pulling her from her stool and standing behind her, holding her in a headlock and backing away from them all.

"I'll break her neck if you come any closer," Inge said to Mireille who immediately stopped. Inge stroked Odette's hair as she talked and she savoured this moment. This group had been a thorn in her lover's side as he tried valiantly to progress and fulfil his dream. They were doomed.

"There's very little potential in this room, bar us three of course. You're nothing and you thought you could take on the Third Reich? No, no, you survived on Georges' coattails and through Eric," Inge said, making it obvious that Eric was a traitor.

"Why, Eric?" Paulette said, her left knee shaking violently and she tried to mask this by deliberately pounding it into the ground. She felt betrayed having imagined they were all in it together and it hit her hard. Gervaise and Margot remained seated, both shaken by the appearance of Inge, a clearly merciless woman and in Margot's trained eye, a 'bit of a hussy' which she whispered to Gervaise, an unhelpful observation. Gervaise had tried to stop Mireille before she had stood up but to no avail and all felt lost to them.

"I have plenty of reasons. Georges should have appointed me leader because I have always been the power of the group. I would have directed us against the true enemy – Britain and America. They're scared of a united Europe and that's their only reason for being here. Most of the policies of National Socialism will benefit France and will at least rid us of the Communist menace." Eric's voice wavered and Paulette raised one eyebrow at this and he realised that he was trying to justify himself to her, not that she was having any of it. Mireille was too focused on Inge, who had hold of her broodmare, to even look at Eric. That bastard would die after Inge but she wanted to deal with her first and get Odette to safety. After this she could put her feet up and stay in bed until she had the baby, afterwards if she wanted. Mireille would work for all three of them.

Eric snorted indignantly, realising how inarticulate he sounded at what was a triumph for him and he raised himself to his full height and looked around the room and attempted to say something clever. "But you want to know the real reason? I have moved on to a powerful coven and I am so ashamed of having been in such an outfit as this that I want to destroy all of the witnesses. Everyone should change friends every few years and in my case I can shed you all without regret." He smiled as he said this, taking control, as Lotte looked at them all furtively. His speech was designed to impress Inge as Eric was aware he had to disown the group completely to ensure his own survival at this hazardous time. Regrets would come later.

"You realise that means that he'll turn on you," Mireille said, Eric's forceful delivery of these words attracting her attention if not her gaze and she tried to reason with Inge. Odette was frantic as she felt the strength of Inge's grip, too shocked to cry.

"In time, but neither of us expects our alliance to be a lengthy one," Inge said. She then whispered huskily in Odette's ear, "What do you want, my dear, a boy or a girl?"

"...Err...I." Odette struggled for an answer and Inge talked over her mumbling and she said,

"I'll take a peek for you." She punched into the left side of her back, her hand raking through flesh as she destroyed mother and child and Odette screamed but nowhere near as loudly as Mireille who charged at Inge. Paulette looked at Mireille thumping Inge, foolishly trying to fight her on a physical level instead of with witchcraft and for one of the few times in her life she looked for escape. Eric and the other woman blocked the front door, Inge blocked the entrance to the back, but there was still the door to the stairs. Paulette tugged at it, telling Margot and Gervaise to follow her and Gervaise stood up in preparation but as Paulette tugged at the knob it would not open. There was no lock and Paulette could not understand it.

"Open up, you fucking fuck!" she said, pulling with both hands before she head-butted the door and screamed, in frustration rather than terror.

"That won't work," Eric said smugly, showing his superiority to theirs. Paulette glared at him and ran across the room towards him, but instead of lunging at him like he expected or trying for the door, she instead turned sharply right, crashing through the window out into the front street. She could feel her arm was slashed to buggery, her cheek too; none of that mattered as at least she was out of the house and able to stand and she ran away. She knew what she had to do. Her body was still damaged from the attack and she limped but she still ran, tripping occasionally but she got straight back up again.

Mireille landed three mighty punches. Inge only needed one, her fatal punch to Mireille's head almost beheading her, the force of it breaking her neck. With Mireille Godet, Odette Piena and child dead in the corner, Inge moved across the room to Gervaise and Margot. Margot had taken her cards out of her bag and was playing a last game by herself, seemingly content. Gervaise pleaded for her life as Inge advanced on her and Margot, looking to Eric as she spoke. They had sometimes quarrelled, but rarely, and mostly they got on well.

"You should have switched sides, Gervaise," Eric said, washing his hands of her, his tone regretful. Her fate was now ineluctable and Eric would not put himself on the line for her.

Margot did not look up, not wanting to break away from her game and she said coolly, "You're going to hell."

"You have to die first for that, prune-face," Inge said. She placed her hands on either side of Margot's cheeks, her thumbs resting behind her ears and Margot screamed briefly as Inge applied pressure until her hands met. Lotte looked away at this whilst Eric looked at the sight and felt squeamish about it. He would never, ever cross this woman. Gervaise retched at the sight before turning frantically to the door which she tried again, opening it on her first attempt. Eric was unsure if the distracting sight of Margot's grisly death had affected his concentration or if Gervaise had forcibly opened the door with her own power, Gervaise equally unsure. She took her chance and ran up the stairs, falling forwards in her desperation to get some distance between herself and Inge, delaying the inevitable.

"Good. I always loved hide and seek," Inge shouted, looking forward to toying with her. Gervaise was as good as dead but Inge noticed that someone else was missing. "Where's that scrawny bitch?" she asked Eric, wanting to completely clean house. She was so focused that she had been unaware of the window breaking and Eric told her and she noticed the curtains blowing outwards.

Paulette was in a state when she came across two Canadians on patrol who helped support her, showing concern. She saw they were armed and she felt a smidgen of regret for they were allies but she had to go and stop Inge so she allowed them to help her and kneed the larger of the two in the groin with all of her might. He went down in a heap and she grabbed his rifle which she had been mindful of and smacked the other in the face with it. He staggered, disoriented by the blow, and Paulette said sorry and ran as fast as she could back to the pub before it was too late.

Gervaise tried to open the window in Georges' bedroom, the roof accessible from the ledge, but found it a struggle as it was very stiff. She could hear Inge patrolling the corridor, kicking in the other doors and taunting her ('little witch, time for a purge'). By the time she forced it open and upward, shattering the pane, Inge had kicked the door in and looked across the room at her, smiling gleefully, her hands dripping blood onto the carpet.

"Please leave me be," Gervaise said meekly, aware that she couldn't exit the window in time – she was not agile and would likely fall if rushed.

"You dug your own grave when you joined this group. What happened? Did the embroidery group throw you out when you found a husband, you priggish bore? Georges Steil must have been a lunatic to try and beat the Nazis with such a band of misfits," Inge said derisively. Inge had things that she wanted to say to every member of the group, Eric having told her about them in detail, but in her anger she had killed Mireille without venting her spleen sufficiently and she made up for it with Gervaise. She had met thousands of women like her before, stuffy bitches who wore cast-iron underwear and envied her for her assets and lifestyle. Unfortunately she was unable to kill the self-righteous puritans every time (mass murder tended to attract attention that even she didn't want) but this once she could and she would enjoy it.

Inge forgot that there was one thing separating Gervaise from the others who had scorned her with their haughty eyes. Gervaise had a modicum of power, a small amount according to Eric, which now proved sufficient to make Georges' cupboard topple down on Inge as she advanced on her. Gervaise had no idea how she moved it (her power tended not to manifest itself so) and she went with the flow instead of questioning it and tried to move other things. She succeeded in making a plate fly at Inge, followed by a pair of shoes and followed by the bed which darted across the room, knocking Inge back. Gervaise gasped in surprise as she achieved this – was the poltergeist activity that centred round her brother one summer some 20 years ago down to her? The hangers came to life from the cupboard, trying fruitlessly to draw blood as they ran over Inge's skin, Inge hurling the small objects away from her and at Gervaise, though they flew straight back at Inge with more force than she threw them with. Inge blamed Eric for not briefing her properly as she found herself driven back out of the door which Gervaise was able to barricade swiftly.

"Bitch!" Inge shouted loudly as she tried to force the door. She tried barging it three times and then hesitated, thinking up a plan.

Paul had birdwatching and fishing, two hobbies that suited him and kept him occupied. Without him Gervaise had found a hobby of her own, a small recreational pastime based on her perfect intuition, which had grown to become important to her and now appeared to have saved her life. She had thought that they'd just use the runes or tarot cards, maybe indulge in reading palms or tea leaves, and the terrorist activities had appalled her (she hadn't intended to get involved in active resistance), but by that stage she was already learning so much about herself that she didn't leave. What the church didn't know wouldn't hurt them and had proved to have helped her – the Christian guilt that she sometimes felt after spells was absent. Gervaise walked to the barricade and touched the cupboard, feeling it with her hands instead of feeling it in her head. She couldn't believe how simple it was to...

Gervaise clutched at her heart as Inge suddenly charged through the wall, creating a huge hole that led to the bedroom she had been using when she slept over. There were a few feet between the two women but all of the objects were behind Gervaise and had to move past her to get to Inge. She was able to direct the smaller items but Inge shrugged these off and grabbed Gervaise by her blouse, pulling her towards her and off her feet so that their faces met.

"Good attempt. I enjoyed it because I needed a warm-up and those three downstairs were sorely lacking," Inge said, smiling happily, as she knew she had control again.

"I can beat you," Gervaise said, realising that she had the potential to defeat her. If she'd only listened to Georges and tried to access all of her power instead of settling contentedly for a sliver she felt she could be the one gripping Inge.

"You're getting above yourself. You could possibly fend me off but defeating the indestructible requires more than spinning some household furniture around. I've been hung and burnt at the stake twice and here I am still. Even tanks couldn't kill me so I doubt a bed will do the job. Well done though. I don't remember most of those that I kill and I will remember you," Inge said, her words meant as a compliment. "Now you wanted to go out of the window..."

"That was excessive," Lotte said, walking with folded arms behind Inge and Eric as they searched the streets for Paulette, the girl who had made Inge aware of the whole resistance, the girl she couldn't break. Lotte felt sick and she was unable to contain her disgust and she wanted Inge to know that she would never be a party to anything like that again.

"Shut up," Inge said, turning to look at her and Lotte was chastened. Inge could kill anyone tonight; she had the bloodlust and Lotte still wanted to live.

"It wasn't excessive. That was impressive," Eric said, feeling on the verge of vomiting at what had befallen Margot, but feeling he had to fawn to Inge. He had been part of the group she had exterminated and at one stage he had opposed the man she grieved so he tried to show her that his loyalties lay firmly with her. Inge was uninterested in anything either of them had to say; she just wanted them there as backup for the main event, her dissection of Laura. It had been nearly 900 years since they last clashed and that would be the approximate length of her suffering or so Inge planned though in practice she would likely go too far and finish her off swiftly. She saw Paulette in the distance and she quickened her pace as the suicidal bitch walked towards her, walking towards her death as Inge was going to rip her head off this time (after calling her a toady and mocking her for believing she was a member of the Pagan Resistance when she was just their thrall). As Paulette drew closer she smiled and raised her rifle and pointed it at Inge who paused and Eric and Lotte walked backwards, looking for cover. Paulette fired, hitting Inge who grinned as the shot hit her cheek, bruising her, but not enough to stop her. The two Canadians heard the shot and they came running round the corner and the one she had kneed in the groin told her to lay down her weapon as he saw her aiming at the unarmed blonde. Paulette looked at him, tried to explain it and then just fired anyway, shooting Inge on the eyelid this time, making her wince and moan in pain. The soldier had his finger on the trigger, but he was averse to shooting women, even those who had killed other women and had hoofed him harder than a bucking bronco. He instead shot the rifle from her hand and he ran to her, knocking her to the ground, and he looked at Inge who was rubbing her eye, moaning about the shot. His comrade (Paulette's blow had left him groggy and as a result he had let his friend take his weapon) saw that he had Paulette under control and he started to walk towards Inge to check on her.

"No, don't go near her! I shot her in the eye and she hasn't even gone down. Do you understand?" Paulette shouted from the ground. She was desperate for them to understand her meaning, for their sake as much as her own. She assumed the others were dead and she did not want them to follow suit.

"Wise words for you, but too late for this one," Inge said, also speaking English and she reached for the soldier and clutched his throat, about to break his neck. She smiled as she did this before she felt intense pain and let go of him, collapsing to the floor. The Canadian soldier at Paulette's side had fired at her, heeding Paulette's example and aiming for her eye (while Paulette's shot seemed to do little damage this still seemed the most vulnerable spot on a freakish creature and caused some pain) and instead of the eyelid he shot her pupil. He blew on his whistle hard as he advanced to his friend who was lying on the ground wheezing, clutching his throat which had the white imprints of her fingers, his windpipe partially crushed. He dragged him back and kept whistling as Paulette picked up the rifle and aimed at Inge again. She was disappointed to find that the rifle was empty. Lotte acted, coming out from the shadows and Eric followed her and they helped Inge to her feet and took her away. The bullet had bounced off her pupil, but it had seriously hurt her and as a stranger to serious pain she reacted badly, crying like a wounded child. They were gone before reinforcements came and the Canadian soldier, who introduced himself to Paulette as Kirk, was too concerned with his friend to go after them.

After 20 minutes medical help arrived with more soldiers and Kirk's friend was taken away and Paulette asked them to come with her to the tavern where she knew there would be bodies. There was a crowd gathered outside standing around Gervaise's battered and bloodied body which had been hurled from the upstairs window into the building opposite. Paulette remained composed and told them that there would be worse sights in the tavern. She entered after Kirk who insisted on going in first and he coughed at the sights, feeling sick but repressing it.

"Sheesh. It's like the murders in the fucking Rue Morgue," he shouted as several other soldiers came in and Paulette looked at the remains of her friends and allies sadly. They had done well, they had made Georges proud she hoped – all bar one who she would see hung. They had tried at least.

As the other soldiers searched the upstairs rooms Paulette said to Kirk who remained downstairs with her, "They won't find anything up there. It was that woman who did it all." She had told him the tale while they waited and after what he had seen of her and now this he believed her.

The other soldiers returned downstairs and the captain said, "Clean up there. You're staggering, Kirk – you want medical attention too?"

"I'll be all right. I thought I was hurt, but not compared to this," he said, shaking his head.

"I am sorry," Paulette said still looking at the bodies. Knocks and punches came with the territory in wartime when hardness was paramount, but for her it felt like the war was over and she did feel bad for hurting him, worse than she did for acts that she had committed that resulted in loss of life.

"Forget it. If you'd have asked we'd have come with you, but I can see why time was of the essence and you couldn't risk us saying no. What I am bothered about is that you go and get yourself checked out," he said, insisting she needed stitches.

"I'm fine, honestly. All I want to do is get back to my room. Will you take me?" she said, wanting to make amends to him in this way and she did not want to spend the night alone.

"How dare they shoot at me?" Inge protested at the top of her voice as Lotte examined her eye as they sat down in the woods. It looked sore but undamaged, which was impressive considering it had been hit by a bullet.

"Your eye is going to be all right," Lotte said, trying to calm her.

"They won't be though. If they win this war I am going to go fucking ballistic," Inge warned, shaking her head in irate anger, close to another paroxysm.

"What will be, will be," Lotte said calmly, trying to abate her anger.

"For you, yes. When I saw you as that plain German wench I saw your potential and I knew you would never realise it. You're too scared to be anything," Inge said, turning on her, sneering at Lotte.

"I'm happy as I am. And falling in love and getting married was scarier than performing any spell and infinitely more rewarding," Lotte said boldly. She was not trying to provoke her, simply explaining why Inge's charges against her were untrue.

Inge said nothing to this and Lotte looked away. Inge was not really mad at her and she turned to Eric and said, "So where exactly does she live?"

"We don't know exactly. Georges would never tell us, but he always returned with muddy shoes and trousers and she mentioned something about a farm once. There is a farm nearby, which has a reclusive owner who's said to be an Englishwoman. I would assume that's the one."

"You would assume that's the one?" Inge said, staring at him contemptuously. "Of course that's the one." She made Eric lead the way to the farm, Lotte lagging behind, becoming entangled in a bramble bush and having to extricate herself without assistance. Inge looked at the exterior of Laura's farmhouse and she looked to Lotte who was panting but had caught up with them.

"Is this the one?" she asked Lotte. Inge's senses were more attuned to those she cared for, those she had lain down with, and she lacked Lotte's intuitive ability unless she was very close to such a person.

Lotte nodded. Spells had been cast from here; one foul one still lingered in the air, a spell of immolation. Her nod was sufficient for Inge to break the front door down and she searched through the house, which she began to wreck, up-turning the dining table, throwing the chairs across the room. She entered the library next and she saw Laura's collection of books on witchcraft and the arcane. This completely confirmed that it was Laura's residence and Inge pulled all three bookcases down, sending the books sprawling across the room. Lotte felt a presence and she kept quiet while Inge, who was tearing up books, suddenly stopped what she was doing and like a cat sniffing out a mouse she looked around for her prey which would not escape her. She followed her senses and walked down the stairs to the wine cellar and basement. Lotte followed her, saying, "She's not here. Let's go."

"Shut up, you soft-hearted fool. You know as well as I do that this house has someone in it," Inge said and she walked to the wall where she knew power lurked behind. Her hands probed the wall for an opening but she was impatient and instead of thoroughly searching for a panel, she punched her right fist through the wall at chest level followed by her left fist. She ripped out the section that remained between her two punches and peeked through at the boy who was backing away in his small room, trying to get as far away from her as possible. She smiled wickedly at him, the boy who Eric had told her about.

The next day Laura was permitted to see Grey again. Grey had confounded the doctors who kept studying him because they were unable to understand how he was recovering so. Laura's spell was slow acting and so his recovery would be though the main damage was dealt with. He was still prostrate and dog-tired but he talked and reached for her hand as he saw her coming, Laura taking his palm in hers.

"I should have died," Grey said to her, overjoyed that he had not, but confused.

"Strange that, isn't it?" she said, her eyebrows raised in overweening fashion as she remained poker-faced. She wasn't going to say it overtly, but he knew.

"I...thank you," he said, tears overfilling his eyes. He was emotional at this, greatly moved, and he tried to smile as his emotions overwhelmed him. She said nothing, but she smiled at him and kept hold of his hand, stroking it lightly. He was loquacious by nature, overly so, and his silence spoke volumes and she enjoyed it.

It couldn't last of course and she didn't really want it to. After several minutes like this with Grey uttering solemn words of life debt which she dismissed, he joked that she would have to come on the trip now, her sharp tongue returning in jest as she told him he couldn't tour the grounds of the hospital, let alone such a vast country. She instructed him that if he wanted her to come with him on a long journey that first he would have to get back in shape and she 'threatened' him with a long stay at her Scottish residence to recover to spare her the 'inconvenience' of travelling with an 'invalid'. She deliberately emphasised certain words to show a false disdain.

"I'm not wearing a kilt though," he said, shaking his head firmly, playing along with her.

"As my patient, at my Scottish home?" she said sharply, indicating she was in charge before she said calmly, "We'll see."

"I've gotten myself in trouble now, haven't I?" he said, pretending to have a sudden epiphany of what the indomitable Laura was like, mock horror at being in her clutches, delivered with a barely concealed smile.

"At last the penny drops," she said, smiling warmly at him.

Grey talked to her of what had happened in the month since he had left her and she listened attentively, especially interested in the details of his shooting and the shooter, Laura convinced that Georges had never met Irwin who was undoubtedly an agent of Inge's. He was interrupted by the nurse, Rosemary Rhodes, who Grey described as 'another lady who doesn't respect me' and Laura saw her smile at this for there was a mild flirtation between the two. Grey knew the delicate reason why she had come over and made a joke of it, presenting himself as the joke in truth, but the two women did not team up to say anything about him. Laura was asked to leave them by Rosemary, and she did, and she saw what this nurse, who she had clashed with at her last visit, thought of Grey. Rosemary was fascinated with his miraculous recovery, but there was something personal too. Laura contained her jealousy, which she recognised was stupid considering she and Grey were not together and she knew his joke was not intentional flirtation, more his way of trying to put them at ease.

When Laura returned to his side she told him of her suspicions about Inge's involvement and she warned him that he was not even safe in the hospital. She spoke gravely, explaining why the quicker he could leave the better, as wearing a kilt in the Highlands was better than wearing a suit in a coffin.

"I don't think he had any powers," Grey said. "I think the stuff about his wife and being a friend of Georges' was a pack of lies and he was strange but... Some of the voices in my head – Linus and Reilus have helped, only I don't agree with their theories." He was taking the matter very seriously as he tried to give her views credence but he doubted it. "I don't see why Inge would want me dead. It's not like I ever achieved anything against her," he said, viewing this as a failing of his. For all of her critical banter, Laura was far more encouraging and supportive than the Pagan Resistance who made him feel useless.

"What are their theories?" she asked, sensing there could be something useful there. She knew how powerful he was even if it was not a power like hers or Inge. He could not cause death through imprecation; he did not have skin harder than diamond. What he had access to was the voices of the dead, legion, and there would be so much he could do with that once his gift was further refined. She could not do that and neither could Inge or Georges or most of the spiritualists who had amused her around the turn of the century. However comprehensive her library was, this man possessed more knowledge inside of him as a channeller than any information archive. The few stories she had heard of his dead friends and their lives and woe entertained her and often there was wisdom there. The dead had died which was a sign of weakness, but she was not closed-minded and knew that any could fall; even Goliath, Tiamat and Morgana died.

"They think that Irwin had lived before as something connected to Inge. You see they both have lived more than once, and I think that colours their judgement as there's no reason to believe that." Grey disagreed with the voices and argued with them without belittling them, but they were adamant and were trying to help him.

"I don't think they're trying to steer you wrong, I think you should listen without being completely tractable, just have an open mind. For now though lock the door to them all. Talking to them is not resting, that'll strain you too much."

"I can't just shut them out," Grey said, unwilling to turn his back on them if he were able as it felt cruel. He was all the disembodied voices had in their darkness; he was their one light and companion.

"I haven't taught you well enough then. If they come into your head tell them you're having a break and don't strain to communicate with them. I pity you in a way. You lack privacy in your own brain, but I think I might be able to help you so that you can talk to them on your terms," Laura said sympathetically. "All that can wait though, you need to physically recover first."

"The way the doctors and the nurses have been around me I won't get chance not to. They keep saying it's miraculous and keep checking and showing other doctors and specialists how I've healed. I think I've become a specialist case study," he said, a little flattered and amused by the attention if not the prodding. His regimen was scrupulously observed and he knew that Laura would likely be banished soon as he saw two doctors coming in the distance who could not keep their hands off his back, looking at it as if they expected it to revert back to its grievous state any second under their vigilant gaze. "If I so much as tried to put a toe on the floor I think they'd point another rifle at me."

"That works for me," Laura said, happy that he was under such close observation which would help him recover quicker and might – no, it wouldn't protect him from Inge if she was determined, Laura corrected herself. She was soon ordered to leave as Grey was told to lie on his front and she told him to take care and he said the same, thanking her again as she left him to it. She visited him every day for the next six days, his only visitor as his unit had progressed further on to fresh battles, leaving him behind. They had heard of his partial recovery and the positive, completely altered prognosis and it had created a buzz and boost. Over these six days Laura saw what Grey meant about the doctors who did keep checking on him, some letting her stay, some telling her to leave in no uncertain terms. It was clear they didn't believe their eyes and Laura wondered if they wanted his lower spine to detach itself from his pelvis again just to restore their faith in medical science. They wouldn't get their wish. Laura was impressed with how well Grey took these constant tiresome interruptions, Grey a far more patient and tolerant person than she was. That nurse – she was in love with Grey, perhaps because of the miracle that had affected her. All had given him up for dead, he had received the last rites, and now he was recovering. Laura saw her kissing her cross twice after talking to Grey, thinking no one could see her. Even stranger, and more revealing, Laura came as she was giving Grey a bed bath and after removing his cross for him she kissed that discreetly before putting it on his bedside table.

Laura had asked Grey why he had given her his cross and she was pleased by his answer. She had felt mild agitation when she received it, tempered by her concern for his health, believing that it might have been an attempt to convert her again. This seemed unlikely to her after the talk they had had after performing the rite where he had seemed completely tolerant and non-judgemental but she could not think why else it was so important to him. He explained that it was his oldest possession and he wanted to leave her something to remember him by and, more importantly, it was her key to getting her hands on his vehicle. His cross was distinctive and had his initials engraved on the back and by presenting it to his parents she would (with a little work) be able to claim his meagre possessions from them. He told her that he understood why the gift might have confused her, and that he tried to explain the reasons to Delgado but was unable to because of the condition he was in. Laura thanked him graciously, for once not adding a putdown.

After staying with him for a week, staying at a small guesthouse (partially damaged but some rooms were habitable) during this time, she had to leave to return to check on Konah and the animals. Grey was doing well and he had such a positive mindset that she knew she could leave him without worries. He had started reading the Odyssey again in bed (for the first few days he was not allowed to even do this) and she told him to make this his most vigorous activity until she saw him again. He asked her what his vigorous activity would be then, playfully rather than crudely, and she told him the caber toss, an indication that she wanted to take him back with her and soon. The doctors wouldn't let him go for an age, she knew that and she understood it for he was still badly wounded, but with Inge doubtless screeching like a dragon with one of many heads removed but even more deadly, she had to take him to a safer environment just in case.

She marched back home thinking of that nurse having Grey all to herself. Her feelings for the man were very confused of late, his near death and sorry state making her question herself. She suspected that this was a case of heightened emotion because of his brush with mortality, rather than love. She had kissed him several more times in the hospital, twice at his request, but that was meaningless and did not set her aflame with desire. He and the nurse were perfectly matched; she could picture them in their suburban house back in America as the neighbours and friends everyone wanted. Laura cared for him, but that was not the same as love. Affection took many forms and she could admit to herself that he was the most important person in her life but that was not such a great distinction. She made friends carefully and very selectively on her own terms and most of these men and women had died off now. There were some villagers in the glens that she got on with, but they knew little of her, unlike Grey who she had been very open with. Her nameless birth, her learning and stories of some of the years from then to now including (some of) her infrequent affairs had all been recounted to him and she knew all of him, but she did from her first sighting of him. She knew what he was then and the essence of who he was but she never dreamed that she could care for him as much as she did. She was going with him abroad, she had promised that and she wanted to now, for a change and to please him. That was arranged and she had no problems with that. It was other things that troubled her, like what followed the holiday.

Returning home she sensed an intruder straight away and Konah's absence. She ran through the open doorway, the door ripped from its hinges, and she looked at the hallway that had her ripped clothes strewn across nearly every inch of floor. She checked in the library – she knew the intruder was in the basement, but she wanted to check on her books first. The room and its contents were decimated but many of the books were undamaged as she took a closer look. Inge had intended to destroy every last one but she had become bored and had been distracted by sensing Konah. She saw *From the Earth to the Moon* was torn in two – she didn't care about the fictional books, it was the arcane manuscripts that troubled her, which Inge had largely destroyed, but this one fictional book's destruction bothered her. She was angry and she walked down to her basement where she saw Eric standing up straight by the wreckage of wall leading to the now empty secret room that still glowed. He trembled as she walked towards him, glowering. She had already been mistrustful of him after his resistance during her spell and now her reservations about him were confirmed. She stood inches from his face and demanded to know, "What happened here and where is he?"

Eric had been scared of Inge when she turned up at his home but he had regained his composure – there was no hope of that here. He felt her power acutely and misanthropy equal to Inge's in her and he knew he was in deep trouble, caught between the devil and the deep blue sea. He did not dare cross Inge, but he was petrified of this woman too. Inge had commanded him to stay once she had retrieved the boy who she had knocked out and was carrying and Eric had tried to reason with her, careful to speak respectfully so as not to rouse her temper further. Inge had told him that she needed someone to remain to tell Laura where to find her and little Konah for the final clash. Eric had suggested leaving a note and then in desperation he had suggested Lotte, talking in French so that Lotte would not understand. As far as Inge was concerned she had no more use for Eric and, moreover, she did not trust him. She trusted Lotte who did have principles and incentive to obey her in her family and she wanted to keep that alliance alive for future use. Even in her anger she wished Lotte her happy ending with her family. Not so for Eric who at one stage had opposed Klaus.

"She gave me no choice. I have done nothing to you or Grey," Eric said, trying to calm her wrath. His position had become so weak as he found himself embroiled in the feud between two ancients who dwarfed his power. His power worked best in a lodge; that was all he had wanted when he had answered Georges' call, before everything got fucked up. Now he was alone with enemies on all sides. He had betrayed the Resistance and, unfortunately, there had been a survivor who would see him executed. Paulette was held in low regard in the town and he could try and deny the allegations but that strategy was too high risk, especially as she was volatile and had demonstrated in her work for them that she was happy to kill. He had considered trying to flee to Germany but even that wouldn't work with Inge's main contact in the Nazi party dead, likely buried with full military honours while Eric suspected his fate would be more ignominious and his body likely to be displayed as a cautionary example.

"Save your justifications for someone who cares. Tell me where they are," Laura said impatiently.

"He's at where Hugo left..." Eric's voice wavered as he delivered the exact line that he had helped Inge devise, little realising he would be saying it to Laura's face, a cryptic clue which she would decipher.

"Just tell me where the bitch is with the child," Laura ordered, placing her right hand on his chest and to his horror it passed through into the middle of him. It was not like Inge's bludgeoning blows through flesh, it was just a tingling he felt as though her hand had become intangible. She stared hard at him and he began to feel pain from her hand and he grunted,

"Notre Dame, Notre Dame." At this confession she gave a slight smile and Eric felt pain and he saw his body turning black and to an ashen powder, originating from her hand until his entire body was reduced to ash on the floor. Laura had been led to believe that Eric was an intellectual; he was also a fool for remaining. If he had fled Laura would have had no inclination to pursue him and he was too insignificant for her to kill through imprecation. Laura thought of Paris, where Grey would long to go but she didn't want him with her this time. She had no love for Konah, no maternal feeling despite their time together. He was scared of her and while she did not encourage this, she did not receive him warmly. She was civil and nothing more. If she had volunteered to look after him it might have been different but old Georges had imposed him on her because of his paternal feelings for the boy.

She had two choices. Inge had infiltrated her house and ransacked and despoiled it and abducted a boy who, regardless of the circumstances, was in her care. Such actions greatly aggrieved her and were sufficient grounds for dealing with her. The battle would be fierce and she fancied she would win – but so did others in history, great men and women who met their own Waterloos. Inge was dense and undeserving of her power, but the fact remained that she possessed might, physically far stronger than she herself was.

Or she could refuse to fight and take Grey back to Scotland immediately. His doctors would fight her but she'd win that battle, no question. He could stay at a hospital in Aberdeen until he was ready to be discharged into her care. The drawback was that Inge knew of her home in Scotland and would search for her there. The French home was ruined now and she doubted she would ever return here so she pondered owning another house in America. It was a shame about Konah, but there were no guarantees he was still alive anyhow. That was what she was doing, she was going to book passage on a ferry to America for two.

She hesitated as she stood at her doorway. He would struggle on such a long journey and she did not dare try overusing her healing hands for fear that his body would become dependent on her powers to stay alive and functioning instead of operating independently. Even if he survived the journey and they stayed safe, there was always the danger of her tracking them down and Laura knew whom she would target first. Grey would not be safe now until Inge was dead, Inge insisting that Laura's friend die to pay for her lover's death. She had to fight her; for Grey, for Georges a little and for her own survival but she admitted to herself that it was not for Konah.

CHAPTER 11 – VIS-À-VIS

The Hunchback of Notre Dame was not Laura's favourite Hugo book nor was Notre Dame Cathedral her sort of place. Witches were not (usually) Christians and she felt out of place as she entered the cathedral where a service was being held. Understanding French, Laura gathered that the service was part commemoration of the lives that had been lost and a celebration of the liberation of Paris and France. The mood was buoyant and wretched, a strange sense of morbidity, of the terrible loss hitting home at this brightest of hours, this blinding bright new dawn, tears of sadness and joy. Laura remained unaffected for this was never her war or people, smiling at those who smiled at her as she walked around the building. She made a shortcut in her own inimitable way in an empty corner, accessing the restricted area and she ascended the stairs, which seemed never ending. She could not detect Inge but that meant nothing for she was aware she was coming and could have used shielding spells. She checked the parapets and the belfry, Quasimodo's haunts, but she found no monsters there. She was sure that Eric had told her what he believed to be true, but she wondered about Inge who in abandoning him revealed what she thought of him. It was only morning and Laura decided to wait on the roof until night when she hoped Inge would show up. A nocturnal confrontation at the witching hour would suit Inge more she realised, Inge one for drama and possessing a sense of occasion.

"Is she there?" Inge asked, as she lay sprawled on the bed in the squalid apartment in the six-storey tenement, which had been her home (and Lotte and Konah's) for the last four days. Inge was calmer now, still in mourning for Klaus, but no longer erupting into overblown histrionics. She cried quietly at times and she did not smile, remaining morose, her grief levelling out, partly quelled by venting her anger on the group. She had even considered the girl Paulette and in a rare coup had empathised with her as the sole survivor, her pining grief making her introspective and pensive, a temporary condition. Lotte was helping her now, taking care of the boy who displayed less fear than Germaine had at her. He had power and Inge figured that was the difference. She had not decided what to do with him yet – she knew what Lotte would want but Lotte did not understand and could not do what had to be done. That was why she was only Frau Wirsing while she was The Inge – The Great Dane as she had been known in her recent past before someone pointed out to her that the expression had another meaning other than the grandiose. She never changed her name, unlike Laura, for she wanted to be a legend and she felt she already was, certainly in her own head.

She had even courted Hollywood briefly, playing a seductress in a minor silent film before she decked a rival diva and work offers were rescinded and she returned to Europe. What did Laura have to compare to her? Inge had lived a full life with dozens of lovers, men of whom history was written, men of power and repute. There was a trail behind her of places she had been, of men's open-mouthed tongues trilling her name in a desperate encore or of men and women who heard her name and defecated themselves in terror. She was a goddess, and Laura? She was just an old, ugly witch who had lived too long and done nothing productive with her time. That was why she killed Klaus, Inge felt, jealousy at what he had achieved in his comparatively short life.

Inge had wanted to kill the inhabitants of a commodious residence but she was half-hearted about everything and in this pliable state Lotte had been able to dissuade her and Inge had actually paid to stay somewhere for a change, at this hovel. It was merely a sojourn as Lotte pointed out and lying on the bed here was little different to lying on the bed of a mansion for she would still be lugubrious though perhaps a little less so.

"She's there now," Lotte said, sensing it. "She's very tough, Inge," Lotte said, warning her as Konah sat on her lap, looking up at her.

"So am I," Inge said languorously, unable to talk with her normal verve and for once she seemed weak. She did not notice this herself and felt assured of victory. Her old enemy, her old acquaintance, her old rival, would die tonight, all of the thoughts of years of torture gone now. Enemies like that you crushed at once for self-preservation's sake. Laura was not lapdog material; she was a wolf.

Laura was calm about the coming storm she faced which would potentially turn this now peaceful city into a war zone. She wondered if the Parisians would pretend not to notice for she found them insouciant and this city, even in peacetime, was no stranger to killings and certainly not unused to women like Inge. She viewed Inge as a glorified courtesan whose best days were coming to a close. Women were starting to step forward to be recognised on their own terms as individuals, not as appendages of men, and rights were filtering their way and even work beyond that of just the menial. For Inge to thrive and prosper she had to be surrounded by men who were absolutely dominant over society, not mildly but imperiously so, and in the world of equality which was hinted at on the horizon, Inge would be lost. There would still be powerful men for her to cling to but Laura knew that the presence of powerful women, powerful for other reasons than vicarious power through fucking – that would unbalance Inge. She would find such women too threatening. Nana died – in Paris, Laura thought, it being a long time since she had read the novel. It was the perfect place for Inge to die too; it was a city of decadence and degradation, of beauty at its most alluring and base, the tower and the pit. The stage was set.

After vespers and after the clergy took their leave Laura left the upper heights of the cathedral and explored the main worship area again. The dead of night would be upon them soon and as Laura walked around the altar with an atheist's clinical gaze, she detected her presence just as she predicted. There was no sign of the boy or anyone else, just Inge walking down the aisle towards her in black silk blouse and (unusually for her) in trousers. She had come to fight, that was clear from her attire and from her military marching, her hard face equally determined. Laura stared at her and jumped down from the altar and stood impassively with her hand on her hips. Inge did not walk all the way to her, though she itched to, leaving several feet between them. Things had to be said, there were issues that had to be addressed before she laid hands on her and they both knew that when they started there would be no chance for dialogue. This was to be no mild-mannered, hair-pulling contest.

"Is the boy here?" Laura said, starting to feel a little adrenaline rushing at the thought of this. Inge began to advance a little and the two began circling around each other, Laura especially circumspect as she knew this could be a trap.

"We'll get to that in good time. You know why you're going to die, don't you, Laura?" Inge said, feeling exhilarated.

"I know why you want to take my life, yes. I would be prepared to talk this through, but I am prepared to fight you," Laura said reasonably.

"We could have come to an arrangement before you killed Klaus. What chance did he have against your sorcery?" Inge protested, taking the stance that Lotte normally would.

"What chance did that Communist group stand against yours?" Laura countered.

"That is your justification for killing my lover? Because I killed some red terrorists?" Inge said, shaking her head. She was not accepting that, it was feeble.

"What about Colin Irwin? Even if you don't know his name, and I know the names don't always matter to you, you know who I mean and what he did," Laura said, mordacious regarding Inge's free and easy sexuality, but turning serious at the end of her sentence.

"Yes. He killed Grey, your lover," Inge said, smiling at what she believed to be true. Laura felt she might believe this and she would not correct her as it kept Grey safe if she believed he had died as she intended. As for Grey being her lover, a notion that had been laughable once was no longer so and she did not correct her on that either.

"Then what is your complaint? You are being irrational. You cannot condemn me for killing your lover after you killed mine first."

"The rules are different for me, Laura, because of who I am. No one touches what is mine without risking being decimated, not even you. I would have left you to have him, but Eric has told me everything about Grey. He was determined to beat me – you can't have thought much of him not to stop him. He set himself up as my enemy and you helped him and that group. That was why I took him from you, to teach you a lesson and to take away your incentive to help the French and the Americans. I was not looking to fight you then," Inge said, cracking her knuckles in anticipation of the punches she was going to land.

"By that logic you have no reason to help the Nazis now. Perhaps we should have talked then, but this was always going to come to pass because of the men who held completely different, I imagine obstinate, views. We have become embroiled in men's battles, their feud, which if you think about it is rather pathetic," Laura observed pithily.

"That sounds like you're trying to get out of fighting to me," Inge said with a slight smile, thinking she had her terrified. She was wrong, Laura was just expressing a sentiment.

"Not at all. All I am saying is that we are fighting for something that neither of us particularly believe, but because of what you did to him, I am willing to fight you."

"I believe in the Third Reich. That's what separates us, Laura, not that that's your real name because you chop and change, don't you? I play a part in this changing world. I take sides; I groom men for dominion. It doesn't even ring true, you helping the Allies. You hide away, that's your nature. You have lived so long and I have only heard four stories about you. There are books written about me, a legend passed down from father to son, the goddess that no woman can compare to. I am a part of history, the men I have loved have names that all know and celebrate, heroes in their homelands and hated in the territories they conquered. I have crammed so much into my years, I have truly lived and the memories I have are more joyous than anything that resides in your brain. What are you, a fucking farmwoman? You're like a nun. You've only had about two lovers in around 1500 years. You're probably shit at sex – you must be because you're my opposite and I excel." Inge revelled in denigrating her and forced a fake laugh as she derided her.

"I find what you have just said fascinating," Laura said, smiling wryly, showing a condescending amusement. "You want to know what I have been doing for my centuries of existence? Unfortunately you couldn't find out my story so easily as anyone could discover yours, for your tales decorate many a brothel wall, male toilets, taverns and dives and bad erotic novels. The world, believe it or not, has more to offer than pulsating cock. Such a statement is sacrilege to your mindset, I understand, but not to mine. The mind has been what I have concentrated on and I have devoted my life to developing my gift and learning. You fell into your gift, born into a practising family, while I have developed mine myself from humble beginnings. For my first few centuries it was a case of keeping my head down and surviving because, as you know, the death feud between some of the men was a bloody, merciless affair. I don't know anyone of our kind who wasn't scared of Octavius," Laura said, referring to an ancient Roman of brutal deviations who used his powers to cleanse the earth in the first millennium of Laura's life.

"Oh, I know!" Inge said vivaciously, forgetting herself and talking to Laura as though she were a friend, this topic interesting her. "I used to lust after him until I met him and he tried to kill me. I don't know what happened to him."

"He died," Laura said, matter-of-factly. "No one is indestructible," she warned.

Laura continued with the point she wanted to make as Inge resumed her hostile stare, which retained a slight smile, the smile of one with sinister plans. "In such a world I felt it was prudent to become as skilled as I could and I used my skills to survive day to day and build up a small fortune. I am satisfied with my own company, but there have been lovers and a husband. Unlike you I won't take whatever is on the market just so that I won't sleep alone. I have to care for the man first."

"I remember you told me about your husband. Some sort of peasant labourer," Inge said disdainfully. "And Steil and Grey. Steil could have been something but he died a failure and I've heard all about Grey from Eric. You seem to be attracted to nonentities."

"Considering you have never met any of them you're not qualified to say that. Grey and Georges are more powerful than any men you've been with," Laura said, getting aerated by the criticism of the men of her past and present and responding impulsively with a weak, 'my boyfriends are better than yours' comment.

Inge laughed out loud disrespectfully, earning a black stare from Laura. "You haven't met any of mine either," she said, stifling her laughter as she spoke before turning serious as she said, "But all of them, even Irwin, top your list. Maybe you can't get quality. It's too late now of course. I would have given you my cast-offs in the past, but not now."

"I would not want the sort of men you have dedicated your life to, the men who you professed to love and then found another while their bodies were not yet cold. I have enough power of my own, mentally and spiritually. I don't rely on my men to fill that gaping void like you do. I select them based on other criteria, which has nothing to do with the size of their army. Yes, my husband was not a wealthy man and he commanded nothing bar two young employees and his home was little better than a barn. I actually loved him though you see and you could never live like that – it has to be ostentatious for you, it has to be someone, no matter how sadistic, who will make what you deem to be an impact. You're a leech. I doubt you help these men at all; you likely sap their strength and hold them back from being what they could be. From what I have heard they tend to die soon after you become involved with them. You probably push them to glory because if they succeed it's more vicarious power for you and if they die taking a risk there'll be another one along soon," Laura said, criticising her now in acerbic fashion. Inge was irate and lunged at her but Laura dodged her blow easily and retreated and kept up her verbal assault as Inge backed her towards an anteroom leading to the first set of stairs.

"And the absolute best thing about your whole demimonde existence – the thing that can make me wake in the middle of the night and burst into hysterical fits of laughter – is your sex life. You boast about your sensualist existence – I don't know how I kept a straight face in London that time we had dinner," Laura said, sneering in her face.

"What the fuck are you talking about?" Inge said, offended and desperate to know what she was referring to. She wouldn't kill her until she knew as she was under her skin now and she needed to determine what she meant. She tried to deduce it herself but this puzzled her and Laura's self-satisfied grin needled her.

"For all that you consider me frigid, I can orgasm and I enjoy it. You cannot say the same..."

Inge interrupted her indignantly. "Of course I can! I've done things with men that you don't even know exist."

"I can believe that and I hope they enjoyed it. Perhaps mentally you enjoy seeing them climax and satisfied because that is all you can get out of it. You aren't the only person to ever receive such a gift or curse. Your body is razor sharp; you are a real iron maiden, but that absence of pain has a negative side. Pleasure no longer exists physically for you. Your body is dull, and all sensation is negated, dead the day you became 'The Inge'. You live as a creature of sex and all it is to you is an action, nothing else. They can ram it in as hard as they like, you're not going to feel it."

"That's untrue," Inge protested vociferously, tears welling in her eyes as this secret was revealed.

"Perhaps you've managed to convince yourself that there's something, but it's merely psychosomatic. If a limb is removed the amputee sometimes feels that the limb is still there, itching in the palm of a removed hand. That's what your itch is, Inge, a phantom sensation."

"Shut up, Shut UP!" Inge shouted as she moved swifter towards Laura who had started to ascend the staircase, still walking backwards. "I was shot in the eye by that little bitch Paulette and that hurt," Inge said (inaccurately though she thought it had been Paulette who fired both shots), pointing out that she was not invulnerable, she could feel.

"Which one because I can't tell? There's no mark. Shot in the eye and no wound. A penis is only made of flesh – I don't think you need a man, I think you need a poker. You might feel something if you use maximum force but you'll need a large supply because you'll break them after using them once." Laura knew she had mentally destroyed her with this revelation which she hoped would make her easy to beat and she kept on taunting her, talking crudely of her own exploits with her husband, taking it both ways, of Georges' tongue and of her skill with her own, the feel of it in her mouth. Considering the length of her life she was relatively chaste (though there were other minor, interim lovers whom Inge didn't know about and she kept silent about them), but when she had found a man (or on occasion a woman) she loved she made up for it. She emphasised her pleasure, her orgasmic joy, detailing acutely each small physical sensation and she saw tears silently stream down Inge's cheeks. Laura was the truly sexual one and while she recounted some of her own lascivious exploits she made sure to refer to Inge's state of stupefaction.

Laura had said too much and Inge lunged at her so suddenly that she nearly caught her and Laura turned and ran up the stairs, looking where she was going. She could hear Inge behind her; thunderous footsteps which threatened to catch her as she fled. She searched for an open space to commence combat as she felt cramped quarters suited Inge better. Laura ran until she found a large room, and with sufficient distance between them she turned around to face the charging Inge and summoned a wind to blow her away. Inge was stalled by the wind but she kept coming, making sturdy advancements. Laura increased the force of her spell to no avail; Inge seeming even more powerful than the last time they fought. Laura was so focused on the spell that she was not retreating and she maintained her faith in her abilities, remaining standing as Inge made it to a few inches from her. Laura had the option of running, but she tried to increase the force of the near typhoon gale as a last stand, unsure of what else to do.

It didn't work and she felt two strong, insensate hands around her throat and Inge smiled again. Laura's critique of her had been unfair. She couldn't feel her lovers but that didn't render the act meaningless or decrease her finesse and she did love them at the time. She did push some for valour, others she did not – it depended if they wanted her guidance and involvement and it varied depending on her faith in them. Laura was no better than she was and no more moral, Inge felt – in fact she was probably worse as she was more calculating. Inge was impulsive and she felt that this excused anything she did as even she accepted that some of her past actions had been unnecessary but had felt right at the time (Odette's death now seemed like a bad deed though Inge put it from her mind by focusing on her narrow hips, the girl and baby not likely to survive the birth anyway). Now she had this bitch in her hands and she tried the same trick she had done on Margot, trying to join her palms. It didn't work, though she could see Laura was in pain, her legs giving way and her mouth agape and Laura sank lower to the floor as Inge maintained her grip. She tried her hardest to crush her neck, but it wouldn't break, Laura performing a defensive spell which wouldn't last forever under this assault. Inge did not press her advantage and instead of keeping hold of her, which would have been the wise course of action, she grew impatient and lifted her up and threw her across the room, Laura sliding into the wall. Inge glided across the room swiftly and kicked her head and she proceeded to kick her across the room. Laura was so focused on protective spells that she could not dare risk an offensive spell and she was looking at ways of tactically retreating. When there was a small distance between them, after a spectacular boot from Inge, Laura touched the floor, which immediately parted and she slipped through, closing it behind her as Inge shouted and cursed at her. Laura fell to the ground, slowing her fall only a fraction with a mild supportive wind before she crashed onto some pews below and she felt completely broken. She longed for the assistance of a charitable Hunchback now but she knew she was on her own, the only one who could defeat this creature.

The problem was she doubted herself after her attempts upstairs and Inge's commanding display. She was 20 times stronger than before. Back then Laura had been inexperienced and her repertoire of spells and gifts had been lacking. Now she had a near complete understanding and harmonious relationship with the other realm and she was still being demolished by a woman who had dedicated her life to pleasures she couldn't feel. To be beaten by Octavius, a man who studied his subject well because of his enjoyment at ripping the pretenders asunder was acceptable, but this was humiliating. She swiftly came to the conclusion that Inge was not acting alone and there was a thin residue of another in the air. Inge had worked with Eric and Laura realised there was another power, another party helping Inge now, combining their might with hers.

Laura hoisted herself onto a pew and sat down, enjoying her slight respite, as Inge had to take the long way down. Laura had the choice of running away, an option she declined to take. If she lost she was dead, but Grey would live. Inge had never even seen him and she believed him dead and would never think otherwise and he would return to America and Inge's base would remain Europe, two strangers who would never meet. If she fled then Inge would come after her and perhaps find Grey. For his sake she stayed to fight, but she waited for the battle to come to her as it doubtless would and soon.

"Sitting down to pray to God? It won't work. We've done too much, all of us, and you're no exception," Inge said, catching sight of her again and sprinting across.

"Let's get this over with," Laura said, standing her ground and summoning fire, which she surrounded Inge with. Her hair frazzled but she progressed and struck her again. She was unstoppable and Laura knew as she was lifted above her head that she could not fight her forever if she merely shrugged off her most potent spells. She was outmatched, pure and simple, and she now knew it.

And then something changed. After Laura was thrown up, nearly hitting the tall ceiling, as she waited to land the complexion changed. She was falling down a great height but she was smiling as she felt that stolen power drifting away. Inge felt it too, the power borrowed from Lotte leaving her from every pore and she shouted her name accusingly as Laura fell in a heap several yards from her.

"Fair fight now," Laura said, getting to her feet, grinning through a busted lip and many, many other injuries.

"I can beat you without her help," Inge said as she ran at her again only this time the scorching fireball made her shriek and fall to the floor as Laura casually walked towards her. Inge gasped in pain – she knew she could feel pain and Laura knelt beside her, looking down at the supine Inge. She felt a pang of sympathy for she could understand her without liking her. Laura said nothing as she drove her hand into Inge's chest and attempted to turn her body into ash. Inge smiled at the sensation, the tingling pleasurable for her though Laura did not smile as Inge proved harder to dispose of than Eric.

"I…I couldn't let her hurt the boy," Lotte said, appearing from the shadows having just entered the building with Konah in tow. He saw Laura who had fed him and looked after him for several months but even though Lotte had been one of his captors, he stayed at her side.

"He's a good boy. I have children myself – they don't belong in these feuds, in war," Lotte said sadly. She had betrayed Inge but it was all over anyway and she had to follow her own conscience, her husband's letter making her think.

Laura ignored her as Inge had her full attention. Laura's hand ached while Inge continued to smile – her hand was being destroyed while Inge thrived! Her attack incapacitated Inge who made no attempt to move and Laura had to decide whether to continue or to cease the fight. Laura retracted her hand out of Inge's body and masked her distress and hid her hand in her sleeve. It was partially withered and would require a spell to fix it. Her hand was the least of her troubles. Laura racked her brain to think of another way to kill her – there were other possibilities but they were not guaranteed to work and she would be too weak to defend herself if they failed. Her most powerful attack had failed and it stood to reason that her less injurious spells would be less effective.

For a brief moment Laura felt grossly inadequate. Perhaps Inge truly was indestructible. She had survived a run-in with the dreaded Octavius – few managed that. Laura knew that she would likely not have been so fortunate as those with similar abilities to her were effortlessly trampled underfoot by him. To be inferior was difficult to stomach, but she still lived and there was the hope of learning something new that would enable her to overtake her in power and Laura clung to this hope. She knew that she could not let Inge know that she lacked the ability to take her life and she pretended that she was 'letting' her live out of mercy.

Laura stood up and said commandingly, "Stand up, Inge. You deserve to die, but I am not going to take your life because Irwin failed in his task. James Grey is alive and I believe he would wish me to be lenient with you so consider this – you live because of the clemency of a man you tried to kill." It was pointless to pretend Grey was dead now – Inge would be around for many more years yet and could find this out and this way Laura could try and deter Inge from going after him again.

"It's time for the war to end. The Nazis are losing, Inge, and I know that you have no time for losers. Germany will be hell by the time they're all done with it so I advise you to leave and start afresh elsewhere. Before I let you leave I want your word of honour that you will not hold any grudges regarding this war. I am giving you, perhaps mistakenly, a second chance but that means you cannot seek vengeance against anyone who you deem has wronged you in this campaign, otherwise…" Laura said, holding out her undamaged hand threateningly.

Inge stood up, clutching her chest with both hands where Laura's ethereal hand had penetrated her. She stared at Laura pensively, saying nothing.

Laura signalled for Konah to come to her and Lotte walked with him, taking him close to Laura. She was almost ready to leave but had a few more things to say to Inge. "Why so sad? Anyone who has lived as long as we have has had bleaker moments than this. Like the men on both sides, we have committed war crimes, but the war is as good as over and all of us, human and superhuman, have to return to our normal lives and forget what has been done. I wish you well," Laura said, sounding sincere even though she wished her dead.

"Cowards seek truces. Admit that you couldn't kill me," Inge said, smiling again as she revealed that she had seen through Laura's bluff. Mercy wasn't part of her repertoire and she knew it, the two of them very similar in many ways. "Fine, bitches, we'll end this battle and go back to killing each other's loved ones instead. I'm going to have fun with your GI and after I tear him to pieces I'll see what Peter's made of, if the Russians haven't done the job for me," she said maliciously, determined to make Laura and Lotte feel the same emotional pain she was going through. She would have killed them too but she was feeling weak and would instead kill those that they cared for first before doing the same to them, Lotte's betrayal instantly ceasing their long alliance.

"Hit her again!" Lotte shouted and the two women realised she was talking to Laura who stared quizzically at her, unsure if she could trust her, before deciding to take a chance, plunging her withered hand back into Inge's chest. Whoever Peter was, he was obviously important to Lotte and Laura felt that this could make them tentative allies against Inge. Laura began to smile now as Inge gasped, Lotte using her power to help Laura destroy her and after two minutes her body decomposed, down to ash. The Great Dane was dead.

Laura forcibly prised Konah's hand from Lotte (Lotte was trying to make him let go of her too with Konah proving resistant). Lotte could see that Laura was displeased with her, despite her switching sides to help her beat Inge. The situation did not fluster her greatly – everything was ruined anyway. She knew in her heart that the Allies had to win the war. It was right, it was just, but the small part of her that was patriotic felt numb at this. She remembered the state of her country and the morale of her people after losing the Great War – what could this demon do to her that would be worse than that?

Laura said (in German), "I don't know whose side you're on and I don't care. I found Inge hard to beat – I could crush you now, even in my injured state. Never cross my path again." After issuing this warning Laura left with Konah.

Lotte had a horrible feeling in her gut that Inge's portentous, final words about Peter would prove true and that Reinald would be gone too and she would be alone – what if she was already alone? She waited a while before leaving the chapel and wandered the streets with no idea of where to go, hugged by rowdy carousers who she smiled sheepishly at, pretending to understand what they were saying. She knew if she spoke a word of German the mob would descend on her at once. She managed to delicately extricate herself from their clutches silently and she thought over her options as her life, like so many others at this difficult time, dissolved into chaos.

Delgado had a 48 hour pass and had known at once how to spend it, choosing to visit Grey who remained behind the lines, now safely residing in a military hospital. Grey was sitting up now, getting a little better every day and he greeted his friend warmly, though chastised him when he heard about his 48 hour pass.

"And you're wasting it here? It's great to see you, Isdel, but get yourself out of here. Tell me how it's going then get drinking."

"It's Corporal Delgado now so as I outrank you I'll decide when I'm going."

"That's excellent news," Grey grinned, shaking his hand, pleased that his friend's potential had been recognised. "Melvin's squad?"

Delgado nodded. "I get to tell Pearce what to do. I haven't abused that…yet."

"You won't either. It's good news for you that I won't be back then 'cause it's a proven fact I never listen to orders or advice. You said about Irwin from the start and I knew better. It doesn't so much matter about me 'cause I'm on the mend, but it stinks Cloisters died for no reason."

"It might not be connected," Delgado said unconvincingly.

"I'm sure he did it. Pass my thanks on to whoever shot him."

"He's injured himself at the moment but he will be returning and I'll pass on your message then."

"Thanks doesn't even cover it. Emphasise how grateful I am, please, Corporal. You aiming higher?"

Delgado grimaced and said, "I'll settle for surviving it. My war isn't over yet even if we are winning. I'm not lying back being fussed over by pretty English nurses," Delgado joked. He added, gravely serious, "Belgium has been very hard."

"You'll survive. My instincts tell me so," Grey said. His powers revealed nothing of the sort, but this white lie was to buck up his spirits.

"I hope so, but it's still a lottery," Delgado said and he told Grey which soldiers had died since he had been gone, Lol Shaw and Victor Sykes the men Grey knew best from the long list. Delgado's words made Grey turn downcast (a combination of sadness at their deaths and disappointment in himself at not receiving their spirits) and Delgado quickly changed tack to try and cheer him up. "Fanelli says when he gets back him and Harvey Baker are going to take you out to a Yankees game to show you what pro baseball is about instead of that Keokuk shit you go on about. His words, amigo, not mine."

"Tell him he's on and that when I'm back on my feet I'll take him on in a game."

"No one thought you would ever be walking again and I saw your injuries, I know it's impossible, but now I can see you're getting better already, fit enough for any expedition. The world's yours to explore now – where's first on the tour?"

"Scotland, I hope. I need to talk to you about Laura," Grey said. He needed to update his friend on the developments, the advancement of their relationship which at the least would leave him with a close friend for life and at best, and Grey, ever the optimist, wanted this, would produce him a wife. Staying true to himself, simple and uncultured as he felt he was, had worked, Laura responding to his lack of artifice and good heart. As he was talking he had another visitor, Laura (with newly dyed black hair) walking through the door of Grey's secluded area and revealing Konah who ran over to leap on Grey, Delgado catching him before he landed on him to Grey's relief. His first question was about Inge, asking her if she was all right.

"Inge won't do anything else now," Laura said, telling him enough so that he would not have to worry. He edged towards her, aching for a kiss and she noticed this and simply smiled at him and pulled away.

"Everyone else is fighting while I lounge around," Grey said to Delgado as a vague explanation and he looked back at Laura, taking both of her hands in his as Delgado began to joke with Konah physically, transcending the language barrier.

"He might be an idiot and a clumsy oaf who gets himself shot by his own men, but thanks for helping him," Delgado said to Laura, appreciating that it was she who had saved his life rather than the doctors.

"She was scared she'd miss out on the sightseeing trip, that's what it was," Grey joked.

"Truer words were never said in jest," she said dryly and she reached into her handbag and produced a small blank book. "I've got my autograph book bought ready for when we meet the stars in Hollywood. You had better introduce me to some." She was accommodating now, ready to accept his journey whatever it entailed and keen to make him enjoy it too.

"Look, Jimmy, I can't stay, but take care, keep that enthusiasm and you'll be back on your feet in no time. I'll take Konah to get a snack and leave you two alone for a bit. You take care of him, Laura," he said seriously.

"I'll be keeping a close eye on him, don't worry," she said sternly, glaring at Grey who smiled back at her disarmingly.

"When you get back to the States, and I know you will, Isdel, get in touch with me. I'll be doing a jig by then."

"So will I when I get discharged. See you, Odysseus. Penelope," Delgado said, looking at Laura respectfully before he left with Konah. Grey had completed the Odyssey now and he appreciated what his friend meant, taking this as his seal of approval. Delgado accepted that Grey adored her and would respond badly to criticism and begrudgingly accepted the union. It was a massive, massive mistake, but he couldn't change his mind and didn't want to part on bad terms and, while he could never approve of witchcraft, at least this time she had used it for good.

"I think I preferred Circe," Laura whispered after he left. She knew herself how hard that must have been for the devoutly Christian Delgado and she knew it was meant to be approbation and she took it as it was intended.

"She has a certain charm. She's not that bad; she's just waiting for the right man and making the most out of the wrong men she meets along the way. By the end she's a pussycat. If you think that's not a good fit, how about me getting compared to Odysseus? That shows he's a good friend, to compare me to a wily battle veteran when we all know that in the short time I've been overseas I've made the odd dozen snafus. That's the best thing about my discharge – I can't do any more harm to the war effort. We'll storm through now without my hindrances. Christmas is the date I'm hoping it's settled for."

"That's not your problem anymore. Oh. Head full of spirits. Okay, I can see why you do want it over quick," Laura said, thinking the matter over.

"It's not just that, but yeah, it'd be nice to have a clear head. Did she hurt you at all?"

"She nearly beat me, but that doesn't matter right now," Laura said, caressing his face with a soft hand.

Satisfied that she would tell him in time Grey said, "I never pictured you like this even in fantasy. Very glam, very chic. More so I mean. We've got a job on our hands making me look dapper so that I don't show you up on our trip," he remarked light-heartedly, making out he was shabby compared to her stylised elegance, different to her previously natural look. Her clothes were different too, less rustic and far more stylish, Laura clad in a (fairly) provocative black dress. The change was not to impress him – Laura knew that to become a more powerful witch she would have to experiment more with the black arts, foul magic that was said to taint (and Laura knew this to be true firsthand) and her change in appearance was symbolic of this. Inge had nearly killed her and Laura felt that the contest should have been one-sided in her favour, not the other way round. Inge was not even her most powerful rival, that honour belonging to another Englishwoman, fortuitously a more levelheaded and generally moderate creature. After struggling against Inge she knew that she stood no chance of defeating her and Laura's goal was to surpass her, not because she wanted to fight her, but just so that she had the option if necessary.

"Your behaviour is more likely to do that than your clothing. You can wear what you want, James, you know I don't care. I decided it was time for a new look for a new continent."

"You look stunning. I look at you and everything else just fades away, and that's not just the elephant tranquilising medication I'm on," he said, as besotted as ever, in buoyant mood.

"I may have to order some of that for Ravensbeck Hospice. I mean Ravensbeck Hospital. I was trying to be funny there with the hospice comment and it fell flat, a little bit too much. In my head it wasn't quite that callous. Erase that. You'll get better, I promise," Laura said, chiding herself for crossing the line, even though he didn't seem bothered.

"You saved me from certain death so I can cope with your gallows humour, even if it is always my head in the noose. Remember to order some bromide as well. With you looking like that you'd best order a few gallons."

"Will do. If just looking at me makes you almost black out then I think you had better recover before getting any further ideas about me. You certainly can't handle me at present," she said, spurring him on to recover quicker with mild flirtation. She would endeavour to make his recovery as quick and enjoyable as possible and she knew he would be a good patient.

"Give me a chance and I will," he said lustily with gusto.

"Get better first then I can contemplate it," she said soothingly. "In the meantime you'll have to settle for this," she said, giving him a full-bodied kiss. Grey reciprocated and the kiss was primal, animalistic as their hands stroked the other, Grey feeling her hair, Laura stroking the back of his neck and hair.

"Settle?" he said breathlessly. "A kiss like that is worth giving your soul for."

"Hmm," she purred, making out she was musing over this thought, but she failed to disturb him and did not intend to.

"About Konah. I'm going to…" Before Grey had chance to try and take responsibility for him, Laura interrupted.

"That's already taken care of. The Pagan Resistance group – I'll tell you all about that when you're out of here, but basically Georges' pub, which he intended for me to have, is now in Paulette's hands and she's agreed to look after Konah. He seems to like her and she was very attached to him when I saw her and I think that's best for everyone," Laura said, sure that this solution worked well for all, even Georges. Konah had been like a son to him and eventually he would inherit his home which seemed fair. Konah had wanted to stay with Paulette rather than accompany Laura to the hospital but Laura wanted to give Grey a chance to say goodbye to him and Paulette had persuaded Konah to go with promises of treats. Paulette was extremely grateful for all that Laura had done for them and for rescuing Konah she would forever receive free drinks if she decided to reopen the tavern.

"I already know a lot about the Pagan Resistance. Eric…he wasn't evil, you know?" Grey said cautiously. He did not want to reproach her, his love for him making him accept behaviour that he would otherwise find unacceptable, but he felt that the matter did need to be addressed. He still loved her completely, only now he held some reservations. Laura's healing hands, which saved him from the grave, sent another man to his doom. They lived in a time when everyone had blood on their hands (especially healers) yet Laura could have refrained. Her situation was not do or die – she chose to blight Eric Girard from existence mercilessly. Nothing that Delgado or the padre had said had deterred his amorous affections for Laura yet this deed planted the first seed of doubt. Eric Girard, who was, if charitable, morally ambiguous, was not worth destroying their love over, yet Eric's anguished words resonated. Grey knew that Laura had probably done what she did through wrath, for him. Even in the name of love such actions were wrong. He knew he was in no position to reprimand her and also knew that doing so would start a heated argument. He still desired making her his wife and wanted to go to Ravensbeck and hoped this stain would fade quickly.

Laura deduced from this, correctly, that Eric's spirit had gone whining to Grey about what happened. "I wouldn't have handled it that way, but it's done," he added, closing the matter, noticing a dissatisfied look on her face. She was noticeably silent as she digested his words while looking as though she was sucking lemons. Bravo, Grey thought to himself – even though the truth needed to be said, perhaps now wasn't the time and he could have handled this matter better. He had thought he'd approached the matter sensitively though her response suggested he'd gone in all guns blazing, which he knew he hadn't. As the damage was already done and she had withdrawn from the conversation he added, "You're taking this as me judging you. I'm not putting myself in that position. All I'm saying is I don't like what happened. This doesn't change anything between us. I'm just sad because what happened isn't something that can be remedied."

"Spirits can be reborn. Work on bringing back St Eric. From Iowa. I withdraw the offer of accommodation. I wouldn't want you to risk your life staying under my psychotic care," Laura said, her words and manner conveying how greatly she felt slighted.

"Laura..." Grey said softly, "You're taking this..."

"Things will never be the same again after my heinous act, surely you see that?" Laura said melodramatically. She stood up and said, "Don't get up, I'll make my own way out."

"You're mad, I get that. Subject closed," Grey said, trying to make peace. He knew he hadn't done anything wrong and didn't want to have to apologise yet if that was what it required to stop her leaving he would do so.

"Mad? Mad and bad? This gets better!"

"Angry, I mean. Stick around until Konah gets back at least, let me try and put a band-aid on this massive crack," he said with a fraction of a smile.

Laura looked at him and her expression turned colder and she said, "You have no idea." With this she left quickly as he called her name down the corridor, shouting louder and louder, apologising too. She heard a loud bang behind her from his direction, which two nurses quickly dashed towards. Laura hesitated and put her forefingers to both eyes and performed a rudimentary spell. She was not going to ever cry in public again. It was too late; this confirmed what she already knew. She had needed some time to think after her fight with Inge, her inability to beat her without assistance affecting her greatly and making her analyse other things. She had been prepared to give Grey a chance and she had questioned this – was he just a replacement for Georges (the two were very similar, Georges slightly more eccentric), was he too moralistic to accept her as she was? She came to the conclusion before she came to the hospital that he would never be able to accept her fully, that he would try and change her or be in denial about certain aspects of her personality. If a little matter like her extermination of Eric Girard troubled him, what would other stories of her past do to him? She had no interest in turning Grey grey. Yet despite reaching this conclusion, upon seeing him again she changed her mind and decided to take him as her lover until he threw moral judgements in her face. She let herself care for him and he chastised her for an act of vengeance she committed largely for him. For all that romantics claimed that opposites attracted saint and sinner never played out well. The saint always tried to redeem the sinner and that wouldn't work in this case.

"No more visitors for you, Grey," the doctor said as he waited for the tranquiliser to take effect. Nurse Rhodes was there too, equally critical of his foolhardy attempt to follow Laura though she retained her personal affection for him while the doctor was less attached and handled all of the soldiers the same. He gave them due respect while cutting them no slack as he knew they'd run wild if allowed to which would not happen in his hospital.

"I fell out of bed," Grey lied. "I was trying to call her back and leaned too far. Don't punish her for my mistake."

"She seemed agitated," Nurse Rhodes said, having passed her on her way out. "She may not come back."

Grey shook his head. "She'll be back."

Had she overreacted? All he had done was express an opinion, and while he disagreed with what she had done, his reproach could hardly have been milder. Yet still it stung. That he had the power to affect her feelings was cause enough to step back from the man. It was not love. It had never been love. All it was, all it had been was a potential dalliance. There had been dozens, maybe hundreds of other potential beaus over the years that never quite made the grade for various reasons. Grey was just another for the list, another also-ran. If he couldn't love her for who she was then she couldn't risk getting any closer to him.

All she had wanted from him was friendship before his persistence paid off and she began to view him differently. The question she now posed to herself was whether their friendship was salvageable. She would answer this question shortly, once she dealt with the intruder in her home. She sensed her from far away and entered the house silently where she found her visitor sat keeled over her kitchen table. Laura recognised her as Germaine Cremont and she relaxed and examined the sleeping girl who looked drawn and gaunt. Laura touched her arm to wake her and Germaine recoiled in fear and immediately broke down in tears.

Laura pulled a chair next to hers and put an arm around her. This was a hassle she didn't need, yet she felt some sympathy for the child who had clearly suffered some great trauma. Ah, yes – she'd met James Grey. "Did the Germans come to your farm on the night they left?" Laura asked gently.

Germaine shuddered and said, "I didn't know where else to come. If she follows me here…Laura, I am so scared."

Laura could just about make out her words through the wailing. "Who do you mean?"

"Inge. She killed my mother and Carol. I'm sorry for just letting myself in. There was no door."

"I know the place was already a tip. You could have helped yourself to any food, you know?" Laura said, commenting on her extreme weight loss.

"I've eaten a bit. I have no appetite."

"That's understandable, but you still have to eat."

"James has left?"

"He went back to fight. What would you like to eat? I'm starving myself, I've just come back from a long trip. I'll cook something small if you like."

"A potato, maybe."

"That's what we'll have. You're staying with me, right? We'll sort out anything else that needs to be dealt with soon enough, but for now, just stay with me, okay?"

Germaine nodded. "I knew you and James would help me. That's what's got me through it. I was hoping he'd be here too. I wanted to say goodbye to my mother and sister too. Too long has passed now. They'll probably be gone."

"Don't underestimate him, he can get spirits from the distant past as well as the recent."

"Not usually. Usually the spirits don't last for more than a few days," Germaine said, remembering the rules Grey had told her. "Even if he couldn't contact them I know he'd still help me," Germaine said, breaking down fully again.

"He's not the best cook in the world so it's best I'm here instead. As you're already upset I'll tell you where James is, to get all of the upset out of the way. Inge tried to kill him too. She sent one of her underlings to kill him and he shot him in the back at point blank range…"

"No!" Germaine cried out loudly.

"He's alive. He's incapacitated but he'll survive and eventually he'll walk again. He's in hospital. That's where I've come from."

Laura made a start on their meal, cooking small portions for both of them as this would seem less intimidating to Germaine and she would be more inclined to eat a little rather than a full plate. Germaine went to the bathroom to wash her face and by the time they sat down to eat she was a little calmer.

"Is he in much pain?" Germaine asked.

"If he is he won't show it. There's been the odd wince or two he hasn't been able to hide. It was a grievous injury. Anyway, don't worry about him. He'll be homeward bound within the next few weeks."

"I'd like to see him before he goes. Not to ask about my family. I wouldn't bother him with that if he's ill. Just to say goodbye and thank him," Germaine said, as tears welled again.

"You don't need to. He already knew you were grateful and he didn't help you for thanks. We're polar opposites, me and James. He helps others because it's the right thing to do."

"You're helping me," Germaine pointed out gratefully.

"Many moons ago, when I was a bit younger than you, an old lady helped me."

"You're not old."

"Next to you and James I'm ancient. If you'd like to see a cripple I could take you there in a couple of days."

"You don't call him that, do you?"

"He takes no offence. If you come with me I'll refrain."

Grey was surprised to see Laura return and before he had chance to speak she said crisply, "First things first, Mr Grey, I think it would be best if we both forget what was said at the last visit."

"Deal." Grey grinned, relieved that they could get back on track. He propped himself up (out of sight of the nurses who hated him doing this, mainly because the doctors gave them earache if they spotted him sitting up) and said, careful not to push his luck as she still seemed a bit standoffish, "Can we seal the deal with a kiss or do I have to settle for a handshake?"

"Neither. My word is enough," she said icily, turning the screw to amuse herself. He truly had hurt her last time and he wouldn't be doing that again. There was no malice in him and she forgave him though he didn't need to know that yet. This man in front of her would probably even feel pity for Hitler at the conclusion of the war when he swung from a rope. His damned empathic nature meant that Eric, Inge and even Irwin became victims to his idealistic gaze rather than the vermin that they were.

"Okay. The docs are sour on me too. I tried to follow you to explain what I meant and apologise. Turns out the spine is connected to the legs. Who'd have thunk it?"

Laura found herself smiling against her wishes and she shook her head and reached into her purse and threw him a packet of cigarettes. Grey caught them and said gratefully, "I wasn't expecting any treats after last time. I know you said you wanted to forget about that; I'd like to clear the air first..."

"Tough shit. If you bring it up again I'll walk out of here and you've proven you can't follow."

"Not true, I've been promised a wheelchair soon, if I behave. Which I have been, mainly 'cause they said if I didn't I wouldn't be allowed any more visitors. I won't bring that up then, if you feel that strongly."

"Don't flatter yourself."

Grey examined his cigarette packet and rattled the contents and put them to his ear and said, "So are these poisoned or booby-trapped?"

"Sorry?" Laura said, quickly deducing his meaning. She came bearing a gift while her words, used primarily to as a defence mechanism, were ripping him to shreds. He seemed in good humour, taking her abuse well, though Laura realised she was laying it on too thick. If they were to be friends she had to lower her defences a little. "If you remember, I told you they were bad for you, so consider them poison."

"Thank you," Grey said seriously, storing them under his pillow. "If we're pretending that visit never happened that would mean the tour of the States is still on."

"By way of Scotland," Laura reminded him firmly, her gaze making him laugh, a contagious laugh that filled his room. "Actually there are three of us going to Scotland. I might be busy around the glens so there will be another nurse to help. Your admirer, Germaine Cremont."

Grey's brow furrowed at this. He wanted to be alone with Laura and he disliked this suggestion. "At the moment I can't do anything for myself, Laura – I don't want a 14 year old girl looking after me. She should stay on her farm." He had feeling in his legs again but he was unable to move them, which meant he would need help with almost everything, and he was uncomfortable with the thought of Germaine doing certain things for him.

"By herself? Besides, she's 15 now. Her mother and sister were killed by Inge," Laura explained. "When I told her about you she was most keen to assist. The girl has nowhere else to go, James, and she needs emotional help as much as you need physical help."

Laura did not need to say this much – as soon as she told him of Claire and Carol's deaths Grey's objections ceased and he felt selfish for thinking of his desires before Germaine's welfare. She would have to come with them, Laura's decision was absolutely correct. "How is she holding up?" he said with concern.

"Not too well. She's here. Do you want to see her?"

Grey nodded vigorously and as Laura stood up to fetch her Grey said, "Not quite yet."

Laura exhaled and looked skyward and said, "Make your mind up!"

"That patience should come in handy when you're looking after me. You know I want to come to Scotland more than anything and I've enjoyed planning it with you, only before we mention it as concrete to Germaine I think we need to check our facts. If they authorised this it would be highly unusual and as I haven't been given my discharge yet…I don't want to mislead her. I'm sure she does want to help me, but I think they're going to insist I go back to the US."

"What do you want?"

"I want to be with you so that's Scotland."

"Then that's what will happen," Laura said decisively.

"I'd love it if it was that simple. Army red tape is tough to cut through. All I'm saying is let's not say it's a definite to Germaine – with you I've talked about it as a harmless reverie because I know if they say no you can shrug it off – you'll probably be secretly glad..."

"I wouldn't be secretly glad," Laura played along, leaving her meaning ambiguous.

"Germaine has no one else bar us. That's cause enough to pity her. She's a lovely girl who doesn't deserve the cards she's been dealt. I have to be straight with her and let her know it's up in the air."

Laura found Germaine was sitting where she had deposited her and she looked up anxiously at Laura. "Is he still alive?" She had convinced herself that he would die too.

"Come and see for yourself," Laura said, leading her to him. Germaine began to cry upon sight of him and Grey opened his arms to her and she fell into his embrace. Laura stood back proudly, believing her matchmaking to be successful. This was a far better mix, with the potential to actually lead somewhere. Two innocents damaged by war in different ways, who Laura fancied would make an attractive couple. She'd be good for him; she already valued both his power and the man wielding it. She was better for him than Laura could be and pushing them together made rejecting him easier. Not easy enough unfortunately as somewhere along the way their feelings had become entangled and her concern for his welfare became an emotional matter rather than an intellectual concern. It was already too complicated now and they hadn't even had sex!

"Can you hear them?" she whispered in his ear.

"No," he said sadly. "I'll work on it. Hopefully they're already at peace."

"If you can't it doesn't matter. I knew it was unlikely. The spirits rarely last for more than a few days," Germaine said, remembering the rules Grey had told her.

"James Grey, how many times have I told you to lie in your bed?" the matron bellowed down the corridor.

"Not now, Matron," Grey shouted back to her. She marched across to him at this remark and Grey said, "I'm not sat right up, I'm just raised up to speak to my visitors. Give a guy a break, please."

"Five minutes," the matron said tiredly.

Once she was out of earshot Laura allowed the laughter that she had repressed to burst forth and she said, "You can't stay out of trouble."

"She'll get over it. Sorry about that, Germaine. You're right, most folk only remain on the spirit plane for a very short time. If they are out there I'll find them, I promise you that," Grey swore earnestly, holding her hands in his as he looked into her tear-filled eyes. Her face crumpled completely and Grey opened his arms to her and hugged her again. The healing process for such huge losses would take time and Grey wanted to help her become the radiant girl that he had seen glimpses of and which Yves had described. She would never be the same but Grey was determined that she could be happy again.

He'd been a bit off with the matron, which he knew he'd hear about later. As he leaned forward to hug Germaine and she held him back tightly, he felt a sharp pain from his lower back, punishment for not following sound medical advice. Laura saw from his expression that something was wrong and she said, "Put the girl down, Grey, or I'll call matron."

Germaine broke away from Grey and reached into her purse for a tissue. As she swabbed her eyes Grey eased himself back onto his pillow and said, "I'd offer you my handkerchief, only it's seen better days and isn't best suited for a lady."

"Thanks anyway," Germaine said, trying to compose herself.

"Thank you. Laura said you were thinking about coming to Scotland to help me get back on my feet."

"Do you mind?" Germaine asked, seeking his permission to look after him.

"Of course not, you're doing me the service by offering to help look after me." It was no time for levity and he was very serious with her, respectful of her loss. "Do you need any help in organising – I truly wish that I didn't have to ask you this question – do you need any help organising the funerals?"

"Laura has helped me with that, thank you."

"What about the farm? Do you need any help with that?"

"The farm can rot for all I care," Germaine said before she reminded herself how important it was to her father. "I can sort that out once you have recovered."

"I can tell we are going to have a bad patient on our hands here, Germaine. He has the makings of a good farmhand – you could do worse – but I would advise against hiring him in his current state," Laura said jokingly, but he deserved the mockery as for him to offer to help her out in his current condition was laughable. Grey had not meant physically grafting on her farm, just helping her come to a decision about what to do with it (whether to rent it out or hire a caretaker) and he sensed that Germaine had understood this.

"I think he'll be a good patient," Germaine said, looking into his eyes affectionately. She was dependent on him and he welcomed the responsibility. He was not confined to solely helping dead spirits – the living deserved his aid too and he and Germaine could help each other. He was still determined to have Laura, even though he saw that she was backing away emotionally from him, but he could be there for Germaine as a friend and Laura as a lover (in due course, definitely not yet), the two not incompatible.

"The only problem is I'm still a soldier. Until I get my medical discharge I don't have the right to go where I want to, which is with you two in Scotland," Grey said gently, noting Germaine's expression change at this worrying news. While she liked Laura, Grey was the one with whom she had formed a connection.

"It's a formality," Laura said reassuringly. "He's not getting out of the trip that easy."

A welfare officer came to see Grey at his request and dismissed Grey's suggestion of immediate medical discharge and recuperation in Scotland. Grey's proposition was so ridiculous that the officer refused to entertain the idea and talked to Grey sternly to discourage the notion. Grey wouldn't back down and kept arguing his case, even though he knew himself it was a lost cause. The US Army shipped their injured soldiers home, irrespective of the soldier's wishes – even if Grey couldn't admit it to the officer, this policy was utterly correct.

"The second you discharge me I'm going to cross the Atlantic and go to Scotland so why not just let me go now?" Grey said, going through the motions, trying his best. He didn't want to disappoint Laura or Germaine, to whom he recognised he was a lifeline. That was how bad her life was, that caring for him gave her some purpose.

"You can do what you want when you're discharged. Until then you're still a soldier and have to obey the rules."

"For all intents and purposes the war is over for me. By the time I'm back on my feet everyone will be back home. What if I take a dishonourable discharge?" Grey said, reluctant to have his army career end this way but prepared to try anything.

The welfare officer shook his head. "That's not going to happen. You're not the first soldier to fall in love overseas, Grey."

"What can you do to help me?" Grey said humbly. "If you've seen situations like this before, what should we do?"

"It'd be easier to get her to come back to Iowa with you than for you to go to Scotland with her. Not that that will be easy either, but I'm willing to try and help you with that. The alternative is absolutely impossible."

"There's another person to come too. A 15 year old orphan I met behind enemy lines who helped me. They're both willing to wait on me hand and foot in Scotland. If I can't go to Scotland then I need both of them to be with me in the States."

"Get real. You're not in a position to demand anything. You're luckier than most. You're a private who came back from near death who should survive the war. Go back to Iowa and in all likelihood you'll get your medical discharge quick provided your parents are willing to look after you, which I'm sure they will be. Accept this, because this is what's going to happen whether you like it or not."

"And Laura and Germaine who helped me in the war are just what...Irrelevant?"

"This Laura is not a refugee. She owns homes here and in Scotland and you say she has plenty of money to look after you. She doesn't need my help or yours. If you'll be sensible I will try and help arrange transport for Laura..."

"And Germaine. I can't leave her alone."

"This isn't my department. Who's the one you're in love with?"

"Laura."

"If you both claim you're thinking about marriage I can try and pull a few strings. Once she's in the US she's on her own – your parents will have to house her if she can't afford her own accommodation. Displaced children are an entirely different ball game."

"She's Laura's ward."

"Legally?"

"She's 15, not 5. Look, I'm sorry for the headache, buddy, but I'm desperate. It's not like I'm asking for anything. Just let me go, that's all I want. I'm still a patriot who wants to get home but I want to walk back on US soil, not be wheeled on."

The welfare officer shook his head. "You can scowl as much as you want, it's never going to happen. I'm here to help you. One day you might realise that we're doing you a favour."

"I get that now. We disagree as to what my best interests are. Throw me a bone."

"Shipping Laura home with you is a big bone."

"It's not enough."

"Then you're going to be disappointed."

Laura decided to visit Grey by herself to make sure he harboured no doubts about convalescing at her Scottish home. If he was homesick or wanted to keep the Army happy she had to respect his wishes – she'd miss him but she had to act in his best interests, which was the only thing that had spared him an affair with her. Despite his moral indignation at her misdeeds, the thought of a fling still appealed (sharing a bed with him, even though their nights were sexless, seemed to have erotic connotations in retrospect, his whole pursuit striking a chord after the fact) but she abstained because he would want her forever and she could not offer him that. She would not see him broken on the rocks like Georges before him. She came away from the visit informed enough to start putting his discharge in motion. They had largely talked seriously for the most part with Grey stating at the end that even if wearing a kilt was a requirement, he still wanted to take this path at this crucial crossroads.

Laura speculated to herself as she left whether Grey's choice made him a wise man or a fool. She would endeavour to be a good friend to him, but by choosing this direction he was veering from 'straight' society towards the life of the outcast. His personality and disposition would at least prevent him from ending up as far on the fringes as she had intentionally strayed.

Grey had made his choice and now it was Germaine's turn. Germaine had seemed keen on the move (though in her highly emotional state she found it hard to be positive about anything) before Grey had alarmed her with warnings that he was not in control of his destiny. Straight after the visit Germaine changed tack and she had gone to stay with one of her school friends and her family with a view of moving in permanently. If she wanted to stay in Maramont that was up to her, though Laura called in to see her upon her return to see if she had changed her mind.

Laura walked with Germaine back to her house, where they could talk privately (the walls at the Farmer house, where Germaine had been staying, were paper thin) and filled her in on the patient.

"He's looking better. They don't like him sitting up, as you know, but he did throughout the visit. We've had a long talk and he's made it abundantly clear that he doesn't want to go back to the States yet. He wants to return on crutches at the least, not rolled back onto US soil. These men and their pride...Basically, the move to Scotland is definitely on."

Germaine could not share Laura's enthusiasm and she said solemnly, "He should go back to his parents. They'll be worried about him if he doesn't come home."

"Even if he was sent home he would be placed in whichever hospital the Army saw fit, possibly hundreds or thousands of miles away from his family."

Germaine looked down at the grass as they spoke, questioning everything. Aiding James Grey's recovery would be something to keep her busy and, crucially, he meant something to her. Quite what she couldn't analyse, but in their few encounters he had impressed her with his inherent goodness at a time when evil dominated. However, as she knew the importance of family more now than ever, she preferred for James' army to ship him home, even against his wishes, for the greater good. She chose to walk away from the offer – he was a lifeline to her, yet she was just a noose to him, a miserable wretch who could never be happy and would unintentionally impede his recovery with her gloom.

"He might be closer than that."

"Possibly. Even if he is, he isn't close to his parents. Nobody in America even knows that he's a medium, and that's a major aspect of James Grey. It's completely up to you what you do. Even if you don't come, me and James are still going to Ravensbeck. We've 'negotiated' terms. He wants to be independent so he won't need that much nursing so don't worry about having to perform any unwholesome duties. He can't take a bath because of his wound so he says he'll hand wash at the sink and he has sufficient upper body strength to climb on and off the toilet without assistance. He'll be dressing himself too – it's important to him that he keeps his dignity. Really he should be helped with all of those things because he's a lot weaker than he makes out but in his position I'd want to be self-sufficient too. The only nursing duty he'll require is having his dressing changed and that's only say a once a week job. I'll be fulfilling more of a housekeeper role – he said maid which is wishful thinking on his part. I'll be cooking for him, changing his sheets and washing his clothes and taking him into the village because the paths are treacherous for him to wheel himself. I can look after him myself – I've handled bigger, uglier and iller men than him before, though you're welcome to come too, if you want. James is very concerned about you."

Germaine's eyes stung at this and she wiped away moisture from her eyes, steeling herself to stop more tears emerging. "I know. He shouldn't waste his energy worrying about me."

"That's the nature of the man, I'm afraid. He said he'd tried again with your mother and sister without luck."

"Too long has passed now. I know it's not to be."

"He'll have tried very hard."

"I know that. Can we stop a moment?" Germaine said as her emotions affected her body and she knelt on the ground, hyperventilating slightly. "When you next see him will you thank him for trying, for everything?"

"Come and thank him yourself. He'll be glad to see you."

"If I come he might talk me into going to Scotland and burdening the pair of you."

"It's your prerogative to stay here with Alison if you wish."

"Her parents have been kind to me. So have you. What I wanted…what would be best would be if my father had never died. After that, what I wanted…James offered to come and help us for one harvest. I looked forward to that, briefly, before Inge destroyed that idea. That was how I wanted to meet him again. I would be older, he wouldn't be a soldier. I'm not saying anything romantic, I know you and James…"

Laura interrupted her and said, shaking her head, "Me and James was always a non-starter. It would never have worked."

"No? I thought we could meet again in calmer times before she came back…we should have moved away. Everything's ruined now, Laura. I don't want to get close to James because I don't want to curse him too."

"Your friend's offer will still be there in a year's time. By then, with any luck, the war should be over and James should be walking. Come with us for the year and after that you can both go home. Don't leave me alone with him!" Laura said frantically, her joke producing a smile.

Two weeks later Laura was given dispensation to take Grey from the hospital as his medical discharge came through. Rosemary Rhodes helped dress him for his trip as they waited for his escorts to arrive and Grey talked about Laura enthusiastically, clearly head over heels in love with her. Rosemary felt that this was a shame. She did not like Laura who she felt was wrong for Grey and she felt that she was a cruel woman who would harangue him and impede his recovery. Rosemary had a big heart and was often touched by her patients, metaphorically speaking, but Grey was different, and she really liked him. The strict matron who had trained her had told her to never become personally involved but tending to someone, seeing a man who was doomed to die summon up the effort to live with courage and dignity – she could not stay detached from that. The other nurses said that it was miraculous and the doctors said it was impossible but all that Rosemary knew was that James Grey was breathing and that was all that mattered. Her intuition told her that it was imperative that he did not leave with Laura and she decided to take her opportunity. While Grey was still technically her patient until Laura came, the fact that he was fully dressed in civilian garb and was finally off his sickbed, now sitting in his wheelchair, (and winding her up by playing about with it) made it seem otherwise and made it acceptable to Rosemary to make her move.

She interrupted Grey, who was excitedly talking about Scotland and all things Scottish, to say, "It is very nice of her to offer to take you in, but I really do think you should heed your army officer's advice about this. Wouldn't it be better to have professional, trained medical staff looking after you until you are ready to look after yourself?"

"I tried coming to a compromise with him. He thinks that getting back to America as soon as possible is what I want or what I should want."

"Off the record none of the medical staff understand this decision. There are over two dozen men healthier than you classified as too unstable to move. Your discharge makes no sense. There's been a mistake," Rosemary said, convinced that something was gravely wrong. Grey's doctors had queried his release and learnt that this controversial decision was not an error.

"Pretend it is a typo, all parties are happy so what's the harm?" Grey said, as surprised as Rosemary by the decision which he wanted processed as quickly as possible before an obstacle came up.

"For a man as injured as you are to be looked after by someone who isn't even a relative or a partner – does Laura have the patience? She doesn't seem to be a terribly compassionate woman. Your recovery is remarkable, but you are still very much an invalid. Perhaps you could stay with her in a few months time and until then let the army continue to look after you. It's their duty."

"With all due respect, you don't really know Laura. She might make it out to be a chore but I know I'll be well looked after. By offering to take this lame duck in, I think she shows a lot of compassion. I would have thought everyone would be glad to see the back of me, no pun intended," he lied, the pun very much intentional. "Besides, Germaine will be helping too."

"Do they understand what is required?"

"Laura's as savvy as they come. She would have considered everything before coming to a decision and I know firsthand that she is a very capable woman. Don't worry about me, Rosemary, I'm looking forward to this." He had been careful to stay level during her critique of Laura – Rosemary was out of line but she was thinking of him and he remained genial.

"Just wiggling your toes causes you to break out in a sweat. To achieve full function will require months of physical therapy. I know of a specialist centre in London."

"Thank you, but everything is sorted. You could do me another favour."

"What is it?"

"Any idea what a haggis is? That's what Laura's cooking for us when we get back and she won't tell us until after we've eaten it."

"Lamb, I think. You're making a mistake, James."

"The alternative is spending weeks or months in hospital where my every need will be tended to – and all of you guys and gals have been great – but where, in some ways, I would be alone. This way's better."

"By severing your connection with the army you might find it hard to return to your country. Travelling is very difficult at present and it's likely that it will be for some time."

"The brass aren't mad at me – it's not like I've been dishonourably discharged. I've made my choice, Rosemary," he said firmly.

"All right, James, I won't argue with you if you're so determined to go with her. Please answer one question for me though. How did you survive?" she asked, desperate for an answer. She viewed him like Lazarus and wanted him to admit it was a miracle.

"Luck. Good fortune. What's that word?" he said, scratching his head, trying to remember one of the many words that Laura had taught him. "Providence," he said proudly.

"You overcame irreparable injuries. That's more than luck or providence."

As Rosemary Rhodes kept pushing him for more details of his recovery, Grey heard another voice who garnered more of his attention. Grey was pleased that Rosemary was talking expansively of faith and miracles, giving him a chance to listen to the spirit.

This is one whacked-out bad dream.

It's not a dream I'm afraid. I'm Grey. What's your name, buddy?

White. Cliff Forrester. I was in the hospital…you are too, yeah? Who are you?

James Grey, formerly Private Grey though I'm now discharged.

Sergeant Forrester though I'm now…dead? Fuck me, this is nuts. If I'm dead why the hell am I still around and why the hell are you talking to me?

Your body is dead, Cliff, or do you prefer Sergeant?

Cliff'll do, you can't salute a corpse.

Your body is dead but the spirit never dies. Because of the suddenness of your death your spirit needs time to adjust, to accept what happened before you are granted peace.

Heaven? There's no way I deserve that, he said, genuinely surprised.

I'll be honest with you, Cliff – I'm not absolutely sure, but I believe that's where spirits go.

You should find out soon enough, boy. I know where I've heard your name. You're the talk of the hospital. You got shot in two and your body rejoined or something.

The story's been embellished a bit. I wasn't shot in two, he said, amused at the tale.

That's what they said and they were astounded by it. I came in 'cause I got shot through the shoulder – stung like buggery but not much worse than a flesh wound – and I died from that and you're still breathing! Good luck to you, I'm not wishing you dead or anything, mate, but whenever anyone makes a miraculous recovery it's always temporary and they just snuff it a little later than expected. That might be why you can hear me, 'cause you're next.

That isn't why I can hear you. I'm a medium, I communicate with spirits and have done for over ten years. I leave hospital today, Cliff, so I should be okay but thanks for your concern, Grey said, appreciative that Cliff was giving his welfare some thought (many spirits could be self-absorbed).

With the English dame? The doctors talked about her too – you know what they're like, they just talk freely in front of us as if we're not there – and in my case I'm not there anymore. Weird shit. The doctors don't want to let you go, they want to take you back to England to do more tests on you. Give me time and I'll remember more. Something about a research facility in the capital. They might have used the word secure or compound. Anyway, she wouldn't have it and she's gotten her own way.

That's Laura, Grey said gratefully. He understood the doctors' intentions and wished that he could help medical science but he knew that his recovery was not down to anything extraordinary in his body for he knew that Laura had healed him even if the doctors still believed that his organs and spine had regenerated naturally. The research would be a waste of time and he realised it was still going to be carried out even without his presence. Over the last week they had taken every imaginable sample from him and, knowing little about medicine and wanting to be a model patient, he had not questioned them though he had wondered why they needed sperm and hair samples (though these had at least been painlessly acquired, unlike the bone marrow).

They reckoned she must have incriminating photos of some of the bigwigs. They're pissed off about it. I reckon they were taking too much interest in you and that's how I died from such a piddling injury. Bastard! Not you, this whole thing.

The war? It's nearly over, this side of it anyway.

Cliff was an easy spirit to deal with and Grey memorised several short messages before he faded away. During this time Rosemary had managed to get Grey to agree to visit her church when he was fully recovered so that she could show off this miracle to the congregation (he would have agreed to almost anything so as to be able to talk to the spirit without interruption). Rosemary said a tearful goodbye to him before Laura arrived as she wouldn't be able to talk freely in her company, and she went to check on other patients, leaving Grey alone to think.

Grey felt enough guilt about not returning to Keokuk without Rosemary making him feel worse about it. All he was really doing was delaying the inevitable. One day he had to return, even if only for a few months. Laura, Isdel, Germaine, Georges and the rest of the Pagan Resistance had accepted him and helped him realise that his dark secret wasn't shameful. He had spent long enough being coy about his abilities – he had long ago embraced his gift privately and he wanted to tell more people and offer his gift to the world, or at least everywhere except

…k, as this would be the hardest place to stand up and be counted. He had … while he recovered to work out the best way of minimising damage while …lling his parents' worst fears. The risks inherent were widespread. Possible …xcommunication, disownment – the chances were he would become a total pariah, pilloried as a heretic or madman. Whether he was hardy enough for this tough path only time would tell but Grey knew with certainty that he would rather be hated for being himself than go back to living a lie. In due course – maybe a year, maybe ten – he was going public and sharing his gift with the world